THE RECLAIMING

THE RECLAIMING

BOOK ONE OF THE KALATHEPTORIS CYCLE

S. MATTHEW MCNALLY

AN OMNIFISC BOOK

ACKNOWLEDGMENTS

No one person writes a book. One person writes a manuscript. The journey from manuscript to book is a collaborative process. There are many people who made this journey with me, without whom this book would still be a manuscript sitting dormant in the dark recesses of my hard drive.

Things that are first go first. Words simply fail to convey the level of gratitude I feel for Benjamin Duncan, John Mills, and Jason Spivey. You guys helped me raise the walls of Tamendad and pave the roads of a much larger world. Your fingerprints are all over this work and without you it simply would not exist. Now it's like the adventure is starting all over again.

Next, no matter how diligently an author may strive to read his or her own work with an impartial eye, it is quite impossible to step outside yourself and read with objective disinterest words you yourself placed upon the page. Thankfully, blessedly, in stepped brave souls who could say with critical aplomb, "Keep this, lose that, tighten this." Steven Buono, Beth Duncan, Jen Huber, Christopher Matthews, Julia Ridgely, Dee Robb and Ben Templeton, I am in your debt.

To my friend, compatriot and guide, Scott James, allow me to simply say thanks for leading the way, brother. And you still owe me a six pack.

And finally to my wife, upon whose shoulders fell the burden of putting up with me during the writing process, and all the incessant, obsessive behavior it entailed, allow me to just say thank you for still being my wife. If you didn't believe in this book, and in me, then this journey would never have begun.

For Lily and Dean.

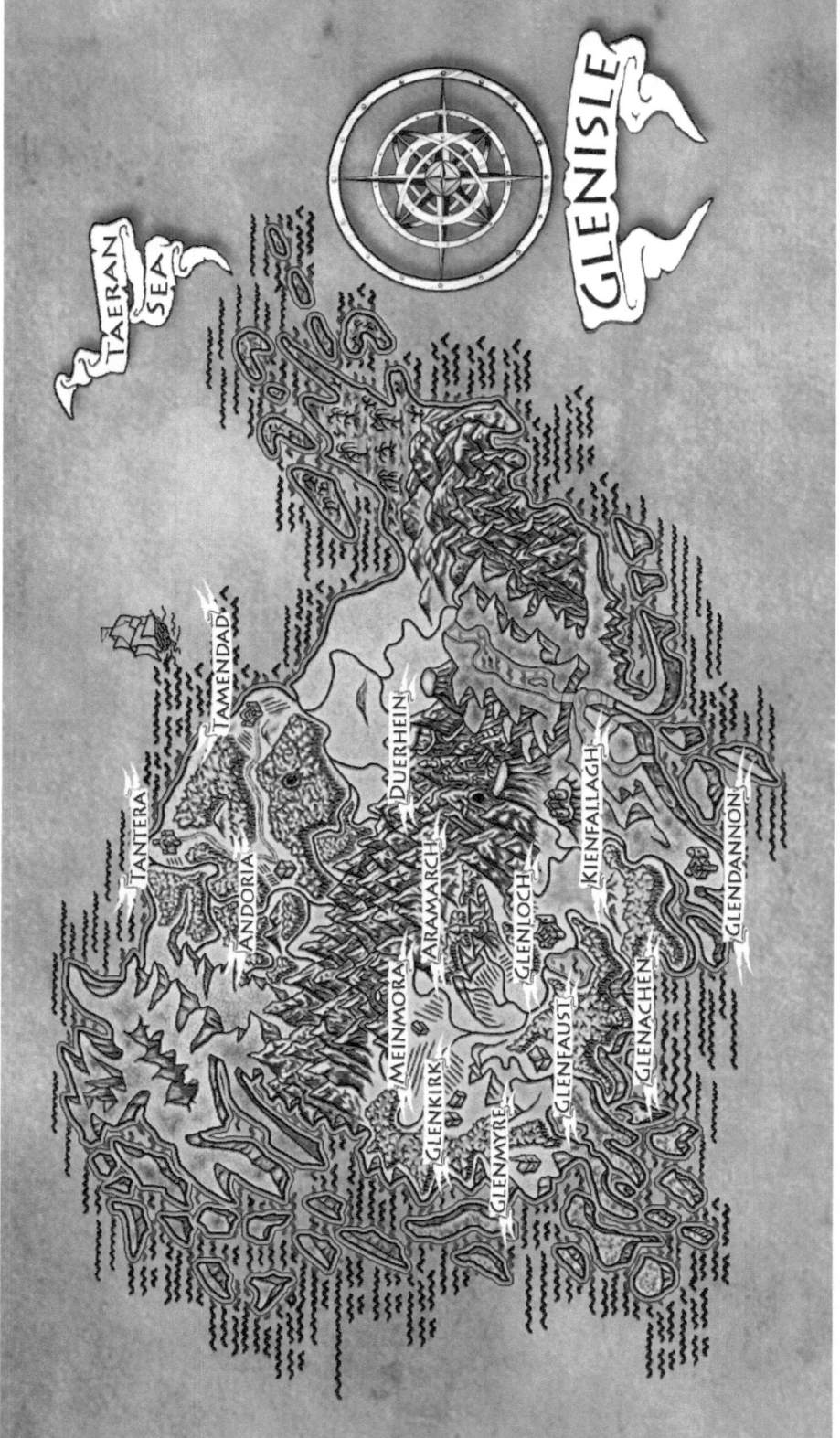

Listen little child
Mind the words I tell
Or the green man come and get you.

Don't wander off too far
In the wood or in the dell
Or the green man come and get you.

And mind yourself at night
By the fire's dancing light
Or the green man come and get you.

Come on little child
Better get yourself inside
Before the green man come and get you.

– Turish nursery rhyme,
from northern Glenisle

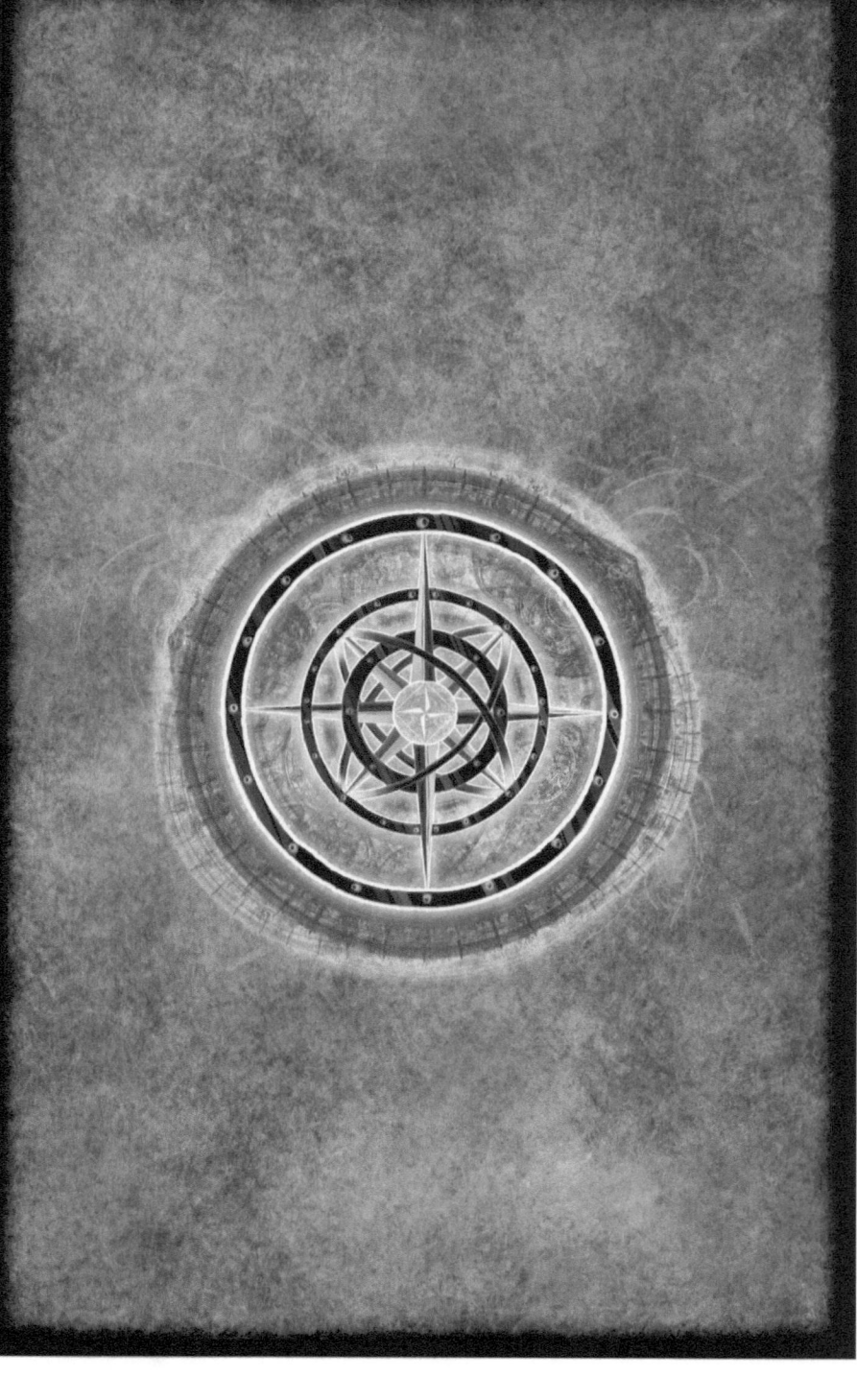

PART I

UNEXPECTED VISITORS

CHAPTER ONE

THE YOUNG NOBLEMAN

There was a story Jonathan Stuart-Camen liked to tell about his son.

William, all of seven years old at the time, had come home covered in mud from head to foot. His white silk shirt was ripped open at the front, half of the buttons missing. His hair, usually well kept by his mother, looked like he had stuck his head out an upstairs window during a gale. What struck Jonathan most about his son's appearance, though, was the fury that burned in his normally benign blue eyes.

"Landowners can rot!" was William's greeting upon seeing his father. To the best of Jonathan's knowledge it was the first time William had ever cursed anyone, let alone an entire class of people, and the words sounded heavy and awkward in his son's mouth. William had also seemed to overlook the fact that his father quite possibly owned more land than anyone else in Tamendad.

"And a pleasant afternoon to you as well, my son," Jonathan softly replied with a smile. "Something vexes you?"

"I was on my way to make my morning devotional," William said, and Jonathan's fatherly smile broadened. The Architessera did not call for boys to begin making devotionals until age twelve, but William took his religion very seriously for a boy so young. "They were right there in the middle of the street, beating up this little girl, younger than me, Father! Younger than me!"

Jonathan thought he could guess the rest, but let his son continue. The telling would be the best thing for William. "She'd accidentally bumped into them and gotten mud on their precious landowners' cloaks." William spat *landowners* like it was foul language. "They were going to beat her with a stick!"

"So you came to her rescue," Jonathan said. It was not a question. His smile was gone now. William needed him to be serious, needed his father to take him seriously.

"I jumped the one with the stick. Tore it out of his hands as he raised it above his head to strike. When he turned and saw who'd done it, his eyes were as big as Nelsie's saucers." Nelsie was the Stuart-Camen's cook.

"What happened next, my son?" Jonathan asked. He was taking his son very seriously now.

"I whacked him in the face with it. Let him taste his own medicine. Then things went a bit fig shaped."

Jonathan could not stifle the laugh that had found its way into his throat. Part of it was the mental image of his own son waylaying a member of what Jonathan himself called the *poppycock rich*, though never in front of William, with his own cudgel. Another part of it was the humor Jonathan found in the certainty that he would have to meet with Governor Chamberlain to explain his son's actions. The poppycock rich would have no doubt turned his son's chivalry into a story of unspeakable battery, unless they were too embarrassed to admit they had been bested by a seven year old.

"The other one started kicking at me like I was a stray dog," William continued without pause, "so I gave him a taste of wood too. Then they both jumped me. I thought they were going to faint when they ripped my shirt and saw the family crest around my neck."

Jonathan mentally crossed off his meeting with the Governor from his to-do list. No one would be stupid enough to admit jumping a nobleman's son, even if provoked.

"I yelled after them as they ran, told them the girl was my sister, told them they'd be put in irons. Anything to scare them." William now paused and took a long, deep breath. Some of the fire had dimmed from his eyes, but not enough.

"I wish I was big enough to use my sword," said William bitterly.

It should be noted that the broadsword was the Stuart-Camen family weapon. The one that hung at William's side had been crafted especially for him by Gunther Moragun, Tamendad's renowned blacksmith, as a present from his father on his fifth birthday. At the time the sword had been almost as long as William was tall, and he had to hold it awkwardly in both hands, one around the grip and the other clenching the basket hilt, to wield it in anything close to resembling the correct form. Some had laughed at Jonathan Stuart-Camen for not giving William a broadsword scaled down to his own size, but the Stuart-Camen method of teaching the broadsword was a family tradition that Jonathan had no intentions of breaking with. And despite William's clumsy style, the boy showed great promise from the very beginning to become an excellent swordsman, perhaps one of the finest of his generation. But that day, standing muddy and disheveled in the common room of his own house, trembling with rage under the gaze of his father, it was the first time William had ever mentioned a desire to use his sword in anger.

Jonathan Stuart-Camen did not, as a general rule, hit anyone so William was taken aback when his father slapped him rather hard across the face. Tears immediately welled up in his eyes, a mixture of pain and fear. His father was suddenly hovering above him, and William felt very small and alone.

"I never want to hear you say that or anything like it again!" his father bellowed.

William was speechless.

After a short while, Jonathan continued, "You have learned well that a sword is not a toy, but it is a testament to my failure as a father that you have not yet learned that neither is it an instrument of revenge. The sword that hangs at your side is a noble weapon. Not noble in the sense that we are noble, because that's all money and politics. It is noble in that how the sword is wielded is a reflection of the man who wields it. You were right to come to the aid of that little girl, William, but did those landowners deserve to die?"

William did not immediately answer.

"Did they?" Jonathan repeated. Now the fire was in his eyes.

"N-no father. I didn't mean... I wouldn't... I'd never..." William trailed off and began to cry. Jonathan softened a little and placed both hands upon his son's shoulders, drawing him close. William looked up at him. His tears had cleared little paths through the mud on his face, and Jonathan could see that the skin of his son's left cheek was red from the slap. He immediately regretted raising his hand to his son. He felt a bit like crying himself.

"I know you didn't, William," he whispered. "But never forget what I told you about your sword. It should never be unsheathed lightly."

"I will never forget, father."

And he never did.

Summer was William's favorite time of year, and this one had been the best he could remember. Being the son of Jonathan Stuart-Camen, the wealthiest horse baron in all of Glenisle, most of William's summers tended to be thoroughly enjoyable. This one, though, was only half over and already he knew it would be one he would remember for the rest of his life. His family schooling was finally complete and he had reached the age of maturity. He drew the attention and respect accorded to a man without having to deal with the everyday hassles and stresses of manhood. He was old enough to represent his father in business and political dealings whenever Jonathan was indisposed, and while William would be the first to admit that such affairs were not his strong suit the taste of authority they brought pleased William greatly. Having not yet married he still lived in his family home, and not being the one in charge of family business left William with quite a bit of spare time. He filled that time pursuing his three great passions in life: the family business of breeding and tending horses, the family practice of studying the broadsword, and the personal pursuit of courting Melissa Tilman.

William and Melissa were a year away from marriage. They had been betrothed for years, since before they had even met each other. Jonathan Stuart-Camen and Winston Tilman had been friends since childhood and had decided very early on in life that they would forever join their two noble Houses through the marriage of their children. The marriage of William Stuart-Camen and Melissa Tilman promised to do well for the prestige of both Houses, increase the wealth and holdings of both, and perhaps even bump them up a notch or two in Tur's political hierarchy. All these details were completely irrelevant to William and Melissa, who were only concerned with the fact that they had the good fortune to be in love with the person they were arranged to marry. Arranged marriages were common in Tur, as were marriages for love, but managing both in one shot was a pretty rare occurrence.

Melissa, a year William's junior, was still bogged down in the tedium of schooling, but she managed to spend at least a little time every day with her future husband. Mostly they just rode their horses up and down the coast or picnicked together on the beach and watched for dolphins, and every now and again they would fall to doing the sorts of things that young people who are in love tend to do. But their favorite thing was just to sit together atop the tallest hill around and just be together quietly in one another's presence. The hill was not particularly tall as hills tend to go, but it afforded the best view both of their little city of Tamendad and of the Taeran Sea, upon the shores of which Tamendad sat. The hill doubtless had a name, probably given by some long-dead cartographer after his mother or daughter or mistress, but no one around seemed to remember what it was. In time it would come to be known as Blood Hill, but that unpleasant business was still a good ways in the future and in the meantime both William and Melissa had come to think of it as simply their hill. So they would just sit there on top of their hill, watching the ships sailing into and out of harbor, keeping an eye out for dolphins, and thinking that if they squinted just so in the right kind of light they could almost make out the coast of the mainland on the other side of the Taeran. And sometimes they would actually talk to each other while they

4

sat there.

This morning was one such occasion. The two of them were sitting together, making sure that as much of their bodies were in contact with the other's as possible, watching the sun finally creep its lazy way out of the sea, when Melissa looked over at her future husband and whispered into his ear, "Do you ever want to leave this place?"

While that was what most people would call a loaded question, William did not hesitate to answer it. After all, Melissa had asked it and nothing Melissa did ever put him on edge. "I will leave it if I have to," he said. "I'll take it as it comes."

She pulled away from him a little bit and he smiled at her, taking in the way the sun shone through her silky brown hair, making it look like it was illuminated from within. Her look at him was contemplative, maybe a little puzzled, but not cross. "You say that quite a bit, that you'll take it as it comes," she said. "Where did you hear that?"

"I got it from my father. When I was little he told me that sometimes we're lucky and life puts us right where we want to be. Then other times our luck will change and we have to go places or do things we might not want to. But there's no sense in worrying about it because it will come as it comes, and worrying about it won't prevent it. The best thing to do is just take it as it comes."

"My love," said Melissa, resting her head once more in the crook of her lover's neck, "I think that might well be the most eloquent thing you have ever said."

"Why thank you," was his reply.

"But it sounds so…passive," Melissa continued with barely a pause. "Like all you do is sit there waiting for things to come your way. Don't you want adventures?"

William chuckled. "Of course I want adventures," he said. "Doesn't everybody want adventures at our age? But my father told me something else, too, and I suspect that it's true. He said, 'The adventures that find you are always better than the ones you go out and find.'"

"Well when those adventures find you," Melissa said coyly, "don't you forget that you will have a wife at home waiting for you."

"Whoever said you would be left at home? I expect you'll be along on a good number of my adventures."

"And if you are lucky," replied Melissa, "I shall bring you along on a good number of mine as well."

And then they both sank back into a comfortable silence; conversations atop their hill were always fleeting things. That was perhaps what William loved the most about Melissa. Almost the whole of his life was taken up by procedure and protocol and all the humdrum decorum that came along with his title. But in Melissa he had found a person with whom he could just shut up and enjoy things without complicating them with etiquette.

Enough time passed in silence for the sun to make its way about a hand's length above the horizon before Melissa planted a soft kiss on William's lips and stood up. The time of her geometry lesson was fast approaching. The two of them tidied themselves, fetched their horses, and rode down the hill into Tamendad.

There are really only a few things that need to be noted about Tamendad. It was either a small city or a large town, depending on who was reckoning it. About twenty-five hundred people lived inside the city proper. Roughly a thousand others, who were too poor to afford their citizenship, congregated together in little mud hovels outside the city wall. The wall itself was about twenty feet high and solid oak, and so far as anyone knew had never been necessary to defend the city from attack. Three smaller gates allowed foot traffic into the city from the northwest, the southwest, and the southeast. The big northeast gate opened into the harbor, where ships came and went all the day long. And, perhaps most importantly, perhaps least, Tamendad was the principal Turish port city on the island of Glenisle, so that anyone coming from the mainland on official business always came through Tamendad.

William and Melissa reluctantly parted ways upon entering the city. The rest of her day was to be spent in the rigorous pursuit of knowledge that would probably serve no practical purpose for the rest of her life. He, meanwhile, was headed home to put in some practice at the broadsword. He cut west down a side street. The Governor's house was in the western corner of town and all the other noble families had stacked their houses up around it as if they thought the family whose house was closest to the Governor's would gain some special favor or position in his administration.

William's house, while not the nicest in Tamendad, was quite lovely. Two stories and twelve rooms of stone and brick, with glass in every window and a chimney on either side. Honeysuckle grew on the south wall, and William associated its sweet fragrance with summer and childhood. A cobblestone walkway led from the street to the front door, above which a rearing stallion, the crest of the House of Stuart-Camen, was engraved into the stone of the archway. Upon reaching the walkway to his home William handed his horse's reins to one of the stableboys who patrolled the nobility's section of the residential district; all of Tamendad's nobility shared a common set of stables with the Governor to save space inside the city.

As William started up the walk to his front door he noticed for the first time that his younger brother Julius was sitting in the yard, legs folded, leaning against the east wall with a book resting open in his lap. Julius was four years younger than William, but it was plain he was destined for greatness. He excelled in his studies, having a particularly strong knack for mathematics and theology. William suspected that before Julius finished his schooling he would have read every book in Tamendad.

Julius turned a page in the book on his lap and decided it was a good place to stop. He lifted his arms above his head, his right wrist grasped in his left hand, and stretched his back. It emitted a slightly audible popping sound and Julius sighed and grunted softly. He looked around the yard and noticed William for the first time. He jumped to his feet and hobbled over, his gait revealing that both his feet had fallen asleep. He shifted clumsily from one foot to the other.

"Good ride?" Julius asked, grimacing.

"Yes, good," replied William. "You know, we do have a number of chairs."

"I like sitting on the ground," Julius replied. "I should have stretched my legs more often." That was Julius. No excuses, no embarrassment, just a simple statement of facts.

"What are you reading today?" William asked, eyeing the tome tucked under Julius's right arm.

Julius held the book in front of him and flipped open the cover, making sure he did not recite the title incorrectly. His dedication to academia put William's to shame. "*A History of the Turish Oracles from Bonaventure to Aedmund*, by Arcumore Jamus Coulings of Westerland." Julius sighed a quick, content sigh, apparently pleased that he had gotten the whole title right. He grinned at William, who only responded by nodding. William had enjoyed theology, but he had downright despised studying the oracles. Upon completing what he thought was a rather exhaustive exposition of every Turish oracle and, of course, Hidalgo Sanctus, it was expected that William take part in the Day of Remembrance, occurring both during Summerfeast and Winterfeast, during which every single name of the more than fifty Turish oracles had to be recited, pausing after each recitation to make the Sign of the Compass. The ceremony could last over an hour if the priests felt like dragging it out, and William had come to think of it as the only blemish on the face of his two favorite times of the year.

7

"Well, as much fun as that sounds like, I have to practice," said William. "After some morning tea," he added. He moved past his brother toward the house, tousling Julius's hair as he went. Julius ducked and pulled away from William's hand, still moving gingerly on feet that were reluctantly coming back to life.

William opened the door to his house and walked in without looking back at his brother, whom he was certain was taking great pains to correct his hair. Reynolds started with a jump from his chair by the door, old Reynolds with his bald head and pressed servant's tunic. William thought of him more as family than anything else.

Reynolds relaxed when he saw it was William. He had given up trying to convince the young nobleman to ring the bell to his own house long ago. "Nelsie has tea on, Master William."

"Thank you, Reynolds. Enjoy your nap."

William came through the common room, past the stairway, through the dining room and into the kitchen. The rest of the house had been blessedly cool, but the wood stove made the kitchen feel like a furnace. Nelsie, the plump and pleasant Stuart-Camen cook, looked up from the bread dough she was kneading. Flour and sweat mingled together to form a paste that dotted her forehead. William greeted her and moved for the kettle on the stove. A cup and saucer sat beside it, a tea ball full of finely cut black waiting inside. William liked Nelsie. She always let him wait on himself whenever he wanted to. He poured steaming water from the kettle into the cup and steeped the tea ball. Blackness oozed from the holes in the metal ball, spreading through the cup like shadow. As he was adding some honey, Nelsie spoke to him.

"Your father's out with the horses. A prize mare came up missing during the night, one that was promised to Winston. You're father's having kittens over it, God knows why. He and Winston Tilman go back well before you were born. He won't think twice about some damn-fool mare jumping a fence, dower or no. But your father's your father, and that's all there is to say about that. Your mother is upstairs reading and sneaking a pipe. Thinks I don't have a nose, she does. I say let the lady smoke, don't do me or no one else no harm. If she smoke-stains her teeth, she's still the best woman this town has in it. Julius is running around somewhere with one of those books of his, going on about his oracles. Reynolds is asleep, of course." Her rundown complete, she went back to her bread.

"Anything else to report?" William asked wryly, blowing on his tea to cool it.

"Just one more thing: nobody likes a smartass." There was a moment of utter silence, then William and Nelsie both erupted into fits of laughter. William took great care not to spill scalding tea all over himself.

"You're one of a kind, Nelsie," said William after regaining his composure, heading out the side door into the yard.

"Thank your stars for that, Will," she called after him. "There's not room in this town for two of me. Bring that cup back when you're done. And mind you don't cut yourself."

"I will and I won't." He pulled the door closed behind him and walked behind the house. He took a sip of tea, then set the cup and saucer on the ground a good distance away from where he would be practicing. He began to stretch out, curling his arms up behind his head and down between his shoulders. He twisted his torso, and noted that Julius was nowhere around. That was another thing he liked about his brother: he gave William some privacy while he practiced, the one time when William could use a break from the distractions of a little brother. Julius was going to be an amazing diplomat one day, and William was thankful his brother would be around to help him out when he became the head of the household.

William put this thought aside with all others and drew the sword from his side. He held its basket hilt an inch away from his nose for a moment, taking a deep breath in through the nostrils, holding it for a few seconds, letting it out slowly through the mouth. Sword and man was all that was left, and the line separating these two tenuous at best. William took up his beginner's stance with eyes still shut. He found it by feel.

He ran through the progressions his father had taught him, fighting his imaginary foes in a clockwork progression. Each phantasm fell before the steady swipes of his blade, and more came to take their places. Invisible assassins surrounded him, approaching him exactly as they always had, exactly as they always would. William progressed through the beginner's sets into the intermediate motions. He added movement to his attacks as his imaginary foes began to dodge and weave through his attacks. He moved to intercept them, using his whole body to swing his broadsword.

Thrust and slash, parry and step. Move with the sword, never against. Always maintain a balance, enough force to carry the sword through the target but never enough to unbalance the feet. Place the sword between you and your enemy. Make it a barrier when it is not a weapon. Keep your distance until your opening appears. Watch the hands, never the eyes. Use the sword's momentum to your advantage. Curve the attack back on itself, twice the slashes without twice the effort. Feel the sword. Above all else, feel the sword.

Off hand, William thought, and transferred his broadsword from right to left. Every move increased in difficulty. It was one thing to appreciate the need for ambidexterity, something else entirely to actually attain it. As William struggled with his off hand, so too did his imaginary assailants begin to struggle. Always they remained just good enough to be in their place when it was time for William to put them down. That was the thing that bothered William the most about solitary practice. Deep down, when you got to the heart of it, it was all bullshit. It kept you focused, but it didn't teach you anything. It was not a method of improvement; it was merely a way to maintain your current level of ability. There were no surprises. The illusory aggressors always pressed their attacks the same way, at the same angles, again and again and again, because they weren't real. They were extensions of the mind, an artificially created focus point, a useful lie. Unless you had a real flesh and blood person in front of you, you were just facing yourself.

William's father had put this in perspective, too. "There are basically three ways to study the sword," he had said. "The first is solitary practice, the second is practice with a partner, and the third is combat. Combat is the best way to learn, no doubt about that, but it is also the easiest way to get killed. Jump right into combat and you'll end up learning more about pain than swordsmanship. Practice with a partner is a good way to learn, because you can mimic combat situations but the person you face is not trying to kill you, assuming you're lucky. Unfortunately sparring partners are hard to come by, and the possibility for injury is still high. One mistake by either man could potentially mean death for both. That fact is true whenever two men face each other with swords drawn. Solitary practice is tedious, and rarely teaches anything new, but at the very least it prevents decline in ability. Plus, you can't die doing it, unless you end up running yourself through. And I think you will agree with me that if you're that inept, you have no business studying the sword in the first place."

And that was that, just one more thing Jonathan had explained to his son with clarity and grace. Jonathan had partnered with William whenever possible, especially during the early part of his training, but his father was a very busy man these days. He still found time to instruct William at least twice a week, but often he had just enough time to demonstrate a new slash or step to his son, watch him try it out a few times, and tell William which points to work on. William was thankful for these lessons, but at the same time he wanted to learn so much more than his father had time to teach him. Jonathan Stuart-Camen had a hundred responsibilities to see to day in and day out, and William sometimes felt guilty for stealing enough of his time to learn a new move. The simple fact was that the time for William to find a master swordsman to learn under was drawing near. Some of his childhood friends had already left Tamendad to become apprentice swordsmen, some traveling to Andoria to learn the longsword from Master Atticus Highcastle, retired lieutenant to the House of Stodlemeyer, some traveling south into the Highlands and beyond to become adept with greatswords or claymores. But William's weapon was the broadsword, and he had no idea how far he would have to travel to find a master to learn under. Certainly at least to Thiston on the mainland, and in all likelihood much farther north. The broadsword was not a rare weapon, but it was relegated mostly to the nobility, where it had become less of a sword and more of an adornment. Most swordsmen preferred the simpler longsword, which cost less and in truth was just as effective except for lacking a hand guard. Finding a master at a nobleman's weapon would be difficult indeed, and would doubtless require quite a bit of travel, and he could not even begin to think about such pursuits until after he and Melissa were married. That was not until next summer, and...

Enough! William thought firmly, coming back to the moment. Outside thoughts had encroached on his mind, as they always did toward the end of his practice. He spared a glance at the sundial in the back yard and noted that two hours had passed, half an hour longer than he had intended. That was good. A man could be forgiven for letting his mind wander after two hours of anything strenuous. Again he brought the basket hilt an inch from his face and closed his eyes, clearing his mind of all thoughts of the sword. Yet another lesson from his father: "When you sheath your sword, leave it there."

William fetched the cup and saucer, drained the cold tea in one long gulp, and headed inside.

CHAPTER TWO

UNEXPECTED VISITORS

William washed up after he was finished with the sword, and by the time he got back downstairs his mother was sitting at the dining room table waiting for lunch to be served. William joined her.

"Hello, Mother," he said. "How goes your reading?"

"It goes well, William," she said with a smile. "Your father will not be joining us."

"Still out looking for that rogue mare? I wouldn't have thought she'd run far if she got out." William knew which horse Nelsie had been referring to. He had helped shoe her.

"Well, your father is determined to look halfway to Tantera if he must. I agree with Nelsie, though. Winston will not hold it against your father if the mare is gone. They have been friends far too long for a runaway horse to come between them, and there are plenty of other good horses he can give in its place." Lyllian shrugged her shoulders as if to say there was no reasoning with Jonathan. William knew this was true.

Julius joined them eventually from upstairs, and they shared a midday meal of warm bread and cheese and roast pork. Afterward Lyllian returned to her reading. William asked Julius if he wanted to play a game of chess but Julius declined, claiming his head hurt from all his reading and he would not be able to mount any kind of offense. William suspected this sudden headache was to save Julius the embarrassment of losing yet another match to his older brother, but said nothing. Julius retired to take a midday bath and William, having nothing better to do, decided to take a walk.

As he approached the landowner's houses he began to sense a buzz in the air. Something exciting had happened, or at least something exciting by Tamendad's standards. William caught bits and pieces of conversation as he strolled.

"...arrived less than an hour ago, every one of them on

thoroughbreds. Dressed like nothing I've ever seen."

Sounds like visitors, William thought. From the description he pictured noblemen from the mainland, hoity-toity braggarts looking down their noses at all the Tamendad folk. If that were the case, though, they would have arrived by ship, not by horse. *Could've brought them along*, William supposed. *Don't want to dirty their bottoms on Glenish horses*. Then he passed a couple of old women talking so excitedly he expected they could be heard all the way across town.

"The leader's as big as a horse, Elsey, and his horse is as big as an ox! And I'll be damned but you can't understand a word he says. Uses the old aye and nay instead of yes and no, and half the time it sounds like he's trying to cough up a hairball!" William was out of earshot before he could hear what Elsey, obviously a much quieter woman than her companion, had to say.

Then he saw them.

They were impossible to miss. The one the old woman had been telling Elsey about, the one she called their leader, was most certainly as big as a horse if not a little bigger. The hulk of a man stood almost a full head taller than William. His chest was as big around as an ale barrel. He had long hair that was somewhere between brown and gray that came down just past his shoulders. Most of it was unkempt, but a single strand of it was braided and hung by the left side of his face. He had a full beard of solid gray, and unlike his hair it looked rather well kept. He wore a plain cloth shirt that could not decide if it was off-white or light brown. A tartan hung across his broad chest, a deep, rich plaid of hunter greens and royal blues, with reds and golds thrown in for good measure. What struck William's eye the most was the mammoth sword that hung on the man's back. William had never seen a claymore before, and marveled that anyone could swing such a sword. It had to be five feet from point to pommel.

William placed the man's age at somewhere approaching fifty or so, based on his gray, but physically he looked like he could overpower any eighteen year old William had ever seen. His undershirt had no sleeves, and the arms that jutted out from his immense shoulders looked absolutely sculpted. The man's thighs, so far as William could see, might very well have been as big around as William's own chest. Every ounce of him appeared to be firm muscle, except for the little bit of a belly that was apparent by the way his kilt hung around his abdomen. *If there's a breed of horse as big as this man*, William thought, *my father needs to breed them as beasts of burden. A team of them could move a castle.*

The big man had four companions, all dressed the same as he but none quite so big. One had a similar build, half a head shorter but just as broad. His hair was a golden brown and hung down well below his shoulders. He had a braid as well, but it hung on the right side of his face. He also carried a claymore, and it looked even larger on him since he was shorter. William thought after looking him over a second time that he had to be the big one's brother, younger by perhaps a decade. Their builds and faces were just too similar not to be kin.

The other three men were much smaller in comparison, though all but one of them were larger than William. One had straight black hair tied back in a ponytail and looked to be twenty-something. Another had curly brown hair that framed his face in a thick mat. That one William could not so easily put an age on, thinking he could be as young as thirty or as old as the leader. The third was close to William's age, perhaps a few years older, and also had brown hair, though his was straight and parted in the middle. William noticed none of these men had braids. He wondered what that meant.

Highlanders in Tamendad, he thought. *Curse me.*

They were walking more or less aimlessly through the main street, looking at the houses that surrounded them. They were friendly, too. They said hello to just about everyone who passed, though they pronounced more like *hulloo*. Most passers-by smiled back at the unexpected visitors but gave them a wide berth, probably more intimidated by the leader's size than by any stories they had heard about Highlanders. William decided to walk right up and introduce himself and offer to show them the sights. He decided, all right, but his feet did not seem to want to move at first. *God, he is big*, William mused, but he doubted these men had come all the way from the Highlands to pick a fight with young noblemen on the threshold of manhood. After he managed to take the first step he found the ones that followed came much more easily.

The big man must have seen him coming out of the corner of his eye, since he was the first to turn. His big toothy grin never faltered, but William could see just an inkling of suspicion in his eyes. William did not let himself hesitate. If he stopped now he might not be able to talk his legs into working again. The others turned their heads as their leader did, and all five men started toward William. They were all smiles, but for an instant an image flashed in William's mind: the brothers loosing their gargantuan swords and slicing him in two, right down the middle; the others hooting and hollering and jumping up and down at the smell of blood; the two brothers plucking his still-beating heart from his opened chest, holding it aloft and screaming a guttural war cry as his entrails littered the streets…

William snapped back to reality and bit at himself for even

entertaining such thoughts. By the time the five Highlanders were close enough to speak he hoped he had regained enough of his composure and color in his face to prevent the men, especially the really big one, from sensing his timidity. He bowed a deep nobleman's bow and spoke with all the authority he could muster.

"Well met, and allow me to introduce myself. I am William of the House of Stuart-Camen, firstborn son of Jonathan and Lyllian. On behalf of my House, my township and its Governor, Lord Geoffery Chamberlain, I welcome you to Tamendad." The nobleman's self-introduction was one of the first pieces of etiquette he had learned; he had made it a hundred times. The Highlanders, however, eyed him like he was a two-headed duck.

After a double take, the big one suddenly moved, reaching forward and grabbing William's forearm. It was already firmly in the Highlander's grasp before William knew what was happening. William tensed, waiting for it to be ripped out of its socket, but the big man was simply shaking it vigorously.

A handshake, thought William. He had heard of the custom before, more common among landowners than nobility. He had never heard of grasping the forearm instead of the hand, but it was quite obvious that what was happening was a variation on a handshake. He relaxed.

"Ah, good t' see ye this morning, lad!" the big Highlander said. He pronounced *good* like *goot*, and the *o* in morning sounded more like an *a*, but William found it hard to believe the old lady he had passed earlier in the street could honestly not understand a word this man said. His accent was deep and guttural, but he was speaking perfectly comprehensible Turish. "'Tis m' turn for an introduction, I suppose, though I hope ye dinnae expect anything so grand as yers." At this the four other Highlanders broke out in deep, guffawing fits of laughter. William's face turned a shade of red.

"Gregor MacDugal o' th' Clan MacDugal." He then gestured to his companions. "This lad is m' little brother, Angus. That o'er there with the black hair be m' cousin Liam MacDugal. Th' one with th' nap on his head is Liam's brother by marriage, Gabrahn Cowan. And this one is a scurvy dog we picked up on our journey and cannae shake off." Gregor said it with a straight face, but his eyes clued William in on the joke. The straight-haired one sprang forward around Gregor and took hold of William's forearm, shaking it violently and flashing a smile that was all teeth. William could tell already that this one was the wiliest of the bunch.

"Dinnae listen t' him, lad, he's a bastard who speaks naught but lies. He'll convince ye that down is up and th' sun sets in th' east if ye let him.

Th' name's Wallace MacConacher, proud member o' th' Clan MacDugal."

Clans. William's father had told him about that once, how the Glenish had clans instead of houses. While William was thinking of this, Angus stepped forward and punched Wallace in the upper arm, hard. Wallace yelped in pain and turned on Angus, rubbing his right shoulder.

"What did ye do that for, cow?" he demanded.

"Ye called m' brother a bastard, and I know for a fact his mother was a married woman. Think twice before ye speak ill o' her again." Angus had a deeper voice and more guttural accent than his brother, sounding like the human equivalent of a bulldog.

"'Twas in jest, fool," Wallace mumbled, still rubbing his shoulder gingerly.

"Aye, so was that punch," Gregor spoke up. "I've seen how m' brother can hit when someone speaks ill o' Ma." All the Highlanders except Wallace broke into more laughter. Wallace just stood there and mumbled murder under his breath.

Gregor shifted his attention back to William. "Ye said…what was it, lad? Ye welcome us t' yer township, do ye? Does that mean ye'd be willing t' show us around it? We've been here for an hour or more and have found naught but houses, pretty though they may be."

"Of course," William answered, "of course. I would be happy to show you everything there is to see in Tamendad. What is it you're interested in, gentlemen?"

"Beer," said Liam.

"An inn," said Gabrahn.

"A bath," said Angus.

"Something for a bruise," said Wallace. More laughter, and this time Wallace himself chuckled a bit.

"All that and more," Gregor said at last, "but first things first. We need a place t' stable our horses, and then ourselves. We've ridden all morning, and 'tis been well since two days gone that we've had a proper meal and a pipe. This town is yers t' show, so lead th' way, lad."

William took a moment to process everything they said they needed, and made a mental list. First things first, as Gregor had said. "Where are your horses?"

"Aye, we hitched them just inside th' wall," said Gregor. "Shall I fetch them?"

William shook his head. "No need. I'll have a stableboy take your horses to the Governor's stables. I assure you they will be quite well taken care of." Gregor and the others assented to this idea, and William went to flag down a stableboy.

"Now for an inn, lad," Gregor said pleasantly once the horses had been seen to. "What's th' best Tamendad has t' offer?"

"The Crown Rose is the best inn in town, probably in all of Glenisle. It's expensive, though," William cautioned. He also wondered how these Highlanders would look in the nobility's local stomping grounds. The mental image was just too priceless to pass up.

"Gold is nae a problem, lad. If this Crown Rose is th' best, let's be about it."

"Aye," said Angus, who did not seem to like talking all that much, "a warm plate and a warm bed would do me well."

"Not t' mention a warm woman t' soothe m' aches and pains," added Wallace, whose right shoulder was now sporting a rather impressive knot.

As William led his new friends northeast through the town he became increasingly aware of the eyes that were upon him. Every person they passed in the street had a look at the newcomers. The more tactful spectators simply gave the men a brief look-over as they passed by, but more than once William spotted men and women who had stopped dead in their tracks and stood with their mouths agape, ogling the Highlanders as if they had a second head or an extra set of arms. William had been surprised to find Highlanders in his own hometown, no doubt about that, but some of these people seemed to have forgotten the fact – or failed to learn it in the first place – that the Highlands began just two days' ride south of Tamendad. The onlookers had curious stares for William as well, though this was curiosity of a different sort. More than one passer-by had seemed a little shocked to find five Highlanders and the son of one of Tamendad's more affluent noblemen strolling across town together as if they had been friends since birth. William realized what these stares meant quickly, and the devious part of him deep down inside was eating it up.

William led the Highlanders past the Antrelican church that constituted the heart of Tamendad's town square and noted that all five of them made the Sign of the Compass along with him as they passed by. He had heard stories that some of the Glenish were pagans, whatever that meant. The fact that these five Highlanders were good Antrelicans like himself made the mental tableau of Gregor and Angus disemboweling him on Tamendad's main street recede even more from the periphery of his conscious mind. Besides Angus punching Wallace over the comment about his mother, unintentional though that comment may have been, the Highlanders had shown no outward signs that they were any more prone to violence than the local citizens. Everyone still seemed leery of the gigantic swords strapped to Gregor and Angus, though, and William thought this understandable. William himself had never seen a sword nearly so big as these, and he had received quite a bit more instruction on swords than the average Tamendader. A sword that size could not be passed off as simple ornamentation as easily as, say, William's own broadsword. Someone who chose a sword as big as a claymore probably felt the need to carry such an immense and intimidating weapon, and William could not think of anything so threatening as to require a five foot blade to deal with. William summed all of these thoughts up by saying, "That's quite a sword you carry, Gregor."

Gregor perked up an eyebrow at the comment, as if he found nothing at all unusual about carrying around a sword the size of a small person. "Oh, aye, I suppose ye've ne'er seen a claymore before, have ye lad? Ah, they make them larger than this in th' Highlands."

"Aye," added Angus, brusquely but not discourteously. "Some Highlanders carry swords longer than ye are tall, William."

"They do at that," Liam piped in. "With blades as wide across as a man's thigh."

William could not begin to imagine it. "How does anyone wield a sword like that?" he asked incredulously.

"Big lads," Gabrahn said, nodding sagaciously as if he had just explained one of life's great mysteries. "Ye know," he added, sounding as though he were talking more to himself than his friends, "young William here really should meet Hamish someday." The other four Highlanders heartily agreed to this idea, though William was clueless as to what exactly they were talking about. When he questioned Gabrahn about who exactly this Hamish was, the Highlander said simply, "One o' th' big lads."

"One o' th' biggest," Gregor spoke up. "Ne'er seen one bigger, truth be told."

"Well, he couldn't be much bigger than you, could he Gregor?" Gregor was by far the largest man William had ever laid eyes on. He had a difficult time imagining that people could get much larger than that, yet the Highlanders all had a chuckle at his comment.

"Oh lad," Gabrahn said, putting an arm around William's shoulder as they walked, "Hamish dwarfs Gregor th' same as Gregor dwarfs us"

William simply shook his head. "I really have to meet him," he finally said.

"Ah, well, ye can probably forget about that unless ye plan t' visit th' Highlands, lad," Gregor said. "'Twould take th' end o' th' world t' get Hamish away from his home. He has nae interest in th' goings-on in Tur or anywhere else for that matter. As far as Hamish is concerned, there's naught worth doing outside th' Highlands. He's happy spending his days tending th' farm and his nights tending Rebecca."

"His wife?" William was almost afraid to ask, but Gregor confirmed it was so. After pondering exactly how to pose his next question, William continued, "Is she…"

"A big lass?" Gabrahn interjected. "Nae, just yer average size o' woman."

"The Four Faces of God smile on her, then," replied William.

They were well past the church now, storefronts and stone buildings coming into view before them as they drew nearer to the docks. These buildings were markedly different from the homes they had seen earlier, simple stone edifices with no sense of frippery. Where the houses had been sculpted and ornamented to please the eye, these buildings were strictly functional in form. Most of these buildings were of only a single story, humble taverns and ordinary businesses that were nonetheless inviting in their austerity. Here and there among the buildings were inns and shops that required an extra story for whatever reason, but even these larger structures exuded a sense of humility. The really fancy buildings had gutters, and the ridiculously extravagant ones had awnings to provide shade and shelter to their patrons. The shops had no-nonsense monikers, usually named after the proprietor. *Gunther's Smithy* was the standard. A thatch-roofed hovel had a wooden sign bearing the word *APOTHECARY* scribbled by hand, which was prosaic but seemed to fit right in. The most creative business title by far was *McRofaly's Magnificent Keepsakes and Aureate Regalia (Precious Hand-Carved Stones for the Lord or Lady)*, belonging to what was actually a rather humble single-story brick building that William thought looked more like a home than a jeweler's shop. Then again, William reminded himself, many of these storefronts were indeed homes as well. Most merchants who were well enough off to afford a permanent building made their workplace serve double duty as their residence.

After only a couple of wrong turns at buildings that looked deceptively familiar William finally caught sight of their destination. "Here we are, gentlemen," he announced, raising an arm and gesturing with an open palm, as if presenting a prize. "The Crown Rose."

It looked more like a house than a business, a two-story building constructed of brick and stone and detailed with whitewashed wood. Trellises overgrown with ivy climbed the side walls. Small chimneys ran along the perimeter of the roof at regular intervals. These vented the fireplaces of the individual inn rooms but gave no smoke now, in late summer. Smoke did escape from the larger chimney that rose from the rear of the building, out of the kitchen, wafting the irresistible aroma of finely seasoned meat over the surrounding area. While the surrounding buildings were packed so tightly together that a man could barely fit in the alleyway between them, the Crown Rose was situated to itself on a lush green lawn of tended grass. A picket fence surrounded the lawn, opening into an arched gateway at the front, where stablehands waited to take patrons' horses upon arrival or fetch them upon their departure. A signpost stuck out from the arch of the gate, the wooden sign proclaiming in bold cursive script that this was indeed *The Crown Rose*. As was common with signs found in Tamendad, an illustration accompanied the inn's title, a picture of a red rosebud with a golden crown hovering above it. A cobbled walk led from the street, beneath the wooden arch, all the way to the front entrance. On either side of this walk were flowerbeds in full summer bloom, and rosebushes grew at regular intervals around the building itself. Truth be told, the Crown Rose would have made a much nicer home than most of the houses in Tamendad.

"She's a right bonny thing," Gregor said. "Ye've led us t' a palace when we asked for an inn."

"Aye, and m' guess is th' food's nae half bad, either," Angus agreed.

The stablehand positioned outside nodded as they passed, and if his look at the Highlanders lasted a bit longer than his look at William, it still did not approach the blatant gawks they had received from the townspeople. There was a certain standard of professionalism that was expected of the Crown Rose staff. The Highlanders nodded to the stablehand as they each passed under the wooden archway in turn, and a couple of them offered a pleasant "good t' see ye" as they passed by. Together the six made their way up the cobblestone walk to the front entrance.

The proprietor of the Crown Rose was a plump and pleasant man by the name of Torrance Mayhew. Master Mayhew was middle aged, bald on top of his head with a line of gray hair curving around the bottom. He had soft blue eyes and a bulbous nose with little red lines that betrayed his love of drink to anyone who knew the signs.

It was Mayhew himself who greeted the six unexpected guests in the common room of the Crown Rose, a well lit antechamber furnished with comfortable benches on which patrons could relax while their tables were prepared. Aside from the main entrance the only other door in the common room was an ornate oak door that led into the main dining room. Mayhew stood behind a small lectern positioned in front and to the left of this door, upon which rested a large leather-bound book along with an inkpot and a quill for the recording of reservations. He was dressed in a black tunic embroidered with gold thread, a fine pair of black breeches, and black boots made of supple leather, the finest formalwear even in the dead heat of late summer. A handkerchief was lying across the top of the lectern, in reach whenever he needed it to dab the beads of sweat from his large forehead. Torrance smiled up from his tome as the door opened, and his smile did not falter a bit as one young nobleman and five Highlanders walked into his establishment. He clasped his hands together in front of himself in a manner that was simultaneously professional and inviting and strode over from around the lectern to greet his customers.

"Young Lord Stuart-Camen, it has been too long since you have graced the Crown Rose with your presence," he said pleasantly and bowed a deep bow, placing one hand on his sizable stomach and throwing the other up in the air behind his ample backside. "And you have brought the talk of the town with you! Gentlemen, may I say to you, *céad mile failte.*"

Gregor stared for a moment. William was not sure exactly what had just transpired, but Gregor's demeanor shifted immediately to extreme cheer as he rushed forward to clasp both hands around Mayhew's forearm, just as he had done with William upon first meeting him. Gregor and Torrance Mayhew now broke into a rather loud conversation in a language that William could make neither heads nor tails of, rhythmic yet guttural. He looked over his shoulder to Angus, who seemed as pleased at whatever had just happened as Gregor was. Angus noticed the perplexed look on William's face and leaned forward to speak softly.

"'Tis th' old tongue, lad. Th' tongue our ancestors spoke. Th' speech is well preserved in th' Highlands and Glens, but we dinnae expect t' hear it spoken among ye Turish." William nodded with a thoughtful look. Gregor and Torrance finished up their brief discourse in the old tongue and the rest of the men gathered around.

"You gentlemen will be needing a table for six?" asked Mayhew, returning to his business tone. "And will you be staying with us tonight?"

"Aye, we'll be needing t' rent yer inn," responded Gregor.

Mayhew narrowed his eyebrows a bit, looking just a tad confused at the Highlander's request. "Yes, you will be needing rooms," he said again, making sure he and Gregor were on the same page.

"Aye, rooms," Gregor clarified. "All th' rooms ye've got. We want th' whole place."

William gave a bit of a start and looked at Gregor with wide, confused eyes. None of the other Highlanders seemed a bit surprised by Gregor's request to rent out the most expensive inn in Tamendad.

"Well," Mayhew said after a thoughtful pause, "I have rented out the entire establishment upon occasion. We have no guests staying with us tonight, though several people do have reservations in the main dining room. You could take your meals in a private dining room if you would like, but there is, of course, the matter of finances. A common room caries a charge of four gold marks by the night, and we have two suites carrying a charge of twelve."

Gregor raised his hand to cut Mayhew off. "Honor yer dinner guests t'night, but dinnae accept any more reservations. M' lads and I would like th' whole place t' ourselves as soon as it be possible." As he spoke he moved his hand to his tartan and retrieved a folded piece of parchment, extending it for Torrance Mayhew's inspection. Mayhew reached out and gently took it from the Highlander's grasp. Unfolding it, he looked it over and immediately began nodding.

"Ah," said Torrance Mayhew, not looking up from the paper. "Yes. Well. I shall see to it immediately. By tomorrow evening the entirety of the facilities will be yours and yours exclusively. For the time being I shall have all the rooms prepared, along with our best private dining room. If you would be so kind as to wait here for a moment, gentlemen, I will set the staff in order." Mayhew returned the parchment to Gregor and excused himself.

"What did you show him?" William asked excitedly as soon as Mayhew had gone.

"Just m' letter o' credit, lad." Gregor said, shrugging his shoulders nonchalantly. He held the letter out to William, who took it and opened it like he expected to find the meaning of life stamped inside. What he did find inside was written in Prima Tonce, the official language of the Antrelican Church, but William was familiar with the layout of a letter of credit. He saw it was authorized by Patrum Carney Gruer of Duerhein, notarized and authenticated by Patrum Antonius Dunleavy, Master Postulant of Tamendad, and signed into the name of Gregor MacDugal of the Clan MacDugal. While not fluent in the Holy Tongue, William had picked up enough Prima Tonce during his schooling to recognize the phrase *kalos signae arumé*.

One thousand gold marks. Try as William might, he could not think of a time in his life when he had seen that amount of coin all at one time, even as prosperous as his family was. Yet he knew how letters of credit worked. Gregor had at some point before leaving his home delivered one thousand gold marks into the possession of Patrum Carney Gruer in Duerhein, wherever that was exactly, and had been given this letter in return. For all intents and purposes, the piece of parchment William held in his hands was worth one thousand Turish marks of gold. His head was swimming a little, and his whole first impression of Gregor and his companions was melting away.

"Gregor, where did you get this kind of money?" William stammered, looking back and forth between the big Highlander and the letter.

"Ah, lad," Gregor said, shrugging his shoulders, "let's just say I'm well off, shall we?"

Mayhew returned to the common room before long, his ample forehead now covered in a sheen of sweat since he had left his handkerchief lying on the lectern. "The preparations have been made, gentlemen. Will you be taking a meal presently or do you wish to retire to your rooms before dining?" Everyone agreed that a break to freshen up was much needed before supping, and the Highlanders were escorted to their rooms by Mayhew himself.

The rooms were all located on the second floor, though referring to it as an actual floor was a bit of an embellishment. The second floor actually consisted of a balcony that ran around the entire perimeter of the main dining room. Every guest room thus afforded a view of the town, since there were no rooms in the middle of the building. This cut down on the Crown Rose's profitability as an inn, but the added ambiance made Torrance Mayhew's rather exorbitant room fees almost agreeable. Gregor and Angus each claimed one of the suites for themselves and left Liam, Gabrahn, and Wallace to choose whichever rooms caught their fancy. Hot water and towels were brought to each of the rooms, and William freshened up in Gregor's suite. After allowing themselves a brief respite, the Highlanders convened downstairs in the Crown Rose's nicest private dining room to take an early supper.

At the center of the room was a large mahogany table set for six. A crystal chandelier hung above the table, its oil lamps already lit although it was only just approaching evening. A bay window gave a view of the flower garden on the east lawn of the Crown Rose, full of lavender and honeysuckle. Tapestries decorated the walls, depicting waterfalls and forest glades.

William and the Highlanders were seated and immediately called for food and drink. Soon the table was a cornucopia of different foods: two different kinds of roast, bowls full of potatoes and beans and cabbage, various soups and breads, pheasant and grouse, venison steaks, an assortment of seafood and a variety of warm, crusty breads. The Highlanders devoured it all with what William at first took for ravenous hunger, but he soon came to realize that the Highlanders simply shared the same passion for good food that they seemed to hold for all of life's pleasures. They ate with a disregard for propriety that would have turned most noblemen's faces two shades of red. William, who had quite a disregard for propriety himself at times, at least for a nobleman's son, very much enjoyed being a part of it. He did not take much from the Highlanders' feast, still feeling full from his lunch at home, but he sampled from this dish and that, finding it all to be delicious.

After their initial furious round of devouring the feast before them, the Highlanders fell to picking at the remains and eventually just took to nursing the three bottles of whiskey they had ordered along with their food. Gregor reclined against the high back of his winged chair and sighed a contented sigh, gazing at the light refracting through the crystal of the chandelier. William saw his opportunity to ask the question he had really wanted to ask all along but had put off because he thought it impolite to ask too soon. He leaned over the arm of his chair toward Gregor, who still was fixed on the little rainbows of light emitted by the chandelier.

"Gregor?" William said in a hushed voice, though not so quiet that the other four would think he was up to something. Gregor came back to reality.

"Food and drink go straight to m' head, lad," he said. "Something ye want?"

"Well, I was just wondering, it's been so long since any Highlanders have visited Tamendad, and then the five of you just show up one afternoon. Don't take this the wrong way, but I was just wondering what brought you all this way?"

Gregor nodded. His manner told William he had been expecting this question to come out eventually, but was glad it had not been the first thing out of William's mouth.

"Ah, well, lad, 'tis a story t' be told, but simple at any rate. It really started o'er Summerfeast a few weeks back, when m' lads and I were hunting together in th' forests around Duerhein, though t' say we were hunting is t' stretch th' truth a bit. Mostly we were sitting in th' woods drinking whiskey, and th' only thing we were shooting 'twas shite. I shall tell ye plain, William, we've all been busy 'round Duerhein o' late, seeing t' King Stodlemeyer's latest round o' taxes for us." William thought Gregor looked almost like he was about to spit as he named the king. "But anyway, th' conversation turned sour, with how much work th' king's demands make for these days and such, and that was when we made th' decision. 'Twas Angus's idea at th' first, as I recall…"

"Aye, 'twas," Angus's deep voice interrupted. William looked to find that Angus and the other Highlanders had turned their attention toward Gregor and himself.

"I merely suggested we could all use a holiday, though," Angus continued. "I dinnae suggest going north."

"Nae, that was my idea," Wallace jumped in. He paused to take a long drink from his whiskey. He nodded as he swallowed the last of it down, looking as though he was agreeing wholeheartedly with himself, and then continued. "Well, I just thought that we had all seen about all th'

Highlands had t' offer, and knew th' Glens just about as well, but we had ne'er taken th' time t' see Andoria or Tamendad."

"Aye," continued Gregor, "and we all assumed there had t' be something worth seeing here, else nae self-respecting Turishman would e'er live so close t' us barbarians." Gregor gave a toothy grin, and the other four all laughed heartily.

Liam spoke up after the laughter had died away. "Truth be told, we were beginning t' think we had made a mistake. Till we met ye, that is."

"Aye t' that, lad," agreed Gabrahn. "William's been more help than we could e'er expect."

"Aye, yer acts have marked ye friend, and we'll nae forget it, lad," Angus said to William, the gruffness of his voice supplanted by the words he spoke. Gregor nodded solemnly and pounded his fist on the table. The others, even Angus, quieted at once and turned their attention fully to the big Highlander at the head of the table. When Gregor began to speak, William understood why the other four followed him. His voice was serious and solemn, and he took great care in stringing his words together.

"We've ridden north from our homes into a strange land, where we were nae certain if we would even be welcome. William has shown us only kindness and offered only friendship, and asked naught in return. Lift yer cups and drink t' him, lads, William Stuart-Camen o' Tamendad, friend and kinsman t' th' Clan MacDugal." The other Highlanders lifted their glasses, after giving Wallace some time to refill his whiskey. Together they all called out, "*Slàinte, sàimhe, gràis*," and drank deeply. William did not know exactly what the toast meant, but he had a pretty good guess.

Kinsman. He liked the sound of it.

After taking their early supper, all retired to Gregor's suite. Angus called for two more bottles of whiskey before they left, both varieties different from the three they had sampled with their meal. Wallace requested a salve for his arm, and muttered under his breath at the jeers this brought from the others. Once up in Gregor's suite, Angus mumbled something to himself about older brothers and how Gregor's suite was larger than his own, though the look in his eyes as he said it was playful. They all settled into the chairs of the central room. Conversation renewed itself, and the bottles of whiskey were passed around. William, who reneged at first when offered the bottles, eventually broke down and took a moderate draught from the darker of the two whiskeys. It burned like liquid fire in his throat but spread out into a warm and cozy feeling upon hitting his stomach. He liked it and disliked it at the same time, and occasionally took a drink when the bottles came around to him. William had been drinking wine with his meals for three years now, but he had only tried stronger drink once before, sneaking it out of his father's study, and he soon found himself feeling just a bit lightheaded and more talkative than he had been anytime in recent memory. The conversation grew louder and became seasoned with expletives, and William's boisterousness increased along with the Highlanders'. Subjects came and went with less and less transition, soon seeming to William as if the topic changed each time anyone in the room thought of one more exciting than the present and blurted it out. When the subject of swords and swordsmanship came up, William jumped on it.

"It's not that I don't think they work," he said, gesturing to Gregor's claymore with his right hand and lifting a bottle to his lips with his left. "It's just...how in the name of Hidalgo Sanctus can you use something like that in a battle? It must be like swinging a lamppost."

"Nae," said Angus loudly, shaking his head in disagreement. "A claymore does more damage than a lamppost, and I speak from experience there."

"He does at that, he does at that," agreed Wallace quickly, and his look said it was not a lie. William would have pursued such a claim at any other time, but with his mind wrapped in a warm blanket of whiskey he brushed it off.

"Well Angus, I'm just saying...my broadsword probably weighs a fifth of what your claymore does, and sometimes it still gives me trouble when I try to double back on a slash. If you don't kill whatever you swing at in one hit, you'd leave yourself wide open to attack."

"Ah, lad, come off it," said Gregor, approaching William from the side. William turned to face the big Highlander, and his world shifted just slightly as he did so. Gregor put a big arm around William's shoulders, swaying slightly back and forth with him. Gregor took the bottle from William and tipped it to his lips. The draught Gregor took was big enough, William was certain, to kill him if he attempted it. After draining half of what remained in the bottle, Gregor loosed a loud belch and continued. "'Tis been m' experience if ye cut something with a claymore and it dinnae die in one hit, ye're pretty much shagged and shorn, if ye catch m' drift."

William was silent for a moment, thinking over what Gregor had just said. He began to giggle. His giggle soon became a snicker, his snicker a laugh, and his laugh an all-out guffaw. Gregor had to hold him upright to keep him from falling to the floor. Everyone in the room laughed, partially with William, partially at him.

William brushed tears out of his eyes with the sleeve of his shirt, and glanced around the room. He was not nearly as intoxicated as some of the Highlanders, though Gregor and Angus both seemed more sober than he. William could not guess how that was possible. Angus had consumed four times what William had, and Gregor twice as much as Angus. While pondering this, his eyes fell to the large window overlooking the streets of Tamendad, and William realized for the first time that the sun had already set.

"I've missed supper," he said. The Highlanders all looked at him.

"Aye, I could do with a bite m'self," said Liam, rubbing his belly. "At least some bread t' soak up th' whiskey."

"No, I mean I've missed supper with my family. Mother will be worried."

Gregor nodded. "Mothers do tend t' worry o'ermuch about their sons, lad. Even when they're full grown."

That was what William liked best about these men. They saw him as a man, treated him like a man. Even though he was treated with respect by his friends and family, and likewise by the townspeople, he was still seen as barely out of his childhood, a man in the loosest sense of the word. The Highlanders, who seemed to judge him more by his actions than his age, treated him as an equal.

"I have to take my leave gentlemen," he said, and was met by a rousing chorus of disagreement. This also pleased him.

"One more drink t' keep ye warm, lad," beckoned Angus, extending a bottle out to him.

"Aye, yer ma will nae be sending th' watch out after ye just yet," said Gabrahn. William was not so certain about that.

"C'mon, lad, the night is young, and so are ye," said Wallace, mischief brewing in his dark eyes. "Th' fun is just starting."

William wanted nothing more at the moment than to bow to their requests and commit to a night of carousing, but the sight of Gregor resolutely shaking his head brought him back to his senses. "Hush yer tongues, lads," Gregor said. "William's a nobleman with responsibilities, and I think we can all understand something o' that." Gregor turned and looked at William. "Lad, 'tis been a hopper, but ye're needed elsewhere and I know how that goes. Stop by on th' morrow, if ye can. We shall be here." He clapped William on the back, and William nodded in return.

"Wallace is right about one thing, though," said Gregor, returning his attention to his kinsmen. "Th' night is young, and there be nae sense in us wasting it in an inn room. We're on holiday, with a whole city t' see. Let's be about it, shall we?"

Upon stepping out onto the balcony, the Highlanders and William became the focus of attention for the entire host down below. The main dining room was packed wall to wall, not a seat left in the house. Torrance Mayhew had obviously capitalized on Gregor's permission to honor dinner reservations that night and packed the house with people eager to catch a glimpse of Tamendad's most talked-about visitors. Some people even broke into applause as the Highlanders came into view. Others were more reserved, and a very few, William thought, looked less than enthused over their presence.

"Ye'd think we were Hidalgo Sanctus in th' flesh," said Liam in a hushed voice, returning the stares of the Turishmen with a level of incredulity.

"Pay it nae mind, Liam," said Gregor, and turned for the stairs. As they descended into the main dining room some dinner guests rose from their seat to approach them. Gregor raised his hand and shook his head and no sooner than he had done so several members of the staff were in motion, showing all the patrons of the Crown Rose back to their seats. Gregor nodded politely to everyone in the dining room and called out a hearty, "Good t' see ye this even." Most of the guests smiled in return. A few shouted their own salutations, but these were lost as Gregor and his companions exited the dining room into the common room with Torrance Mayhew in tow. Once they were all alone Gregor turned his attention on the proprietor of the Crown Rose.

"Well, Mayhew, I'm glad we could make ye some coin t'night." There was only a hint of exasperation in his voice.

"I took the liberty of fetching your horses from the Governor's stables, so they will be available to you at a moment's notice," said Mayhew, and it was painfully obvious he wanted to change the subject. "Will you be needing them?"

"Nae, we shall see th' city afoot t'night."

Wallace requested that more whiskey be waiting in Gregor's suite upon their return, and then the Highlanders and William left the Crown Rose together.

"We part ways," Gregor said once they were in the street. "Th' Four Faces o' God smile on ye, William. I hope t' see ye on th' morrow." The other Highlanders offered similar sentiments, then turned and headed deeper into the heart of the trade district. William stood for a moment to watch them go, wanting nothing more than to follow after and experience the underbelly of Tamendad. Instead he sighed once, turned around, and headed for home, only his thoughts to keep him company.

CHAPTER THREE

THE MISSING MARE

During the day the trade district of Tamendad overflowed with tourists and townspeople alike, wandering through the bricked streets, peering this way and that, browsing through the shops for eccentricities. It was a markedly different place by night, William found, when the respectable people had long since retired, and the sailors and off-duty constabulary came out to join the merchants themselves and claim the district for their own. Every tavern was filled with raucous customers hefting frothy mugs of ale.

William made his way through the streets of the trade district, looking in through the window of each tavern he passed. In each was to be found a boisterous celebration of life and friends and drink that he had never dreamed of before tonight. He almost expected to see Gregor, Angus and all the Highlanders at the center of attention in each tavern he passed by, though he knew they had headed the other direction upon parting outside the Crown Rose. It was just that they would fit so well in any of the barrooms he saw. They belonged in this environment. *Not like you. This is not your world. You had better enjoy it while it lasts.* William shrugged off the thought. There was no sense getting bent out of shape over it.

The boisterousness of the taverns was offset by the dark silence of the storefronts, which had long since been locked up tight for the evening. The merchants themselves were out either celebrating a good day's business or drowning their sorrows. The look of the dark, dead buildings unsettled William slightly. He was unaccustomed to any place looking so empty. Even when everyone was fast asleep in his part of the residential district there would always be at least one lamp lit in every house just in case of late-night visitors bringing important news. Some of the larger homes kept the entire ground floor as bright as day, and the Governor's house was always alight. The darkness of the storefronts that surrounded William made them look abandoned, almost made the whole district seem like a ghost town. William could not be terribly frightened by the looks of them, though, because throughout his entire walk out of the trade district he was surrounded by a muddled sea of drinking songs and sailor's shanties that drifted out into the streets from every tavern and mixed into an indistinguishable carol of inebriation. The sound warded off any visions William might have otherwise had of a deserted Tamendad, continuously insisting that everyone in the district was alive and well and very, very drunk.

The storefronts and taverns began to thin out and William saw the church up ahead. He considered for a moment stopping to make a devotional but quickly decided that doing so would go much more smoothly when his thoughts were no longer adrift on a current of Highlands whiskey. He was not drunk – at least, he didn't think he was – but there was a slight stagger in his step and he was certain anyone who came within arm's reach of him would be able to smell what he had been up to. He respectfully made the Sign of the Compass as he passed under the church's steeple and continued on his way home.

Before long he saw the silhouette of his home come into view ahead, barely illuminated by the soft glow of the lamps that lined the streets. The common room on the ground floor was well lit and there was a glow in the window of his father's study. William swallowed hard as he turned onto the cobbled walkway of his house. The front door opened as he stepped up to it, Reynolds's wrinkled face smiling at him from across the threshold.

"Welcome home, Lord William," the old butler said, escorting him inside. William heard Reynolds sniffing the air softly as William passed him. There was little doubt the butler could smell alcohol on him, but the smile never left his lips. It was not the butler's place to discipline him. "Your mother and Julius have taken to bed for the evening, but your father is waiting for you in his study. He requested a word with you upon your return."

"Is he upset, Reynolds?" William's eyes were pleading. He wanted very much to hear that his father was not cross. It would make climbing the stairs to his study much easier.

"He is upset about something, Lord William. Lord Jonathan has been upset all afternoon." Reynolds's words seemed to add a weight of fifty pounds to William's shoulders. "I do not think you are the only thing bothering him, though. He came home upset over something well before you missed dinner."

"Great. Thanks, Reynolds." William was looking up the stairway as he spoke.

"Shall I have Nelsie prepare you a plate for when your business with your father is complete?"

"No, I'm fine," said William, sounding distant. "Get some sleep. It's past your bedtime." William heard Reynolds harrumph behind him as he started up the stairs. The butler always got an offended air about him whenever anyone insinuated that he slept too much, but he never argued about it because he did, in fact, sleep too much.

Badgering Reynolds did nothing to lift William's spirits. He could not imagine that his father was seriously upset over his tardiness, but Reynolds had been the Stuart-Camen butler since long before William had been born, and if anyone was able to tell that something was bothering Jonathan Stuart-Camen, it was Reynolds. The steps creaked slightly under William's boots as he slowly took each one. The upstairs hallway was dark, the sconces already extinguished. William could make out the rectangle of light at the end of the hallway that was the door to his father's study. It had been years since William had been afraid of the dark, but each step down that hallway was a trial.

When he found himself in front of the entrance to his father's study, William took a deep, soothing breath. It was not enough to keep his heart from skipping a beat as he raised his hand to knock. He paused there for a moment, holding his hand motionless before rapping his knuckles against the oak thrice. He was unaware that he was holding his breath. There was no immediate answer. Just as William prepared to knock again, he heard his father's voice from inside.

"Come in, William."

William opened the door and the sweet smell of pipe tobacco greeted him. Stepping into the room, William saw his father sitting behind his desk, holding his favorite pipe in his left hand and swirling a glass of brandy in his right. He had that look about him that he always got whenever he was lost in deep concentration, a look that William could only describe as distance, as though he were a million miles away even when he sat within arm's reach. Jonathan motioned to one of the chairs that sat before his desk. William had a seat in it.

"I hear from half the noblemen in town that you made some interesting new friends today," said Jonathan, trying his best to give his son a warm smile. William could tell it took some effort.

"Aye," replied William. "I mean, yes. Five Highlanders, all from someplace called Duerhein. I supped with them this evening at the Crown Rose. They rented the whole place to themselves, Father! Gregor, the one who leads them, had a letter of credit for a thousand gold marks!"

Jonathan nodded. "Gregor MacDugal of the Clan MacDugal," he said when William was finished. William was somewhat surprised that his father knew Gregor's full title, but kept quiet for the moment. His father continued after the briefest of pauses. "You made some influential friends today, William, though I doubt you had any idea you were doing so. The Clan MacDugal is one of the most powerful clans in Glenisle, and Gregor MacDugal is a very prominent member. Some might even say he heads the clan, though the head of a Glenish clan is more difficult to determine than the head of a Turish noble house. Either way, he holds more sway in the politics of Glenisle than anyone in this town holds in the politics of Tur."

William had absolutely no idea what to say in return to that. Gregor was obviously rich – William figured out that much upon seeing his letter of credit – but he had assumed Gregor was just a well-to-do landowner. Until now he had no idea he had spent the afternoon with one of the most important men in Glenisle. He wanted to ask his father a thousand questions about it. In the end, though, he could not think of a suitable way to initiate such a line of questioning and decided the timing was inappropriate anyway. He quickly changed subjects.

"Father, I'm sorry I missed supper. I was conversing with Gregor and his friends and totally lost track of time. I hurried home as soon as I realized the hour." William squirmed slightly in his chair. He hated making excuses to his father.

Jonathan's expression did not change from the contemplative look he had worn since William had entered. "Conversing," he said, staring absently ahead. He took a long draw off his pipe and exhaled slowly, the smoke encircling his head like an angel's halo. "Yes, Highlanders have an interesting way of conversing, don't they, son? In my experience it almost always involves quite a bit of liquor."

William shifted uncomfortably in his very comfortable chair. He wanted to protest, to object, to look his father squarely in the eyes and say that he was of age, a man and no longer a child, and that there was nothing wrong with a nobleman sharing a common cup with gentlemen he was entertaining. But there was a part of him deep down inside that was always reduced to a diffident child whenever his father's steady gaze fell upon him.

"I'm sorry, father," he mumbled, looking squarely at his knees.

"There's no need to be sorry, William," his father said, and there was a consoling quality to his voice that William was relieved to hear. "I was younger than you are now when I had my first serious drink, and I can tell by the look of you that you imbibed in much greater moderation than I did. Most boys your age would have overindulged to the point of having to crawl into this library on their hands and knees."

William laughed. His father did not.

34

"Father, if it isn't my lateness or my drinking, what is bothering you? Reynolds said you wanted a word with me?"

Jonathan took a sip of brandy and cleared his throat. "I'm certain your mother told you that a prize mare came up missing this morning." It went without saying that if Lyllian had failed to mention this, Nelsie would certainly have not.

William nodded. "The one that was to be dower for Winston. I heard."

"Well, we found her this afternoon." Jonathan gave William a grim look.

"Dead?" William asked.

"Worse than dead. Mutilated. We found what was left of her strung up in a tree."

William's heart sank. "Someone stole it?" he asked. It was very unlikely that particular horse had been taken at random. If someone had snuck onto Jonathan Stuart-Camen's land to steal that particular horse, it most likely meant someone had objections to the marriage.

"No, I don't think so. Part of the fence had fallen where we kept her, and I believe she most likely jumped it herself. That one always had spirit in reserve. Whoever did it probably just came across her in the open."

William had trouble picturing it. He had never ridden the mare himself but he had handled her and knew how much fight she had in her. One person had no chance of bringing her down. Two would have had the fight of their lives. It would have taken a group of at least four or five.

Something clicked in William's head. He did not like where this was leading. "Why would anyone slaughter a good horse?" he asked, reluctant to approach the subject that sat mocking him in his mind.

"I don't know. She had made it a good way from here, so I doubt it was anyone from town. A lot of the carcass was missing, and I would almost say whoever killed her did it for food, except for..." His father paused to take another sip. "There was quite a mess. It was savage. Barbaric." William winced at the last two words.

"Killing a purebred mare for food? That's stupid. There's no reason..." William found great difficulty in expressing his thoughts.

"No, there isn't." His father shook his head and clamped the stem of his pipe between his teeth, chewing on it absently.

"Father..."

That was all William could say. He could not find the words. There was a long, uncomfortable silence in the study. William found his mind roaming toward unsettling thoughts. He mirrored his father's troubled

35

expression. Both father and son sat not looking at each other, each lost in his own thoughts.

"I do not want you to mention this to anyone, William," his father said, breaking the silence at last. "Right now the only people who know are the people in this house. And Winston," he added after a pause. "I talked to him as soon as I got back to town, and we have already agreed upon a replacement mare, though Winston insisted it was unnecessary. No reason for me to lose two of my best mares, he said. His mother should have named him Agathas, because the Face of Beneficence smiles through him."

William could see how uncomfortable his father was. He and Winston had been fast friends since boyhood. He had promised the mare to Winston as a gift, and even though Winston had been more than understanding about the situation William knew how much his father despised leaving his promises unfulfilled. "Anyway, everyone who knows about it as of now can be trusted not to jump to conclusions. But if word gets out, some people might start getting suspicious of the wrong people for the wrong reasons."

"I understand, Father. I won't mention it to anyone."

"Good. It's better that this remains strictly a family affair."

William pursed his lips, taking a deep breath through his nose. He had to ask the question that was burning in his mind. Regardless of the answer, he had to know. "Father, you don't believe Gregor and the other Highlanders did it, do you?"

"No," his father replied, and his lack of hesitation reassured William. "No, I do not believe that for one moment. But," Jonathan was suddenly very, very serious, and William's eyes widened, "there are some people in this township who would believe it, and without cause or justification. So my advice, son, is to keep silent on the matter if you want to protect your new friends."

William nodded earnestly. He thought of the image he had allowed himself to dream up, of how even he had suspected the Highlanders to be brutally, barbarically violent before he had really gotten to know them. He also thought of how a lot of influential people in Tamendad would not rethink this initial suspicion, no matter how likable Gregor and his friends turned out to be. "I will not speak a word of it to anyone," he said at last.

"Very good. Now, I have some business to be about. You have had quite a full day. I'm sure you want to wash up and retire for the evening."

"Yes, Father," said William respectfully, rising from his chair. He moved to the door.

"Goodnight, son," his father called after him, not looking up from his desk.

"Goodnight, Father," William answered, pulling the door behind him as he exited his father's study.

William did in fact want nothing more after speaking with his father than to wash up and retire for the evening, but he lay awake staring at the ceiling long after he had stripped off his clothes and climbed into bed. A hundred different thoughts filled his mind. Gregor and the other Highlanders were not responsible, could not be responsible. Still, if they had not killed the mare, who had? Maybe they had seen something, anything, on their ride north to Tamendad that could be useful in finding the culprit, but William could not even broach the subject with Gregor. Or could he? He was supposed to keep silent on the matter to protect Gregor and the others from false accusation. William could not see how telling Gregor himself about the mare could put him and his friends in any danger. Unless, that was, they had actually been the ones who did it, in which case mentioning it to Gregor might actually put William in danger. William shook this idea off. Deep down inside he knew that they would not do something like that. He simply had to ask Gregor and find out what, if anything, he had seen on his ride north to Tamendad, but that meant breaking his word that he would not speak of it outside the family.

Every corner William turned in his mind led to even more difficult questions. When sleep finally did come upon him it was fitful and restless, filled with bad dreams of screaming, mutilated horses and innocent Highlanders locked in stocks. William rose from his bed the next morning still uncertain as to the proper course of action. He filled the washbasin with cool water and submerged his face in it. The cold rush cleared his senses and snapped him to awareness, but did nothing to answer his many questions or settle the queasy feeling in the pit of his stomach. He pulled on clean clothes and made his way down to breakfast. Perhaps he could discuss it further with his father, though for the first time in his life William was uncertain that this would be of any help.

As he descended the stairs the aroma of cooked sausages and hot tea greeted him, and he suddenly found himself to be very hungry. He entered the dining room to find himself the last member of the family down for breakfast. His father sat sipping a cup of tea, leafing through the morning's first letters. His mother was discussing something with Reynolds, who still had sleep in his eyes, but she looked up and bid William good morning upon his entrance. Julius sat with his elbows on the table, flipping idly through *A History of the Turish Oracles from*

Bonaventure to Aedmund. William had never been allowed to read at the table, but Jonathan and Lyllian had long since given up on trying to keep Julius's books out of the dining room. William took his place at the table, and Reynolds placed a plate before him. William ate hungrily.

"Letter from the Governor for you, son," said William's father, barely looking up from his reading.

William almost choked on a bite of potato. "From the Governor?" he repeated, as if he thought his hearing was off. "Why?"

"I do not make it a practice to read other men's mail," replied Jonathan.

William smiled in spite of himself. He liked being called a man, especially by his own father. Reynolds came forward and handed William a folded parchment, the letter in question. William studied it intently. It bore two different seals of red wax. The first was the Rearing Lion, the Royal Crest of the House of Chamberlain. The second was Governor Chamberlain's own personal seal, a fig tree with a serpent coiled around the trunk. William ran his hand over them, as if to make sure they were real.

"When did it come?" he asked without looking up from the letter.

"Less than an hour ago," he heard his mother say. "It came at first light."

Julius sat with his arms crossed over his book, staring intently at William. "Must be pretty important, brother. What are you waiting for? Let's see what it says."

"Now, now, Julius," Jonathan said, folding his own letter and laying it down on the table. "A man's letters are his business and his alone. What's on that paper is William's concern, not yours."

Julius looked for a moment like he might protest, but in the end just said, "Sorry, William. I didn't mean to overstep."

"No, it's okay. I don't mind. It's just, you know, my first letter of official business." William shrugged his shoulders. He felt silly. He ran his thumb under the edge of the parchment, releasing the seals, and unfolded the letter.

To Lord William of the House of Stuart-Camen, of Tamendad

From the desk of Lord Geoffery of the Royal House of Chamberlain, Governor and Right Ruler of Tamendad, written this Twenty-Sixth Day of Luthane, the Year Nine Hundred Eighty-Nine Posteriori Cataclymian.

Peace and greetings unto you, Lord William. I pray this

38

letter finds you in good health and good cheer. It has been brought to my attention by one of my advisors that we have received five most distinguished guests from Duerhein, in the Highlands to the south. It has further been brought to my attention that you have taken upon yourself the commission of acting as guide to the city for these gentlemen. If I may say so, Lord William, you take after your father in your hospitality and generosity.

My purpose in writing this letter is to express the hope that you will deliver unto these five gentlemen my invitation to dine with me at my house this evening, so that I may officially welcome them to our township. As you have already made the acquaintance of these gentlemen, I feel that an invitation offered by you would set them more at ease than an invitation offered by one of my messengers who would to them be but a stranger. Dinner shall be served at sundown, with brandy and tobacco to follow. An invitation is, of course, extended to yourself and your family. I eagerly anticipate your response.

Signed,

Geoffery of the House of Chamberlain

Governor and Right Ruler of Tamendad

William looked to his father. "Does Governor Chamberlain know about the missing mare?" he asked. Julius tore his eyes away from his book at hearing this question, looking first to William, then to his father, then back to William again. Jonathan and Lyllian looked at each other for a moment, and William's mother shook her head slightly.

"Not that I am aware," Jonathan said.

William nodded, looking over the letter a second time. "Well, we're all invited to dinner with the Governor tonight. The Highlanders are to be the guests of honor."

"It's high time I had a night off for a change," came Nelsie's voice from beyond the kitchen door. Everyone in the room laughed. Even Reynolds chuckled a bit, under his breath.

William hurried to get through his breakfast plate and bid his family a good morning. He did not want to keep the Governor waiting any longer than he had to. It was a pleasant day in Tamendad, the sun shining brightly and a northeastern wind bringing in the salty scent of the sea to season the air. When he reached the Crown Rose he noticed a new sign hanging below the nameplate on the arched entrance to the courtyard, which read *Reserved for Private Use*.

The streets around the Crown Rose were fuller than usual, teeming with people who had a gleam of intrigue in their eyes. Everyone watched the edifice with great interest, hoping to catch a glimpse of Tamendad's most talked-about visitors in years. William started up the cobbled walkway to the Crown Rose's entrance, feeling all the envious eyes upon him. Some of the most important people in town had to muck about the streets hoping for so much as a glimpse of the Highlanders, and here this whelp of a nobleman was strolling right into their inn as if they had all been fast friends since birth. William savored every step.

The front door of the Crown Rose was unlocked and unattended, and William let himself in. There was no one waiting in the common room, which did not surprise William seeing as though Torrance Mayhew had no reason to be expecting patrons. As he stepped through the doorway into the main dining room, William received a bit of a shock. One of the larger tables in the room was overturned, centerpiece and utensils strewn about carelessly on the floor. The gentle sound of snoring was coming from behind the table. Aside from whoever was snoring, the main dining room appeared deserted. William cautiously crept his way toward the overturned table, his hand involuntarily gripping the hilt of his broadsword as he went. As he passed the capsized table, the unconscious forms of Wallace and a woman William had never seen before came into view. She was pretty, probably somewhere in her middle twenties, with sandy brown hair disheveled around her face. They were both wrapped in a bed sheet and, so far as William could tell, were both naked underneath. William stood there for what seemed like a good little while, just staring. Finally he shifted, moving to place his hand on Wallace's bare shoulder. He shook gingerly, trying to rouse the sleeping Highlander. Wallace did not respond. William shook a little harder, and had to duck out of the way as Wallace bolted upright and took a wild swing in William's direction, all without opening his eyes.

"Bastard swine…nae respect for a lad…makes five this week." The incoherence in Wallace's voice told William that the Highlander had absolutely no intention of waking up anytime in the foreseeable future.

"He's just sleeping it off, honey," a sultry-sweet voice said. William jumped slightly, before he realized Wallace's lady companion was stirring. "He drank more last night than I've seen a man drink in a good while. My name's Loraine." The sandy haired woman extended a graceful hand, and William shook it lightly. Now that he reconsidered it, he realized he had met Loraine before. She was a member of the waitstaff at the Crown Rose.

"Charmed, madam," William said politely, making sure to keep his eyes focused firmly upon hers, and not upon any other part of her. "What happened last night?"

"Oh, the boys just had some fun entertaining some off-duty constables and it got out of hand," she said as she stretched. "Angus claimed he could wrestle three men at once, and the constables called him out. They're still down at the church getting patched up if you want to visit them."

"Oh, um, no," William said, scratching the back of his neck and surveying the main dining room. "My business is actually with Gregor. Is he in his suite?"

"Sure is, honey. You can go on up."

"Thank you. It was a pleasure meeting you, Loraine. Again, I mean." William turned to go, but stopped after only a few steps. He looked back to Loraine. "Is Master Mayhew upset over the damages?"

Loraine laughed a chirping laugh. "He was at first, but he had a long talk with Gregor about it. Gregor told him to tally up the cost of the damages, add ten percent, and put it on the bill. Torrance hasn't said a peep about it since." William nodded, and chuckled a bit. He climbed the stairs up to Gregor's suite.

"This had better be damned important, whoe'er ye be," came Gregor's voice from inside, even gruffer than usual, when William knocked. The big Highlander did not sound happy, and there was a perturbed expression on his face when he threw the door open. He was wearing his kilt and nothing else. At first William was afraid Gregor was about to rip his head off, but Gregor's angry expression melted upon seeing who it was.

"Ah, William, good t' see ye this morning!" Gregor grabbed William's forearm and shook vigorously. William smiled brightly in return.

"Good morning, Gregor. I hope I didn't disturb you."

"Nae, lad, Chelsie's still sound asleep. That lass cannae hold her liquor, 'tis a shame. Nice girl all the same, though." Gregor had a sly look about him.

"Chelsie?" William asked. He didn't really wonder all that much though.

"Aye, one o' th' cooks. Bonny little thing, she is. But enough o' that. Come in, lad." Gregor threw an arm around William and practically dragged him inside before he had a chance to accept or decline the offer.

"So what brings ye out this morning, lad?" Gregor asked as he and William sank down into two of the overstuffed chairs.

"Official business, actually," said William. "You and the others have been invited to dine as guests of honor with Governor Chamberlain tonight."

Gregor nodded, running his fingers through his beard. "Aye, sounds wonderful, lad. I look forward t' it."

William gave Gregor the details and sat a while longer, making small talk. Then he excused himself after politely declining breakfast. Once he was gone, Gregor sat back in his chair and sighed deeply. He had an uneasy feeling. It had been haunting him for a while now, and he could sense it in his lads, too. No one had mentioned it, but it had been there since well before their arrival in Tamendad, lingering on the fringes of the mind.

There was just something about that butchered mare they had come across in the woods that shook him to his core.

Chapter Four

More Unexpected Visitors

The sun was lazily approaching its bed on the western horizon, bathing all of Tamendad in long shadows. The peddlers in the open air market were bargaining last-minute sales at highly discounted prices, accepting that at this point in the evening any amount of coin in the pocket was preferable to carrying unsold goods back home for the night. The lamplighters were just beginning to make their rounds through the city, staving off the encroaching darkness with artificial illumination. Soon the warm smell of burning tallow would fill the streets, hinting at the scent of roast meat and vegetables and hopefully enticing some townspeople and visitors to take their supper at a tavern.

In his master suite at the Crown Rose, Gregor MacDugal stood before the full-length dressing mirror, adjusting his tartan across his chest. His kilt and tartan were freshly washed, as was his best cotton undershirt. His *duál* hung neatly at the left side of his face, the tip tightly wrapped with a bit of red leather to mark him the head of his family. The rest of his hair was neatly combed and tied back at the base of his neck. His beard was also combed and neat, and all of him smelled pleasantly of spices and bath salts. Gregor finished fidgeting with his tartan and glanced at his claymore, still resting upright in the corner of the room. He sighed. He still was uncertain about whether or not to wear it. In Duerhein, and anywhere else in the Highlands, a man would appear a fool arriving at a dinner invitation without his family sword. So far as Gregor could tell, it was not much different here among the Turish. He had noted that William wore his broadsword everywhere he went, and he had also noticed other well-to-do people strolling through the city streets with weapons at their hips. But he was also fully aware of the uncomfortable looks he received when he wore his claymore in public. These Tamendaders had come to accept broadswords and longswords as just another fashion accessory, but Gregor's great blade put them at alarm.

A knock at the door drew Gregor away from his thoughts. He opened the door to find Angus standing there in the hallway, a mirror image of himself except for the height difference and the tan leather strip that wrapped the end of his *duál*. Angus did not have his claymore either. He entered the suite and moved to the table, pouring himself a dram of whiskey. Gregor could tell his brother was nervous. Angus rarely drank before suppertime.

"Are ye wearing yer claymore t'night, brother?" Angus asked between sips.

Gregor was relieved that Angus was uncertain over protocol as well. It told him he was not making a mountain out of a molehill. "I dinnae know," he replied, after some hesitation. "What do th' other lads intend?"

"They're all going armed, but their weapons dinnae draw th' looks ours do, brother. Some people look at us like we were monsters or madmen when we have our swords with."

Gregor took a deep breath, looking once again to his sword in the corner. "Aye," he said at last, and the firmness in his voice seemed to startle his brother, who almost choked on his whiskey.

"Aye what, ye goat?" Angus said, sending his brother a smirk and wiping the whiskey from his chin. "It took an hour t' tend m' beard, and now I'll show up with it reeking o' liquor like some village drunkard."

Gregor did not acknowledge his brother's comment. "Aye, I'm wearing m' claymore t' dinner, and so are ye. We're MacDugal, and we wear MacDugal blades. Half this town saunters around armed and nae a person raises an eyebrow o'er it. We should be extended th' same courtesy."

Angus, who had moved to the washbasin and was now washing his beard, simply nodded, thoughtfully. "Aye, that's true." That was the end of it. Gregor strode resolutely to the corner of the room and snatched up his claymore. Once the strap was in place over his chest a look of relief immediately spread over his face.

"Damn tartan ne'er lays right without m' baldric under it," he said. The weight on his back was reassuring, and he needed reassurance for the subject he was about to broach. "Angus," Gregor said, hesitating in spite of himself.

Angus became immediately serious at the tone of Gregor's voice. "Aye, what is it, brother?"

"I intend t' tell th' Governor about that butchered mare we saw on th' ride," Gregor said, only a hint of uncertainty in his voice. Angus did not reply immediately. "Something about it has been bothering me since we came across it," Gregor added.

"Gregor, ye're head o' th' family, and more than that ye're m' older brother, and I'll defer t' any decision ye make, but I dinnae think it a good idea. We already discussed this. If we mention it t' anybody, especially th' Governor himself, we'll likely be suspected as th' ones who did it. As friendly as e'eryone seems here, ye know as well as I that there's suspicions t' be found beneath e'er smile. Ye've heard th' stories some o' th' Turish tell about our people. They think us barbarians at best. M' advice, if I be allowed t' give it, brother, is t' nae mention it unless th' Governor brings th' subject up. If ye're th' one t' bring that conversation t' th' table, it'll look like ye're trying t' distance yerself from it."

Gregor just nodded while Angus spoke. He knew his brother well enough to know that once Angus got on a roll, it was best just to shut up and let him finish. He did not talk much, but when he did, it came in torrents. After Angus had said his piece, Gregor spoke up. "Ye're m' brother and I love ye, Angus. I respect yer opinion in all I do, but I disagree with ye now. Whate'er did that t' that mare, 'twas nae a simple beast. That mare was nae killed for food, but for pleasure plain and simple. Whate'er killed it is dangerous, Angus, and it happened close enough t' this town that th' townspeople should know about it. The Governor has nae reason t' suspect us of anything, and from what I hear he's a good man. If he does suspect us…ah, well, he can get buggered."

"Aye, brother, as ye see it." That was what Angus always said when Gregor made a decision he did not agree with.

"All right then," said Gregor, giving himself one last look in the mirror. "Go strap on yer claymore, and then fetch th' others. I shall be waiting outside with th' horses."

"We're riding our horses t' th' Governor's?" Angus asked. He sounded surprised. It wasn't much of a walk.

"Aye, brother," Gregor responded. "We're going t' arrive in style, and show these Turish how barbarians do it." Gregor flashed a wink toward his brother as they both left the suite. Angus laughed as he made his way across the balcony to his own suite.

The main dining room had been set right again, and appeared as immaculate as ever. Only a handful of the waitstaff was on duty, as Gregor had informed Torrance Mayhew that he and his lads would not be dining there that night. Gregor made his way outside and down the cobbled walk, calling to the stablehand to bring the horses up. Gregor had been waiting for perhaps five minutes, standing where the walkway met the street with his arms crossed over his chest, smiling at everyone who passed and disregarding the uneasy looks his claymore brought, when he heard the voice calling to him.

"Escuse me there!"

Gregor turned in the direction of the voice, which was coming from down the street in the direction of the docks. The man waving and walking briskly toward him was short, trim and most definitely not Turish. He came up perhaps to Gregor's chin, if that. He had black, wavy hair down to his shoulders and a mustache of the same color which curved around the sides of his mouth and blended into the neatly trimmed whiskers on his chin. His complexion was that of a dark suntan, and he wore a very handsome smile. He was well dressed in black breeches and a billowing white shirt of silk covered by a vest the color of a fine wine, with golden embroidery in a flowing pattern. His well-polished black boots were turned down at the top. He wore a duelist's sabre on his left hip and a parrying dagger on his right, both finely crafted and bejeweled.

The man walked right up to Gregor and bowed low. He looked dignified even in humbling himself. He straightened and looked Gregor right in the eyes. He was a full head shorter than Gregor, and yet the way he carried himself, the confidence that bordered on cockiness exuding from him, made Gregor feel like the man's eyes were meeting his own straight on.

"*Compagno*, can you tell me whether es true someone has reserved this Crown Rose all to themselves?" He had a breathy accent, and he stressed the *wh* sound to almost ridiculous levels. It was obvious that Turish was not his first language.

"Aye, 'tis true," responded Gregor, pointing up to the sign above his head that said as much. "Why do ye ask, sir?" The curiosity was thick in his voice.

"Allow me to esplain myself," the black-haired man said. "My name es Julio Franco Francisco Ferdinan." Gregor's eyes widened a bit more at the mention of each successive name, and the black-haired man obviously noticed. "You may call me Ferdinan," he added. " I just arrived here by ship, and I have nowhere to spend the night. The gentlemen at the docks directed me here, saying es the best in town, but along the way I overheard mention that the entire establishment had been rented out for personal use. I was hoping I was misinformed. Tell me, do you know where I may find this man who has the place to himself, so I may discuss with him the possibility of procuring a room and a meal for myself?"

Gregor extended his hand. "'Twould be me. Gregor MacDugal o' th' Clan MacDugal, at yer service, sir, and a fellow stranger t' this town." They shook. "If I may be so bold," continued Gregor, "where do ye hail from, sir?"

"Of course," Ferdinan replied. "I come from Conquia, across the Melteric Ocean."

"Conquia, aye. Ye're a long way from home." Gregor felt compassion for Ferdinan. His own home was only two days' ride away, and Tamendad still made Gregor feel like a stranger in a strange land. He could only imagine how the Conquian felt.

"That I am, *compagno*. That I am." Ferdinan smiled ruefully, and made a sound halfway between a laugh and a sigh.

"Tell ye what, lad. Come inside with me, and I shall tell th' owner t' give ye anything ye want. Yer dinner is on me t'night, and if ye need a place t' stay ye can have yer pick o' rooms. M' lads and I are only taking up five. Come on, then." Gregor patted Ferdinan on the back, taking extra care not to overdo it and send the Conquian flying off balance, and started back up the cobbled path to the front door. Ferdinan did not move for a moment, standing at the intersection of street and walkway with a look of pleasant surprise on his face, then hastened his step to catch up to his much larger companion.

"You honor me with your hospitality," he said with a genuineness in his voice that told Gregor the man was not saying this simply out of custom.

Gregor dismissed the compliment. "Ah, 'tis nothing, lad. I have long held th' belief that th' true measure of a man is how he treats a stranger in need." Ferdinan nodded thoughtfully.

The big Highlander led the Conquian into the Crown Rose, where a liveried servant came at once to attend to whatever was needed. Gregor gestured to Ferdinan as he addressed the attendant. "This is..." Gregor paused, and gave Ferdinan a flustered sidelong glance. Ferdinan jumped right in without missing a beat, bowing extravagantly.

"Don Julio Franco Francisco Ferdinan, of Conquia," he said, just as extravagantly as his bow. Gregor nodded, as if agreeing that that really was his companion's name.

"Aye, and he's t' be m' personal guest t'night. Inform Master Mayhew that Master Ferdinan here is t' be given anything he requests, and th' charges are t' be added onto m' bill." The servant said he would see to it, and ran off to do just that.

"Does this mean you cannot honor me by accompanying me at dinner?" There was a heartfelt regret evident in Ferdinan's voice.

Gregor shook his head. "Unfortunately, lad, I cannae. I have business elsewhere in town t'night, but I hope ye enjoy yer dinner. Th' food is good here, and th' service is excellent."

"I am sure it will be wonderful. I very much look forward to future conversations. God goes with you, *compagno*." With this, Ferdinan bowed deeply once more, and departed into one of the adjoining private dining rooms.

Nice lad, Gregor thought, watching him go. *But with all that bowing, his back must be killing him.* A ruckus upstairs drew his attention away from the Conquian, and he saw his four traveling companions making their way down the stairs. Angus was in the lead, and the three bringing up the rear were as well dressed as the brothers. "'Tis about time, lads," Gregor said with a note of exasperation. "What kept ye?"

"Ah, Gregor, these two are worse than th' worst woman could e'er hope t' be," Liam said, gesturing to Gabrahn and Wallace. "Ye'd think they were planning t' court the Governor." Gregor chuckled, but Gabrahn and Wallace did not look amused.

"Who was that?" Angus asked under his breath, nodding his head in the direction Ferdinan had gone. He had a mildly suspicious look about him.

"A Conquian with more names than most men have patience. Calls himself Ferdinan. He just arrived by ship and I'm letting him take his dinner here t'night." Gregor's explanation did not seem to put Angus at ease, but his brother did not mention it further.

The Highlanders departed the Crown Rose together to find their horses waiting for them. If the Highlanders had drawn stares from the townspeople before, it was nothing compared to the looks they received now that they were all together, armed and dressed to impress. None of them made any sign that they noticed the attention, except Wallace, who made ridiculously cordial bows to anyone who stopped for a look, calling out "m' lord," or "m' lady" as they passed. The Highlanders mounted their steeds, and together they made their way toward the Governor's house.

Geoffery Chamberlain, Governor and Right Ruler of Tamendad, stood looking himself over in the full-length mirror of his bedchamber and fidgeting with his neckerchief. He was a thin man with sandy brown hair for the most part, neatly kept, and the gray that spread out from his temples matched the gray of his eyes rather perfectly. He was the only man in Tamendad who wore spectacles, little squares of glass held together by wires stretched back over his ears. He was dressed formally in dark colors, breeches and a long surcoat of dark gray over a shirt of royal blue. This neckerchief, the third he had tried on, was burgundy, and he thought it looked no better than the others. He wiped the sweat from his brow with the back of his hand and slid the neckerchief off, going back to the hunter green one for the moment.

"Highlanders in Tamendad," he said absently to the uncomfortable-looking man in the mirror. "First time in three generations."

That, not the color of his neckerchiefs, was what occupied the bulk of his mind. Since the Stodlemeyers had taken the throne, Turish relations with the Glenish had been in steady decline. The Chamberlains had not been particularly fond of their neighbors to the south, but had for the most part left the Glensmen and Highlanders to their own devices. Archibald Stodlemeyer and his predecessors, on the other hand, had displayed an open contempt for the denizens of Glenisle, so much so in fact that the seventy or so miles between Tamendad and the Highlands might as well have been seventy thousand. Now five Highlanders had ridden north with all the appearances of extending a hand of friendship. Not just any five Highlanders, Geoffery Chamberlain constantly reminded himself. This was Gregor MacDugal and his advisors that were coming to dinner. There was no mistaking that this was the most important dinner Geoffery had attended in a good while. If things went well it could foster improved relations between the Glenish and…well, if not all of Tur then at least with Tamendad, and perhaps with the House of Chamberlain. If things went poorly…

"It's Elysia, father." His daughter's voice startled him back to the present. He had not noticed her reflection in the mirror, standing in the doorway behind him and smiling. He turned to look at her, and his worries were stayed for a moment. Elysia, his little tomboy of a daughter, was a full lady now. She was wearing a beautiful gown that brought out the red in her auburn hair. She was smiling, but there was a look of questioning concern in her eyes. She did not have to ask.

"I'm fine, Elysia," Geoffery told his daughter, trying his best to mask any nervousness in his voice. "Just driving myself crazy over which neckerchief to wear."

"The green one," she said without pause, stepping into the room. "The burgundy clashes, and the blue is too close to the color of your undershirt."

"You have your mother's eye," Geoffery said wistfully. He did not speak of his wife very often, even this many years after her death. He still missed her very much. Geoffery tied the green neckerchief in place around his throat, for good this time. Elysia stepped between him and the mirror and took both his hands in hers.

"Where was your mind just now?" she asked.

"You could always read me like a book. I'm just flustered over the unexpectedness of all this. Five Highlanders showing up out of the blue, and the Conquian ambassador should be arriving tomorrow. I just feel stretched a bit thin."

"There is no one better suited to the task than you, father. Don't worry." Her look reassured him, the way her mother's look had done so many times in the past. Geoffery admired her gift for diplomacy.

"Okay. I won't." He kissed his daughter on the cheek.

"Good. Now come on. Our guests will be arriving any moment."

Geoffery gave himself one last look in the mirror after Elysia had moved from in front of it. He straightened his surcoat and flattened his green neckerchief, which he now saw was indeed the best choice of the three. He left his bedchamber and went to await the arrival of his dinner guests.

William and his family arrived while the sun was still flirting with the western horizon. Governor Chamberlain greeted each of them cordially, and William basked in the moment when the Governor personally thanked him for his services. After exchanging a few pleasantries with the Governor, the Stuart-Camens were escorted to the sitting room by one of the house servants, where they were offered aperitifs and entertained by a group of minstrels while they awaited the guests of honor.

Governor Chamberlain stood waiting at the main entrance of his home as Gregor and his men arrived on horseback. Geoffery's eyes widened as he took in Gregor's bulk, but being the accomplished diplomat that he was, he had plenty of time to regain his composure as he crossed the lawn to meet them. The five men had just dismounted and were handing the reigns of their horses over to the stablehand when Geoffery came within speaking distance.

"Greetings to you from all of Tamendad, Gregor, *moirear* of the Clan MacDugal, and to all your companions." The Governor extended his hand, as did Gregor in return, and the two grasped forearms. "I am Geoffery of the Royal House of Chamberlain, Governor and Right Ruler of Tamendad, and I bid you welcome on behalf of my city. You honor me with your presence this night."

"Peace and greetings t' ye, Governor Chamberlain, from m'self and from all th' Clan MacDugal. Ye honor us all with yer warm invitation, and we gladly accept." Gregor did not particularly care for all the protocol involved in meeting a magistrate, but he was very pleased that Geoffery Chamberlain knew enough of the old tongue and the old traditions to call him *moirear*, a lord. It was a courtesy he did not expect.

Gregor set about introducing each of his companions, starting with his brother Angus. Governor Chamberlain extended warm greetings and grasped forearms with each of them. He honored Angus by referring to him as *tànaiste*, second in command, and the others by hailing them *comhairadh*, advisors. Each in turn thanked the Governor graciously for his invitation, and Gregor could tell they were all very pleased to be addressed in the old ways.

Once the introductions and formalities were out of the way, Governor Chamberlain and the Highlanders made their way into the house. Everyone convened in the grand dining room, which reminded Gregor and William of the dining room they had supped in at the Crown Rose if it had been scaled up to fit five times as many people. Servants dodged and weaved around one another with great dexterity to bring appetizers and wine to the dinner guests, and the musicians from the sitting room had relocated to provide a pleasant musical accompaniment to dinner. William introduced his family to Gregor and the Highlanders, and Gregor was relieved that these introductions and greetings were less formal than those he had had with the Governor.

Dinner was presented in four courses. The dinner conversation was pleasant but uneventful, as it was considered inappropriate in both Turish and Glenish circles to discuss serious matters over food. Julius asked several questions about life in the Highlands, and Gabrahn and Wallace took quite a strong liking to the boy. Liam fell into a conversation with Elysia and William's mother, while Angus, who admitted to breeding horses himself, talked trade with Jonathan. William was ecstatic to find that this left Governor Chamberlain and Gregor to himself. Their conversation dealt mostly with anticipations of what this year's harvest would yield, a very brief history of Tamendad as told by its Governor, a brief lighthearted parley between William and Gregor over whether or not a hand guard was an essential feature of a good sword, and a recount of the Highlanders' ride north from Duerhein, during which Gregor took great care to say nothing that would hint at the unpleasant discovery it had brought.

After dinner was eaten and the plates and platters cleared from the table, Governor Chamberlain suggested the dinner party adjourn back to the sitting room for tobacco and brandy. William knew that this meant Gregor, Jonathan and the Governor would be separating themselves from the others, probably retiring to the Governor's own study, to attend to what the Turish referred to as *noblemen's business*, which was exactly the sort of thing that was not discussed over dinner. Everyone else at the table had apparently made this connection as well, because everyone except Gregor and Jonathan rose from their seats, thanked the Governor graciously for the wonderful meal, and moved for the sitting room.

William offered his thanks to Governor Chamberlain for the meal, then turned to Jonathan and said, "Father, send word when you are ready to take leave and I shall have the horses sent for." He bowed politely to the three men still seated at the table, and turned to join the others.

"Does this mean you will not be accompanying us, William?" the Governor called after him.

William wanted to yell in affirmation, but his nobleman's sensibilities allowed him to manage a more civilized reply. "My apologies, Lord Governor, I was unaware that I was invited. It would be a great pleasure to join your company." William begged pardon from the Governor and went to tell his mother that he would not be joining her immediately. She smiled proudly, but said only, "Very well, son. Have your father send word when he wishes to retire." William kissed her on the cheek, and he and Julius exchanged excited winks before he rejoined the other men. Together they made their way up to Governor Chamberlain's study, on the second floor.

Governor Chamberlain set about filling brandy glasses, while William, Jonathan and Gregor entertained themselves by looking about the leather-bound tomes that filled the shelves.

"Brandy, William?" The Governor honored him by offering him the first glass poured. William was uncertain what to say. He glanced sidelong at his father, who nodded very subtly, before accepting, but he politely refused when offered a pipe. William had never much taken to tobacco. He found it hurt his lungs and burned his lips. Gregor, Jonathan and William each took a chair before the Governor's desk, and the sweet smell of pipe tobacco, which William did not mind as long as he was not the one smoking it, began to fill the air. William swirled the brandy in his glass the way he had seen his father do it. Last night's escapade with the Highlanders aside, this was the first time he had ever had a drink in the presence of men. The brandy was sweeter and spicier than the Highlands whiskey had been, but it still spread that same pleasant warmth across William's stomach as he sipped it. After a brief repose from conversation, it was Gregor who finally broke the silence.

"Gentlemen, I have a question I cannae find a way t' approach gracefully, so I shall just ask it and let ye think me daft if ye will. Are ye aware of any horses that may have come up missing lately?"

William looked to his father, who looked every bit as surprised as he did. Gregor did not notice this at first, because his attention was held by the Governor's reply.

"Well, I am unaware of any missing horses, but a few head of cattle were recently stolen from the local Thalison stock," Geoffery said, with a moderately perplexed look on his face.

"What?" asked William and his father simultaneously.

"Yes," the Governor explained, "someone broke a section of fence along Raymund Thalison's pastures and took six of his heifers. I have sent out scouts to search the surrounding countryside, and they should be returning the morrow."

Jonathan did not seem to know exactly what to say to this, so it was William who spoke. "Gregor," he said, great importance in his voice, "what made you ask about horses?" He chose his words carefully. He had made a promise to his father not to mention the mare to anyone outside the family, and he still intended to keep it.

Gregor hesitated slightly now that all eyes were upon him, but he began telling the tale of how he and his companions had come across the mare the previous morning, of how it had been butchered and the remains strung up in a tree, and of the strange markings carved into what was left of its hide.

"We didn't notice the markings. Scavengers had picked away most of the flesh by the time we found it." Jonathan was speaking more to himself than anyone else. Everyone in the room looked at him, and he uncomfortably met each of their stares in turn. "The mare was mine," he continued at last. "She was discovered missing yesterday morning."

William felt like his mind was a stampede of thoroughbreds. "Governor, the place where Lord Thalison's fence was broken, did it look like it had collapsed on its own?" Jonathan perked up as his son asked this question.

Governor Chamberlain, who apparently had been lost in his own thoughts for the past few moments, started a bit upon being addressed directly. He took a draw off his pipe, and spoke with the stem of it still clenched between his teeth. "So far as I have heard, William, there was no mistaking that the damage to Lord Thalison's fence was man made. The wood was splintered and cracked, and in places it looked like it had been chopped by an axe."

"Then I don't think my mare was stolen," Jonathan said. "A section of my fence had fallen, probably from the heat and humidity, and I think the mare jumped it herself."

"Aye," said Gregor, the loudness of his voice startling the other men, "and I'd wager whoe'er did that t' yer mare was th' same who took this Thalison's cattle as well." Gregor finished his brandy in a gulp and clamped his teeth around the stem of his pipe. "But who?" It was the question burning in each of their heads. No one answered immediately.

"I have four riders out, and I should have their reports by midmorning. In the meantime, I am going to increase the guard tonight by a quarter, just as a precaution. We will know more by tomorrow afternoon." There was a finality to Governor Chamberlain's words. Their conversation drifted to somewhat more pleasant topics, but each of the men seemed to have trouble concentrating on whatever subject was at hand. After less than an hour, Jonathan and Gregor sent word to the other dinner guests that they would be retiring soon. Governor Chamberlain accompanied them down to the common room, where the entire dinner party was reunited, and the lengthy process of bidding everyone goodnight and dismissing them began. After everyone had exchanged their goodbyes and left the Governor's house, they found their horses waiting for them.

"That was quick," Lyllian said to her husband as they approached the coach they had come in. She could plainly see the lines of concern spread across Jonathan's forehead.

"We'll discuss it at home," Jonathan said, kissing his wife on the forehead. There was no crossness in his voice, just a note that told Lyllian whatever the matter was, it was something to be discussed in confidence. She nodded and patted her husband's hand.

A few paces away, Angus was quietly querying Gregor as to what had been discussed in the study. William, who was walking behind his mother and father, could barely overhear a handful of Gregor's responses, but he knew Gregor was telling his brother about Raymund Thalison's heifers, and he thought Angus looked relieved.

"I said ye were worried for nothing, brother. Governor Chamberlain dinnae even hint that he suspected us of anything," Gregor reassured Angus, under his breath.

"Aye, and if those cows were taken days ago, he has nae reason to." Angus added. The Highlanders had reached their horses, but Gregor made no move to mount.

"Are ye coming, brother?" asked Angus, already in the saddle.

"Nae, 'tis a fine night and I have some things t' think o'er, so I think I shall walk. Lead m' horse behind ye, and have it stabled. I shall be along directly."

"Aye, brother, as ye see it."

The Highlander's horses were close enough to the Stuart-Camen's coach for William to overhear what Gregor had said. "Father," William said, hesitating, "I think I will offer Gregor some company, if he will have it."

Jonathan looked thoughtful for a moment, then nodded. "I think that is a very good idea, son. I'll see you at home." Lyllian told her son to be careful, and he kissed her on the cheek. He closed the door to the coach, and it followed after the Highlanders

"Care for some company on your walk, good sir?" asked William.

"'Twould be a pleasure," replied Gregor kindly.

They walked mostly in silence, and what little conversation they made had nothing to do with rustled cattle or butchered horses. As they came to the smaller landowner's houses, Gregor said, "'Tis a pretty town,

William."

William nodded. "It's home," he said simply.

"Aye, and 'tis done ye well. But then again, ye've done it well, too." Gregor kept looking straight ahead, down the street, but he could see William's grin out of the corner of his eye.

"What about your home, Gregor? Tell me about Duerhein?"

"Ah, well, lad, where t' begin?" Gregor was unaccustomed to talking about his home, since most people he came into contact with on a regular basis already knew it well. "There are really two Duerheins, t' be true about it. Th' one takes its name from th' other."

"Two?" asked William, looking up at the big Highlander with quiet interest.

"Aye, one Duerhein is a town nae bigger than this, perhaps a bit smaller truthfully, in a valley o' th' Highlands two days' ride south o' here. Th' other Duerhein is m' family castle, which th' town is built around."

"How long has the castle been in your family?" William asked, waving to a member of the constabulary as they passed by.

"Oh, a ways back, probably ten generations." To be honest, Gregor thought that was a conservative estimate, but he had no real way of telling. Duerhein had always been associated with the Clan MacDugal. One was synonymous with the other.

William furrowed his brow and pursed his lips. He decided it was best to just stop beating around the bush and ask. "Gregor, are you the head of your Clan?"

"Nae, lad," Gregor said, and William was glad that the big Highlander did not seem to mind William's interrogation. "Tavish MacDugal is the *ceann-cinnidh* o' th' Clan MacDugal, but I am th' head o' th' Duerhein MacDugals, and the Duerhein MacDugals sometimes hold th' ear o' Tavish MacDugal. Do ye kennit, lad?"

William nodded, though in all honesty he was more confused than before. So far as he knew, there was no distinction to be made between the Stuart-Camens of Tamendad and the Stuart-Camens of any other city in Tur. The notion that the Duerhein MacDugals were thought of differently than other MacDugals was alien to him, but he did not really feel like pursuing the matter. He already had enough on his mind without a crash course in Glenish politics.

The tolling of bells began to rise in the soft night air. Gregor listened to them for a moment, then turned to William. "Why are they ringing th' church bells, lad?" he asked. William had stopped walking, and Gregor thought he looked a little pale.

"Those aren't church bells," said William. "That's the alarm!"

CHAPTER FIVE

AT THE GATES

The sound of town criers scrambling through the streets began to rise, and William and Gregor found that they had both started running without realizing it. Fragments of the criers' calls met their ears.

"They're at the northwest gate! To arms! To arms!"

William was surprised to see his broadsword in his right hand. He had no memory of drawing it. He distantly noted that Gregor had his claymore drawn as well. The street to the northwest gate was full of people moving in both directions. Terrified-looking people sprinted through the streets toward William and Gregor, away from whatever force was trying to gain entrance to the city. Armed men and women dodged through this exodus of townspeople along with Gregor and William, trying to get closer to the source of the disturbance, trying to see what exactly was going on. The sounds of combat came from up ahead, steel ringing against steel, screams of men losing blood and life. Constables pressed forward, moving to engage head-on whoever was attacking Tamendad. William's feet could not carry him fast enough. His heart was in his throat. He felt like he might vomit.

"Close the gates! Close all the gates!"

Dear God, why is this happening?

"Get more archers on the walls!"

William screamed. His legs burned. His lungs felt like he was breathing acid instead of air. After too many minutes, the northwest gate came into view.

The gate was slowly drawing shut, but the opening between the doors was still plenty wide enough for men to fit through. The doors were heavy and took precious time to close, time William feared they did not have. William forced his legs to carry him faster. Gregor was with him, stride for stride, running with his claymore lifted above his head. William did not notice the wild look on Gregor's face. He was too busy focusing on what lay ahead.

"What in God's name are they?" Gregor yelled, not slowing his stride.

Monsters. No. This isn't happening.

The things pouring through the northwest gate were shaped like men, fought like men, but they were most definitely not men. They had skin the color of moss and exaggeratedly sloped shoulders. Their bottom jaws stuck out much too far, and tusks protruded from them. They wore hardened leather breastplates and fought with curved swords, and howled and hooted like wild animals. Horror seized William as he realized the monsters outnumbered the men almost two to one, and more were coming through the gate with each passing moment. There were already at least fifty in the street ahead, and a good number of men already lay wailing and bleeding in the streets. If the intention of these beasts had been to take the town unawares, as William was almost certain it was, then they were doing a fantastic job of it. Even the guards who were still uninjured moved slowly, clumsily, as if they could not quite make themselves believe what they were fighting against.

Gregor increased his run to a speed that no man his size had any business possessing, leaving William in his dust. His great family sword held at the ready, Gregor plunged headlong into the chaos that engulfed the northwest gate.

Gregor screamed and let his claymore fly, a graceful, deadly arc of Highlands steel. When it was over, Gregor stood above two halves of what had previously been one of the invaders. He raised his claymore high above his head, the blade now a wet crimson. Two more of the monsters charged for Gregor, their screams full of hate and fury over what had happened to their fallen comrade. They were angered by the slaying of one of their own. Somehow, deep down inside, Gregor found relief that they displayed such human emotion. Humans had weaknesses. Maybe these things did too.

Gregor's blade flashed twice in the lamplight, and the two newcomers shared their comrade's fate. One had lost its head, the other its left arm and the left half of its chest. Blood flowed down Gregor's arm from a fresh wound, but he paid it no heed. It was barely more than a flesh wound, and what little pain it provided only fueled Gregor's battle rage. Wherever he swung his claymore, the hoots and howls of the creatures gave way to moans and wails. He charged forward, carving a path into the midst of the invaders.

William stared briefly at the three dead things dropped by Gregor's sword.

They bleed. They die.

He screamed as he launched himself forward into the fray, and one of the monsters rose up to meet him. William's blade seemed to move on its own, meeting the thing's attack in mid-stroke and pushing it aside, then slashing its stomach open. The monster's eyes widened in shock as its innards slowly became its outards. It slumped to the ground like a rag doll. William had no time to let the sight register in his mind. Another invader took the first one's place, snarling and slashing at William's face. Somewhere deep down in the eternally logical part of William's soul, he marveled at how remarkably unlike the imaginary foes of his practice sessions these things were. They bobbed and weaved, parried and regrouped, pressed advantages that his phantasmal attackers would never dream of pressing. They were living, breathing things. This was real. They wanted to kill him.

William's blade found true once again, and red blood gushed from the wound he had inflicted on his opponent's throat. William had no time to think, no time to react to the gruesome sights that met his eyes. There were always more invaders, more monsters that William still could not quite convince himself really existed, waiting for their turn to try to kill him.

The sound of the bar slamming into place on the closed doors of the northwest gate was sweeter than any music, but too many invaders had found their way into the town. A quick glance around told Gregor and William that more constables had fallen than monsters, and the invaders were beginning to break through what little containment the guardsmen could manage. Things did not look good. A scream brought William back to the here and now, and if he had had time to think about it, he would have thought it sounded somehow similar to Gregor's battle cry. One of the monsters was making a bull rush right for him, bearing down on him at great speed. William had little time to react. His instinct told him to try a spinning sidestep with a sweeping blow toward the creature's head, a move he had only tried alone on the beach, when there was no real danger. There was no time to weigh options. As the invader came within arm's reach, William twisted on his feet, sweeping around to the monster's left side and following through with his sword. For a moment he thought it had worked. Then a pain he could never have imagined exploded in his side, and a sickly wet warmth began to spread where the beast had cut him open. He knew without looking at it that it was a serious wound. It hurt too bad and bled too freely not to be. William stumbled and fell to his knees, gripping his side. When he removed his hand to inspect it, it was drenched in his own blood. The monster rounded on him, and William saw he had only managed to nick its shoulder. It approached. William tasted fear and bile.

"*Thorak rakuth, Abuneth,*" the creature snarled at him through a sneer, closing to within striking distance. William raised his sword and tried to get to his feet, but found he lacked the strength. He was not sure if it was pain, shock or terror that kept him on his knees, but he was pretty certain the end result would be the same. The monster raised its blade high.

I love you, Melissa. I love you, Father. I love you, Mother. I love you, Julius. I don't want to die. Please.

More screaming, and blood splashed on William's face. He thought at first that the end had come for him, entirely too soon, but marveled when he realized there was no pain. His would-be murderer lay in two halves, sliced in twain just above the navel. Angus towered above William. His claymore was covered in blood. He had the same wild look about him that William had failed to notice on Gregor.

"Ye're hurt. Can ye stand?"

"Yes," William replied without thinking, and he found he spoke the truth. His side erupted in fresh pain with every step he took, but there would be time to deal with that later, when the city was safe. William surveyed his immediate surroundings, and found himself encircled by Highlanders. Gregor had regrouped with the others, and all five now fought together. Liam, Gabrahn, and Wallace all wielded longswords that bulged slightly in the middle of the blade, suggesting the look of a teardrop. None of their blades were clean. Gregor was splattered in blood from head to foot, and it was impossible to tell how much was his and how much had once belonged to his enemies. The creatures kept their distance from the Highlanders, despite the taunts and jeers the Highlanders yelled at them.

"Ye're okay, lad?" Gregor called over his shoulder to William, his eyes not leaving the invaders that lurked just out of reach.

"I'm fine," William said, trying to sound resolute.

"Good. Let's do some damage, lads." The Highlanders pressed forward, leaving William at the rear of the fray, and the monsters recoiled before them.

William spotted the man with black hair, dark skin, red and gold vest. He was armed with sabre and parrying dagger, and looked more like he was dancing than fighting. There was no time to wonder about it. The invaders' numbers had been cut in half, and the late-arriving guardsmen had turned the advantage in the townspeople's favor, but the monsters had now shifted tactics from divide and conquer to doing as much damage as possible before the inevitable. They had the look of cornered animals. William reentered the fight.

Don Julio Franco Francisco Ferdinan, Ambassador of the Conquian Throne, had been out for what he had hoped would be a relaxing evening walk through this new city when the frantic tolling of the alarm bells, a sound that transcended any language barrier, told him something was amiss. Now he stood shoulder to shoulder with the locals in defending this town from the beasts attempting to force entry.

Ferdinan was ultimately disappointed with the challenge these green monstrosities offered. At first look he had thought them frightful, but once he had engaged them at the sword he found them to fall like leaves in autumn. For all the clumsy awkwardness with which they wielded their swords they might as well have been armed with feather dusters. Anyone well versed in the art of swordplay would have had little trouble dispatching these things, and Don Ferdinan was a consummate swordsman. He suspected he could handle these things easily enough with only his parrying dagger, and that in his off hand. Perhaps if four or five ganged up on him at once he would have been hard pressed to escape without a nick, but Gregor and his *compagnos* were doing an excellent job of preventing the things from banding together in groups any larger than two or three, and only then for a few moments. These Highlanders had little grace about their manner in battle, but they fought with a passion that Ferdinan deeply respected.

At this point, Ferdinan was simply toying with the pathetic creature he found before him. He had studied its moves enough to know that it basically had two: swing and duck. Ferdinan's own sabre danced and weaved through the creature's defenses, and his parrying dagger provided more than enough protection to ward off the creature's desperate attacks.

"You fight with all the grace of a three-legged goat," Ferdinan said loudly. He seriously doubted the thing could understand him, but he knew the constables and armed townspeople, especially those wounded but still fighting, would be bolstered by his confidence. He found it awkward taunting in a foreign language. The Turish tongue had none of the grace that made Conquian ridicule an art form. It sufficed, though. "If this es all you bring against me, what in the world possessed you to try taking this city?" The creatures eyes were wide with fear. This game of cat and mouse had served its purpose. It was time to end it. The monstrosity's sword went flying out of its grasp with a flick of Ferdinan's parrying dagger.

Sidestep, parry, thrust, twist.

Ferdinan ran the creature through the throat. He dispatched it quickly, honorably, the way he had been taught, the way he taught others to do it. The monstrosity's eyes widened, focusing on nothing, as it dropped to the ground.

"Not on my watch," said Ferdinan. He made the Sign of the Compass as the thing died, then turned his attention to where it was more needed.

For the first time since drawing his claymore, Gregor MacDugal expanded his focus beyond what was immediately in front of him. The arrival of his companions, along with the surprisingly proficient Ferdinan, had turned the tide of the battle, and what few invaders remained alive in Tamendad were being stalked like prey. Eight men with bows had made their way onto the wall by now and were calling down to the townspeople below that the creatures still left outside the gate were retreating.

The monsters left outside the wall when the gate had finally drawn shut had apparently tried to carve their way into the city. Parts of the wall and northwest gate would have to be repaired, but the overall damage was only moderate. The situation was more or less in hand, but Gregor's immediate surroundings were not pretty. Men and women lay bleeding and dying in the streets, their bodies intermingled with the corpses of the fallen invaders. Wails and whimpers engulfed the area immediately around the northwest gate. Without diverting too much of his attention to counting the fallen – the immediate situation still held too much potential for danger to lose oneself completely in thought – Gregor guessed that perhaps twenty townspeople were down. Of those twenty, perhaps a third made no sound or movement. Others were wounded but still on their feet, a look of cold horror spreading across their faces, due as much to what had just happened as to whatever injuries they had suffered.

William was pulling his broadsword from the chest of one of the fallen monsters when Gregor spotted him. His entire left side was a rich crimson, but his walk told Gregor the wound could have been worse. "Ye fought well, lad," Gregor said, and William jumped slightly as though startled by the big Highlander's voice. Gregor softened his tone a bit. "Most lads freeze up th' first time they draw steel and mean it. Ye should get t' th' church and have that cut dressed and sutured. Leave th' cleanup work t' us."

William had his hand pressed firmly against his left side. His wound did not appear to be bleeding freely any longer, but it was still serious enough to require a healer's care. William made no sign that he was prepared to leave, though. He stood fast, and looked all around him with the wide-eyed, emotional look Gregor had seen on too many young faces, the look of a man who was seeing the reality of war for the first time. William looked like he did not know whether to cry or scream.

"What are they, Gregor? What the twist are they?"

Gregor could think of no suitable reply but the truth. "I dinnae know, lad."

"Es this something that happens regularly around here?" asked a voice that Gregor knew but William did not. The big Highlander and the young nobleman turned to see Ferdinan striding toward them, confusion blending with exasperation on his face. He noticed William's blood-soaked clothing. "Do you need help, *compagno*?" he asked with concern in his voice.

"I'm…" William found he could not say he was fine. That was just too great a lie. "Not right now. Who are you?" Under normal circumstances, William would never have been so forthright.

Ferdinan arched an eyebrow, but obviously did not think William's brusqueness rude. "My name es Julio Franco Francisco Ferdinan." Ferdinan bowed as he spoke. "You may call me Don Ferdinan. And who are you?"

William told Ferdinan his name.

"Es a pleasure to meet you, William." He pronounced it *Wheel-yum*. "Under the circumstances, I think es a good idea for you to see a healer. I will escort you to the church personally."

William opened his mouth to protest, to insist that he was fine and wanted to stay, to help in whatever way he could, but Gregor interrupted him.

"Aye, a good idea, Ferdinan. He's lost a good deal o' blood. The lad's probably still high from battle, and he's likely t' pass out as soon as he starts t' come down. I'll nae have a man who fought so bravely having a ditch for a bed tonight."

"Well spoken," Ferdinan agreed.

"You two know each other?" William asked.

Gregor replied, "We met this afternoon," at the same time Ferdinan said, "We have been acquainted." Without giving him a chance to say anything further on the matter, Ferdinan turned William down the street toward the church and started walking alongside.

"Where are you from, Ferdinan?" William asked, grimacing with each step.

"I am from Conquia, across the ocean."

"The Land of Hidalgo Sanctus?" That was the first thing William had learned about Conquia, that Hidalgo Sanctus, the Reformer of the Antrelican Church, had been born there.

Ferdinan smiled warmly at William. "Sí, the Land of San Hidalgo. The capital city es named after him."

"I have always wanted to see the cathedral he built," William said. He found talking about anything other than the nightmare at the northwest gate helped him forget about the pain that burned in his side, and he did have a genuine interest in the Great Benefactor.

"Oh, es a magnificent sight to behold, and to think he built it in two days makes you realize how favored he was by God." Ferdinan's manner told William that the Conquian was very proud of his nation's history. After a short pause, Ferdinan continued by saying, "I think you would fit in well in my country."

"Why do you say that?" William asked.

"Because you fight so well to be so young," Ferdinan explained. "Es been my esperience that very few Turishmen study the art of swordplay, but you wielded your sword with honor and passion tonight." William had no idea how to reply to that. Honor had been the last thing on his mind while he had been fighting, and he had felt more fear than passion. The two walked the rest of the way in silence, Ferdinan keeping a watchful eye on William, ready to jump to his assistance at a moment's notice if the young nobleman appeared to stumble.

When they reached the church they found it a hub of excitement, with town criers and personal messengers running in and out, and priests anxiously looking over the injured who came on foot or stretcher. Ferdinan insisted on staying by William's side until he was actually in the personal care of a healer, despite William's continued insistence that he was fine. "I gave my word," Ferdinan said simply, and that settled it, at least in the Conquian's mind.

"William! Oh, thank God!" Jonathan Stuart-Camen came running through the crowd of the church and embraced his son tightly. "I feared the worst. Thank God you're alive." William made no reply, just sighed very deeply against his father's shoulder. He needed that hug more than anything else in the world at that moment. After the embrace ended, William introduced Ferdinan. Jonathan thanked the Conquian profusely for seeing his son safely to the church.

"Es nothing," Ferdinan replied, bowing.

"They hit the southwest gate, too," Jonathan said to both William and Ferdinan, and to neither. "We got the gate closed before any of them got in, but they attacked the gate itself. They had axes and picks. They had almost cut through, but they pulled back as soon as the ones at the northwest gate began to retreat. When I heard you were at the northwest gate, William, I..." Jonathan's words trailed off. He had tears in his eyes.

"Lord Stuart-Camen, come, let's have a look at that cut," said Patrum Albermarle, the church's Master Healer, as he approached. He led William and his father off to a private room after they had said their good-byes to Ferdinan. The room was just big enough to hold the cot, washbasin and chair that furnished it. Patrum Albermarle stripped William of his clothes, giving him a loincloth to wrap himself in, and washed the cut. The water, which was oily and smelled of pungent herbs, stung like liquid fire on William's wound.

"It is deep, but it does not look very serious," the Master Healer said. "The Face of Beneficence smiled on you this night, my son. I have already seen much worse. A few days of rest and you should be fine." Patrum Albermarle stitched up William's side and applied a poultice that was hot and cold all at the same time, then left William and his father alone. William was glad that his father was the only one there to see him cry.

CHAPTER SIX

THE WANDERER

Great, thought Colvin. *I'm dreaming again.*

It was the sound of metal on metal, the incessant *clink clink clink* of hammer on anvil that set the tempo of life. The heat was overwhelming, and sweat covered his tanned and leathery skin. He still had six horseshoes to make before he could take a break, and already the sound and the heat were driving a wedge into his psyche. But it was not real sound. It was not real heat. His muscles ached. That much was real, though not because of working at a forge. They ached from weeks of sleeping propped up against a tree or, failing that, the biggest rock he could find. His mind had no problem translating his pains to suit the dream. His mind was underhanded like that. In a way, he hated his mind.

A rooster out in the lane refused to shut up. Colvin was well aware the sun was up. He had been well aware that the sun was up since it rose over the eastern horizon, five hours ago. The rooster took no chances, though. The rooster's commission in life was to inform the world that the big bright ball was in the sky. For all the rooster knew, it alone possessed the knowledge that the big yellow thing was visible, and it set about its task of reminding any living thing within earshot of this fact at intervals of thirty seconds or so. Colvin hated the rooster. He hated it because of the sound it made. Roosters did not, contrary to popular belief, *cock-a-doodle-do*. *Cock-a-doodle-do* was a cute sound. The sound the rooster made was like a thousand forks being scraped across a thousand stoneware plates, or perhaps more like the sound Colvin assumed a stray cat would make if used as a doorstop. He hated the rooster because it did not have to make horseshoes. The rooster didn't have to work for its supper. It didn't have to *pull his weight*, Loran Rothwald's favorite expression. It didn't have to go to bed with aching muscles because Loran Rothwald was too lazy to forge a single horseshoe now that Colvin was around. It didn't have to worry about whether or not Loran Rothwald would eventually figure out that it was sleeping with his daughter. Colvin hated the rooster for all these reasons, for all these concerns he had to deal with but from which the rooster was ignorantly, blessedly free. Mostly, though, he hated it because it was a part of the dream.

He heard screaming from down the lane. He could not make out the words, but he knew who it was. He knew because he had already lived all of this. The dream was just a reminder, a savage replay of how he came to be homeless and penniless. *Always today,* Colvin thought, looking around the forge. *Why does it always start on this day? Why can't it ever start on one of the days I had sex with Rosie?* He never got to relive that part of it in his dreams. He only got to savor the bad ending to it all, over and over again. The screaming grew louder. It had been at this point, when it had all actually been happening for the first time, that he realized the voices belonged to Loran Rothwald and his daughter, Rosie. Colvin's heart began racing and his palms, which had previously been the only part of him that had not been sweating, began to do so now. The sensation – fear mixed with excitement – was there, but it was disconnected. It was a part of the dream, a mere echo of how he had felt at that moment. At the time, he had been terrified. Now he was, at most, mildly flustered.

The voices drew nearer. He could clearly make out a few of Loran Rothwald's words now. "…bastard's going t' die. You hear me, bastard? You're going t' die!" Colvin had honestly believed, at the time, that Loran spoke the truth. Rosie's words were a jumble of emotional sobs and pleas on behalf of Colvin's life. One feeling that had not faded at all since that day was Colvin's regret for putting Rosie in a situation like that. She was a good girl. Almost beautiful, and not just physically. That part of it could not be denied, of course. She had a body to die for, or at least Colvin had thought so up until that moment of his life. Now the bitter irony of that saying slapped him hard across the face.

"Where are you, bastard?" Loran Rothwald screamed above the wails of his daughter. Colvin had not appreciated how downright stupid this sounded coming out of Loran's mouth until long after he had escaped from his would-be executioner. Loran Rothwald knew exactly where Colvin was. Loran Rothwald had set Colvin to work in the forge personally that morning.

Terrified as he was, Colvin appreciated that his situation provided him with few options. He could try to hide, which was beyond impractical given the confined space of Loran Rothwald's forge, or he could meet the storm head-on. He decided in favor of the latter option and walked out into the lane.

I really hate the sound his jaw made when I broke it.

Loran Rothwald's rage increased tenfold when he saw Colvin emerge from the forge. The middle-aged man broke into a run, screaming at the top of his lungs, fury blazing in his eyes. He was charging straight for Colvin.

"You've turned my daughter into a whore, you bastard! A no-good wretch of a whore! Who'll marry her now that she's been spoiled by the likes of you? You're going t'–" Colvin assumed *die* was to be the next word out of Loran Rothwald's mouth, had he been given the chance to complete his sentence. There was a disturbingly wet crackling sound as Colvin's right hand connected squarely with Loran Rothwald's jaw. Colvin was not fully aware he had thrown the punch until he saw Loran sprawled on the ground before him, both hands clutched firmly to his jawbone, which now met his skull at a grotesque angle. Loran kicked his feet wildly in pain, rolling around on the ground. His threats were immediately replaced by whimpering mumbles, almost impossible to interpret due to the difficulty he suddenly found in speaking.

"I took you in. I took you in when nobody else would. I gave you a home."

It was at that moment Colvin saw the old blacksmith for what he really was: a balding, moderately overweight father of two, an over the hill blacksmith growing too old and tired to tend his own forge, and a moderately dislikable louse who had nonetheless given Colvin a temporary home in return for free labor. All things being equal, he deserved having his jaw broken no more than any other man Colvin had ever met.

"I'm sorry," Colvin said, speaking more to Rosie than her father. Rosie's look of shock, eyes wide, mouth hanging open, did not change. "I'll be going, now."

"I spit on your grave, bastard," said Loran Rothwald.

Colvin sighed. He left them there in the lane, Rosie wiping away tears and tending to her injured father, Loran Rothwald alternating between wailing in pain from the throb in his jaw and bleating out curses after Colvin.

Well, we make the beds we lie in.

The smell of rotgut informed Colvin that the dream had shifted on him. He knew where it was heading. Whenever it started with Loran Rothwald's forge, it always continued on to this. All his dreams found their way here eventually.

The forge and the lane were gone. He was in the little two room hovel with Malcomb and Doris. Malcomb, gaunt faced, slack jawed, sat at the makeshift table, which was really just a large, irregularly shaped piece of wood balanced on a barrel head. He gulped his cheap liquor out of a tarnished pewter tankard, his sunken eyes staring blankly out the open window. Doris sat as far away from Malcomb as she could get and still be in the same room with him, hunched down in a corner and peeling potatoes that were more green than brown. She had her hair up in the impossibly tight bun she always wore, salt and pepper hair stretched back so taut Colvin swore one day her face would split right down the middle. She looked like a cat and had no chin, though she frequently reminded anyone who would listen that she had been a real looker in her day. She wore one of her many dresses with the high neck and hem just flirting with the floor. Colvin wondered how long it had been since Malcomb had seen Doris naked, but he did not wonder this often. Malcomb had very little need to see Doris naked, because Malcomb had been sleeping with Lorna Mae Cooper for several years. Doris was well aware of Malcomb's infidelity, but did not lose sleep over it since she had been sleeping with Eldridge Cooper, Lorna Mae's father, for just as long.

The thatch-roofed hovel smelled of shit and boiled turnips, a smell that Colvin still to this day associated with Malcomb and Doris and, subconsciously, with death. Norbert, the mange-covered tabby cat, sat on the floor beside Doris, watching everything with the jumpy nervousness that Colvin assumed it had learned by watching its owner. It walked with a severe limp due to Malcomb's tendency to kick it across the room when he was drunk. Malcomb also walked with a severe limp, due to Doris's reaction whenever Malcomb kicked Norbert. Nobody raised much of a fuss when Malcomb kicked Colvin.

Colvin had lived with Malcomb and Doris for the first twelve years of his life, but they were not his parents. They both had a tendency of reminding him of this fact whenever they were in particularly foul moods, which in Colvin's experience was an almost daily occurrence. Colvin had no idea who his real parents were, just that they had abandoned him when he was still a babe and Malcomb and Doris had taken him in. Colvin could not decide whether he hated Malcomb and Doris more than his real parents, or vice versa. He had never met his real parents, though, which made it somewhat easier to hate Malcomb and Doris. At least he could pretend his real parents had a valid reason for abandoning him. So far as Colvin could tell, Malcomb and Doris acted like they did simply because they were assholes.

Malcomb drained the last of the liquor from his tankard, let out a rancid belch and refilled the tankard halfway. Colvin looked up from the dead runt of a chicken he was plucking to watch this. Whenever Malcomb drank like this it meant he was intending to either have sex with Lorna Mae or beat Colvin.

Boy, it's time for you to go.

70

"Boy, it's time for you to go," said Malcomb, not shifting his eyes away from the window. Colvin wanted very badly to believe he did not know what Malcomb meant.

"Where do you want me to go, Malcomb? I already took the beans to Carson's farm and got your whiskey from Emmett Shayle."

"We just can't afford feeding three mouths anymore. You're more trouble than you're worth. You've been more trouble than you're worth since we took you in, but if you stay any longer you'll eat us all into poverty." Malcomb took another long swig from his tankard. Doris did not look up from her potatoes. Norbert sat back on his haunches and started hacking up a hairball. Colvin called Malcomb a drunkard and a lousy son of a bitch. Just like the punch that dislocated Loran Rothwald's jaw, he didn't realize he had done it until he saw the effects. The next thing he knew, he found himself being thrown around by his shirt collar, getting slammed into the mud walls as hard as Malcomb could manage. Colvin was very thankful the shanty's walls were made of dried mud, because it made being thrown against them much more bearable than if they had been brick or stone. Besides the momentary brain-jarring flash of pain that occurred at the moment of impact, a person could get thrown against one of those mud walls all day without any serious adverse effects.

Doris only reacted by shifting out of the way when Malcomb slammed Colvin into the wall right next to her. All three of them were accustomed to this sort of thing happening in their home. This time, however, Colvin did something he had never done before. Colvin fought back.

Colvin formulated the plan in its entirety the moment before he slammed into the wall next to Doris. He had never been one to overstrategize. The familiar blinding burst of pain washed over him as he sunk an inch into the mud of the wall, but receded just as quickly as it had come. Malcomb pulled him forward again, and Colvin's hand snaked out with lightning quickness toward Doris. The paring knife she used on her potatoes was small but razor sharp. Malcomb's inebriated brain did not immediately register that Colvin had a weapon, but it became quickly apparent to him when Colvin used it to slice deep into his forearm. Malcomb screamed in pain, releasing Colvin and clamping his hand over the cut. Blood flowed freely between his fingers. Doris screamed in horror, though Colvin would later debate with himself over whether this was out of concern for her husband or just sheer shock that something so out of the ordinary had happened. The latter seemed much more plausible. Norbert voiced his general feelings about what was transpiring by arching his back, raising his hackles and hissing, all while still trying to dislodge his hairball. Colvin backed slowly away from all three of them.

"You little bastard!" screamed Malcomb. "I took you in! I gave you a home!"

"Do you two realize how much you bastards completely messed up my life?!?" Colvin screamed in reply. "I still dream about this shit! I'll probably dream about it until I die! I haven't lived here for years, and I still can't trust anyone!"

"Well, we can't be held responsible for that," said Doris, her voice much more reasonable in the dream than it ever had been in real life.

"She's right, Colvin," added Malcomb, calmness in his voice despite the blood still flowing from his forearm, which had now turned black and viscous, more like tar. "Our shortcomings as adoptive parents cannot be to blame for your inability to connect with other people on anything more than a transient level. There's no denying we did a number on you during your childhood, but that doesn't mean the damage is irreparable. You have to take charge of your own life and stop blaming the people who gave you a raw deal."

Colvin shook his head disbelievingly. "I hope you rot, both of you. I hate you most of all."

You have to wake up right now.

Well, okay then.

Colvin began the long, tedious journey up from the dreamworld. His dreams were always reluctant to let him go, and this one held a firmer grip than most. His hate began to melt away, and he willingly left it behind. He always left his hate in his dreams. It served no purpose in the real world. In the real world, hate just turned a person into a cynic and an asshole. In his dreams, though, hate helped him distance himself from all the bad things, helped him convince himself he was not like the bad things. It helped him disarm the power the bad things still held over him, little by little. It helped him remember that he was better than the bad things, and that was a very important thing to remember.

Slowly but not reluctantly, Colvin opened his eyes and brushed back a lock of his blood-red hair from his face, coming back to reality. For the moment, that reality consisted solely of the point of a scimitar hovering menacingly six inches in front of his face. Colvin blinked a few times, blurriness receding from the corners of his vision. He focused intently on the blade. He wanted to believe he was still dreaming, but there was little hope in that thought. The blade was too crisp, too undeniable to belong to the surreal underworld of his dreams. He trailed his eyes up the length of the blade. It was sharp, but not as sharp as it could have been if great care had been taken with it, and a few tiny specs of rust dotted its length.

Colvin would probably have never noticed the rust had he not been given any opportunity to inspect the sword at such close proximity. The sword remained in place, too close for comfort but not yet drawing blood. Colvin thought it safe to assume that since whoever was holding the scimitar had not yet slid it into his face, he probably was not in immediate danger of that happening now. The fact that he had woken up at all told him the swordsman was probably more interested in threatening him than killing him, at least for the time being.

Colvin tore some of his focus away from the sword itself, moving his eyes to the hand that held it. The hand was wearing a tight-fitting green leather glove. No, that was not quite right. It looked like a green leather glove at first, but Colvin realized he could see fingernails on the hand. The hand itself was green. So was the forearm. Colvin's eyes darted all over the form of the man holding the sword, taking too little time to ascertain any specific details about him except that every inch of exposed skin was the color of pea soup. Colvin blinked again. The man's shoulders were much too rounded, and his arms were too long. He was moderately bow-legged. He had a dramatic underbite, out of which protruded two fangs so long they had to be called tusks. His nose was flat and slightly upturned. His hair was a greasy mottled mess of a shade Colvin could not discern. Whatever he was, he was not a man. Colvin was not entirely certain he was a he at all.

"This is new," was all Colvin could think to say. The green thing cocked its head to one side, looking down at him with pallid yellow eyes. Colvin met those eyes, and the green thing took half a step away from him. Colvin had come to expect this reaction or something similar whenever he met someone's gaze, or in this case, *something's*, for the first time. Colvin's eyes were beyond intense. They were bluer than the sky, blue the color of ice and steel. An old soothsayer in the village before Loran Rothwald's, a blind and half crazy old maid, whom everyone in the village scoffed at in public and handed coppers to in private, had called them wolf's eyes, and had told Colvin that they were the reason for all of his hardships. Colvin did not quite buy the idea that everything bad that had ever happened to him was due to the color of his irises. He was well aware, though, that his intense stare made it difficult for people to feel comfortable around him, at least until they got to know him and realized that deep down he was basically harmless, if a bit emotionally scarred. At any rate, his eyes had put the green thing slightly off kilter, and he appreciated that this could turn out either in his favor or against it. The green thing regained its composure and grunted threateningly at Colvin, as though the sword it held was not threatening enough.

"*Lorthok*," the green thing said, waving the point of the sword back and forth in Colvin's face. Colvin just blinked in return. There was a long, drawn-out silence, followed immediately by another long, drawn-out silence. Halfway through the third long, drawn-out silence, the green thing spoke up.

"*Lorthok!*" it said again, more forcefully than before, adding emphasis by jabbing the sword in Colvin's general direction.

Colvin shrugged his shoulders in the most non-aggressive manner he could manage. "I don't know what that means," he said simply. Now it was the green thing's turn to blink at him. It had a look on its face as though it were pondering a difficult riddle.

"I'm just gonna take a gamble and assume you want everything I have," said Colvin, making absolutely certain he did not make any sudden movements. That tended to be the motive at issue whenever a man found himself on the wrong end of a sword. "Well, I don't have anything. You picked the worst person in Glenisle to try and rob."

The green thing just stood there, still as stone, not understanding anything. Eventually, Colvin was certain, it would grow weary of the communication barrier and dispatch him as soon as it became clear Colvin could serve it no purpose. So Colvin's mind raced to find some purpose he could serve.

"Are you hungry?" Colvin asked, making a gesture of putting food in his mouth. He hoped his simple sign language was enough to break through, and sure enough a light dawned in the creature's xanthous eyes. It nodded.

"Sure, I can find you something to eat, but I have to get up from leaning against this tree first, and I don't want you to put that sword through my face, okay? I'm just gonna stand up real slow, and keep my hands in the air where you can see them. Okay?" Colvin kept his body completely still, raising his hands very slowly, his palms turned outward toward his captor. It nodded at him, though Colvin was almost totally certain it had understood two or three of his words at best.

"*Lorthok*," it said a third time.

"Yeah," Colvin said, slowly rising to his feet. "Lorthok." He was pleased to find that the green thing backed off a bit, giving him room to stand. Colvin took a brief moment to stretch out his aching muscles, making sure his posture in no way insinuated he was raising a hand against his captor. Although this was undeniably the worst situation Colvin had awoken to in recent memory, it could have been worse. He had found himself taking orders on the wrong end of a sword before, though it had always been a relatively normal-looking human being holding the sword. Still, Colvin was relieved to find that the green thing, whatever it was exactly, explored other options of procuring food before just turning Colvin into breakfast. To Colvin that meant it might be possible to reason with his captor and bargain for his life. The apparent language barrier that existed between him and the green thing might put a damper on that, though.

Colvin set about his task of gathering food for his kidnapper. In light of not knowing the thing's real name, or even if it had one, Colvin found himself referring to it in his mind as Lorthok. It was as good a name as any. He walked in front, Lorthok bringing up the rear, the rusty scimitar between them. Colvin had scavenged for his food for most of the last five years of his life and it had long ago become second nature to him, so his mind wandered as he searched for tubers and wild fruits. His back was to his kidnapper, but he had stolen a good look at the green thing while standing up and stretching, and he had already begun the almost involuntary process of sizing up an enemy. Lorthok was tall, with a stout and muscular build, but it was less than half a head taller than Colvin, and he guessed it wasn't much stronger than him, either. He really didn't have enough knowledge about Lorthok to posit a guess, but based solely on the greed with which it accepted and devoured what Colvin offered, apparently without even considering that Colvin might be trying to pass off something poisonous, he assumed it was probably weak with hunger. It had a mean look to it, but that half step backward it had taken upon meeting Colvin's eyes told him that it could be intimidated, perhaps even frightened under the right conditions. After what felt like about half an hour foraging through the trees, Colvin decided there was little doubt he could take Lorthok in a fair fight. However, Lorthok had a sword and all Colvin had was his good looks, which would be severely damaged when Lorthok put its sword through Colvin's face upon his making a hostile move. For the time being, Colvin resigned himself to the gross unfairness of his present circumstances.

Colvin was almost overjoyed when he came upon a largish patch of mushrooms. He had been walking for well over an hour with the point of Lorthok's scimitar poking occasionally into his back, which he found to be a genuinely horrible motivating technique. His back hurt both from the flesh wounds he had accumulated and all the bending over to root for tubers or pick wild berries. He plucked one of the mushrooms from the bunch, sniffed it and nibbled from the tip. He nodded to Lorthok and handed it the mushroom, which was the system he had worked out for communicating something was safe to eat. Lorthok gobbled the fungus down hungrily and turned its attention to the other mushrooms still on the ground, though it kept the scimitar pointed at Colvin. Lorthok plucked the mushrooms one by one, shoving them into its tusked mouth.

Colvin looked away from his captor, taking in what under normal circumstances would have been a perfectly lovely summer day. He had learned quickly that he did not enjoy watching the thing eat. The tusks made it impossible for Lorthok to close its mouth while it chewed.

"So listen, Lorthok," Colvin said, stretching his arms out over his head, "you've got quite a spread there to keep you occupied for a while, and my back is killing me, so I'm going to take a load off. I'll take your not killing me as a sign that you're okay with that." Colvin stretched out on a fallen tree trunk a few feet away from where Lorthok was gorging itself. Lorthok kept a wary eye on him, but concerned itself primarily with the mushrooms.

The tree trunk was moldy and slightly damp, leaving a moist imprint on Colvin's backside as he settled down onto it, but it felt good to be off his feet. Colvin crossed his right leg over his left and rubbed his bare foot. The bottom was thick with calluses from lack of shoes. The dull ache in his feet had been with him for so long he almost did not notice it anymore. He took in his surroundings, glad to be doing so for the first time all day without worrying about whether or not what he saw was edible. The rolling hills around him were lightly wooded, and the distant scent of brine informed him that he was close to the coastline. He was three months out of Loran Rothwald's village, and could have made it to pretty much anywhere in Glenisle in that time, but it was summer, the land offered up plenty of food to those who knew how to look for it, and Colvin felt he could use some time to himself, to sort out his priorities, as it were. Still, he had been making a halfhearted attempt to make his way gradually north toward the Taeran Coast and was pleased to find that he was drawing near. Summering out in the wild would be no problem, but winter would bring on a whole new slew of problems. Colvin had planned to find himself close to Tamendad or Tantera when the weather began to turn, in hopes that he could barter his services in return for room and board through the dead season.

A sudden hunger pang rumbled in Colvin's stomach, and he gripped at his abdomen with both hands. He had been in the company of Lorthok all morning and had handed over every morsel of food he had come across. He had a sneaking suspicion that Lorthok would not take kindly to him holding some of his discoveries back for himself. Without drawing attention to himself, Colvin began to lackadaisically examine his immediate surroundings, hoping to find something edible within arm's reach that he could hoard for himself. There was nothing to be found, and his heart sank just a little. He had survived off tree bark before, he reminded himself, but a quick inspection of the tree he sat upon revealed not an inch that was not either sodden or rank. There was nothing fit for human consumption besides the mushrooms, and he was not about to ask Lorthok for one of those. Colvin spoke up to take his mind off his hunger.

"So, Lorthok, where you from originally?" Lorthok replied only by raising an eyebrow, the stem of a mushroom hanging out of its slightly gaping maw. There was silence for a moment. "Really?" Colvin continued. "I hear it's lovely there this time of year. So…wife and kids? Or husband and kids? Can't really tell which is more appropriate, and I wouldn't really want to find out anyway. Myself, I'm more of a loner. Never really had a relationship that didn't end badly. Usually overprotective fathers. I'm sure you know what that's like. I doubt many fathers take to you when you come around to court their daughters. Or to eat them, as the case may be. I'd like to settle down someday though, find a nice girl and raise up a family. Own a little patch of land, plant some beans and corn, live life the way God intended. Roof over your head, three square meals a day, no waking up to find an ugly green bastard pointing a sword at your face. Yes sir, a man could get used to that."

Lorthok watched Colvin with a confused interest, bits of mushroom clinging to the corners of its mouth. It was taking its time with the mushrooms now, chewing each one slowly, appearing to savor each bite. When the last one had disappeared down its gullet, Lorthok waved its sword in a way that told Colvin it was time to go.

"*Rokah*," it said, wiping crumbs off its leather breastplate.

Colvin nodded, standing up from his log and stretching out one more time. "Best conversation I've had in a month," he said.

The same as before, Lorthok propelled Colvin onward through the hills at the point of its scimitar. Colvin continued the hunt for sustenance, but slacked off a bit upon realizing that Lorthok was shoving more and more of the morsels Colvin handed over into the leather pouch dangling by its hip. At first Colvin was relieved to take a break from foraging. Ultimately this just gave him more time to ponder his situation, though, and he soon started to worry. Lorthok was stuffed to the brim with nuts and roots and berries, and most especially mushrooms, but had given Colvin no sign that it was going to release him from service anytime soon. Lorthok's belt pouch would also be brimming with food before too long, at which point Colvin's usefulness would begin to wane in Lorthok's eyes. Eventually the sun would begin to set, and Lorthok would grow tired for the evening, and there was little hope in Colvin's mind that his kidnapper would simply trust him not to do anything rash or dangerous while it was sleeping. Colvin followed this line of thinking through to its logical conclusion.

"One of us is going to die." He did not realize he had said it out loud.

Colvin took a deep breath. Anger, not fear, flashed through him. He had faced the potential for death too many times to really be scared of it anymore, even if the thing that threatened him now was monstrous in appearance. He was being used as slave labor until his usefulness was exhausted, then he would be slaughtered like cattle. Colvin realized that Lorthok had no reservations about killing and eating a man. He had figured that out a little more each time he had looked into its cold yellow eyes. Lorthok just wanted to use him as much as it could before doing the inevitable.

Colvin had not been aware until now that he was clenching his fists. His knuckles were white with tension. His anger was getting the best of him. It had a nasty habit of doing that at the most inopportune times. More than once he had flown off the handle and put himself in a position where the risk of bodily harm was very high, and he owed it more to sheer dumb luck than anything else that he had made it out of each of those situations with only minor injuries. He wanted to keep his hostility in check, but a part of him somewhere deep down inside, a part that was always rational, told him that if he were to make a move against his captor, it would be smartest to do so on the spur of the moment, without giving it a chance to anticipate what was coming. Colvin felt his heartbeat pick up and his stomach muscles tighten. It was an old, familiar feeling. The task at hand was going to be difficult. He had fought armed people barehanded on occasion, and had the scars to prove it. More often than not, those skirmishes had ended with him running as hard and as fast as he could to escape his opponent. With any luck, Lorthok's bowed legs would make that possible now, too.

His strategy came upon him so suddenly, it almost formed itself. He played it out in his mind's eye. One deft motion, a spin and a step to the left, coming around and beside the blade. He would lay into Lorthok's head as hard as he could, hopefully dazing his captor enough for it to loosen its grip on the sword. Colvin would let the blade drop. Retrieving it might open himself up enough to give Lorthok an opportunity he couldn't afford. Besides, he was good with his hands. That would do it. Assuming he could turn around in time to sidestep the attack he knew would be coming, everything would work. If he could not get out of the way of Lorthok's blade…well, in that case he would die here and now as opposed to later at Lorthok's campsite. Colvin took a deep breath. Best not to overanalyze things. Best just to do it now, before the resolve breaks. Mentally, Colvin prepared himself. He would do it on the count of three.

Colvin burped and tasted rotten eggs.

His anger and his resolve ebbed for a moment. His stomach rumbled with something that he could not quite make himself believe was hunger. It felt too similar to nausea. There was not much of it, just a hint, but Colvin's mind was already working, reexamining every bite of food he had taste-tested for Lorthok. He stopped dead in his tracks when he remembered the joy he felt when he came across the patch.

Did those mushrooms have purple spots on the caps?

It took a moment for him to realize that the poke in the back he always felt whenever he slowed his step did not come. He looked back over his shoulder. Lorthok looked even greener than usual, its free hand clamped tightly to its abdomen. The scimitar hung limply by its side. It had a glazed look in its eyes, not appearing to see Colvin at all. It groaned a low, rough gurgling sound. Colvin's eyes widened.

It ate the whole damn patch.

"Are you okay?" he asked timidly. Lorthok dropped to its knees and vomited brutally in reply. Colvin jumped out of the way, narrowly avoiding being befouled. He could hear the thing's stomach rumbling and cramping. Lorthok looked up at him with a mixture of surprise, contempt and fear in its eyes. It wretched again, and farted at the same time. Bile dripped from the corners of its mouth. It looked more pathetic at that moment than any creature Colvin had ever seen. Lorthok doubled over, curling up into a fetal position, and heaved once again. The stench was overwhelming, and Colvin plugged his nostrils shut. The thing was whimpering and groaning between dry heaves now. Colvin just stood there gawking, having absolutely no idea what the twist to do. He wanted to run, to get as far away as he could now that his captor had suddenly taken ill, but something kept his feet planted. His own stomach bitterly protested the little nibble of poison mushroom Colvin had given it. He could only imagine what Lorthok was going through. In spite of himself, Colvin felt pity for the thing.

"You would have killed me, you know," Colvin said, sounding rather stupid with his nose plugged up as it was. As soon as he said it he realized he was not so certain of it anymore, now that an opportunity for escape had presented itself. It was conceivable that Lorthok would have kept him around only long enough to fill its pouch, then sent him on his way. He could not be certain which outcome was more likely, but now that he was in no immediate danger he found the one to be as plausible as the other. The more he thought it over, the more his vision of Lorthok running him through before making camp for the evening seemed like the first stages of a hostage's panic. Of course, there were no guarantees. Lorthok might well have been planning to do Colvin in when it was done with him. Colvin was thankful he would never know for certain.

Lorthok wailed and gnashed its teeth. Colvin approached the thing slowly. "You ate way too many of them," he said slowly, carefully, as if he thought enunciating his words clearly could break down the language barrier. "I should have noticed the purple marks, but I didn't. Five of those mushrooms would have been enough to make a strong man bedridden for a week. You ate at least twenty of them. You're going to die." Lorthok's eyes widened as if the thing actually did understand what he was saying. Its eyes shifted to its scimitar, laying on the ground a few feet out of its reach. There was no hostility in those yellow eyes, only pleading. Colvin sighed.

"Yeah, I wouldn't want to go this way either," he said, moving over to the sword. He picked it up slowly and wiped it on the grass, cleaning the vomitus from it. He looked at the rust-dotted blade for a moment. His life always seemed to come down to doing things he had absolutely no desire to do. He moved to stand directly above his captor, raising the sword high above his head. Lorthok's eyes widened, and its pupils contracted. It was bracing for the inevitable. At that moment, it looked more human than it ever had.

"I'm sorry. I honestly didn't mean to poison you." The tarnished steel still glinted in the sunlight as Colvin swung it resolutely home. The swish of blade through air gave way to a sound like a hatchet cleaving wood. Lorthok's head rolled away from its body. The thing's blood was red, Colvin was only mildly surprised to see.

Colvin cleaned the blade as best he could. A sword could come in handy, if only for trade. Colvin hoped he would only have to use it for trade. He also took the pouch half full of food. That would come in even handier than the sword. When he was done, Colvin considered burying Lorthok, or at least crossing the thing's arms over its chest, but finally decided that his desire to avoid touching the filth that covered the thing overrode any sense of respect for the dead. Colvin set out in the direction he vaguely assumed was north, leaving Lorthok to its eternal rest.

"Quite a morning," he said.

Chapter Seven

Rebuilding

Daylight came to Tamendad as it had every morning since the township's founding, but it was a day unlike any other. The streets still were filled with townspeople going about their business, the marketplace still abounded with peddlers hawking their wares and shoppers searching for bargains, the church bell still rang out to announce God's gift of another day, but a certain undefinable something hung heavy in the air, a feeling that suggested some small measure of the city's spirit had been lost. Laughter was rare that morning. Few people smiled. Many paused briefly here and there in the streets to kneel and make the Sign of the Compass before the houses whose doors bore the swath of black silk that announced a family in mourning. Everyone went out of their way to be kind and respectful whenever a constable came past on his rounds. People looked at bandages as though they were military decorations of valor. And absolutely no one went near the northwest gate who did not have orders to do so. People avoided the southwest gate, too, but this was mostly just to give room to the men who were charged with repairing the damage there. The sight of its splintered wood sent shivers down the spines of some passers by, a reminder of the siege that had come so close to devastating success, but no one had drawn their last breath there. The battle had been fought at the northwest gate, where the ground had been hallowed by men who gave their lives defending the city, where no townsperson now approached out of respect for the fallen, and where the bricks of the street were still a slightly wrong shade of red.

The doors to the city remained closed that morning for the first time in as long as anyone could remember. The gates of Tamendad rarely closed these days, and on the rare occasions that they did it was usually done just to ensure that the hinges had not frozen with rust. Before last night, the doors had never been drawn closed due to the threat of attack. Now each of the four were securely barred, and twenty-five armed men stood watch at each. Not all these men were constables. Many were just common townspeople who had volunteered to give up hours of their time standing guard. More people had volunteered to join the city watch last night than had done so in the past six months. Amon Jefford, Tamendad's Captain of the Guard, had to set up a post outside the church where men and women could line up and wait their turn to explain why they wanted to wear a constable's longsword. By the time the sun peeked over the horizon that morning, Captain Jefford's man had been interviewing prospective constabulary, one after another without interruption, for eight consecutive hours.

The repair effort had been underway practically since the monsters had called their retreat. Even more people had volunteered for the repair effort than for the constabulary, so many in fact that quite a good number had to be politely sent away, dragging their feet as they went. The central command of the repair effort had been set up at the southwest gate, where the damage was most severe, and Ferdinan stood in charge of the whole effort. Quite a few thought this a bit odd, since no one was entirely certain who, exactly, he was, but no one questioned his authority. Everyone followed his orders partially because he had been the first person in all of Tamendad to meet with the Governor after the attacks, in a private meeting that had lasted most of the night, but people also followed him just because he seemed to exude authority. He had a way of giving orders that made people want to follow them, that made people think what he had just ordered them to do was the most obviously important thing they could possibly be doing at that moment.

Ferdinan had not slept a wink last night. He had headed straight to the Governor's house after leaving William at the church. One of the Governor's personal guards had tried to block his path at the door, insisting that the Governor was seeing absolutely no one at the moment, but Ferdinan had prevailed in that match of wills.

"I am Don Julio Franco Francisco Ferdinan," he had announced, "King's Ambassador of Conquia, and more than this I am a man who just drew steel and helped defend this city from an army of creatures I would have never believed were real if I had not seen them with my own eyes. The Governor es especting my arrival tomorrow, but I am here now and I will see him now. Unlike you, I am not so willing to sit idly and wait for these...*things* to come back, hoping that the Governor's house still stands tomorrow so that I may see him then, when his overzealous doorman with an inflated sense of self-importance es willing to let a man who can offer much-needed advice pass." Ferdinan's icy stare penetrated right through the guard's glower, and the guard sent word after only a brief hesitation to ask if the Governor would see his caller.

"You have a serious problem, Governor," Ferdinan had announced as he entered Geoffery Chamberlain's study minutes later. The meeting had lasted three hours, with a notice from the Governor that the two of them were to be interrupted only for the most serious of emergencies. Toward the end of the meeting, even Governor Chamberlain had found himself agreeing with Ferdinan's "suggestions" without really even thinking them over all the way. Ferdinan had such an aura of confidence about him and his suggestions made such good sense – that the central command of the repair efforts be positioned at the southwest gate, not only because the damage was worse there but because the northwest gate should remain more tranquil out of respect; that two watchmen should be posted at every sentry point; that the Governor himself should make an open address to the people as soon as possible to assuage their fears as much as could be done; and so on – that Geoffery Chamberlain, whom no soul in Tamendad ever second-guessed, found himself following Ferdinan's every word like the enamored page of a great and charismatic knight. As daybreak approached, a knock at the study's door interrupted the Governor and the Conquian, the first interruption since Ferdinan had entered. A weary-looking constable entered, looking ill at ease.

"Report," said Governor Chamberlain and Ferdinan at the exact same time. The Governor looked at Ferdinan with a raised eyebrow, but the Conquian did not seem to notice. After the constable had looked both men over with a touch of curiosity, he delivered his message.

"Your Lordship," the man in armor said, then hesitated, looking at Ferdinan. "Your Lordships," he began again, "I apologize for the interruption, but I deemed this matter serious enough to intrude. The lookouts posted around the southwest gate discovered something lying just outside the gate not long ago. They would have seen it earlier, but the moonlight was poor and their focus was directed at a distance, and–"

"Yes, yes, get on with it," the Governor chastened. He had not slept, and his temper was short.

"Sorry, Your Lordship. What they discovered was a burlap sack. It must have been left by the invaders during the attack, or when they started to retreat. And in the sack…" The constable faltered.

"Go on," said Ferdinan, standing with his arms crossed over his chest.

The constable drew a deep breath. "The sack held four severed heads. The four scout riders you sent out in search of Lord Thalison's cattle, Governor."

Governor Chamberlain slumped into his chair. His report had come early.

❖   ❖   ❖

No one knew exactly what had been said in the meeting, only that very important people had been kept waiting while Ferdinan spoke to the Governor, and that the Governor had given Ferdinan certain authority within the township. Now Ferdinan strolled around with his arms folded over his chest, a determined look on his face while he inspected the repairs to the southwest gate. It was admittedly slow going, seeing that strong lumber was a relatively rare commodity within the city walls. Governor Chamberlain refused to send out a party to harvest trees until he had confirmation that the invaders were nowhere to be found, and he was understandably reluctant to send out scouts. Still, the volunteers did all that they could with what they had, working their fingers to the bone and doing their best to keep out of the constabulary's way. Ferdinan made certain not to press anyone too hard and to constantly praise the townspeople's efforts, but beneath his resoluteness he constantly calculated the city's weakness to another attack. If the invaders returned soon, there was little doubt the southwest gate would fall quickly, and Ferdinan knew from his reports that the condition of the northwest gate was only slightly better. Ferdinan did the only thing he could think to do, and hoped for a miracle.

For the first time in a long while, William awoke after the sun was already in the sky. He was in his own bed, back in his parents' house. He wanted nothing more than to convince himself that everything about the night before – the invaders that looked like monsters, the screams of the wounded, the *blood* – had been a dream, but the bandage still wrapped tightly around his midsection stood as an insurmountable reminder of the reality of it all. The intense stabbing pain he had felt in his side the night before had given way to a dull, disconcerting ache that began in his left side and spread out to envelop his whole body. He could tell that Patrum Albermarle's treatment had already begun to work. He groaned as he sat up in bed.

"Good morning, my love," Melissa's voice greeted him. She was sitting in a chair at the foot of his bed that had not been there the night before. She could not mask the concern in her eyes. She smoothed her dress as she stood up, and moved over to sit on William's bedside. She ran her fingers across his cheek. Her touch was pleasant and warm.

"How long have you been sitting there?" he asked, taking her hand in his and kissing her knuckles.

"Oh, I lost track of time. I came as soon as I heard. Reynolds and your father helped move that chair in here for me. You slept like a babe through the whole thing." She chuckled and tousled his hair, but the concern was still in her eyes. "How do you feel?"

William hesitated. The truth was that he felt like shit. His wound itched, the ache that had replaced the sharp, stabbing pains left much to be desired, and he had a beast of a headache. He did not dare tell his betrothed all that, though. She was already terribly worried about him. "I have been better, my love, but I'll manage." That seemed to be true enough without giving too much cause for alarm.

Melissa nodded. "I'll have Reynolds bring you up some breakfast."

"No, don't bother," William said before Melissa had a chance to rise from the bedside. William swung his feet over the edge of the bed and planted them on the floor, making sure his loincloth did not reveal anything to his future bride. "I'll grab a bite to eat on my way out."

Melissa grabbed William's hand, less of a gesture of affection than a means of preventing him from standing up. That was just as well. William was not entirely certain how much difficulty trying to stand would present. "Where do you think you are going, my love?" she asked. With the inflection of her words, she might as well have just come right out and told William he was not going anywhere.

"There is too much to be done in this town today for me to waste any more time in bed, Melissa." His manner was gentle, but resolute.

Melissa shook her head slightly. "Patrum Albermarle said you needed at least a few days of bed rest before you were up and around again. You'll reopen your wound if you try to help with the repairs." Melissa was halfway between instructing and pleading.

"So the repairs have already started then? Good."

"Oh, William, you are impossible. I should give you something to make you sleep." She sounded like she would almost do it.

"Melissa, my love, I give you my word I will take it easy. Nothing strenuous, just lending a hand wherever someone needs it."

Melissa sighed. She knew there was no reasoning with William when he got like this. She reluctantly acquiesced, and waited outside his bedroom while he dressed. They descended the stairs and entered the dining room together, William limping noticeably as he went.

"Good morning, Lord William," Reynolds said while preparing a plate for each of them. "Your mother is out helping with the repairs, and your father left this morning to stable and safeguard the horses."

"They just let him go?" William sounded exasperated. He was obviously troubled by the news that his father was beyond the safety of the city walls.

"Governor Chamberlain has suggested no one leave the city, but he has not forbidden anyone to do so," Reynolds explained. "People can still come and go as they please, though they must announce themselves and their business at the gates before passing through."

"Don't worry, William," Melissa said. "My father went along, and they took a good number of strong men with them, all of them armed. Father promised me they'd turn back at the first sign of trouble."

William was relieved that his father was not alone, but he was still uneasy about it. "By the time we saw the first sign of trouble last night, it was almost too late." Melissa winced at her betrothed's words. She did not like to think about how close William had been to the attack.

"Lord Jonathan left strict orders that you were not to leave the house, Lord William," Reynolds said, changing the subject. "I suppose that will not stop you, though."

William almost laughed. At least the old butler knew enough not to try talking William out of it. Reynolds sat a plate of poached eggs, bacon and toast before William and Melissa, and excused himself. William cleared his plate greedily, as though he had not eaten in days. He had not even realized he was hungry until he had taken the first bite, and before he knew it his plate was completely clean. He waited for Melissa to finish her breakfast, impatiently wondering if she was stalling intentionally, before he rose from the table. Melissa rose and walked with him.

"Where are you going, my love?" he asked.

"You are not the only one capable of lending a hand, William, and at least I am whole."

William did not even dream of offering any objections. For one thing, Melissa was as stubborn as he was, perhaps even more so, when she made up her mind. For another, William suspected the repair effort would need as much help as it could get. Together they sat off for the southwest gate.

"William, es good to see you again," said Ferdinan, smiling and walking briskly toward the young nobleman and his betrothed. He smiled even more brightly at Melissa, taking her hand and kissing it. "And to you, my lady, good morning." William felt a small flash of jealousy. He did not think Ferdinan had meant anything by it, but William barely knew him, and he was just so…charming.

"You are in charge of the repairs, Ferdinan?" William asked, as much to bring the Conquian's attention back to him as anything else.

"Sí," Ferdinan replied simply. "You have come to volunteer? I am glad to see you are feeling well enough to…how do you say?…*chip in.*"

"Whatever I can do, Ferdinan. I'm here to help."

"Wonderful," Ferdinan said, clasping his hands together. "The men at the northwest gate are in need of assistance, and it will raise their spirits to be led by a man who fought there."

William blinked. "Led?" The word sounded strange in his ears. He did not think he had heard Ferdinan correctly.

"Sí, William, I need someone I can trust to oversee the repairs to the northwest gate. You are a nobleman, and you have the respect of the townspeople for what you did last night." Ferdinan spread his hands in a way that suggested he thought putting William in charge of the northwest gate was the most obvious course of action imaginable. "So, what are you waiting for?"

"Uh…"

"Excuse me, Master Ferdinan," Melissa said politely, "but I have come to offer my services as well. If I may make a request, I would also like to be assigned to the northwest gate."

Ferdinan made a move that was something between a nod and a bow. "Of course, my lady. William will need assistance with leading the men, and I think perhaps he will also need someone to make sure he does not overdo it. I practically had to drag him kicking and screaming to see a healer last night, and I do not think he would take great care not to reopen his wound if left to himself."

"Am I supposed to just walk up and tell everyone I am in charge?" William asked. He sounded like he still could not quite believe what Ferdinan had asked him to do.

"They will know," Ferdinan said, a mysteriously convincing quality in his voice. "And they would follow you even if I had not put you in charge." William's eyes widened. He could not imagine why people would follow him.

"Thank you, milord," Melissa said, wrapping her arm around William's.

"Es nothing," Ferdinan replied, bowing elegantly. Melissa curtsied, and William stammered out a thank you.

"No, thank you, William," Ferdinan said, that same mysterious quality in his voice again, and then turned his attention back to the southwest gate.

Melissa gently led William back the way they had come. They walked in silence for a while, only speaking to return the greetings of those who spoke to them. William did not notice the unusually large number of people who stopped to bid him a good morning, or the respect bordering on reverence with which they did it. Melissa noticed, however, and squeezed her betrothed's arm tightly. Pride swelled her heart, but there was a fear present within the pride. A good number of heroes' wives ended up widows, and she and William were not even wed yet.

"He has no idea what he's doing, putting me in charge," William said quietly to his lover.

"I think he knows exactly what he's doing," she replied, patting his hand.

William fully expected the men at the northwest gate to laugh at him when he told them he had been placed in charge of repairs there. A boy of his age had no business ordering around fully grown and fully capable men, no matter what Ferdinan said. He tried thinking of some way to word it that would not offend the men he presumed to lead, but as it turned out he was not even given a chance to speak. Men began to turn and stare as William and Melissa drew near the northwest gate. A murmur ran through the crowd of people working there, and everyone stopped to look as soon as they heard what was being said. The man who had been giving orders before William had arrived began to approach. He was a big man, stout and strong with tanned skin and brown hair, and looked to be of middle years. William readied himself to deliver Ferdinan's order, but the man started talking before William could get the first word out.

"Lord Stuart-Camen, you honor us with your presence, sir," the man said, and then dropped to one knee. William looked at the man with surprised eyes, then turned to look at Melissa. She was smiling brightly at him, her look seeming to say, *you see?* "My name is Merrik, Lord, and I stand ready to follow whatever you order."

"Merrik, get up. Get up." Merrik got to his feet, and William addressed him. "I have come to help with…I have come to oversee the repairs."

"Tell us what to do, Lord," a young man about William's age called out from the small crowd of onlookers. William saw him, saw his willingness to serve, willingness to do whatever William told him. William hesitated. He had no idea what he should tell them.

"Show me what you have done so far," he said at last, and was surprised by the determination he heard in his own voice. That was a good start. Merrik led William and Melissa to the wall, and began to explain what had been done, what had yet to be done, and why. William listened intently, and started formulating plans. He had the look of a leader. Melissa held William's hand tightly in both of hers.

Manhood suits you, my love, she thought.

❖　　❖　　❖

Colvin stood atop the hill overlooking the town, blinking and rubbing his eyes. He was not certain whether it was Tamendad or Tantera he was seeing, since he had never seen either of them before in his life.

Regardless of which city it was, he was genuinely surprised to find himself so far to the north. He had climbed this hill, the tallest one around, because he suspected it would afford a decent view of what lay ahead of him. He had not expected to find the sea on the other side of it.

He could not make out many details about the city by the sea, only that it was surrounded by a sturdy wall and all the gates appeared to be closed. Colvin could not decide if it was good fortune or ill to stumble upon the town like this. On the one hand, he had not felt safe since his run-in with Lorthok that morning, and having a city wall around him would no doubt help ease his worries. On the other hand, cities tended to be dirty, smelly places, and the people in them tended to be much less friendly than people who made their homes in thorps and hamlets. Colvin had never had much luck appealing to the kindness of village folk, and he was not entirely sure how he would ever manage in a city. He stood atop the hill, debating with himself for several minutes. In the end, his need for a sense of safety overrode any pragmatic concerns of how he would maintain his livelihood. If he ran into another of Lorthok's race – or worse yet, a whole group of them – he felt relatively certain that he would not have much of a livelihood left to maintain. He started down the hill toward the city gate closest to him.

Colvin began to notice that something was not quite right with the town before him. For starters, it had appeared from the top of the hill that all the gates of the city were shut tight. So far as Colvin had heard, though he admittedly had not heard much, neither Tantera nor Tamendad shut their gates during the day, and Tamendad was not known for shutting its gates at all. As Colvin got a bit closer, he saw that the gate itself looked like it had seen better days. Good-sized chunks of wood had been cleaved from it, and several other places were splintered. All in all, it looked like a very large and very angry dog had vented some of its frustrations on it. Colvin wondered how safe he would be in this city after all.

"State your name and business!" a voice called down to him from the top of the wall as he approached. Colvin looked up to see two men standing on little platforms atop the wall on either side of the gate. The sentries wore shirts of chain, with swords sheathed at their hips and a bow and quiver slung over each of their shoulders. The voice belonged to one of the guards on the right side of the gate.

"Um, my name is Colvin, and I really don't have any business, I just want to enter this city," Colvin said, uncertainly. "Which city is this, by the way?"

The guard did not immediately reply. Colvin could see that the guard was saying something to the other man that shared his platform. The gatekeepers probably did not receive a lot of visitors who did not know which city they were seeking entrance to, Colvin mused. "You seek entrance to Tamendad, good sir," the guard finally called down to him. "Be advised that no man may be allowed to enter these gates with a drawn weapon." Colvin looked at Lorthok's scimitar. His scimitar now, he reminded himself. He had been carrying it for so long he had forgotten he had it in his hand.

"What should I do with it?" Colvin asked. The guard failed to stifle his laughter. Colvin wanted to punch him.

"I suggest you sheath it, sir," the guard said.

"I don't have a sheath."

"Well, then just stick the blade between your trousers and your belt, and be careful not to cut yourself."

Colvin shrugged his shoulders, and slid the blade of the scimitar underneath the length of rope that was holding his pants up. He looked back up at the guard when he had finished. "Good enough?" he called up.

"Open the gate. One to enter," the guard called down to someone inside. There was a metallic sound of a wench being turned, but nothing happened immediately. Enough time passed to make Colvin wonder if the guard had just been taunting him before the gate began to lurch open, and even then it appeared to do so with great reluctance. The doors opened barely wide enough for Colvin to squeeze through between them. As soon as he was on the other side, the same voice called down from above. "One has entered. Close the gate." The wenchmen busied themselves with reversing their previous course of action. Colvin wanted to ask exactly what had happened to the city, but he was whisked through the gate and into the city streets by the watchmen posted there before he even had a chance to open his mouth.

Colvin found himself standing in the middle of a wide bricked street. There were houses on either side of him, though the ones to his left looked a bit nicer than the ones to his right. Up ahead and way down the street, he could see a large building that he thought was probably a church. He could not be certain, however, because the open pavilion tent that had been set up right in the middle of the street partially blocked the view. A couple of tables and a handful of chairs sat underneath the roof of the tent, and men and women were continuously coming and going around it. They all seemed to be talking and listening to one man in particular, a man with dark skin and darker hair, who was wearing a red vest with gold embroidery that was the nicest article of clothing Colvin had ever seen. The man was obviously in charge here, and Colvin's curiosity demanded he speak with someone who knew what was going on.

Colvin walked up to the tent, right up to the dark-skinned man who was sitting in the nicest chair at the nicer of the two tables. The man was inspecting a piece of paper and did not say anything at first. Colvin cleared his throat to get the man's attention.

"Something I can help you with?" Ferdinan said, looking up from the report he was reading. "Have you come to volunteer?"

Colvin had never heard anyone talk the way this man did, like he could not decide whether he wanted to talk or breathe. In a way, his accent was beautiful. "Volunteer for what?" Colvin asked.

Ferdinan arched an eyebrow. "For the repair effort."

"Oh, well, sure, I guess," Colvin said. "Say, exactly what happened here, anyway?"

"You have not heard?" asked Ferdinan, his voice incredulous.

"I just got here," replied Colvin. "I'm not from Tamendad."

"The city fell under attack last night. Es probably your good fortune you were not here. What es your name?"

"I'm Colvin."

"Colvin what?" Ferdinan asked.

Colvin scratched his head and shrugged his broad shoulders. "Just Colvin."

"You do not have a family name?" Ferdinan asked. Colvin could tell this man had never heard of such a thing.

"I don't have a family," Colvin said simply. Ferdinan nodded, saying nothing. He had a look in his eyes that came close to pity.

Ferdinan stood up from his chair and bowed to Colvin, introducing himself.

You've got plenty of names for the both of us, Colvin thought.

"Where are you coming from, Colvin?" asked Ferdinan, rubbing the whiskers on his chin as he spoke.

"Well, everywhere and nowhere, really. I'm a bit of a wanderer." Colvin shuffled his feet a bit. He did not like being asked about these sorts of things.

Ferdinan's look was suddenly curious. "I have to ask you, did you see anything...*unusual* on your way to Tamendad?"

"Well, um, yeah." Colvin just decided to spit it out, regardless of how stupid it sounded. "A green thing with tusks held me captive and made me find food for it until I accidentally fed it an entire patch of poison mushrooms."

Ferdinan nodded, and did not look like he thought Colvin was crazy in the slightest. "Those were what attacked the city," the Conquian explained. "How many did you see?"

"Oh, just the one." Colvin could barely imagine what it would look like, an army of Lorthoks storming the city. No wonder everyone seemed so curt. They were probably still in shock.

"You are certain you only saw one? Es very important." Ferdinan could barely mask the desperation in his voice. The Governor still hesitated to send out scouts, and here a man had strolled right up to him with the information it would have taken a scout at least a day to gather. Miracles happened.

"Yeah, trust me, I'd remember seeing more of them," said Colvin.

Ferdinan could not contain his smile. "And you came on foot from the southwest?"

"More or less," Colvin replied. "I kind of ambled all over the place."

"Even better," Ferdinan said. "Your help would be invaluable at the northwest gate. William Stuart-Camen es the man in charge there. If you will escuse me, I have to speak to the Governor." Ferdinan bowed deeply, then patted Colvin on the shoulder, smiling, and walked briskly toward one of the side streets that broke away from the main avenue. Colvin stood under the pavilion for a moment longer, not entirely certain what had just happened. He gave himself a shake. It appeared no one was going to show him the way to the northwest gate, so he decided to look for it himself.

CHAPTER EIGHT

GETTING ACQUAINTED

Ferdinan hurried through the streets of Tamendad, moving just quickly enough that he could still manage to appear dignified. His run-in with the red-haired young man, whose name he could not quite recall even this soon after meeting him, had been a godsend. Now he just had to discuss with the Governor what the young man with intense eyes had told him and send out a party to hew some trees from the wooded hillsides, and Tamendad would have more than enough strong lumber to restore the walls to their original condition. He felt like his feet could not carry him fast enough. It would be improper for an ambassador of the Conquian throne, not to mention the man in charge of the repair efforts to the city, to be seen running through the streets. Such a sight might start a panic. Still, Ferdinan had to measure his steps carefully to keep from involuntarily breaking into a jog.

Once he arrived at the Governor's house, he strode right up to the front door and let himself in, not even acknowledging the guards posted on either side of the main entrance. The guards made no move to stop him. They knew well enough from hearing about what had transpired that morning that Don Ferdinan came and went as he pleased, and was not a man to be held up for any reason when it looked like he was calling on business. Ferdinan took the stairs to the second floor two at a time, and walked right up to the entrance to the Governor's study, where the guards posted outside barred his way.

"Governor Chamberlain is in a meeting with Captain Jefford, and they are not to be disturbed." It was the same guard whom Ferdinan had given a tongue-lashing that morning, and he looked like he was deriving no small amount of pleasure from delivering this news.

"Es an emergency," Ferdinan explained, and moved to step around the guards blocking his path. They sidestepped to intercept him again.

"The Governor gave strict instructions that he was not to be bothered while meeting with Captain Jefford, for any reason," the guard said, smiling. His companion had a worried look on his face.

"This es unacceptable. I must speak with the Governor now. It cannot wait."

"It will have to, because no one is getting into this room while Captain Jefford is still inside. You can wait in the sitting room. It should not be much longer." Ferdinan felt an urge to punch him in the face. The Conquian began tapping his foot instead, and crossed his arms over his chest. There was a tense moment of silence.

"Very well," Ferdinan said at last, spinning on his heels and moving toward the sitting room. He muttered curses under his breath in his own language as he walked away.

The sitting room on the second floor of the Governor's house was furnished with comfortable, overstuffed chairs and benches, and beautiful tapestries hung on the walls, depicting different scenes of the city itself and the countryside that surrounded it. Here and there, a portrait of one of the previous Governors adorned the walls. A table by one of the windows overlooking the noblemen's houses held glasses and a bottle of brandy. It was a perfectly lovely place for a man to bide his time while waiting, but Ferdinan despised being made to wait no matter how nice his environs. He did not bother having a seat. He stood with his hands clasped together at the small of his back, peering out the window at the city below him. A servant in livery entered the sitting room.

"May I bring you something while you wait, sir?" the servant asked meekly, as though he expected to be yelled at. Word had obviously begun to spread about Ferdinan's second run-in with the overzealous guard.

"A glass of red wine, please." Ferdinan did not look away from the window as he spoke. He heard the servant turn and exit the room without a word.

The city down below looked like all was perfectly well within it. This window faced the southeast, and neither of the damaged gates could be seen from it. In the streets below, stableboys waited to be called upon to fetch horses for the noblemen and landowners. Men and women were coming and going with a quickness to their step, but if Ferdinan had not known about the events of last night he would have thought their haste was due to some pressing matter known only to themselves. Here and there a constable made his rounds through the city streets, obviously made uncomfortable by the reverential stares he was receiving. In a strange and distant way, the sight made Ferdinan think of his own city, across the ocean, and the way its streets looked from the window in his own study. Losillas was a long way away.

Ferdinan heard the footsteps of the person entering the room, and

S. MATTHEW MCNALLY

nodded to himself over how prompt the servants saw to their duties here. He did not immediately look away from the window.

"Master Ferdinan," came the woman's voice, sweet yet professional, "I heard about your encounter with my father's guard." Ferdinan turned his gaze from the window and saw a young woman with auburn hair and fair complexion standing in the middle of the sitting room. He knew her at once to be Elysia, the Governor's daughter, from the stories he had heard of her, but he had never actually lain eyes on her until now. She was wearing an embroidered green gown that brought out the color of her eyes, and she had her hands clasped together in front of her. She was beautiful. Ferdinan tended to think all women were beautiful, each in her own unique way, but Elysia had an aura of gentle confidence about her that was rare to find in the fairer sex. Ferdinan bowed formally, his right hand pressed against his abdomen and his left extended in the air behind him. He moved toward her, and when his eyes met hers she looked like she was about to take a step backward. Ferdinan gently, gracefully extended his right hand and took her left in it, raising it to his lips and planting a soft kiss between the first and second knuckle.

"Lady Chamberlain, es very gracious of you to see me in person, but an apology es unnecessary. I understand that your father es a very busy man right now, and everyone must wait their turn to have a moment of his time."

"That is very kind of you, Master Ferdinan," Elysia said, smiling politely. She was absentmindedly trailing her fingers over the spot Ferdinan had kissed on her hand. "There is still no excuse for the way you were spoken to."

Ferdinan smiled, shrugging his shoulders slightly. "The guard and I have a bit of a history. I spoke rashly to him this morning, and he es just making the most of an opportunity to get back at me. Es human."

"You are a very understanding man," Elysia said. "Many of my father's visitors would not have as much patience."

"Patience es a virtue, my lady, and a necessary one for ambassadors to possess."

"Yes, of course. You must miss your home quite a bit after your tour of our kingdom. If I may be so bold as to request a moment of your time, would you sit with me and tell me of San Hidalgo?" She gestured to one of the benches, a smile barely curling the corners of her lips. Ferdinan bowed again, less grandiosely this time.

"I can think of no better way to spend my time than conversing with such a lovely woman, Lady Chamberlain."

"Call me Elysia, Master Ferdinan," she said, curtsying, blushing.

"Very well," Ferdinan replied, moving toward the bench, "but then

95

you must not call me Master, for God es the only one worthy of that title."

"Well spoken, sir," Elysia acquiesced. Ferdinan waited for Elysia to seat herself before joining her. Once they were both on the bench, slightly closer to one another than practicality forced them to be, Ferdinan began his story.

"To begin, I actually hail from Losillas, not San Hidalgo."

"Oh, I just assumed you were from the capital city, since you were an ambassador of King Altores," Elysia explained.

"An understandable assumption, but certain duties tie me to Losillas," Ferdinan said.

Elysia nodded. "I have heard that some of the finest swordsmen in the world are trained in Losillas," she said, trying her best not to eye the duelist's sabre at Ferdinan's left hip.

"Sí, Losillas es one of the few remaining places where swordplay es still studied as an art form. Men travel great distances to study under the grand masters." A servant entered the sitting room, gently setting a glass of wine on the end table beside Ferdinan and taking great care not to interrupt the conversation. Elysia told the servant she did not require anything with a dismissive wave of her hand, not looking away from Ferdinan.

"It sounds terribly violent," she said.

Ferdinan shook his head while sipping from his goblet. "No, no, not at all. *Decusé* es the first lesson a student of the sword learns."

"*Decusé?*"

"The closest word in your language would be honor, but even that fails to capture the essence of *decusé*. The sword es a weapon, but the use of that weapon need not be recklessly violent. When two swordsmen face each other in a duel, es an unspoken understanding between them that neither will do anything unfair or underhanded to gain advantage. Es a match of pure skill between the two, and the better swordsman will be triumphant." Ferdinan took another sip of his wine before continuing. "And when a duel es to the death, es ended as quickly and painlessly as possible. Es no reason to prolong suffering."

"That is an interesting philosophy," Elysia said, and she realized that she had scooted a bit closer to the Conquian without knowing it.

"*Decusé* es the only philosophy worth following, Elysia. Es what separates men from beasts. Es the smile of Tactus."

"The Face of Consonance?" asked Elysia.

"Sí," replied Ferdinan. "*Decusé* es the way God intended man to live. Es the path to perfect harmony between the soul and God."

Ferdinan's eyes met Elysia's, and the two just sat there for a moment looking at each other. Ferdinan thought about how easy it would be for a man to lose himself in those big, beautiful, blue-green eyes. *She is the Governor's daughter,* he reminded himself harshly.

Elysia gave herself a shake, bringing herself back to reality. Her thoughts had not been entirely ladylike. "And what about when a swordsman faces an opponent who fights dishonorably?"

"You butcher them like dogs," Ferdinan replied levelly. "Without mercy. Without remorse."

Elysia stared into Ferdinan's dark eyes in silence. The measured ferocity of Ferdinan's response had shocked her, but she was somewhat ashamed to admit it had also excited her to a degree. She found herself at a loss for what to say.

They were interrupted before she had a chance to respond. The guard who had taken such great pleasure in making Ferdinan wait had entered the sitting room, and he had the look of a man who had just received a stern talking-to. "Master Ferdinan, Governor Chamberlain will see you now," he said meekly.

Ferdinan smiled at Elysia, and looked back to the guard. "Tell the Governor I will be with him in a moment."

This man, Colvin thought, *is an idiot.*

There was little doubt that the young blond-haired man with the bandage wrapped tightly around his midsection was William Stuart-Camen, since he was the one everyone around the northwest gate seemed to be listening to. That in itself seemed odd, since he looked to be perhaps even younger than Colvin, and there were many men following his orders that looked to be at least twice his age. What really caught Colvin's attention, though, was that William had obviously sustained a major injury and looked more like he should be in a sickbed than out helping with repairs.

"You come to volunteer?" a voice asked from behind Colvin. He turned to see a rather largish man of middle years standing with his hands on his hips.

"I suppose so," Colvin said. He pointed to the blond man. "Is that William Stuart-Camen?"

"Yeah, that's *Lord* Stuart-Camen," said the man. "He's in charge here, but there's no need to bother him. He's got a lot on his plate. You look like you'd make a good, strong runner. Go fetch a wheelbarrow and start bringing supplies to whoever asks for them. If you have any questions, look for me. My name's Merrik."

Colvin nodded. "Sure thing, Merrik." Merrik nodded in return, and then diverted his attention elsewhere. Colvin sighed as he set about looking for a wheelbarrow. *Lord* Stuart-Camen. That was fantastic. He was probably some high and mighty, holier-than-thou type. Colvin did not look forward to getting acquainted with him. His experience with nobility had been limited, but what few times he had come into contact with the upper class they had usually been taking food out of the mouths of hard working men and women who could barely keep themselves afloat. He was mulling all this over so deeply that he almost tripped over the wheelbarrow before he saw it. He began making his rounds, asking the men and women repairing the gate and wall what they needed, then fetching it for them from the nearest supplies stock house. It was monotonous, boring work, but the townspeople seemed to think well of the volunteers, and Colvin thought he might just have discovered how he was going to find a meal and a place to sleep that night.

Hours passed. Colvin continuously ran back and forth, to and from the stock house, the wooden handles of his wheelbarrow raising blisters on his palms and the bricks of the street scraping up the bottoms of his bare feet. He barely had a moment's rest. It seemed someone was constantly needing something, and he had counted only two other runners servicing the whole northwest gate. One was an older man, probably about Merrik's age, who seemed gruff and whom Colvin had no real desire to get to know. The other was around Colvin's age, but smaller and more wiry, with brown hair tied back in a ponytail and wearing only a pair of trousers and padded leather shoes. Colvin would have done just about anything for those shoes. He had not had a pair of shoes in months.

After about three hours of nonstop running, sweat pouring down his face and stinging his eyes, Colvin finally decided to take a little break. He was not tired, exactly, but there were no clouds in the sky to shield him from the intensity of the summer sun, and being right next to the sea made it so humid he felt like he was swimming more than walking. Colvin paused to draw a bucket out of the nearest well, drinking as much as he could from it and dumping the rest over his head. The water tasted slightly salty, but it was cool and refreshing nonetheless. He brushed his drenched hair back from his face, and saw that the young runner with the brown hair had stopped to have a drink himself.

"Oi, I'm Dennis," the young man said, turning the crank to make the bucket descend. "I haven't seen you around here before."

"No, I just came into town today. My name's Colvin." Colvin extended his hand, and Dennis shook it with the one that was not turning the crank.

"You picked a great time to play tourist, Colvin." Dennis flashed a grin.

"That's what it's starting to look like," Colvin replied. "You're from here, then?"

"Born and raised," Dennis said. The rope that connected bucket to crank was now fully extended, and Dennis began the somewhat slower process of bringing it back up.

"They really keep us going, don't they?" Colvin gestured to the men and women making various repairs to the northwest gate.

"Yeah, well, I'd want to get it finished as fast as possible too. No telling when those things might come back."

They stood in silence for a few moments, neither seeming to know exactly what to say about that. It was the fear that everyone in town shared but no one mentioned, that those things might come back as soon as night fell again. There was not much that could be done to the walls and gate without a good supply of lumber, but anything that could be done would help. Dennis drew the full bucket from the well and lifted it to his lips, what water he could not manage to get down his throat running down his chest and trousers instead. When he was done, he sighed and tipped the bucket over his head like Colvin had done.

"Well," Colvin said at last, "we could always throw mushrooms at them."

"What?" Dennis asked, and laughed the half-laugh of someone who was not quite certain if the person he was talking to just tried to make a joke.

"Never mind," Colvin said. "Long story."

"Well, I suppose–"

"All right, gentlemen, break time is over. Let's get back to work." The voice came from over Colvin's shoulder. Colvin turned his head to see William Stuart-Camen walking toward him.

"We still have a lot of work left to do today, and the quicker we get it done the better," William explained as he approached. Dennis nodded vigorously and quickly moved to fetch his wheelbarrow, but Colvin was not so quick.

"Of course, Lord Stuart-Camen," Dennis said as he rolled his wheelbarrow past. He looked back over his shoulder at Colvin, obviously surprised that he was not snapping back to work.

Colvin folded his arms over his chest, not moving. William gave him a questioning look, which Colvin mistook for contempt. Colvin's temper always had a way of getting the better of him, and his first impression of William had not been a good one. "What's your problem?" he said.

William did not immediately reply. This was the first time all day one of the workers had responded to him the way he had feared they might.

"I mean, I'm out here working my butt off," Colvin continued, "not to mention how hard everyone else is working, and the only time you talk to me is to yell at me for taking a drink of water? Meanwhile you're out here half dead, with a bandage all that's holding you together, so I know you can't be chipping in that much." Colvin tried to make himself shut up, but once he got started he usually could not stop.

Anger flashed in William's eyes. In the back of his mind, he had been waiting to hear that speech all day. "I was merely saying we've still got a lot to do, and none of us has time to stand around. We have to get that gate back in order as quickly as we can."

"Oh, well, yes sir, commander, sir," Colvin replied. He feigned a military salute, doing as good a job of it as anyone who had never actually seen a military salute could. The look that spread across William's face made Colvin instantly regret his words. He had been expecting anger. He could deal with anger. Colvin had a long and glorious history of royally pissing people off. William's look, however, was one of pure hurt, as if Colvin's words had cut him to the bone. Colvin pushed the wheelbarrow past William, cursing himself under his breath as he went.

"Oi, runner!" William called after Colvin. Colvin took a deep breath before turning around. He braced for the storm he felt was sure to come.

William walked up to Colvin. "What's your name?"

Colvin sighed his name. *At least a jail cell is a place to sleep*, he thought.

"Why aren't you wearing shoes, Colvin?" William asked.

After only a slight pause, Colvin replied, "I don't have any." William's question had thrown him for a slight loop.

"Well, I can't let you be a runner in bare feet. You'll cut yourself up terribly with all the debris lying around."

Colvin wanted to punch William. This guy wasn't going to throw him in jail, he was going to take away Colvin's only hope of scoring a meal and a bed. "You know what? You can go–"

William called for the foreman before Colvin could finish his instructions. "Oi, Merrik, come here please." Some distant and detached part of Colvin's mind noted with moderate interest that William had said please. Merrik quickly made his way over. Colvin cursed under his breath.

"Merrik," William said as the foreman approached, "see to it that Colvin here gets a good pair of boots."

"Right away, Lord Stuart-Camen," Merrik said, and turned quickly to see to William's command.

Colvin shrugged his broad shoulders. He had failed at every

opportunity to figure this William Stuart-Camen out. "I can't afford to pay for a pair of boots," he said.

"Then consider them a gift," William said simply.

Colvin blinked. It was the first time in his life anyone had ever given him anything with no strings attached. He had no idea what to say, but William did not give him a chance to say anything. The young nobleman just patted him on the back, smiled, and walked away.

William's smile did not falter. Colvin's words had stung him, but he had stuck closely to his father's teachings. Meeting hostility with hostility might seem the natural course of action, but nothing got under a man's skin more than thanking him after he spit in your eye.

Afternoon passed into evening rather quietly. The biggest news in town was that a party of men had been sent out to harvest trees from the surrounding hills, though no one was entirely certain if it had been Governor Chamberlain or Ferdinan who had made the order. William stayed at the northwest gate until Melissa all but dragged him away, insisting it was time to rest. Colvin went out of his way to keep out of William's view while the young nobleman was still in command. Each step in his new boots reminded him of how he had shot off at the mouth. He genuinely was sorry for what he had said to William, but Colvin had never apologized for anything in his life. There had never really been a reason to, before today. Every time Colvin had ever badmouthed someone, it had been for genuinely good reason. He really was not sure how a person went about saying he was sorry. All he knew was that he wanted to put off finding out as long as possible.

Dennis had not had much to say to him after word had spread about the impromptu confrontation with William, nor had anyone else. Colvin began to feel like he had seriously stepped in it this time. It was one thing that he had insulted a man who for all intents and purposes seemed to be an honestly likeable fellow. It made matters worse that in doing so, Colvin had ostracized himself from quite a few people who would have otherwise probably been willing to spring for the cost of a meal and a decent place to sleep that night, had he asked nicely. Colvin replayed the events of the afternoon that had led up to his confrontation with William over and over in his mind, wondering at which point he had formed the wrong opinion of the young nobleman. In the end, he decided to blame Merrik's insistence that *Lord* Stuart-Camen was much too busy a man to bother meeting someone like Colvin, though he did this mostly because it was easier than blaming himself.

A new shift of volunteers arrived as the sun was just beginning to signal its slow-moving retreat toward the western horizon, and many of these newcomers, who were blessedly unaware of Colvin's earlier outburst, were quite friendly with the red-haired wanderer as they passed by. Colvin gladly relinquished his wheelbarrow to the short but stocky gentleman who requested it from him. As glad as he was to have new boots without having to pay for them, they were still new boots, not yet broken in, and the dull ache that stabbed through both his feet made each trip to the stock house a little more unbearable than the one before. In the back of his mind, Colvin wondered if that had been part of William's intentions. Either way, it did not really matter. He'd had those boots for only a matter of hours, and already they were his most prized possession.

Colvin left the northwest gate in pretty much the same condition he had found it, despite all the efforts of the assiduous volunteers, and went out in search of a place to fill his stomach and rest his head. So far, all he had seen of Tamendad were private residences, and rather nice ones at that. He had no idea which way would take him into the trade district, where he hopefully could barter his services for a meal and a warm, dry corner to curl up in, so he picked a direction at random and started walking.

It became quickly apparent that chance had steered him wrong, as he soon found himself surrounded by yet more private houses, the most extravagant he had seen thus far. Well-dressed lords and ladies eyed him suspiciously in his pauper's rags, with an oddly curved sword suspended at his hip with a length of hemp rope. Colvin grew increasingly uncomfortable, but measured his steps carefully so as not to break into a run. Running would only draw more attention to himself, and probably convince the wrong sort of people that he was up to the wrong sort of business, and that would land him in the stocks before he had a chance to explain himself. Colvin wanted desperately to put a good amount of distance between himself and anyone wearing a nobleman's crest, but he was rapidly discovering that the streets that ran through this part of the residential district had a deceptively labyrinthine quality about them, and before he even knew what he was doing Colvin found himself hopelessly lost.

Don Julio Franco Francisco Ferdinan of Losillas was making his way through those same streets, coming from his latest visit to the Governor's house. This time, however, he had not been visiting the Governor. He was returning from his evening tea with Elysia Chamberlain. Ferdinan had never heard of referring to tea as a meal before coming to Tur. If any beverage deserved to be elevated to that status, in Ferdinan's mind it was assuredly wine. But the custom had presented Ferdinan another opportunity to get to know the Governor's daughter. Tea had lasted almost two hours, and he and Elysia had discussed everything from the hierarchical structure of the Conquian monarchy to Elysia's favorite places to take her afternoon rides, and Ferdinan's head was still adrift from his time spent with the young Lady Chamberlain. Ferdinan tended to enjoy the company of women in general. He found that they did indeed tend to live up to their appellation as the fairer sex, each of them possessing a grace and delicacy, not to mention a frequently undiscovered reserve of inner strength, which any man would be hard-pressed to duplicate. When Ferdinan made the claim that all women were beautiful, as he regularly did, more often than not he was referring to this inner beauty rather than the mere physical sexuality that most men fawned over. It would be downright foolish to allege that physical beauty was not an endearing charm that drew Ferdinan to many women, but the Conquian ultimately found what lay beneath the physical level, deep in a woman's soul, to be what truly fascinated him.

His general adoration of women aside, something about Elysia appealed to Ferdinan in a way few women could. She was demure yet knowledgeable, and exuded a confidence that was rare even among men. She was ambitious, yet she did not desire power simply for power's sake. She possessed a level of wit and intuition that eluded many women twice her age, yet she still had all the exuberance of youth. The two hours they had spent together over tea, discussing whatever topic floated through their minds and gradually inching closer and closer to one another, had seemed like mere minutes, and Ferdinan's mind was focused on everything except where he was going.

It was at that point, with Ferdinan strolling absentmindedly through the streets with his hands clasped together at the small of his back, and Colvin continuously having to talk himself out of panicking, repeating over and over to himself that there had to be a street that led away from all these noblemen's homes, that the two spotted each other. Ferdinan waved at the young man with red hair, who was still too far away to be dignified in calling out a greeting.

Colvin breathed a deep sigh of relief. He had only met Ferdinan once, and very briefly, but it was a friendly face, belonging to a person who was less likely to turn him in to the constabulary for prowling around the noblemen's homes. After taking such great care to meter his steps, Colvin allowed his pace to quicken a bit, hastening to close the distance between himself and the well-dressed man with the funny accent.

What es his name? Ferdinan thought. *He told me his name twice, and I even said it back to him. Es something with a C. Corvin? Coldwin?*

"Man, Ferdinan, it's good to see you," Colvin said when the two neared to within speaking distance.

Ferdinan panicked as the young man addressed him by name. Custom dictated that he do the same in return or risk appearing flippant, and yet still the name escaped him. He went with the first thing that popped in his head. "Sí, es good to see you again as well…Cave…man?"

Ferdinan buried his face in his hand. Of all the possible names that started with *C*, he had just called his new acquaintance a caveman.

Colvin just stood and blinked. Suddenly, something fell into place in his brain. "Oh!" he exclaimed, more loudly than he had intended, and Ferdinan opened his eyes to look at him again. "No, no, it's Colvin. *Colvin.*"

"Sí! *Colvin!*" Ferdinan repeated the name forcefully, trying to drill it into his brain. The Conquian shrugged his shoulders and gave an exasperated look. "My sincerest apologies, Colvin. Es been a busy day, and my mind es scattered."

"Don't worry about it," Colvin replied. "I'm so glad to see you. All the buildings here look the same, and people were starting to give me the evil eye."

"The evil eye?" Ferdinan asked. "What es this evil eye?"

"I mean they were starting to get suspicious, you know? Some stranger in rags running around the streets in front of all the rich people's houses, it kind of raises alarm."

"Well, Colvin, from what I heard of your hard work at the northwest gate today, these people should be honored to have you in their presence. Tell me, have you dined yet tonight?"

Colvin's stomach rumbled at the mention of dinner. He had lived off sour wild berries and barely edible tubers for so long he had almost forgotten what real food was like. "Actually, I was just looking for a place to eat." No need to clue in his obviously more affluent friend about the depths of his poverty, Colvin figured. At least not until they were close enough to a tavern that Ferdinan's sympathy might merit a charitable plate of roast meat and potatoes.

"Come, come," Ferdinan said, clapping his hand on Colvin's broad shoulder. "Dinner es my treat tonight. I was just on my way to the Crown Rose."

Colvin felt like dancing. He would get his first real meal in over a month, and it would not cost him a copper mark. Just to make conversation, Colvin asked, "Is that a good place to eat?"

Ferdinan pursed his lips momentarily, appearing to ponder the question much more than Colvin thought such a simple inquiry merited. "Es acceptable," Ferdinan replied at last, nodding.

Together, the two new acquaintances made their way across town toward the Crown Rose. Colvin found his journey much easier with Ferdinan as his guide, soon realizing that one of the reasons he had been having such a difficult time finding his way out of the residential district was because the streets there ran in different directions than they did in any other part of town. Before long they reached Tamendad's main street and began to leave the private residences behind them. As they passed the church Ferdinan bowed to one knee, making the Sign of the Compass with great reverence. Colvin also made the Sign, but more so just to go along with Ferdinan than out of any deep sense of spirituality. It was not that Colvin was particularly irreligious, just that when a man spent the majority of his time trying to figure out exactly how he was going to survive for another day, loftier considerations like religion tended not to play an important role in his daily routine. Colvin thought it wise not to mention any of this to Ferdinan. Not only might it offend his companion's religious convictions, it might also jeopardize his promise to pay for Colvin's dinner.

They made small talk while they walked together, mostly just commenting on benign topics like the weather. Ferdinan complimented Colvin on his new boots, which made Colvin play the entire fiasco at the northwest gate over once again in his mind. Colvin could see Ferdinan occasionally eyeing the scimitar supported by a length of rope at Colvin's side, but Ferdinan never voiced whatever thoughts he had on that subject. Before long, they both arrived at the whitewashed archway of the Crown Rose.

"Well, here we are, Colvin," Ferdinan announced. Colvin looked up at the sign hanging from the archway, nodding, not wanting to admit he could not read the words on it. The illustration made it abundantly clear Ferdinan was not lying.

As he approached the doorway of the Crown Rose, Colvin noticed that the place seemed pretty dead, as taverns tended to go, but he said nothing about it. Ferdinan said the place was acceptable, and Colvin assumed his companion was much more competent than himself in judging an establishment's quality.

Ferdinan led the way into the Crown Rose with Colvin in tow. Ferdinan seemed to be considerably less impressed with the grandeur of the Crown Rose than Colvin found himself to be. He thought immediately upon entering the main dining room that it had to be the nicest place he had ever set foot in. He felt entirely out of place.

Only two tables had people sitting at them, though there were enough servants standing around to wait on a packed house. Three Highlanders sat at the smaller table, with enough food and drink in front of them to satisfy six men. Two larger Highlanders, each as big as a bear, sat at the other table, but it was the much younger man that Colvin focused on. Of all the restaurants in Tamendad, Ferdinan had led him to the one where William Stuart-Camen was taking his dinner that night. The pretty girl who had spent most of the day by his side at the northwest gate was still by his side now, and their table bore a spread of food unlike anything Colvin had ever seen. William seemed to be locked into a conversation with the bigger of the two Highlanders at his table, and he did not immediately notice the newcomers. Colvin thought he might still have time to slip out unobserved when Ferdinan saw fit to make an escape impossible.

"*Compagnos!*" the Conquian exclaimed, and Colvin jumped. "I want you to meet the young man who made it possible for me to persuade the Governor to send out a logging party."

This is not happening, Colvin thought, but Ferdinan clasped a hand on his shoulder and led him right to William's table. Colvin avoided making eye contact.

"This es Colvin," Ferdinan said, his firm inflection on the name indicating that he never intended to forget it again. "He arrived in town today and immediately volunteered to assist at the northwest gate. He will be joining us for dinner."

"Ah, Colvin, lad, good t' meet ye," Gregor exclaimed, leaning forward in his chair to grasp Colvin's forearm.

"This es Gregor MacDugal," Ferdinan introduced, "and his brother, Angus." Colvin nodded politely, still not looking at William. "And you must have met William at the northwest gate."

Colvin was just beginning to nod his head when he heard William say, "Actually, no." Colvin looked at the young nobleman with surprise. William was smiling, as was the young lady sitting to his right. "I'm afraid we were so busy at the gate today that I failed to really get to know everyone I was ordering around. It's a pleasure to make your acquaintance, Colvin."

"Uh, the pleasure is mine, Your Lordshipfulness," Colvin said. He was still uncertain how exactly one addressed a nobleman.

"Thank you, but please, it's just William."

Colvin nodded. After the rest of the introductions, Ferdinan and Colvin filled two of the empty chairs at the table. Colvin was trying his best to be polite, but he eyed the food on the table like a starving animal.

"What are ye waiting for, lad? Dig in before it gets cold." Gregor did not have to give any more encouragement. Colvin filled an empty plate with slices of roast and steaming vegetables, and several hot, crusty rolls. He did not bother with the knife and fork that were in front of him, but only Ferdinan really seemed to notice. He answered questions between bites, mostly just recounting his encounter with Lorthok that morning. Eventually the conversation shifted its focus away from the newcomer, which relieved Colvin since he did not particularly enjoy talking about himself, and moved on to the more general affairs of the township.

"Governor Chamberlain finally saw reason and agreed to send out scouts tomorrow," Ferdinan informed them. "We are sending one out on horseback in each direction at first light."

William stayed quiet, but wondered if anyone else had noticed Ferdinan say *we* instead of *the Governor*, and what they thought about it if they had.

"We have every constable fit to stand patrolling the gates tonight," Ferdinan continued, "and the lookouts have reported nothing unusual on the horizon. I doubt those things will come back tonight." He sounded confident, but he made the Sign of the Compass after he had finished speaking.

"Well, with what the logging party brought in this evening, we should actually be able to start making real progress on the walls and gates tomorrow," William said. "I could definitely use your help again tomorrow, Colvin."

"I'm here to help," Colvin said, shrugging his shoulders.

"What ye really need t' be concerning yourself with, Ferdinan, is training all th' people ye have wanting t' sign up for th' constabulary. M' lads and I must've had twenty men here t'day, asking if we could give them pointers on how t' fight. Most dinnae even have their own weapons."

"There are not enough swords to arm everyone who wants to fight," Ferdinan said, shrugging his shoulders as he took a sip of wine.

William sat up when he heard Ferdinan say this. "Gunther is working as hard as he can to repair all the swords that were damaged in the attack, and he'll start making new ones as soon as he's done with that, but he's only one man."

"Well," Colvin interjected, "I could give him a hand. I know my way around a forge." Everyone at the table turned to look at him. Everyone except Angus, who was swirling a glass of whiskey and seemed to be lost in his own thoughts.

"You do?" asked Ferdinan.

"Well…yeah. I was an apprentice blacksmith for a while." Colvin did not think it necessary to reveal the details of how his apprenticeship under Loran Rothwald had ended.

"Well why did you not mention that when we met?" The look on Ferdinan's face almost made Colvin question why he had not said anything about it, as if it was common practice to walk up to people he had never met and announce that he had experience working at a forge. Colvin did not answer, though, because he thought the reason was obvious enough: Ferdinan had not asked.

"Well, William, it looks like you will have to do without Colvin at the northwest gate tomorrow," Ferdinan said at last. "His services are needed elsewhere."

Colvin had mixed emotions about working at a forge again. The work itself was rather rewarding, the feeling Colvin got from creating something tangible from a lump of raw metal. Still, forges tended to remind him of Loran Rothwald, and how their relationship had turned sour.

Angus's gruff voice brought Colvin around from his musings. "And before 'tis all o'er," Gregor's brother said, still focused on the rays of light refracting through the whiskey in his glass, "perhaps his services will be needed on th' battlefield." No one said anything to this at first, but it was a thought on all their minds. Even if those things did not come back tonight, they would come back eventually. That was a foregone conclusion.

"Well, I can fight," Colvin said at last. "I don't really know how to use a sword, but I'm good with my hands."

"Aye, lad," said Gregor, "ye look like ye pack a pretty mean punch. Tell ye what. M' lads and I shall be practicing our fisticuffs out on th' beach on th' morrow's morn. What say ye come down and have a round with us?"

"Sure thing," Colvin said. His rambunctious side was eager to see just how well he would fare against Gregor and his boys. Colvin had met a couple of Highlanders before, but he had never had a chance to scuffle with one.

Everyone left matters of repairing and defending Tamendad behind, moving on to more pleasant conversation. Everyone at the table, even Melissa, imbibed a few spirits, and things at the Crown Rose became much more laid back. At some point, a playful skirmish broke out between Liam and Wallace over some comment that no one else in the dining room overheard, and the two Highlanders rolled around on the floor, pinning and locking each other in a number of uncomfortable-looking positions. The waitstaff waited patiently just out of harm's way for the men to calm themselves so that they could set about righting whatever the brawl had put wrong. Part of Colvin wanted to join in right then and there, but he reserved himself, instead taking part in a conversation with William and Melissa. Colvin was both pleased and embarrassed to find that his initial opinion of William Stuart-Camen had indeed been way off the mark. The guy ended up being genuinely friendly, and quite approachable to boot. They both discussed their childhood, each marveling at just how different the other's had been. William and Melissa both listened with great interest as Colvin recounted some of the places he had visited. Colvin in turn listened attentively to William's recounting of his family schooling. Colvin had always longed for knowledge, but formal education had always remained out of his grasp. As evening passed on into night, William inquired of Colvin if he had a place to stay.

"Well, um, honestly, no," Colvin replied. "I was gonna try to barter for a bed somewhere."

"Lad, there be plenty o' beds here at th' Crown," Gregor interjected, having overheard. "Ye're free t' take one up t'night."

Colvin was just beginning to agree enthusiastically when William interrupted.

"Actually," the young nobleman said, "and I mean no offense, Gregor, but I would like to offer Colvin quarter with my family. There is plenty of room at my father's house."

Colvin looked at William and hoped his expression was not as wary as he felt at that moment. It was one thing for William Stuart-Camen to offer to wipe the slate clean after the two of them had gotten off on the wrong foot. It was quite another, and a level of generosity Colvin had never before encountered, for a nobleman to open the doors to his own house for a vagabond. Without wanting to seem discourteous, Colvin met the young nobleman's very kind offer with a very quizzical, "Why?"

William leaned closer to Colvin, which in its own strange way made Colvin even more uncomfortable. "For one, you need a place to stay. That much is simple. For another, I feel I wronged you at the gate today. You deserved a drink of water without a half dead nobleman getting on your case about it."

With that, Colvin was dumbfounded. He had played the incident by the well over in his head a hundred times since it had happened, and not once in all the replays had Colvin felt like it had been William who had done the wronging. "Well, you gave me the boots," Colvin shrugged. If the young nobleman felt some debt was due over his behavior, those boots should have paid it in full.

"The boots were a gift of necessity," said William. "You needed them to do your job properly. This is a debt of gratitude. You volunteered for repairs upon first setting foot in Tamendad. Your knowledge of the surrounding countryside convinced the Governor it was safe to send out loggers, and when they returned safely it further convinced him to send out scouts. You're a stranger to town, and yet you've probably done more for Tamendad today than any of its citizens. If nothing else, I would feel better if tonight you laid your head under the roof of a home. I feel like Tamendad owes you that." After a pause, he added, "I feel like I owe you that."

And that was how Colvin, a penniless wanderer, went from waking up with a monster's sword in his face to sleeping in a nobleman's bed, all in one day.

CHAPTER NINE

LITTLE LESSONS

The night passed without so much as a hint of trouble. The watchmen on the wall reported nothing more exciting than an obstreperous owl that was eventually silenced by the arrow of one of the more easily perturbed lookouts. Daylight brought a whole host of volunteers to relieve the guard, and most of the constabulary relinquished their posts gratefully, still having not fully adjusted to their nocturnal assignments. The volunteers who took their place were green and fidgety, but they were dedicated to defending their homes.

As the sun was just barely clearing the horizon that morning, the northwest gate of Tamendad opened wide enough to allow five men on horseback to exit the town. Once they were through, the men separated, each moving in a different direction of the compass. No scouts were dispatched to the north, northeast, or east, since the Taeran insulated Tamendad against attack from those directions, but every other direction was covered. The lookouts posted on the city's walls watched them go, waving and wishing them godspeed, and calling out to the townspeople below when the scouts had ridden out of sight. The scouts would ride all day today and ride back tonight. They were to return with haste if they encountered anything unusual. Ferdinan had done all he could to persuade Governor Chamberlain to send the scouts out farther, insisting that there would be little opportunity for Tamendad to prepare against an attack by the time any aggressors were within a single day's ride, but the Governor insisted it would have to do, for now. What even the Governor did not know was that Ferdinan himself had convinced the scouts that were set to ride out the next morning of this fact, and had persuaded them to ride half again as far as the scouts were riding today, against the Governor's orders.

The departure of the scouts was the most exciting event in Tamendad that morning, with several townspeople coming out to see them off and wish them well. Once the riders were outside the city walls, the townspeople fell back into their normal morning routines. Peddlers set out their wares for inspection in the marketplace, noblemen and landowners moved through the streets seeing about whatever pressing business this morning brought, and the shops and taverns of the trade district opened their doors to the first customers of the day.

In his master suite at the Crown Rose, Gregor MacDugal sat on the edge of his bed. His elbows rested on his knees, and his head in turn rested in his hands. He made a rumbling noise in the back of his throat that sounded somewhat like a dying ox. Chelsie was still fast asleep on her side of the bed, her sleep still too well insulated by liquor for Gregor's rousing to wake her.

"Curse th' drink," Gregor muttered into his palms. The pounding ache in his head made his eyes feel like they were going to pop out of their sockets, and his mouth tasted like he had licked a dead skunk. The curtains of the bedroom were drawn tightly shut, but what little light snuck its way through the miniscule openings in the fabric was enough to make Gregor wince. Every movement, no matter how slight, brought on a fresh wave of queasiness. It was almost enough to make him swear he would never drink again, but he had never made such an oath and refused to do so now. He would never swear an oath he had no intention of keeping. With a total disregard for his personal sense of well being, Gregor stole a quick glance around the bedroom. The world seemed to rotate slowly around him as he did so. Everything was in disarray. One of the overstuffed chairs in the bedroom was overturned. A half-empty bottle of amber liquid lay on its side, a good portion of its contents now pooled around it, soaking the rug and making the whole suite smell of whiskey. The tapestry that had served as the main decoration in the bedroom lay crumpled in the corner. Gregor sighed. It would take a good number of the staff quite a while to set everything in the suite right again, and he knew the rest of the guest rooms looked about the same. Last night's revelry was going to be quite expensive.

Gregor slowly stood up from the bed, the throb in his head vehemently protesting every movement. He made his way over to the washbasin, filling it with wash water and dunking his head into it. It helped, but not much. He wiped the water from his eyes when he was done, then grabbed the other pitcher of water, the one that was meant for drinking. He did not bother with the cups; he just lifted the pitcher to his lips and chugged. His stomach objected to having anything put in it, but allowed the water to stay put at least for the moment. Gregor exited the bedroom and moved into the common room of his suite, which was in slightly better condition. No furniture was overturned, but some detritus littered the floor, and Gregor's kilt and tartan were strewn across the daybed. Gregor snatched it up and started wrapping it around himself, hoping that Chelsie had been the only other person in the room when he had taken it off. He could not quite remember.

The knock at the door made Gregor feel like iron spikes were being driven into his skull. "Aye, just a bit," the big Highlander called out, making the last loop around his abdomen with his kilt. He wondered who was calling at this hour. The lads probably would not be stirring until he stirred them, and the waitstaff knew well enough not to even think about disturbing the Highlanders while they were sleeping off a night of hard drinking. Gregor had a sinking feeling that it might be Torrance Mayhew calling, this latest round of damages to his establishment enough to make him rethink the deal he and Gregor had agreed upon. Even more than this, he feared it was someone coming to inform him that the city had fallen under attack again, but that seemed unlikely. The knock was entirely too irresolute to come from a messenger bearing such important news. Whoever it was, Gregor was not going to find out just standing there in the middle of the common room. He moved to the door and opened it wide.

Ferdinan looked like death warmed over. He had large dark circles under both eyes. He stood with his left hand braced against the door frame, and he looked like he would collapse if he tried to move it. His hair was disheveled around his face, and he was not wearing his vest. His shirt was not tucked in. He fairly reeked of a sickly-sweet combination of wine and liquor. "Es the last time I ever let you talk me into…what did you call it? *A bit o' fun?*" Ferdinan tried his best to mimic Gregor's accent as he said the last four words, failing miserably to sound anything like the big Highlander but managing to sound hilarious nonetheless. Gregor began to chuckle until the pain it caused him registered in his brain. He groaned and rubbed his temples.

"Ye look like I feel, lad," Gregor said, moving aside so Ferdinan could come through the doorway. The Conquian's steps were very delicate. He looked like he might fall down at any moment. He made it to the nearest chair and slumped into it.

"What in God's holy name happened last night?" he asked, rubbing his eyes laboriously.

"I dinnae rightly recollect most of it, lad, but I know it all started t' go south when ye tried t' teach us that flatfooted dance o' yours." Gregor poured Ferdinan a glass of water from the drinking pitcher in the common room. Ferdinan accepted it gratefully, but took measured sips.

"My better judgment should have told me you Highlanders were not suited to dance the fandango. What happened after that?"

"Well, I remember at one point ye made a wager with Wallace that th' chandelier would have nae problem supporting yer weight," Gregor replied, easing into a chair himself.

"I would never do anything of the sort," Ferdinan protested. Gregor smirked. "And admit it," Ferdinan added under his breath.

Gregor laughed heartily despite the pain it brought. "Ye're one of a kind, lad," he said, and he meant it. Ferdinan was one of the few men Gregor had met who had been able to match him drink for drink, and the Conquian had still managed the manual dexterity when it was all over to attempt teaching one of the prettier female servants how to tango before retiring to one of the empty rooms for the night.

"Thank God for that, Gregor," Ferdinan said, finishing off the last of his water. "I do not think the world would know what to do with two of me."

"I know what ye mean, lad," the big Highlander replied. The two men sat in silence for a few moments, each waiting for the agony in his head to subside. When it became abundantly clear that this would not be happening anytime soon, it was Gregor who spoke up. "Well, lad, stay here as long as ye like, but I told Colvin I'd meet him on th' beach this morn."

Ferdinan nodded, and got up from his chair. He drew a deep breath, in through the nose and out through the mouth, and Gregor was amazed at the transformation that seemed to take place in him. His hangover appeared to melt away. Besides the bags under his eyes, Ferdinan looked right as rain. An eye as well trained as Gregor's, however, could easily tell it was just a facade. Deep down, Ferdinan was still as miserable as when Gregor first opened the door to his suite. Gregor admired the Conquian's willpower.

"I have to be getting to the southwest gate myself. I have duties to attend today as well." Ferdinan forced a smile, and managed to actually make it look pleasant.

Gregor nodded. "Aye, lad. I shall see ye this even, but dinnae expect another party. Old men need time t' mend after such merrymaking."

"Well then, es our good fortune we still have our youth," said Ferdinan with a smirk. He headed for the door.

"Mind ye dinnae cut yerself on th' way out," said Gregor in parting. "I doubt th' servants have picked up what's left o' th' chandelier."

The beach was deserted except for the five Highlanders all trying to beat the sense out of one another. Colvin straightened his clothes – his new clothes – for about the fiftieth time since dressing that morning. The white cotton shirt and well-tailored trousers had been lying across the back of the chair in his bedroom when he awoke that morning, and when Colvin conferred with Reynolds he learned that they were indeed yet another gift from William Stuart-Camen. Colvin had been smiling ever since. It had been years since Colvin had had new clothes, real clothes, made in a tailor's shop out of good fabric. They fit his body much better than hand-me-downs or patchwork garments ever could. He had wanted to thank his host for them personally before heading out to the beach, but Reynolds had informed him that Lord William had set out for the northwest gate before first light. Colvin made certain before he left the Stuart-Camen household that Reynolds would deliver his debt of gratitude to William in his stead, whenever the young nobleman returned.

The Highlanders on the beach were all fighting barehanded, locking and pinning each other in the sand. Curses and yelps of pain filled the air. Gregor was squaring off against his brother, which was apparently just fine with the other three lads, who were all having a go of it together. Gregor was the first to notice Colvin's approach. "Ah, lads," the big Highlander called out, "we have company." Everyone turned to look in the direction Gregor was pointing except Angus, who capitalized on his brother's inattention by tackling him to the ground and locking his muscular arms around his brother's throat. Gregor growled and coughed as he tried to pry Angus's meaty arms from around his windpipe. "Ye nerveless cur!" he snarled, "When I get free I'll stomp yer arse good."

"If ye get free," Angus taunted. Gabrahn, Liam, and Wallace had all shifted their attention back to the brothers, and were whistling and jeering over Gregor's predicament. It was rare that anyone got the better of Gregor in a round of fisticuffs, even his own brother. Colvin worked hard to stifle the laugh that wanted to escape from his throat. He was not nearly close enough to the Highlanders to be overheard yet, but there was little doubt in his mind that Gregor would eventually get free somehow, and Colvin wanted to do nothing that might direct the big Highlander's anger toward him when it happened.

"I'm warning ye, Angus, let me go," Gregor said, but the choked sound of his voice and the deep crimson color his face was turning prevented his words from carrying any hint of serious threat.

"I'll let ye go when I put ye out, or when ye can get free yerself, brother." Angus had a determined look on his face that made it clear he had no intention of letting his brother wriggle out of his current predicament. He increased his leverage on the hold to add emphasis to this fact.

"Dinnae say I dinnae warn ye," Gregor spat, his eyes starting to bulge slightly. Both of the big Highlander's arms shot upward, the butts of his palms crashing into his brother's temples. Angus immediately broke the hold, blinking repeatedly and stumbling backward. He crashed onto his backside in the sand, trying to stand up but failing at every attempt. He found his legs had suddenly turned to jelly. The other three Highlanders turned their jeers toward Angus, hoping that Gregor had not really noticed they had ever been directed toward him. Gregor picked himself up and started brushing the sand from his tartan, his face slowly returning to its normal color.

"That was quite a move," Colvin said, coming within speaking distance.

"Ah, thank ye, Colvin. 'Twas nothing," he said.

"Nice threads ye got there, lad," said Liam, walking over to join Gregor and Colvin.

"Thanks," Colvin said, smiling brightly. "William gave them to me."

"Ah, a good lad that William is," said Gregor. "Ye're fortunate t' have fallen in with him, ye are."

"Come t' have a go at it, Colvin?" Wallace called out, cracking his knuckles. "Or did ye just come out t' shoot th' shite?"

Colvin smirked.

"This one's mine first," Liam said, staring right at Colvin.

"Aye, ye and Liam have a tussle," Gregor said, patting Colvin on the back. "I want t' see how ye handle yerself."

Colvin nodded, pulling off his new shirt. He folded it and laid it on the sand, not wanting to chance it getting ripped. Colvin and Liam stood a few feet away from each other, and the others gathered around to watch. Angus, who had finally managed to get his legs working again, stumbled over to join his brother.

"'Twas a good shot, brother," he said, his eyes still not quite back into focus yet. Gregor nodded.

"First one with a knee down loses," Liam said, stretching his arms above his head.

"Sounds fair to me," Colvin agreed. He raised his clenched fists and readied himself. The other Highlanders started whooping at the two combatants as they approached one another, mostly just calling for Liam to kick Colvin's arse. Liam ducked inside on Colvin, throwing a punch that was meant for his midsection, but Colvin spun out of the way and managed to drive a fist into Liam's side. The Highlander grunted in pain as Colvin stepped away and raised both fists again. Liam moved forward once again, and Colvin managed to just duck under the punch aimed for his head before it landed, planting first his right fist and then his left into Liam's abdomen. Liam slumped slightly, the wind partially knocked out of him, and Colvin raised up quickly, trying to connect an uppercut to his opponent's chin. Liam pulled back enough so that the blow just grazed him. The Highlander finally managed to land a punch, driving his fist into Colvin's sternum. Pain erupted in Colvin's chest, making his breathing difficult. Colvin still had his right arm raised from his attempted uppercut, and he now brought it down swiftly, his elbow connecting with Liam's forehead. The Highlander's stance shifted slightly, wavering. The blow had dazed him for a moment.

"Aye, lad, ye've stunned him! Finish him off!" Gabrahn was cheering on Colvin now instead of his kinsman. Liam tried to back off, but Colvin kept right on top of him. Liam raised his arms over his face, more concerned at the moment with defending himself until he regained the totality of his senses than with trying to press any semblance of an attack. Colvin's fists flew at his opponent, most just connecting harmlessly with Liam's forearms but a few shots sneaking past his guard. Liam began to stumble, and his hands dropped in an attempt to catch his balance. Colvin's left hand snaked out and grabbed Liam's tartan, pulling him in. His right fist flew, connecting solidly with the side of the Highlander's face. Liam's body went limp for a moment, and he collapsed on the sand. He looked up at Colvin with wide, blinking eyes that were filled with astonishment.

"Aye, lad, that's th' way!" Wallace called out. "He dinnae know what hit him!"

Colvin took a deep breath and tried to wipe away sweat from his brow that was not there. The whole thing had lasted less than thirty seconds. These Highlanders fought at a furious pace, launching themselves totally into the attack. Colvin knew enough not to boast about his victory. He suspected it might very well have been him lying in the sand if Liam had managed to land the first punch. He extended his arm and helped his opponent to his feet. Liam shook his head quickly, trying to clear his senses, then clapped Colvin on the shoulder.

"Well done, lad," the black-haired Highlander said. "Ye're quicker than ye look."

"Aye lad, let's ye and I have a go now," said Wallace, moving quickly forward.

"Nae, lad," called Gregor, holding up a hand. "Colvin fairly manhandled Liam. I have a feeling he'd downright embarrass ye." The laughter this comment brought made Wallace fume, but he kept quiet. "Besides," Gregor continued, "I have him next." Gregor's smile was all teeth, and all the other Highlanders broke out into raucous jeers at this. All except Liam, who simply clapped Colvin on the shoulder once again, nodded solemnly and said, "Good luck, lad."

Colvin swallowed hard. "Go easy on me, Gregor," was all he could think to say.

"Ah, lad, ye dinnae seem t' have any trouble with Liam. Surely an old man like m'self shall present ye nae boggle."

Colvin sighed. Looking Gregor over, he thought he would stand a better chance trying to wrestle a den of mountain lions with raw meat strapped around each of his limbs. "First one to a knee?" he asked in an exasperated tone of voice.

"Aye," Gregor replied. Both men raised their fists. Colvin steadied himself. He was pretty sure he had no chance of besting Gregor, but his only hope was to catch Gregor off guard like he had managed with Liam. He stepped forward quickly, and was amazed when his fist sailed right through Gregor's defenses and landed squarely on his jaw. It was a good, solid punch, at least as strong as the one that had destroyed Loran Rothwald's jaw, and Gregor's head snapped around with it. Colvin was filled with hope for just a moment, until Gregor turned his face back toward him. A deranged smile spread across the big Highlander's face. Colvin completely forgot about trying to catch Gregor with a flurry of blows, forgot about trying to catch him off guard, forgot that for one brief moment he had thought he had a chance to win this fight.

"Oh, aye!" Gregor said, nodding, and the wild look in his eyes grew even more intense. Colvin tried his best to back up as quickly as he could, but he had no time. Gregor's punch landed squarely on the side of Colvin's face. His eyes felt like they would explode. The whole world danced and shimmered around Colvin, then faded away completely. Colvin was vaguely aware of feeling himself land on the beach. He tumbled into darkness.

When he came to, he thought he had only been out for a few moments but had no way of knowing for sure. Howls of laughter met his ears. "Ye spun him 'round like a bonny top!" he heard Wallace exclaim. Colvin groggily pushed himself up and raised slowly to his feet. Gregor lent him a helping hand, steadying him when he finally stood upright again.

"I dinnae jar ye too much, did I?" the big Highlander asked.

Colvin was very, very glad Gregor had decided not to gloat. "I'm okay," he said. "I think."

"Sorry about that, lad. That punch o' yers got th' best of me."

Colvin nodded. "I could say the same thing about yours."

Colvin was glad to find that none of the other Highlanders were lining up for an opportunity to try beating him senseless anymore. The ease with which Gregor had dispatched him had apparently been enough to satisfy everyone's curiosity over just how good he really was. Gabrahn, Wallace and Liam all fell back to roughhousing with one another, but Angus seemed to have no desire to go another round. He appeared to have almost fully recovered from Gregor's blow, but his eyes still went crossed every now and then, and an occasional stagger found its way into his step.

Colvin barely had to ask Gregor to give him some pointers on barehanded fighting before the big Highlander agreed, and Angus lent a hand as well. The six men spent almost a full hour there on the beach, with Colvin rapidly learning every move the brothers demonstrated for him – or on him, if he was unfortunate. Gregor and Angus both commented on how deftly Colvin moved for a big lad, though Colvin could not quite feel big next to Gregor and Angus. Still, there was something in what they said. Colvin had always had a gracefulness that seemed out of place belonging to someone with a blacksmith's build. Colvin took a few moments to impress his new friends with the backflips and handstands he had picked up during the times in his life when he had to play jester to earn his meals. Colvin laughed along with the Highlanders, heckling even more loudly than the others whenever someone tried and failed to duplicate one of his acrobatic moves. Gregor and Angus knew well enough not to even attempt them. It was approaching midmorning when Ferdinan's arrival interrupted their fun.

"I had a feeling I might find you gentlemen still out here," the Conquian called out playfully as he approached. He was smiling, but Colvin thought he seemed a little tense, the grimace on his face too exaggerated to be caused only by squinting in the sun. "I hope you had an escellent workout this morning, but I am afraid I have come to steal Colvin away from you." This comment was met with general protestations from all the Highlanders except Gregor, who just nodded.

"Ah, lad, 'tis been a hopper, but yer services are required elsewhere," the big Highlander said.

After fetching his shirt and saying his goodbyes to the Highlanders, Colvin followed Ferdinan back toward Tamendad. "Gunther es especting you," Ferdinan said as they walked together. There was something in the Conquian's manner that seemed just a little off.

"Are you all right?" Colvin asked. Ferdinan looked at Colvin, and his facade dropped for just a moment. Colvin thought Ferdinan looked like he was about to vomit.

"I feel...how do you say?... sick as a dog. Gregor talked me into having a few rounds with him last night, and the situation quickly got out of hand."

Colvin nodded. "Why don't you go back to the Crown Rose and sleep it off?"

Ferdinan looked at Colvin like he had just spoken blasphemy. "I have responsibilities that cannot be postponed because of my discomfort," he said sternly.

"I didn't mean anything by that," Colvin explained, and was a bit surprised to find that he genuinely did not want to offend Ferdinan. Usually he only went out of his way to avoid stepping on people's toes when he stood to gain something from it.

"I know, Colvin. I beg your pardon. I have a bit of a quick temper this morning."

Colvin nodded, and the two made more pleasant conversation as they trekked back to Tamendad's northeast gate. The guardsmen atop the wall called out for the gate to open as soon as they spotted Ferdinan and Colvin approaching. The gate opened just wide enough for the two men to walk through single file, and closed quickly after they had entered the city.

"Well, you should not have any problems finding your way to the blacksmith, and I am needed back at the southwest gate," Ferdinan said.

"Actually...I might need some help," Colvin said sheepishly.

"Oh, es very close to the Crown Rose, Colvin. Es got a sign hanging right outside of it. You cannot miss it."

Colvin hesitated after Ferdinan had finished speaking, but Ferdinan noticed the embarrassed look on his friend's face. "What es troubling you, Colvin?" he asked.

"Um...Ferdinan...I can't read," Colvin said.

Ferdinan stopped in his tracks. "You cannot read?" Ferdinan obviously thought Colvin's illiteracy bizarre. "Did your parents not teach you when you were a boy?" There was a momentary silence, and Ferdinan's face turned a deep red from embarrassment. "Colvin," he stammered, "I am sorry. I forgot about you not having a family."

"That's okay, Ferdinan," Colvin said. His being an orphan really seemed to bother Ferdinan more than himself. After this many years of self-reliance, Colvin was pretty well adjusted to being on his own.

Ferdinan insisted on showing Colvin to Gunther's shop personally. Colvin made mental notes as he went, making certain that he would be able to find his way alone next time. He did not want to bother Ferdinan any more than he had to. Before long, Ferdinan and Colvin stood in front of the small stone building that bore the sign reading *Gunther's Smithy*, though Colvin had to take Ferdinan's word on this. Colvin bid Ferdinan goodbye, and headed for the front door. The familiar sound of hammer striking anvil floated out through the open windows. Colvin knocked forcefully on the door, making sure the owner would be able to hear it over the sounds of the forge. The sound of metal on metal faded. He heard movement inside. The door opened.

Colvin's first thought was that Gunther was a little person, but he only thought this for a moment. Gunther stood not even five feet tall, but he was just as broad as a normal-sized man, if not a little broader. He had long gray hair, tied back behind his head with a thin strip of leather, and a long, flowing beard that came down past his belly, the end of which was also tied together with another leather strip. He wore plain clothes of neutral tones, lots of dark browns and grays, and a good, sturdy pair of square-toed workman's boots. In a way, he reminded Colvin of a scaled-down version of Gregor, though Gunther's nose was much more bulbous than the big Highlander's and his arms were longer in proportion to his body. His muscles were not quite as well defined as Gregor's either, but he was actually stouter. He had fierce eyes the color of the sea. Something about his appearance reminded Colvin of a block of stone.

"You must be Colvin," Gunther said. His voice sounded like a frog had crawled down his throat years ago and set up permanent residence there. "I'm Gunther." The short man extended his right hand, and Colvin shook it. Gunther had an amazingly powerful grip. "C'mon in, son. We got a lot of work to do."

Colvin stepped into the smithy. Tongs and hammers of every shape and size hung on the walls. Three different anvils sat on the floor, each a different size than the others. The forge itself looked like it had been built right out of the ground, a furnace of worked stone and wrought iron that put Loran Rothwald's to shame. A large pile of weapons rested beside the forge, consisting mostly of swords but containing the occasional dagger or pole arm. The workshop was hot, but not as hot as Colvin expected it to be. Three of the walls bore two open windows, and there were several open vents in the ceiling that could be shuttered closed in case of bad weather. Everything in the workshop was set a bit lower than Colvin was accustomed to, positioned to be at a comfortable height for the shop's owner, but Colvin thought he could manage. The largest of the three anvils would accommodate him rather nicely, and all of the tools themselves were of normal size.

Gunther stood in the middle of the shop, looking Colvin over. "I was told you got experience," he said gruffly.

"I was an apprentice blacksmith for a while," Colvin replied. "I mostly forged horseshoes, but I did some other stuff too."

"Ever work on weapons?" Gunther picked up a sword from the pile of weapons laying by the forge. It bore several rather nasty nicks and a slight bend. "It's a little different than makin' horseshoes."

"I've re-tempered a couple of daggers before," Colvin said, shrugging his shoulders. "And I'm a pretty quick learner."

"Good. You'll need to be." Gunther wasted no time in setting Colvin to work, but he was a much more patient and understanding mentor than Colvin would have guessed. Colvin claimed the largest anvil as his own, and Gunther stayed with him for a while, showing him the proper technique and correcting him when he made a mistake. Colvin had never been one to respond well to criticism, but Gunther had a way of showing Colvin what he was doing wrong without making him feel like an idiot. Colvin tried hard to get everything right the first time. He wanted Gunther to be pleased, though he was not really sure why. After only two days in Tamendad, his way of thinking had already changed significantly.

Pretty soon Colvin was at it alone, hammering out the dents and nicks from the weapons that were not too badly damaged. Gunther kept all the weapons in need of major repair to himself, and Colvin was glad to see this. Working on weapons was indeed quite different than the type of metalworking Colvin was used to, and he didn't think he would be able to handle much more than the petty mending jobs Gunther threw his way, at least not yet.

Gunther's workshop was plenty big enough for the both of them to work comfortably around each other, and Colvin frequently forgot that he was not alone at the forge. The only constant reminder that he was in the presence of another person was the makeshift harmony that arose when the ringing of his hammer strikes intermingled with those of Gunther's. In a strange way, Colvin found this sound much more pleasant than the incessant *clink clink clink* he remembered from working in Loran Rothwald's forge.

Gunther and Colvin rarely spoke to each other while they worked, but every time the short, bearded blacksmith patted Colvin on the back and muttered a gruff, "Good work, son," Colvin felt like he had grown another inch. Before long, the rays of the noonday sun began to shine down directly through the vents in the ceiling, and Colvin found that he was working up quite a sweat. Gunther handed him a leather cord without saying a word, just nodding, and Colvin accepted it with another nod, tying his red hair back with it. Every so often Gunther would take a break and step through the only other door in the workshop besides the main entrance, always returning quickly with two cups full of fresh, cool water. By the time the sun was just starting to think about calling it quits for the day, Gunther hung his hammer up on the wall and signaled for Colvin to do the same. It had been a good day's work.

"We'll have to wash up before dinner," Gunther said. "The wife hates it when I come to the table and stink up the whole house."

Colvin nodded, grinning. After working with him all day, Colvin had grown to genuinely like the way Gunther did things, and the promise of his second free dinner in as many days was music to his ears. Gunther exited the workshop through the main entrance, and Colvin followed close behind. Gunther led him around the side of the building, where a squat rain barrel rested against the wall. Gunther peeled off his soaked shirt, and Colvin noted that the short blacksmith's form did indeed bear a striking resemblance to a solid block of granite. Gunther began sloshing the water out of the barrel with his hands, rubbing it under his arms, across his chest and through his hair. Colvin did the same, and found the water to be cool and refreshing against his sweaty skin. After they had both washed up, Gunther continued around the building, which was considerably larger than it looked from the front. There was another doorway in the rear, and a little patch of tilled soil, on which grew a fairly decent crop of tomatoes, potatoes and beans. Several empty barrels were stacked against the back wall, next to the doorway.

When Colvin followed Gunther through the door, he was not surprised to find that the rear of the building served as the blacksmith's home. Colvin found himself in the room that served double duty as both kitchen and dining room in Gunther's home. A sturdy oak table with four chairs sat in the middle of the room. Two more barrels sat in one of the corners, but unlike the ones outside these were full of liquid. One held water, and Colvin was pretty sure the other held beer. A wood stove sat under one of the windows. All manner of cooking utensils hung on the walls all around the room. There was a large cast iron kettle hanging in a fireplace that reminded Colvin of Gunther's forge, and one of the homeliest women Colvin had ever seen was tending whatever the kettle held. She was short, even for a woman, but was still taller than Gunther. She had a large wart on her left cheek, and a few wiry hairs grew out of it. Her gray hair was tied back into a bun, and Colvin could not help but think of Doris. He cringed slightly when the woman at the fireplace turned to look at him. At first glance she looked like she was about to yell at the young newcomer, but her lips quickly curled into a broad smile that improved her looks dramatically.

"Well bless me, I had no idea Gunther was bringing company to supper!" The old woman's voice was sweet and melodious, much more pleasant than her physical appearance would have suggested. She wiped her hands on her apron and hung her ladle on a peg sticking out from the mantle, and moved toward the two men. Colvin thought the light of the fireplace must have been playing tricks on him when he had first seen her. This woman was certainly by no means attractive, but she was not nearly one of the ugliest women he had ever met. "Sweet God!" she exclaimed as she came close. "Your shirt is soaked right through with sweat! Let me fetch you a clean one." The old woman moved quickly through the doorway of the kitchen, into another part of the house. Colvin looked to Gunther, who was chuckling softly to himself.

"That's the wife. Her name's Gertrude." Gunther moved to the fireplace and retrieved the ladle, dipping it into the kettle and drawing out a small helping of what looked like beef stew. The smell of it made Colvin's stomach rumble with hunger. Gunther slurped it down and grunted with pleasure. "Bonny good cook," he said while he chewed.

Gertrude returned before long carrying a black shirt, and she all but stripped Colvin's off of him. The shirt was a little too broad in the shoulders, which was a feat in itself, and came down only to his navel, but it was well-made and cut from good fabric. Colvin seated himself at the table at Gertrude's insistence while Gunther busied himself with dipping three tankards into one of the barrels in the corner. He placed one of the frothy mugs of beer in front of Colvin when he was done, and the young apprentice took a long draught from it. It was undoubtedly the finest brew Colvin had ever sampled. Gertrude brought him a large bowl of stew and a large chunk of bread to go with it. The stew was chock full of vegetables and large pieces of beef, and Colvin wanted nothing more than to devour it ravenously, but he managed to restrain himself until Gunther and Gertrude were both seated at the table.

"Where's Gangis?" Gunther asked, blowing on a spoonful of stew to cool it and gesturing toward the empty chair at the table.

"He volunteered to be part of the day watch," Gertrude said. "He'll be relieved at sundown."

"Is that your son?" Colvin asked between bites.

Gunther nodded. "He lends a hand at the forge when I need it, but mostly he just dreams about becomin' a soldier. I'm sure you'll meet him eventually before all our work's done."

The three made pleasant conversation while they ate, and everyone at the table had a second helping of Gertrude's hearty stew. After the last morsel of bread had been used to sop up the last drop of soup, Gertrude cleared the table while Gunther retrieved a leather pouch from one of the cupboards. When he opened the pouch, Colvin could smell the sweet smell of tobacco. "Care for a smoke?" Gunther asked, pulling a whole dried leaf from the pouch and stuffing shredded tobacco into it. Colvin accepted, and Gunther handed him the first rolled cigar. Colvin enjoyed a smoke with Gunther and his wife, only mildly surprised that Gertrude joined them, and insisted on helping Gertrude straighten up the kitchen before bidding them goodnight.

Chapter Ten

A Forced Sense of Normalcy

Another night passed without incident, and daylight brought the normal morning routine to Tamendad. The city guards were not quite so weary-eyed when the volunteer watchmen came to relieve them, and the volunteers themselves seemed more at ease with their commission. For the second straight day, all excitement was focused on the scouts. Several townspeople crowded in the town square around the five fresh riders who were set to depart that morning, wishing them well and giving them small gifts of wrapped sweetcakes or flowers. Some of the prettier girls in Tamendad offered kisses for good luck. None of the scouts refused.

Other townspeople gathered around the northwest gate and waited patiently, more or less, for the return of the scout riders that had been dispatched the previous morn. These men and women also bore small gifts, and a fair number of pretty girls waited to do a bit more than kiss the men who had risked their lives, but an anxiousness hung over the entire crowd. The scouts might return bearing news of impeding doom, or worse yet, they might not return at all. The tension around the northwest gate came to a head when one of the lookouts atop the wall announced, "A rider approaches!" Not a soul was breathing as the doors of the northwest gate creaked open just wide enough to allow the man on horseback to pass through. He was young, but not very young, with a shaggy mop of hair the color of honey and tanned skin covering his lean but muscular form. He had the unmistakable look of exhaustion about him, as did his mount. All eyes were upon him, and he shifted uneasily in the saddle as he met the gaze of the expectant townspeople.

A soft murmur ran through the crowd, the first words spoken since the lookout's announcement. The group of people that had gathered in the middle of Tamendad's main street parted slightly, and Julio Franco Francisco Ferdinan emerged from their midst. The Conquian walked with a determination to his steps, and the look on his face was as firm as stone. The scout dismounted as quickly as his weary limbs would allow and moved toward Ferdinan. Silence fell once again as the two men met. Ferdinan stood with his arms crossed over his chest, a posture many important people in Tamendad had become well acquainted with of late. Ferdinan said nothing. The look in his eyes asked his question for him. The people in the crowd stood on tiptoe and craned their necks.

"Nothing to report from the southeast," the rider said. The northwest gate erupted into a sea of cheering applause. Townspeople rushed forward to greet the scout rider, and he accepted them all as graciously as a man who had gone without sleep for a day could manage. Soon his arms were full of small, wrapped bundles, and his cheeks and lips were red from all the kisses he had received. The townspeople's throngs of adulation had quickly separated the scout and Ferdinan, but this was just fine with both men. The scout was enjoying being hailed as the hero of the moment, and Ferdinan had learned all he could from this man. Now he had to wait for the reports from the others.

The four remaining scout riders returned at irregular intervals, but the last rode into Tamendad less than an hour after the sun had risen. Each scout had the same look of exhaustion, and each announced the same, "Nothing to report," when he fell under Ferdinan's gaze. With every passing report, the response of the crowd grew louder, not softer. When the fifth and final scout reported encountering nothing to the west, a jubilation spread through all of Tamendad like ripples on a pond. As soon as the final scout was accounted for, the five fresh riders set out upon their quest and the cycle began again. In the meantime, though, all of Tamendad would celebrate its newfound certainty that it was safe, at least for another day.

William arrived at the northwest gate early that morning eager for another day overseeing the repair effort. He found that he was settling into his commission far more easily than he had originally expected, aided in no small part by the fact that the volunteers actually doing the repairs were eager to follow his lead. He was also encouraged by the fact that after two days his sutured wound felt as though it was starting to set up a bit, not healed by any means but stable enough that William felt comfortable actually sharing some of the burden himself rather than just walking around managing the effort from over everyone's shoulders. If the men and women working to mend the gate had seemed willing to serve him before, they became downright enamored with him when he actually started swinging a hammer. The sight of a nobleman rolling up his sleeves along with commoners to reach a common goal carried more weight than William's pep talks and encouragement ever could. William was careful not to overdo it, as he had promised Melissa at great length he would, but once he started contributing to the repair effort with more than just orders and encouragement he found his station became so much more cathartic. It was as though through helping heal the city's wounds he was somehow healing some of his own.

Progress at the northwest gate continued at a steady pace, but that morning's work was filled with frequent interruption. William allowed the workers a moment's break to celebrate whenever a town crier came bearing news that another scout had returned to Tamendad without encountering any hostile forces. William's own heart rejoiced with each announcement, and by the time the news of the fifth scout's return was carried to the northwest gate William felt like dancing in spite of his wound. The scouts had brought assurances of safety that would last only a single day, but that certainty of one day was enough for the townspeople who desperately needed something to cling to. William found himself so ecstatic over the news that he simply could not call for the volunteers, who had all fallen to cheering and dancing and embracing one another, to get back to work. He just stood there smiling with his hands on his hips, occasionally giving a shout or a whistle of his own, and embracing the sense of safety the scouts' reports had brought, no matter how fleeting.

Colvin was up and out early as well that morning, arriving at Gunther's smithy when the sun was barely up. Gunther greeted Colvin with a smile that was surprisingly warm for the gruff smith, and sat Colvin down at the kitchen table, putting a plate of beans and toast in front of him before letting him get to work. Colvin was just finishing up his breakfast, Gunther lazing in the chair beside him and sipping from a tall tankard of beer, and Gertrude tending the morning's laundry, when the town crier made his way through the lane in front of Gunther's shop proclaiming the safe return of the first scout. Gunther and Gertrude looked at each other, Gunther nodding and a smile barely curling the old woman's lips. Colvin grinned to himself. The two had said more to each other with that one look than most younger couples would have been able to say with a thousand words.

Gunther and Colvin got to work as soon as Colvin had his breakfast down, and the harmony of twin hammers on anvils met Colvin's ears once again. Like the day before, Colvin found the work difficult but rewarding, and he discovered that mending the simple cuts and nicks on the weapons seemed much easier with only one day of experience behind him. Both Colvin and Gunther let their hammers fall silent whenever a town crier came past in the street outside, and with every account of a scout bearing no news, Colvin and Gunther would look to each other and grin. When the fifth crier came past, proclaiming with great enthusiasm that the final scout was accounted for and that he, as well, had nothing to report, Gunther shut his eyes tight, took a deep breath, and let his lips curl into a full smile. Gertrude came bursting through the door that connected the workshop with the rest of the residence, and the old wife carried three mugs overflowing with frothy brew.

"Woman, I've told you to stay out of my workshop," Gunther said, but he snatched up one of the tankards all the same.

"Oh shut up, you old toad," Gertrude exclaimed, and her voice was full of joy. "I've just heard the best news I can recall in a good while, and I'll be stripped naked and switched like a whelp if I don't celebrate it." She shoved a mug of ale into Colvin's left hand, since he was still holding his hammer with his right. "You're lucky I'm a married woman, you young thing you," Gertrude said with a wink. "The news has set my old heart a-racing, and God only knows what I'm likely to do." The smile dropped from Colvin's face, and his eyes went wide. Gunther bellowed with loud, guffawing laughter, and had to set his tankard down on his anvil to keep from spilling his beer.

"Wife, you're gonna scare away my new apprentice if you're not careful," he said. Colvin relaxed a bit, but he still kept a wary eye on Gertrude. The three lifted their tankards together and drank to the good news.

While the whole town reveled in its newfound, though temporary, sense of safety, the nexus of the celebration was the Crown Rose. Gregor MacDugal and his lads whooped and hollered with news of each returning scout, and with news of the fifth scout's entry into the city Gregor opened the doors of Torrance Mayhew's establishment wide and invited all inside to celebrate. Gregor offered to buy a round for any man or woman who wanted to drink to the occasion, though he had to explain more than once that only the first drink was on him, and the purchase of any future rounds was the responsibility of the imbiber. Tables and chairs were cleared from the floor of the main dining room to make way for an impromptu dance floor, and soon Gregor and Angus were demonstrating the proper way to dance the jig and the Highlands fling. Even Torrance Mayhew joined in the dance, too overwhelmed with the morning's news to much care about whatever damages having such a large number of people crammed into the dining room might cause. *Besides,* the aging proprietor thought, *I might as well have a little fun on Gregor's coin myself.*

Ferdinan joined in the festivities at the Crown Rose, tearing himself away from the southwest gate when he heard of the celebration the Highlanders were hosting. Ferdinan was received with great enthusiasm, cheered like a hero by the townspeople in the Crown Rose when he made his entrance. He bowed formally and called for a glass of the best wine Torrance Mayhew had to offer. His eyes widened slightly when the pretty girl tending the bar sat a bottle of fine Conquian red before him. He knew it by vineyard and vintage, and it was considered exquisite even by Conquian standards. "I was not especting *this*," said Ferdinan, smiling.

"Master Mayhew reserves it for special occasions," she explained. "And for special guests." Her smile was flirtatious, to say the least.

"Would you care to dance, my dear?" Ferdinan said, bowing and extending his hand. The bartendress curtsied.

"I would love to," she replied.

The feeling of elation ran throughout Tamendad all day, but most of the festivities had died down well before the midday meal. The streets of Tamendad began to thin out a bit as the day wore on, with many of the peasants leaving the walls of the township to return to their homes of mud and thatch outside. Several of these men and women had grown tired of sleeping on the floor of the church or, failing that, on the lawn outside it, and the promise of just one day of safety was enough to coax many of them back to their homes for the time being. With the township no longer overflowing with people, everything seemed almost normal inside it. Guardsmen were still posted at every gate, and the gates themselves remained closed when no one was passing through them, but quite a few more people departed the town on business or pleasure than had dared to the two days prior.

William left the northwest gate as morning began to give way to afternoon, putting Merrick back in charge of the repair effort in his absence. His wound was finally beginning to ache from the hammering, and although he could have remained at the northeast gate to oversee the effort his resolve to do so faltered once he realized that Melissa's theology lesson would be ending soon, which would afford them the opportunity to take their lunch together. All the morning's celebration had left him missing the person he most wanted to celebrate with.

He found the church full of men and women offering up prayers of thanksgiving and petitioning for continued safety for the town, and it took quite a while before he finally found Melissa. In truth, it was

Melissa who found him, sneaking up behind him and snaking her arms around his waist, planting a kiss on his cheek. The young lovers embraced in a tight hug and laughed together, sharing their joy and relief from the morning's news. They waited patiently in line to kneel before the Master Postulant and bring their prayers of thanks before God, then left the church together, deciding to pack a picnic lunch and eat together atop their hill. They talked of everything except danger to themselves and the city, and when the mood came upon them unexpectedly they both fell to kissing each other passionately, lying together on the patchwork blanket they always brought along on their picnics. They both knew anyone could see them there on top of their hill, but for once in their lives they simply did not care.

They walked back down to Tamendad together, hand in hand, and were almost upon William's house before they realized something was unusual. "Those are two of the Governor's guards," Melissa said, gesturing to the two armed and armored men positioned in front of the main door of the Stuart-Camen home. "What's going on?"

"I have no idea, my love," William said. He tried to sound self-assured, but he suspected his worry came through in his voice. He quickened his step toward his family's house, and was glad Melissa did likewise without having to be asked. The guards bowed as William and Melissa approached the front door.

"Good afternoon to you, milord, milady," the two guards said in unison, and then the one whose insignia marked him of lower rank fell quiet. The higher-ranking guard continued on, "The Governor and Master Ferdinan are expecting you, Lord William."

"They are?" William heard himself ask. He looked to Melissa, and found a peculiar reassurance in the fact that the look on her face bespoke a comparable level of confusion to his own.

"Indeed," the superior officer said, and opened the door for the young lord and lady. William and Melissa gave each other one more uncertain look before stepping inside. They found both Governor Chamberlain and Ferdinan sitting in the common room. The two men stood and smiled as the young couple entered. William just stood there and blinked, his brow furrowed. The Governor had never been in his house before.

"William, es good to see you again," Ferdinan said, and then added, "And you as well, Melissa." Both young nobles smiled at Ferdinan, but both still looked confused as ever.

"Lord William, I hear you have been doing good work at the northwest gate," Governor Chamberlain said.

"I thank Your Lordship," William said, bowing before the Governor.

"Lady Melissa, I understand you had your concerns over letting

William oversee that part of the repair effort," said the Governor.

For all her usual poised calmness, Melissa started a bit when the Governor addressed her. "Only because of his injury, Your Lordship," she replied, managing quite well to mask the nervousness in her voice. "I had no doubts of his ability to lead the effort."

"Well," Ferdinan interjected, "es probably a great relief to you then that he will no longer be in charge there."

William's eyes widened. When he looked to Melissa, he saw that her eyes were as wide as his own.

"Have I done something to displease Your Lordship?" William asked, trying to keep emotion out of his voice.

"No, William," Governor Chamberlain said, "not at all. I am simply reassigning your duty."

"I do not understand," Melissa said, and William was glad she had said it for him. He was not sure he could even manage to speak at the moment, he was so baffled.

Ferdinan spoke up before the Governor had a chance. "We are raising a militia," he said, "and we need you to assist with their training."

William had absolutely no power to stop the smile that spread across his face. Melissa was positively beaming at him. Still, there was the question. "I'm...*honored*," William said, "but surely there are men more qualified than myself."

"Yes, there are," said Ferdinan, and William faltered at the Conquian's bluntness, "but all those men are members of the constabulary. They cannot spare the time it takes to train others."

"My father–" William began, but the Governor's words cut him off.

"Your father is now a lieutenant in the constabulary, William, and I'm afraid he will now have even less time to spare than usual."

"It was actually your father who suggested you," added Ferdinan, "and I totally agree with his recommendation."

"I graciously accept, Lord Governor," William said, bowing. He felt Melissa grab his hand and squeeze it, and he smiled . "Now if you will excuse me, gentlemen," William continued as he rose from the bow, "I have to practice."

Melissa and William said their goodbyes to Governor Chamberlain and Ferdinan, who were shown out by Reynolds. The guards snapped to attention as the door of the Stuart-Camen home opened, and followed down the walk after the two men. When they got to the cobbled street that ran in front of the Stuart-Camen home, Governor Chamberlain and Ferdinan both stopped to converse for a moment.

"Are you headed back to the southwest gate now that our business with young Lord Stuart-Camen is finished, Don Ferdinan?" the Governor asked.

Ferdinan shook his head. "Actually, Governor, there es something I need to discuss with you first," the Conquian said, and he had a serious look.

"Yes, of course, I always have a moment to spare for the Conquian ambassador. What is it?"

"Es something that should be discussed in private," Ferdinan said.

The Governor arched an eyebrow.

"You intentionally disobeyed an official order!" Governor Chamberlain's normally composed voice boomed off the walls of his study. He was standing behind his desk, both hands firmly planted on its surface, where he had been sitting only moments earlier. "If you were any other man, I'd have you arrested and thrown in irons!"

"I disobeyed your order to protect your township, Governor," Ferdinan spat, standing with his hands on his hips. "Any reasonable man would have seen that a day's ride was not enough warning to be useful."

"That was not your decision to make," the Governor said through clenched teeth, and the level tone of his voice added more emphasis than any scream could have.

"I made it my decision," Ferdinan retorted in an equally measured voice.

"You are treading very dangerous waters, Don Ferdinan."

"Perhaps," Ferdinan said, narrowing his brow, "but so es your city. If it were not for me, your town would probably not even have enough lumber to begin fixing the gates yet. If it were not for me pestering you to send out scouts, we would not even have the knowledge that we are safe for another day, what little good that does us. And if it were not for me taking my case to the scouts themselves and making them see reason where you would not, Governor, then the second attack would take us all completely by surprise when it came."

"We are not even certain there will be another attack," the Governor said, though his voice did not have quite as much resolve as it could have.

"There will be, Geoffery," Ferdinan said, without hostility. "We are intelligent men. We both know whatever those things were, their attack was no isolated incident. If we are going to prepare for what comes next, we must take risks. Timidity might get your people killed."

"So might temerity," the Governor replied.

"Perhaps," said Ferdinan, shrugging his shoulders, "but at least with temerity we will go down fighting."

Governor Chamberlain held Ferdinan's stare for a good while before looking away. He sighed deeply and rubbed his eyes, and for a moment his weariness shone through. Ferdinan wondered if the Governor had gotten more than a couple of hours of sleep since the attack. Governor Chamberlain collapsed more than sat down in the chair behind his desk, and stared off into space in the general direction of the window. "Why do you question every decision I make?" he asked.

"I question everything, Lord Governor," Ferdinan replied. Geoffery perked up just a bit at his words. It was the first time in a while that Ferdinan had addressed him properly. "Only questioning men find solutions to the problems that face them."

There was silence again in the Governor's study. Governor Chamberlain sat in his chair, staring at nothing, lost in thought. Ferdinan stood rubbing his right hand over the whiskers on his chin, his eyes fixed on the Governor. Neither man spoke for some time.

"Who are you, Don Ferdinan?" the Governor finally asked. "You're obviously a bit more than you let on to be."

Ferdinan stood still a moment, then nodded subtly. "I am an ambassador of the Conquian throne. I am also more than this, but my duty to King Altores prohibits me from revealing more about myself."

Governor Chamberlain shifted his gaze and looked at Ferdinan, nodding slightly. "Duty has a way of tying our hands," the Governor said, though the sound of his voice conveyed that he was speaking as much to himself as to the Conquian.

Ferdinan's posture became a bit more relaxed. "The Conquian word for duty es *reposidad*, which comes from the word that literally means to bind oneself."

"You Conquians have a way with words."

Ferdinan grinned empathetically. "You must trust me," he said, and the Governor straightened a bit in his seat. "You have no reason to trust me, other than that you know me to be a man of duty and honor, like yourself, but you must trust that what I do, I do for the good of your city." Ferdinan's stare was as unyielding as cold steel, but Governor Chamberlain held it without flinching. The pause lasted only moments, but seemed to stretch on for an eternity. Finally, the Governor nodded.

"You and I have strikingly different outlooks on many issues, Don Ferdinan, but you have given me no cause to doubt your intentions."

Ferdinan nodded as well, earnestly. "Thank you, Lord Governor," he said, and bowed slightly. "Now I would also like to discuss why you have not yet addressed the townspeople as you said you would…"

❖   ❖   ❖

Afternoon gave way to evening, and Colvin once again had dinner with Gunther and Gertrude; Gangis was once again absent from the dinner table, as his schedule that day had been filled with errands to run outside the city walls. Gunther and Colvin had made a considerable dent in the pile of weapons needing repair, and both had worked up quite a hunger in the process. Gertrude put plates piled high with scallops and whitefish in front of her husband and his new apprentice, and Colvin gobbled down the seafood ravenously. It was his first time eating fresh seafood, and he found it to be much better than the heavily salted fish that was common farther inland. The three did not have beer with this meal. Instead, Gunther disappeared down the stairs into the basement of his home and emerged with a dusty glass bottle. The wine Gunther produced, which he took credit for making himself, smelled slightly of honeysuckle and tasted a little like apples and spice. It fit the meal perfectly, though Colvin found it hard to believe Gunther had made the wine himself. It was so delicate compared to the beer he kept on hand.

Colvin stayed to help Gertrude straighten up after dinner once again before excusing himself, and then began making his way through the streets of the trade district. He moved roughly in a direction that would take him toward William's home, but would also carry him close enough to the Crown Rose to justify stopping in for a drink if Gregor and the others were up to anything. He was a bit surprised when he found all five Highlanders out on the front lawn of the Crown Rose, practicing fisticuffs and grappling techniques.

"Have ye heard th' news about th' militia?" Gregor asked, wiping sweat from his brow, when Colvin had joined them.

"Gunther said they were thinking about raising one," Colvin replied. He had not heard anything beyond that.

"Aye, well, 'tis official now. Ferdinan stopped by earlier this even with all th' details. Th' Governor's going t' make th' announcement on th' morrow. Th' lads and I have been asked t' assist in training th' men and women."

"We're just brushing up a bit," Liam added. He had a bit of a shiner under his left eye. Colvin thought it best not to bring attention to it.

"That's great!" Colvin said. "I can't imagine anybody better suited to the job. You'll have the recruits whipped into shape in no time."

"That's th' hope, at any rate," Gregor agreed. "Come in and have a drink with us, lad?" Colvin agreed with minimal persuasion. Soon Colvin and the Highlanders sat sipping whiskey and recounting the events of the day. The Crown Rose had been restored to almost normal condition, though a few small sections of the floor in the main dining room would have to be replaced and Colvin noticed the chagrined look on Gregor's face when he asked what happened to the chandelier. When Colvin was close to finishing off his glass of whiskey, Angus spoke up.

"So are ye going t' volunteer for th' militia?" he asked. All eyes focused on Colvin, and the red-haired man shifted a bit uncomfortably in his chair.

"Ye'd be a great help t' us, lad," Gregor added. "Ye're good with yer fists, and I'm sure ye could help us teach th' greener men a thing or two with that tumbling o' yers."

"Well...uh...I hadn't really thought about it."

"Ye should, lad," Angus told him.

"Aye, ye'd be a real asset," Gregor agreed.

Colvin felt like he might actually be blushing. That was one of the nicest things anyone had ever said about him. "Well, I'd like to, but Gunther's keeping me really busy," Colvin explained. "If I can find the time, though, I will."

"Ah, well, as for that, lad," Gregor began, then hesitated to pound the last of his whiskey before continuing, "th' Governor shall nae even be making th' announcement until th' morrow, and it should take at least a day t' get e'eryone who volunteers sorted. Perhaps by th' time we're actually ready t' begin with training proper, ye shall nae have so much work t' tie ye down t' th' forge."

Colvin nodded, but said nothing immediately. After taking a few moments to think it over, he spoke up. "I'll talk to Gunther about it tomorrow." All the Highlanders seemed quite pleased at this, and talked Colvin into having another dram before he finally departed the Crown Rose.

He whistled to himself as he walked through the streets of Tamendad, making his way across town toward William's house. He was standing at the beginning of the Stuart-Camens' walk before he knew it, and allowed himself a laugh at his own expense. Just two days ago the streets in this part of the residential district had been enough to send him into a panic. Now he found his way through them with barely an upward glance, and his mind lost in a dozen different thoughts.

Reynolds opened the door for Colvin when he knocked, and the old butler smiled. "Master Colvin, how has the day treated you?" the butler asked as he escorted Colvin inside.

"Not bad, Reynolds," Colvin replied. "How about yourself?"

"All is well. You have a caller, sir."

Colvin hesitated at Reynolds's words. "I do?"

"Yes, sir. He came perhaps half of an hour ago. He is waiting in the common room for you." Colvin furrowed his brow, but said nothing more to Reynolds, turning and walking into the common room. A well-dressed, elderly gentleman was sitting in a chair, his hands folded delicately in his lap. He had wiry gray hair that appeared to ardently protest any effort the man made to keep it combed. Other than his wild hair, though, the man was a picture of propriety. The man stood and nodded slightly, not quite enough to be considered a real bow, when Colvin entered. Colvin returned the gesture as best he could.

"You must be Colvin," the elderly gentleman said, his voice sounding quite formal. "My name is Stewart Salvington. I am an instructor in the faculties of reading and writing."

Colvin blinked. "I don't understand."

Master Salvington looked puzzled. "The good Don Ferdinan has procured my services to aid in your instruction of the written word," he explained.

"Oh." Colvin felt like he should say more, but nothing came immediately to mind.

"I have been told you are a busy man, Colvin, but you will have to free at least one hour, preferably two, from your schedule every evening. The written word can be quite a difficult subject for some to grasp, and it seems the older the student, the more difficult his task. Where would you like to take your lessons?"

Colvin shrugged his shoulders. "I have a room upstairs. We could use that, I guess."

Stewart Salvington snatched up a brown leather satchel from beside the chair. It was well worn, and looked to hold more than a few books. "Excellent," the old instructor said. "Lead the way."

Colvin climbed the stairs to his first reading lesson.

The next day, Luthane gave way to Anteron, marking only half a month remaining of summer. It also marked the first church service since the attack on Tamendad, and the church in the town square was filled as never before with townspeople offering up thanks to God that the creatures had not come back, and pleas for mercy on the souls of those who lost their lives. The names of every person who had been killed in the attack were read and the Sign of the Compass made after each. Then Master Postulant Dunleavey read a rather poignant passage from the Architessera:

The mind of man comprehendeth not why the Face of Dissonance must at times smile. Against the grin of Animas the fool cries, "God hath abandoned us!" But a man's left hand would sooner abandon his right. All that riseth must fall at length, but all that falls shall riseth again. That which is whole shall be torn asunder, and that which is torn asunder shall be rebuilt. Such are the ways of God and man, for the face of man is but one, yet the Face of God is Four in One. At times Agathas and at times Paraxis. Tactus this day, Animas the morrow. Hear, abide, and take comfort that the Face of God is always smiling.

The words had never carried such weight as they did that morning.

Gregor and all his lads attended the church service that day, as did Ferdinan, and the Master Postulant also said a prayer giving thanks for the presence of these men and the assistance they had lent in defending the town, and beseeching the Face of Beneficence to smile upon each of them and keep them all safe. Gregor and the other Highlanders were obviously embarrassed by the attention, each of them muttering something along the lines of, "'Twas nothing," when the focus of the churchgoers was on them. Ferdinan was obviously more comfortable in the spotlight, nodding respectfully and making the Sign of the Compass when the prayers were said in his name.

Governor Chamberlain made an open address to the townspeople immediately after the church service, officially announcing the creation of the militia. There were entirely too many people who volunteered for the constabulary for Captain Jefford to ever be able to properly train and outfit them all, the Governor explained, so all those who volunteered would be formed into a militia. The militia would be charged with assisting the constabulary in defending Tamendad from outside aggression, but would not be vested with the power to police the city. Members of the militia would receive no pay for their services, but they would be fed during their training, given quarters within the city if they lived outside the wall, and if unable to provide their own munitions they would be outfitted with proper armaments, either swords to those who showed promise at them or what the Governor referred to as improvised weaponry.

"That means pitchforks and quarterstaffs t' those o' ye who dinnae know," Gregor added at this point, lightening the mood.

No one was very surprised to see that Ferdinan stood with the Governor throughout the entire speech, and even took it upon himself to answer a few questions the townspeople shouted out once the Governor concluded his remarks. Once all the questions were answered, the Governor set up scribes outside the church, commissioned with recording the names of anyone who wished to volunteer for the militia. Before the end of the day, those scribes began to wish that they were being paid by the name.

While the rest of the town was filing into the church that morning, Colvin was making his way to Gunther's smithy. In a way, he thought that fitting. The closest he ever felt to the Divine, which admittedly was not particularly close at all, was when he was making something with his own hands. Creativity was, after all, the single most Godlike quality a man possessed, or so the Church taught. At any rate, Colvin felt much more spiritual working with hammer and anvil than sitting in a pew.

He received a few strange looks, walking away from the church when everyone else was walking toward it. Most everyone in the town knew that he had been assigned to help out Gunther, though, and that the pressing need of solid weapons was enough to excuse a man from worshiping. Colvin waved amiably to all the passers-by, and almost all of them returned a wave and a smile his way. Life in Tamendad had proven to be much more agreeable than Colvin would have ever let himself imagine.

He walked on, turning the last corner before coming to Gunther's workshop, and noticed the scratching, grating sound that was coming from the smithy. That in itself was nothing odd. Gunther was just using one of his grinding wheels. What Colvin found strange about it was that Gunther was taking time to grind down a weapon, something simple enough for Colvin to have no problems with, when there were still a good number of seriously damaged blades in need of the master blacksmith's attention.

Colvin approached the smithy, and took a moment to focus his attention on the sign that hung outside it. He was pleased that after just one lesson, he knew with certainty that the first letter was *G*. He could not make out any of the others yet, but that one letter filled him with pride. That was a rather alien feeling, but he liked it. His first assignment from Stewart Salvington was to be able to arrange a series of letters so that they would read *Gunther's Smithy*. He already had one of the fourteen letters down.

Gunther was inside, working at a grinding wheel as Colvin had suspected, but he was not alone. Another man was with him, much younger and slightly taller than the blacksmith. The other man had black hair and a black beard, neither so long as Gunther's, and was just as broad as Colvin if perhaps half a foot shorter. His bulbous nose and gray eyes, in addition to his unmistakable stature, identified him immediately as Gangis.

Gunther and Gangis looked to be taking turns sharpening axes at the grinding wheel, but the axes they sharpened were certainly in no need of repair. Gunther's axe was double-headed, sturdy-looking but intricate, and it looked like it weighed a good stone or more. The axe Gangis held had only a single head, but it was counterbalanced with a mean spike that Colvin immediately appreciated could do just as much damage as the axe blade. Another wicked spike, this one looking more like a spearhead, adorned the base of the haft, just below the grip. Both weapons were truly terrible-looking and the way both men handled them, even when just sharpening them, made Colvin think both men knew a thing or two about putting them to use.

Gunther stopped spinning the grinding wheel and looked up from it when Colvin entered. "Colvin! Glad you're here!" Gunther said. "I want you to meet my boy, Gangis." Colvin and Gangis shook hands, and when Gangis said, "Pleased to meet you," Colvin thought the young man's tone sounded like Gunther's voice had gone on a diet. Gangis and Colvin both expressed that they had been eager to meet the other. Colvin found it difficult not to grin like a fool when Gangis mentioned that his father had spoken at length about how much help his new apprentice had been while Gangis was occupied performing watchman's duties. Gangis in turn looked pleased when Colvin mentioned how much his parents boasted about their son's dedication to protecting the town.

"Those are nice axes you both got," Colvin said once the introductions were out of the way, but his compliment also carried a question.

"My old friend Gregor MacDugal paid me a visit last night," Gunther began, and the blacksmith paused at Colvin's look of confusion upon his referring to Gregor as an old friend. Gunther went on to explain that he had once worked as a blacksmith in Duerhein during his "younger days." This made Colvin wonder just how old his new mentor really was, because William had told him that Gunther had been Tamendad's blacksmith since before he was born. Colvin figured it might be considered impolite to bring that subject up, though, so he kept his mouth shut. Gunther recounted his visit with Gregor, which had revolved around what Gregor and Colvin had discussed the night before. The Governor was forming a militia. Gregor wanted both Gunther and his son to join, and both men had agreed. "Not to boss you, Colvin," Gunther said when he had finished relating his story, "but I wanna encourage you to do the same. The militia could use another good, strong man like yourself."

Colvin was flattered, and a bit relieved that he had not even had to broach the subject of the militia with his new mentor. "Yeah, I was actually thinking about joining the militia myself, but I was worried about all the work we've still got to do."

Gunther nodded. "We're gonna have to bust our asses, that's for sure.

Gregor said they're gonna take tomorrow to get all the volunteers for the militia sorted out. I figure if we lower our shoulders we should be able to plow our way through a good chunk of this shit before trainin' starts. Besides, I'm pretty good with an axe. I won't need to spend much time trainin' after I've worked the rust out." Colvin could not be sure, but he thought Gunther had winked as he said it.

All five scouts returned to Tamendad before afternoon began its transition into evening, and they brought with them a second wave nothing to report. This was met with no less excitement than the day before, but the level of celebration did not come close to reaching the frenzied elation of the previous day. A third group of riders was dispatched, and these would ride the furthest yet, this time with the Governor's support. The repair effort continued, with Ferdinan overseeing the southwest gate and Merrik the northwest. Landowners and noblemen came and went on business. The last of the men and women slain in the attacks were buried. Tamendad's marketplace bustled with activity. Many fathers took their sons fishing in the Taeran Sea for the first time in days. Lovers walked hand in hand through the streets. Children played games. Old women gossiped. Old men told dirty jokes over tankards of ale. More people volunteered for the militia. Life, as it has a tendency to do under even the most unusual of circumstances, went on.

CHAPTER ELEVEN

THE PRIDE OF TAMENDAD

William ran through the progressions for what felt like the hundredth time. In fact, it might well have actually been the hundredth time. He had lost count. He had been at it for at least three hours, maybe more. He could not be entirely certain. He had lost track of time long ago. His left side was quite tender, and he had to be mindful not to put too much stress on the stitches as he walked through the movements, but so far as he could tell the injury had done nothing to hamper his abilities as a swordsman. As for that, he was hardly surprised. William had been running those same progressions for so long he felt reasonably certain that he could manage them even if he lost a limb.

This, however, was a little different. As William ran these progressions he became increasingly aware that for the first time in his life he was not simply running them for himself. Each move, each slash, each parry, each feint would have to be taught to another student of the sword, and he was the one who would have to do the teaching. The progressions were second nature to William, as much a part of him as his family name, and he had started to take them for granted. Now faced with the prospect of having to teach others how to use the sword William found a need for absolute perfection had started to arise in him. Mistakes that he would have shrugged off in the past, missteps that he would have forgiven himself, poor form that he would have accepted as simple fatigue now all became completely inexcusable. If he were to do this thing, if he were to take simple farmers and townspeople, put a sword in their hands and somehow by the grace of God turn them into honest swordsmen, then he as their instructor had to be the embodiment of excellence.

This need was of two natures. For one, his students deserved it. They were coming before him to learn. It was his duty to teach, just as his father had taught him. If he were to demand less than perfection of himself, it would be a disservice to his students. For the other, there was no doubt in William's mind that if his students, several of whom were certain to be quite a bit older than he, were to take him seriously then he had to present them no opportunity to question his ability. William Stuart-Camen was not a master swordsman, and no one would present him as such to the militia. But he was competent. Every move he made with his sword in his hand would have to portray that competence. And so he plunged back into the forms yet again.

He could not be certain who was drawing the most stares, he with his marathon practice session or the Highlanders falling all over one another and thumping each other with quarterstaffs. Either way, there was an assortment of strange sights to entertain anyone who passed by the Crown Rose this evening. While he had not been paying close attention to the Highlanders' actions, William had grown to appreciate their skill in combat. Everyone he talked to who had witnessed their practices had described the Highlanders' way of fighting as ragtag or undisciplined, but it was apparent that everyone who made such accusations had spent no real time studying their ways. The way they handled themselves in a fight was indeed disconcerting to those who watched them – or fought them, for that matter – but that was exactly the effect they strove for. For one thing the Highlanders were quick, quicker than any other men of their size William had ever seen. They used that quickness to their advantage, launching themselves wholeheartedly into an offensive. Once they really got going, it was almost impossible for an onlooker to stay focused on what the Highlanders were doing. Most made the assumption, obviously erroneous, that since they could not stay focused on what the Highlanders were doing, the Highlanders themselves could not possibly be focused on what they were doing either.

For another thing, the Highlanders were completely malleable in their fighting style. This was what gave William the most trouble in really understanding their tactics. Everything the young nobleman had learned about swordfighting he had learned through his father's method of progressions. Every slash, every parry, every movement he knew how to use was structured. It was all a collection of formal techniques. The first thing he had learned from his father was that there was a proper and an improper way to do anything with a sword, and the goal of a good swordsman was to learn the proper technique for everything. Improper techniques got men killed. All these notions of propriety and sound methodology clashed with everything the Highlanders did in battle. So far as William could tell, Gregor and his lads did not have a formal technique for anything they did. Each of the Highlanders had his own distinct way of wielding the quarterstaff. Liam tended to grip his staff with both hands close to one of the ends, using a backhanded striking technique that reminded William of sweeping a broom. Wallace, on the other hand, gripped the staff firmly in the middle with both hands and twirled it in a continual blur of slashing strikes. Gabrahn tended to thrust and stab with his quarterstaff more than anything else, and he had a deadly, almost pinpoint accuracy in finding the vital areas. Angus and Gregor actually seemed to share a similar style at the quarterstaff, but similar only insofar as it was really no style at all. They attacked with an amalgam of strikes, incorporating Liam's sweeps, Wallace's spins, and Gabrahn's thrusts with yet other types. Sometimes they swung the staffs the same way they swung their claymores. Sometimes they used the staffs to trip their opponents. Sometimes they did not even use the staffs as weapons, instead using them as barriers to keep their opponents out of striking distance. Not surprisingly, Angus and Gregor seemed a bit more skilled at the staff than the others, and Gregor a bit more skilled than Angus when it came down to it. Yet even that advantage seemed based more on simple experience than any edge the brothers' particular pseudo-style might have given. Each Highlander's individual method was pretty much on par with the others' as far as efficacy of style was concerned.

William came to the end of his progressions and sheathed his sword. He was thirsty, and his mind was wandering. He was not certain if he was done with practice for the evening – he would make that decision later – but for the moment he needed a respite. A member of the Crown Rose's waitstaff approached William as soon as he showed signs of taking a break. The servant carried a round tray with cups of fresh drinking water. William nodded his thanks to the servant as he took one of the cups from the tray, and thought not for the first time that the servants employed by Torrance Mayhew conducted themselves with even more professionalism than many of the servants under the employ of Tamendad's noble families. William took a long sip of water, and looked up to see Gregor taking another cup from the servant's tray. The big Highlander was also short of breath and sweaty, but he gave the servant a friendly, "Thank ye, lad," just the same before turning his attention to William. "'Tis a pleasure t' watch ye practice yer swordsmanship, William," he said between sips. "Ye're going t' be an asset in training th' militiamen."

"Thank you, Gregor," William replied. "Your words honor me. If I do half so good a job at training them as you and your lads do, those things don't stand a chance."

"Ye shall do a fine job, lad," Gregor said, watching the other Highlanders continue with their sparring session. Angus was taking on Liam, Wallace and Gabrahn all at the same time, and not doing a terrible job fending for himself. "Ye're a good man, William. Th' militiamen shall be lucky t' have ye."

"Thanks, Gregor," William said. "We're all lucky that you and your friends are here. You've done so much."

"Ah, lad, any good man would do th' same," Gregor dismissed. The two men stood in silence for a moment, watching the others scuffle about. The three younger Highlanders eventually managed to bring their opponent down, though Angus had managed to fend off his opponents for much longer than William would have ever though possible when fighting three-against-one. "Ye know, lad," Gregor began, but then hesitated for a moment and eventually continued with a dismissive, "Ah, ne'er mind."

William looked at Gregor with a curious interest. "What is it, Gregor?" he asked.

Gregor was silent for a moment longer before replying. "Well, 'tis just that I was thinking, and dinnae take this th' wrong way, but perhaps ye should allow me and th' lads t' give ye a few pointers on fisticuffs. Now that's not t' say ye need any help in knowing how t' handle yerself in a fight, mind ye, just that th' lads and I think it might do ye well t' know a few holds and a couple o' ways t' strike barehanded in addition t' yer broadsword."

William nodded. "That would be great," he said. "I think it would really help me branch out a bit with my technique."

"Aye, lad, that's what I was trying t' say," Gregor agreed.

"Actually, Gregor," William continued, "there's something else I've been meaning to ask you about." William was not sure why he was nervous to ask Gregor the question he intended to ask.

"Aye, and what's that?"

"Well, actually I was wondering if it would be possible to learn the old tongue."

Gregor had a mildly surprised look on his face from the question, but nothing that approached disapproval. "Why would ye want t' learn th' old tongue, lad?" Gregor asked.

William shrugged his shoulders. He gave the only reason he had. "Because I respect you and your ways."

Gregor gave William a thoughtful, solemn look. "Lad, ye honor me. 'Twould be a pleasure t' teach ye. It shall nae be easy t' learn, though, I must warn ye."

William nodded his understanding.

The two men stood there a while longer, and were soon joined by the other Highlanders. They spoke mostly of the militia and what the next day would bring. According to Ferdinan's latest report, the Governor's announcement that morning had resulted in a stampede of volunteers to such an extent that by the time all the names had been recorded, nearly one in ten citizens of Tamendad would be charged with defending it. The entire next day would be spent dividing those volunteers into two groups: those in need of combat training and those who were already fit to serve without. The group in need of training would then be divided again into two subgroups. Those who either owned a sword or showed enough promise with one to be given one of the few Tamendad had to offer would train at the blade under William's instruction. The Highlanders would train the other group, the rough and tumble types, men and women big on heart but short on experience. If time permitted, Gregor and his lads would also give William's group a few pointers on hand-to-hand combat and more unorthodox tactics in an attempt to make them more well-rounded soldiers.

If time permitted.

Those three words scared William more than anything else in Ferdinan's report.

❖   ❖   ❖

Colvin arrived at the smithy before the sun was even in the sky the next morning, and yet as he walked up the cobbled street toward the workshop he was only mildly surprised to hear the peal of hammer against anvil already ringing in the cool darkness of the pre-dawn air. Colvin had never met anyone with Gunther's work ethic, a trait that Colvin could have easily found incredibly annoying in someone who drew attention to it but one that made him like the short blacksmith better than perhaps anyone he had ever met. To meet Gunther Moragun was to know instantly that he was a man who had found his true life's calling in metalworking and savored every opportunity he had to practice his craft. Colvin hoped that one day he might find something that brought his life such a sense of purpose.

Colvin entered the workshop without knocking, not wanting to interrupt Gunther from his work. Gangis shared the shop with Gunther, and both father and son had worked up a sweat that told Colvin they had already been at it for quite a while despite the ungodly early hour. He wondered if Gunther had slept. If he had, he probably resented the time away from the forge.

"Decide to sleep in this mornin'?" Gunther said without looking up from the glowing blade he was hammering.

Colvin's only reply was a smirk the blacksmith could not see. He set himself to work, and the ring of his hammer joined those of the other two men in the workshop. He soon lost himself in the rhythm of the forge. The vibrations that ran up his forearm with every strike of his hammer set a tempo to the work, an improvised metronome to set the pace. The ringing peals of hammers on anvils sounded deceptively like bells tolling in unison. The ethereal quality of the sound seemed fitting, a choral testament to the creation that was continuously happening in the workshop. Colvin's mind buzzed with excitement over it all. Loran Rothwald had never come close to instilling in Colvin this level of passion for the blacksmith's craft. Then again, Loran Rothwald was not half the blacksmith Gunther was. Probably not even a quarter.

There would be no breaks today, a decision the three smiths had all come to unanimously and without discussing it with each other. There was much work left to be done on the weapons damaged in the attack on the city, enough to keep three men busy for a full day and probably more, but it soon became apparent that the smithy's workload was much heavier than they had originally realized. Mere moments after the sun began to light the eastern horizon, not a quarter hour after Colvin had arrived, the door to the workshop was opened by the first townsman bringing in his own personal weapon in need of repair. This was to remain a recurring and increasingly frustrating theme throughout the day, so that no matter how hard Gunther, Gangis and Colvin worked, the pile of weapons yet to be repaired stayed about the same size. These newer arrivals thankfully required less effort than the weapons that had been damaged in the attack, as they had mostly just spent years hanging on walls or tucked away in attics and had fallen into disrepair through their lack of care and use.

There was no real way to measure the time as it passed, except to keep track of the sun's slow progress across the sky. The open vents of the ceiling made that possible, but it required entirely more patience than Colvin possessed. The fierce-eyed apprentice preferred to just lose himself in the hammer strokes and focus completely on the moment. He had never felt so deeply philosophical in his life as when he worked at Gunther's forge. He did not mention this to Gunther – he could not even begin to imagine what words he would use to convey that message – but in a way he knew Gunther understood how he felt. There was no mistaking the look in Gunther's eyes when whatever it was he was working on began to take shape. Underneath the short blacksmith's coarse exterior was a man who relished every sculpting strike of hammer against glowing steel.

Colvin was so focused on the moment that he almost did not notice the door of the smithy open. A woman entered the workshop. She was not particularly short for a woman, but she was closer to being short than tall. She had a fair complexion and her straight black hair came down to just above her shoulders. She wore a plain gray shirt with short sleeves

146

that laced at the collar, along with a pair of plain trousers the color of charcoal and a pair of square-toed workman's boots not unlike Gunther's. She was not ravishingly gorgeous, but Colvin found her appealing in a way he could not quite describe. He watched her from the moment she entered the workshop, but she did not even glance in his direction, not even when she crossed right in front of him. She moved toward Gunther and placed a hand delicately on the short blacksmith's broad shoulder. She moved with a grace that could never rightfully be called daintiness. It was more like simple, cool elegance. Gunther turned his head quickly when he felt the physical contact, and the look in his eyes was fierce at first. He was not a man who liked being interrupted while he worked. His scowl morphed instantaneously into a smile when he saw who it was.

"Well hello there, Melinda" he said in his rough yet amicable voice. "What brings you out this way?" Colvin was no longer hammering at the glowing sword blade that lay on his anvil. He was listening intently.

"Sorry to bother you, Gunther," Melinda said. Her back was to Colvin now. He wished he could see if she was smiling. He had a gut feeling she had a pretty smile. "I know you're busy as a bee right now. I was just wondering if I could borrow a pair of your smallest tongs. The bolt broke on mine." She brushed her hair back behind her left ear as she spoke. Colvin absentmindedly did the same without realizing it.

"Sure thing, hon," Gunther replied. "You know where they are." Melinda nodded and turned toward the rack that held the smallest of Gunther's tools.

"Afternoon, Melinda," Gangis said as she passed by him on her way toward the tool rack, giving her a friendly nod. She returned the greeting, then set her attention on the various tongs hanging on the rack in front of her. She snatched up a pair and pocketed them, then turned toward the door. She was moving back toward Colvin. If he was going to say something to get her attention, his opportunity had now presented itself.

He wanted to say something memorable. He wanted to say something witty and charming. He wanted to say something that would impress her. What he ended up saying was, "Oi." He smiled his best smile and silently berated himself for being so scatterbrained. It wasn't like him to stumble over his words in front of girls. His single spoken word managed to catch her attention, though. She stopped and turned to him, looking him over like she had just at that moment noticed he was in the same room with her. Her look seemed to appraise every inch of him. Her eyes, which Colvin now saw were brown, widened slightly as her gaze met his, but it was hardly the startled reaction his steely eyes were so frequently met with. She returned his smile, and he saw that her smile was like the rest of her: not stunning, but attractive and mysteriously endearing.

When she smiled, she looked like she knew a secret she would never tell.

"Oi," she said in return. The briefest of moments passed before she continued on her way out the door of the smithy, calling out, "Thanks again, Gunther" over her shoulder as she left. Colvin was not certain, but he thought that she had used that moment to look him over once more. It made him feel like an awkward adolescent to admit it, but he hoped she had liked what she had seen.

"Who was that?" Colvin asked when she was gone, trying to sound as disinterested as possible. Both Gunther and Gangis looked up from their anvils at him, and both looked like they were trying very hard to suppress a smirk. Gangis, at least, said nothing.

"Melinda's a friend of mine," Gunther said, returning his attention to the glowing blade lying on his anvil. "Silversmith. Got a table in the marketplace where she sells her wares." Colvin nodded silently. He wondered to himself how long he would have to wait for an opportunity to visit the marketplace.

The three smiths' day together at the forge was a good one. They had been working at such a breakneck pace that they had not given themselves even a moment to really appreciate the progress they were making. But as the last dying rays of the sun were extinguished from the western horizon and the star-dotted blanked of night spread itself over Tamendad, Gunther sighed a deep sigh, wiped the sweat from his brow and said, "Kill the forge." Only then did Gangis and Colvin realize that the nicked sword Gunther had just finished mending was the last of the weapons damaged in the attack. All that remained – though there were many – were the weapons that townspeople had brought in at regular intervals over the course of that day, what Gunther referred to as "spit and polish jobs."

After washing up they retired to the kitchen where Gertrude was just finishing up a special dinner of venison and seafood, a celebration of all their hard work. Gunther rebuffed his son when Gangis moved to start dipping out tankards of beer from the keg in the kitchen, muttering something about a special occasion and disappearing down the stairs to the basement. He returned with a smaller keg that had a pour spout and filled four tankards with a rich, dark stout. He took credit for brewing it himself.

Once the heaping plates were on the table, everyone raised their tankards and Gunther led a succinct but meaningful toast. "All of us proved true when a challenge reared its head. I couldn't have made it through without both of you. Now's the time to enjoy our accomplishments. Ganugamon's pride." Everyone clicked tankards together over the table, spilling a bit of the stout's frothy head on the

148

food below, and echoed Gunther's sentiment of "Ganugamon's pride." Everyone except Colvin, who was not really sure exactly what that meant. He would ask about it later. Now was the time to feast.

Colvin had three plates of venison steak and some rather insect-looking creature that everyone else at the table identified as crab. It could have been called mule vomit, for all Colvin cared, and he would still have eaten mounds of it. Once the seemingly impregnable shell was cracked, the tender, flaky meat inside was the most succulent thing Colvin had ever put in his mouth.

The four sat together for almost two hours, sharing good food and good conversation. Gunther told a number of anecdotes from his long career as a blacksmith, some of which had the other three at the table laughing so hard tears rolled down their cheeks. Gangis played a ditty on the pipe flute, a talent Colvin would have never imagined the burly young blacksmith possessed until he pulled the instrument from his pouch and started playing it. Gertrude provided a vocal accompaniment to her son's music in a twangy, warbling voice that seemed to fit perfectly. Colvin also provided a bit of dinner entertainment after only minimal goading, doing jumps and backflips and handstands that brought applause and whistles from his three companions. It was all the most fun Colvin had had in a long time, perhaps in his entire life. The regretful look in Gunther's eyes when he finally announced, "We've all got a busy day tomorrow," along with how hesitant everyone was to actually start clearing the table told Colvin that his sentiments were shared. Once all the scraps were thrown out and the dishes stacked for washing, Colvin bid Gunther and his family a good night.

Night gave way to day. As the sun began to illuminate the eastern horizon, men and women began filling the town square around the church. Some had swords at their sides. Others carried pitchforks and staffs and a varied assortment of other items that could improvise as weapons. Some carried nothing with them besides an eagerness to learn how to defend the city. All came together that morning, though, from different backgrounds and different walks of life to become the first militia ever raised in Tamendad.

There were also other people in the town square, spectators who took an interest in seeing for themselves the men and women who would be charged with assisting the constabulary in defending the city. The onlookers kept their distance, though, sticking close to the edge of the square as per the Governor's orders. Townspeople were welcome to watch the militia train, but no one was permitted to interfere.

In the heart of the town square, on the steps of the church, a small group of men stood shoulder to shoulder. Governor Chamberlain and Don Ferdinan stood together in the center of the line. Gregor MacDugal and the other Highlanders stood with them, as did William Stuart-Camen. Captain Jefford was also present, standing at attention beside the Governor. Once all the militiamen had filled the square, the Governor spoke.

"The township of Tamendad owes each of you a deep debt of gratitude," he announced. "You have selflessly given your time and your abilities to assist your home in its hour of great need. You ask for nothing in return but instruction on how to better serve your fellow townspeople. I am truly blessed to govern a township of such valiant men and women. It is with this sentiment in mind that I hereby name you *The Pride of Tamendad*." The crowd erupted in thunderous applause and raucous whistles and cheers. Gregor grave a shrill whistle and the other Highlanders boisterously applauded the Governor's proclamation. William clapped. Captain Jefford and Don Ferdinan stayed still as stone, looking over the men and women gathered in the square with a calculating look in their eyes.

"Militiamen! Attention!" the Captain of the Guard exclaimed in a commanding voice, and the applause tapered off. The men and women of the Pride of Tamendad stood tall, chests out, abdomens tight. They almost looked like real soldiers. "Form ranks!" the Captain announced, and the militia began dividing itself into three groups.

Ferdinan cursed softly, under his breath. The order had been seen to promptly enough, but sloppily, without discipline or direction. At first no one seemed certain exactly where their group was supposed to form ranks at, and those few people with the initiative to signal for other members in the same group to fall in around them did not take the time to see if anyone else in their group had done the same elsewhere. Some militiamen appeared to wander aimlessly, not asking where they were supposed to fall in either because of pride, stubbornness or embarrassment. A few people had forgotten exactly to which group they had been assigned. The whole process was given a nudge in the right direction when Gregor announced that everyone to be trained without a sword should fall in around him, and William followed suit for the people who were to be trained with swords. That left out everyone who had been declared already fit to serve, which not surprisingly had been the group having the smallest amount of difficulty following the order.

The look Ferdinan shared with the Governor and Captain Jefford said all that had to be said. An order to form ranks in a group of that size should have taken perhaps to the count of ten, if the commander was feeling generous. When all three groups were separated and standing at attention, more than ten times as long had passed.

There was no questioning that the men and women of the Pride of Tamendad were dedicated, and there was also no denying that there was some talent there. Ferdinan was confident the militia could indeed live up to its name, given proper training. But time was running out. Everyone in the town could feel it. The latest scouts had passed Tantera and Andoria and nearly reached the Highlands before circling back to Tamendad, and still found nothing to report. In its own queer way, that was more unsettling than discovering a whole hoard of the things that attacked Tamendad. A group that size of such monstrous creatures should have been impossible to miss, and if they had scattered during the retreat that should have made it all the easier for at least one to be spotted. That the invaders had managed to seemingly disappear implied they were cunning beasts, which were the most dangerous kind. It also implied that they had a plan to follow for their retreat, since trying to manage such an impressive disappearing act on the spur of the moment would have proven a logistical nightmare. With this in mind, it was foolish to think that the invaders would not come back, and it was a foregone conclusion that when they did come back, they would strike skillfully and strategically.

Ferdinan looked over the Pride of Tamendad once more. Gregor was beginning to address his rabble of militiamen. William was leading his group away from Gregor's, putting enough distance between them that what Gregor and the Highlanders were saying and doing would not distract the militiamen he was trying to instruct. The group of people who were deemed fit to serve had already begun to break up. Some of them, the ones who had other business to see to, were leaving the town square quietly, making sure not to interrupt anyone's training. Some of the others fell in with one of the training groups, volunteering to lend the instructors a hand when and if they needed it but mostly just standing quietly and being mindful.

Ferdinan made the Sign of the Compass. The Pride of Tamendad. The fate of the town was in their hands.

Gregor pounded the end of his quarterstaff on the bricks of the town square. The four other Highlanders did the same, and the percussion of staffs on street cut off the whispered murmurs running through the crowd. This group was slightly larger than the group of aspiring swordsmen. It was larger in the sense that it held more bodies than the sword group, and also in the sense that its members were physically larger than the other group. There were some real brawlers in the band of militiamen Gregor looked over, even if they did not realize it yet. His job was to teach them.

Silence fell over the crowd, but the Highlanders continued the rhythmic tapping of their staffs. A few members of the crowd looked uneasily at one another. It was not entirely clear to many if this was some sort of Glenish ritual or just a device to catch and hold the people's attention.

The entire group of people flinched as Gregor began a chant in his booming voice. It had no words, just a sepulchral series of hoots and growls. The other Highlanders picked up the chant with their leader, each throwing the timing slightly off so that no two of them were making the exact same noise at the exact same time. As each Highlander added his voice to the guttural chorus it became increasingly clear that whatever was happening had to be a Highlands tradition. Instead of making the chant seem that much more disjointed by joining in, the addition of each voice gave rise to an undulating, pulsating harmony. The sound of it threatened to beguile anyone who listened too attentively. It sounded tribal. It sounded violent. And as quickly as it had started, it was gone. The Highlanders did not fade out the way they had joined in. Instead, all fell silent as soon as Gregor stopped. The last beat of staffs striking brick seemed to hang thick in the air for long moments. No one spoke. A few did not even breathe.

"I am nae a man who believes in much o' what th' Turish hold t' be military sense," the big Highlander began. He spoke loudly, but not as loudly as he could have. He wanted the militiamen to strain to hear him. He wanted them to hang on every word like it might unravel the grand mysteries of life and God. So far he was doing an excellent job of it.

"Howe'er," he continued after a pause, "'tis a good idea that ye should have a military name for yer division. Now all together, ye are th' Pride o' Tamendad, though only time shall tell if ye are worthy o' that particular title." Some militiamen looked uncertainly at one-another. Gregor's voice had not carried a tone of doubt, merely that of a simple statement of fact, but his words were strikingly different from the encouraging remarks of Governor Chamberlain. "Separately, this group shall be known as Fist Division. Th' other group in training," Gregor gestured in the direction William had gone with his men, "shall be known as Sword Division. Finally, those men who dinnae need training shall be called Shield Division."

The names were as good as any, Gregor supposed. He had helped come up with them, along with William and Ferdinan. Gregor paused now for a moment, looking over the crowd before him. A few of them whispered the name to themselves. Some did not seem to care for it, but the general sentiment seemed positive. He allowed his men a moment to get acquainted with their new title before proceeding.

"WHO ARE YE?!?" Gregor bellowed suddenly, and a few of the militiamen jumped in surprise.

Silence. Gregor sighed.

"Fist Division," came the lone voice. It had been stated emphatically, like it was the most obvious thing in the world. Gregor found the source. Colvin was easy to spot with his height and his hair the color of blood. He was not smiling. He was incredibly serious. Gregor nodded. He was glad Colvin was in Fist Division. Honestly the lad should have been put in Shield Division, but Gregor had asked him as a personal favor to go through the training with Fist Division. Gregor intended to use Colvin more as an assistant than train him as a militiaman. He was just glad to have the guarantee that one man under him knew what the twist he was doing.

"WHO ARE YE?!?" Gregor asked again.

"Fist Division!" Colvin exclaimed this time, and he had accompaniment. About a fourth of the division had caught on. The reply was met with all the Highlanders butting their staffs against the ground once and saying something sounding like *Ah-woo*.

"WHO ARE YE?!?" The question was repeated as soon as the sound of the Highlanders' call had faded.

"FIST DIVISION!" This time almost everyone said it, and more than half had been screaming. Another pounding of staffs. Another *Ah-woo*.

"WHO ARE YE?!?"

"FIST DIVISION!!!" everyone screamed. Five quick strikes of staff on brick. Another *Ah-woo*, this time from some of the militiamen as well.

"Damn right," Gregor said. "Now let's get t' work, lads. M' name is Gregor MacDugal o' th' Clan MacDugal, but I'm certain most o' ye already knew that." Gregor introduced each of his lads. He started with Angus, but made no mention that they were brothers. In fact he said nothing about any of the other Highlanders that would draw more attention to him than the rest. "We are nae th' leaders o' Fist Division," Gregor said after introductions were out of the way. "In fact, we are nae even members o' Fist Division. We cannae be, since we dinnae hail from Tamendad. We're Highlanders."

"Too bleeding right we are," said Wallace, and even Gregor could not help but chuckle. The other Highlanders whooped it up a bit in support of their kinsman's sentiment.

"We have a saying in th' Highlands, so we do," Gregor continued after the others had quieted down. "Come th' morrow or th' grave. Some o' ye may have heard it. Either way, that saying tells ye everything ye need t' know about th' Highlands way.

"Now we all heard yer Governor, wise and just man he be, say that all ye lads were asking for was instruction on how t' better serve yer township. Well, me and m' lads here are going t' give ye that instruction, and we're going t' make damn sure ye take t' it. We're going t' teach ye how t' fight, come th' morrow or th' grave.

"I know ye shall tell me ye already know how t' fight. Ye've been fighting since ye were a wee lad. Ye came out o' yer mother's womb fighting. Well, I shall tell ye plain that ye're full o' shite. Now ye probably know how t' scrape. Ye possibly know how t' scuffle. Bugger all, ye might even know how t' tussle. But chances are ye dinnae know th' first thing about how t' fight. Nae unless ye've e'er faced another man and known that if ye dinnae kill him, ye would scale th' summit. Unfortunately, lads, 'tis exactly th' situation we find ourselves in. This city is under attack. Aye, 'tis true there's been but one attack yet, and that was six days gone, so some o' ye may have convinced yerselves that ye're in th' clear. Well, I shall nae abide th' spreading o' lies in m' presence. Deep down, ye all know as well as I that we have nae seen th' last o' those green beasts." Gregor paused. He wanted his last words to really sink in. The one thing that threatened to undermine the training he and his lads would give was if the militia did not take it seriously. The men and women of Fist Division were obviously unsettled by Gregor's words, but their looks told that they knew the big Highlander's claim was true. Every one of them did know, somewhere deep down inside, that the invaders would return eventually.

"So let's just roll over and die, shall we?" Gregor went on, shrugging his broad shoulders. "Save th' beasts th' trouble o' breaking us. Accept our fate without raising a fuss. We shall all just lie down like a whipped bitch and wait for th' inevitable t' happen, what say ye?"

Silence. Gregor was met by a host of blinking, taciturn faces. The big Highlander shook his head. "I dinnae bloody think so. Ye lads are what stands between those beasts and this city. Yer city. They're out there somewhere, planning, scheming t' take Tamendad by force. And I can promise ye this: if those things be capable of any thought at all, they're thinking that ye're all going t' cower like dogs when they return. They expect t' stroll right through th' gates and take all th' town has t' offer without anyone raising so much as a finger. They think ye're weak, they think ye're lazy, and they think ye're scared. That's why they're playing this waiting game with ye, lads. They're trying t' make ye sweat. Well, what say ye, lads? Are we going t' just let them have th' city?"

"NO!" Fist Division roared.

"Are ye going t' learn how t' fight?" Gregor asked.

"YES!" Fist Division affirmed.

"All right then. M' lads and I are all here t' teach. But I shall warn ye, th' task before ye shall be difficult. We are nae yer mothers, and we dinnae intend t' coddle ye. Ye are going t' endure more pain and lose more sweat and tears in th' next few days than ye e'er thought yerselves capable. Ye're going t' get bruised. Ye're going t' get battered. Ye might even bleed a little. But I want ye always t' remember this: howe'er bad ye think I hurt ye, howe'er much ye might want t' quit, always remember what it is ye're doing here. Ye are nae fighting for money, and ye are nae fighting for glory. Ye're fighting t' defend yer home. If ye think this training hurts ye, I promise ye, as God as m' witness, 'tis nothing compared t' what those beasts shall do t' ye when they come back if they find ye unable t' defend yerselves. Oh, and one more thing on that matter. If ye e'er feel like I'm asking ye t' give too much, there are some fresh graves in this city's graveyard. I suggest ye visit them, and reconsider exactly how much it is I'm really asking ye t' give."

Another moment of silence as Gregor let his words sink in.

"Now with that out o' th' way, we can begin th' training proper. I can see that some o' ye have brought spears and pitchforks along with ye. That's good. Those things can do more damage in a fight than most men might think, affording ye know how t' use them, o' course. Now all o' ye who have such weapons, ye shall be learning from Gabrahn how t' best make use o' them. As for the rest o' ye, it shall be th' quarterstaff that yer instruction shall focus on. Th' staff may perchance be God's preferred weapon, seeing as though He saw fit t' make them both so useful and so plentiful. I see some o' ye have brought staffs with ye, so I suppose ye already know a thing or two about how useful a stout shaft o' wood can be in a fix. As for the rest o' ye, 'tis yer lucky day. Ye get a gift." At Gregor's signal, Angus moved to the steps of the church and retrieved one of three large bundles wrapped in cloth, as long as a man was tall. When he returned, Angus dropped the bundle to the ground, and it made a loud *clack* when it hit. Opening the bundle revealed that it was full of sturdy-looking staffs. All the Highlanders began barking orders at Fist Division, and unarmed men and women came forward one at a time to receive their issued weapon. Only a handful looked uncertain.

Once everyone was in possession of a weapon and back in ranks, Gregor began to speak again. "Now th' first thing ye must learn is..."

❖   ❖   ❖

"...that a sword can be as dangerous to the wielder as to his opponent," William finished his caveat. Sword Division stood at rapt attention, hanging on his every word. "Unless, of course, you know how to use it. I know you all are eager to forge ahead and learn how to use a sword, but we are going to start off slowly. We have to, if you want to

155

learn correctly. Rushing your training will likely accomplish nothing except getting you killed, and you are all too valuable to take risks with. The first lesson you're going to learn is the proper way to stand."

It was almost imperceptible, but William picked up on the undercurrent of general impatience that ran through the militiamen standing before him. He sympathized with them, remembering how anxious he had been when he first started learning the sword. He wanted to assure them all that the lesson on proper stance would be brief, that they would all soon enough be learning slashing and parrying techniques, but he kept quiet. For one thing, he was intent on teaching these men and women using the same methods his father had used with him. For another thing, William thought it wise not to mention that training would be sped along because no one was really certain how much time they had left.

The young nobleman began his instruction on the proper way to stand when wielding a sword. Weight balanced approximately evenly on both feet. Right foot forward and right knee slightly bent, assuming the swordsman was right-handed. Torso turned slightly, but not quite profile. Dominant hand held forward, approximately level with the sternum. Off hand either touching the outer thigh to keep it out of the way or extended slightly behind the body for balance. William demonstrated the form as he gave his instructions. He was not surprised that his militiamen picked up quickly on the proper stance. There was indeed some real potential in Sword Division.

William dropped his stance while ordering his students to maintain theirs. He began to walk full circles around each of his students, examining every aspect of their form. He made comments and minor corrections, but mostly he found that everyone had gotten it pretty much right on the first try. He spoke more words of praise than correction. He also noted that his words carried a great deal of weight with his men. They already respected him, before he had even really begun to do anything as their instructor to earn their respect. It was undoubtedly because of the stories that had spread through Tamendad about his actions at the northwest gate on the night of the attack. He commanded a great deal of respect now wherever he went in town, but there was more to the sense of importance with which his men listened to his comments than simple hero worship. A good number of competent soldiers had fallen during the attack on Tamendad. That this young nobleman had survived with only one significant wound to show for it indicated that he knew what he was talking about.

"Your feet are spread just a bit too wide apart," William said to the man he had just finished orbiting, "and your right hand needs to come up a bit." William patted the man on the back and moved on to the next person in line, but he had not moved far enough away to keep from hearing the man he had just critiqued mumble, "Yes, your highness," under his breath. The militiaman William was approaching had obviously heard it too, because he stiffened and made a concerted effort not to look in the direction of the man who had said it. William stopped in his tracks and spun on his heels, locking his gaze on the mumbler. The man's eyes widened slightly in a moment of surprise, but this was quickly replaced by a forced look of cool defiance. William strode up to him, not stopping until their faces were barely a hand apart.

"I'm sorry, what was that?" William asked, crossing his arms over his chest.

The mumbler set his jaw firmly and drew himself up, putting his hands on his hips. He said nothing.

"What's your name?" William demanded. The forcefulness of it surprised even himself.

"Balen," the mumbler answered without much pause.

"I didn't tell you to drop your stance, Balen."

Balen sighed and resumed his previous posture but it was obvious he was intentionally being sloppy, to let William know it was a half-effort at best.

"Balen, if you have something to say to me, come out and say it like a man. Don't whisper behind my back like a willful brat."

Anger flashed in the mumbler's eyes, and he dropped his stance once again. "You've got a lot of nerve, boy," he said.

More than a few people gasped when they heard Balen's words. Under normal circumstances, no one would think a thing about Balen calling William *boy*; the mumbler was at least fifteen years William's senior. But no one spoke to a nobleman with such flippancy. Still, William never lost his composure. The young nobleman could see out of the corner of his eye that everyone was now completely focused on his confrontation with Balen. How he handled himself with this insubordinate was critical.

"You're dismissed, Balen." He said it with all the emotion a man might be expected to show when sending an underdone steak back to the kitchens.

Balen blinked. "What?" He came close to stammering.

"I have no use for a man like you in Sword Division. You're a waste of my time, and you're dismissed. Perhaps Gregor MacDugal could whip you into shape, assuming he'd even let you join Fist Division in the first place, but I simply don't have the time or the patience for it. Now get out of my sight."

Balen did not move. "What are you going to do," he said, "have the constabulary remove me?"

"No," William replied, "I think I can manage that on my own." His right hand came to grip the handle of his sheathed broadsword, but his even stare never faltered from Balen's eyes. The mumbler tried to look skeptical, but he could not hide the dilating of his pupils or the quickening of his breathing. After the briefest of hesitations Balen began the long, embarrassing walk out of the town square, muttering under his breath as he went. William did not spare a glance in his direction. His men snapped back to attention when he turned to address them.

"You are here to learn," he said, "and it is my pleasure to teach you all that I can. But I refuse to teach anyone who does not take my lessons seriously. You will approach your training with a certain level of commitment and respect. Do I make myself clear?"

"Yes sir!" Sword Division exclaimed in unison.

"Good. Now let's get back to work."

CHAPTER TWELVE

DECUSÉ

Don Ferdinan sat in the Governor's chair, behind the Governor's desk, in the Governor's study. Mid-afternoon sunlight poured through the open windows. The breeze smelled of city and saltwater and the ripe botanical smells of late summer. A goblet of red wine sat just within arm's reach on the desk. Numerous papers and parchments were scattered across the desk as well, some written in Turish, some in Conquian, some in Prima Tonce. The one he was reading at the moment was in Turish. He read it over for the third time. He spoke Turish fluently, but reading it was another matter. He had it pretty much figured out, though.

> *To Lord Geoffery of the Royal House of Chamberlain, Governor and Right Ruler of Tamendad.*
>
> *From the desk of Lord Fitzsimmons of the Reigning Royal House of Stodlemeyer, Governor and Right Ruler of Tantera, written this Third day of Anteron, the Year Nine Hundred Eighty-Nine Posteriori Cataclymian.*
>
> *I must express my deepest sympathies for the tragedy that has befallen Tamendad. I can assure you that you and your people are in my prayers nightly.*
>
> *In regards to your request for assistance, the township of Tantera gladly pledges fifty well-made longswords and an additional twenty-five halberds. These shall be sent with armed escort as soon as the shipment is gathered and set in order. You may expect to have them in your hands by 13th Anteron. I pray that you find no need for their use, but I hope that they prove beneficial should the need to use them arise.*

Unfortunately, due to the stealthy and unpredictable nature of the attack on Tamendad, I fear that I cannot spare a single trained soldier. Tantera has been on high alert since we received first word of the attack, and at present I need every member of my constabulary both to protect the city from outside aggression and to keep the peace within. Perhaps it might avail you to seek assistance of manpower from Andoria, or from Thiston across the Taeran Sea.

My prayers, and the prayers of all Tantera, continue to be with you during these trying times. If you need anything else, please do not hesitate to ask.

Signed,

Fitzsimmons of the House of Stodlemeyer

Governor and Right Ruler of Tantera

Ferdinan rolled the letter up and slid it back into its cylindrical case. He tossed the case haphazardly back onto the desk, where it landed among a dozen other indistinguishable cases, and picked up the goblet of wine. He sighed deeply, watching the wine slosh around as he swirled the goblet in his palm. He had suspected no other answer when he had sent the letter to Tantera, but it was still disheartening to find his suspicions confirmed. The least Governor Stodlemeyer could have done was acknowledge that Don Ferdinan, not Governor Chamberlain, had signed and sent the letter. Then again, if Fitzsimmons Stodlemeyer honestly thought that letters had not already been dispatched to Andoria and Thiston, he probably was not a very bright man to begin with. If he further thought Tamendad could afford to wait around until the thirteenth of Anteron for the weapons that had been promised, he was undoubtedly a bona fide imbecile.

Ferdinan gulped down the last of his wine and picked up a random uncased parchment from the desk. It did not particularly matter which of the various letters and reports he turned his attention to next. They all demanded his attention, and they would all be seen to sooner or later. Reclining in the large chair, Ferdinan began reading. He was pleased to see it was a report on the progress of the Sword Division of the Pride of Tamendad, penned by William Stuart-Camen. William's style was concise and prosaic, and presented Ferdinan with little difficulty in deciphering the usually puzzling, sometimes pedantic Turish language.

Sword Division was making astounding progress after only one day of training, William reported, and there was little doubt that all militiamen in the division would soon be demonstrating a competent level of skill with the sword. The greatest challenge seemed to be getting the men and women to embrace the military structure of the militia. There was just too much staunch individualism in the people who had volunteered for the militia to turn them into a unified military force in the time allotted. Accepting this hindrance to military unity, William estimated that Sword Division of the Pride of Tamendad would be capable of adequately performing its duties within a week's time.

At the bottom of William's report, after the young nobleman had signed his name, there was a postscript:

> *On a personal note, Colvin continues diligently in his studies with Stewart Salvington every night, no matter how exhausted he is after his days at the forge with Gunther or training with Gregor. He frequently brings his elementary reader to the dinner table with him, on those increasingly rare occasions that he dines at my house, and just about every conversation I have with him is seasoned with a good number of questions about which letters make which sounds, and why all words require at least one vowel. I asked him if he wanted me to send along word of his gratitude in this letter, but he instead requested my assistance in other ways.*

There was one more page to the report, which Ferdinan found blank except for three words, printed in the middle of the page:

> *Thank you, Ferdinan.*

The handwriting was strong and simple, not at all like William's sweeping nobleman's script. Great care had obviously been taken in the transcribing of each letter, so that each one was of perfect form. Ferdinan smiled more broadly than he could remember smiling since his arrival in Tamendad, perhaps since his arrival in Tur. William's postscript and Colvin's note told him more about what was going on in the township than all the other reports and letters combined. They reminded him that everywhere in the city lives were being lived while all the rest of this awful business was going on. It put things in perspective, and made it a bit clearer why he was going without sleep to orchestrate the military defense of a township he had not even heard of a month prior.

The door of the study opened, and Governor Chamberlain entered. The Governor took three long steps into the room before he stopped, staring at the Conquian sitting behind his desk. His arched eyebrow told that he had not been expecting to find Don Ferdinan here when he entered his own study.

Ferdinan looked up from William's report and nodded, giving no indication that he thought anything odd at all about using the Governor's study in his absence. "We can espect no aid from Tantera. They pledge nothing but weapons, and even that promise will take nine days to fulfill. I doubt the reply from Andoria or Thiston will be any different, assuming they even send one."

The Governor stood quietly for a moment, looking Ferdinan over with an unchanging expression of bewilderment. "I was unaware," he said at last, "that I had sent out requests of aid."

"I did not want to take up any of your precious time with such trifling matters, Lord Governor," Ferdinan explained.

"Would you mind if I sat down, Don Ferdinan?" the Governor asked, though there was very little question to his words.

"Of course, Governor, feel free," Ferdinan said, and gestured to the three chairs that sat in front of the desk. Governor Chamberlain might have lost his temper if Ferdinan had seemed even slightly imperious in his suggestion. Instead, the Governor just harrumphed and took a seat in one of the chairs he had never bothered to sit in before. It was really quite comfortable.

"Anything else you need to inform me of, Don Ferdinan?"

"The militia es progressing well in training, the southwest gate es estimated to be seventy-five percent repaired, the northwest gate es back at full strength, Captain Jefford reports that the constabulary stands ready to act at a moment's notice, and the most recent vintage of red from New Bellehaven es surprisingly good."

The Governor nodded. "Good to know," he said.

"Now if you will escuse me, Governor," Ferdinan continued, standing up, "I am on my way out."

"Business to attend to?" Governor Chamberlain asked, standing as well and moving around the desk to claim his chair before Ferdinan was even finished vacating it.

"Pleasure for once, actually. Visiting a friend."

"Well, you certainly deserve a moment of peace, Don Ferdinan. Your work ethic is quite astounding," the Governor said, settling into his chair like an animal protecting its territory.

"Thank you," Don Ferdinan said. "A good day to you, Governor."

Ferdinan stepped out of the study, closing the door behind him. Governor Chamberlain shifted his attention to the numerous reports and letters that lay scattered on his desk and sighed. His own chair suddenly seemed less comfortable.

❖   ❖   ❖

Clink, clink, clink.

Colvin found working at a forge alone again brought with it a mishmash of strange feelings. Every strike of his hammer called up memories of Loran Rothwald, of Rosie, of curses and broken jaws. Strangely enough, the forge seemed hotter without Gunther and Gangis in it. The ring of steel against steel did not seem to carry the soothing, melodious tone Colvin associated with working under the tutelage of the short blacksmith. It was much more like the sound from his dreams. Colvin involuntarily glanced around the workshop from time to time to assure himself that he was indeed in Tamendad, not the old village. He felt silly. He felt like a little boy.

This was Gunther's smithy, not Loran Rothwald's. Gunther was not there at the moment, and neither was Gangis. Both father and son had been called away early that morning to assist Jonathan Stuart-Camen with what had turned into a veritable epidemic of thrown shoes once the horses had been allowed out of the stables to graze and run for the first time since the attacks. But it was the same workshop he had come to feel comfortable in and perhaps even love a little bit over the past few days, and it was in Tamendad. Colvin could not quite bring himself to call Tamendad his home – it had been so many years since he had called anywhere home – but the township felt more secure than any place he had been in recent memory. He had made friends here. Honest to God friends. People who did nice things for him and did not ask for favors in return. People for whom he did favors anyway. He could not quite remember the last time he had had a friend.

Clink, clink, chink, clink.

He had so many friends now, more than he could count on one hand. So many people had given him so much, and quite a bit of it had been without him even asking for it. William, of course, was the best example of that. William probably could have had Colvin thrown out of town for the way he had treated the young nobleman at their first meeting. William had instead ignored Colvin's behavior and opened up his family's home to the wanderer. He had also provided Colvin with an entire wardrobe free of charge. All done out of the kindness of William's heart, all done expecting nothing in return.

All his friends had demonstrated selflessness, though. Gunther had

163

fed him more home-cooked meals in his few days at the forge than he had eaten in months before entering Tamendad. The short blacksmith had even offered to let Colvin stay in his home. The only reason Colvin had declined the offer was because he knew that no matter how much Gunther insisted otherwise, his presence would be a burden on the blacksmith and his wife, whereas he could stay at William's house without anyone really even noticing.

Gregor and the Highlanders welcomed him whenever he came around, always offering food and drink and a bed to sleep in if he needed it. They had given him the sturdy oak quarterstaff that he was slowly learning how to use. And Gregor had given him one doozy of a black eye.

Ferdinan had procured for him the services of Stewart Salvington, a gift for which he would always feel indebted. Yet Ferdinan had not so much as mentioned the lessons with Master Salvington since they had begun. Colvin had decided that was probably because of the embarrassment he had shown when he had admitted his illiteracy to Ferdinan.

So many friends, and he wanted to do nice things for each of them. Not because they had done things for him, but because they all deserved nice things. Colvin felt blessed.

Clink, chink, clink, clink, chink.

None of his friends were with him at the moment, though. He was alone at the forge. He should have been training with Fist Division. To be honest, at that moment he would have much preferred to be training with Fist Division. But Gregor had released him from training that day. The agreement had been that one man would always remain at the forge repairing weapons even after the Pride of Tamendad began training. The vast majority of the time that would be Gunther or Gangis, since both of them had been deemed ready to serve. But today both father and son were off shoeing horses. That left Colvin, the only other blacksmith in Tamendad, alone at the forge.

He felt lonely. It was a strange and alien feeling. During all the time he had spent alone over the past several months he had rarely felt lonely. He was accustomed to being by himself most of the time. Even when other people were around him, he tended to keep to himself. Now, after less than a week in Tamendad, he was unsettled by the absence of others. The town was changing him in ways he did not understand, in some ways he did not even notice until the change was complete. He wasn't even certain exactly who he was anymore. His whole definition of himself was in flux.

The uncertainty he found in his waking hours was accompanied by a blessed tranquility during sleep. The dreams had not returned since the day he had awakened to find himself Lorthok's captive. The surreal underworld of his dreams, and all the bad things it contained, seemed distant now, as if Tamendad was somehow acting as a buffer. When he dreamed now, which he rarely did, it was about the sorts of benign things other people told of dreaming about: being able to fly, walking down the street and discovering that he had forgotten to dress himself, falling from a great distance only to wake up the moment before impact. Colvin had never had dreams like that before. He did not hate them.

Chink, chink, clink, chink, clink, clink, chink.

The glowing sword blade on Colvin's anvil was taking its new shape nicely now, after giving some initial resistance. Colvin felt a bit guilty for spending so much time on reforging one sword when there was other work for him to be doing, especially because the sword he was working on really did not need to be reforged at all. A few minutes at the grinding wheel, an oil bath, and a polish job would have sufficed. But something in the sword called out to Colvin. He had not been sure when he had started work on it if he had learned enough under Gunther to manage reforging a sword by himself, but he did not seem to be having any problems with it now. It was looking less and less like the sword he remembered seeing in Lorthok's hand with each stroke of his hammer.

Colvin put down his hammer, taking a short break to wipe the back of his hand across his forehead. Sweat dripped into his eyes, blurring his vision for a moment. It was dreadfully hot, even for a smithy. Summer was refusing to die gracefully, choosing instead to lash out with as much heat and humidity as it could muster in protest of its inevitable transition into autumn. Colvin snatched up the cup of fresh water resting near him when his vision cleared, drinking deeply from it.

Chink, chink, chink, chink, chink.

Colvin straightened as he noticed the sound for the first time. He was so used to hearing multiple strikes of steel against steel while he worked that it had not even registered in his mind until now. The sound was coming from outside in the street, and it was growing louder. There were voices discernible under the sound as well.

"Hold still, you son of a bitch!" someone was saying. Colvin quickly thrust the glowing blade into the barrel of saltwater. It screamed and hissed as it was immersed, and steam bellowed. Once it was sufficiently cooled, Colvin tossed it aside and hurried out of the smithy. He feared he would see an army of Lorthoks attacking the city. What he saw instead was Ferdinan fending off the attacks of a very angry-looking man. The man was swinging an iron rod at Ferdinan, and Ferdinan was using both sabre and parrying dagger to defend himself. Ferdinan stole a quick glance in Colvin's direction, and in doing so communicated that he was having no real trouble evading his attacker's blows.

"Colvin, es good to see you again," Ferdinan called out, returning his attention to his assailant.

Colvin began to act without even realizing he had decided to do anything. Moving to flank Ferdinan's attacker, Colvin cracked his knuckles and announced his presence.

"You best back off," he called to the man with the iron rod. The man did not even acknowledge Colvin's presence.

"Es kind of you, Colvin, but unnecessary," Ferdinan said, still not taking his eyes from the attacks aimed at him.

"Shut up, you bastard!" the man said. "You're going to die!"

Some part of Colvin, a part that kept him calm and collected, snapped. The words were too reminiscent of Loran Rothwald, brought too many bad memories and emotions boiling immediately to the surface. Colvin advanced.

"Colvin, no!" Ferdinan exclaimed, his eyes widening, but it was too late to back down. Ferdinan's attacker turned, rounding on Colvin. The iron bar flew, aimed right at Colvin's temple. Ferdinan screamed, the first time he had lost his composure during the entire skirmish. If the blow did not kill Colvin outright it would probably leave him mentally crippled for the rest of his life. Ferdinan launched himself fully at Colvin's aggressor, but he knew he was too late. He could not save Colvin from the crippling blow.

Except the blow never landed.

As Ferdinan lunged forward, he was vaguely aware of Colvin's movements. Colvin planted his feet and leapt, flipping backwards away from the attack. The iron bar sailed through the air where Colvin's face had been a moment before. Colvin planted his hands on the ground and sprang back onto his feet, standing ready to defend himself. The hilt of Ferdinan's sabre connected with the spot where the man's spine met his skull, and the man crumpled to the ground. It had all happened in less than a heartbeat.

Ferdinan and Colvin both stood breathing heavily, looking at each other.

"What esactly were you doing?" Ferdinan demanded, exasperation in his voice.

"Me? What the twist were you doing?" Colvin threw up his hands in disbelief. "Who is he, and why was he trying to kill you?

"Oh," Ferdinan said. "Well. Es a long story."

"Supposing you tell it?" Colvin replied.

"He es Elizabeth's husband," Ferdinan said at last.

166

"Who's Elizabeth?"

"She keeps the bar at the Crown Rose. We have been having an affair for a few days, though she did not think to mention to me that it was an affair at all." Ferdinan's words were a mixture of irritation and bewilderment. Both of these feelings increased when Colvin began laughing. "What es so funny?" the Conquian demanded.

"An angry husband?" Colvin said. "I'm sorry, I just thought it was something more serious than that."

"Es been my esperience that an angry husband can be quite a serious thing to deal with," Ferdinan said

Colvin's laughter died away, but he kept a derisive smile on his face. "I thought you and the Governor's daughter were an item," he said with a hint of a tease in his voice.

"Where did you hear that?" Ferdinan asked, almost demanded. His tone wiped the smile from Colvin's face.

"It's just the word around town, Ferdinan. Sorry if it's a touchy subject."

Ferdinan shrugged his shoulders. "I was just unaware anyone knew about it, es all. Elysia and I have tried to be discreet."

"So you really do have something going on with the Governor's daughter?" Colvin asked. He had thought the stories were just so much gossip and rumor, something to take the townspeople's minds off more serious matters.

"I am not sure what your *something going on* means, but Elysia and I have been seeing each other privately. I do not see what that has to do with Elizabeth's husband, though." Ferdinan gestured to the unconscious man lying in a heap as he spoke.

It took a while for Colvin to find the right words. "Ferdinan, usually if you're with someone, that person is the only person you're with. Especially if it's the Governor's daughter." Colvin wondered if monogamy wasn't the rule in Conquia. He knew next to nothing about the country, but he found such an idea hard to believe.

Ferdinan looked perplexed. "Es not like Elysia and I are…what es the word you Turishmen use?…*courting*? We enjoy each other's company, but she has made it quite clear she has no desire to pursue a commitment with me or any other man at this point in her life. None of the women I am seeing at the moment are looking for anything serious. I would never lead a woman to think I offer anything but companionship."

"Exactly how many women are you seeing, Ferdinan?" Colvin asked.

"A gentleman does not discuss such things, Colvin," Ferdinan answered.

"No offense," Colvin said. "I just wanted an idea of how many more angry husbands you might have to deal with."

Ferdinan sighed. "I do not make it a practice to have affairs with married women. There are no words to describe how angry I am at Elizabeth for not telling me she was married. I would never have pursued her had I known."

Colvin believed Ferdinan. The Conquian looked genuinely upset. The two men stood in silence for a moment, before Ferdinan changed the subject. "That was quite a spectacular move," he said.

"Oh, the backflip?" Colvin replied. "Just a little something I picked up during my wandering days." He found himself speaking of his wandering days as if they had been a part of his life long left behind. He reminded himself he had been a wanderer mere days ago.

"Most men would not have been able to get out of the way of that attack," Ferdinan continued, quite serious. He obviously did not think of Colvin's acrobatics as a jester's act.

"Yeah, well, thank God I'm not most men, right?" Colvin shrugged and cleared his throat. He could not figure out why Ferdinan's attention was making him uncomfortable, but it probably had something to do with the way the Conquian was looking him over like a stablemaster appraising the quality of an alleged thoroughbred.

Ferdinan was in deep thought. He said nothing, inspecting Colvin from the crown of his red-haired head to the square toes of his workman's boots. He had never considered the possibility before now, but he would have never thought Colvin capable of the maneuver he had just seen the young man perform, either. Such nimbleness rivaled that of a good number of accomplished swordsmen, perhaps even Ferdinan himself. Well, no, Ferdinan decided immediately, that would be stretching it a bit, but nonetheless, Colvin had real potential. And the idea of taking a man from such humble beginnings under his wing appealed to the eternally poetic part of Ferdinan's soul.

"Have you ever studied the sabre, Colvin?" Ferdinan asked.

"Well, uh, no," Colvin replied, blinking. "Never really had the chance." Nor had he ever, before that moment, even considered the possibility that the chance might at any point in his life be presented to him.

"I suspect you would do esceedingly well at it," Ferdinan said. He was scratching the whiskers on his chin with his right hand. "Of course, es the question of where we would find you a good sabre. Turish sabres tend to be balanced all wrong for swordplay, and es no time to procure a Conquian sabre. And es going to take a lot of your time, which I hear you have very little of these days. And es going to be very difficult, even for someone as gifted as you. The sword never comes particularly easy at first, no matter how talented the student. And all this assumes you would actually be interested in studying—"

"Ferdinan, I'd love to. It sounds great," Colvin interrupted. The more Ferdinan talked about how difficult it was going to be, the more excited Colvin grew over the prospect.

Ferdinan half-nodded, half-bowed in agreement. "I am a busy man, as are you, but studying the sabre takes time, especially at the start of it. Two hours every afternoon. Gregor will escuse you from Fist Division under my care after the noon break, and we will practice in the courtyard of the Governor's house, where the wall will separate us from any intrusions. We will begin as soon as we can find you a sword." Ferdinan's last sentence did not sound hopeful. Colvin glanced for a moment at the sabre Ferdinan had sheathed at his left side, and a thought popped into his head so suddenly the young apprentice would have sworn it hadn't even originated in his own head.

"I have an idea, Ferdinan. C'mon." Colvin stepped over the unconscious form of Elizabeth's husband and reentered Gunther's workshop. Ferdinan followed suit without immediate question. When the Conquian entered the smithy, Colvin was already holding Lorthok's blade up for inspection.

"Will this work?" Colvin asked. Ferdinan took the blade from Colvin, looking it over attentively. He spent several minutes on the blade, turning it this way and that, slashing it through the air and weighing it in his hands before he answered the question.

"Es curved adequately, and es made from good steel, no question. The weight es a little off, though es difficult to say by how much, and the tip es not shaped correctly for piercing, but all that can be fixed. Reshape the tip into a piercing point and reduce the weight by perhaps a quarter, perhaps even a third. Do you think you can have all that done by tomorrow?"

"Not a chance," Colvin replied.

Ferdinan looked at Colvin in a moment of surprised silence. "I admire your honesty, straightforward though it may be," Ferdinan said. "Well, you cannot spend two days in a row out of training. But I have a suspicion that Gunther would have no qualms about making the necessary corrections. He has taken a liking to you. I will have a talk with the blacksmith when he returns from Lord Jonathan's stables. In the meantime, you get back to work. Tonight we will go out on the town to celebrate the beginning of your training as a swordsman."

It all sounded wonderful to Colvin, but none of it so much as the talk of celebrating.

❖   ❖   ❖

The Sailor's Song was not Ferdinan's kind of place. There was sawdust on the floors, many of the tables were just vaguely round pieces of wood attached to a barrelhead, the wine was dipped out of a keg, and the whole establishment smelled of sweat and brine. In spite of all that, Ferdinan was having a wonderful time there. Part of it was Colvin's infectious enthusiasm. The red-haired apprentice reveled as though he had not had a night out in years.

Colvin had, in fact, never had a night out like this, but he kept that fact to himself.

Another part of it was that despite the bad wine and bad decor, everyone in the place was as friendly as could be. The Sailor's Song was frequented by seafarers, no surprise there, but it was also popular with the constabulary. A good number of militiamen were also present this night. That mix of clientele made for some boisterous merrymaking. The clincher, though, was that the serving wenches were downright beautiful, and they all seemed to be quarreling over who got to attend to Ferdinan and Colvin.

"I think that one likes you," Colvin told Ferdinan, pointing to the ample-chested blonde who had brought the latest round of drinks to their table.

"You might show promise at the sword," Ferdinan said, "but when it comes to women you are as blind as a bat. Es clearly you she had has taken an interest in."

"Me? How can you tell?"

Ferdinan sighed the sigh of a man who is charged with explaining that up is not down. "When she came to the table, she gave you your drink first, and looked at me only long enough to make sure she would not spill mine on me as she sat it down. She was talking to you when she asked if we needed anything else. When I replied that we were fine for now, it took her a moment to realize what I had said—"

"But she smiled at you, and she blushed," Colvin interrupted.

"Because she was embarrassed. She had forgotten I was even at the table. And when she finally turned to leave, you were the last one she glanced at."

"How did you pick up on all that?" Colvin was obviously impressed.

"Attentiveness es one of the true marks of a great lover," Ferdinan explained. "Es as important during the pursuit as during the actual romance. Perhaps even more so."

Colvin nodded. "What else?"

"Escuse me?" Ferdinan said, arching an eyebrow.

"What are the other true marks of a great lover?" His thoughts had for some reason turned to the black-haired woman named Melinda. He was surprised to find himself on the edge of his seat.

"Ah," Ferdinan said, smiling and nodding. "Attentiveness es the first, but no more important than the others. Es merely the first step in the pursuit. Next es confidence. Confidence es an important one, no doubt. There es nothing most women find more desirable in a man. Even if a man does not have looks, which es obviously not a problem for the two of us, confidence can win him over with many women. Then there es honesty, also very important. Never mislead a woman, never make false promises, never withhold the truth. Those are the tactics of cowards and fools. Honesty requires that you make your feelings clear at the beginning. If you are not interested in anything serious, es your obligation, your duty as an honorable man, to let a woman know before any feelings develop. Do you understand?"

"Right, right," Colvin said. "Don't string them along. Next?"

Ferdinan chuckled. "Next comes selflessness. A great lover, like all great men, always places the other before the self. Es often said that true love can occur only when a man and a woman both care more about the wellbeing of their lover than of themselves, and es true, to a degree."

"Selflessness," Colvin agreed. "Gotcha."

"Finally, and perhaps most importantly, es passion. There are no great lovers who are not passionate lovers. I would go so far as to say there are not even any competent lovers who are not passionate lovers. Even a selfish, lying louse of a man can satisfy women, occasionally, if he has passion. Passion carries a man a long way. Es true in all of life, not just with romance."

"Okay," said Colvin, trying to keep everything straight in his mind. "Let me see if I've got it. First is attentiveness. Next comes confidence. Then honesty. Then there's selfishness...I mean selflessness, sorry, and then passion, the most important of all." Colvin repeated it to himself. *Attentiveness, confidence, honesty, selflessness, passion. Attentiveness, confidence, honesty, selflessness, passion. A-C-H-S-P.* Colvin did not realize until much later that night, while he was lying awake beside the blonde serving wench, whose name turned out to be Meena, that he had successfully guessed the first letters of each of the words.

Morning brought another day of training for the Pride of Tamendad, and a whopper of a hangover for Colvin and Ferdinan. Neither man let it slow him down that much, since there was work to be done. Ferdinan spent the day receiving reports, sending letters, giving orders, and doing other sorts of administrative things. Colvin spent the entire day training with Fist Division, and Gregor and the other Highlanders gave him all kinds of grief when they learned he had a hangover. Colvin took it all with good spirits, and beat the crap out of Wallace during a sparring match to vent his frustrations. When the day was over, Colvin and Ferdinan went carousing together yet again. This time it was a petite oil merchant named Autumn that Colvin wound up sharing a bed with by virtue of hitting all the true marks of a great lover. As Colvin lay awake next to his lightly snoring conquest he could not help but feel guilty about bedding two different women in two days, but by morning he had come to terms with it, having gone over the past forty-eight hours rigorously in his mind and assuring himself that he had at all times been attentive, confident, honest, selfless, and dear God had he ever been passionate.

The next day, Gunther sent word to both men that the alterations to the sword were complete. Colvin and Ferdinan hurried to Gunther's shop to inspect the finished product.

"Es amazing," Ferdinan said, holding the handle of the scimitar-turned-sabre and making lazy circles in the air with the blade. "Gunther, you are an artist."

Gunther grunted. "Well I don't know about that, but I'm good at what I do."

"Tell me what you think, Colvin," Ferdinan said, handing the sword over to his newest pupil. Colvin was slightly reluctant to take it. He knew nothing about swords. Ferdinan was much more qualified to assess its quality. Ferdinan stood firm, though, with the handle of the sword pointed toward him, and Colvin eventually took hold of it. The two most obvious differences, noticeable just from looking at the sword, were that the handle now sported an arched hand guard and the blade was considerably thinner with a piercing point at the end. But when Colvin took hold of the sword and felt it in his hand, a host of differences, all invisible to the eye, became apparent. The balance of the sword was completely different. Its weight felt to be half of what it was, and it was now evenly distributed along the entire length of the sword instead of being concentrated toward the end of the blade. It required nowhere near as much effort to swing now, and gave much less resistance to a change in direction.

"Wow," Colvin said.

"Didn't have enough time to do everything I wanted with it, but it's as close to a duelist's sabre as I can get without meltin' down the whole thing," the short blacksmith explained, tugging on his beard. "Should be good enough to learn on, anyway."

"Gunther, es nothing short of amazing what you have done," Ferdinan said. "Es so much better than anything I was hoping for."

"I do what I can," replied Gunther dismissively, but there was no mistaking the grin the spread across the short blacksmith's face.

Ferdinan thanked Gunther once again and he and Colvin turned to leave the workshop, but they were stayed by Gunther saying, "Wait, Colvin, I got something else for you." Gunther retrieved a leather pouch that was lying on the anvil Colvin usually used, and he pressed it into Colvin's hands without another word. Confused, Colvin opened the pouch and pulled out the contents, and he could not keep his face from lighting up. He pulled the leather gloves on immediately and punched the air a couple of times, getting a feel for them. The dagger blades riveted into place on the backs of the gloves were razor sharp, and were attached to the gloves so well Colvin suspected they would never come loose no matter how hard he punched. They were not particularly pretty things – Colvin doubted any gloves with dagger blades jutting from them could ever really be very pretty – but they were undeniably of the highest craftsmanship. The gloves themselves were sturdy treated leather, and looked like they probably cost the better half of a gold mark. The dagger blades were riveted and stitched in place with heavy thread, secured on the back of each glove. The base of the blades were covered with another piece of leather so that the blades looked like they grew right out of the glove.

"Gregor said you were good with your hands in a fight, and I thought you might be able to use them," the blacksmith explained.

"Shit yeah!" Colvin said.

"Don't mean to step on your toes, Don Ferdinan," Gunther continued. "I've got no doubt you'll turn Colvin into a fine swordsman. I started makin' these before you ever asked me about the sabre."

"No, no, es good," replied Ferdinan. "You have given Colvin another option. In times like this, a man needs all the options he can get." The Conquian eyed the gloves a bit longer and added, "Es a very good idea, Gunther. Arm an unarmed man without asking him to change the way he fights. Tell me, do you think we could make more of these for the militia?"

Gunther tugged at his beard for a bit, thinking it over, before he wrinkled his nose and grunted. "Doubtful," he replied gruffly, obviously wishing he could give a different answer. "If we had the time and the materials, sure. But those are blacksmith's gloves, the heaviest cowhide. Can't use nothin' lighter or the blades would rip right right off with the first good punch. I doubt there's more than a dozen pairs of gloves that strong in this whole town. They're expensive, and there's just not enough demand for 'em."

Ferdinan nodded. "Es a pity. Once again you have proven yourself a master artisan."

After leaving Gunther's smithy, Colvin and Ferdinan headed toward the Governor's house for Colvin's first lesson in swordplay, pausing just long enough for Colvin to deliver his new dagger gloves to his bedroom at the Stuart-Camen household. Colvin felt his heartbeat pick up a bit as they approached the stone wall running around the perimeter of the Governor's home. His heart was nearly racing when they came to the main courtyard. When Ferdinan said, "Let us begin," Colvin thought it might burst right out of his chest.

"Relax," the Conquian said, his voice soft and reassuring. "Es nothing to worry about. We will begin at the beginning. Normally, your instruction in the sword would begin with a lengthy lesson on *decusé*, the foundation of all swordplay. Unfortunately, time es an issue for us, so we will just have to skim over the basics. What are the five marks of a great lover?" Ferdinan snapped off the words of his last sentence like a general barking orders. Something in his voice made Colvin stiffen.

"Attentiveness, Confidence, Honesty, Selflessness, and Passion," Colvin answered, his words coming so quickly that each one clipped the one before it.

"Good," Ferdinan said. "These are essentially the same characteristics of *decusé*. Now I'm going to run through this quickly, so pay attention. Attentiveness es self-esplanatory. If you are not attentive with a sword, you die. Simple, no?"

Colvin blinked.

"Confidence es an easy one too. You cannot be timid with a sword. You must be bold, confident of your abilities as a swordsman. This es as true for beginners as for grand masters of the blade, and there es a subtle point to be learned there. Being confident does not require you to know everything that can be learned about the sabre, only that you are thoroughly comfortable using what you do know. Understand?"

"I think so."

"Good. Passion es also easy to esplain. If you reduce swordplay to a simple series of movements, a set of mechanics to memorize, and study it as though it were simple geometry, you will fail. If, however, you approach the sword with passion, strive to make the sword a part of yourself, pursue swordplay like you would pursue a beautiful woman–"

Colvin grinned roguishly.

"–then you will succeed. But the others – honesty and selflessness – how do you apply these qualities to the sabre? Es harder to esplain than attentiveness, confidence and passion, but still simple. Honesty, as applied to swordplay, means that you will use no dishonorable tactics to gain an advantage. No throwing sand in the eyes. No attacking a man who cannot defend himself. No causing your opponent to suffer unnecessarily. In short, honesty as applies to the sword es an unspoken understanding that you have sworn to follow the rules of honor.

"Now, that brings us to selflessness, perhaps the most difficult quality to attribute to swordplay. When it comes to being a great lover, selflessness means putting another person's needs before your own. Does that mean you should put the needs of your opponent before your own? Escuse me for saying so, but that sounds like a perfect way to wind up dead."

Colvin chuckled in agreement.

"Selflessness, as applied to swordplay, means that you relieve yourself of all notions of greatness, all aspirations of fame and fortune, all dreams of ambition right now, at the start. You do not study swordplay for what it can bring you. You study swordplay because es a worthy pursuit. You stand to gain nothing from it but a knowledge of the art."

There was a moment of contemplative silence. Colvin faced his instructor rapt with attention, running over in his mind all Ferdinan had just told him. It was a lot to take in in such a short amount of time.

"That, Colvin, es *decusé* in very brief summary. Now I have gone over with you in a matter of moments what most all beginners are supposed to spend the better part of their first week of lessons learning. I do this for two reasons. The first, which I have already mentioned, es because time es an issue. The second es because I already know you are an honorable man."

"Thank you, Ferdinan," Colvin said.

"Es nothing. You have proven your honor to me, and the rest of the town for that matter. But hear me now. Just because we skim over *decusé* in our lessons does not mean you can let the words go in one ear and out the other, understood? Whenever you think of the sword, thoughts of *decusé* follow. You cannot have one without the other. *Decusé* es the foundation upon which all of swordplay stands. Try to remove it and everything falls apart."

"I won't forget that," said Colvin.

"Good. Now with that out of the way, we can begin with the actual art of swordplay." Ferdinan drew his sabre, and with only a look told Colvin to do the same. Colvin complied.

"Assume the stance," Ferdinan said.

"What?"

"Assume the stance," Ferdinan repeated.

"How?"

"Assume the stance." Ferdinan's words were firmer now.

Colvin protested, "But I don't know–"

"Assume the stance!" Ferdinan was on the verge of shouting. Colvin, confused as ever, tried his best to mimic the stance he had seen William use when practicing the broadsword. It felt like he got it approximately correct, but Ferdinan began shaking his head immediately.

"Wrong!" the Conquian shouted. Colvin clenched his jaw. "Assume the stance!" Ferdinan demanded once more.

"I don't know how!" Colvin screamed in reply. "Tell me what I did wrong!" A couple of the Governor's personal guards passing close by on their rounds eyed the two of them warily, but continued on their way once they recognized Don Ferdinan.

"You only did it on the outside," Ferdinan explained, the edge gone from his voice. "Now try again. Assume the stance."

Colvin sighed, but tried once again to mimic the posture of William Stuart-Camen. Once again, Ferdinan said, "Wrong." Colvin did not move. He tried harder.

"Better, but still wrong," Ferdinan said.

Colvin tightened the stance until his muscles felt like tightly coiled springs.

"Let it go, Colvin."

The red-haired apprentice blinked at Ferdinan's instruction. What, exactly, was he supposed to let go? He said nothing.

"You must let it all go," Ferdinan continued. "All your worries, all your fears, all your hate. You must let all the bad things go."

Colvin felt like he had been punched in the gut. How did Ferdinan know about the bad things?

"The proper stance comes from within," said Ferdinan. "Only when your mind assumes the proper stance will your body be able to follow. You must clear your senses of everything. You and your sword, only those things are real. All else es pushed aside. Now, assume the stance."

Colvin closed his eyes.

"Assume the stance!"

Colvin breathed deeply.

"I said assume the stance!"

It all started to slide away.

"Assume the stance, you son of a bitch!"

Anger flashed in the corners of Colvin's mind. A brief mental image of Colvin punching the short, arrogant Conquian came...and went. The anger faded.

Colvin assumed the stance.

"Good."

Colvin opened his eyes when he heard Ferdinan's compliment. Neither man smiled.

"You are a quick learner, Colvin. Most men work long and hard on developing the strength of will to let go."

Colvin made no reply.

"Well, we are moving along wonderfully," Ferdinan said. "Now we learn to use the sword."

Colvin suddenly found that his schedule was stretched almost to the breaking point. He awoke at dawn and breakfasted with the Stuart-Camens. After breakfast he reported to the town square for Fist Division training, where he stayed until the midday break. After the break, he left the square and met Ferdinan in the courtyard of the Governor's house for two hours of swordplay lessons. Once that was over, he returned to the town square to finish up Fist Division training. Afterwards he returned to the Stuart-Camen home, washed up, helped Nelsie a bit with dinner and had his evening reading lesson with Stewart Salvington. Then he usually supped with the Stuart-Camens, talked with William for the better part of an hour about anything except the Pride of Tamendad and then headed into the trade district. As often as not, Ferdinan accompanied him. Colvin's life had become more structured than it had ever been, yet he had never had so much fun.

He was becoming quite popular in the trade district after hours. Several of the bartenders knew him by name and he was surprised to find that he had become almost as popular with the ladies as Ferdinan. Almost. Each night brought a different woman, each beautiful in her own way. Some he slept with, some he didn't; that decision was ultimately the woman's to make. Colvin was a bit surprised to find that he really did not have much of a preference. He supposed that since the sex was plentiful, it didn't need to be perpetual. The ready availability of it curbed his appetite a bit, so to speak. The sex was good, no denying it, and it was refreshing not to have to worry about anyone's father finding out about it, but ultimately Colvin found he enjoyed spending time with a woman regardless of whether or not he slept with her at the end of the night.

What he enjoyed the most was talking, really *talking* with them, about important things. They would talk about their thoughts and desires. They would talk about their aspirations and their fears. They would talk about what they wanted out of life. And the more Colvin talked with them, the more he realized that each woman was a unique individual, with thoughts and hopes and dreams that belonged to her and her alone. There was something captivating about each one of them. He found he cared about them, all of them. It was not love, but it was a genuine concern. Whenever a woman expressed feelings that ran deeper than his own, which happened more than once, Colvin was very careful in explaining that he could not offer more than friendship and compassion. A few tears were shed, a few objects were thrown in his general direction, but overall his honesty was well received.

The mornings were becoming colder and darkness was falling earlier. Summer was in its death throes and autumn waited patiently to stake its claim. The morning of 9th Anteron found Colvin sitting at the breakfast table with William and his family. Colvin was rolling a sausage back and forth on his plate with his fork, not really paying attention to the conversations going on around him. He had spent the previous night in the company, and the bed, of a barmaid at The Dancing Serpent, one of Tamendad's seedier alehouses. Her name was Jennias, but she went by Jen. More than anything else in the world she wanted to own a tavern of her own. She also wanted to see Wexford before she died. She wrote exceptionally bad poetry, and she knew it, but her father liked her poems so she kept writing them. She didn't believe in marriage, most likely because her mother had left her father for another man after fifteen years together. Jen was at least ten years older than Colvin, with a seemingly inexhaustible reserve of sexual energy. Morning had come much too early. Colvin was still not fully awake, and still a little drunk, but he perked up when he heard Lyllian mention she would have to send Reynolds to the market to pick up some lamp oil.

"I'll do it," Colvin said, more loudly than he had intended. Everyone at the table turned to look at him. Colvin shrunk a bit in his chair.

"What was that, Colvin?" Lyllian asked with a kind smile. William had really wonderful parents, the kind Colvin sometimes imagined the ones who had abandoned him were like.

"I said I can make a run into the market for some lamp oil, if you'd like. So you don't have to send the butler." Colvin tried not to look too eager, just someone offering to lend a hand.

"That would be very kind of you," Lyllian said, nodding. She had Reynolds fetch a small coin purse and told Colvin to buy something for himself with whatever was leftover. When Colvin politely objected, Lyllian insisted. "Consider it payment. It's only fair." What passed for fair in the Stuart-Camen household was a damn sight better than what was considered fair in Colvin's world.

When breakfast was over Colvin helped clear the table, as he always did, and then headed out for the market. As he was walking down the cobbled path in front of the Stuart-Camen home, he heard William calling after him from the house. The young nobleman had mischief in his eyes, and it looked strange on the normally upstanding young man.

"Are you going to ask to court her?" William asked as he reached

Colvin on the walk. He was speaking so softly he was almost whispering.

"Who?" Colvin asked, trying and failing miserably to feign ignorance.

"That silver merchant you're interested in," said William.

Colvin furrowed his brow. "Who told you about that?"

"Ferdinan," William said. "Over tea the other day."

"Ferdinan?" Colvin said. "How did he find out?"

"He heard it from Gregor," William explained.

"And how did–" Before Colvin could even get the sentence out all the way, he remembered Gunther talking about his friendship with Gregor MacDugal. Colvin cursed under his breath.

"Sorry, I didn't mean to upset you," William said.

"You didn't," Colvin said, "I'm just not used to everyone knowing my business."

"Well, are you?" William asked again.

"Common folk don't *court*," Colvin replied, trying to avoid the subject.

William rolled his eyes. "You know what I mean," he insisted, and he had the look of a stubborn child. "Whatever you want to call it, are you going to do it?"

Finally, Colvin nodded. A smile spread across William's face. "Good luck," he said, patting Colvin on the shoulder.

"Uh, thanks," Colvin replied. The idea that a nobleman was interested in his love life was just a bit unsettling.

"Let me know how it goes," William said before turning and heading back into his house. Colvin stood there for a moment, scratching his head, then turned and went on his way.

It was Colvin's first visit to Tamendad's market, and he was highly impressed. Row after row of tables and booths sprawled out in all directions. The air was full of the sounds of hawking and bargaining. All assortment of goods were displayed, without any apparent order to the layout. A nice canvas-covered booth displaying a variety of fine scarves and neckerchiefs was neighbored by a gnarled old man missing one eye who promised anyone who came within earshot that his potions could heal any malady in half the time of the best Antrelican healers. A toymaker peddled his wares right beside a table sporting a gruesome array of knives not intended for kitchen use. Colvin spotted two competing perfume merchants with adjacent tables who looked like they might come to blows at any moment. Colvin paused for a moment at the small booth of a bookseller, and again at a vintner's table. Mostly he just wandered, keeping an eye out for both lamp oil and the silversmith named Melinda. He found the oil first and purchased a cask of it, haggling with the merchant until he agreed to cut his price in half and have it delivered to the Stuart-Camen home at no extra charge. The coin purse Reynolds had given him held three times the oil merchant's original asking price, and that left Colvin with a tidy sum of money to work with.

The silversmith was considerably more difficult to find than the oil. There were probably over five hundred tables and booths competing for space in the marketplace; Colvin was looking for someone he had met only once, briefly. There were no clocks or sundials in the market, and the din of commerce made it impossible to hear a town crier unless you were standing right beside him, but Colvin guessed he probably had an hour before having to report to the square. There was no real way to systematically search the market, so Colvin just wandered.

Strangely enough, he heard her before he saw her. He was stuck in the middle of a crowd of people trying to squeeze through a narrow lane between two rows of tables set up entirely too close together when he heard someone say, "You must be raving mad if you honestly think that's a fair price." In itself, that was nothing unusual. A thousand similar sentences were being spoken in every direction. What really caught Colvin's ear was the reply of, "Well, if I am raving mad, do you think it's a good idea to upset a lunatic?" For one thing, hardly anyone would try to haggle like that. For another, it was undoubtedly *her* voice. Colvin was not sure why he was so certain, but he began to push his way against the current of the crowd just the same.

He saw her as soon as he emerged. She was sitting three tables down, haggling with a well-dressed man over the price of a jewelry box. She was wearing the same clothes she had been wearing in Gunther's shop, all grays and blacks, trousers instead of a skirt. Colvin moved toward her table, and before he got there the well-dressed man had already stormed off in the other direction. She did not see Colvin approach.

"Oi," he said, figuring it had worked well enough the first time. She turned her head quickly toward him, and a moment passed before a look of recognition spread across her face.

"Oi," she replied with just a hint of a smile.

"I'm Colvin."

"I'm Melinda. What can I do for you Colvin?"

Colvin looked over her table. All manner of things were displayed on it: lockets and charms, bracelets, rings, chests and boxes, snuff cases, hair combs, even a couple of daggers. Such a wide variety of goods, yet all crafted in a similar style. She was very talented at her trade.

"I was hoping you could help me out," he began. "There's this girl I kind of fancy, and I'm hoping to get to know her a little better. I want to get a small gift for her, a little trinket to let her know she's caught my eye."

Melinda nodded, brushing her hair back behind her ear exactly as she had in Gunther's shop. "Well, obviously you don't want anything too personal or romantic. Do you know what sorts of things she likes?"

"Not really, no," Colvin said. "Do you have any suggestions?"

Melinda looked thoughtful for a moment. "I'd probably go for a bracelet if I were you. It's jewelry, so she'll probably like it, but it's not as presumptuous as a ring or a necklace."

Colvin looked over the bracelets on her table. They were all pretty. "Which one would you suggest?" he asked. Melinda hesitated for a moment. The one she picked up had a band about as wide as a finger. It had black etching and an opaque stone of light green in the middle.

"This one's pretty and affordable," she said, handing Colvin the bracelet.

"How much?"

"Seven silver marks," she said.

"That's gotta be twice its weight," Colvin said, raising an eyebrow.

"Extra for the etching and the stone," she explained.

"I'll give you four," Colvin said.

Melinda was not smiling. "Seven," she said coolly.

Colvin smirked. "Five."

Melinda crossed her arms over her chest. "Seven."

"Six," Colvin said. "Six is downright charitable."

"Seven," Melinda repeated.

"Okay, seven, but that's my final offer," Colvin warned.

A smile threatened to turn the corners of Melinda's mouth up. "You drive a hard bargain, Colvin," she said.

"I'm no fool," he replied. He retrieved his coin purse, which was hanging by a leather cord around his neck, under his shirt, resting against the small of his back.

Melinda gave him a questioning look. "Do you always carry your money like that?" she asked.

Colvin shrugged. "You can never be too careful," he said. He counted out seven silver marks and handed them over, taking the bracelet and pocketing it. "Thanks for your help."

"Don't mention it. I hope she likes it."

Colvin nodded and moved back into the crowd of people passing by. He stole a quick glance at the sun. Less than half an hour until training began. He was cutting it close. He started to loop his way around the market as best he could, given the haphazard setup, and stopped at a table long enough to pick up a black velvet bag, which set him back

181

another silver mark. He could have talked the price down by at least a few coppers, but he was running out of time. He dropped the bracelet into the bag and pulled the drawstrings shut and continued his circuit of the marketplace. He was operating purely by memory and he made a couple of wrong turns, but he still had more than a quarter of an hour left when he spotted Melinda's table for the second time. She was haggling with a brunette who looked to be a merchant herself. Politeness dictated that Colvin keep quiet until the bargaining was complete, but Colvin had no time for politeness. He walked quickly to her table.

Confidence, he thought. *Act with confidence. There's nothing most women find more attractive.*

"Oi," he said when he arrived at her table. She had not seen him approach this time either, and she turned impatiently toward him.

"Look, I'm in the middle–" she began, but fell quiet when she saw him. Impatience gave way to confused curiosity on her face. "Oi," she replied, and the word was spoken almost as a question.

Colvin produced the small black bag. "I got this for you," he said.

She slowly took the bag from his hand. When she found the bracelet inside, she could not hold back her smile. She definitely looked like she had a great secret when she was smiling.

"Can you hold on for just a second?" she asked him. He nodded, and she immediately turned her attention back to the merchant woman. "Okay, okay," she said. "You can have it for two and a half." The merchant woman did her best to remain professional, handing over two gold marks and five silver and picking up the largest jewelry box on the table. Melinda and the merchant woman bid each other a good day with a simple nod, and then Melinda turned her attention back to Colvin.

"You just cost me five silver marks," she said.

"Well then you should have no trouble forgiving me, since I just made you fourteen silver marks," he said wryly.

"How do you figure?"

"I paid you seven marks for a gift that was for you," he explained, gesturing to the bracelet still in her hands. "You can sell it again and double your profit."

"You're forgiven," she said.

"Normally I wouldn't rush this so much," he said, "but I have to report for training in about, oh, right now, so–"

"You're in the militia?" she interrupted.

Colvin nodded. "Fist Division. Anyway, I was wondering–"

"Would you like to have dinner with me tonight?" she interrupted yet again.

Colvin stood in mid-syllable for a moment, his mouth hanging open.

It was the first time a woman had ever asked him to dinner. He liked it. "Yes," he said.

"Where?" she asked.

Colvin pondered for a moment. He had not thought that far ahead. "Are you familiar with the Crown Rose?" he asked at last. Melinda nodded, that confused curiosity returning. It made her look pretty damn cute. "Meet me there a half-hour after sundown," he said. She looked like she was about to say something, but at the last moment she decided just to nod in agreement instead.

"Great," Colvin said. "Now I've really gotta hustle. Remember: Crown Rose, half-hour after sundown. See you then." He smiled, winked at her, then left the marketplace as quickly as he could.

CHAPTER THIRTEEN

THE CALM

William tapped out for the fifth time in a row. The lock Gregor had him in made his leg feel like it was about to snap at the ankle, the knee and the hip, all at the same time. He gritted his teeth to keep from crying out from the pain, and slapped his palm on the ground, signaling surrender. For the first time, his tapping did nothing to stay Gregor's hold on him.

"Nae, lad," the big Highlander said, his voice full of concentration. He was walking a fine line with the pressure he was applying to William's leg, not enough to break or tear anything but enough to make it hurt like the devil. "How do ye say *mercy* in th' old tongue?"

William screamed in spite of himself and cried out, "You're going to break my leg!" His leg felt like it was being sent through a cider press. Still Gregor did not relent.

"I'm nae going t' break anything, lad, save perhaps yer spirit. Now how do ye say it?"

"I don't remember!" William yelled. His vision was getting cloudy. The pain was bringing tears to his eyes.

"Ye've nae been studying," Gregor said through clenched teeth. William was stronger than he looked. The young nobleman was threatening to wriggle free of the hold. Gregor was not having any serious trouble maintaining his grip, but he had to concentrate to make sure William did not end up breaking his own leg in his attempt to escape. "Mayhap I've been too lenient with ye as a teacher." Gregor increased his leverage on William's leg. He had to be very careful now. Any more pressure and something would probably break.

The pain roared through William's whole body. His leg felt like it was on fire. His stomach knotted. His hands went numb. His head swam. William closed his eyes tightly and screamed a string of words that made even Gregor want to blush. Yet William found that with the exquisite pain came an accursed clarity of mind, like a part of him was closing itself off from sensation. That part felt cold and logical and just out of reach. William did not think of the word; the word was violently thrust into his consciousness by the detached part of his mind.

"*Ioch*!" William screamed. "*Ioch, ioch, ioch*!!!" The strangest thing was that even after screaming it, he was not sure whether he had spoken the word in the old tongue or in Turish. The searing pain in his leg subsided immediately, replaced by a steady, throbbing ache. William opened his eyes and wiped them with both hands. Gregor was already standing, extending a hand to help the young nobleman up. William grasped it firmly and found himself standing a moment later. Gregor patted him firmly on the back.

"Th' ache shall nae last long, and it shall be gone quicker if ye walk it out."

William nodded and said nothing, standing on one leg and bending his aching knee to stretch it out.

"Now then," Gregor continued, "if *ioch* means mercy, how would ye ask someone, such as a man about t' break yer leg, t' show ye mercy?"

William stood in silence. He was both thinking the question over and standing guard against another assault from Gregor, which he feared might come if he got the answer wrong. Finally, he answered, "*Iochadagh*."

Gregor nodded. "Aye, though that's an older usage. The preferred form would be *iochmoradagh*, since ye would probably want t' be sure th' person knew 'twas yerself ye were asking mercy for." William made a mental note of the usage rule, and swore by the pain in his leg that he would never forget it.

"What the twist are you two talking about?" came Colvin's voice from the crowd of Fist Division members. Gregor and William both turned to see the red-haired young man making his way toward them. Colvin was smiling like a dog in a butcher shop.

"Lessons in th' old tongue," Gregor said, looking Colvin over suspiciously.

"Ah," Colvin said. "Everyone's learning things, it seems." He looked like he could break into song and dance at any moment.

"She said yes?" William asked, half a question at best. Colvin simply nodded.

Gregor perked up at hearing this. "Ah, congratulations lad," the big Highlander said. "When are ye meeting her?"

"Tonight," Colvin said.

"Where are you taking her?" William asked.

"Aye, that's a good question," Gregor interjected before Colvin had a chance to reply. "Ye best be careful where ye go, lest ye be cornered by one o' yer other lady friends while ye sup with Melinda."

"I'd thought of that, actually," Colvin said, "and I was hoping you wouldn't mind letting me take her to dinner at the Crown Rose."

"O' course ye can take her t' dinner at th' Crown!" Gregor replied with a broad grin. "I shall tell th' lads t' behave themselves t'night and have Mayhew set up a cozy dining room for two."

"Thanks, Gregor," Colvin said. "So what's with all the people?" Colvin gestured to the crowd filling the square. Members of Fist, Sword and Shield Divisions were all present, along with other men and women who did not belong to the Pride of Tamendad, all jumbled together into a mob of people.

"Did you forget we're starting everyone on barehanded techniques this morning?" William asked.

Colvin blinked. "No way. It couldn't be... What day is it? It's not the ninth already?" It was almost inconceivable that the Pride had been training for a week. Time passed much more quickly when it wasn't spent trying to figure out where your next meal was coming from. "Well whaddya know," he finally said.

The church's main bell rang once, signaling the start of training, and all the instructors started separating everyone by division. Starting that day, the training sessions before the midday break were no longer restricted to militiamen. Any townsperson who wanted a few pointers on how to better defend himself was allowed to attend, and the entire morning training session was devoted to basic barehanded techniques. The session after the midday break was to remain unchanged, each division training separately and away from the public.

Gregor was the unquestioned leader of the training session that morning. The other Highlanders and Colvin assisted him, as did William, who had learned a thing or two about wrestling over the past week through his lessons under Gregor, lessons that were usually spent quite literally *under* Gregor. Fist Division was a step or two ahead of everyone else. The Highlanders had finished up training their men in the quarterstaff a couple of days ago, and the members of Fist Division had already learned the most basic elements of hand fighting. Gregor had done this so that the members of Fist Division would be able to help out their fellow militiamen in picking up the basics, and also to let them have a moment of glory for themselves. Fist Division was as well-respected as either of the other two divisions, but it was undeniably comprised of more rough and tumble types, the sort of people others tended to think might not be very bright. Every time a Sword or a Shield asked a Fist about the correct posture or the best way to throw a punch, it bolstered the confidence of Fist Division as a whole.

Training went well that morning, and the Pride of Tamendad was quick in learning the basics of unarmed combat. As the sun approached its peak overhead, Gregor called for the midday break. With an hour to themselves, the militiamen dispersed from the square to grab a bite to eat, a cool drink, a smoke or whatever else was fancied. Gregor and the Highlanders headed to the Crown Rose to take their lunch. William dropped in on Melissa at the church. Colvin headed toward the Stuart-Camen home to grab a quick bite on his way to meet Ferdinan at the Governor's house.

"Something es distracting you today," Ferdinan said as Colvin carefully retrieved his sabre from the nearby rosebushes. "It was not this easy to disarm you on your first day of lessons."

"Sorry," Colvin said, snaking his hand between the thorny stems. He pulled his sword from the bush without a single scratch to show for it and walked back over to Ferdinan.

"So what es the matter?" Ferdinan asked when he was once again face to face with Colvin.

Colvin sighed. "It's a girl."

Ferdinan nodded and pursed his lips together in an expression that was almost a smirk. "I see," he said. "Well, it was just a matter of time."

"What was?"

"*El prím amor*," Ferdinan replied. "First love."

"Hey now, I'm not saying I'm in love," Colvin said. "I just fancy her."

Ferdinan shook his head. "You misunderstand. *El prím amor* es like… puppy love. Es mostly infatuation."

"Oh," said Colvin. He felt much too old to be accused of puppy love. "So, who?"

"Her name's Melinda. She's a silversmith. She's got a table in the marketplace. She's got these big brown eyes that you just get lost in, and this great smile that makes her look like she knows something. She's just…real."

Ferdinan nodded. "Are you going to tell her about the others?" he asked. It was like the Conquian had read Colvin's thoughts.

"Honesty is the third characteristic of *decusé*," Colvin replied absently. It was what he had been telling himself all morning.

Ferdinan nodded once again. "Es sometimes difficult, being honest. But I can tell you this: any relationship built upon a foundation of dishonesty es doomed to crumble. If you are serious about this woman, you must follow the tenets of *decusé*."

Was he serious about this woman? He didn't even really know her. Colvin said, "You're right," without even realizing it.

"May I give you a word of advice, Colvin? About women, I mean?"

"Of course," Colvin said. He was always anxious to hear any words of wisdom from Ferdinan.

"A woman es like a sword. Remember that."

Colvin stood silently, awaiting the explanation that would make Ferdinan's words explode with meaning and insight. That explanation never came. Ferdinan just grinned, looking like he had imparted the meaning of existence with his words. Colvin furrowed his brow.

"What?" he asked.

"A woman es like a sword. Now let us get back to work on your parrying technique." Colvin opened his mouth to say something, but no words came out. He sighed in confusion. Then he assumed the stance, and all external considerations fled.

Melinda closed up shop in the market early that evening and made her way into the trade district. It would have been inaccurate to say she was nervous. It took considerably more than a dinner date to make her nervous these days. But she was terribly out of practice when it came to this sort of thing. She needed some advice and something pretty to wear. She was heading to talk to the one person she could think of who could provide both.

The sign in the window of *McRofaly's Magnificent Keepsakes and Aureate Regalia* announced that it had already closed for business that evening, but it did not deter Melinda from walking right up to the front door. She gripped the rope of the bell and began the procedure. Two fast rings, then a mental count to four. Two more fast rings, and another count to four, followed by a single ring. McRofaly only opened his door after hours for people who rang the bell like that, and Melinda was not aware of anyone else in Tamendad besides herself that knew the secret ring. She waited. She could hear the last toll of the doorbell still resonating inside, but there were no sounds of motion. There was no light in any of the windows, either, but there was still a little daylight left. It was unlikely that McRofaly was not at home. He rarely went out in the evenings.

Finally Melinda heard a stirring inside, accompanied by the sound of McRofaly asking who it was from behind the door. She wanted to ask him just exactly who the twist he thought it was, but instead she replied, "It's Melinda," loudly enough to be heard through the sturdy door.

"Just a moment," came the reply. More sounds of stirring from within, then the sound of the door lock unlatching. McRofaly opened the door. His hair was a mess and his clothes were wrinkled. He looked haggard. "I dozed off at the kitchen table," he explained without her asking. "Come on in."

The front door of *McRofaly's Magnificent Keepsakes* led into the room that served as the actual shop. This room was all polished tables and finery and overstuffed chairs where really big spenders could sit and sip tea while McRofaly displayed his jewelry for their inspection. The room was immaculate. It was where dust went to die. Melinda followed McRofaly through the shop and into the back of the house, the part that served as McRofaly's domicile. Stepping through the doorway that joined the two parts of the house was like stepping into another world. Unorganized stacks of paper were piled everywhere. Opened books were propped up against whatever would support them. The cold wood stove was serving as a makeshift desk during the warm months, supporting a cup full of quills, an inkpot, and a thick stack of blank parchment. Gem cutting tools were littered across the counter, and several small, wooden cases were stacked one on top of another in the corner. McRofaly's living space was a shrine to disorganization. And yet still not a speck of dust anywhere. Melinda joked that McRofaly kept his house cleaner than soap.

McRofaly cleared a stack of books and papers from a chair at the table. "Have a seat," he said, and moved to the fireplace before Melinda even had time to take a step. "Do you want some tea? I can make a fire and have the water boiling in no time."

"No thanks, I don't really have time," she said.

McRofaly turned to look at her, smoothing his wild black hair. He scratched at his beard. "Plans tonight?" he asked.

"I'm having dinner," Melinda said evenly. "With a man."

McRofaly laughed out loud. "You?" he said. Melinda had daggers in her eyes. McRofaly noticed. "That didn't come out right," he said. "It's just, how long has it been?"

Melinda hesitated before answering. At first she had to think about it, and then she was embarrassed to answer. "Two years," she said.

"And what did you end up doing to him?" McRofaly continued.

"I broke his nose," Melinda said. "But that was only because he was only interested in one thing," she added defensively.

McRofaly smirked. "We are all only interested in one thing," he said. "Some of us just conceal it more effectively than others. So who is the lucky man who has breached your outer defenses?"

Melinda sighed. "His name is Colvin. I think he's Gunther's new apprentice. He's...very easy on the eyes."

McRofaly smirked again. "So what is it you're wanting to borrow? Probably a necklace, since I see you already have a bracelet. Is that my jadestone set in it?"

Melinda looked down at the bracelet Colvin had given her. "Yeah, it's yours," she said. "How did you know I wanted...? Yeah, a necklace. Something that will match the bracelet."

"Brown garnet," McRofaly said.

"What?"

"Brown garnet," he repeated. "It will compliment your eyes." He moved to the corner and retrieved the case stacked fourth from the top. It had no markings. McRofaly never marked anything. He just remembered where everything was. He set the case in front of Melinda and opened it, pulling out a necklace. "White gold chain, to match the silver. The stone is two and a half carats, big enough to be pretty but not enough to be gaudy. Get it back to me sometime tomorrow." He dropped the necklace into her hand.

"Thanks, McRofaly," she said.

McRofaly nodded.

She stood, pocketing the necklace, and gave McRofaly a kiss on his forehead, which barely came up to her lips. She assumed he was so reclusive because he had always been teased about his height, or lack thereof. She was about as wrong as she possibly could have been.

"Try not to draw blood," he said as he walked her to the front door. She did not look amused.

"Good night, McRofaly," she said as she stepped out into the street, sending him a smile as she departed. McRofaly returned the sentiment. When she was gone, he closed the door, turned the lock, secured the chain and put the bar in place. Then he returned to his kitchen, pulled open the trap door and descended the stairs into the basement no one knew he had.

"You're sure you don't mind?" William asked for the fourth time.

"I am totally, completely, wholeheartedly sure that I don't mind," Colvin replied. "Beyond any shadow of a doubt. I have never been more certain of anything in my entire life. Ever."

"Well, we can always have dinner somewhere else if you want us too. I know Melissa would not mind in the slightest."

Colvin sighed. He looked William in the eyes, and placed both hands on the young nobleman's shoulders. "Hear me now," he said. "You and Melissa are going to have dinner at the Crown Rose tonight. I have no problem with you having dinner at the Crown Rose tonight. I *want* you to have dinner at the Crown Rose tonight. Do you understand?"

"Yes."

"Good."

"What do you think of the clothes?"

"Are you kidding me?" Colvin said, turning to look himself over in the mirror once more. "I feel like royalty." He ran his hands over his shirt. "What did you say this stuff's called?"

"Silk," said William.

"It feels like...a cloud," Colvin said. "Like a cloud spun into cloth." *C-L-O-U-D*, thought Colvin.

"I've never seen a green cloud," said William.

Colvin smirked. "I like the color on me. I've never worn anything that wasn't white before. Unless you count sweat-stain tan. The breeches are a little snug, though."

"Only because they're new leather. They'll stretch."

"They feel like they've got me in a death grip," Colvin said, widening his eyes a bit to make it clear which part of him he was referring to. William chortled, but Colvin didn't think it was very funny.

Silk shirt. Leather breeches. *Another* new pair of boots. "I'm costing you a fortune," Colvin said.

"Don't worry about it," William replied. "What's one less outfit for me? I already have too many. How was your lesson with Master Salvington?"

"He says I'm making good progress. We're going to start on sentence structure soon."

William nodded. "Nervous?" he asked.

"About what?" Colvin lied.

"I had better be going," William said. "It's almost dark, and Melissa will be expecting me."

"Yeah, me too," said Colvin. "I want to get to the Crown Rose a little early, make sure everything's set up."

"Okay," said William as he walked out of Colvin's room. "We'll see you there." Colvin nodded. When William was gone, Colvin looked himself over one more time in the dressing mirror. His clothes probably cost more money than he had ever hoped to see in a lifetime.

You're still just a worthless little vagabond, the well dressed man in the mirror told him. *Melinda's going to take one look at you and laugh in your face.* Colvin tried not to listen. *You think a change of clothes is enough to do anything for someone like you? What a pathetic piece of shit you are.*

"The girls in the trade district like me," Colvin whispered. He knew it was a mistake as soon as he did it. That voice rarely came to him while he was awake, but when it did it was just best to ignore it. Acknowledging it only made it stronger.

The voice laughed at him It was the voice of Malcomb, and of Loran Rothwald, and of a dozen others. It was his own voice, too. *You think so? You're just so pathetic that they felt sorry for you. You're worthless. Why do you even bother going on?*

I don't believe you, came another voice. This one was strange, unfamiliar. *You're lying.* It sounded like Ferdinan. And Gregor. And Gunther. And William. *Be quiet.* And it sounded a little like himself, too.

I will NOT be quiet! I will NOT, I will NOT, I will NOT!!!

Colvin closed his eyes. He assumed the stance. Both voices faded to nothingness. When he opened his eyes, he saw only the nicely dressed red-haired man staring back at him in the mirror. He breathed deeply. The air smelled sweet. Colvin tied his hair back in a ponytail and then left for the Crown Rose.

The rider kept to the shadows as much as he could, and rode like mad when he was forced to cross a clearing. He had shaken the things trailing him, and it had been at least an hour since he had last heard them in the distance behind, but he was still taking every precaution. If he scaled the summit before delivering his message, his death would merely be the first of hundreds.

He rode with his bow in his left hand, an arrow nocked. He shot at anything that moved. He had already killed two raccoons and had a near miss with an owl. He was just a tad bit jumpy. Being trailed by monsters did that to a man.

The position of the moon told him nearly three hours had passed, give or take, since spotting them. He could have almost been back to Tamendad by now if he had not been spotted. His pursuers had chased him all over the countryside, and he had spent what felt like an eternity playing a demented game of cat and mouse. He had slipped the noose, though, at least for the moment. He estimated he was perhaps another hour from Tamendad, maybe two, assuming a straight course and steady progress. He was tired, and his horse was exhausted, but sleep was the furthest thing from his mind. He had to survive. He had to reach Tamendad. Failure was too costly to consider.

He sat on his horse at the edge of a copse of trees, staring out into the openness beyond. The moon was full and provided plenty of light to see by. The next opportunity for cover lay at least a half-mile ahead. In the distance between he would be vulnerable. His eyes strained against the darkness. He thought he could make out all manner of moving shapes, but it was just his mind playing tricks. He *would* be vulnerable during that whole stretch, though, and there *could* be anything out there in the darkness waiting for him. Unfortunately he had no alternative. He would just have to ride like a madman and pray that whoever might be out there waiting was a horrible shot.

"You're a damn fool for being spotted," he whispered into the night. "But then, you're a total genius for getting away from them. It all cancels out in the end." He tightened his grip on the reins. No more time for hesitation. He kicked his heels hard against the horse's flanks, snapped the reins and rode like mad.

The entirety of Turish courting custom was centered around food. A couple could not rightly be said to be courting until they had shared a meal together, and the meal shared said everything about the seriousness of the courtship. A breakfast signaled a courtship that might last a month at the outside, as both the courtiers were actively informing the other that they simply wanted to get this business out of the way because they had more important things to do that day. A luncheon was the standard choice, typically taking place in the lady courtier's home and preferably with her family present. A dinner was serious business, a private dinner downright scandalous. Under courting custom, by asking Melinda to join him at the Crown Rose, Colvin might as well have proposed marriage on the spot.

Colvin knew none of this, of course, because as he had rightly pointed out to William that very morning, common folk did not court. Not in the truest sense of the word. Courting included contracts and formalities and negotiations of the two families and a host of protocols and etiquette that had to be followed. Courting was always wrapped up in power and money and holdings and continuing the lineage. Common folk got to slip that particular noose and just get right to the point.

Nobles and landowners courted. Common folk ate.

Colvin was starving as he stood waiting at the archway at the end of the Crown Rose's walk. He had been too nervous to do anything more than pick at his lunch, and the hearty aromas of the trade district were making his mouth water and his stomach growl. He could think of nothing except the feast that awaited him inside. Then he caught sight of Melinda making her way up the cobbled street toward him and for a moment he forgot that food existed.

She wore a formal gown with a a plunging neckline that did not so much show off her breasts as simply let anyone who looked at her know they were there. The gown looked new, though in fact it was quite old. It had hung untouched in her wardrobe for years. Her workman's boots had been replaced by leather slippers that were all straps. Those were new, and they hurt her feet. She wore only two pieces of jewelry: McRofaly's brown garnet necklace and the bracelet – her bracelet – that Colvin had given her. She had little white flowers in her hair.

Colvin bowed in the Turish fashion as best he could, and felt a fool. "Milady," he said.

"I'm no lady," Melinda replied, then made a funny face as she realized how that sounded.

"I like your necklace. It brings out the color of your eyes."

"Thank you," she replied. "It's on loan."

"Shall we?" Colvin gestured toward the cobbled walk leading to the main entrance of the Crown Rose. They started up the walk together.

"I thought Gregor MacDugal had this place reserved all to himself," she said, looking the building over.

"He does. Gregor and I are good friends."

"Oh really?" Melinda asked. "How long have you known him?"

"About two weeks," he replied. Melinda arched an eyebrow.

The door opened just as Colvin was about to reach for the handle. Torrance Mayhew himself ushered the couple into the common room of the Crown Rose. The rotund proprietor was absolutely beaming. He was dressed as he always was, in the finest formalwear. He bowed low as Colvin and Melinda stepped through the doorway past him.

"Colvin," the owner said, "so good of you to visit us again."

"Thank you," Colvin said. *Gregor or Ferdinan? Which one put him up to this?*

"As always, we have a bottle of our finest red awaiting you," Mayhew continued.

Ferdinan, Colvin thought. *Definitely Ferdinan.*

"Madam," said the proprietor, delicately gripping Melinda's hand, "welcome to the Crown Rose. I am Torrance Mayhew, proprietor, and if there is anything I can do to make your visit with us more pleasant, please let me know. Now would you like to be shown to your private dining room?"

"Actually, if it's okay with you, Melinda," said Colvin, "I was thinking we could have a drink before dinner and I could introduce you to everybody."

"A drink sounds good, but who is everybody?" Melinda said with a curious glint in her eyes.

"Gregor and the Highlanders. William Stuart-Camen and his intended, Melissa Tilman. Don Ferdinan is having dinner with Elysia Chamberlain. Honesty I think he just brought her to get under Elizabeth's skin."

"Who is Elizabeth?" Melinda asked. She was quite impressed with the company Colvin kept, but she was trying not to show it.

"She's...oh, uh, I probably shouldn't really mention that. It's a sensitive subject with Ferdinan. Forget I said anything."

Melinda nodded. "Yes, by all means, a drink before dinner," she said both to Colvin and Torrance Mayhew.

The owner of the Crown Rose straightened at once and smiled brightly at the two of them, clasping his hands together in front of him. "Wonderful," he said. "This way, please." He turned and led them through the door into the main dining room. It was considerably darker within than Colvin remembered, the central chandelier being conspicuously absent. Everyone was sitting at one grand table, and they all turned their attention to the approaching newcomers. Colvin began the lengthy process of introductions.

"Melinda, this is Don Julio Franco Francisco Ferdinan of Losillas," he said, "and this is the Lady Elysia Chamberlain." Both Ferdinan and Elysia stood, he bowing, she offering her hand.

"Melinda, a pleasure to meet you," the Conquian said. Elysia said a pleasant hello, and Colvin's eyes widened a bit as he really noticed her appearance for the first time. She had her hair done up, and her strapless, flowing gown was a far cry from the rather prim dresses Colvin usually saw her in.

"And this is Lord William Stuart-Camen and Lady Melissa Tilman," Colvin continued. Both young nobles stood. William bowed and Melissa curtsied.

"Milord, milady, an honor to meet you," Melinda said.

"Oh please, just call me Melissa," the young noblewoman said, smiling.

"And I'm just William," the young nobleman added. "Whenever someone addresses me as *Lord Stuart-Camen* I always think my father's standing behind me."

Colvin introduced the Highlanders next, all except Liam and Wallace who were not present. Gabrahn, Angus and Gregor all stood when Colvin introduced them, gripping Melinda's forearm gently and exchanging pleasantries. Gregor was the last to be introduced, and the big Highlander bowed low to Melinda, his fist over his heart, and, smiling, said, "Any friend o' Colvin's..." Melinda noticed with a smirk that he did not finish the sentiment.

Colvin and Melinda joined the others at the large table. Colvin called for a glass of wine, and all the Highlanders looked quite pleased when Melinda ordered a whiskey. They all sat there together for a while, making small talk, exchanging stories and steering the conversation away from any mention of militia or monsters. Colvin eventually got around to asking Gregor about where Liam and Wallace had gotten themselves off to.

"Ah, dinnae take it personal, lad," Gregor explained, looking a bit rankled. "They're both still young lads, and a quiet evening with friends dinnae much tickle their fancy. They headed out on th' town for th' evening." Colvin nodded. He didn't take it personally at all. If he had not been having dinner with Melinda, he probably would have gone with them himself.

Melinda and Colvin finished their drinks and politely excused themselves from the common table, signaling to Torrance Mayhew that they were ready to be shown to their private dining room. Master Mayhew showed them to a small dining room just large enough to be cozy for a party of two. The ceiling was draped with wine-colored fabric that billowed out from a small brass chandelier that hung in the middle of the room. The walls were painted the color of cream, but artwork hid most of it. A single window overlooked a small flower garden illuminated by hanging lanterns. The table was small and round, with a pillar candle surrounded by dried flowers as a centerpiece. The room was custom-made for romantic dinners.

"I hope you like seafood," Colvin said as he held Melinda's chair out for her.

"Oh, I can't eat seafood," she said as she slid into her seat. "It makes me terribly sick. I swell up. Sometimes it's so bad I can't even breath."

Colvin looked like he had been punched in the gut. "Oh," he said. "I'm really sorry. I was told this place is famous for its seafood, so that's what I ordered us. Let me go see if the cooks can change the menu."

Melinda patted Colvin's hand lightly. "I'm kidding," she said. "I love seafood."

"Dirty trick," Colvin said with a smirk. He took his seat across from her. A servant brought them wine and bread while they waited for dinner to be served, and now that they were alone they finally got around to the topics they had not wanted to broach while in the company of the others. Melinda asked the questions first, and Colvin found himself recounting his entire life's story, with emphasis on the last few months. He left nothing out, not Malcomb's beatings, not the affair with Rosie Rothwald, not even his soirees with Ferdinan. He didn't volunteer any extra information, but he answered all her questions truthfully. Even during what Colvin considered the worst parts, Melinda just nodded and looked thoughtful. She never seemed offended or angry. By the time the servant brought in the first tray of steaming crab and shrimp, Colvin felt like he had dictated his memoirs. He snatched up a crab and proceeded to dismember it.

"Enough about me for a while," he said. "What about you?"

"What about me?" she said demurely, batting her eyes while dipping a chunk of claw meat into drawn butter. Colvin had to laugh at her.

"Where did you grow up, for starters?"

"Well, I was born and raised just outside Benson's Hold, on the mainland. My parents were farmers, good people but boring as dirt. I left home when I was fourteen."

"Then what did you do?" Colvin asked.

"I traveled. First just in Tur, then later I headed across the Melteric for a while."

"What brought you back?"

"I got homesick," she said, shrugging. "Just a poor farmer's daughter, right?"

"There's no shame in being homesick," Colvin said. For just a moment, less than a moment, he saw something in her eyes. Weakness? He didn't think so. But he knew it was a part of her few people ever saw. He thought it might have been the sexiest thing he'd ever seen. "So then you came to Tamendad?" he continued.

She shrugged. "It's where the boat finally docked. I could make enough money here to survive."

"So where did you learn silversmithing?" Colvin asked.

"Parland," she replied after draining her wine.

"So that's the secret to your success? Foreign techniques?"

Melinda widened her eyes in mock surprise. "You guessed it," she gasped. "Of course now I'll have to kill you."

"Of course. More wine before murder?"

"Please."

They talked while they ate, sharing childhood memories and adult aspirations. Melinda was interested to hear how a self-avowed vagabond had come to keep such distinguished company. To that question, Colvin answered that he really had no part to play in it. Beginning with Ferdinan on that first day in town, everyone had just taken to him. He was simply the beneficiary of extreme good fortune, for once in his life. Colvin in turn wanted to hear how a fourteen year old girl had managed to fend for herself in the big, mean world. Melinda said it was because she always looked and acted mature for her age, and nobody ever really questioned her as long as she carried herself like an adult.

Sometime later another servant entered the dining room carrying a tray with two plates on it. The servant set the plates on the table, then spun on her heels and left the room before Colvin could ask the question burning in his mind.

"What the twist is this?" he asked. The thing on his plate looked like no creature he had ever seen before. It had a long, cylindrical body a shade of red so intense it looked unnatural. On one end of its body was a fanned tail and on the other was what passed for the thing's face, with eye stalks and antennae. It had claws on the ends of its arms, sort of like a crab's but bigger and nastier. Colvin wondered which of his friends had played the prank of sending these things to his table.

"It's lobster," Melinda said. "You've never had it?"

Colvin just shook his head, shifting his gaze from Melinda to the thing on his plate and back again. He could vaguely recollect some mention of lobster when he had discussed the menu with Torrance Mayhew that afternoon. At the time he had not wanted to admit he had no idea what Master Mayhew was talking about. He regretted his silence now.

"It's like crab, but better," Melinda said. "Here, I'll show you how to do it." Melinda walked Colvin through the procedure of getting to the edible parts of his lobster. If eating crab was messy, eating lobster was downright grotesque, with all the pulling and ripping and cracking. When it was all over, Colvin stared at the pieces of white meat lying on his plate: two arms, two claws, and one tail. Most of the ugly creature sat in pieces discarded in the large bowl that held the inedible parts of the meal.

"Try it," Melinda coaxed. She had that secretive smile again. Colvin sliced off a piece of the tail. "Dip it in butter," Melinda interrupted before he had a chance to get the bite in his mouth. "It's better that way." Colvin dunked the meat in his drawn butter, then ate it. Before he even swallowed, he knew he had found his new favorite food.

"Oh my God," he said, slicing a second bite before the first one was even all the way down.

Melinda's smile brightened. "I'm glad you like it," she said. "It's one of my favorites." Colvin just nodded, chewing.

They both ate their lobster, Colvin pacing himself to avoid talking with his mouth full. When the lobster was gone they shared a desert that was set on fire before it was served. They found themselves finished with their meal long before they were finished with their conversation.

"Would you like to go for a walk?" Colvin asked as they both stood from the table.

"I would love to," she said.

They found the wine flowing freely when they reentered the main dining room, and everyone looked to be enjoying themselves quite a bit. Gregor and Ferdinan tried to talk them into joining them for an after-dinner drink, but the big Highlander and the slight Conquian fell silent when they realized Colvin was angling for some quality time alone. Colvin and Melinda bid everyone goodnight and headed out into Tamendad. They strolled aimlessly, without a destination in mind. They talked as they walked, about whatever topic presented itself. Sometimes they just walked quietly, side-by-side, but the silence was not uncomfortable. They took in the lamp-lit sights of the trade district, and their stroll was serenaded by a chorus of drinking songs from the taverns. A few passers-by recognized Colvin and said hello. These were mostly militiamen, but a few were regular patrons of Gunther's smithy. Melinda noted to herself that everyone who said hello seemed happy to see Colvin. He had become quite popular during his short time in Tamendad.

"So tell me about Parland," Colvin said, marking the end of another comfortable silence. "Where exactly is it?"

"Oh, it's on the continent, across the Melteric," she replied. "It's north of Conquia. I assumed since you and Don Ferdinan were friends that you knew about Parland."

"Honestly, I didn't even know about Conquia until I met Ferdinan," Colvin replied.

Melinda chuckled. "Parlanders are renowned traders. They're known the world over. No matter how far you travel, you're bound to find someone who can speak Parlandis. If you want something, a Parlandian trader probably has it to offer, and if not, chances are he could get it for you."

"How long did you live in Parland?"

"Not long," she said. "A couple of years. Then I came to Tamendad."

"How long ago was that?"

"Four years," she said. Colvin nodded thoughtfully.

Their aimless stroll had brought them out of the trade district, and the familiar sight of the town square lay ahead. Colvin made the Sign of the Compass as they approached the church.

"Devoted Antrelican?" Melinda asked.

"Oh, uh, not really," Colvin replied. "Just something I picked up from Ferdinan." He glanced sidelong at her, wondering if he was broaching the bounds of impropriety. "You?" he asked.

Melinda hesitated. "I haven't been to church in years."

"Why?" Colvin asked.

Melinda made a face. "I didn't expect to be discussing this tonight."

"I'm sorry," replied Colvin. "I didn't mean to offend you."

"No, it's fine." Melinda looked contemplative. "Look," she said, "obviously this all had to come from somewhere. There has to be something behind it. But at the same time, I've seen bodies of children that died of starvation lying in gutters. There is no shortage of horror in this world. Just look at those things that attacked the city. Sometimes it feels like your prayers just never get heard. Like either God isn't listening at all, or his compassion is arbitrary. So what's the point?"

"Wow," Colvin said.

"What?"

"You just described almost exactly how I feel. I've never been able to put it in words."

She stood looking at him a moment, biting the corner of her lip in a way that made Colvin go weak in the knees. Then she shocked him by reaching out and taking his hand in her own.

"Come on," she said.

They walked on in silence, hand in hand, both of them lost in thought. When they were past the church, Colvin spoke up again. "You know," he said, "we're close to the residential district. Would you like to see where I live?" The words sounded strange coming out of his mouth, but he really was starting to feel like he lived with William's family.

Melinda stopped walking and looked at him with an unreadable expression.

"Are you asking me to retire to your chambers, good sir?"

And there it was, the moment of decision. Never mind that Colvin had not been asking what she thought he was asking. The idea was out there now, and there was no covering it up. Colvin stood scratching the back of his neck, looking at everything but her. He had fallen into it with his carelessness; it had happened too soon.

Confidence is the second trait of decusé, he thought. He looked into her eyes, his smile not lessening his seriousness.

"Yes," he said. "But I want you to know I don't expect anything."

An eternity passed.

"I'd love to," she said.

Colvin began to breathe again.

He led her through the labyrinthine streets of the residential district, past the landowners' homes. He knew the way to William's house like the back of his hand now, and the two of them stood at the walkway of the Stuart-Camen household not a quarter-hour later.

"A beautiful home," Melinda said, looking it over.

"Thank you," Colvin replied, not entirely certain why. In all effect she could have been commenting on an inn he was staying at. He could take no credit for its quality.

Colvin opened the door himself, not bothering to ring the bell. As he expected, Reynolds was fast asleep in the high-backed chair just inside the common room, snoring lightly. Other than the unconscious butler, the entire downstairs floor appeared deserted. Colvin looked back at

Melinda, first pointing to Reynolds, then holding his finger to his lips. Melinda nodded her understanding. Together the two of them crept their way across the common room, taking great care with their silence. With each step Colvin exaggerated his movements more and more, taking large steps, walking only on the balls of his feet, bringing his arms up to his chest with hands arched like claws; a caricature of a cat burglar. Melinda clamped both hands over her mouth, but it was not enough to stifle her laugh. What escaped between her fingers sounded like muffled coughs, but her eyes were wide and her hands could not completely hide her smile. The look of her made Colvin laugh too, and by the time they neared the top of the stairs they were both nearly guffawing, tears running down their cheeks. Colvin motioned for Melinda to follow him, and they made a mad dash for his room. Colvin threw the door open and practically dove inside; Melinda followed close behind and closed the door quickly behind her. The oil lamp by the bedside was lit and the bed had already been turned down. Colvin collapsed onto it, burying his head in a pillow to mute his laughter. It passed after a few moments, and Colvin sat up to see Melinda leaning against the door, her hands pressed to her abdomen, trying to regain her composure. Her laughter, too, was dying away. Colvin stood, wiping tears from his eyes, and walked to her, flashing his best smile. She slapped his arm playfully.

Then she kissed him.

She ran her fingers through his red hair, pulling his face closer to hers, and covered his mouth with her own. Her tongue snaked into his mouth. He felt the vibrations of her moan against his lips.

Passion is the fifth and most important trait, he thought distantly. He would have no problem with that. He took her into his arms and met her tongue with his own, biting her lower lip, kissing down her jaw line to her chin. Her breath came in heavy gasps. She licked her lips. He pressed his forehead against hers and kissed her mouth again.

Later he would vaguely remember scooping her up in his arms and moving toward the bed, but at the moment he simply found that they were both lying together, with no memory of how they had gotten there. His arms slid around her waist. He was pressing against her now, and she moved her leg gently back and forth, grinding against him through the leather of his breeches. He moaned into her mouth, and he could feel her smile against his lips. He cupped her breast through the fabric of her gown and ran his thumb in loose circles around her covered nipple. She arched her back against his touch.

God, he thought, *I've done this before. Why does this feel so different?*

Nothing existed except the two of them. There was no militia, no lessons on swordplay or the written word, no Crown Rose, nothing. Even *decusé* seemed distant, hazy. The feel and the smell of her was all that was real. He felt drunk. He knew only one thing with any certainty: he wanted that gown off of her. He slid his hand up from her breast, curling his fingers around the strap of her gown. He looked into her eyes. She stared back at him. Slowly he slid the strap over her shoulder and down her arm. Her collarbone was revealed to him, and he thought it was perfect. He leaned forward, kissing along its length. He heard her sigh deeply, contentedly, throwing her head back into the pillow. He moved his lips down, kissing the top of her breast. She moaned.

He wanted to uncover her breasts completely, to slide her gown all the way off, now, and drink in her nakedness, but he made himself wait. Patience was an essential feature of passion. He kissed his way across the neckline of her gown, which now barely covered her nipples, then back up her neck, up her chin, to her mouth. Their tongues swirled. He thought he might burst. He pressed hard against her leg. Her eyes fluttered open, and her lips curled in that delicious smile. His left hand slid slowly up her body, tickling across bare flesh as he reached her shoulder. He hooked his thumb on her other strap and gently began to slide it down her arm, exposing more of her to him inch by inch.

Melinda sat up so suddenly she almost butted heads with Colvin. In one motion she was up off the bed, pulling the straps of her gown back into place on her shoulders, heading for the door. "I have to go," she said, not slowing down, not looking back. Then she was gone, pulling the door shut behind her.

Colvin sat on the bed, stunned. "What the twist?" he asked the door.

A moment passed in confused silence, then Colvin was up straightening his clothes and going after her. Reynolds was just getting to his feet as Colvin quickly descended the stairs, a deeply confused look on the old butler's face. Colvin did not look entirely on top of things himself, for that matter.

Reynolds gestured in the general direction of the front door. "You just missed her, Master Colvin," he said. "She let herself out without saying a word. She looked as though she was in a terrible rush." Colvin looked from the butler to the closed door. He felt like he should at least have had an inkling about what had just happened. "Is everything all right, Master Colvin?" Reynolds asked. Colvin turned to him. The butler still had sleep in his eyes.

"Fine, Reynolds, everything's fine. Sorry to wake you," he said, then he was out the door and in pursuit. He spotted her right away. Melinda had not even made it to the end of the street yet. He quickened his step to a jog and called out to her when he drew near. When she heard him she slowed but did not stop. She made a point of not looking at him when he fell into step beside her.

"Did I miss something?" he asked, gently placing his hand on the small of her back. She stiffened at his touch. He pulled his hand away. There was an uncomfortable silence, the first of the evening. The echoes of their footfalls on the bricked street were deafening. When it became clear she was not going to answer him, Colvin sighed and said, "I'll walk you home." Melinda barely acknowledged him.

They walked in silence, Melinda directing their course since Colvin had no idea where she lived. She led him out of the residential district, past the church, back into the trade district. She did not say a word to him, leaving him to his thoughts while they walked. His mind was a muddled sea of confusion. Melinda was the embodiment cool calmness, at least externally. Inside, her whole world trembled.

Oh God, she thought, *don't let him try anything. I couldn't handle it if he tried anything. Why did I throw myself at him like that? So stupid. I can't let him find out. Please. I couldn't handle it...*

There was a small section of houses and apartments, too small to be considered a residential district, nestled in the eastern corner of town between the trade district and the marketplace. It was to a humble three-room house in this section of town that Melinda led Colvin in silence. When they finally stood before its front door, Melinda nodded in its direction. "This is me," she said. Those were her first words since leaving Colvin alone in the bedroom, and each one of them sounded labored.

Colvin half-nodded, half-bowed. "Goodnight, milady," he said, smiling as much as he could manage, relatively certain he would never see her again except in passing. He wondered what had gone wrong.

"That's it?" Melinda said, her voice a mixture of surprise and relief. "You really just walked me home, and that's it?"

"What were you expecting?" he asked.

Her expression was unreadable, but somehow Colvin knew what she was thinking, knew what she had been afraid of when he followed after her.

"I told you I didn't expect anything," he said in little more than a whisper.

Melinda touched his cheek. She did not even realize she had done it until her hand was against his face. She looked at him with those intoxicating brown eyes.

"It was just...too much too quickly back there," she said, and he nodded. "Come and see me in the market tomorrow if you can, and we'll have lunch."

Colvin told her he would. She kissed him on the cheek, where her hand had been, before she went inside.

Colvin stood silently, staring at the closed front door of her house for a long moment after she had shut it behind her. He shook his head. This had been, beyond a shadow of a doubt, the strangest evening he had spent in quite a while. Ferdinan's words from earlier that day came back to him. *A woman is like a sword.* He stood there, thinking long and hard about it. He looked it over from every angle he could think of. *Nope,* he thought at last, *still doesn't make a damn lick of sense.*

CHAPTER FOURTEEN

THE STORM

It took some coaxing from everyone at the table to convince Gregor to fetch his Highland pipes after he admitted he could play. At first the big Highlander had been resolute in his refusal, but an hour of pleading and half a bottle of whiskey had loosened him up tremendously, and now he was putting on quite a show. The warble of the pipes was strange, unlike anything any of the people not wearing kilts had ever heard before, but everyone was enjoying the music.

Ferdinan did not know quite what to make of it at first, but once the Conquian realized the rhythm of Gregor's ditty was perfectly suited to a slightly modified fandango he began to cut a rug. Elysia did her best to mimic Ferdinan's movements, but mostly she just managed to stomp her feet, jump up and down a bit and laugh at herself. Elizabeth was glowering at them from behind the bar. William and Melissa danced as well, not even attempting anything that resembled what Ferdinan was doing, mostly just spinning in a circle and shuffling their feet. Gabrahn and Angus clapped their hands and slapped the table in time with the music. Gabrahn commented that he wished he could find a fiddle. The main dining room of the Crown Rose was filled with laughter.

Gregor came to the end of his latest tune, *Young Alpin Courts a Bonny Lass*, and threw back another dram of whiskey. He had sampled this one before. It was distilled in Seamus Shaugnessy's land, about a day's ride southwest of Duerhein. Old Seamus knew how to make magic with malted barley.

Everyone in the Crown Rose called for another song, even the waitstaff. "Hold yer bloody horses, ye slave drivers," Gregor said, pouring himself another whiskey. Honestly he was enjoying the attention. It had been a while since he had been talked into playing the pipes, and he would have gone on all night if he could have.

"Come on, Gregor," William said, his arm around Melissa's waist.

"You're not winded already are you?" The young nobleman was grinning like a rogue.

"Lad, are ye in need of another wrestling lesson?" Gregor replied, giving William a level look that said he meant it.

William tried to hide how hard he swallowed at Gregor's words. "Whenever you're ready," the young nobleman said. "Take all the time you want. No rush."

Gregor licked his lips and placed the double-reed of the melody pipe between them and picked up the tune of *Dammaugh Off to War*, a somewhat more somber melody suitable for slower dancing. William took Melissa into his arms, and the young couple twirled their way around the dining room, whispering things to each other that only young lovers ever say. Ferdinan and Elysia also danced together, Ferdinan holding her hand against his chest. He saw Elizabeth leave the room from the corner of his eye. He was satisfied with his retaliation. There was no need to torment the woman, just get back at her enough to let her know how he felt about what she had done. Thankfully Elysia had been more than understanding about the situation. Of all the women Ferdinan could have brought to dinner, the one Elizabeth was powerless to do anything about was the Governor's daughter.

"Thank you, my lady, for all your help," Ferdinan said to her as they danced.

"My pleasure," she told him, grinning. "I have to say, I'm having a wonderful time."

Ferdinan smiled at her. "As am I. But then, I always have a wonderful time when I am in the company of a beautiful, intelligent woman."

"Don Ferdinan, are you trying to flatter me?" she asked coyly.

"That depends," he said.

"On what?"

"On whether or not es working." He laughed, as did she, and they continued on their way around the makeshift dance floor.

It was William that first noticed Colvin sneaking in the door like a man arriving late for church. He looked like he had no idea what was going on. "Colvin!" William called out, waving him over, "Come join us! Tell us about your evening!" The wince on Colvin's face as William spoke his last sentence told the young noblemen he might have just stuck his foot in his mouth.

Everyone bid Colvin a boisterous welcome, and he was offered a drink three times before he even sat down. Gregor brought *Dammaugh Off to War* to a premature end and joined everyone else at the table. A full glass of whiskey was set in front of Colvin, and it quickly disappeared down his throat. He winced a bit at the burning sensation.

"Thanks," Colvin said. "I needed that."

"Es anything you want to talk about?" asked Ferdinan.

Looking around the table, Colvin realized all eyes were on him. He looked down at his glass, realizing it had been refilled, began to lift it to his lips, hesitated, and set it back down on the table.

"You know," he said, "sometimes women are—"

He never had a chance to finish his sentence. The door leading to the common room flew open, and a town crier entered. He was out of breath.

"All militiamen...report to...the town square," he gasped, then hesitated just long enough to make sure he had been understood before turning and departing as quickly as he had come. Everyone around the table was on their feet before the door closed behind him. Gregor, Angus and Gabrahn headed upstairs to fetch their swords. Everyone else moved for the door.

"Get home as quickly as you can," William said to Melissa. "Shutter the windows and bar all the doors. And absolutely do not come out until you hear the all clear." He looked deep into her eyes. They were filled with fear, but she stood resolute.

"Be careful, my love," she told him.

"I promise you I will," he said. They kissed, embraced each other tightly, then parted ways. William focused all his effort in holding back tears.

"All my weapons are at your house," Colvin said, falling into step beside William after Melissa had gone. William was glad to have something else to think about.

"I'm sure we'll have time to fetch them, whatever is going on."

"It would probably be smarter for me to run and get them now," Colvin said. "Just in case." He nodded in the direction Melissa had gone.

William wanted to smile and cry at the same time. "Be careful," he said. "Make her run. Don't let her give you any *unfit for a lady* crap. She won't slow you down." Colvin nodded and put a hand on William's shoulder for a moment, saying all that needed to be said with just his look. William patted Colvin on the back, and then the red-haired wanderer was off, running after Melissa.

"Do you have any idea what this is about?" Elysia asked Ferdinan, and William listened intently for his reply.

Ferdinan was leading the way, so no one could see the troubled look on his face. "One of the scouts was taking longer than anticipated to return," the Conquian said. "It might have something to do with that."

"Why wasn't the Pride informed?" William asked, almost demanded. He could not quite explain his agitation, or why it was directed at Ferdinan at the moment.

"We put the constabulary on alert and tripled the watch, but we did not want to inform the militia, or any of the other townspeople, until we had something to tell them."

"I received no word of the alert," Elysia said.

Ferdinan chose his words carefully. "Es because you are technically not in the chain of command," he said. "This was a matter of security, so it was only told to those who needed to know." Elysia still did not look pleased, but she nodded her understanding.

"You could have at least put the Pride on alert along with the constabulary," William said.

Ferdinan looked back over his shoulder at William. "The Pride of Tamendad es always on alert," he said. William held the Conquian's stare for a moment, then finally nodded.

The Pride of Tamendad was already beginning to form ranks when Ferdinan, William and Elysia arrived in the town square. From the look of it, about half its members were already present with more filling into the square with each passing moment. Everyone was armed, either with sword or quarterstaff, and a palpable nervousness hung over the crowd. Men and women fidgeted with their weapons. More than a few people were explaining their theory about what was going on to whoever would listen, and no two theories were particularly congruent. Just about everyone had the unmistakable look of fear. Yet everyone was doing exactly as they were supposed to, exactly as they had been instructed to do if – when – something like this happened.

Governor Chamberlain stood atop the church steps with his hands tucked behind his back, silently surveying the activity in the town square. Ferdinan and Elysia made a beeline for him while William fell in with Sword Division. Geoffery spotted Ferdinan and his daughter walking toward him, and his calm demeanor broke for a bare moment. He walked swiftly to them, turning his attention first to Elysia. He embraced her tightly.

"You must get home quickly, child," he said, his voice strained with poorly masked emotion. "My guards will escort you."

"The Governor's guards protect the Governor, father," Elysia replied, her large, slightly damp eyes offsetting the calmness of her voice. Her father, however, was having none of it. He ordered two of his guards to accompany her home and not to leave her side for any reason. Elysia knew her father well enough not to argue the point. She embraced him once more and began to depart the square. After only a few steps she hesitated, looking back over her shoulder.

"Don Ferdinan," she said in a whisper, but Ferdinan still heard and turned to her.

"Lady Chamberlain?"

"Please be careful," she said.

They stared at each other for a moment, and Ferdinan nodded solemnly. "I promise you I will. Do not fear. God will see us through this." Elysia nodded as well, and continued on her way to the Governor's house.

Order asserted itself quickly once the Highlanders arrived, Gregor and Angus and Gabrahn all barking orders to Fist and Sword and Shield alike. Colvin was one of the last to arrive, and he took a moment to find William and tell him that he had seen Melissa safely home. Soon after, all three divisions stood side by side by side, facing Governor Chamberlain and Don Ferdinan, waiting for someone to put their fears into words. Governor Chamberlain looked over the Pride of Tamendad, taking in the sight of their frightened yet determined faces. He looked to Ferdinan and sighed. Ferdinan nodded reassuringly. The moment of reckoning had come. A hush fell over the crowd as the Governor prepared to speak.

"A scout has returned from the southwest, reporting that he encountered and was pursued by a band of the creatures responsible for the attack on Tamendad. The scout reports that the creatures were moving toward the city." A murmur ran through the Pride. There were a thousand questions running through their minds. "The scout rider estimated the creatures were two hundred in number, but he warns he did not have a good look at them before he was spotted and pursued. There could very well be more of them. With the time the scout took in evading his pursuers, he estimates the creatures might be no more than an hour away."

The silence was deafening.

"What are our orders?" came William Stuart-Camen's voice. The young nobleman stood tall and resolute, his voice firm. Everyone waited anxiously to hear the Governor's reply.

"Shield Division will assist the constabulary at the gates," the Governor said. "Sword Division and Fist Division will stand ready here, in the town square, as reserves. When the constabulary is in need of you, they will send runners. Understood?"

"Yes, sir!" almost everyone shouted in unison.

"Don Ferdinan will instruct Shield Division on where to go. The rest of you stand ready. Anyone who has need to fetch anything, go now and hurry back. Tell your loved ones to stay inside and bar their doors." The Governor made the Sign of the Compass. "The Four Faces of God smile on us this night," he said, then turned and left the town square. A few militiamen hurried off to retrieve weapons or armor. Ferdinan ordered

Shield Division into four equal groups, sending one to each gate. The Conquian then surprised everyone by falling into rank with the men and women in the town square.

"Good t' have ye, lad," Gregor told Ferdinan when the Conquian approached.

"Likewise, Gregor," Ferdinan responded, looking over Fist Division. The men were on edge, but they had a hungry look about them. Ferdinan and Colvin spotted each other. Colvin was in the process of putting on his dagger-gloves. Ferdinan looked at the sabre hanging disregarded at Colvin's side. Colvin shrugged. Ferdinan did the same.

"No offense, Ferdinan," Colvin said when he came within earshot, "I've just had a lot more experience with my bare hands."

"Of course," Ferdinan replied. The Conquian did not look offended, but Colvin was afraid Ferdinan might feel slighted. He felt strange that he was concerned with such things when the town was about to come under attack.

"So what do we do now?" Colvin asked.

Ferdinan and Gregor both replied at the same time, "We wait."

It was the longest hour of Jonathan Stuart-Camen's life. Each moment of it seemed to stretch on forever. William's father stood in silence at the northwest gate with the ten constables under his command. Both his hands rested on the hilt of his broadsword. His men were shifting their weight from foot to foot, stretching their muscles, occasionally yawning. The other constables around the northwest gate did the same. It had become a waiting game. Even in their boredom, however, the constables were constantly vigilant. The presence of the militiamen Don Ferdinan had sent as backup helped hone the constables' senses. Trained, armed constables were not about to be shown up by militiamen when it came to preparedness. As if sensing the challenge from the constabulary, the Shields were going out of their way to be on their guard, and they seemed ready to pounce at any moment. Jonathan was glad both groups were on the same side.

Watchmen and archers were posted all along the city wall, peering out into the night, hoping and dreading to catch a glimpse of movement. They were all perched behind tower shields, watching the surrounding countryside through small arrow slits. With Governor Chamberlain tripling the watch, and the archers supporting the watchmen, men were packed tightly along the length of the wall. Only a handful of men had the luxury of a lookout platform; most had to balance themselves on the wall itself. Two and three men crowded behind a single tower shield, and extra arrow slits were still being added to some shields with one of the many small saws being passed around by the watchmen and archers. Even with their close proximity and the added hassle of cutting new arrow slits in the barriers, every man on the wall kept both eyes continuously on the horizon, watching for any sign of movement. The watchmen showed no signs of boredom, not that Jonathan expected them to. Watchmen spent hours atop the walls scanning the distance for signs of trouble every time they were on duty. They knew how to sit and wait for hour after uneventful hour without falling prey to listlessness or letting their thoughts wander. They were trained to pay attention, even when there was nothing to hold their attention.

"I wish they'd stop stalling and just come on with it," Jonathan heard one of his men say. He did not have to look around to know it was Laerian, the youngest constable under his command. Laerian was barely twenty, a constable for less than a year. His father was a Lieutenant of the Guard, and one of Captain Jefford's closest men. Laerian wanted nothing more than to follow in his father's footsteps, and the young constable's head was still filled with damnfool notions of adventure and daring-do. He was a good soldier though, young and strong and equally proficient with sword and bow. And he was fiercely loyal. Jonathan turned and fixed the young man with a stare.

"Be careful what you wish for, constable," Jonathan said. Laerian snapped to attention and cried out, "Yes, sir!" Jonathan returned his attention to the gate, and to the men atop the wall. He sympathized with the young constable. Jonathan was old enough to be Laerian's father, yet he too was anxious for whatever was going to happen to just go ahead and happen. Part of that had nothing to do with youthful foolhardiness. The danger was coming, and it was inescapable. Each moment that passed without incident was just a prolonging of the inevitable.

At that moment, as if they had been reading Jonathan's mind, the watchmen atop the wall began to call down to the men below in a chorus of alarm. They all used different words, but the same general message was expressed: there was movement in the distance, and something was approaching. Everyone around the northwest gate snapped to attention. Hands instinctively gripped sheathed swords. The archers began nocking arrows. The militiamen from Shield Division tensed, holding weapons ready.

"Give me a number," called up Commander Pilfrey, the highest ranking officer at the northwest gate, singling out a lone watchman with a pointed finger. His deep, resonant voice was urgent but bore no sign of fear. Commander Pilfrey was getting on in years, and he had spent the better part of his life in uniform. The younger constables joked that he could command his way through the end of the world without his nerve breaking.

"It is too far and too dark to estimate with any certainty, Commander," the watchman replied.

"I understand that, constable," Commander Pilfrey said, "but I need a rough guess for a preliminary report. You may refine the number later."

The watchman turned back to the horizon and took another long, hard look out into the darkness. All eyes were on him; all ears were awaiting his reply.

"Perhaps three hundred," the watchman finally called down. Everyone except Commander Pilfrey tensed. The Commander called for a runner and sent word of the initial sighting and estimate of forces. Then, with a wave of his hand and the utterance of a single word, the constabulary erupted into a wave of activity. Atop the wall bowmen readied themselves, positioning arrows through slits, awaiting the order to draw. In the city below, unit commanders gave the orders for men to draw their swords and began maneuvering them into formation. The constabulary's liaison to the militia carried orders to the members of Shield Division on where to stand and what to do, and the militiamen listened attentively. Everyone prepared for the battle at hand.

"Loose swords!" Jonathan called to his men, pulling his own broadsword from its scabbard. He thought about Lyllian and Julius and the servants. They were at home, upstairs, the lamps extinguished, the doors barred, the windows shuttered, as he had instructed when the constabulary went on alert. "Forward! Step lively!" He thought of William standing with Sword Division in the town square. The rest of his family was as safe as they could be under the circumstances. William was out here with him, in the open, exposed to the danger. Part of him wanted to run to the town square and find William, then flee Tamendad as fast as they could run. He clenched his hand tightly around the grip of his sword. "Halt! Stand ready!"

An infinity of time passed. Worlds could have been created in that time; civilizations could have reached their zenith and died away. The entirety of the cosmos stretched out with each breath, and all the soldiers at the northwest gate of Tamendad stood balanced on a razor's edge. The air was thick. The chill of a night on autumn's doorstep did nothing to prevent men from sweating. Steel glistened in the lamplight. No man so much as cleared his throat.

"It's them!" a watchman cried out, his voice slicing through the silence like the voice of God. "I count three hundred and fifty!" Nervous looks were exchanged along the wall as well as down below. Almost double what the scout rider had originally estimated.

"Give me confirmation," Commander Pilfrey called up.

"Three hundred and fifty," another watchman called out. "A good count."

"Good count," another watchman echoed.

"Good count," came yet another voice.

Please watch over my family. Jonathan thought. *Please watch over William. Please let me see them again. Agathas cut Paraxis this night.*

Commander Pilfrey called for another runner and sent word of the latest numbers, then turned his attention back to the wall. "Bowmen! Draw at six hundred paces. Loose at four." A host of voices from atop replied in the affirmative. The Commander turned his attention to the foot soldiers. "Should the gate give way," he said loudly enough to be heard by both constabulary and militiamen, "fight like you mean it."

Howls went up from outside the walls, distant but quickly drawing nearer. "The enemy approaches at a run!" a watchman called down. "They carry a ram!"

"Stand ready, men," Jonathan said. His words were not meant just for the ten men under his command. He looked at the constables all around him and saw faces of stone, soldiers ready for war. How much had Tamendad already changed since the first attack? How much had already been lost? Could it ever be regained?

"Ready!" the commander of the bowmen exclaimed, and all the archers drew back. The enemy was six hundred paces from the wall.

A silence that seemed to bite at the soul followed, excruciatingly long yet painfully short at the same time.

"Loose!"

How could anything cover two hundred paces so quickly? Arrows zipped away into the night. The howls continued, but a few fell silent. More arrows were drawn from quivers and nocked. Again the commanding bowman gave word to loose, and more arrows streaked down from the wall toward their targets. Then the beasts were at the door. The northwest gate lurched once as the ram struck home. The new wood creaked and groaned in protest. A few of the tower shields fell away from the wall, and the constables below watched in horror as the lookouts and archers who had taken cover behind those shields were riddled with arrows from outside the wall. Some fell backwards into the protection of the city wall and lay on home soil as they gasped their dying breaths. Others tumbled forward, into the sea of monsters waiting outside. Their deaths came much more swiftly.

"Get those men down!" Commander Pilfrey was screaming. "Get them off that bleeding gate right now, before we lose them all!" Perhaps it would not take the end of the world after all.

Another strike of ram against gate. The wood bowed slightly, and sawdust fell. More shields fell away atop the wall, and more men fell one way or the other. The constables inside the gate watched it all unfold in wide-eyed terror.

Jonathan was distantly aware of hearing Laerian say, "What the twist is that?" Jonathan looked, and watched the single, flaming arrow sail up, up, up, farther than any arrow should have been able to sail. It seemed almost to pierce the heavens, and then it erupted into a brilliant ball of light. All the men around the northwest gate gasped.

"That's a signal if I ever saw one," Jonathan said. "Be ready for anything." His stomach tightened. This was going to be a long night.

He was known, to those few that knew him, as Tharl. In his language it meant *sneaky one*. It was not his birthname. His birthname had been Baloth, which meant *little foot*. He had earned the right to be called sneaky one by proving true during his testing, when the age of ascension came upon him. He had taken to the Over, the world of the paleskins, as all young ones did when they sought their man-names. Nikoth, *broken tooth*, had been his assayer. Surly old Nikoth had followed him into the Over and watched with great delight as he shadowed a paleskin, falling upon the lightsider and sliding the dagger between its shoulder blades before it even knew it was being pursued. Baloth had become Tharl at that moment, when Nikoth had proclaimed him a man and spoken his man-name for the first time, though it was not until he and Nikoth had carried the body back down into the Under that Tharl had enjoyed his ascent ritual. The blood of his paleskin had tasted sweet and metallic on his tongue.

All that was long ago, shrouded in the past. Nikoth was long dead now, along with most of Tharl's childhood friends. Many of them had not survived their testing. Of those that had, some had been lifted up when the gods demanded immolation. Others had fallen more recently, during the *rukh*, the preparation. The gathering of knowledge about the paleskins and the Over had claimed a good number of sturdy warriors. But it was of little consequence to Tharl how his childhood friends had died. He had no contact with those few who still lived, and he wanted none. *Dah*, childhood, was gone. The *rukh* was almost complete. Soon would come *Abuneth*, the reclaiming. Tharl had his part to play in all of it, and it was a most important part.

"Kor," Tharl whispered into the shadow, speaking only to himself. He spoke the name with so much reverence he might have been naming one of the Ancient Ones. And as for that, why not? What had the Ancient

Ones done to reclaim all that had been stolen? What had they done at all, besides demand the blood of good warriors, blood that might have been shed recovering what had been lost? Kor promised to do what even the Ancient Ones had failed to do. Why not exalt his name even beyond those of the Ancient Ones?

The trick, Tharl knew, was to make it to the wall without being seen. Once he was there, he would be in little danger of being discovered. Paleskin sentries tended to set their sights at a distance and ignore what lay right beneath their pointy noses. With his back against that wall he could sneak all the way to his destination without fear of being spotted. But his back was not against that wall now. His back was hundreds of feet away from the wall along with the rest of him, crouched down as low to the ground as he could make himself. To get to the wall he would have to pass through exactly where the paleskin spotters would be focused. It helped that they were probably as blind as lurbets. All paleskins tended to be, especially in the dark. Still, they would be edgy tonight, looking for anything that moved in the darkness. The attacks would draw their attention elsewhere, but he would need luck to reach his target. Sneaking would not be effortless with the cargo he carried.

He patted the barrel softly, stroking his calloused green hand over the wooden sides of it while he waited for the signal. It was not terribly large, but it was cumbersome. It took effort to carry it tucked under his arm, and it slowed him down. He would have to rely exclusively on stealth to deliver his cargo. The most difficulty would come in crossing the few hundred feet of open terrain before reaching the first of the huts that crowded the city wall. All of those huts would be deserted. That had been learned by watching how the paleskins had responded to the first assault. There would be no one to spot him in those huts, and with all the cover they provided he could carry a torch through them without the paleskin sentries spotting him.

Tharl could feel his heartbeat in his throat. Somewhere out in the darkness, on the other side of the city, Kor was watching, waiting to learn of the results of Tharl's effort. The fulfillment of the *rukh* and the beginning of *Abuneth* was in his hands. All hope rested on him. He had to succeed. Failure would doom them all, doom *Abuneth* before it began. His was the most important part to play, and Kor himself had chosen Tharl to play it. Kor had honored him by visiting him personally to ask. That conversation had been filled with talk of duty and self-sacrifice, of the glory of *Abuneth* and what it would mean for their people, and of the honor of *narkoth akuul*, a meaningful death. How could he have done anything but agree when Kor laid it out such? His name would be spoken as a hero when they told his story. His grandsons' grandsons would be revered for their bloodline. He would find the highest honor in bringing the paleskins' doom down upon them.

He saw the signal, the great blast of light that rivaled even the sun. The warriors had engaged the gate on the other side of the city. The distraction was set. Tharl's moment of greatness had come. He remained low to the ground, shuffling forward like a dog on its belly, rolling the barrel in front of him. The front of his clothes were soon soaked; the dew had already set. That was just as well. The dampness made the fabric even darker, more difficult to spot when he could finally take to his feet again. He had to be very careful with his cargo, though. Too much moisture would ruin it. Kor had been emphatic in that point during his instructions. Every few feet, Tharl paused long enough to wipe the sides of the barrel with his hands, drying it off as best he could. It would be fine. It had to be fine.

Tharl kept his face down as he crawled, not wanting to chance the moonlight catching the whites of his eyes for the paleskins to spot. It would have been much smarter to attempt this when the moon was young, but the *ardah* had demanded that this be the night, claimed the Ancient Ones demanded it. Kor had not been pleased with that, but he had relented in the end. Kor needed the ardah on his side to accomplish what had to be done, and the ardah held closely to the old ways. The Ancient Ones demanded that this be the night, so this was the night. Never mind how much more difficult it made Tharl's job, or anyone else's for that matter. The Ancient Ones could rot, for all Tharl cared. He would follow Kor into the afterworld and beyond.

He had halved the distance that separated him from the first of the mud hovels surrounding the city wall. Pushing and crawling, pushing and crawling, wiping the barrel off and starting again. His muscles were still as fresh as when he had started. He could have crawled all night.

How much time had passed since the signal? Not much, bare minutes at most. The desire for quickness and the need to be careful were at war in Tharl's head. The sound of his heartbeat drowned out all else. He kept his eyes low, focused on his cargo in front of him. Push and crawl, push and crawl, wipe down the barrel and start again.

Tharl reached the first hut.

He sprang to his feet and stretched his muscles. Plenty of vigor left in them. The hardest part was over. He snatched up the barrel and tucked it securely under his arm, then peered around the corner of the hut. No more than twenty feet separated this one from the next, and the closer he got to the wall the more tightly packed they would become. He was too close to the paleskins to crawl now. He would have to dodge from building to building on foot. Tharl took a deep breath and stepped out from behind the cover of the hut. He moved quickly, striking a balance between speed and silence, and did not stop until his back touched the wall of the next hut. He listened for the alarm that would come if he had been spotted. No alarm came. Tharl smiled. He dodged quickly to the next hut without hesitation. Still no alarm. From hut to hut, cover to cover he went until soon there was barely enough space between the buildings to walk. He could have strolled casually then without fear of the paleskin sentries, but necessity spurred him onward. Before long he left the last hut behind him and put his back against the wall. Tharl sighed with great relief. He would reach his destination and deliver his cargo. There was no doubt of that now.

Tharl crept silently around the perimeter of the wall, and his mind wandered. He dreamed of what would happen after his orders had been carried out, after he had secured his place in the story of *Abuneth*. His mind was filled with images of his people swarming the streets of the paleskin city, wiping out all of its wretched inhabitants. Tharl smiled. It was a sweet dream, Kor's dream, the dream of all their people. That dream was about to come true.

Tharl continued to skirt the wall, making his way toward the sea. It was eerily calm. He could hear nothing that indicated his people were attacking the gate on the other side of the city. From where he stood, all seemed peaceful.

The first sounds of chaos to meet his ears came not from the battle across town but from the docks ahead. Word of the invasion had spread and sailors now scurried, preparing their ships to cast off. Captains argued with crewmen about whether or not to finish loading or unloading the last of the cargo before taking to the sea. The harbormaster was trying desperately, and failing miserably, to get the frightened sailors to listen to his orders. The smaller, faster ships which had already cast off were colliding haphazardly with each other as they left the docks, some threatening to capsize, because nobody wanted to wait his turn to flee. A few fistfights had broken out. The docks were in bedlam, and it was music to Tharl's ears. The paleskins would spare no warriors to quiet the tumult at the docks, and the sentries on the wall would never spot him in the middle of such chaos. Tharl kept close to the wall as he rounded the last corner, the docks coming into view. He walked at a quickened pace. His target was ahead. He neared the great northeast gate of Tamendad. His cargo felt light as a feather under his arm.

A paleskin whose dress indicated he was a sailor approached him, eyes filled with the madness of riot. The paleskin held a club and had a look about him that suggested he was searching for someone, anyone, to bludgeon. He neared within a few feet of Tharl, close enough to make out the features of his intended target, and stopped dead in his tracks. Stupefaction replaced the madness in his eyes.

The paleskin said something in its filthy tongue, but Tharl could not understand his words. Only Kor and the ardah had ever bothered to learn the wretched paleskin tongue; only they had the need too. Tharl bared his teeth and snarled. The paleskin stood still as stone, eyes wide, mouth agape. Tharl roared. The sound was deafening, unmistakably inhuman. The crotch of the paleskin's pants grew dark with wetness before he fell limp from fright. Tharl cursed himself. His anger had gotten the best of him. He had drawn the attention of some of the other paleskin sailors. Worse yet, the sentries would have heard. Tharl broke into a run. The gate was less than a hundred feet away.

He reached the gate just as the shouting started from above. He did not know the specifics of what the sentries were screaming at him, but he could guess the general meaning. There was no time to care. Tharl dropped to his knees before the gate, setting the barrel upright in front of him. He trimmed off half the length of the fuse with the claw of his right thumb. It had to be done quickly, with no chance for the paleskins to reach him in time. He retrieved his flint and steel.

"*Thorak rakuth, Abuneth*," he whispered to the barrel. *What I do, I do for the reclaiming*.

It took three strikes of flint on steel to make a decent spark, seven to make one that caught the fuse. It smoked and hissed as it burned. Tharl watched the glowing ember travel along the fuse. The wheel was in motion. He had succeeded. *Abuneth* was begun.

An arrow from above struck Tharl in the arm. Others pierced the ground around him. He laughed through the pain. The paleskins had been too slow in fetching their bows. They were as dead as he was.

The flame disappeared down the hole in the barrelhead.

"*Narkoth akuul*," he told the night.

Tharl's world was consumed by fire and pain.

❖   ❖   ❖

The northeast gate exploded.

❖   ❖   ❖

The blast was heard all over Tamendad, and the full moon was blackened out by the smoke. When it began to clear, all that remained of the northeast gate were charred, splintered chunks of wood dangling from warped, smoking hinges. Bodies, some whole and some in pieces, littered the ground. The air was thick with sulfur and blood and burnt flesh. A few of the smaller boats around the docks had capsized from the blast. Sailors who had been thrown overboard during the explosion swam to shore, only to turn right back around and try to reboard their vessels. Nobody wanted to get too close to where the gate had been only moments ago. Tamendad had become completely accessible from beachside. Whatever was out there in the darkness would be coming to the northeast gate, and soon.

At the northwest gate, the few watchmen and archers still clinging furiously to the wall began screaming wildly to the soldiers in the town below. "They're on the run!" they screamed. "They're heading for the blast! Run! God's sake, RUN!"

The constabulary and the militiamen ran. Jonathan screamed a curse and told his men to keep up with him. They had to make it to the northeast gate. There was no way the gate still stood after the blast they had just heard. How many soldiers had survived the blast? Was anyone still alive at the northeast gate to hold the city? How long to get there? Jonathan ran until his leg burned in protest.

Screams filled the night air. Some were screams of terror, coming from behind the shuttered windows of the buildings. A few fools had thrown open their shutters to get a look at what was happening. Every time Jonathan spotted one of these, he screamed for the fool to get back inside and bar his windows. Very few people disobeyed. Other screams came from the soldiers running through the streets with weapons drawn and ready. There was fear in these screams, no doubt, but iron determination drowned it out. The screams were battle cries of men whose homes and families were in danger. Fear had to take a backseat to the unflinching need to defend one's home, or the battle was already lost. The speed with which the soldiers moved through the streets said that none of them were apprehensive to engage the enemy. At least not now, when the gauntlet had been thrown down. They ran like mad, until their legs burned and their throats threatened to clench shut. They ran as fast as any men ever had.

But they were not going to make it.

The invaders had known exactly what they were doing, and they had achieved their objective with perfection. They would reach the gate first, because they had given themselves an insurmountable advantage. While the constables and the militiamen would have to dodge around buildings and wind through the streets, the invaders had a roughly straight shot, right around the wall and into the city. Somewhere in the deepest, darkest part of his mind, Jonathan Stuart-Camen knew this. Most all of them knew it. The savage irrefutability of it stared them in the face.

The cry went up all over town, meant mostly for the constabulary but intended for the townspeople as well.

"Sword and Fist advance to meet the enemy!"

"Oh God, NO!!! WILLIAM!!!"

Jonathan found a speed he never knew he had.

It was a straight shot from the town square to where the northeast gate had once stood, and they had started moving as soon as they heard the explosion. They were no longer Sword Division and Fist Division. They ran together as an intermingled mass, swords and quarterstaffs held ready. They had received barely a week's training. Most of them hardly knew how to use the weapons they held. They were the greenest soldiers in Tamendad, and they were rushing headlong into the front lines of a war.

Gregor, Colvin and Ferdinan ran together, close to the front. William was back in the crowd a bit, still managing to keep some of his men together with him. They were in sight of where the gate should have been. Smoke still bellowed from the small crater the blast had caused. Bodies littered the street, and most of them did not move. A few constables and militiamen were stumbling to their feet, doing their best to wipe blood from their eyes and ready their weapons. The howls of the approaching enemy were growing louder. They were drawing near the gate.

"Time to make our stand," Ferdinan said, loud enough for only Colvin and Gregor to hear. The Conquian had sabre and parrying dagger drawn, and a look in his eyes neither Colvin nor Gregor had ever seen before.

"We're going *through* th' gate, lads!" Gregor cried out to the Pride. "We cannae wait for them! We have t' hold them. They cannae reach th' gate!" All the Highlanders bellowed. War cries rang up from the Pride of Tamendad. They were about to earn their name.

"Stay as close to me as you can," William told the men around him. "We'll fight back to back if we have to." He gripped his broadsword so tightly his knuckles were white. He was going back into the abyss. This time he was ready. This time Tamendad was prepared to fight back. "Tamendad stands!" he screamed. The words felt right. It was as good a battle cry as any.

"Tamendad stands!" his men echoed.

"Tamendad stands!" The cry filled the night. Everyone picked it up.

Colvin heard it. It struck something deep within him. He clenched his jaw. His blood burned. Lorthok's people were coming to take Tamendad away from him. They could not have it. "Tamendad stands!" he screamed.

"Tamendad stands!" cried Gregor and all the Highlanders.

"Tamendad stands!" screamed Ferdinan.

The line was drawn.

They cleared the gate.

They met the enemy.

The invaders were rounding the last bend of the wall as the Pride of Tamendad spilled out of the city. Their howls grew louder as they spotted the Pride. They advanced at a sprint. The front lines collided, and they were all engulfed in the tumult of war. Gregor barreled through the invaders' line, cutting them down, spinning his claymore so quickly the eye could barely catch it. Heads and limbs fell away where his sword struck.

Ferdinan danced with cat-like grace, weaving through the monsters, slicing, piercing, putting them down. He used his parrying dagger to turn their own attacks against them.

Colvin punched once, and ran Lorthok through the eye. Three rapid strikes to the abdomen disemboweled the creature. He rounded on the next Lorthok. It was preoccupied with another Fist, trying to cut its way through the young militiaman's quarterstaff-barrier. Colvin stepped behind it, reaching around and sliding the blade of his dagger-glove across its throat. It dropped. Colvin spun on his heels just in time to plant both fists, both blades, up and under another Lorthok's ribcage.

William and his men fought together, their blades cutting way through the enemy. William ran the progressions and spilled blood with his blade; his men followed with him. He watched out for them, and they for him. They fought as one force, one great multi-headed beast.

"Th' Pride must hold, lads!" Angus screamed, and William was vaguely aware that the Highlander was somewhere near. "Make them fight ye, lads! They cannae reach th' gate!"

William spotted Angus. His claymore was a deep crimson. Liam and Gabrahn fought with him, and their tear-shaped swords were wet with blood as well.

The whole of Sword and Fist were in the fight now, and those who had survived the blast at the gate were with them, yet more invaders were joining the battle with each moment. The odds were shifting. Now for every three Tamendaders, there were four green-skinned monsters. Soon it would become two invaders to every militiaman. Then it would become even worse, as casualties began to mount. More men were down every second, clenching wounds, trying to stifle bleeding. The scale was already starting to tip in the invaders' favor. The Pride of Tamendad was beginning to slide down a slippery slope toward defeat.

How long? How long had they been fighting? How long until they were routed? Could they do enough?

"We have to pull back!" someone yelled.

"Nae!" screamed Gregor. "We have t' hold, lads!"

"If we don't pull back, we're dead!" came another voice.

"Then so be it," whispered the big Highlander.

"Reinforcements approach!"

The town criers had taken atop the wall to deliver their message to the Pride, screaming as loudly as they could to be heard over the din of battle. The invaders loosed arrows on the criers. A few were hit. They fell to their deaths still screaming their message.

"Reinforcements approach! They can be seen! They're coming!" The arrows did not silence the message.

"Fight for your city!" Don Ferdinan screamed. "Fight for your families! Fight for your homes!"

"Tamendad stands!" William screamed.

"Tamendad stands!" echoed Colvin.

The war cry went up again. The Pride of Tamendad pressed forward. William had lost too many men to count. Angus, Liam and Gabrahn had all been cut. Gregor was a bloody mess, and Wallace was no better. Blood flowed into Colvin's eyes from a gash across his forehead. He had another on his arm. Ferdinan had lost his parrying dagger. He bled from his side. Sword and Fist had lost a fifth of their number. They fought on with courage they did not know they had.

Sometime later – moments, hours, no way to tell – reinforcements arrived. Suddenly the cry of "Tamendad stands" was simply louder, fiercer, and there were more men there than had been a moment before. Constables and Shields fought their way into the front, making themselves a buffer. Sword and Fist began to fall back and spread out, making sure no invaders got around the edge of the battle to reach the gate.

William heard someone call his name. He turned. His father was with him.

"Are you hurt?" Jonathan asked, looking his son over quickly. William was bleeding, but from nothing more substantial than flesh wounds.

"No, Father."

"Stay with me."

"Yes, sir."

Father and son pressed forward. Their men fell in together. They wedged into the front line. Broadswords struck home. Two generations of Stuart-Camens relieved invaders of the burden of living.

Colvin met up with Gregor.

"Where's Ferdinan?" they both asked. They shared a concerned look.

"Nae time t' worry about that, lad," Gregor said. "He can fend for himself. Are ye all right?"

Colvin nodded. The cut on his forehead was starting to clot. He could almost see clearly.

"All right, stick with me lad," Gregor said. They began to advance together. A good number of men followed them. A group of invaders, perhaps twenty in number, broke through the line ahead of them. They closed on Gregor and Colvin. Gregor raised his claymore. Colvin assumed the stance. They pressed forward, into the attackers' charge.

Angus fought alongside Liam and Gabrahn, and a good number of Swords and Fists followed after them.

Wallace and the men who followed him held close to the docks, preventing any invaders from skirting around the fight.

Ferdinan led a charge of thirty fresh men into the heart of the invading force. He had picked up a dagger from a fallen constable. It was not designed for parrying, but it did in a pinch.

So it went. Everyone was bloodied. Men were dying all around. Against an army of monsters, still outnumbered, their backs against a wall, they were holding the gate. Then, a moment or an hour later, the monsters began making their final push. It began with a rolling wave of howls and screams and barking sounds from that spread out over the invaders from the middle, and suddenly they were all throwing themselves against the front line, tearing into constabulary and militiamen with scimitars and polearms and bare hands. They wailed and howled as they came, all of them screaming the same nonsense words.

"*Abuneth!*" the monstrosities cried. "*Thorak rakuth, Abuneth!*"

The line threatened to break.

From the rear of the fray, Angus rallied the troops. "This is it, lads!" the Highlander called. "This is their big push! Hold them now and we've won th' day! Remember what ye fight for! Tamendad stands!"

A hundred similar cries met him. Angus began the charge. "Forward, lads! Turn them back!"

Angus's charge met the enemy. The entire battle became the front line. All the Highlanders pressed forward with their kinsman. Ferdinan followed. So did Colvin. William and his father were right there with them. Blood was let. Men and monsters died. Two great waves crashed against one another. Everything fractured. Strategy was lost. No one who made a stand there by the docks outside Tamendad's shattered northeast gate, whether constable or militiaman, was ever able to give an accurate account of that last great push to save their homes. The moment was consumed by the haze of fury and violence.

At some point during those lost moments, Gregor was heard yelling, even above the roar of the fighting. "Angus! Angus!" the big Highlander cried. "*Bràidir!*" The sound of his voice made even the invaders cringe.

When sanity finally began to return to the northeast gate, the monsters were in retreat.

Atop a hill, hidden by darkness, two creatures stood overlooking Tamendad, watching what was unfolding outside the city. Their dark green skin helped hide them from prying eyes. One was dressed in animal skins with feathers tied in its hair, an unshod staff folded under its arm. The other wore a breastplate of boiled leather riveted with metal strips, two sheathed scimitars crisscrossed over its back. The armored one was a full head taller than its companion. They spoke together in a language that would have been understood by no one in Tamendad.

"You have underestimated the paleskins' resolve, Kor," the ardah said. "They have raised an army to defend themselves. They will not fold so easily."

Kor made a noise in the back of his throat something like a pig's grunt. He watched his people retreating from the city below, falling back into cover of night. He would rejoin them later. "It is of little consequence," Kor replied. "The reclaiming is begun." A moment passed in silence. Kor turned to face the ardah. "The Ancient Ones gave you no sign of this?"

The ardah locked his gaze on Kor. Neither flinched.

"I saw no sign," the ardah said. "It was not the will of the Ancient Ones for Tamendad to fall tonight. That is apparent now."

Kor said nothing further about it. How long until the ardah's Ancient Ones would allow another strike? If the Ancients were unreasonable, Kor would not wait for them. He felt certain he could move the warriors himself, without waiting for the ardah to speak the will of the Ancient Ones. The paleskin city was wounded. The death strike would have to come soon. He had waited too long after the first attack, but that was no fault of his own. He had had to wait for the ardah to relent, for the accursed Ancient Ones to give their blessing. His people had their first taste of *Abuneth* now. Even after being routed tonight they would be hungry to return, anxious to fell the paleskin city. Kor would not have to abide the old ways much longer.

"Let us return home, Kor," the ardah said when the last of the surviving warriors had faded into the darkness. He turned and began to walk away.

"Not our home much longer," Kor said. From the corner of his eye he saw the ardah flinch. Kor allowed the smallest grin to upturn his lips. Did the ardah feel his hold over their people slipping? Could he sense that the old ways were dying? Would he guess what was happening before it was too late, both for the Ancient Ones and for himself?

Kor and the ardah withdrew, back toward the nearest gateway into the Under.

Abuneth was begun.

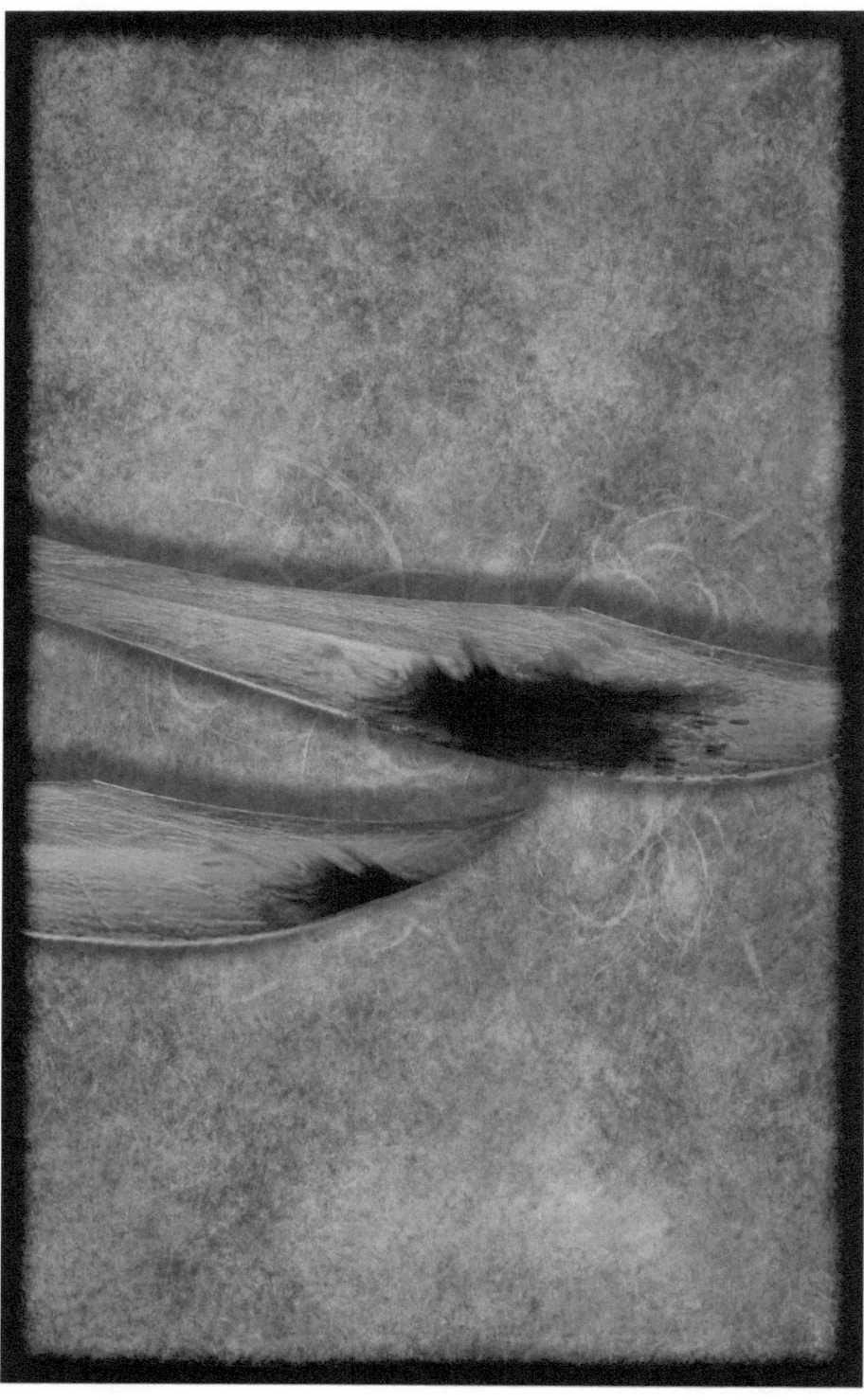

PART II

DESPERATE MEASURES

CHAPTER FIFTEEN

AFTERMATH

"Angus!"

Gregor knelt over his brother, pressing his hands hard against him, trying to staunch the flow of blood. Angus was bleeding from so many places it was difficult to tell what was a wound and what was not. His kilt and tartan were soaked through. His breaths were coming in ever more ragged gasps. His eyes were starting to shift in and out of focus. Angus reached up with a trembling hand and touched his brother's face, smearing blood in the big Highlander's beard.

"I am nae going t' make it, brother," Angus whispered. His voice sounded choked and wet.

"Aye, ye are, brother," Gregor insisted. "Ye're going t' be fine. I just have t' stop th' bleeding and then I shall get ye t' th' church and th' healers shall patch ye up. Ye're going t' be fine." Gregor's voice sounded choked as well. Wallace, Liam and Gabrahn were all kneeling there with the brothers, all of them wiping away tears and saying absolutely nothing. An occasional sniff was the only sound they made.

"Look me in th' eyes and tell me that," Angus said. He began to cough, and blood sputtered from his lips and dribbled down his chin.

Gregor's face scrunched up tight. His lip quivered. Tears began to roll down his cheeks into his scraggly beard. "Nae," he whispered. "Nae, nae, nae, nae…" He was no longer trying to stop the bleeding. He put his large arms around Angus, pulling his brother close, nestling Angus's head against his barrel chest.

The other Highlanders found they could not even look at him. They hung their heads. Their shoulders convulsed with quieted sobs.

"Dinnae cry, brother," Angus whispered. "I shall be among our kinsmen soon. I think…I have…th' better lot."

"As ye see it brother," Gregor said, doing his best to wipe the blood from his little brother's face. He remembered watching Angus take his first steps. He had been there when Angus had broken his arm falling out of that accursed apple tree their da had forbidden them to climb so many times. He had stood groomsman at his brother's wedding. Who would tell Kila how her husband had died? He would, of course. It was his duty, both as head of the family and as Angus's brother. He would tell her. He would.

"I shall tell...our parents...ye love them," Angus gasped. His eyes were starting to roll back in his head. "So cold..." he whispered.

"Ye shall be warm soon, brother," Gregor whispered, running his fingers across his brother's face. "Lie still and relax, Angus. Ye shall be warm soon." Gregor could no longer see his brother's face. His tears had blinded him.

"I see Da." Angus was fighting hard just to whisper now, struggling for the breath just to say three words.

"Aye, brother. Go t' him," Gregor said. The words caught in his throat. He could not hold back his tears. His whole body rocked with his sobs. "Tell him I miss him."

"Do...nae...cry," Angus said, words barely audible. He was smiling. He was going home. Every MacDugal who had gone before him reached out to help him across the gulf. Generations of his kinsmen waited to embrace him. His parents were right there before him, arms spread wide. Da looked so strong, so handsome, not at all like he had looked on his deathbed. Ma looked young and beautiful. She was smiling. She beckoned him. He would be with them in a moment. He had to tell Gregor how wonderful it was, how strong and healthy everyone looked. He could hear his brother's sobs, feel him trembling. Why was Gregor crying? This was wonderful. It was bliss. It was peace, true peace, like nothing he had felt before. He was as light as a cloud. He was floating. His heart was filled with joy. He had to tell Gregor there was nothing to cry about. Where was Gregor? Why couldn't he see him?

"Do...nae..."

He crossed the gulf.

He was gone.

Gregor wailed. The other Highlanders' voices joined his. It was the sound of pain, of suffering, of death. It was the sound of loss. Liam, Gabrahn and Wallace all hugged each other tight. They sobbed together. Gregor clenched Angus's motionless form tight against him. He buried his head against his little brother's chest. His heart broke there, outside the shattered northeast gate of Tamendad.

Ferdinan was there the next moment, throwing his arms around the big Highlander, sobbing with him, sharing his pain. "I am here," Ferdinan whispered to his friend, over and over again. "I am here. I am right here, Gregor."

Gregor let go of his little brother and latched on tight to Ferdinan. He wailed again.

Ferdinan began to pray, in Turish so Gregor could hear. "May the Four Faces of God smile upon you. May He hold you tight in His arms. May He lift you up and exalt your name. May you find peace forever, now that your suffering es at an end." The Prayer for the Fallen of Battle.

"May th' light o' God shine upon yer soul forever," Liam added through his tears.

"May th' hand o' th' Creator wipe away all yer tears," said Wallace, sobbing.

"Lay down yer sword, kinsman," Gabrahn added, wiping his eyes. "Ye dinnae need it where ye're going."

Gregor pulled his face away from Ferdinan's bosom. He looked at Angus. His brother looked so peaceful, like he was sleeping. He was really gone. Gone forever. Taken. Ripped away.

"When I reach th' summit, may yer face be th' first I see on th' other side," Gregor told his little brother.

Sometime later, William and Colvin were there with them, embracing, crying, grieving together. Gunther and Gangis were there too, wiping tears from their eyes, their hands resting on Gregor's shoulders. Friends mourned together. No one else approached them. Whenever a man thought about trying to, the look Ferdinan or Colvin or William or any of the others gave him was enough to make him back respectfully away.

Others also mourned outside the northeast gate. Fathers knelt beside dying sons and sons beside dying fathers. Brothers and sisters bid tearful goodbyes. Some died alone, calling out to God as their last moments in this world slipped away. Many were long dead. A gruesome array of body parts littered the ground, hands and limbs and heads and entrails. A stench hung in the air that would remain for many days. It was the smell of death.

Many more men and women lay on the ground clutching wounds that were not mortal, staunching blood, staring up at the stars and wondering what the twist had just happened. The majority of the crowd were walking wounded, and no one had escaped injury altogether. A fortunate many had rode out the battle and earned only scrapes and nicks, but everyone would have scars to show from this night. The Antrelican healers arrived only moments after the invaders had retreated, fanning out into the crowd and beginning the long, arduous process of stitching wounds and applying poultices. Other priests, not trained in healing, came from the church as well and began the equally burdensome task of administering last rites. The most badly injured waited nervously to see whether the priest who finally came to tend them would be carrying a healer's bag or a Sacred Compass for the death sacrament.

Yet while all the mourning and weeping was going on there beside the docks, men and women were celebrating, too. Cheers and whistles mingled with the wails and sobs. Some people were actually dancing. Every now and then a man or a woman with a bow would shoot an arrow in the direction the invaders had fled, and more than a few people would call out into the darkness what those monstrosities could go do with themselves. Men embraced openly without regard for what others might have thought. Some of the female constables and militiamen allowed a few men to steal kisses. There were few moments when someone was not crying out, "Tamendad stands!" The revelers were respectful of those who were grieving, keeping their distance from them, but there was much to be joyous about. Tamendad had been defended from a real, full-on assault. The enemy had been turned back. They had won the day.

Gregor and his friends stood together as the priest performed Angus MacDugal's last rites. Everyone crowded around the big Highlander, putting their hands on him, helping support him as the priest spoke. The death sacrament was performed in the Holy Tongue, but every practicing Antrelican knew what the words meant.

It meant a loved one was gone.

Everyone stood in silence, heads bowed. Everyone except Gregor. Gregor stared at the face of his brother, so peaceful, so terrible. Angus did not look like he was sleeping, and Gregor did not know how he had ever thought he did. His little brother looked unnatural. He looked hollow. He did not look human at all. Angus's body was an empty husk, just so many pounds of worthless flesh. The spark of life was forever gone from it. What made Angus *Angus* was gone out of the world. Gregor felt more alone than he ever had in his life, more alone than when his wife had died, more alone than when his own parents had died. Angus should have still been here. He had not been sick. There had been no warning that he was going to die. He was here, and then he was just gone, taken by the last desperate push of those wretched beasts.

Why dinnae ye fall back? Gregor thought. *Ye saw them coming, brother. Ye saw th' line start t' break. Ye saw them coming through. Why did ye stand, brother? Why did ye dig in? Why dinnae ye fall back just a little? Just a little?* Gregor knew why. He had witnessed it. The line had almost broken. Those beasts had found a fissure and had started to press through it, right toward Angus. If Angus had fallen back, even just a little, the beasts could have skirted him. Gregor knew that; Angus had known that. So Angus did what Gregor would have done, what any Highlander would have done. He stood. He dug in. He made the beasts face him. He bought enough time for the fissure to be sealed up. And he died making sure the line held.

Tamendad stood because Angus MacDugal fell.

The priest made the Sign of the Compass and moved on. There were many more dead men and women whose souls awaited their last rites. As soon as the priest was gone, Gregor spoke.

"Fetch wood," he said, looking to the other Highlanders, and he sounded as though the fate of the world depended on it. Everyone gave a start at his words, and at the iron quality of his voice. Liam, Gabrahn, and Wallace all looked at each other, then at Gregor. "Aye," Liam said, and the three of them went off to do as they had been instructed.

After a moment of confused silence, Colvin said, "I'll help," and followed after the three Highlanders.

"Me too," said William, doing the same. Gunther and Gangis followed suit without speaking. Gregor stood and watched them go. He turned to look at Ferdinan. The Conquian looked back at him. That look expressed more about pain and grief and understanding and, most importantly, about friendship than any words ever could. Gregor started walking back toward Tamendad. Ferdinan followed by his side. They walked together. They each drew strength from the other's mere presence.

They reentered Tamendad, headed for the trade district. The town was in an uproar. Some people danced in the streets while others still hid behind shuttered windows and barred doors, refusing to believe the attack was really over. Townspeople desperately searched for a town crier or, failing that, implored the constables attempting to restore order to tell them what had happened. The constables turned a cold shoulder more often than not, their attention focused on the hooligans who had turned to looting during the confusion. Few people approached Gregor and Ferdinan. Their appearance was enough to dissuade all but the most desperate inquisitors. Gregor was covered in blood from head to toe, and it was quite plain to see that most of it was not his own. Ferdinan was sporting a most impressive slash across his right side, where his shirt had turned a rich crimson. In addition to looking so roughed up, it was obvious both men had been crying. Most everyone steered clear of them. To those few brave souls who did approach and ask what had happened at the gate, Gregor said simply, without meeting their gaze, "Th' battle is o'er and th' enemy has fled. Go home t' yer family." No one refused to accept his account, and everyone followed his suggestion.

Gregor and Ferdinan walked to the Crown Rose. They had to wait for the waitstaff to remove the tables and chairs they had used to bar the door from the inside before they could enter, and then came the unavoidable period of question and answer, during which Gregor and Ferdinan had to reassure all the servants along with Torrance Mayhew himself that yes, the battle really was over, yes, the constabulary and the militia really did repel the invaders, and yes, the northeast gate really was not there anymore. Not surprisingly, Master Mayhew and his servants found that their questions lost a great deal of urgency when it came out that Angus MacDugal had been killed during the attack. That news was met with somber silence. A few of the servants wept, as did Master Mayhew. Chelsie hugged Gregor tightly. He hugged her back, but found he had no more tears to cry at the moment. The woman's embrace was comforting, though. He drew strength from it. He was beginning to realize how many friendships he had formed in Tamendad. A detached part of him wondered why it always seemed to take tragedies to make a man realize important things like that.

After a moment of shared grief, Ferdinan sent the servants away. The Conquian knew that Gregor would never do it himself. The Highlander's heart was even bigger than the rest of him. He would have stayed there with them, letting them weep and ask their questions about how it happened until he was drained of all strength. Ferdinan had no such compassion for them. All his compassion was focused on Gregor at the moment. The Conquian was polite but insistent that this was not the time or the place. The servants scattered, and most of them bore understanding looks as Ferdinan shooed them away. Chelsie was the last to go. She had been hugging Gregor the whole time. She pressed her forehead to his.

"I'm here if you need me," she whispered to him.

"I know, lass," he replied. And he did know. A lot of people were there for him.

When Chelsie had gone back to the kitchen, Ferdinan and Gregor were once again alone. Gregor told Ferdinan thank you with his look, and Ferdinan nodded once. "I have t' fetch something from m' suite," Gregor said.

"I will be here when you are done, Gregor," Ferdinan told him.

Gregor nodded.

The Highlander climbed the stairs to his suite, and the weight of the world bore down upon his shoulders with each step. When he entered, he found the common room tidier than he had left it. The waitstaff had apparently worked off some of their anxious energy by straightening the rooms after barricading themselves inside the inn. It was funny the things some people did in a crisis. Gregor could not imagine taking the risk of dying with a feather duster in his hand rather than his claymore. But then, he was a warrior, born of a great line of warriors. It was in his blood. Not everyone was meant for the warrior's life, and thank God for that. A world full of warriors would be a desolate place indeed.

Gregor's pipes were laid neatly on the daybed of the common room. He moved to pick them up. From the corner of his eye he saw movement in the bedroom. His claymore was in his hands in an instant, and he charged headlong into the bedroom before realizing he had simply caught a glimpse of himself in the dressing mirror through the doorway. He was barely able to choke back the war cry that had already begun to rise in the back of his throat. He felt a bit of a fool, chasing after looking glasses lurking menacingly in the shadows. He was very glad Ferdinan was not there to see him. When his embarrassment passed, he finally took a good look at himself in the mirror and realized that he looked a fright, covered in blood from head to toe. How much was his? Surprising little, it turned out. His whole body was covered with nicks and cuts, but he had sustained no injury worse than a simple flesh wound.

Neither had Angus, before the end...

He forced himself away from those thoughts. It was too fresh in his mind. He would deal with his memories later. There was work to be done. He filled the washbasin and washed the blood from his face and arms. It did not accomplish much; his skin was still ruddy after he was done, and the blood stains would probably endure for a week or more, but he felt better once some of the blood was washed away. He retrieved his pipes and left the suite.

Ferdinan was waiting in the main dining room, as he had promised he would. Descending the stairs from the balcony, Gregor really noticed the Conquian's injury for the first time. Blood no longer flowed freely from Ferdinan's side, but he still kept his right hand pressed firmly against the wound. His whole right side was blood-drenched. His outfit was ruined. Not that Gregor really gave a damn about that, but the big Highlander knew Ferdinan would find that almost as upsetting as the actual injury.

"We should get ye t' a healer, lad," Gregor said as he rejoined Ferdinan.

Ferdinan pursed his lips and shook his head. "After," he said somberly.

"Aye," Gregor said. "After."

❖   ❖   ❖

Much wood had been gathered when they returned to the northeast gate. Most of it had come from the remains of the gate itself, though there was a bit of driftwood thrown in as well. The pile was almost as tall as Gangis, and all the men were still gathering wood when Gregor and

Ferdinan returned. Gregor noticed that someone had laid out Angus's body so that he looked to be more comfortable, his hands crossed over the hilt of his claymore, which had been laid gently on his chest. Gregor was glad to see that. Everyone was looking at Gregor and his pipes. The Highlanders understood. The others did not.

"Thank ye, lads, this should do nicely," Gregor said, gesturing to the wood pile. He set his pipes delicately on the ground a few feet away, then took a long, deep breath. "Let us build th' pyre."

Together they set about their task. Of the nine men gathered there around the body of the fallen Highlander, Colvin, William, Gangis and Ferdinan had no experience with building a funeral pyre, but no man professed his ignorance. The Highlanders all knew exactly what to do, and Gunther also demonstrated a knowledge of the subject, and together they were able to walk the four novices through the construction. Other men and women began to take notice of what was happening, and many realized for the first time what price Angus MacDugal had paid. As the nine friends continued to build the pyre, other constables and militiamen started to gather around, bowing their heads. Silence spread over the crowd like a wave. The only sound was of the Antrelican priests still giving last rites. Every now and again Gregor or one of the others would catch a whisper of explanation from the crowd. The specific words varied from report to report, but the general message was always the same: Angus MacDugal was dead; a funeral pyre was being built.

Some people did not know how to react to that. The practice of burning the dead had been heard of, but few in Tamendad had ever actually witnessed it. Antrelicans usually buried their dead; Hidalgo Sanctus had taught that it was the best way. The Glenish were one of the few surviving cultures that still practiced cremation, and it was generally viewed as a holdover from their pagan roots. Those thoughts occurred to William, and Colvin, and Gangis, and most especially Ferdinan as they helped build the pyre, but the men kept their reservations to themselves. The Architessera did not proscribe cremation, and even if it had, no one was about to broach that subject with Gregor.

The pyre was finished in less than half an hour. When it was done it resembled an oversized bed frame, eight feet long and five across, rising three feet off the ground. It looked so delicate that a decent wind should have been able to level the whole thing, but once the last stick had been put into place Gregor slapped his palm hard against the top of it, and not a single stick budged. The four novices were a bit amazed that Gunther and the Highlanders knew how to build such a thing from memory, without a detailed construction plan and using whatever wood lay close at hand. When Gregor saw that the pyre withstood his test, he nodded once and said, "This shall do," speaking to no one in particular. He began stuffing handfuls of brush and wood chips into the frame for kindling, and the eight others followed suit. Then it was done, and the pyre was ready.

Gregor turned his attention from the pyre to the body of Angus. The big Highlander gently uncrossed his brother's hands from over his sword, picking up the claymore and turning to his three kinsmen. Liam, Gabrahn and Wallace all straightened under Gregor's gaze. He approached them with sword in hand. He signaled out Gabrahn, who was standing in the middle.

"M' brother's sword now belongs t' Gabrahn Cowan o' th' Clan MacDugal," Gregor said. "He shall wield it in accordance with th' traditions o' th' Duerhein MacDugals."

"I shall wield it with a heart o'erfilled with pride, and I shall remember," said Gabrahn.

"Fetch yer baldric and hanger, kinsmen," said Gregor.

Gabrahn nodded and turned his gaze upon Angus. For a moment Gabrahn appeared on the brink of tears again, but he found his resolve and went and knelt beside Angus's body. He began to delicately remove the baldric from around Angus, and as he did, he spoke to Angus softly, so that only the men who had built the pyre were close enough to hear. "I take yer sword now only t' hold it for a little while," Gabrahn said, "and I shall return it when next we meet."

When the baldric was removed from around Angus's chest Gabrahn put it in position over his own, and Gregor helped place Angus's sword on it. The claymore looked positively gargantuan on Gabrahn's back, and yet at the same time the sword seemed to fit him in a way. Once the sword was on his back, Gabrahn returned to stand with Liam and Wallace. Both men placed a hand on Gabrahn's shoulder, and Gabrahn found reassurance in the gesture.

Gregor looked at the body of his little brother for a long moment. A host of memories flooded him. Angus's first step. His first word. His obsession with the forbidden apple tree. His fascination with birds and butterflies and anything else that could fly and his insatiable thirst for understanding of how they did it. The first time Angus had tried to pick up a claymore. The excitement in Angus's voice the first time he told Gregor he had decided to propose marriage to Kila. The tears Gregor and Angus had shed together standing by Da's deathbed. The image of the first monster's sword sliding into him, the first of many. His insistence, even at the very end, that Gregor should not cry. Gregor relived a lifetime's worth of memories encapsulated in a single moment. All that remained of Angus in this world was contained in those memories.

"Someone help me move him," Gregor said. William, Colvin, Gunther, Gangis, Liam, Gabrahn, Wallace and Ferdinan all moved to assist, and they were not the only ones. Everyone who was gathered together there around the pyre by the northeast gate took a step forward and offered their help without saying a word. The nine men who had built the pyre hoisted up the body of the fallen Highlander, and the constables and militiamen who were closest to the nine reached forward and laid their hands upon them. Those who were too far away to reach simply laid their hands on whoever was standing directly in front of them, and soon all the men and women there were embracing, sharing their strength. At the head of the embrace stood Gregor MacDugal, and he held in his arms the limp body of his little brother.

Gregor laid Angus upon the pyre. The wood groaned slightly under the weight, but held firm. Gregor crossed his brother's arms over his chest and straightened his brother's hair, paying special attention to his *duál*. He smoothed out ruffles in Angus's tartan. He made Angus look as peaceful as he could. He knew it was his last opportunity to look after his little brother.

Ferdinan wept at the care Gregor took in his actions, at the delicateness of Gregor's touch. The sight of it sang to the Conquian's heart. Colvin put an arm around Ferdinan's shoulders, and William took Ferdinan's hand in his own.

When Gregor had finished tending to his brother he turned and looked over the people there. He addressed his kinsmen and friends, but spoke loudly enough that everyone there might hear him.

"'Tis written that a man's soul is eternal, but his body is as insubstantial as ash and air," he said. A few of the priests who were still attending the wounded there, either by dressing their wounds or performing the death sacrament, looked startled by the big Highlander's words. No one would have thought Gregor MacDugal to be learned in the Architessera. "Our kinsman," Gregor continued, "m' brother, Angus MacDugal, is dead. His soul continues on, and though 'tis nae our place t' know th' fate of a man's soul, I shall have words with any man who dinnae abide that Angus has reached th' summit." A moment passed in silence. Most people did not even breathe. "But his body is left behind," Gregor continued, "a cast-off shell devoid o' purpose, and so, in accordance with what is written, we reduce his body t' th' ash and air to which it is so akin. Such is th' way o' th' Clan MacDugal. May God's mercy shine upon us."

The big Highlander commissioned his three kinsmen to find fire and bring it while he readied his pipes to play. Most of the fires from the blast had already burned themselves out, but it was not difficult to find a place where a small one still burned, or, failing that, embers which still glowed hot enough to easily be stoked back to flames, and it did not take long at all for the three Highlanders to return carrying lit torches. They took up positions around the pyre, with Gabrahn standing at the head. They all looked to Gregor. He nodded.

"Light!" Gabrahn yelled, and he thrust his torch into the heart of the pyre. Liam and Wallace did the same. Smoke began to billow from it as the kindling caught. The first flames appeared quickly and began to spread. Gregor began to play. It was the saddest sound any man there had ever heard, sadder than any song should have ever been. It had been said that the violin was the sound of an angel weeping. If that was the truth, then what Gregor played on the Highland pipes was the grieving wail of God himself. Grown men shed tears unabashedly as they watched the body of Angus MacDugal burn. Even the priests found need to dry their eyes. They pyre began to burn so hot, with flames leaping several feet into the air, that the crowd had to back away from it. The pyre's roar became a steady accompaniment to Gregor's pipes. He continued with his playing of *Coming Home to Duerhein*, the funeral dirge of the Clan MacDugal. He had played that song too many times, for too many young men taken too soon. Now he played it for his own brother, something which in his darkest nightmares he had never dreamed of doing. He found tears he did not think could still be in him, and they trailed down his cheeks into his matted beard while he played.

Sometime later, it was over. The pyre eventually collapsed and burned itself down to cinders long after the body of Angus MacDugal had been eternally committed to ash and air. When it was done, Gregor all but ordered his friends to the healers. They obeyed, dragging the big Highlander along with them. The crowd dispersed. No man who had witnessed Angus MacDugal's funeral ever again spoke an ill word about the practice of cremation, not even the priests, and many of the witnesses had fierce things to say whenever anyone spoke unflatteringly of the act of burning the dead.

There were two things Kor hated about the Under.

The first was that it stunk of sulfur and guano. The sulfur was their own doing. Kor's people did not need as much light to see by as paleskins did, not by a far cry, but just like any sighted creature they were helpless in complete darkness. They kept as few fires burning as possible, the bare necessity, but sulfur and pitch were the only readily available combustibles in the Under, and the smoke had nowhere to go. The stench of it seeped into hair, clothes, everything. It burned the eyes and the nostrils, and it caused a most wretched, hacking cough after a time.

The guano was no fault of theirs, just an unavoidable fact of life in the Under. The bats usually kept their distance from the fires, but generations' worth of bat droppings lay in heaps in any direction. What was worse, the accursed stuff was edible if not particularly palatable, one of the few readily available food sources in the Under. Kor's people actually had to go out and gather the foul stuff and bring great basketfuls of it back. Kor was certain it was a curse from the Ancient Ones, making guano edible. No matter how sweet it sometimes smelled, no matter how much it sometimes tasted like fruit paste, when it came down to it, Kor's people were still eating shit.

The other thing about the Under that Kor hated was that everything was made from one of two building materials: mud or stone. Stone was favored for its strength and durability. That might not have been the case if Kor's people had been capable of turning mud into stoneware, but firing up a kiln would have meant producing so much smoke and noxious fumes that no one would have been able to get close enough to use it. So stone was the material of choice. Hard stone. Cold stone. Uncomfortable stone. The stone was as plentiful as the bat shit.

There was iron too, of course, little veins of it running all throughout the Under, but it was reserved exclusively for the making of *morchas* – the swords the paleskins called scimitars – in the forges that lay much deeper below, near the very Heart of the World, where the liquid rock flowed. The ardah had claimed those forges were an ancient abandoned vileness of the Ganugamosh and advised Kor to leave them alone. Kor had almost agreed, but in the end the promise of those forges was enough to outweigh any repulsion Kor felt at the thought of using Ganugamosh creations. The decision to use those forges had ultimately been the difference in making *Abuneth* a reality. With them, morchas came as quickly as Kor could get iron to the forgeworkers. Those forgeworkers melted and tempered and hammered and sharpened even now, replacing the morchas damaged or lost in the attack that night. The wheel of *Abuneth* was turning at full speed.

The sacrifice's death rattle brought Kor back to the moment. The young warrior lying on the altar – more stone – had been wailing for so long that the silence sounded odd when it finally came. The altar and the floor were covered in blood. The walls were splattered with it. Some had even gotten on the ceiling. This sacrifice had fought. Kor had to stifle a smile at that. His people were beginning to cast off the old ways for themselves, without him even leading them to it. The ardah, as drenched in blood as the altar, pulled his knife from the sacrifice's chest. He turned his eyes on Kor. "The immolation is complete. The Ancient Ones are appeased."

You just cost me one of my best warriors, you old-minded fool, thought Kor. He bowed his head before the ardah. "May the Ancient Ones be appeased by all that we do," he said. The ardah nodded. Kor exited the Place of Offering, leaving the ardah to the gruesome business of what was done with a sacrifice after it was dead. Kor found that humorously symbolic, the ardah dwelling among the dead while he himself turned his attention upon the living. Kor chuckled to himself lightly as he walked down the dark corridor, leaving the sanctum behind him.

He was greeted by a throng of warriors all crowded together, awaiting his return. They all began to howl as soon as they saw him, and cries of *"Thorak rakuth, Abuneth!"* echoed all around. Kor threw his head back and howled with his people. He clapped the closest warriors on the shoulders or punched them in the arm. He celebrated with them. There was much to celebrate, even if they had not taken Tamendad this night. They had attacked the paleskins for the first time in generations. They had moved into the Over together, as an army, and stormed out of the darkness screaming war cries. They were no longer relegated to shadow. They no longer hid in holes underground. They had revealed themselves fully to the paleskins. They had waged war. There was much to celebrate indeed.

Kor raised a fist into the air, and the warriors fell silent at once. They stood rapt with attention waiting to hear Kor speak. Kor looked over his warriors, the army of the reclaiming. A good number of them bore injuries, but none of them appeared maimed. They still held the euphoria of battle. Most of them would have probably followed Kor right back to the gates of Tamendad at that moment had he asked them to. Kor considered it for a moment, but dismissed the thought as quickly as it had come. It was too soon. Better to give at least some small measure of rest to warriors who had fought so hard. Kor lowered his fist. Some of the younger warriors were actually standing tiptoe and craning their necks to better hear. Even the eldest warriors, some several seasons older than Kor, looked anxious to hear Kor's proclamation.

"Abuneth kul!" Kor yelled. *The reclaiming is upon us!* Kor's words were met with a roar of howling cheers. Celebration broke out in the corridor once again, and it lasted for a long while. Warriors waited their turn to come before Kor and kneel and kiss his feet. Every warrior who had a mate offered her to Kor to use as he saw fit. A few cut themselves and caught the blood in small cups, presenting it to Kor to drink, the highest sign of allegiance among their people. The warriors were in a

fervor. Kor had led them into a new beginning. The Under was filled with the sounds of celebration as it had never been before.

It took the return of the ardah from the Place of Offering to still the crowd. The warriors bowed their heads before him, and Kor did the same. The ardah was fingering his necklace of teeth. Kor despised that necklace more than anything else about the ardah. Each of those teeth represented a young, strong, able-bodied warrior that had died on the altar instead of the battlefield. Each one of those sacrifices could have died for something more meaningful than the Ancient Ones' contemptible demands for immolation.

"The Ancient Ones have been appeased," the ardah said.

"When will we strike the paleskins again?" asked a young warrior with fire in his eyes. The ardah obviously did not care for the question, nor for the young warrior asking it without showing the proper reverence. Kor had a suspicion that the next time the Ancient Ones called for a sacrifice, it would conveniently be that warrior they chose. Then again, perhaps the next one to lay on the altar in the Place of Offering would be the ardah himself.

"Soon," said Kor, answering in the ardah's place. "Soon."

William winced as the healer continued stitching the wound on his upper arm. So far he had had four wounds sewn up: two on his left leg, one on his abdomen, and one on his chest. He also had two cuts on his left arm, one of which the healer was currently suturing, and another on his right. None of his seven cuts were nearly as bad as the one at his side had been, but they all hurt like the devil, thanks in part to the poultice the healer applied to each one after he was done sewing it up.

The wooden bench William sat on was brutally uncomfortable. He would have much preferred a bed to lie in, like the one he had all to himself the last time he visited the healers, but tonight all the beds were filled with the seriously injured. The patchwork jobs like William had to make do with the benches. Men and women were crowded together on them, waiting their turn for their wounds to be cleaned and stitched up. The healers were going to have their hands full for quite some time.

William looked at Colvin, who was sitting beside him on the bench. Another healer was stitching up the gash on Colvin's left arm. Aside from the nick on his forehead, the cut on his arm was the only injury he had sustained. In that way he had been very lucky, but that one wound was worse by far than any of William's seven. It had cut almost down to the bone, and the healer was busy stitching the muscle back together before even thinking about getting started on closing the flesh up. The most repulsive thing about it was that the healer had to open the wound wider so he could get to the muscle inside, so now the laceration ran almost halfway around the circumference of Colvin's arm, the skin stretched wide so the healer could see what he was doing with his stitchwork. The healer had applied some sort of paste that had made Colvin's arm feel cold and go completely limp, and as long as Colvin did not look at what the healer was doing, he was completely oblivious to what was happening to him.

"I've never seen anything like that pyre," William said to Colvin, trying to help the red-haired man keep his mind off the stitches he was receiving. "Have you?"

Colvin shook his head. He found he still could not really talk about it. Angus's cremation had been the first time in years he had cried. Before that, he had not even been certain he was still capable of it anymore.

"The Glenish tend to hold nothing back at funerals," Jonathan Stuart-Camen said. Jonathan was sitting on the bench across from William and Colvin. His wounds had already been sutured, but he was waiting until the healers had finished with his son. "They tend not to hold anything back at any time, for that matter."

"They are a beautiful, passionate people," said Ferdinan through clenched teeth. The Conquian was sitting beside Jonathan with his shirt off, his right arm raised high above his head. Yet another healer was stitching up the deep wound just above his hip. The blood had been cleaned away before the healer began his needlework but his entire side was still stained a soft red, and fresh blood oozed slowly from the wound as it continued to close with each stitch. Ferdinan was obviously in a considerable amount of pain, but he had thrice refused the numbing salve that had been used on Colvin's arm. The salve was a precious commodity among the healers, and Ferdinan insisted they save it for those who needed it more than he. "Es interesting so many Turishmen think of them as pagan barbarians."

"Turishmen tend to fear what they don't understand," William said.

"All men fear what they don't understand," said Colvin, staring off into space. He wasn't sure if what the healer had used to numb his arm was starting to wear off, but he was becoming aware of the sensation of the thread sliding through the biceps in his left arm. There was no pain involved, just the feeling of needle and thread stitching muscle back together. It was an entirely disconcerting sensation. Colvin assumed the stance to block it out.

"That's very true," Jonathan said. "Sad, needless to say, but true."

"Perhaps the Turish should spend some time developing an understanding of Gregor's people," Ferdinan mused. William, Jonathan and Colvin all nodded their heads in agreement.

"What do you think Gregor will do now, Ferdinan?" William asked. Jonathan and Colvin turned to look at the Conquian, as did almost everyone sitting within earshot. That was one of the biggest questions running through Tamendad's collective mind at the moment. No one knew exactly how Gregor MacDugal would react to his brother's death, but everyone knew the big Highlander would do something, and it was likely to be something big.

Captain Jefford was suddenly standing there with them before Ferdinan had an opportunity to weigh in with his opinion on the subject. To say that Tamendad's Captain of the Guard looked haggard would have been a most polite understatement, but there were no sutured wounds on Jefford's body. He had been standing in charge of the constables at the southeast gate, where Jefford himself had anticipated the attack to come, and he had not made it to the northeast gate before the invaders had called their retreat. Don Ferdinan and Jonathan Stuart-Camen knew that that, more than anything else, was eating away at Captain Jefford from the inside.

"My apologies for bothering you while you are in such a delicate position," the Captain said, directing his words mostly to Ferdinan but meeting the gaze of Jonathan, William and Colvin as well.

"Es nothing, Captain," Ferdinan said. "What do you have for me?"

"The Governor wishes to see you at once, as soon as you are done with the healers. He says he has much to discuss with you."

"As do I with him," Ferdinan replied. "Anything more?"

"Not for you specifically, Don Ferdinan," Jefford said, "but I do carry a message for Lord Stuart-Camen."

"What is it, Captain?" Jonathan asked, rising to his feet and standing at attention.

Captain Jefford blinked. "I'm sorry, Lieutenant. I meant the other Lord Stuart-Camen. At ease."

"Yes, Captain?" William said. "I would stand and salute, but..." He gestured to the healer stitching up the wound on his arm.

Captain Jefford nodded. "Sword Division is on high alert tonight. You and your men are to assist the constabulary at the damaged northeast gate until sunup."

William did not say it aloud, but he was of the opinion that calling the northeast gate *damaged* was akin to saying Angus MacDugal was a bit under the weather. The northeast gate was gone, and Tamendad was wide open to attack. "Yes, sir," the young nobleman said.

"What about Fist Division?" Colvin asked.

Captain Jefford turned to him. The Captain looked at what the healer was doing to his arm and winced. "Fist Division is to stand down," Jefford told him. "Get some rest, Colvin. We'll need fresh men to depend on in the morning."

Colvin nodded, feeling a little surprised that the Captain of the Guard knew him by name.

Captain Jefford turned to go, then hesitated for a moment. "Oh, Lieutenant Stuart-Camen, I forgot. I do have some news for you. Patrum Albermarle said that Constable Laerian should be fine. The sword did not hit any organs. Albermarle did not go as far as calling it a miracle, but the look in his eyes said it all."

Jonathan nodded, relieved. "Thank God," he said. Laerian had taken a blade for him in the heat of those final chaotic moments of battle. Jonathan had carried the young constable to the church himself.

Captain Jefford nodded, then left the four of them sitting there. Jonathan stood, straightening his constable's uniform. William was still not used to seeing his father in that uniform. No matter how good of a swordsman Jonathan was, William could not make himself think of his father as a soldier. "I had better see where I'm stationed tonight," Jonathan said. "Are you all right, son?"

William nodded. "I'm okay, Father."

"I will try to get stationed at the northeast gate with you," Jonathan said.

William nodded again. Having his father there would make the night pass much more easily.

"Your father es a very good man," Ferdinan said to William after Jonathan was gone.

"I know," he replied.

The healers finished stitching up Ferdinan's side, Colvin's arm and William's multitudinous wounds at about the same time. Colvin still had practically no use of his left arm, and he thought it was just as well that Fist Division had the night off. His rag-doll arm would have been about as useful in a fight as a breastplate made of pillows. It felt like it had just gone ahead and decided to die without waiting for the rest of his body to follow suit, but the healer assured him he would have total feeling back in his arm by sunup.

"You will have to escuse me, but I must meet with the Governor," Ferdinan said as he buttoned his shirt back up. Half of the silk was the original white, flowing fabric, and the other was a stiff, rich crimson. Ferdinan ran his fingers over the large hole in the fabric just over his stitches. He sighed. "Another shirt ruined. At this rate I'll be wearing Turish-tailored clothes before all es said and done." Colvin smirked at William, and William focused all his energy on not laughing. "I will catch up with both of you tomorrow," Ferdinan continued. "Be careful at the gate, William. And Colvin, try to get some sleep. God goes with you, *compagnos*." With that, Ferdinan was gone.

"I'll walk with you to the gate, if you don't mind," Colvin said to William.

"I don't mind at all," William replied. "I could do with the company. I don't really feel like being alone right now."

"Me neither," sighed Colvin.

They gladly left the benches behind them. Their backsides had grown quite numb from them, and their first few steps were more of a waddle than a walk as the blood began to circulate once again.

"My ass is as numb as my arm," Colvin said.

As soon as they were in the sanctuary, William nudged Colvin in the arm. Colvin did not immediately notice. William did it again, harder, and Colvin's arm dangled limply, swaying back and forth. Colvin looked at his useless arm, then at William.

"Sorry," William whispered. "Look." He pointed into the sanctuary.

Colvin's eyes followed the line of William's pointing. The Highlanders were all sitting together in one of the pews toward the back of the church. They sat in silence, staring at the ornate Sacred Compass resting on the altar. They were the only ones seated in the pews. Everyone else in the sanctuary was crowded close to the front, around the Master Postulant or one of his underlings, awaiting their turn to make their prayers. Colvin and William both jumped a little when Gregor began to speak.

"God, ye saw fit in yer infinite wisdom t' take m' brother Angus t'night. I dinnae question ye, God, but I dinnae ken ye, either. He was so young. He had so much life left t' live. M' heart is breaking, God. I miss m' little brother so much. I dinnae know what t' do without him. In so many ways, Angus was m' anchor. He was th' rock o' th' family. He held us all together and made us hear reason even when we dinnae wish. He was kind, and gentle, and loving. He was a good husband t' Kila, and I know he would have been a good father had ye e'er seen fit t' bless Kila with a child. And as a brother, he was more than I deserved. I feel so lost without him. Please take care o' him. Keep him safe and warm. Watch o'er him until I get there. This is what I ask o' ye."

William turned to Colvin. "What is he doing?" the young nobleman asked.

"He's praying," Colvin said, though he did not sound absolutely certain about that himself. William arched an eyebrow. Colvin shrugged, but with only one shoulder. Praying without kneeling before a priest was unheard of. Only lunatics claimed they could know the Four Faces of

God and speak to them directly. Nothing in Gregor's prayer had sounded insane – just very, very sad – but it abided none of the Antrelican doctrines of prayer. It was a total disregard for church protocol, and yet it was without doubt the most heartfelt prayer William and Colvin had both ever heard.

"Shouldn't you be getting to the gate?" Colvin whispered after he had William had shared an introspective moment. William nodded, though reluctantly, and he and Colvin left the church together.

Once they were outside, William asked the first of a hundred questions burning in his mind. "How can they pray like that, without a priest?" he asked. Colvin eyed him a bit suspiciously. "I don't mean that the way it sounds," William said quickly, "I just mean that's so different from everything I've ever been taught about prayer."

Colvin did another one-shouldered shrug, then took a moment to look contemptuously at his left arm and sigh before responding. "I've stayed in a couple of villages too small for a church before, and the people there just had one of their own act as the postulant for the other villagers' prayers. If the postulant doesn't have to be a priest, maybe Gregor's people think you don't even need a postulant at all."

"But how would God hear prayers without a postulant?" said William. He was growing more confused by the moment. Could God hear prayers prayed without a priest? If God was really omniscient, then He certainly should have been able to hear prayers like Gregor's. That prayer had certainly been more important than many William himself had prayed before.

"God's supposed to know everything, right?" Colvin said, echoing William's thoughts. "Maybe he just…hears. I don't know." This was a conversation Colvin would have never dreamed of having just two short weeks ago. He would have been more worried about finding food and shelter than debating whether a priest was a necessary component of having your prayers heard by God.

"It was beautiful," said William. He had a funny, soul-searching look in his eyes.

"Everything the Highlanders do is beautiful," Colvin said. He was starting to get a little worked up himself. "They're just so…*poetic*. They're sort of like Ferdinan. They do everything with so much passion." Colvin had a brief mental image of Ferdinan in a kilt and tartan. He would have burst out laughing if the subject he was discussing with William had not been so serious.

"They take it as it comes," said William with a surprisingly knowing quality to his words.

Colvin looked at him with an arched eyebrow, throwing around in his mind what William had just said. "Yeah," he said, nodding. "Yeah, that's it. That's *exactly* it, William. They take it as it comes. Nice way to put it."

"Thank you," William said.

When they reached the northeast gate they found it overflowing with armed townspeople. Most were either constables or militiamen, but a good number were just regular Tamendaders brandishing a strange array of weapons that looked to be of questionable quality. A few stumbled around, betraying their inebriation. It was amazing how willing some men became to take up weapons after the liquor had been flowing. Most of the self-commissioned soldiers appeared to be behaving themselves, but a few were a bit overzealous, trying to convince anyone who would listen to follow them out into the darkness to hunt down the beasts like the dogs they were. Not surprisingly, the drunkest vigilantes were the most adamant supporters of forming a lynch mob. Colvin and William looked at each other.

"I think this is going to become a regular problem around here," Colvin said.

"I'm afraid you're right," replied William.

A constable quickly approached the two of them on foot, looking quite frazzled. William waved to him, and the constable waved back. "Thank God you're here, Lord William," the constable said when he drew near. "They're giving us a spot of bother, and most of them refuse to leave. All they're accomplishing right now is making our job difficult. Maybe some of them will listen to you."

A little ways off, closer to where the northeast gate had stood mere hours ago, a man – farmer, by the look of him – was hoisting a pitchfork into the air. "Come on, you pansies, follow me to glory!" he exclaimed to the crowd. William clenched his jaw, and Colvin noticed that the young nobleman's left hand came to rest on the basket hilt of his broadsword.

"I will have a word with them," William said coolly. The young constable nodded, looking appreciative.

"Try not to kill anyone," Colvin said. He was almost entirely joking.

CHAPTER SIXTEEN

A COUNCIL OF EIGHT

The head was beginning to stink.

McRofaly had done quite a good job in keeping it preserved, but at twelve days there was just no keeping it from heading south. The eyes had already shriveled up and rolled back deep into the oversized sockets. The ears were about to fall off. The gums were practically gone, and McRofaly suspected he would have been able to lift the two large tusks right out of the jawbone with his bare hands. The green, leathery skin had started to break open in places, the hair was falling out, and it filled the basement with the nauseating smell of decay. McRofaly did not dare touch it. He was not finished studying it and he could not risk damaging it in any way, especially now that it had rotted to the point that the slightest touch might cause irreparable damage. McRofaly needed it intact to learn all he could from it: cranial dimensions, dental structure, estimated brain mass, visual acuity – that was pretty much out of the question now that the eyes were turning into raisins – overall circumference and a host of other details most people would have found too grotesque to contemplate. None of it disturbed McRofaly all that much. Certainly what he had been forced to do in his pursuit of knowledge over the last two weeks had turned his stomach a few times, and he had found that a liquid diet suited him well these days. But ultimately, what he did he did for understanding, and McRofaly was the type of man who would do anything for understanding.

The head was quickly reaching the breaking point, though. At first it had been easy enough to deal with. McRofaly had just kept a clothespin on his nose and that was that. But one of the more disturbing things about decaying body parts, as McRofaly was well aware, was that being around them could make a man sick even if he could not smell the stench. In time, the eyes would start to burn and the skin would break out in terrible rashes and boils. It was because whatever agent caused the decay would spread to any nearby living hosts. McRofaly would not be able to keep the head much longer. That was a pity, considering how difficult it had been to liberate the corpse of one of the invading creatures of its head without being noticed. Perhaps after his academic quest was at an end he could pickle the head and keep it in a jar as a sort of trophy.

Business at *McRofaly's Magnificent Keepsakes and Aureate Regalia (Precious Hand-Carved Stones for the Lord or Lady)* was, for lack of a better word, dead. War had a tendency to do that to businesses that specialized in what the common man considered luxury items. Tamendaders were more interested in things like weapons and armor and buying foodstuffs in bulk quantities to hoard for use in a disaster than in the purchase of fine jewelry. McRofaly's business had been down since the first attack on the city, and the jeweler had already decided there was no pressing need to open his doors that morning. The facade of *McRofaly's Magnificent Keepsakes* remained closed up, cold and uninviting, and it fit right in with most of the other storefronts in that little section of the trade district, where moderately successful merchants operated their businesses out of their own homes. Black funeral swaths were as common as open doors. A good number of merchants had run off to join the militia when it had been announced, and after the battle the previous night business in the immediate area was way down. McRofaly expected no customers, and no customers came.

McRofaly sat at the large table in his basement, pouring over the latest addition to his library. The tome laid out in front of him was one of the bulkiest in his collection, several hundred pages in length, and the leatherbound book fairly reeked of dust and mold. The book itself had been outrageously expensive; having it delivered from Andoria had cost him a small fortune. The investment had been worth it to ensure the secrecy of the transaction. The scout he had struck the bargain with had absolutely no interest in academia, and McRofaly could rest relatively assured that the rider had not even bothered to glimpse at what he had been carrying. Even if the scout had snuck a peek, the author of the book had used such archaic and convoluted terminology that anyone without a good amount of experience studying arcana would have been hopelessly lost. McRofaly had no trouble following along with *A Compendium of Extraordinary Beasts*, though. He had been studying works like that since he was barely old enough to manage the strength to open them. His secret basement was stocked with a wide assortment of arcane lore acquired not only over his own lifetime, but also over the lifetime of Esten, the man who had overseen his instruction in the pursuit of arcanology. McRofaly's library was not very big, just three small shelves piled full of books and scrolls and maps, but as far as the rarity and value of what it contained, McRofaly's personal library rivaled even that of Governor Chamberlain. Unlike the Governor's personal library, no one besides McRofaly knew his existed. Such precautions were necessary for men like McRofaly, who studied the arcane. Certain religious authorities held the belief that the arcane was tantamount to the occult, and more than a couple of the books in McRofaly's collection could have gotten the jeweler tried as a heretic. McRofaly had no desire to die at an Inquisitor's hands, so he held closely to the last instruction Esten had given him before the old sage had died: "For men like us, McRofaly, trust is just another word for suicide."

Even for someone as well versed in the study of the obscure as McRofaly, *A Compendium of Extraordinary Beasts* was slow going. The problem was that there were just so damn many extraordinary beasts described in it. Whenever McRofaly thought he was finally on the right track with a certain species, he would find some minor characteristic – inverted knee joints, an extra set of limbs, a tail, a third eye, whatever – that simply did not fit with the creature whose head rested on the table in front of him. He had thought that once the book arrived it would be a rather simple endeavor to find a species that matched the physical characteristics of what had attacked Tamendad. As it turned out, there were a dozen species that nearly matched the traits of the invaders, but not a single one so far that hit the mark dead on. Of course, McRofaly had only managed to get about a quarter of the way through the book in the four days since it had come. The author of the compendium, some random scholar who called himself Loriallis, had a penchant for extensive diagrams and heavily annotated footnotes, and an annoying tendency to reference other works he had penned which McRofaly did not own. Loriallis was forcing McRofaly to work at a snail's pace, and McRofaly despised the man for it.

McRofaly sat back in his chair and took a long drag from his pipe. The smoke burned his lungs, but it felt infinitely better than the air that was soiled from the decaying head. He held the smoke in his lungs and put the pipe down, running his hands through his dirty black hair. He had forgotten to bathe since the book arrived. He had a tendency to do that when he was engrossed in his studies, and he forgot to eat almost as often. Not that he could really make himself eat with that hollow-eyed head staring at him. Ever since the eyes had started to go, McRofaly thought it looked downright creepy. It reminded him of something, but he could not put his finger on exactly what. He exhaled and took a moment to straighten his clothes, a mostly useless gesture. He had worn those clothes for four days now. He felt filthy.

He heard movement from upstairs, a scuffling across the floorboards in his kitchen. In an instant he was up from the table and ready to defend himself. His heart was pounding in his chest, as much from the skunkweed in his pipe as from his fear. He neared the steps that ascended from the basement into the kitchen, and just as he was about to start his way up his intruder appeared at the top of the staircase.

"How the twist did *you* get in here?" he said. The cat just meowed at him and started gliding down the steps. It was emaciated; each of its ribs were clearly visible under its matted black fur. McRofaly wished the damn thing could speak, so it could tell him how it kept getting in. McRofaly prided himself in the security of his home, but this annoying little furball seemed to come and go as it pleased. The last three times that McRofaly had slept, he had woken to find the thing curled around his feet, purring like it had just eaten a dozen canaries. The cat joined McRofaly in his secret basement and rubbed its head against the jeweler's leg, purring deeply. McRofaly looked down at it and sighed. He did not know how it kept coming back, but he did know why. The first time it had gotten in it had eaten the whole bowl of skunkweed right out of his pipe. McRofaly was not much of an herbalist, but he knew skunkweed would do for catnip in a pinch. He might as well have given the cat a twenty pound salmon. He was never going to be rid of the damned thing.

The cat jumped as if it could read McRofaly's thoughts. It took a moment for McRofaly to realize where the thing was heading. The cat was on the table and halfway to the head before McRofaly could react. "Oi!" he yelled. "That's mine! No! Dammit, cat, get down!" McRofaly lunged for the cat and planted his foot right on his walking stick lying on the floor. He cursed as he felt himself lose his balance, and suddenly he was no longer vertical. He slammed hard against the table. The cat scrambled, and books and papers went flying. The head began to roll. McRofaly screamed, righting himself as quickly as he could. The head was perilously close to the edge. It began to topple. It rolled off the table. McRofaly leapt for it. He scooped it into his hands just a moment before it hit the floor. It was safe.

McRofaly looked down at the head in his hands. It stared back at him with its hollow, raisin eyes. Revulsion clawed at the pit of McRofaly's stomach. He retched and let the head fall. The sound it made as it hit the floor – sort of like an overripe melon thrown against the side of a building – sent him over the edge. He sprinted upstairs out of his basement and emptied the contents of his stomach into the washbasin on the kitchen counter. When he was done he wiped his mouth with a towel and scrubbed his hands for a good while, then threw the contents of the washbasin out the window. There was no need to have that stinking up the place in addition to the head. Then, once he had composed himself, he returned to the basement. The cat had managed to chew the nose off of the head and was making a meal of it. McRofaly doubled over once more, dry heaves racking him. Thankfully his stomach had nothing left to lose. He shooed the cat away from the head, and found his prized trophy ruined. The face had split right down the middle, one of the tusks was broken, and one eye lay hanging out of its socket, dangling by a sinewy cord. McRofaly managed to get the head into a burlap sack without actually having to touch the foul thing, then threw the sack into the corner. He would deal with that foulness later. For the moment he busied himself with the much more pleasant task of straightening up the non-organic things that had fallen from the table during all the commotion. He picked up *A Compendium of Extraordinary Beasts* from the floor. It had miraculously survived the fall without being damaged. He laid the book carefully back on the table, then bent down to retrieve some of the other loose papers and quills that littered the floor. As he did so, something in the book caught his eye. McRofaly straightened and looked at it. It was a diagram – a very highly detailed diagram – of a head. Two tusks jutting from a pronounced underbite, a flattened nose, deeply set eye sockets, cranial circumference of approximately twenty-eight inches. The diagram was hand-drawn in black ink, but Loriallis's exhaustive footnotes specified the exact shade of green of the beast's leathery hide, a color somewhere between that of pea soup and forest moss.

McRofaly sat down at his table and leafed through the entry. He noted with a detached sense of interest that it was well past the halfway point of the book. It would have probably taken him another two weeks to get to it. McRofaly quickly scanned over the diagrams detailing the physiological characteristics of the beast. It was bipedal, roughly humanoid, with sloping shoulders, elongated arms and a body mass approximately fifteen percent greater than that of an average man of equal height. No inverted knee joints, no extra limbs, no tail, no third eye. McRofaly began to laugh – a giddy, high pitched noise. He quickly scanned the section on the beast's social and cultural habits. Finding exactly what he had expected to find, McRofaly clapped the book shut and stood up from the table. He could not stop laughing. The cat was in the corner, sniffing at the sack. McRofaly gripped the scrawny black thing by the nape of the neck, tucking the *Compendium* neatly under his other arm, and headed up the stairs into the kitchen. He closed the trap door behind him and set the cat gently on the floor. It looked up at him and meowed, its tail straight up in the air slithering wavily back and forth.

"Good kitty," McRofaly said. He rummaged through his cupboards and retrieved a sizable hunk of salted fish. He tossed it, and the cat pounced on it before it had even hit the floor. "I don't have any milk, so water will have to do for now," he said, setting a saucer on the floor beside the fish. He scratched the cat behind the ears. It completely ignored him. Its whole world at the moment consisted of dried herring. McRofaly left the cat to its feast. First, a bath and a change of clothes were in order. Then it was straight to the Governor's house to present his findings.

❖   ❖   ❖

William had never felt anything so entirely good as dunking his head in that particular rain barrel. The cold rush of water completely enveloped his head, simultaneously relaxing and invigorating him, waking him up and washing away so many of the stresses of the longest night of his life. Beyond its purely therapeutic qualities, the rain barrel also managed to completely insulate him against the outside world. Inside the barrel, all was dark and quiet. All the sounds of commotion were muted. He had the barrel all to himself, his own private little world without nervous militiamen and overzealous, inebriated townspeople eager to make heroes of themselves or die trying.

It had taken William and the rest of the commissioned men the better part of two hours to clear the vigilantes from the northeast gate. They had not gone quietly. The more the constables and militiamen insisted that the vigilantes go home and sleep it off, the more obstinate and impertinent they became. Toward the end, the self-appointed saviors of Tamendad became standoffish with the constabulary and militia. They accused the soldiers of being soft, weak and afraid. They had called the Pride of Tamendad useless and the constabulary a bunch of overpaid pansies. Then they started in on the insults about family members. William knew it was all just drunken brazenness, that the alcohol had channeled those townspeople's fear into effrontery, but that understanding had not kept the vigilantes from progressing from verbally abusing the guards to physically harassing them, and the young nobleman had felt some small measure of satisfaction when he had authorized Sword Division to use force in apprehending the troublemakers.

The night was rather uneventful after all the vigilantes had been put under custody of the constabulary, but the small hours had passed with frustrating slowness and everyone at the northeast gate had been on edge the whole night, jumping at even the smallest noises out in the darkness. Sunrise had seemed forever in coming, but now the sky was lit and William's watch was over. He was exhausted. He wanted to go home and collapse into bed and escape into the blessed obliviousness of sleep for as many hours as he could manage. He could not do that just yet, though. First he had a meeting to attend at the Governor's house. Word of that had come just before sunrise. Governor Chamberlain had called a war council, and William had been appointed to attend as the representative of Sword Division. William had mixed emotions about that. He was honored to represent his division of the Pride, but the words *war council* had really driven home to the young nobleman that what was going on in Tamendad was no longer a simple matter of defending the town against aggressors. William's city was at war, and he was caught up right in the middle of it.

For the briefest of peaceful moments, none of that mattered while William had his head underwater. All that mattered was that the rainwater had quickened him and loaned him the strength to go on a little longer without sleep. He would have probably stayed there with his head in the barrel for an hour or more if he could have. As it was, his lungs were already beginning to burn from lack of air. He pulled his head from the barrel with some amount of reluctance and wiped the water from his face. As soon as he did, all the stresses and demands of Tamendad rushed in to resume their place on his shoulders. William straightened his clothes and the sword by his side. He had had his brief respite. Now it was back to business. He turned back toward the wounded gate to go look for his father, but Jonathan was already walking toward him, waving. William waved back. His father looked no better than he did. Then again, there was no reason that he should. They neared within speaking distance.

"Shouldn't you be off to the meeting, William?" Jonathan said, looking at the position of the sun over the horizon. "You're going to be cutting it close."

"Yes, Father," William said, sighing the words unintentionally. He sounded like he had just been told to eat his cabbage.

His father eyed him with concern. "Are you all right, my son?" Jonathan asked, putting a hand on William's shoulder.

William sighed deeply. "I'm fine, father, just feeling the weight of the world at the moment."

Jonathan nodded. "You're doing a wonderful job, William, dealing with all these stresses at your age. You have earned a lot of people's respect, and that includes my own." Jonathan hugged his son.

"Thank you, Father," William said. The words did not take away his burdens, but they made them feel strangely easier to carry.

Father and son parted ways, and William headed toward the Governor's house. The sight of the fractured northeast gate had depressed him to no end throughout his entire watch, but the sight of the residential district almost crushed him. Black mourning swaths hung all over. No matter which way William turned his head, one was always in sight. He hoped that the whole of the town did not bear as many funeral banners as he saw around him at that moment. The sheer numbers would have been unbearable.

As he neared the Governor's house, William noticed a short, well dressed man bickering with the guard at the front gate. He was shorter even than Ferdinan and a bit on the scrawny side, with straight black hair and a trimmed beard. He had a long walking stick in his right hand and a large book folded under his left arm. William did not recognize the man, but he had no problem recognizing the guard. It was the one who had gained quite a reputation as a self-important nuisance for giving Don Ferdinan such a hassle after the first attack on Tamendad. If the short man was trying to gain entrance, he had his work cut out for him. William approached cautiously, doing his best not to draw attention to himself. That did not require much effort, as both the guard and the short man were focusing all their attention on the other. Their bickering was becoming heated. William drew close enough to overhear their conversation.

"You *have* to let me in!" the short man said. "You don't understand!"

"I understand two things, sir," the guard replied. "First is that you're trying to get into the Governor's house, and second is that *nobody* gets into the Governor's house this morning who was not sent for. I'm sorry, but that's Governor's orders."

"But the Governor would have sent for me if he knew what I had to tell him," the short man retorted.

The guard shrugged his shoulders. "If the Governor knew what you had to tell him, then he wouldn't have to send for you," he said smugly.

The short man's mouth dropped open, and he looked at the guard with a mixture of exasperation and disgust. "That makes *absolutely no sense!*" the short man said excitedly. "If the Governor knew what I had to tell him, the only way he would know is if I had told him, and the only way I could have told him is if he had sent for me. But the Governor *doesn't* know what I have to tell him, and so he hasn't sent for me."

"And that's exactly the reason why you can't go in," said the guard.

William scratched his head and tried to reason his way through what he had just heard. It gave him a headache.

"Look," said the short man, regrouping, "you're making this much more difficult than it has to be. There's nothing paradoxical about it. I have to see the Governor, because I have information he needs! I know what those things that attacked the city are! I already told you that!"

"And I already told you, sir, that no one is getting into the Governor's house that was not called for by the Governor himself. I'm just doing my job. Now I'm afraid I have to ask you to leave, or I will have to have you removed."

The short man's face tightened up into a most horrible scowl, and for a moment William was afraid he was going to use either the book or the walking stick – or both – on the guard's head. William stepped quickly forward. "Excuse me, gentlemen, excuse me," he said loudly as he drew near the two men. "I could not help but overhear your conversation."

The guard bowed before William, muttering a greeting, but the short man was glaring at him like he had just burst in on a private dinner. "Who are you?" he snapped at William. The guard shot the short man a most uncivil look.

"I am William Stuart-Camen, a commander of Sword Division." Technically that was not true. The Pride of Tamendad had no titles of rank. Then again, William had indeed issued commands to a good number of people since the previous night's attack, and those commands had been followed, so he supposed he was justified in calling himself that.

The short man nodded impatiently. "What do you want?" he said.

The guard straightened and took a step toward the short man. "You show some respect, or I'll teach it to you," he barked. The short man rounded on him. William threw up his hands and stepped between the two men, pushing them apart.

"Whoa," he said, "it's okay, let's just calm down." He looked at the guard. "It's all right. Tensions are running a little high this morning. Everyone's on edge. No harm done." The guard was looking past William, still focused intently on the short man, but he muttered, "Yes, milord," all the same.

William turned to look at the short man. "May I have a word with you?" he asked.

The short man nodded apprehensively. "Well it doesn't look like I'm going anywhere else at the moment," he said, still glaring at the guard.

"Good," William said, practically pulling the short man away from the guard. They walked a little ways down the length of the wall that surrounded the Governor's house, where they could talk without the guard overhearing. Once William felt certain he and the man were out of earshot, he cut right to the chase. "I'm meeting with the Governor as part of a war council this morning, and I might very well be able to get you inside. What's your name?"

The short man perked right up, seemingly forgetting all about the guard for the moment. "McRofaly," he said.

"Your full name," William clarified.

"That is my full name."

"McRofaly is a surname," William said.

"It's the only name I have," McRofaly insisted.

William shrugged. "Okay, McRofaly, did you mean what you said about knowing what those things are?"

"I never lie about what I know," McRofaly lied.

"Why are you just coming forward now?" William asked.

"I have my reasons," McRofaly answered.

"And I suppose that whatever you know, there's no way you're going to tell it to me and let me deliver it to the Governor."

"You are a wise man, Lord William," McRofaly said. Strangely enough, there was not a hint of sarcasm in his voice.

"Okay, I'll get you in to see the Governor, but you hear me now. If I find out you are lying about this, I will make sure you get thoroughly acquainted with the smallest, dingiest holding cell the constabulary has to offer. Understand?"

McRofaly did not flinch. "Perfectly," he said.

"Okay, then follow me and please, for God's sake, don't say anything snide."

McRofaly simply nodded. He and William walked back to the front gate together. The guard straightened, eyeing first McRofaly, then William. He did not look pleased.

"Master McRofaly will be accompanying me inside," William said confidently but not arrogantly.

The guard was taciturn. He did not look pleased. "Very well, milord," he said curtly. "Proceed."

William bowed and thanked him before passing through the gate. Much to his surprise, McRofaly did not even look in the guard's direction as he passed by. The two men walked side by side into the Governor's house and, after asking a liveried servant where the war council was meeting, proceeded up to the third floor of the house. The third floor was the most luxuriously furnished and extravagantly decorated. The Governor's bedchambers were located on this floor, as was his daughter's, but most of the rooms were devoted to meeting with advisors, liaisons, dignitaries, and ambassadors, and it was obvious that Governor Chamberlain spared no expense in making such guests comfortable. Lush tapestries and rare paintings adorned the walls, and a number of overstuffed benches and mahogany tables provided comfort in the hallways. William had no problems finding the room in which the war council was meeting. As soon as he reached the door to it, he turned to McRofaly.

"You'll have to wait here a moment," William told him.

McRofaly arched an eyebrow. "Why?"

"I can't just show up to the meeting with an uninvited guest. I'll have to ask the Governor if he will listen to what you have to say."

McRofaly rolled his eyes. "My God, do you people want to find out what you're fighting or not? This is insane."

"Calm down, calm down," William pleaded. "Listen, it's just protocol. How would you feel if someone just showed up uninvited at your door and tried to barge their way in?"

"They wouldn't be able to barge their way back out again," McRofaly said evenly.

William was not certain exactly what that meant, but he was pretty certain that he did not want to find out.

"Okay, all right, fine," McRofaly added at last. "But I'm helping myself to a brandy." He gestured to the decanter resting on the nearby table.

William opened his mouth to say something, then changed his mind and decided just to nod instead. He turned and entered the meeting room.

The room was a large rectangle, with windows all along the southwest wall. The center of the room was occupied by a large, circular oak table, above which hung a crystal chandelier. Ten high-backed, winged chairs sat around the table, and six of these were occupied. Governor Chamberlain sat with his back to the windows, so that he could see whoever entered the room. Don Ferdinan sat to the Governor's right and Captain Jefford to the Governor's left. The presence of those three men needed no explanation. Gregor MacDugal sat in the chair beside Ferdinan. He was there as the representative of Fist Division. Gunther sat one chair removed from Captain Jefford, and he was representing Shield Division. Colvin sat next to Gunther, and would have been unable to provide a decent reason for his presence if anyone asked him. All Colvin knew was that a messenger had shown up before daylight that morning telling him to be at the Governor's house by an hour past sunup, so here he was. William took the seat to Colvin's right. Everyone in the room was looking at him. Suddenly he felt like a little child.

"My apologies for my tardiness," William said, looking around the table.

"Think nothing of it," the Governor said. "We are all aware of the long night you've had, Lord William. Now that we are all here, we can set ourselves to the business at hand. First things first. Captain Jefford, could you please advise the war council of the latest numbers?"

Captain Jefford straightened in his chair. He had large, dark circles under his eyes. He picked up a parchment from the table, but he barely glanced at it as he spoke. "The preliminary reports from the attack estimate a total of sixty-six dead." Everyone at the table except the Captain, the Governor and Ferdinan gasped. Colvin shook his head. Gregor clenched his jaw. William closed his eyes and sighed. Gunther cursed. "Of that sixty-six, eighteen were constables, forty-one were militiamen and seven were town criers. Those numbers are likely to increase as the most seriously wounded continue to scale the summit. Also, preliminary reports currently hold the number of enemies killed at forty-eight. That number is also likely to increase as more bodies are located. We suspect a few corpses from both sides might also have been carried out on the tide."

"Thank you, Captain," Ferdinan said.

"Any questions?" asked the Governor.

Colvin meekly raised his hand. "Um, my question doesn't actually have anything to do with Captain Jefford's report," he said. "I'm just not entirely clear on exactly what I'm doing here."

Suddenly everyone in the room was talking at the same time. Gregor said, "I asked for ye t' be here, lad," at the same time Ferdinan was saying, "I requested your presence, Colvin." On one side of Colvin, William was explaining that he had asked for Colvin to be there, while on the other, Gunther said, "I thought you'd be good to have around for this," in his characteristically scratchy voice. Across the table from Colvin, Governor Chamberlain was trying to run down the list of everyone who had asked for the red-haired wanderer to sit on the war council, and although Colvin could not be entirely certain in all the commotion, he was pretty sure he heard Captain Jefford saying, "I was actually wondering about that myself." Silence fell in the room as everyone realized that everyone else was talking. Colvin looked around the table with wide, confused eyes.

"Oh," he said. "Okay."

A moment passed in silence, with everyone looking at everyone else.

"Aye, well," said Gregor at last, "I was at least one o' th' ones who asked for ye t' be here this morning, Colvin, and I shall explain m' reasoning. I have an announcement t' make." All eyes shifted to the big Highlander. He met everyone's gaze in turn. "Immediately after this war council, m' lads and I shall be leaving Tamendad on horseback and returning t' th' Highlands."

Silence.

Ferdinan placed a hand softly on Gregor's shoulder.

Governor Chamberlain nodded solemnly. "I understand, Gregor."

Gregor arched an eyebrow. "Oh really, Governor?" he said. There was something odd in his voice. "Tell me, what exactly is it ye understand?"

Governor Chamberlain squirmed slightly under Gregor's gaze. The way the big Highlander was looking at him was disquieting. The Governor spoke very delicately. "Gregor," he said, "you have paid as hard a price as anyone in Tamendad, and you have paid it defending a city that is not even your own. After the events of last night...after the loss you have endured...no one is going to question your motives if you chose to–'"

"Tuck tail and run?" Gregor interrupted. "Oh nae, Governor." His voice was calm, and disturbingly level. "M' lads and I are nae leaving for good. What those bastards did last night ensured that I am in this t' th' bloody end. M' lads and I are going t' ride back t' Duerhein, aye, and when we get there we're going t' rally th' troops. I plan t' march th' armies o' th' Clan MacDugal down their wretched green throats. Those bastards took m' little brother from me, Governor. I intend t' teach them a lesson in pain."

Everyone at that table silently thanked God that Gregor MacDugal was on their side.

"Now I cannae speak for anyone else, but th' reason I asked for ye t' be here, Colvin," Gregor said, turning his attention on the red-haired young man who was now sitting with eyes wide and mouth agape, "is because I'm leaving Fist Division in yer hands."

Colvin nearly choked. "Wh-what?" he sputtered.

"Fist division be yers, lad," Gregor repeated. "I've made m' mind up on th' matter. I want ye t' take m' place."

"Why?" Colvin asked. Part of him hoped he did not sound ungrateful, but another part of him was too surprised to care.

"Because ye're th' best man I've got. Ye teach those lads in Fist as much as I or any o' m' kinsmen do e'er time we train. They listen t' ye and they respect ye, and they shall do more o' both after last night."

The entire war council was looking at Colvin. William was not exactly smiling, but his look was close enough to it to make Colvin shift uncomfortably in his seat. On Colvin's other side Gunther was nodding his head in an infuriating manner, demonstrating his agreement with Gregor's decision. Captain Jefford and Governor Chamberlain were staring at him expectantly, awaiting his answer. Ferdinan was looking at him as well, and out of everyone at the table only the look Ferdinan was giving Colvin bolstered him in any way. The Conquian's look demonstrated both understanding and compassion. Only Ferdinan seemed to realize how difficult what Gregor was asking would be. Colvin could not even bring himself to look at Gregor. What the big Highlander was asking him to do was...well, it wasn't *impossible*, but it was pretty damn close. Colvin had enough trouble keeping his own life in order. There was no way he would ever be able to organize all of Fist Division. Even if the militiamen did listen to what he said, the job was just too big. Only Gregor could manage to hold that rowdy group of farmers and rapscallions together. And besides, that was entirely more responsibility than Colvin was asking for. Sure, he would fight those monsters and do his part to make sure Tamendad was as safe as possible for as long as possible, but being put in charge of Fist Division would completely bind his hands. He would be caught up in this war to the bloody end, as Gregor had put it. Not that Colvin was planning to desert anytime soon, but he had no intentions of dying for Tamendad either, and after the previous night's attack there was no denying the possibility that when it was all over, Tamendad would be wiped off the map. Colvin had to keep his avenues of escape open. There was no way he could take control of Fist Division. Simply no way.

A memory bubbled to the surface of Colvin's mind, a moment in the heat of battle. The invaders were pouring out of the night. Colvin stood ready, assuming the stance in both body and mind. The creatures were coming to take Tamendad away from him. They could not have it...

Sitting at the table of the war council, Colvin's eyes widened. It was more than just a memory. He had almost relived it. Everyone at the table was still looking at him, waiting for his response. Colvin looked out the window. There were hundreds of people in the town below who felt the same way, hundreds of people willing to fight for their homes who just needed someone to tell them how to do it. How would Fist Division hold together without Gregor? Who would hold it together? Colvin knew what Gregor said was true. The men and women of Fist Division did listen to him, and they did respect him. They would most likely follow him, too. Could he really take that much responsibility upon himself?

Another memory followed the first, latching hold to Colvin's brain: Malcomb's words, words never spoken in the real world, words from the underworld of his dreams.

Your inability to connect with other people on anything more than a transient level...

"I'll do it," he said.

Gregor nodded. "Thank ye, lad." He sounded as though he had not had a doubt that Colvin would accept. Obviously Gregor was not the best judge of character. William clapped Colvin on the back and congratulated him. Gunther pounded his first once on the table and loudly told Colvin, "You're gonna do great. I've got all the faith in the world in you." Colvin did his best to nod and act appreciative. He was feeling a tad bit nauseous at the moment.

Ferdinan's voice cut through Colvin's congratulations. "Gregor," the

Conquian said, "how many men do you think you will be able to rally, and how long do you espect your return to take?"

All eyes focused on Gregor, and Colvin felt no small amount of relief at no longer being the center of attention. The big Highlander gave his beard a thoughtful tug and ran his big fingers down the length of his *duál* before answering.

"Well, if I had naught concern for th' safety o' this city, I would nae return until I had gathered enough men t' crush those beasts like th' fist o' God. As it turns out, though, I have grown quite fond o' Governor Chamberlain's township here, so I dinnae intend t' leave ye high and dry for so long. When I reach Duerhein I shall rally what men I can in two days. That might be as few as only a couple o' hundred bodies, but if fortune favors us it could be that number thrice o'er."

The image of between two and six hundred Highlanders storming the battlefield, all fighting with the same ferocious intensity of Gregor and his kinsmen, danced through the minds of the men who comprised the war council. Gregor could almost read their thoughts.

"Now I shall warn ye," the big Highlander said, snapping the other men from their violent daydreams, "what it takes a group o' four men two days t' cover on horseback will take four days at th' least t' march a small army o'er. With th' two days spent rallying men, we're talking about a stretch of eight days, nine mayhap, before I return."

No one said anything for a moment, then Captain Jefford said, "There was a stretch of twelve days between the first and second attacks. Perhaps those monsters won't even show themselves again until after you are already back with us, Master MacDugal."

Ferdinan shook his head. "I do not think we should even hope to be so fortunate."

"I agree," added Gunther. "Better assume we're gonna have to hold this town against attack at least once before Gregor gets back. At least we won't be kiddin' ourselves."

Governor Chamberlain nodded somberly. "I believe at this point it is a foregone conclusion that our aggressors will attempt another invasion soon. The ferocity of last night's attack was on an entirely different level than the attack nearly half a month ago. I think it is safe to say that our enemy's resolve has escalated. While I sympathize with Captain Jefford's optimism, we must prepare for the worst. It is our task to devise a strategy to hold Tamendad at least until Gregor MacDugal can return with reinforcements. Suggestions?"

The seven men sitting at the table looked at each other in silence. "Governor, if I may," said Captain Jefford at last, "the northeast gate is completely destroyed and the city is wide open to attack. We lost over fifteen percent of our standing forces last night. It is my concern that Tamendad might well be indefensible, especially considering that we do not even know the nature of the beasts we are trying to defend it against."

"Actually," blurted William, "something has come to my attention that might be of assistance there." Now it was William's turn to feel six pairs of eyes focused on him.

"What do you bring before us, William?" asked Ferdinan, his tone communicating the urgency that everyone at the table felt.

William nervously cleared his throat. "Well, on my way here this morning I met a man who claims to know what those monsters are. He says he knows how to fight them."

"And you have reason to think his word es credible?" Ferdinan asked.

William hesitated slightly before answering. He really knew absolutely nothing about McRofaly. The sense of urgency McRofaly had displayed in trying to argue his way past the guard at the front gate would have been difficult to fake, though. "I have no hard evidence that what he says is true," William said, "but I believe him regardless."

Ferdinan nodded. "I implicitly trust your judgement, William. I believe we should hear what he has to say."

"Who is this man?" Governor Chamberlain asked, straightening himself in his chair. "More importantly, where is he?"

"His name is McRofaly, Lord Governor, and actually, he's waiting just outside, in the hallway."

McRofaly was one more brandy away from being drunk. Whoever William Stuart-Camen was talking to inside that meeting room, they were taking their sweet time inviting him in. If they were going to make a man with such important information wait, then he was going to take full advantage of the free drinks. He sat on the bench nearest the meeting room, walking stick propped up against the wall beside him. He held his brandy in his left hand, while his right was idly flipping the pages of *A Compendium of Extraordinary Beasts*, which was lying open on his lap. He was skimming the entry on the velusharok, the only known hexapedal herbivore in existence. According to Loriallis, the velusharok had a head on either end of its body, and it excreted waste through an orifice in the center of its underbelly. Also, brewing a tea from the clippings of the velusharok's claws was purported to yield an aphrodisiac of legendary proportions. McRofaly thought the velusharok sounded most interesting. Unfortunately its only known natural habitat was an island several hundred miles off of Conquia's northern coast, a trip he had neither the time nor the resources to make. He took a sip of brandy and began to skim the entry on the velusharok's mating habits, the understanding of which required a thorough familiarity with basic geometry and a strong stomach. His reading was interrupted when the door of the meeting room opened and William Stuart-Camen joined him in the hallway.

"Well it's about time," McRofaly said, looking up at William as the nobleman drew near.

"Oh my sweet God, how much did you drink?" William almost screeched when he saw the half-empty decanter sitting on the floor beside McRofaly's bench.

McRofaly thought William seemed a little tense. "Don't worry," McRofaly said, closing his book. "I've only had a couple. The bottle was only three-quarters full when I found it. I'm fline."

"You're *fline*???" William tried to scream and whisper simultaneously.

"What?" said McRofaly.

"You just said you were *fline*," said William. He was feeling a touch flighty at the moment.

"Did I?" said McRofaly, looking thoughtful. "Well, nothing to get so worked up over. Just a slimple sip of the tongue."

"I'm doomed," groaned William, rubbing his temples. He suddenly found he was getting a headache.

"William, for the love of God, calm down," McRofaly said, getting to his feet. "I'm kidding."

William looked at McRofaly with wide, desperate eyes, his hands still firmly planted against his temples. "You're kidding?" he asked, almost begged. "You promise you're kidding?"

McRofaly sighed. "I promise. Do you honestly think I would get drunk before addressing the Governor's war council? I've had just enough to loosen me up a bit and curb my nerves. I assume you're finally ready for me?" McRofaly snatched up his walking stick and headed for the door to the meeting room.

"McRofaly?" William said, a touch of impatience in his voice.

McRofaly turned to look back at William with an equal measure of impatience. "What?" he demanded.

"Leave the brandy."

McRofaly looked first at the drinking glass still in his right hand, then at the young nobleman standing with his arms akimbo. "No," he said, shrugging, then turned and nonchalantly proceeded into the meeting room.

When McRofaly entered the meeting room he paused for a moment to really take notice of the six men seated around the table. The six men in turn straightened to look at the short, well-dressed man who had just barged in. McRofaly could identify most of the people at the table on sight. Everyone in Tamendad knew what Governor Chamberlain looked like, and the same could be said of Captain Jefford. The physical description of Gregor MacDugal was almost as widely known. McRofaly guessed that the dark-skinned man with the hair the color of jet had to be Don Julio Franco Francisco Ferdinan. McRofaly knew Gunther Moragun from Tamendad's merchants' guild. That just left the young man with red hair and steely eyes, and McRofaly had absolutely no idea who he was or why he was attending a meeting with what were perhaps the seven most important people in Tamendad at the moment.

McRofaly swept his view over the six men and slightly bowed, muttering, "Good morning." Everyone at the table nodded and returned the sentiment. Before the conversation could go any further, William walked briskly into the room and positioned himself between McRofaly and the table, trying his best to pretend that nothing at all peculiar had just happened. McRofaly sidestepped around from behind William so that the young nobleman no longer blocked his view.

"So–" McRofaly began, but it was the only word he managed to get out.

"Gentlemen, may I introduce Master McRofaly," William interrupted, paying no attention to the sidelong look McRofaly was giving him.

There was a moment of uncomfortable silence.

"Lord William tells us that you may be able to shed some light on the nature of our enemy," Ferdinan said once the moment had come to an end.

"Indeed I will be, Don Ferdinan," McRofaly replied, bowing.

"Please," Governor Chamberlain said, "have a seat and share your knowledge with us." Out of everyone in the room, McRofaly knew Gunther best so he took the seat next to the short blacksmith. He sat his brandy and book on the table and neatly laid his walking stick on the floor beside his chair. William also reclaimed his original seat, and while the young nobleman was settling back in, McRofaly busied himself flipping open *A Compendium of Extraordinary Beasts* to the right section. Then he took one more sip of brandy and looked around the table once more. The Governor's war council sat on the edges of their seats, their collective attention focused intently upon him. If McRofaly had not been mildly inebriated, he would have been terrified. As things stood, though, he felt loose as a goose.

"The creatures that have twice besieged our town are frequently referred to as goblins or bogeymen by the fanciful tales that grow from man's imagination," McRofaly began.

William suddenly felt like he might vomit. He had brought a man before the war council who was going to waste everyone's time telling the types of stories young children told to frighten their friends and siblings when the lamps were put out at night.

McRofaly could feel the skeptical looks sent his way, but he pressed on. The facts would speak for themselves. "As is often the case, however," he continued, "a lack of genuine knowledge has created a warping of the truth. There is nothing supernatural about the creatures that attacked us. They are not bogeymen. The name by which they are known among those learned enough to study them is *goruk*."

Gunther's eyes widened. "Goruks," he whispered to himself, and it was spoken half as a statement, half as a question. The short blacksmith's voice was a blend of surprise and contempt. His was by far the most expressive reaction to what McRofaly had said.

"Something ye'd like t' add, Gunther?" Gregor asked.

Gunther, who had been lost in his thoughts, started a bit at being addressed. The short blacksmith looked around the table and ran his stubby fingers through his flowing beard. "My people tell stories about the goruks," he said. "There's legends say we fought a lot of bloody wars with them before the Great Burden, but they haven't been seen in years. Personally, I thought they'd all but died out." Gunther seemed uncomfortable talking about it. He shifted in his seat and avoided making eye contact with anyone but Gregor. McRofaly was giving Gunther a very suspicious look, but the blacksmith did not notice.

"All right then," Governor Chamberlain said, "What can you tell us about these goruks and how best to stand against them, Master McRofaly? You as well, for that matter, Gunther."

Gunther cleared his throat at being addressed by the Governor, and he almost sounded nervous. "I don't know much of nothin', just a bunch of myths and stories," Gunther said so gruffly that it came out as a near-grumble. He still was not looking anyone in the eyes for more than the barest of moments.

McRofaly leaned back in his chair and crossed his arms over his chest. "I, on the other hand, can tell you just about anything you want to know about them," he said with a mysterious sparkle in his eyes. In the next moment, the war council was engulfed in a torrent of questions.

"How do we fight them?" Captain Jefford asked.

"How can we hold the city against them?" Governor Chamberlain said.

"Why did our scouts not spot them?" asked Ferdinan.

"What's th' easiest way t' kill them?" Gregor demanded with a disturbing gleam in his eyes.

269

"You're sure it's goruks?" Gunther implored.

"Where do they come from?" William asked.

McRofaly raised both hands, gesturing for the men to still themselves. He was grinning widely. They were in the palm of his hand. He stood to gain much from being the man who informed the war council how to best face their enemy.

"What does *lorthok* mean in their language?" Colvin suddenly blurted out.

"What?" McRofaly asked, turning to look at Colvin with a furrowed brow.

Colvin returned the stare in equal measure. "What does *lorthok* mean in their language?" he repeated.

McRofaly's jaw dropped open slightly, and he began to thumb through the entry on goruks in the *Compendium* despite his certainty that he would not find the answer to that question. The other members of the war council exchanged confused looks with one another. McRofaly could not decide if he wanted to laugh, or curse, or both. Out of all the possible candidates, the mystery man had been the one to ask a question he could not answer.

"Well," McRofaly said, "I'm not entirely certain. Just out of idle curiosity, why do you ask?"

"Oh," Colvin said, straightening in his seat, "well, I've just been wondering about it since one of them said that word to me when it took me hostage."

"Ah," McRofaly said, nodding sagaciously and focusing all his effort on not reacting the way he wanted to react to what the red-haired young man had just told him. "I can see how that could pique one's curiosity. Unfortunately I am not thoroughly familiar with goruk modes of speech. My knowledge about them is of a more generally cultural nature."

"No problem," said Colvin.

McRofaly forced a smile around clenched teeth, turning his attention back to the council as a whole. "As far as your other questions, I have the answers for all of them," he assured.

"Excellent," Governor Chamberlain said. "Most importantly, Master McRofaly, how do we hold Tamendad against them?"

"Actually, Your Lordship," McRofaly replied, "I mean no disrespect by saying this, but the most important question that has yet been asked is William Stuart-Camen's."

"It was?" William asked, and he sounded like he could not quite believe it.

"Most definitely," McRofaly said. "Through an understanding of where goruks *come from*, as you put it, William, all of the questions about how to face them as enemies will be answered."

"Very well then, Master McRofaly," Governor Chamberlain said, sounding just slightly irritated, "can you tell us where these goruks come from?"

"With all due respect, Your Lordship, that question would become much easier for me to answer if we could relocate this meeting to your library."

The Governor was a bit surprised by McRofaly's request, and his look showed it. For a long moment Governor Chamberlain simply sat there quietly, strumming his fingers against the tabletop, looking thoughtful. McRofaly was putting an effort into not overstepping his bounds, but the Governor and his war council had to be made aware that McRofaly held the knowledge they required and that in this circumstance knowledge was most definitely power. McRofaly also knew, though, that Governor Chamberlain was not a man who allowed others to manipulate him, even subtly. Geoffery Chamberlain had to decide how much he was willing to give to get what he needed.

After a near-eternity of awkward silence, Ferdinan leaned over and whispered something into the Governor's ear. McRofaly wanted desperately to know what the Conquian was saying, but he resigned himself to looking as disinterested as possible. Governor Chamberlain and Don Ferdinan exchanged whispered comments for a few moments before the Governor once again turned inward with his thoughts.

"Very well, Master McRofaly," the Governor finally said, and McRofaly bowed as a sign of gratitude.

The council adjourned down to the library.

CHAPTER SEVENTEEN

THE MAKESHIFT TACTICIAN

"So what is all of this about?" William asked McRofaly as side by side they descended the flight of stairs leading to the ground floor.

"I already explained it," McRofaly answered without sparing a glance in the young nobleman's direction. "It will be easier for me to answer questions about the goruks if we are in the Governor's library."

"But why?" asked William.

McRofaly shot William a sidelong glance and sighed. He hated having to explain his intentions to anyone, and he did not entirely trust William Stuart-Camen. The young nobleman had been helpful, certainly, but he was still a member of the ruling class, and in McRofaly's experience there was no shadier lot to be found than the nobility. "Because a brief lesson in history and geography are in order, if my suspicions are correct," McRofaly said, and his tone was one that might have been used in telling a five year old to keep quiet.

They continued down the stairs together in silence. McRofaly was straining to overhear what Gunther and the red-haired man were talking about. Those two were keeping to themselves, walking a few good steps behind William and McRofaly, who were in turn walking a few good steps behind Governor Chamberlain, Captain Jefford, Don Ferdinan and Gregor MacDugal. McRofaly could not make out a word of what Gunther and the mystery man were discussing, but it was quite obvious that it was a sensitive subject. Perhaps McRofaly's suspicions about Gunther were correct. For the longest time McRofaly had believed that the short blacksmith was simply what he appeared and nothing more. It was, after all, a completely believable hypothesis. There were plenty of perfectly normal people who just happened to be really short. Little people, they were generally called. Some people called them midgets. The truly tactless called them dwarfs or spivs. Gunther Moragun was certainly stouter than most little people, but that did not necessarily mean he was not a perfectly normal person. Then again, a normal person would not have had such a startled reaction to the mere mention of goruks. A normal person would not have heard legends of wars against the goruks before the Great Burden. And a normal person would not have spoken of *his people* as Gunther had.

Was it possible that Gunther was indeed what McRofaly suspected? The prospect was fascinating. And yet the mystery of Gunther Moragun was not what was foremost on McRofaly's mind. McRofaly found that his thoughts were gravitating toward the man with whom Gunther was talking in hushed tones. What kind of question was it to ask what *lorthok* meant in the goruk tongue? It had no bearing on anything. It had been without a doubt the silliest question McRofaly had ever heard. And yet it had completely floored him, thrown him for the loop of a lifetime. What kind of man asked a question like that? Obviously a man who had been taken captive by a goruk, but that just raised the question of what kind of man got taken captive by a goruk and lived. The red-haired man was an enigma, something McRofaly could never have predicted and probably could not have prepared for even if he could have predicted it. And out of everything in the world, there was nothing that fascinated McRofaly more than an enigma. He could not just come out and ask the mystery man what his story was, so he did the next best thing under the circumstances.

"Who exactly is the red-haired man, anyway?" McRofaly said, gesturing over his shoulder.

"Huh?" William replied. His mind had wandered, trying to puzzle out exactly what McRofaly had meant, talking about geography and history lessons. So far he had not come up with anything.

McRofaly rolled his eyes and gestured more forcefully back over his shoulder. "The red-haired man?" he repeated. "Who is he?"

"Oh. That's Colvin. He's only been in town a couple of weeks. He's a house guest of mine, actually."

"*Colvin.* Where have I heard that name before?" McRofaly muttered, talking more to himself than to William.

William answered nevertheless. "He's a member of the Pride of Tamendad, a pretty important part of Fist Division. He'll be in charge of Fist while Gregor is gone."

McRofaly shook his head slightly. "No, that's not it," he said. "Wait a minute. Where is Gregor going?"

"To the Highlands, to bring back reinforcements."

"That's good to know," said McRofaly, but he sounded distant. He had heard Colvin's name somewhere else, sometime recent. Why did he remember hearing the name spoken in his own home? He had not had a customer in days, and the only other person who had been by recently was…

"Melinda," McRofaly said suddenly as a gear started turning in his brain.

"What?" William asked, musing to himself that this McRofaly was a strange character indeed.

"Colvin knows Melinda."

"You know Melinda?"

"We're acquaintances," McRofaly replied.

"Small world," said William.

"Tiny."

Gunther was the last man out of the meeting room, and he found Colvin waiting for him in the hallway. "What's eating you, Gunther?" Colvin asked him, voice full of concern, as soon as he was out of the meeting room. Gunther sighed and slumped his shoulders, and Colvin thought the short blacksmith looked like a cat that had gotten caught trying to open the canary's cage.

"I'm actin' like a damn fool, that's what," Gunther replied, shrugging. "It's just somethin' I though: was dead and buried in the past."

"Would you like to talk about it?" Colvin asked, doing his best to imitate Ferdinan's diplomacy.

Gunther laughed a little. "Bit young to try playin' mentor to me, aren't you, Colvin?" Gunther chuckled. "I suppose you're confused right out of your head with all that you've heard this mornin'. C'mon. I'll explain on the way down to the library."

They started down the hallway together. Gunther was quiet for the first few steps, mulling over where to begin his story. Colvin waited patiently for the short blacksmith to find his words.

"Suppose it all comes back to what I said about *my people*. That's as good a place as any to start." Gunther hesitated for a moment and looked at Colvin, who was listening intently. The face of the red-haired young man was a mixture of compassion and inquisitiveness. "What I'm about to tell you is gonna sound strange," Gunther began, "and you might think I've gone mad, but it's the honest truth." Gunther took a deep breath before continuing, and Colvin was about ready to jump out of his own skin from anticipation.

"I'm not human," Gunther said.

There were no words to describe the look that spread across Colvin's face except to say that it was the look a man can only have when one of his friends has divulged that he is, in fact, not human. Gunther was actually rather familiar with that look, and knew what it meant immediately, so he was prepared when Colvin looked at him with wide, confused eyes and said, "What?"

"I'm not human," Gunther repeated. "I know what that sounds like, but it's the honest truth."

"But if you're not human, what are you?" Colvin asked. It was plain from the sound of his voice that he was not quite buying what Gunther was telling him.

"My people are an ancient people," Gunther replied. "Some say we're even older than mankind. I don't know. Our oldest legends mention men, so probably not. Not that it really matters, anyway. The important thing is that while your people built their world aboveground, we were doin' the same beneath the surface. We are the Ganugamosh, descendents of Ganugamon, He Who First Carved the Way."

Colvin still did not quite believe what Gunther was saying, but his incredulity was beginning to subside, and a thousand questions were taking its place. "So why don't you live underground?" he asked.

"My family left the homeland four generations ago," Gunther said with a note of what almost passed for melancholy in his voice. "Every now and then that sorta thing happens, for whatever reason. We make good metalworkers and stonemasons. We have to, livin' underground like we do, and our work is usually in high demand among lightsiders."

"Among what?"

Gunther chuckled. "Sorry," he said. "That's what we call your people."

"Oh," Colvin said. Was he actually starting to believe it? "So is Gertrude a… Ganugamosh?"

"No, no, she's human," Gunther said. "I'm the first from my family to marry a lightsider. That's why I can't ever go back to the homeland."

"You can never go back to your home?" Colvin asked. Yes, he was starting to believe it, God help him.

"Oh, I can go back, but I can never *really* go back. Not for good, because my business is all wrapped up with lightsider business."

Colvin nodded. "So Gangis…"

"Is a halfblood."

"Does he know?"

Gunther sighed. "He knows the name of our people, some of our legends. I tell him what he wants to know. We don't talk about it much. It's never really been a part of his life. He looks at it like it's all ancient history, interestin' to hear about but not important in the here and now. He should know more." It obviously made Gunther uncomfortable to say that.

They had made it down the stairs to the first floor now, and they walked together in silence for a few moments. Colvin was having a surprisingly easy time accepting the notion that Gunther was not human now that his initial reflexive disbelief was fading away. After all, the goruks, whatever they were, were most certainly not human. At least the Ganugamosh were friendly and honorable, if Gunther was any indication. "What do your legends say about goruks?" Colvin asked at last, and Gunther grimaced.

"They're bad," Gunther said. He was gravely serious. "A lot of our legends were lost during the Great Burden, but enough survived to tell that goruks are nasty, brutal beasts…violent…savage." It unsettled Colvin to no end when he realized that the peculiar inflection he heard in Gunther's voice might just be fear.

From up ahead in the hallway leading to the Governor's library, McRofaly suddenly, loudly said, "Melinda." Both Colvin and Gunther arched an eyebrow and shared a confused look.

Governor Chamberlain, Captain Jefford, Don Ferdinan and Gregor MacDugal had all been brisk in exiting the meeting room, and through everyone keeping pace with Gregor's large strides the four men had soon put a good amount of distance between themselves and the others. Once they were alone, it did not take Governor Chamberlain very long at all to make his feelings known. "I do not think I entirely trust this McRofaly," he said. "No, I do not believe I trust him very much at all."

Captain Jefford nodded to himself. Ferdinan said nothing. Gregor shrugged his broad shoulders.

"I shall tell ye this, Governor," the big Highlander said. "I know just about e'er family line in Glenisle, and I have ne'er heard any mention of a family or clan by th' name o' McRofaly. Take that for what it might be worth."

"That is certainly interesting," the Governor said.

"Personally, I feel we have no reason to distrust McRofaly at this point," Ferdinan said. "He has not told us anything yet. I suggest we withhold judgement until he has been given a chance to present his case."

"He might be wasting our time, Don Ferdinan," said Captain Jefford.

"Es apparent by your own words to the war council that we are at a loss for how to deal with these goruks, Captain," Ferdinan replied. "Do you have a suggestion for how we might better spend our time?" Captain Jefford remained silent, but his look was shooting daggers in Ferdinan's direction. The Conquian seemed oblivious to the Captain's glower.

"We have a saying in th' Highlands," Gregor interjected. "A liar ties his own noose. If ye listen t' McRofaly's story long enough, any holes in it shall become apparent as they fall under scrutiny. A man can fake his way only so far before his fabrications come back t' bite him in th' arse. On th' other hand, if his stories hold up, then ye know what he speaks is truth."

"We could all use a little more Highlands wisdom in our lives, Master MacDugal," said Governor Chamberlain, to which Ferdinan whispered, "Amen."

Gregor chuckled. "Ah, well, as for that, Governor, 'tis what we've been trying t' tell ye Turish for years. I just hope this man dinnae take too long making his explanations so that m' lads and I can ride while there's still plenty o' daylight left."

The Governor looked mildly surprised. "I had assumed you would skip McRofaly's lecture so that you might be on your way, Gregor."

"Oh nae, Governor," Gregor replied. "Let it suffice t' say that I have a vested interest in finding out all that I can about th' goruks. 'Tis good t' know yer friends, but better t' know yer enemies." No one could deny the sagacity of that pearl of wisdom. "I shall tell ye this, though," Gregor continued. "If it turns out that McRofaly is wasting our time, he shall wish that he hadn't."

Ferdinan silently hoped that McRofaly was telling the truth, for his own sake.

"Master MacDugal," Captain Jefford began, obviously taking great care in choosing his words, "please know foremost that I am deeply sorry for what you have endured. However, as Captain of the Guard I must think of Tamendad's safety at all times, and it would be such an incredible help to the defense of the city if you could leave just one of your men here while you ride to Duerhein…"

Gregor cut the Captain off. "Thank ye for yer kind words, Captain, both for me and for m' lads. If it were up t' me, Liam, Gabrahn and Wallace would all be staying behind while I rode t' Duerhein m'self, but th' lads would nae hear o' that, and I know enough t' nae bother wasting m' time trying t' convince them when their minds are made up. I cannae blame them for wanting t' make th' ride. Angus was their kinsman." There was no hiding the raw emotion in Gregor's voice as he spoke his brother's name. Captain Jefford nodded, and that was the end of the matter.

The four men walked the rest of the way to the library in silence. They had just arrived at the door when from behind them they heard McRofaly say, "Melinda." Everyone turned and gave the short, well dressed man a quizzical look.

"Small world," William said as they reached the doorway to the library and met up with the four men standing before it.

"Tiny," McRofaly said, and flashed a smile at the Governor and his companions. Colvin and Gunther joined them a few moments later, and McRofaly flashed them a smile as well. The look he got in return from Colvin was hovering somewhere between curiosity and suspicion.

The eight men entered the library. "Well, now, Master McRofaly, here we are," the Governor said, and McRofaly clapped his hands and replied, "Why yes, indeed we are," without missing a beat. While the other seven men all watched, McRofaly set about the task of gathering what items he needed from the shelves. McRofaly had never been inside Governor Chamberlain's library before, but he was thoroughly familiar with libraries in general and had no trouble finding what he sought. Soon he had piled a good number of maps and books and scroll cases on the small table in the middle of the room. While McRofaly gathered his materials, he glimpsed briefly up at the Governor and said, "At some point I will need to speak with the scout who spotted the goruk army headed toward Tamendad last night, so it might save time to send for him now, in advance."

McRofaly had already returned his attention to gathering items from the shelves when the Governor finally replied, "Actually, Master McRofaly, I intend to see for myself if your story has merit before I grant any more of your requests." McRofaly turned from the bookshelves and locked eyes with the Governor. Neither man said a word. The Governor was an image of reserved calm. On the other hand, there was no overlooking the irritation behind McRofaly's eyes. A good number of thoroughly uncomfortable moments passed. Aside from William nervously clearing his throat, the library was engulfed in overwhelming silence. At long last, McRofaly nodded impatiently and said, "Very well then. Let us begin, shall we?" He set his attention on the books and papers stacked on the table and retrieved a scroll case that bore so many markings of age it bordered on ancient. "This is an original draft of Tamendad's town charter, and as it belongs to the Governor himself, I assume it includes a detailed historical account of the township's founding?"

Governor Chamberlain said, "What does the town charter have—"

"If we are to determine whether or not my story has merit, I must be allowed to tell it in the manner that best suits me," McRofaly interrupted.

Anger flashed across the face of Governor Chamberlain for the briefest of moments. He took a deep breath to compose himself and forced a nod. "Very well," he said. "You are correct in your assumption."

McRofaly nodded as he opened the scroll case and retrieved the papers within. He began leafing through the charter, skimming over the early history of Tamendad. "It might take me a moment to find what I'm looking for, but I suspect it will be near the beginning," he muttered distantly, not taking his eyes off the charter. "Ah! Here we are. I will read it for you so you do not have to all crowd around to see it." McRofaly cleared his throat and began to read aloud the entry he knew he would find.

"*Second Daimont, Year Seven Hundred Thirty-Seven Posteriori Cataclymian. Construction of the Church continues at good pace, and the town wall continues to go up as King Chamberlain continues to send lumber from the mainland. Patrum Demmias is kept busy treating an outbreak of hives among the men. His dual roles as Master Postulant and Master Healer are taxing him greatly. He is a great man to bear such responsibility.*

"Well, this is all irrelevant. Let me skip ahead to the important part...

"*The evening patrol reported spotting and giving chase to green men in the surrounding woods. Arrows were loosed by both sides, but the green men had disappeared into the woods before the patrol could draw near enough to engage them in hand combat.*

"The entry goes on, but it contains nothing of further importance." When McRofaly looked up from the town charter he was met with the sight of seven stunned faces.

"May I please see that?" Governor Chamberlain asked, gesturing to the page in McRofaly's hands. McRofaly acquiesced, and politely handed it over to the Governor for inspection.

"I will be damned," Geoffery Chamberlain whispered to himself as he read the entry. Ferdinan was reading it as well, over the Governor's shoulder, and he looked like it was taking every ounce of the Conquian's resolve to remain calm.

"Governor, es difficult for me to understand how you were unaware of this, in the charter of your own city," Ferdinan said with forced evenness.

For the first time in a long, long while, Geoffery Chamberlain looked sheepish. He had to put considerable effort into holding Ferdinan's gaze. "It has long been believed that the mention of *green men* in Tamendad's charter was a reference to the native Glenish and their pagan customs. To be honest, I had forgotten the mention of it was even recorded. The thought had not occurred to me until just now that it might mean something different," the Governor said delicately. Ferdinan said something in Conquian that sounded unpleasant.

"Actually, 'tis an understandable assumption, Julio," Gregor said. "Many o' th' Dammaugh still hold t' th' old beliefs even t' this day. Belief in th' green man is widely held even by th' Antrelican Glenish.

'Twould nae surprise me t' hear that th' Turish referred t' us as green men at th' first."

William and Colvin gave each other a look of surprise, though their intrigue had little to do with Gregor's talk about the green man. That had been the first time they had ever heard anyone address Ferdinan by his first name.

In response to Gregor's words, Ferdinan simply shrugged and said, "Still would have been good to know."

"There is more," McRofaly said, rustling the remaining pages of the town charter to recapture everyone's attention. "But before I go into that, will the Lord Governor reconsider my request to call for the scout rider?"

Without hesitation, Governor Chamberlain called for one of his servants and gave instructions to have the scout brought to the library with all possible speed. Once the servant had left them, McRofaly returned his attention to the town charter, recounting to the war council more of its stories about green men and the havoc they wreaked during Tamendad's founding. He read only the relevant parts, for brevity's sake, but noted to himself with interest that Patrum Demmias eventually had a nervous breakdown. According to the charter, the green men returned on 7th Daimont, this time leading a sneak attack in the early hours of the morning. They fled back into the woods as soon as Sir Isaac Dan, Tamendad's founder, rallied his men for a counterattack. After that incident, three days could not pass without another skirmish erupting, usually with the green men leading a sneak attack during the night. By 20th Daimont, all construction in Tamendad had halted and all men were commissioned by Dan to assist in the fighting. Heavily armed patrols were sent deep into the woods to search for the green men's stronghold. The early Tamendaders sustained heavy casualties, as the green men were reported to use "dishonorable, barbaric, and savage tactics," and that they "defiled the dead and wounded in unspeakable ways." As McRofaly read those lines, many members of the war council glanced in Gregor's direction. Those unflattering words had long been believed to have been written about the native inhabitants of Glenisle. If Gregor took offense to them, though, he showed no outward sign of it. The big Highlander was listening intently, paying particular attention to Dan's accounts of battles with the green men.

McRofaly continued with his abridged narration of Tamendad's early history. On 24th Daimont, Dan's men discovered the green men's stronghold in a dense patch of forest approximately fifteen miles south of Tamendad. On 26th Daimont, Sir Isaac Dan himself led every man under his command in a charge against the green men, and after a long and bloody battle Dan's forces won the day. Dan estimated that about half of the green men were killed, and the other half scattered. They never returned after the battle, and the construction of Tamendad soon resumed.

"So as you can see," said McRofaly once he was finished reading, "this is not the first time Tamendad has had to deal with goruks. They have been with us since the beginning." McRofaly rolled up the town charter and slid it back into its case, taking care not to damage the brittle paper. "Any questions?"

"Where did they go?" William said, while most of the other men asked the same question in different words.

"All the charter says is that they were scattered," McRofaly said. "They were never spotted again, at least not by anyone who had a chance to make record of the sighting. There are a good number of stories from the colonization of northern Glenisle of people getting lost in the woods and never being seen again. Some of those disappearances may very well have been goruk handiwork. But as far as documented sightings, we have none. Thus we know they did not remain in northern Glenisle. That leaves us with two possibilities. The first is that they went south. Gregor, are you aware of any stories from the Highlands about encountering this sort of creature around the time the Turish began colonizing?"

Gregor looked thoughtful for a moment. "Nae," he said, "naught that I can recollect, and I am fairly well versed in Highlands lore. Th' only beasts we have mention of encountering during that time were th' Turish themselves."

The Governor arched an eyebrow.

"As I expected," McRofaly said. "That leaves us with only one possibility. After the battle with Dan's men, the goruks went beneath the surface." There was a moment of silence, during which the war council expected McRofaly to say something further and McRofaly failed to do so.

"What esactly do you mean, *beneath the surface*?" Ferdinan asked.

"Goruk physiology makes the creatures equally adept at living underground as above. In fact, the proportion of subterranean goruks to land-dwelling goruks is believed to be around one-to-one."

"How do you know all this?" Governor Chamberlain asked.

"Let it suffice to say that I am a student of the obscure," McRofaly replied. After a brief hesitation, Governor Chamberlain nodded. McRofaly pulled a large, rolled-up paper from the stack of things and unfurled it on the table. "Now this you will probably have to crowd around for," McRofaly said, and the other seven men all squeezed together around him. The paper was a map of Tamendad and the surrounding areas, ending probably ten miles or so before the Highlands began. "Now Dan was not entirely clear in his account, but I believe that his men discovered the goruk stronghold somewhere near here." McRofaly pointed to a spot on the map where two decently large streams intersected southwest of Tamendad. "The soil there would be fertile enough for a moderately large pre-agrarian culture to sustain itself."

"The goruks are pre-agrarian?" Governor Chamberlain asked.

"Yes," McRofaly said. "Did I forget to mention that?"

"Yes, you did," the Governor said.

"Oh. Sorry. Yes, they are pre-agrarian. Scavengers, mostly. Some strains demonstrate a rudimentary understanding of horticulture."

Colvin furrowed his brow. He found it nearly impossible to believe anyone could actually spell words as long as the ones McRofaly was bandying about. Just trying to reason out the spelling of *pre-agrarian* threatened to give him a headache.

"There are no trees there," William said suddenly. "The town charter said the green men were found in a forested place."

McRofaly nodded. "Most of the smaller forests, including this one, would have been harvested out during Tamendad's completion, as well as the founding of Tantera and Andoria."

"Never wise to harvest somethin' til it can't be regrown," Gunther muttered.

"We know that the goruks did not reach the Highlands," McRofaly continued, "so they must have found a way underground before getting that far south." McRofaly scanned the map for a few moments, and most of the others craned their necks to attempt doing the same. "Here," McRofaly said excitedly and pointed to a spot on the map a few miles west of the intersecting streams. "This is the nearest cave to where the goruks were discovered by Dan, and it's still several miles north of the Highlands. Governor Chamberlain, does this cave lead far underground?"

"I am not certain," the Governor replied. "That cave has never been extensively mapped."

McRofaly cursed under his breath, more out of frustration than anger.

"That cave opens up into caverns that stretch across this whole island," came Gunther's gruff voice. Everyone in the library looked at Gunther with great curiosity, most especially Colvin and McRofaly. Gunther looked around at the seven men. The sheepishness the short blacksmith had displayed earlier had been replaced with an unflinching resolve. "Trust me," he said.

Before anyone had a chance to respond, the door of the library opened and a man entered. He was young, twentyish, with an angelic face counterbalancing an otherwise weathered appearance. He was tall and beanpole thin, but not gangly in the slightest. "Lord Governor, I came as quickly as I could," the man said, and he sounded slightly out of breath. He glanced around quickly at the other men in the library, but his attention stayed mostly fixed on the Governor.

"Ah, thank you for being so prompt," Governor Chamberlain told the man, then said to the rest of the war council, "Gentlemen, may I introduce Ian Morlocke, the scout rider whose bravery and quick-wittedness saved Tamendad."

Morlocke smiled, and he resembled a bashful teenager when he did it. "You flatter me," he said. "How may I serve?"

"A simple question, Master Morlocke," said McRofaly. "Could you please indicate on this map where you were when you first spotted the invaders moving toward Tamendad?"

Morlocke looked to the Governor, and the Governor nodded. Morlocke made his way over to the map lying on the table. Everyone else moved back a bit to give him room. Morlocke studied the map for a long moment and said nothing at first. He scratched at his chin and hummed a little.

"Well, keep in mind that it was dark, so I didn't exactly have my bearings," he said at last.

"An educated guess," replied McRofaly. "Please."

Morlocke looked indecisive for a moment, then placed his finger on the map. "There," he said with surprising firmness. "Maybe not *right* there, but close."

Everyone in the library shared an excited look. Ian Morlocke had just pointed to a spot within five miles of the cave.

"You are certain of this?" Ferdinan said. "Absolutely certain?" The Conquian was as serious as anyone there had ever seen him.

"Yes sir, Don Ferdinan," Morlocke replied, obviously curious about what all the fuss was over. "I was on my way back to Tamendad, and I remember passing this cave a little while before I saw them. The look of it in the moonlight gave me the creeps."

The war council's reaction was animated. There were more than a few whispered curses. Gunther slapped his hand down on the bookshelf and Gregor began cracking his knuckles. William began to chuckle, not entirely certain what he was laughing about. Captain Jefford muttered, "We've got them." Governor Chamberlain was just looking at McRofaly with an unreadable expression. Ian Morlocke was nearly beside himself at this point, and said, "Pardon me, but what is all this about?"

Ferdinan stepped up to Morlocke and patted him firmly on the shoulder. "You may have very well just saved your city for a second time," he said. Ferdinan, Governor Chamberlain and McRofaly took turns filling Morlocke in on the goruks, Tamendad's early history, and the significance of the cave. Morlocke's eyes grew wider with each word.

"I can lead men to that cave," Morlocke said hastily once the explanations were over with. "I could do it blindfolded."

Ferdinan once again patted Morlocke on the back, but this time there was a more fatherly quality to it. "Do not rush headlong into uncharted territory, especially when es full of things that want to kill you." Morlocke reluctantly nodded. "In time you might get your chance," Ferdinan continued. "For now, you must keep all of what you have heard to yourself. Es an order."

"Yes sir," Morlocke said.

"Don Ferdinan knows what he's talking about," William added. "I spent most of last night trying to prevent a bunch of drunkards from storming off into the night after the goruks. Imagine how many men and women might charge right into a slaughter if they knew about this cave."

Morlocke nodded somberly, eyes wide and full of concern.

"That will be all, Master Morlocke. Thank you for all your assistance," Governor Chamberlain said. Morlocke sprang to attention and bowed to the Governor before making his exit. Once Morlocke was gone, the Governor turned immediately back to McRofaly. "Why have the goruks come back now, after two and a half centuries of reclusion?"

McRofaly cleared his throat. "I cannot answer that question, Lord Governor," he said. "Fortunately, though, it is an ultimately meaningless question."

"What do you mean?" the Governor asked.

"It is irrelevant to ask why the goruks have chosen this moment to resurface. Their reasoning is probably based on a number of political, religious and cultural subtleties that have no bearing on the particulars of our situation. What matters is why they have chosen to come back at all, regardless of when they chose to do it, and the answer to that question is obviously to reclaim what they feel was taken from them when Tamendad was founded."

"'Tis a blood feud," Gregor said, mostly to himself.

"That makes them a much more formidable adversary," said Ferdinan. McRofaly nodded.

"So what do we do?" Captain Jefford asked.

It was time for McRofaly to earn his keep. He cleared his throat again and cracked his knuckles. Everyone was focused intently on him. He jumped right into it. "The first thing we have to deal with is the northeast gate. The goruks know it was completely destroyed, so they will focus future attacks there, at least at first. Subterranean goruks are uncomfortable in bright light, so attacks will come at night. First, every night, build two great bonfires at the northeast gate. The light and heat will deter them. Build those fires no matter what. If we have to send out parties to harvest lumber, send them close to midday, when they will be in least danger of an attack. If it rains, douse the bonfires in alcohol and lamp oil to make them burn. Those fires are essential. And for God's sake, make sure they are far enough removed not to threaten the walls.

"Second, gather as many carts and wagons and crates as possible. The more the better, the heavier the better. Anything that will impede entrance to the city. Position all of them just inside the northeast gate. If any sailors actually stay docked after last night, tell them they will have to use another gate to enter the city.

"The next thing to address is the city guard. Rework the schedules of the constabulary and the militia so that ninety percent are on duty throughout the night. Ten percent will be enough to raise an alarm if the goruks actually try to surprise us with a daytime attack. At night, station half the men at the northeast gate and the rest throughout the city. During the day, station all the soldiers at the northeast gate. Holding that gate is our top priority. Also, concerning the guard, I know we took heavy casualties last night. Fortunately, the goruks have not yet had an opportunity to discover how many were killed. It is unlikely that they would send a scout out last night, when they knew we would be most on guard. Ideally, we would bury the casualties within the city walls to conceal their number, but there is simply no space for that. So instead, we must bury them all in a communal grave."

"Many families of the deceased will object to that," Governor Chamberlain said.

McRofaly nodded. "You will have to make a speech about it, Lord Governor. Tell the townspeople that the deceased are being buried communally as heroes, to commemorate what they did for Tamendad together. Say that a plaque will be made listing all the individual names after the current conflict is resolved. If there are still a good number of families who refuse, you will simply have to make the mass grave an executive order. This is war, and war quickly becomes ugly even off the battlefield.

"We must also do what we can to make our forces appear greater than they are. I suggest stuffing clothes full of straw so that they look like men. Position them around town. After last night, there are a lot of weapons with no one left to use them. Put weapons in the straw men's hands so that they look like guardsmen. They will have to be kept away from the walls, because the facade will only hold up from afar, but it should serve to make it appear that we have more men than we really do to any goruks who manage a glimpse into the city."

"What happens if the trickery es discovered?" Ferdinan asked.

"That would be manageable," McRofaly replied. "If the goruks discovered the straw men, they would likely become overconfident. That could work to our advantage, because Tamendad still has a formidable force defending it. Underestimating what the constabulary and militia are capable of could be costly for the goruks.

"The next matter is the townspeople themselves. Governor Chamberlain, when you make your address about the communal burial, you should also mention everything else that has been discussed here, with the obvious exception of the cave. The townspeople must be brought up to speed on what it is we are facing in this war. After last night's attack, rumors are no doubt starting to spread. If left to their own devices, the townspeople will soon have painted the goruks as the specters of our nightmares made flesh, and I can assure you that as stories of the goruks' fearsomeness grow, the townspeople's resolve to stand against them will diminish proportionately. The people of Tamendad must know that the goruks are flesh and blood, and that they bleed and die just as easily as we do. More importantly, for reasons of morale, they should know that Tamendad has faced this enemy before and persevered. They must believe that this enemy can be defeated. Last night's stand helps, but there is still much to be done. Also, the townspeople should stay as far away from the northeast gate as possible, both for their own safety and for the safety of the guard. The townspeople could distract the constabulary and the militia if they're allowed to just come and go as they please. And this decision is ultimately yours, Lord Governor, but I wholeheartedly suggest placing restrictions on who can enter and leave the city.

"That brings us to the cave itself. The most obvious solution would be to cave it in. Do we have the means to do that?"

Governor Chamberlain and Captain Jefford looked deeply contemplative for a long moment. Eventually, both men shook their heads. "I do not believe so," Governor Chamberlain said. "At least, none that would allow us to collapse the cave without alerting the goruks in plenty of time to stop us."

"As I expected," McRofaly said.

"Black powder could probably do it," Ferdinan mused. Everyone except McRofaly looked at Ferdinan as if the Conquian had just said that flibberting gibbets could probably do it.

"What exactly is black powder, lad?" Gregor asked.

"Es a...how do you say?...*combustible*. Es very rare, very costly to make and very, very powerful."

"I've heard stories of black powder," McRofaly said. "If the stories are true, it should most certainly be able to collapse that cave. Do you have any with you, Don Ferdinan?"

"Regrettably, I do not," Ferdinan replied. "Es a rare commodity, even in Conquia. The flagship of the Conquian Armada keeps a small supply onboard, but es probably back to Conquia by now. It would take several weeks to have some sent."

"This will all be over in several weeks, one way or another," McRofaly said. "So collapsing the cave is out. That leaves us with really only one option. That cave must be under surveillance at all times, day and night. There must always be a scout watching it, with orders to return to Tamendad and warn us immediately if anything stirs. Obviously we must have men on this that we can trust not to say anything of it to anyone. Morlocke seems like a good man. I would suggest putting him in charge of the surveillance effort. Let him choose the men he wants under his command, but make sure he knows you have the final say on the matter, Governor. Like I said, we cannot afford to let word of this cave get out, so we must be very selective in who we allow to watch it. Also, we will need men who can watch the cave without being spotted. The goruks cannot yet be aware that we know where they are hiding. We must not tip our cards too early, or we would be throwing away a number of tactical advantages that we cannot afford to lose."

There was a long moment of silence in the library.

"May I please have a glass of water?" McRofaly asked at last. "My throat is bone dry."

Governor Chamberlain immediately called for a servant to bring a pitcher of drinking water for Master McRofaly.

"For a citizen, you make an amazing tactician," Captain Jefford said.

"Thank you," McRofaly replied. "I try."

CHAPTER EIGHTEEN

HOPE

Liam, Gabrahn and Wallace had their belongings packed and the horses saddled. There was a buzz around the Crown Rose, not only from the men and women who passed by in the street to ogle the Highlanders preparing to depart, but from the waitstaff of the Crown Rose itself. The Highlanders were leaving. In itself, that was more than enough cause for despair. The Highlanders had twice played a major role in defending Tamendad from invasion. Losing them would be devastating to the war effort. But the despair was counterbalanced by the spreading knowledge of why the Highlanders were leaving. Liam, Gabrahn and Wallace had not wanted to make it known that they were riding for reinforcements, but it became quickly apparent as they prepared for their journey that the townspeople had to be told something; otherwise the situation would have quickly grown out of control. Before an hour was up, news of Highlander reinforcements was spreading like wildfire throughout Tamendad. As is wont to happen, the story grew with each retelling. Some townspeople claimed that reinforcements were already on their way. A few swore that they had already arrived. The foolishly optimistic were spreading word that the Highlanders had already intercepted the invaders on their way to Tamendad and had killed them all. Whenever Liam, Gabrahn or Wallace was asked about it, they would always set the record straight as to what exactly was going on, but for the most part they just busied themselves with getting ready for their ride. The horses had been well kept and had grown restless, ready to run. They would get their wish soon.

Gabrahn was just strapping the last saddlebag into place when Gregor and Ferdinan walked up the cobbled path to the Crown Rose, and Gabrahn communicated his frustration with all the stories running wild around town by just shaking his head, rolling his eyes and sighing. Gregor patted Gabrahn on the back and nodded. "People tell fanciful tales when luck runs hard," Gregor told him, and Gabrahn nodded, still looking frustrated. Gabrahn was still wearing Angus's claymore on his back, and with each passing hour that he wore it, the great blade looked more and more like it belonged on his back. He had not taken it off since the funeral. He had even slept with it on, which was no small feat to accomplish without suffering serious injury.

"We're ready t' ride," Gabrahn said, patting his horse on the flank. The stallion neighed and shuffled its rear hooves a bit at the pat as if to say he was ready to go. "Liam and Wallace are inside, making sure we dinnae forget anything. I'll fetch them."

"Nae," said Gregor. "I shall do it. Make sure th' horses are ready."

Gabrahn nodded and said nothing, turning his attention to checking straps and buckles he already knew were secure. Gregor and Ferdinan continued up the path and into the Crown Rose. The common room was empty, as usual, and they walked straight through it. In the main dining room the waitstaff were doing a good job of looking busy despite the fact that they really had nothing to be doing. Everyone turned when Gregor entered. There were a good number of questioning looks. No one said a word. Liam and Wallace descended the stairs empty-handed. They looked tired, even though they had slept. When they saw Gregor down below, they hurried to him.

"Everything's ready t' go," Liam said. "Shall we ride?"

"Aye," Gregor said. "We've work t' do. But first I need t' find Master Mayhew, so that I might settle up with him."

"That will not be necessary, Master MacDugal," came the voice of Torrance Mayhew from behind Gregor. Gregor turned and saw the proprietor of the Crown Rose standing in the doorway that led to the kitchen. Gregor walked over to him so that the two of them could speak privately.

"What exactly do ye mean by that, sir?" Gregor asked.

"I mean we will settle your bill when you come back to stay with us again," Mayhew said. "Which, may I add, I hope is very soon."

"That's a lot o' money we're talking about, lad," Gregor said. "I shall not lie t' ye, there's a chance I might not make it back t' pay ye, if m' luck turns sour and I happen across a group o' those beasties on m' way t' th' Highlands. 'Twould probably be in yer best interest t' go ahead and settle up with me now."

"Then I suppose your unsettled bill will have to serve as your inspiration to stay alive, because I really quite insist on the matter," Mayhew said.

"Master Mayhew, sir, ye're a good man, and I thank ye kindly," Gregor replied.

"The Crown Rose will always have a room for you, Master

MacDugal. Anytime." Gregor nodded and gave Torrance Mayhew a pat on the shoulder. Mayhew nodded firmly in return. "Godspeed, Gregor," he said.

❖   ❖   ❖

While Gregor was speaking privately with Torrance Mayhew, Ferdinan took the opportunity to have a word in private with Liam and Wallace. "Es very brave of you to make this trip with Gregor," he said quietly. Liam and Wallace looked at each other.

"What exactly do ye mean by that?" Wallace asked.

"I mean es brave of you to go with him, to make sure he es safe."

"Did Gregor tell ye that?" Liam said. He looked a little concerned.

"No," said Ferdinan. "I figured it out for myself. Es obvious when you really think about it. The two of you, and Gabrahn as well, are honorable, selfless men. Under normal circumstances, I know the three of you would choose to stay here and help the city fight this war. But you also know the pain Gregor es enduring, and you know that if you let him ride to the Highlands alone, he es as likely to charge headlong against those creatures himself as he es to actually make it to Duerhein and rally men to fight. You are good friends to go with him."

"Thank ye, Ferdinan," Liam said. "Ye are so good a judge o' character I suspect ye have some Highlands blood flowing somewhere in yer veins."

"Es highly unlikely, though it would be an honor to share the blood of so high-minded a people. The only reason I bring this subject up es because I hope to give you a word of advice for your journey, if I may." Ferdinan was speaking in little more than a whisper now to make sure that Gregor could not overhear him.

"O' course," Liam said, equally quiet.

"There es a cave to the southwest of here. Gregor knows of it. Es where those monsters – they are called goruks – have their stronghold. If Gregor mentions heading for it or shows any signs of veering toward it, you must do whatever it takes to restrain him. Es for his own safety. His wound es too fresh. His loss may cloud his judgement." Ferdinan was the embodiment of urgency. Liam and Wallace both nodded somberly.

"Aye, we shall keep that in mind," Liam said. "Ye are a good man, Don Ferdinan. I can see why Gregor thinks so highly o' ye."

Ferdinan and the Highlanders had no chance to say anything further on the matter, because at that moment Gregor rejoined them. "Well, that's settled," the big Highlander said, rubbing his hands together. "Let's be about it, shall we, lads?"

"Aye," Liam said. "We've burned a fair amount o' daylight already."

291

"I will ride out with you a ways," Ferdinan said.

Gregor looked him over and nodded. "It shall be good t' have yer company for a while, lad," Gregor said.

They departed the Crown Rose and found Gabrahn outside explaining to yet another townsperson that no, reinforcements were not already on the way regardless of what stories were going around. It was obvious the townsperson was desperately trying not to believe what the Highlander was telling him. Gabrahn gave up on trying to convince the man and made his way over to join his kinsmen. "Hopeless," Gabrahn said, looking at Gregor. "We had better ride soon if we're t' get some men back here in time t' satisfy th' locals."

"Aye, there's nae need t' keep th' good men and women o' Tamendad waiting. Mount up, lads." The Highlanders took to their mounts. Ferdinan borrowed a stallion from the Crown Rose's stables. Together the five men rode to the southwest gate. The crowds in the streets parted before them, looking up at them as if gods were riding through the streets of Tamendad that morning. There was unmitigated desperation in the faces that looked up at them, and Gregor could see it as plain as day. Gregor MacDugal and his lads were Tamendad's Great Hope. They would ride off into the lion's den without regard for personal safety, and they would return with a host of warriors to turn back the invading armies. They would save the day. They had to, because if they did not, the alternative was unthinkable.

"I dinnae like th' way they stare at us," Gabrahn muttered just loudly enough to be heard by his companions. The townspeople's expectant looks were unnerving him.

"Ah, Gabrahn, that's easy t' fix," Wallace said. "Just pretend they're all a bunch o' pretty lasses."

"And how is that supposed to make it better, lummox?" Gabrahn asked.

"Well now, Gabrahn, if they were all pretty lasses, then ye could rest assured that they would all be looking at me instead o' ye," Wallace explained. Ferdinan laughed heartily at that.

They were surprised to find Governor Chamberlain awaiting them when they reached the southwest gate. A group of townspeople had also gathered there, and the bricked street was littered with flowers for their horses to walk on. All the constables present at the southwest gate sprang to attention when the Highlanders came into view. It was nothing short of a hero's sendoff. Gregor reigned in, and the Governor approached his horse. The big Highlander did not dismount. He did not want to seem rude, but he was in a bit of a rush.

"Master Ferdinan, have you decided to accompany *Moirear*

MacDugal to the Highlands as well?" the Governor asked.

"No," Ferdinan replied, "I am just riding out with them to see them off. I will return shortly."

The Governor nodded, then turned his attention to Gregor. "This will be brief," he said. "I know you are eager to be underway. I just wanted to tell you, on behalf of Tamendad, but more especially on behalf of myself, thank you. We owe you a debt of gratitude that can never be repaid." A murmur ran through the crowd at what the Governor did next. Geoffery Chamberlain dropped to one knee before Gregor's stallion and bowed his head. He did not stay down long, only a few moments, but the message was clear. Gregor was not quite sure what to say. Thankfully, the Governor did not give him time to say anything. "Godspeed, Gregor MacDugal," Governor Chamberlain said loudly. "I pray you return to us safely, and swiftly." The Governor then turned toward the gate and exclaimed, "Gatekeeper! Open the gate! Five to ride forth." The southwest gate slowly began to creak open.

"Fortune kiss ye and God keep ye, Governor," Gregor said.

"Amen," the Governor said.

Once the gate was opened wide enough, Gregor gave the signal and snapped his reigns, leading his lads out of Tamendad. The crowd erupted into cheers, but the sound quickly faded behind them as they rode through the gate. The rolling hills of northern Glenisle met them, and they covered them at a full gallop. They crested the hill that William and Melissa had shared so many picnics on and Tamendad disappeared behind them. The horses ran fast and free, overjoyed to be out of the stables. They were full of spirit. It would be needed.

Ferdinan rode with the Highlanders for a good while, until they came to a place that he and Gregor recognized on sight though neither man had ever lain eyes on it before. A stream carved its way through the land from east to west, while another one did the same from northwest to southeast. Gregor reigned in at the place where they intersected. The whole area was covered in wildflowers and berry bushes, and several tubers poked their heads up through the black soil. The air was sweet there, vibrant and full of life. There were no trees around, but it would not have taken long to cultivate an entire forest in that rich soil. It was as pastoral a setting as any of the men had ever seen, and Liam, Gabrahn and Wallace could not understand why Gregor and Ferdinan looked so uneasy. The big Highlander and the Conquian were looking all around as if they expected a trap to be sprung at any moment.

"This was where it all started," Ferdinan said. He could almost hear the war cries and the clang of steel against steel echoing through two and a half centuries to find his ears. A chill ran up his spine. His skin was covered in goosebumps. He was not scared, not quite, but this place was just a little too real for him.

"Aye," said Gregor after a time. "This was where it started. And it ends back there, in Tamendad. I promise ye that, lad." Ferdinan and Gregor looked at each other for a long time.

"You will be in my prayers," Ferdinan said.

"Aye, and ye in mine," Gregor replied. "This is where we part ways, m' friend."

"For a little while."

"Aye, a little while."

Gregor and Ferdinan dismounted and embraced. If such a thing was possible, Ferdinan was actually squeezing harder. When the two men broke the hug, Ferdinan's eyes were glassy. "You must be careful," the Conquian implored.

"Aye," Gregor said, mounting his horse again. "And ye must hold th' city till I return. Tamendad must stand. It must." *I will nae let Angus have died in vain.*

"God goes with you, *compagnos*," Ferdinan said, raising a hand to the Highlanders. Gregor returned the gesture. A light breeze picked up. The sun disappeared behind a cloud. A fish splashed in the water, trying to catch a fly on the surface. Time stood still for a moment. Then Gregor snapped the reigns, and his horse charged across the stream and out into the countryside. The other Highlanders followed.

Ferdinan stood there for a moment and watched them go. Once they were out of sight, he made the Sign of the Compass, wiped the tears from his eyes, and headed back toward Tamendad.

The Pride of Tamendad did not train that morning, due in part to the fact that two of its divisions had been up the entire night. An announcement was made soon after the Highlanders had departed that Colvin was taking charge of Fist Division, and the red-haired wanderer was a little surprised at the reaction with which the announcement was met. There was a good degree of downheartedness in Fist over the loss of the Highlanders, as Gregor and his lads had become well respected, but the overall consensus was that Colvin would make an adequate replacement until the Highlanders returned. Not a single person objected to Colvin being put in charge, even though he was one of the youngest men in Fist Division, and an outsider to boot. Gregor had been right about how well liked and respected Colvin was among the men and women of Fist Division.

Colvin met briefly with Fist Division that morning to fill them in on what was going on with Gregor and his lads, and to do his best to prevent anyone from thinking the Highlanders had abandoned them. There was almost none of that sentiment going around, as everyone in Fist Division had already heard the stories of reinforcements. As Colvin spoke to them, he was continuously amazed at the way everyone was paying attention to him, heeding his words and promptly agreeing with everything he said. They were following him, a homeless boy with a shady past who up until about two weeks ago had no prospects for the future. He did not command their attention quite so easily as Gregor had, but they followed him just the same.

Once his address to Fist Division was at an end, Colvin walked around town for a while, just trying to process how much had happened to him since stumbling across Tamendad. The last two weeks had been a whirlwind. In some ways it felt like he had been in Tamendad barely more than a day. In others, it seemed like a year had passed since waking up to Lorthok's scimitar in his face. He was a different person now than he had been then. The old Colvin was fading away. The man who was taking his place was strange and alien and uncharacteristically optimistic about the future, especially in the middle of a war.

It was midmorning, perhaps ten o'clock, and Colvin still had plenty of time to kill before meeting Melinda for lunch in the market. He was not even certain the market would be open that day, after the events of the previous night, but he had every intention of making good on his invitation from Melinda. Even with all that had happened since, he was still completely bewildered by the dark haired silversmith. Melinda was not like any woman he had ever met before. If only he could figure out if that was a good thing or a bad. After pondering these thoughts for a while, Colvin looked up to realize that he had walked in a circle and was now right back in the town square, in front of the church. It was still abuzz with the activity of mending the damages, both physical and spiritual, of the previous night's attack. Colvin was inside the sanctuary before he even realized he had decided to go in. So many prayer candles had been lit that there was not enough room for them on the dais that usually held them, and several had been set up on the floor around it. Puddles of white wax covered almost everything in that corner of the sanctuary. Flowers had also been laid haphazardly among the candles. Some of these had already burned down to ash. Others were encased in wax. A few small trinkets, personal belongings of the deceased, had been laid among the prayer candles as well, in the hopes that they might help remind the Creator of who exactly that particular prayer candle had been lit for. Colvin found the scene uplifting and heart-wrenching at the same time. He did not bother trying to find a candle to light. He knew he would not find one. Besides, there were more pressing prayers to be heard than anything he would come up with, he was certain. At the front of the church, standing before the altar, Master Postulant Dunleavy looked to be on the verge of collapse. Had he been at it since the attack? How much longer did he intend to tend the flock? How much more could he possibly have left to give?

Colvin settled down into a pew near the back of the sanctuary. He watched in silence as the line of townspeople waited their turn to say their prayers. No doubt many of them had already been before the Master Postulant at least once already, but when it came to ushering your loved one's soul into the next world, who was to say how much prayer was enough? Colvin felt the curious tug of grief on his heart as he sat there watching, and he wondered why. He had not lost anyone in the attack, unless he counted Angus, but even then he had really known Angus for only a few days, and Gregor's brother was not a man Colvin would have called a close friend. Certainly he was sad the Highlander was gone, but it was not like he had lost a member of his family. For that matter, he did not have a family to lose. He was a wanderer, an outcast, alone in the world, self-reliant and self-assured. He was free.

Well, not so free now, he thought. *Not now that you're in charge of Fist Division. You're locked into it now, just like the rest of them.*

Just like the rest of them. Colvin suddenly realized why his heart was grieving. He was sharing the townspeople's pain. He was feeling their loss. He was a part of the town now, if not officially then at least in spirit. What affected the town affected him and, to a degree, vice versa. For the first time in Colvin's life he had the sensation of belonging to something larger than himself. The feeling was unqualifiably strange. Even more peculiar was the sensation, distant and elusive, that the larger thing he was a part of was in turn a part of something larger still. He felt like he was on one strand of an expansive web, the weavings of which he knew he would never, in all likelihood, be able to comprehend. It made him feel very small, and yet at the same time it made him feel strangely essential in a way. His eyes focused on the Sacred Compass. He felt something stir within him, somewhere deep inside. He rose from the pew and moved to stand in queue for the Master Postulant. He found the prayers he had to pray had suddenly grown in their urgency.

The news of the Governor's speech took precedence even over the rumors about Highlander reinforcements coming to save the day. By the time the sun reached its peak overhead, the town square was packed with men and women and children standing shoulder to shoulder, all trying to squeeze closer to the steps of the church to better hear what Governor Chamberlain had to say. Nervous chatter ran through the crowd in waves. When the Governor finally emerged from the church and took his place on the top step, the height of the crowd grew by a few inches as everyone stood on tiptoe in hopes of catching a better glimpse of him. Silence fell like a stone. The Governor cleared his throat and began to speak.

"People of Tamendad," he proclaimed, "we are at war. An enemy has arisen out of our past to confront us once again. As it was before, this is not a war that we declared, but it is one that we will fight with steadfast resolve, and we will win. Just as Tamendad vanquished this enemy before, we will vanquish it again. We will not fail."

"When did we face this enemy before, Lord Governor?" a man close to the front called out, just as Governor Chamberlain knew someone would. The Governor recounted the stories of Tamendad's distant past, of Sir Isaac Dan and the goruks. He told them everything except where the goruks went once they had been scattered, and thankfully no one in the crowd thought to ask that question. Geoffery Chamberlain did not feel comfortable about the prospect of lying to his people, but he would have without hesitation if anyone had asked that question. Ferdinan and McRofaly were right. The townspeople could not know about the cave. Not yet.

Just as McRofaly had predicted, Governor Chamberlain could see some of the terror drain from the faces in the crowd as he explained all that he knew about what the goruks were. The simple ability to place a normal name on the creatures, instead of having to refer to them as *the invaders* or *the monsters*, seemed to bring their fearsomeness down a notch in the minds of the townspeople. The knowledge that they were an enemy Tamendad had faced and triumphed over before dispelled any notions that they were supernatural or invulnerable. The crowd was rapt with attention as Governor Chamberlain recounted how Sir Isaac Dan led a group of inexperienced soldiers against the goruks and scattered them into the wind. That had been accomplished before construction of the town had even been completed, before a constabulary had been set up, long before a militia had been raised. The Governor could see the hope swelling up in the crowd as he told the stories of how Dan's men repelled the goruks. Tamendad was facing a normal, mundane enemy, made of flesh and blood, who could be defeated and had suffered defeat in the past. That did more for the spirits of the townspeople than the rumor of ten thousand Highlanders brandishing flaming claymores could have, because it was unequivocal fact.

Governor Chamberlain went on to explain the measures that were going to be taken to defend the northeast gate. The crowd seemed to think the bonfires and the obstacles were both good ideas, and the knowledge of how many men would be standing guard at the wounded gate put the people as at ease as they possibly could have been under the circumstances. No one seemed to have any qualms about staying away from the northeast gate, either, just as Governor Chamberlain had expected. The townspeople would most likely have kept their distance from that gate anyway, even if the Governor had not requested it himself. It was a sight most people wanted to avoid. They took the news that travel out of Tamendad would be restricted almost equally well, with only a few people disapproving. Very few people had any desire to leave the relative safety of the city walls, fractured though they may have been, to venture out into the countryside where the goruks might be lurking. Some people were skeptical about the prospect of the straw men, but no one openly objected to it. The townspeople were willing to go along with any idea that might help keep the goruks at bay, no matter how farfetched it sounded. As Governor Chamberlain expected, the announcement of the communal burial drew the most mixed reaction. It helped that the Master Postulant had said the church would support burying the dead in a mass grave, but a good number of people still objected to the idea. Governor Chamberlain followed McRofaly's suggestion and told them that it was being done to honor the fallen in memory of the sacrifice they had all made for Tamendad, and that a marker would eventually be created listing each individual name, but he also explained that it had to be done to hide Tamendad's losses from the goruks. The townspeople deserved to know that. Geoffery Chamberlain had never been a man to try to sway popular opinion by playing on the emotions of the people. Surprisingly enough, explaining that the mass grave was necessary for tactical purposes actually won more people over to the idea than talk of honoring heroes. The war was bringing out the tougher side of Tamendaders, and many of them understood full well that sacrifices were going to have to be made if the city was to be defended. By the end of the Governor's remarks, the group that was still adamantly opposed to a communal burial were a small, although vocal, minority that contained surprisingly few family members of the deceased. Unless they swayed an impressive number of people over to their side, Governor Chamberlain felt relatively secure that he would not have to invoke his authority to ensure the communal burial, for which he was thankful.

The Governor concluded his address by reiterating that the war would be won, and that the goruks would learn that Tamendaders were still made of sterner stuff than they. A hundred questions rose up from the crowd as the Governor turned to leave the town square, but he did not take the time to answer them. He had to much left to do that day. A few cheers and whistles broke out from the crowd, but mostly the people just discussed what they had been told. The crowd reluctantly dispersed, still eager to hear more, know more, and be reassured that the war would be won. A few people tried to laugh about the idea of straw men defending the city, but most were in no mood for humor. One of the Governor's pages announced that written accounts of Sir Isaac Dan's experiences as well as all known information about the goruks would be posted throughout the town, and that seemed to please a lot of people.

Governor Chamberlain returned quickly to his home, and he found Don Ferdinan waiting in his study when he arrived there. The Conquian looked tired. Then again, just about everyone in the Governor's house that morning looked tired. Governor Chamberlain and Don Ferdinan exchanged a somber look. The Governor sighed deeply.

"Es begun," Ferdinan said. "Es much to be done."

"That is an understatement," the Governor replied.

"Ian Morlocke has already submitted his list of potentials, and he claims he es ready to begin watching the cave immediately. The names on the list seem reasonable. Es waiting your final approval, but I told him to go ahead and assemble his men. He wants to set up an outpost for his men a few miles from the cave. I think es a good idea, if we can find the right spot. It will be less noticeable than us constantly sending scouts into the area."

"Agreed," Governor Chamberlain said. "Well done, Don Ferdinan."

"Thank you, Geoffery," Ferdinan said. He poured two glasses of brandy, and sat one of them in front of the Governor. Geoffery looked first at the glass, then at the Conquian who had just taken a seat.

"Early for brandy, isn't it?" the Governor said.

"Not for men who have been up all night," Ferdinan replied. The Conquian took a sip and breathed hard through his nose as the burning liquid landed in his stomach. Governor Chamberlain did the same. "You should get some sleep," Ferdinan said after a few moments had passed quietly. "You look like shit."

Governor Chamberlain stared into the amber liquid in his glass, his eyes full of weariness and worry. "I have a feeling none of us will be getting much sleep in the days to come," he said.

Half the tables in the marketplace were empty, and the faces of the people there, both merchants and shoppers, had the detached look of sleepwalkers. It was obvious that everyone there would have rather been somewhere else, but some people had shopping to do that just could not be put off, and most of the merchants who set up their tables and booths that morning were ones who simply could not afford the luxury of a day off, even with the most unusual circumstances they found themselves under. Pretty much every table and booth that sported wares was dedicated to the bare necessities, either foodstuffs or lamp oil or the like, and a sizeable portion of the merchants that were open for business in the market devoted at least a part of their space to daggers or knives or other items that could be used for self-defense in a pinch. Those things sold just as well as the foodstuffs and oil, if not better.

Being in the market made Colvin very uncomfortable, being surrounded by so many gaunt-looking faces and vacant expressions, a world that was still in shock. He hurried through the sprawling lanes of tables and booths as quickly as he could, operating from memory. He was not surprised when he found Melinda's table bare and uninhabited. He just hoped that it was because she had decided not to open up shop that morning. The chances of her being hurt in the attack were slim, but the possibility was there and the uncertainty gnawed at Colvin's stomach.

He found his way to her house with barely any trouble, just a couple of wrong turns and one brief pause to retrace his steps. A small wisp of smoke rose out of the thin chimney – it was a little brisk that morning – and the sight and smell of burning cedar was a relief. Colvin knocked on the door and was further relieved when he heard her muffled voice from inside, calling out that it would be just a moment. She opened the door and her eyes widened slightly when she saw who it was. She looked like she was surprised to see him. "Hungry?" he asked.

"Oh," she said. It was all that she said. She just stood there in the doorway staring at him.

"Oh?" he said at last. "Oh what?"

"I mean..." She hesitated.

What the twist was going on? "What?" he said again.

"I was worried that something might have...I mean, I just thought when I didn't hear from you after the attack that maybe...I thought maybe you had been hurt."

Her face was unreadable. He thought he could hear concern in her voice, but there was something else, too. Was it accusation? Could it have possibly been accusation? That made no sense at all.

"I kind of figured that after the way our evening ended you wouldn't want me dropping by in the middle of the night," he said. He shrugged, and it pulled the short sleeve of his shirt up above the stitches on his arm. Her eyes went to it for a moment, then returned to his face. He was glad for that. She had seen that he *had* been hurt.

She nodded. "Would you like to come in?" she asked. He said yes, and she opened the door a little wider so he could step through. The inside of the small house was warm, not hot, and brightly lit. There was an old chair pulled up close to the fireplace, and a book was resting upside down on the right arm. The bed pushed up against the west wall was unmade. The implements of her trade were scattered all over the room, trays containing chunks of raw silver, molds for casting jewelry, etching tools, a few random gemstones. The house had a well-lived-in look to it that made it feel cozy to Colvin. The air smelled like her. "Listen, about last night," she began, and then hesitated, trying to find the words. "Before the attack, I mean. At William's house."

"You don't have to explain anything," he said. "That's not why I came."

"Oh," she said.

"There's that word again."

She looked uncomfortable.

"Do you want me to go?" Colvin asked. He hoped that she would say no, but in a way it would be easier if she just said yes. At least it would be less confusing.

"Why did you come, then?" she asked, ignoring his question. She crossed her arms over her chest, then thought that might make her look standoffish, so she dropped her hands to her side. That felt unnatural, so she put her hands on her hips. That, she decided, made her look even more standoffish than crossing them over her chest, so she dropped her left arm to her side and put her right hand on the back of her neck. That seemed a rather benign stance, so she stuck with it.

"Because you invited me to have lunch with you," Colvin said at last, looking her over like he thought she might be going mad. That notion had actually occurred to him, truth be told.

"Can I just say that I'm sorry I led you on last night and I'm sorry I gave you the wrong idea about my intentions and things just moved too quickly and I'm sorry." It all came out in a jumble, but she obviously felt better after she said it.

"Oh," Colvin said. "Okay. I thought…" He trailed off. They looked at each other, both of them giving the other an unreadable look.

"You thought what?" she asked.

"Nothing. I understand. Can we still have lunch?"

"Sure," she said. "I'd love to. Any suggestions?"

"Well, the Crown Rose is out," he said. "Gregor left this morning, and I doubt I could get us in there without him."

"I heard about that," she said. "Do you think he'll be safe?"

"I would worry more about the goruks, if I were you," he replied. He was pretty sure he was joking.

"Well, that's okay," she said. "Don't get me wrong, it was a wonderful dinner last night, but that place is a little above my usual fare. I know a place that serves a pretty good plate of roast and potatoes. They know me there."

"Roast and potatoes sounds good to me," Colvin said.

The tavern Melinda led Colvin to was really just a hole in the wall with a wood stove and a couple of rickety tables, but the meat was tender and the potatoes were fresh and the beer tasted like Gunther himself had brewed it. They had the place to themselves, which was fortunate since the place was so small that the presence of another couple would have made it feel overcrowded. They talked over their lunch, but Melinda was putting a noticeable effort into steering the conversation away from anything that even bordered on romantic or flirtatious. She spent a good quarter of an hour discussing the weather, and perhaps ten minutes commenting on how if the price of raw silver continued to rise she might have to learn another trade. Whenever Colvin would pay her any sort of compliment, even one so benign as saying her hair looked nice, she would thank him, always very politely, and immediately change the topic to something more neutral. When lunch was over, he offered to walk her back to her house but she politely declined, claiming she had some errands to run. They parted ways without so much as a handshake or a mention of when they might get together again. After being treated like a war hero by almost everyone he had come into contact with that morning, Colvin had no idea how to interpret Melinda's cold reception. He wanted to ask her, but he did not dare. In her mood, that might have been enough to kill any chances of ever seeing her again. In a way, Colvin thought at the moment that might not be so bad, and yet still something about Melinda compelled him, even when she was as unreceptive as she had been over lunch. Colvin decided the next best thing to asking Melinda would be to ask Ferdinan, but when Colvin arrived at the Governor's house he was informed that Don Ferdinan was getting some much needed sleep and was not to be disturbed, not that Colvin would have disturbed Ferdinan from his sleep for so piddling a matter anyway. News that Ferdinan was asleep depressed Colvin even further, though, since it meant that he would not be having his lesson in swordplay that afternoon. He had been looking forward to it all day, certain that it would help clear his mind. Instead, Colvin got talked into helping move the many crates and carts and wagons that had to be in place at the northeast gate before nightfall, as well as gathering spare lumber from around town for the bonfires. The work kept him occupied, but it was mostly mindless and allowed his thoughts to dwell on all that had happened, and by the time he was finished with it he was beginning to slide into a deep funk. Around four o'clock that afternoon he was ordered to bed and informed that he was being placed on night duty beginning immediately. He took his lesson with Stewart Salvington early that evening and then went to bed, where he lay awake, tossing and turning, thinking about goruks and war and the mixed signals that women sometimes gave, waiting and dreading for night to fall.

CHAPTER NINETEEN

MAKING A STAND

By nightfall, *goruk* was the new buzzword in Tamendad. Everyone was working it into conversation as much as they could. It was almost as if people believed that by saying the word, the creatures were somehow robbed of their power. In the inns and taverns of the trade district, men and women spoke loudly about the goruks over tankards of ale and mead as though they had long years of experience dealing with the beasts. Tales of Sir Isaac Dan became the favorite of the local bards and storytellers, and accounts of Tamendad's founding fetched a good number of performers a full purse and a few rounds of free drinks. Every alehouse that evening played host to a man or woman who was at least a competent enough storyteller to recount *The Battle of Tamendad*, which was what everyone was calling Sir Dan's routing of the goruks. No sooner than the tale was finished, often with embellishments of how numerous the goruks were, how few Dan's men were, and how easy a time they had of winning the day, someone would call out for an encore performance. The storytellers were always quick to oblige, so long as the coin and the drinks kept coming their way.

The boisterousness of the trade district was offset by the somber mood that enveloped both the town square and the northeast gate. The gardens surrounding the church had been converted into a makeshift morgue, with the covered bodies of sixty-eight men and women lying in rows on the grass. The mass grave had taken longer than anticipated to dig, and by the time it was ready the sun had been sinking toward its bed on the western horizon. Antrelican custom dictated that a corpse could only be buried while the sun still hung in the sky, so rather than try to rush through the ceremony at the expense of the dignity of the deceased, the Master Postulant had decreed that the bodies of the sixty-six people who had been killed in the attack as well as the two that had passed away during the course of that day would be placed outside the church for the night and buried in the morning. The sight of sixty-eight shrouded corpses decorating the church's gardens was disturbing enough while the sun was still up. In the moonlight, it was macabre. Most people avoided the town square, going well around through the empty marketplace if they had business on the other side of town, and those townspeople going to the church to light more candles or say more prayers put great effort into hurrying to and from the church and not catching a glimpse of the sight on the way.

On the northeast side of town, two bonfires and a host of crates, carts, wagons and other assorted bulky items stood in place of a functioning gate. The only people there were constables and militiamen. Everyone else kept their distance. The taverns closest to the gate did not even open that evening. Part of it was because the Governor had instructed everyone to keep their distance. Another part of it was the simple truth that no one wanted to be too close to the wounded gate when night finally fell again. Even some of the most seasoned constables were visibly unsettled by this assignment. There was a certain strength to be found in the almost ridiculous number of people standing guard at the northeast gate, a number far greater than had ever been stationed together on the same assignment before, but that only did so much to curb the anxiety that came with knowing that when the other shoe finally dropped, they were going to be right on the front line. But McRofaly's ideas would offer no small amount of protection. The two bonfires roared and blazed like a blast furnace, and so many obstacles had been piled up in front of the fractured gate that the guard would have time to sink a dozen arrows into any invading goruks before the beasts made it halfway through. It was just that the sight of the missing gate made Tamendad feel vulnerable, no matter how many bonfires and obstacles were piled up in front of it. Without two sturdy wooden doors and a stout iron crossbar, the northeast gate looked like an open sore on the city's face.

No ships were docked in Tamendad's harbor that night. A few captains had actually stayed docked throughout the day, thumbing their noses at the goruk threat, but as soon as evening began to wane and dusk approached, even those hearty seafarers cast off for safety's sake. The ships, four or five big ones with perhaps as many smaller darters in the mix, all huddled together now a few hundred feet out to sea, lookouts still up in the crow's nests peering into the darkness, ready to give the word to hoist anchor and sail even farther out to sea at the first sign of goruks. With the empty taverns behind them and the empty docks in front of them, the guards at the northeast gate felt utterly abandoned. It was a very dark night.

The men and women at the northeast gate had been bolstered by the news that Don Ferdinan was going to be standing guard with them. The

Conquian had made that announcement at sundown, and without first consulting the Governor about it. Ferdinan felt it was important for everyone, soldiers and townspeople alike, to know that even though he was of a different nationality and swore allegiance to a different king, he was going to be there for them and with them throughout the entire crisis. When Ferdinan showed up at the northwest gate shortly after darkness fell and the bonfires were lit, everyone had to admit that he looked much better after getting some sleep. The bags that were now permanently in place beneath his eyes had at least been deflated a bit, and he had the characteristic spring back in his step. William, too, had benefited greatly from a few blessed hours of unconsciousness. Colvin, on the other hand, did not look so well kept. When all the tossing and turning and sighing and deep contemplation was factored out, he had gotten about one hour of decent, restful sleep that evening, and even that had been plagued by dreams. They had not been nightmares, exactly, more like unconscious extensions of his waking confusion, but they had served make what little sleep he had gotten useless nonetheless. Colvin was not complaining, though. His worst day in Tamendad was still a hundred times better than his best day alone in the wilderness.

Colvin did get his swordplay lesson that day, after all. He and Ferdinan practiced together at the northeast gate. It gave them something to do, a way to take their minds off the disquieting tedium of their assignment, and it was certainly a better way to pass the time than sitting and counting the hours until an attack that might not even come. Colvin was actually starting to get the hang of swordplay, more or less. He pretty much had rudimentary parrying down pat, and his offensive technique was coming along every day. Ferdinan was obviously pleased with his pupil's development, and that night's swordplay lesson consisted mostly of a continuous sparring match, a lighthearted back-and-forth that allowed Colvin to show off what he had learned. Ferdinan took great care not to upstage the red-haired young man too badly. It would have been poor form to make Colvin look bad, not only because Ferdinan considered him a friend but also because Fist Division now looked to him for leadership. The playful contest between Colvin and Ferdinan drew the attention of a good number of guardsmen, even some of the commanding officers who should have been telling everyone to focus on their duty. No one really wanted to focus too heavily on this particular duty, though, and a match of skill against two of Tamendad's most mysterious figures provided ample entertainment. William watched his two friends square off as well, but his interest was more than simple distraction. His attention was firmly fixed on analyzing each move, each strike, each step. William watched to learn all that he could.

Colvin's sword went sailing out of his hand, and the tip of Ferdinan's sabre came to rest against his throat. Colvin tensed reflexively. No matter how many times Ferdinan disarmed and covered him, Colvin could never quite make himself accept that he was in no real danger. Having a blade at his throat made him nervous, no matter how much he considered the man wielding that blade a friend. Ferdinan smiled slightly and shrugged his shoulders, pulling his sabre away from Colvin's throat. "What did you do wrong?" he asked.

Colvin also shrugged. "I got overconfident?" Colvin said, pretty certain it was not the correct answer.

"Esactly the opposite," Ferdinan replied. "You second-guessed your move. My left side was completely open for a moment, but instead of going for the opening immediately, you held back because you doubted your ability. By the time you decided to follow through I had reset my stance and your opportunity was lost."

"Sorry," Colvin said.

"Do not apologize to me. You are the one who es dead."

Colvin chuckled softly. That was what Ferdinan always said. "Shall we go again?" he asked.

"Actually, I was wondering if maybe I could have a go at it," said William. Ferdinan and Colvin looked at the young nobleman, then at each other.

"Would you mind?" Ferdinan asked Colvin.

"Oh, not at all," Colvin answered. "Go ahead, William. You'll give him a lot more of a challenge than me."

William and Colvin exchanged places. William drew his broadsword and readied himself. Standing off a little ways, watching intently, Colvin really noticed for the first time how different William and Ferdinan looked when they assumed their stances. William looked rigid, firm, sort of like a statue of rock. Ferdinan, on the other hand, appeared flexible, limber, like a coiled snake ready to strike. Yet both men looked like they knew what they were doing; Ferdinan a bit more so than William, but that was most likely attributable to greater experience, not greater natural ability. *How can two people look so different when they're both doing the same thing?* Colvin wondered.

"On your guard, William," Ferdinan said, shifting his weight back and forth from foot to foot and holding his sabre ready.

"On your guard, Don Ferdinan," William replied. His heart was racing from excitement. He was about to spar with a real, honest-to-God swordsman, and it was someone other than his father.

Ferdinan made the first move, a straightforward lunge and thrust that William easily deflected. William's imaginary foes had made that move against him a thousand times, and Ferdinan's was no more difficult to deflect. William countered with a slash at chest level, and doubled the attack back toward Ferdinan's face. The Conquian leaned back out of the way of the first attack, then stepped forward and ducked under the second, rising up with a well-timed thrust toward William's abdomen. William sidestepped and pushed the attack low and aside, then fully extended his sword arm, using his broadsword as a barrier while he regrouped. Ferdinan fell back a couple of steps as well, bouncing slightly on the balls of his feet. William admired his grace. His movements were so smooth that sword and swordsman were often indistinguishable.

William pressed forward quickly, hoping to catch Ferdinan off balance. He brought his sword up, aiming high. Ferdinan was defensively set in the blink of an eye. The Conquian was quick. At the last moment, William feinted, dropping his blade and coming in from underneath. He felt certain his attack would land, or at least would have landed if he had actually been trying to hit Ferdinan, but in the space of a heartbeat Ferdinan had moved out of the path of the attack and was spinning around William, trying to flank him. William grunted in frustration. That was almost exactly the same move that William had wanted to use against the goruk that had injured him in the first attack, the move that had earned him the wound that still itched maddeningly at his side and threatened to never heal quite right, and Ferdinan had just executed it to perfection. William spun on his heels, and luck more than skill brought his broadsword into position to deflect an attack from Ferdinan that he had not even known was coming. Ferdinan cursed softly under his breath, appreciating that his advantage had been foiled by random chance, and tried to double back and come at William with a slash to the abdomen. Again steel rang against steel as William countered that attack as well, and this time it *was* skill that guided the young nobleman's blade. Ferdinan fell back, out of William's reach, and recaptured his balance.

William furrowed his brow at the move. Ferdinan had had the offensive. Why had he given it up so quickly? Cautiously, William approached his opponent. Ferdinan made no move forward, just stood ready, waiting. William set himself. Ferdinan flashed a smile. William came in with a thrust toward the chest. Deflected. He pulled his sword back with the force of Ferdinan's parry, rolling it into a slash across the midsection. Dodged. He sprang forward into a series of thrusts to the head, the chest, the torso. All deflected. A feint to the torso, then a swipe toward the face. All he hit was air. William saw it then, at that moment, and he did not hesitate. There was an opening, an undefended spot on Ferdinan's right side. He lunged for it...

William was no longer holding on to his sword. It sailed through the air and landed in a nearby wagon. Ferdinan sheathed his sabre and bowed. William just looked with wide eyes. "How did you do that?" he asked. "I never saw you set up to disarm me."

"Es because I let you set yourself up," Ferdinan replied.

Before William could follow up on that, he realized that there were a number of people applauding. He looked around and saw that most of the onlookers were clapping and whistling and smiling. A young Sword came up and retrieved William's broadsword from the back of the wagon and brought it to him. When he handed it over, he bowed and politely said, "That was very impressive, sir."

"Right up until my sword went sailing into the night," William replied.

"Well," the Sword said, "I doubt there's anyone else in Tamendad who could last much longer against Don Ferdinan." He returned to the crowd of guardsmen before William could think of anything to say in return. He felt a clap on the back and turned to see Ferdinan smiling brightly at him.

"You are remarkably talented, William," he said. "I knew from seeing you fight the goruks that you knew how to use a sword, but after seeing you duel I think you have the makings of a consummate swordsman."

"Thank you," William said. It was perhaps the nicest compliment anyone had ever given him. "But what did you mean when you said you let me set myself up?"

"I studied you," Ferdinan said. "That was what I was doing when I fell back and let you take the offensive. I was watching your moves, deciphering your weaknesses. I realized that you always loosen your grip when you slash from your left to your right, so I used that against you."

"I do?" William asked incredulously. "I didn't know that."

Ferdinan nodded. "Es why it worked. You have to find something your opponent es unaware he does. That way he cannot do anything to counter it."

"That was amazing!" said Colvin as he walked up to join the Conquian and the young nobleman. "Fantastic! I've never seen anything like it."

"Thank you, Colvin," Ferdinan said. "Now tell me, what did you learn from it?"

Colvin scratched the back of his neck, thinking the question over. In all actuality, he had learned quite a bit from watching Ferdinan and William spar. He had learned that there could be more than one correct way to do something. He had learned that a difference of appearance did not necessarily imply a difference of essence. He learned to always look for his own weaknesses, so that other people would not find them for him. He learned to make sure to keep a firm grip on his sabre when slashing from left to right. He was not sure that any of those things were what Ferdinan was looking for, though. But he had to say something. "Well, uh…wait, what's he doing here?"

Colvin pointed down the bricked street in the direction of the town square. Ferdinan and William turned to look, and saw Ian Morlocke and Captain Jefford hurrying up the street toward the northeast gate. There was little guess as to which man Colvin had been referring. Colvin, William and Ferdinan walked out to meet them, telling the rest of the guards to stay put. They met up with Captain Jefford and Ian Morlocke a couple of hundred feet away from the gate, far enough from any potential eavesdroppers that they could speak without having to worry about keeping their voices down.

"They're on the move," Morlocke said as soon as the five men were all together. He was deadly serious, and quite a bit out of breath.

"How many?" Ferdinan asked.

"I counted about a hundred," Morlocke replied so quickly that his response almost clipped the end of Ferdinan's sentence. "Nowhere near the number that came last night."

"They think we're weakened," William said. "They think it'll just be a mop-up effort." There was anger in the young nobleman's voice.

"Perhaps," Captain Jefford said. "But if that were the case, don't you think they would just open the flood gates and try to swarm us with everything they have?"

Colvin shrugged. "Maybe what's coming at us is all the able-bodied soldiers they have left."

"Let us pray to be so fortunate," Ferdinan said. "Were you spotted?"

"No," Morlocke replied without hesitation.

"You are certain of this?"

"Absolutely, sir."

"Good," Ferdinan replied. "This will sound odd, but you are going to have to ride back out, and this time you are going to have to let them see you. Do not get close enough to endanger yourself, just close enough to be spotted. We cannot allow them to find us prepared for an attack unless they encounter a scout between there and here. Otherwise they might grow suspicious that we have found their stronghold."

Morlocke nodded, as did Captain Jefford. "Good plan, sir," Morlocke said.

"Thank you. How far away are they now?"

"I rode straight here as soon as I saw them. They were all on foot, so I would estimate at least another three hours, probably four," said

Morlocke.

"Good. Let them spot you when they are an hour away, then get back here as quickly as you can. That will give us plenty of time to be set for them."

Morlocke nodded, said his goodbyes and turned to go. Everyone bid him Godspeed and implored him to exercise caution. When he was gone, the four members of the war council turned their attention to each other. "It seems we will not have to wait long to appraise McRofaly's defense strategy," Captain Jefford said.

"Es possible this might work to our advantage," Ferdinan replied. "If we turn this attack back easily, we might buy some time before they decide to attack again."

"So, what are our orders?" Colvin asked.

"Safe to assume they'll be coming for the northeast gate," said William. "May I make a suggestion?"

"Of course," said Ferdinan. "We all value your opinion, William."

"Well it seems to me that if they think a force of a hundred is going to be enough to take the city, they won't be expecting much resistance. If they don't encounter much resistance before they reach the gate, we might be able lure them into a false sense of confidence and trap them."

"Interesting," Captain Jefford said. "What do you suggest?"

"Let's position all our archers in the front, right behind all the obstacles. Have them crouched down, so the goruks won't see them at first. When the goruks get past the bonfires, *if* they get past the bonfires, they'll be trapped. Our archers rise up, loose their arrows, and it's like target practice."

Ferdinan looked thoughtful for a moment, then nodded.

"Good idea, man," Colvin said.

"Sounds like a plan to me," Captain Jefford said. "I'll inform the Governor."

Ferdinan, William and Colvin returned to the gate. They found the men there in a state of anxious anticipation. They had not been able to hear any of what had been said, but an impromptu conference between Tamendad's Captain of the Guard, a scout rider, Don Ferdinan and two important members of the Pride of Tamendad could only mean one thing. When Ferdinan made the announcement that goruks had been spotted heading toward Tamendad, the guardsmen had the look of men who had just gotten official confirmation of something they already knew anyway. There was a nervousness in the crowd, undeniably, but there was also a peculiar sense of relief. Most of the men and women stationed at the gate had already faced the goruks at least once before, and some had been present during both attacks. The actual fighting itself was not quite so terrible as the agonizing waiting game that many feared would have to be played before being called upon once again to fight for their homes. The enemy was on its way. The waiting game was over before it had even really begun.

Ferdinan, William and Colvin ran through the plan several times. Extra bows were fetched and distributed to anyone who had any experience in the use of one. Ranks were formed, archers in front, foot soldiers behind. The commanding officers continuously pep-talked the men to keep their spirits up. A few men recounted stories of the previous night's battle as if it was an event long in the past, tales of heroic stands and goruks being cut down like wheat. It did not take long for Gregor's name to be mentioned, and with Gregor's name came Angus's. A few different people who had been fighting close to Angus when it happened recounted their experience of it. More than one of those people's lives had been spared because of what Angus MacDugal did. Jaws were clenched and grips tightened around weapons as people talked about the sacrifices the Highlanders had made for Tamendad. From somewhere in the heart of the crowd, an anonymous soldier, impossible to tell whether constable or militiaman, yelled out, "Fight for Angus MacDugal!"

Colvin wished he had been the one to think of saying that. He echoed the sentiment, yelling, "For Angus!" Ferdinan followed suit, and he looked as though he were fighting hard to keep his eyes from tearing up. William said the same, as loudly as his lungs could scream it. Someone somewhere called out another name, another person lying dead under a sheet in front of the church. Another life stolen by the goruks. Yet another name came from up ahead, in the midst of the archers. There were some tears flowing now, and some rolled down William's cheeks as he called out the names of men who died fighting under his command. Each name bore its way into the heart of every man and woman there, and before long all sixty-eight names had been spoken. It did not take long for the names of those killed in the first attack to be called out as well. It was a testament to grief, and a reminder of what everyone was fighting for. And, of course, soon the call of "Tamendad stands!" filled the night air along with the names of the departed. Constables and militiamen railed against an enemy that was still hours away. They screamed. They howled.

They readied themselves for battle.

Three hours later, the northeast gate was a markedly different place. No one said a word. Everyone stood rigid in their ranks, focused on the gate in front of them. They were engulfed by the cold, unnatural calm that comes only before a fight for survival. When a town crier came bearing news that the goruks were less than an hour away it did not even seem to phase them, except that a few jaws were more tightly clenched and a few brows more narrowly furrowed. Ferdinan went over the plan with the constables and militiamen once more, just to ensure that there were no last moment questions about exactly what everyone was supposed to be doing. Then they waited, together.

In a way, that final hour lasted an eternity, each moment a stomach-churning torment of unending suspense, yet at the same time it seemed to pass in the blink of an eye. Visual confirmation of the enemy came just before midnight. Captain Jefford, who had joined the men shortly after Morlocke's second return to Tamendad that night, relayed the message. "This is it," he yelled to the crowd of men and women standing ready at the gate. "The enemy has been spotted coming over the horizon. They will be here momentarily. It is time to make our stand." No one said a word. They just stood ready.

Somewhere out in the distance, a lone howl pierced the night. Silence followed for a moment, and then another howl, still distant yet closer than before. Then two howls. Then four. Then a dozen. Then a hundred. The enemy was coming back out of the night, and Tamendad stood ready. Sometime later, no more than a few minutes, a town crier sprinted up the street toward the northeast gate. He screamed his message loud and clear, announcing that the enemy was making a beeline for the northeast gate. Howls and snarls echoed in the night, growing louder with each passing moment. "Archers, down," Ferdinan called out, and every man and woman with a bow took a knee. Everyone else stood ready, muscles tense, weapons drawn, teeth clenched. The bonfires burned. The carts and wagons and crates stood to do what the fractured gate no longer could. The people of Tamendad waited to face their enemy once again. The howls and screams neared, audible through the gate. They were clearing the last corner, and picking up speed from the sound of it. They were growing falsely confident.

"As soon as the first one comes into sight," Colvin called out, "shoot every last one of the bastards. And if they start to break through the barrier…well, then I guess we get to have some fun." A few people actually laughed. Colvin laughed with them. He looked at William, standing beside him. William caught his gaze, a look of determination in his eyes. "Scared?" Colvin asked.

"About enough to piss myself," William replied. "You?"

"Shitless," Colvin said, grinning like a madman.

"Good feeling," William said.

"The best," Colvin agreed.

If the bonfires did anything to deter the goruks, they did not show it. They came leaping through the flames, snarling and screaming, "*Thorak rakuth, Abuneth!*" at the top of their lungs. Every now and then some random article of clothing would catch fire, and once one thing was aflame the whole beast went up, wailing and flailing its arms until it eventually stumbled to the ground and did not move again. Most, though, rushed through the fires madly and then started the trek over the obstacles they found just within the city gate. That obviously unnerved them a bit, and it was clear from the expressions on their tusked faces that they had not been expecting it. Then the trap was sprung.

"Now!" Ferdinan screamed. "Archers up! Loose!"

A host of bowmen rose up from behind the last line of wagons and carts, drew a bead, and loosed. The *swish* of arrows flying free filled the night air for a moment, followed by the hollow *thunk* of those arrows finding their mark. Goruks stumbled and fell, clutching the arrows that jutted from their chests and heads and arms, wailing in pain. The goruks just behind the front of the pack stared in wide-eyed disbelief at their fallen comrades, and at the archers who had felled them. In another moment the archers had bows nocked and aimed again, and a second volley flew and found its way home. More hulking green forms dropped, some with the shafts of multiple arrows jutting from their corpses. The goruk battle cry was lost in a sea of screams and confused chatter. A few still came on, trying and failing to hasten their step through the rigged obstacle course, and were quickly dispatched by the archers' arrows. Most turned and fled back into the night from whence they had come. Once more the archers drew aim and loosed, and a few straggling goruks received arrows in the back for their sloth. The echoes of fearful howls and screeches began to dissipate into the darkness. The men and women at the northeast gate looked around at each other in confused silence. No one had yet processed what had just happened. There was no conceivable way that it had actually been that easy.

"Tamendad stands!" William screamed. The night was filled with cheers and howls and laughter and the sounds of people crying, a jumble of noises of celebration and relief. It was too good to be true, but it was true nonetheless. No one had been hurt. No one had died. It was an unconditional victory. William hugged Colvin tightly, and Colvin, wide-eyed and in disbelief, hugged back as best he could. Colvin looked around at the scene before him, trying to accept the reality of it but failing to make himself believe it. Victory was theirs. The enemy had been turned back.

"Should we give chase, sir?" a young, enthusiastic-looking constable yelled to Don Ferdinan above the din of the crowd. A good number of people fell silent and looked to Ferdinan to hear what he would say. Colvin was one of them. So was William.

Ferdinan quickly dismissed the question without even conferring with Captain Jefford. "No," the Conquian replied. "We must not leave the gate undefended. Let them go back to their home and spread word of what they encountered here. Besides, as fast as those cowardly dogs were running, it would take us all night to catch up to them." Ferdinan's words brought a fresh outburst of raucous cheers from the crowd, but both William and Colvin could tell there was something bothering the Conquian. With a subtle gesture, nothing more than a tilt of the head and a slight wave of the hand, Ferdinan told them that he wanted a word with them. They both signaled their comprehension and snuck away from the crowd a bit so they could talk in some semblance of privacy. In the fervor of the celebration, none of the constables or militiamen noticed the three men's departure.

"What is it, Ferdinan?" William asked as soon as they were alone, his voice full of concern.

"Es too easy," Ferdinan replied, keeping his voice low. "Not to insult your strategy, William, but they turned and fled as soon as they realized they were meeting resistance. They did not even consider trying to find cover and fight back. They just retreated."

William looked perplexed. Colvin, on the other hand, was nodding.

"What does it mean?" William asked.

"Well, it could be a trick," said Colvin. "They might be trying to give us false confidence. What do you think, Ferdinan?"

Ferdinan scratched at the whiskers on his chin for a moment. "Es possible," he said at last, "but I doubt it. From all we have seen and heard, there es no reason to believe the goruks are stupid. I do not think they would send a hundred of their own into a slaughter just to instill false confidence."

"Maybe they underestimated how ready we'd be to face them," Colvin mused.

"Well, we know one thing for sure," William said. "McRofaly's defensive measures passed their first test with flying colors. Even if those goruks had kept coming, the archers would have been able to drop them all before a single foot soldier would have even had to raise a weapon."

"Sí," Ferdinan said, "es a solid defensive setup. But now the goruks are going to know about it, and they are going to start planning around it." The three men shared a grim look over that thought. "I am going to apprise the Governor about what happened here," Ferdinan continued after a silent moment. "I assume Geoffery will want to meet with his war council after this, so I will probably see you in the meeting room in a few hours. Enjoy the rest of your watch, gentlemen." Ferdinan bowed deeply and bade them goodnight before departing. William and Colvin stood and watched him go.

"Did you notice he referred to the Governor by his first name?" William asked.

"Oh yeah, I noticed," replied Colvin.

"Someone once got thrown in the stocks for an entire day for doing that."

Colvin sort of laughed. "I guess it's true what they say."

"What's that?"

"War makes for strange bedfellows."

William thought that over a bit, then looked at his new friend for a long while. Colvin looked back at him, equally thoughtful. "You can say that again," William said, giving Colvin a pat on the back.

Chapter Twenty

Desperate Measures

That morning's sunrise was the most beautiful sight any of the men and women at the northeast gate had ever witnessed, not just because of its pleasing aesthetics but because of what it meant. The sunrise itself was breathtaking on its own merit, the type that only occurs at the nexus of summer and autumn, when the sky explodes into a tableau of reds and oranges and purples just before the sun peeks its head above the eastern horizon. But what made that particular sunrise even more moving was that with it came the knowledge, solid and irrefutable, that all the goruks had thrown against Tamendad throughout the entire night had been a single hit and run attack, during which the hit had never really had a chance to occur. Tamendad had been seen safely through another night without a single soul being lost. The guardsmen at the northeast gate, as well as all over the city, applauded and cheered the coming of the sun, but most were entirely too tired after a long night on duty to muster anywhere near the level of enthusiasm they had displayed when the goruks had been sent screaming back into the night. The much smaller day guard arrived at the northeast gate not even a quarter of an hour after the sun was in the sky, and the night guard was visibly relieved to see them.

Once dismissed, the men and women of the night guard headed eagerly for their homes and, more specifically, their beds. Colvin and William had no such luxury. As expected, a messenger had arrived at the gate about an hour before dawn instructing Colvin and William to report to the Governor's house immediately after they were off duty for a meeting of the war council. William took the news decidedly better than Colvin. After spending two nights in a row on guard duty, the young nobleman was nearly adjusted to a nocturnal schedule. Colvin, on the other hand, had had one hour of sleep in the past twenty-four, and while he was not quite on the verge of collapse, he was pretty damn tired and not particularly in the mood to do anything other than lose consciousness for a few hours. He felt certain he was too tired even to dream; he needed to just phase out of reality for about eight hours and wake up refreshed and replenished, and in a much better mood. Sleep would be a couple of hours longer in coming, though, and there was nothing to do about it besides suck it up and take it with a smile.

McRofaly usually preferred to eat alone. For one thing, having a companion at a meal meant having to clear another place at his kitchen table, which could potentially mess up the intricacies of his filing system for days. For another, McRofaly just did not like having anyone in his personal space. It made him nervous. It was unsettling enough to deal with the customers that came into his shop. Having someone in the same room as the trap door was almost enough to give him a shaking fit. But he almost trusted Melinda – almost – and when she had shown up at his front door that morning under the pretense of shopping for some semi-precious stones to use in her craft it had been obvious that she had something else on her mind. It had taken almost no coaxing to get her to agree to stick around for breakfast, and she had made the discovery, known to very few people, that McRofaly was actually a pretty good cook.

"God, I don't know what I'm doing," Melinda said, putting another forkful of eggs and peppers in her mouth.

"Melinda, you've been to dinner with two men the whole time I've known you," McRofaly said. "Of course you don't know what you're doing." He found it sort of humorous that Melinda had come to him for advice of this nature. Romance and courting were two subjects he knew almost nothing about. He was doing his best to be helpful. "Does he seem like someone you'd pursue a courtship with?"

"I don't know," Melinda sighed, thumbing her hair back over her ear. "He seems nice enough, I guess. I'm not even sure I'm interested in anything romantic at all. And assuming I was, I certainly don't know if I'd be interested in anything romantic with someone like Colvin."

"Someone like Colvin?" McRofaly asked demurely.

"Oh come on," Melinda said, stabbing at a sausage on her plate. "Everyone in town knows that Colvin spends almost all his free time with Don Ferdinan chasing skirts like they invented the concept. That's the last kind of man I need to get involved with."

"Then why did you see him again after your dinner date with him?"

"It was just for lunch," Melinda replied. She sounded defensive. "Besides, he really does seem nice. I'd like to get to know him, just as friends." Melinda jumped a little bit when the black cat sprang up on the table in front of her and snatched the last sausage from her plate. In one swift motion McRofaly rose from his seat, scooped the cat from the table, and placed it gently on the floor.

"No, Sococo," he said, "I told you, you eat on the floor."

Once the sausage had disappeared down its throat, the cat rubbed itself up against Melinda's leg. Melinda reached down and scratched it behind the ears. Sococo purred contentedly and licked his chops. "I thought you didn't like animals," she said.

"I didn't. I do now."

"What changed your mind?" She pulled her hand away and Sococo batted at her leg with his paws and meowed, voicing his objection to the cessation of ear-scratching.

"He helped me find something I was looking for," McRofaly replied. He scooped up Sococo and cradled him like a baby, scratching his stomach and behind his ears simultaneously. If it were possible for a cat to grin like a fiend, Sococo was doing it. "God, I have to get going," McRofaly said, looking out the kitchen window. "I've got to meet with the war council this morning."

Melinda nodded, standing and wiping away the stray crumbs that had landed on her shirt. "Do you want me to help you straighten up?" she asked.

"No, that's okay," McRofaly said, depositing Sococo at his feet. "This place practically cleans itself."

"Okay, well, thanks for lending a sympathetic ear," Melinda said, gathering up the stones she had purchased.

"No problem. He must really be something to have you so worked up."

Melinda sighed, again. "Yeah, well, I just wish I knew if he's just after another conquest."

"Don't worry," McRofaly told her. "I'll have a word with him."

The war council was an assortment of haggard-looking faces that morning. Governor Chamberlain and Don Ferdinan, who had pretty much given up sleep for other pursuits, looked like they always did, which was to say they looked exhausted almost beyond repair. Captain Jefford looked nearly as beleaguered, but he had had a solid six hours of sleep the previous day, so his reserves were running just slightly fuller than the Governor's or the Conquian's.

Gunther had a cantankerous air about him, though it was admittedly difficult to distinguish between it and his normal gruff demeanor. The short blacksmith was still upset that he had not been stationed for duty at the northeast gate. It had been explained to him more than once that Tamendad could not afford to put all its best soldiers at the northeast gate, since that would weaken the defenses of the other three gates. Gunther had wholeheartedly agreed with the practicality of that idea, and had grudgingly gone along with his assignment to the southwest gate, but it was quite obvious that not playing a part in turning back the attacking goruks was weighing heavily on his heart.

Colvin's stare was almost vacant, the look of a man in desperate need of sleep. It was obviously taking great effort for the red-haired young man to focus on any one thing for more than a few seconds, and every now and then his eyes would begin to slide slowly shut and his chin would begin to dip down toward his chest until either Gunther on his left or William on his right would plant an elbow into his ribs. Every time that happened Colvin snorted and bolted upright, rubbed his eyes, looked sheepishly around the table, and apologized even if no one had really noticed him starting to doze off.

William did not actually look all that bad, but more than one person at the table noticed a hardness to the young nobleman's face that had not been there just a few weeks prior. William Stuart-Camen had done a lot of growing up over the course of the previous two weeks, perhaps too much.

McRofaly was the one man at the table who looked right as rain, dark hair combed back neatly, beard evenly trimmed, all of him smelling of bath salts and oils. He was downright vibrant compared to his six fellow war council members, and they all hated him a little for it.

"Let us not dally," Governor Chamberlain said once everyone was situated at the table. "Three things saved us last night. The first was Master McRofaly's defensive design. The second was Lord Stuart-Camen's tactical setup. And the third was dumb luck." The Governor paused to drive this last point home. "One thing is obvious," he continued after a while. "Last night's attack was not a serious attempt by the goruks to gain control of the city."

"What the twist was it, then?" Colvin said, sounding a bit more demanding than he had intended. "Sorry, that came out wrong," he added hastily. "What I meant to say was, what the twist was it, then? I mean... forget it."

Governor Chamberlain almost laughed. He deferred his answer to Captain Jefford, who straightened in his chair as he spoke. "From all we have gathered, it appears that last night's attack was along the same lines as the first attack on Tamendad. Both attacks ended as soon as the goruks met any serious resistance, with a good number of goruks retreating as quickly as they could back into the cover of night. Most likely, it was an attempt to gauge our military strength and the defensive tactics we are using."

"I agree," said McRofaly. "Goruks tend to study their enemies in an attempt to discover weaknesses that can be exploited." William glanced sidelong at Ferdinan when McRofaly said this, but the Conquian seemed not to notice.

"We were very fortunate to not lose a single soul last night," Governor Chamberlain said. "But we cannot hope to be so fortunate in the future. The fact that the goruks attacked us two nights in a row confirms our fears that they intend to escalate a full-scale war against us. Measures must be taken to circumvent as much damage as possible. I have conferred with Captain Jefford and Don Ferdinan about this, and we have reached a most important decision, one that will affect all of you deeply."

"What is it?" Gunther asked, and the apprehension in his voice was shared by William, Colvin, and McRofaly.

"We are evacuating Tamendad," said Ferdinan. He said it in much the same way that a man might say he had to go to the market to pick up some flour.

"What?" William nearly screamed, and he was not the only one. Colvin, Gunther and McRofaly all had strong reactions to Ferdinan's proclamation. Gunther was the most animated, pounding his fist hard against the table.

"We're givin' up?" the short blacksmith cried in disbelief. "We're just gonna roll over for these goruk swine? I can't believe what I'm hearin'!"

"Then perhaps you are hearing the wrong thing," Governor Chamberlain replied, the cold levelness of his voice a counterpoint to Gunther's fiery passion. "Don Ferdinan spoke the truth. We are evacuating all townspeople not directly involved in the effort to hold the city. I have had correspondence with Governor Stodlemeyer of Tantera, and he has agreed to take them in until this war is finished. But no, despite what it might have sounded like, we are most certainly not giving up."

"How do you plan to relocate so many people?" asked McRofaly. By the tone of his voice it was plain that he appreciated the difficulty involved in such a task.

"I have discussed this matter with several ship captains," Governor Chamberlain said, "and I have procured the services of seven passenger ships. We will sail as many people as we can up the coast, since that is the safest means of transportation."

"A passenger ship could carry perhaps a hundred people at most, if you packed the deck and all the cargo holds shoulder to shoulder," said

McRofaly. "Seven ships, that's seven hundred people at best, less than a third of the population. What about the rest?"

"Tantera es sending a shipment of weapons to assist our cause against the goruks," Ferdinan explained. "Es scheduled to arrive in two days. Governor Stodlemeyer es sending a small armed guard to escort the shipment, to ensure it does not fall into goruk hands. Those who cannot fit onto the boats will return to Tantera on foot with the armed guard."

"It's not going to be enough," Colvin said, mumbling through his exhaustion.

"What was that?" Ferdinan asked.

"What's Tantera sending to protect the shipment?" Colvin said. "Five, maybe ten guards, I'd guess, just because the Governor isn't going to want to spread his own forces too thin. However many he sends, there's no way its going to be enough to defend hundreds of people marching up the coast."

"You're smarter than you look," Captain Jefford told Colvin. Colvin shot the Captain a glowering look, and the Captain looked a bit startled. "God, I'm sorry, Colvin," he said. "That did not come out right at all. I'm a bit tired. You'll have to forgive me. I just meant that I wouldn't have expected someone who grew up in the countryside to pick up on things like that so easily."

"No problem," Colvin said. "We're all tired. And thanks."

"Well, Colvin, you are correct," Governor Chamberlain interjected. "We cannot depend on Governor Stodlemeyer's guards to provide adequate protection for the townspeople. Once the weapons shipment arrives, the townspeople will return to Tantera with the armed guards that escorted it, and Shield Division will accompany them. All except you, Gunther. We need you here to serve as blacksmith for the war effort."

Gunther did not look very pleased about the decision, though it was difficult to say whether his objection was against Shield Division being sent out of the city or him not being allowed to accompany them. Whatever he had to say on the matter, he kept it to himself for the moment, sitting in his high-backed chair with his arms crossed over his chest.

William's look of pained concern made it obvious that he just could not envision an evacuated Tamendad, and that his thoughts were focused on the friends and loved ones he would have to say goodbye to. It did not soothe him when it came out that the nobility and the landowners would be first to be offered space on the passenger ships, which meant that all of William's closest acquaintances would be making the trip to Tantera in the safest possible way. If anything, that knowledge only served to make him angry. Why, after all, should wealth and title insulate people against the danger that common men and women faced? Space on the ships should be assigned through a lottery system. That was really the only fair way to do it. William did not want to turn the war council into a debate on the inherent unfairness of the Turish class system, but he also could not keep an opinion he held so strongly to himself. Once the young nobleman had stated his case, so eloquently and cogently that even a member of the oldest noble family would have heard him through before calling him a fool, Governor Chamberlain gave him a look that almost bordered on rueful.

"You are your father's son, and you should take that as the highest possible compliment," Governor Chamberlain said. "Please at least let me explain why it must be done this way. The seven ship captains with whom I have made arrangements were none too eager to involve themselves or their crews in this conflict. Getting them to agree to terms required the promise of a sizable sum of coin, far greater per passenger than it would normally cost to ferry a person up the coast. The only people who would really be able to afford their asking price are nobles and landowners. I can assure you, William, that whatever space is left on the ships once everyone has had a chance to procure their own passage using their own coin will be filled to capacity, with the expense coming out of Tamendad's own coffers, and that space will be assigned through a lottery."

"They're *profiteering*?!?" William exclaimed. The young nobleman looked around the table, and most of the war council looked back at him with the same uncomfortable look that most men had when they had just told their children that fairies did not really leave nuts and fruits and candies for them during Winterfeast. That was not the look Ferdinan was giving William, however, and William certainly noticed it. Ferdinan's look was peculiar and a little unsettling, and William felt almost certain that it contained something close to admiration. Whatever it was, it was left for discussion at a later time.

"War profiteering is an ancient practice. You could almost say it's the world's second oldest profession." McRofaly's interjection tore William's attention away from Ferdinan, and the young nobleman looked at McRofaly with a hint of curiosity encroaching on the outrage that was evident on his face.

"What's the oldest?" William asked. As soon as that question was out, Gunther began to guffaw. Colvin widened his eyes and furrowed his brow at the same time, a genuinely perplexed expression, and, not knowing exactly what to say, just stretched out the single syllable of, "Uhhhh." Captain Jefford smirked. Governor Chamberlain was smiling like he had just heard something very, very funny. McRofaly looked as though he was about to say something, but Ferdinan cut him off before he had the chance by saying, "Es something to be discussed later. For now, let us focus on matters surrounding the war." William was thoroughly confused, but he relented just the same.

"Speaking of matters surrounding the war," McRofaly said, "I have a few points to bring before the council, if I may."

"Of course," said Governor Chamberlain. "Your opinion is highly valued, Master McRofaly."

Yeah, now you say that, McRofaly thought. "I have been studying the plans of the city, and as I feared I might, I discovered that we cannot depend on the city wall to hold against a full-scale charge. The oak the wall is made of is as sturdy as any wood can be, but no variety of wood can hold a candle to stone. The fact is, this wall was never meant to stand up to an assault. It was built to dissuade the Glenish from attacking. King Reginald Chamberlain the Constant commissioned its construction in the hopes that the Glenish would balk at the sight of a fortified city."

Captain Jefford, Governor Chamberlain and Don Ferdinan all wore grave expressions, and Gunther, Colvin and William obviously found the news troubling as well. "Any suggestions on how to deal with this problem?" the Governor asked.

"We must send out patrols," Ferdinan said before anyone else, even McRofaly, had a chance to respond.

"We're already doing that, Don Ferdinan," Captain Jefford said.

"No, Captain, I am not speaking of scouts. I mean we must send out armed patrols to keep watch around the city, to engage further goruk attacks before they can reach the walls."

"If we put guards outside the walls, that will weaken the defenses at each gate," William said.

Ferdinan shook his head. "Since the attack two nights ago, nearly a hundred more people have volunteered to help defend the city. If we put most of the new volunteers on day guard and assign the most capable to night duty to make up for the loss of Shield Division, es possible move some men outside the gate without compromising our interior defense."

"We will have to send out a logging party," Governor Chamberlain said. The six other men of the war council all looked confused over the Governor's apparent non sequitur. "I will not send men and women out against the goruks without assisting them in any way I can," the Governor explained. "I intend to light up the countryside with bonfires."

"Probably wouldn't be a bad idea to build a few spiked trenches for the patrols to fall back to if the fightin' starts to turn rough," Gunther added. The Governor nodded his agreement.

"If we are sending out loggers, wouldn't it be smarter to use that wood to try to rebuild the northeast gate?" asked William.

McRofaly and Governor Chamberlain both shook their heads simultaneously, and each hesitated a moment, seeming to defer to the other for an explanation.

"It's not possible," said McRofaly finally. "Rebuilding part of the wall would be one thing. That's just shorn tree trunks braced together with support beams. But the main gate of Tamendad would be a massive undertaking."

"We repaired two gates after the first attack," William retorted.

"Repaired," countered McRofaly. "Not rebuilt. Both those gates still stood, they had just suffered damage. At the northeast gate we would be starting from scratch. It would require a master carpenter and a work crew of dozens, complete with work horses, pulleys, scaffolding... It would be difficult even under normal conditions."

"Master McRofaly is correct," said the Governor. "The task is simply too grand to attempt while we are at war. Make no mistake, we will repair the northeast gate, but not until this goruk threat is put down. The setup we are presently using to hold the northeast gate will suffice for now."

William nodded. He had lived in Tamendad his whole life, and yet found himself only appreciating just how much effort had gone into building the city now that he was in danger of losing it. That thought would have made him laugh if it did not make him feel so much like crying.

"There's also the matter of who gets assigned to the patrols," Captain Jefford said. "If I may, Lord Governor, I do not believe we should send out any new volunteers on patrol until they have at least a few days of proper training behind them. Also, we have a fairly significant number of guardsmen still nursing injuries from the battle at the northeast gate. I would suggest that all the fighting injured be stationed within the walls."

"Wise suggestions, Captain. Draw up the patrols as you will. You have never steered me wrong," Governor Chamberlain said. "Now, what else do you bring before the council, Master McRofaly?"

McRofaly folded his hands and looked around the table, and he looked almost apprehensive. "Two suggestions on how we might deal with future attacks, Lord Governor," he said with all the cool confidence he could muster. He knew his ideas would not be received warmly, if they were received at all, but they were well-reasoned plans, and McRofaly was certain they would work. Well, nearly certain, at any rate.

It seemed prudent to McRofaly that he should lay out the more radical of his suggestions first. That way, if it were rejected out of hand his second suggestion might seem all the more reasonable in comparison.

The faces of the war council members grew steadily more incredulous as McRofaly laid out the points of his first plan. Captain Jefford did not appear to think very highly of it. Unsurprisingly, Ferdinan looked to be the most receptive to the idea. Once McRofaly had explained the plan in detail, taking great care to highlight all the precautions that would be taken for safety's sake, the war council was engulfed in silence. Governor Chamberlain's brow was furrowed with deep contemplation. It took a good while for him to respond.

"That plan presents entirely too much danger to the townspeople for me to authorize it," the Governor said at last. "Once the town is evacuated, however, all bets are off. What is your other suggestion?"

"Secondly, Lord Governor, I want to scout a few areas between here and the cave. Personally."

"Why?" asked Ferdinan before Governor Chamberlain had the chance. "To what end?"

"I have been studying the maps in the library, and I have found a few locations that might lend themselves to an ambush against the goruks on their way to the city."

"Ambushing an enemy goes against the rules of war," Captain Jefford said.

McRofaly looked at Jefford, nodding, his smile just the slightest bit condescending. "You are correct, Captain, but as I understand it, the rules of war exclusively govern conflicts between humans and other humans. They have nothing to say about conflicts between humans and goruks."

Captain Jefford looked like he was about to say something in response, but instead just sat back in his chair and nodded. In truth, the usually disimpassioned Captain of the Guard found a sense of savage pleasure in the idea of ambushing the goruks.

"The smartest time to do it would be on the day that Tamendad is evacuated," McRofaly continued. "Assuming the goruks even keep an eye on the city during the day, there will be so much commotion that day that it would be easy for a goruk spy to overlook a couple of extra scouts sneaking off into the countryside."

"A *couple* of scouts?" the Governor replied. "Who do you intend to accompany you?"

"Ah, yes, well, this would obviously be a rather dangerous scouting mission," McRofaly said, "and I think it is reasonable of me to request a companion to provide for my safety. I would suggest that Colvin be sent along with me."

Everyone in the room looked at Colvin, and they all noticed for the first time that the red-haired young man was slumped in his chair, his chin resting flat against his chest, which rose and fell with the steady, deep breaths of unconsciousness. William and Gunther had both been too absorbed in their own thoughts to notice Colvin doze off, and they both planted an elbow into his ribs to rouse him. He jumped up in his chair from the sudden, rough contact, blinking repeatedly and taking quick glances around the table.

"Huh? Whazza? Oh, sorry," he mumbled, wiping the sleep from his eyes and reddening a bit around the cheeks.

"Master McRofaly has requested that you accompany him on a scouting mission, Master Colvin," the Governor explained. "What are your feelings on the matter?"

"Today?" Colvin asked, the desperation in his voice making it evident that he sincerely hoped such was not the case.

"No, you would be going out the day after tomorrow, when Tamendad is evacuated," Governor Chamberlain replied.

Colvin looked across the table at McRofaly, and the relief he felt over not having to put off sleep for a scouting trip was supplanted by his suspicion of the man. Colvin could not put his finger on it, but there was just something shady about him. Colvin had been around far too many unsavory characters not to notice McRofaly's more peculiar traits, like how his eyes always told more than his stories did. "Why me?" he said at last.

"I have a few reasons," McRofaly replied. "It's widely known that you were a wanderer before coming to Tamendad, so you know how to survive the wilderness. You also possess a familiarity with the area that Tamendad's best scouts would be hard pressed to match. You're skilled at combat, with bare hands as well as various weapons. You're resourceful. You're courageous. And just about everyone in this town respects you after knowing you for only two weeks, so you must be an upstanding, dependable sort of fellow."

Colvin's ears burned from all the compliments McRofaly had heaped on him. He halfway believed they were sincere. "What exactly is this scouting mission for?" Colvin asked the Governor. He was embarrassed to ask, since it drew even more attention to the fact that he had fallen asleep during the council meeting, but he had to know before he could make a decision.

"Master McRofaly believes he might be able to find a location suitable for setting an ambush against the goruk forces on their way to Tamendad."

Colvin took a deep breath and looked at McRofaly through narrowed eyes. There was no denying that McRofaly was holding secrets. Then again, who wasn't? Colvin wondered how well-respected he would be if a few of his ever got out. Despite what secrets McRofaly might have been holding back, there was also no denying that he was dedicated to assisting the war effort. And the tactical advantage of an ambush was just too great to pass up.

"I'm in," Colvin said.

"Excellent," said McRofaly and the Governor simultaneously.

Governor Chamberlain and Don Ferdinan slumped into chairs on opposite sides of the desk in the Governor's study. The meeting of the war council had just concluded, and both men were in desperate need of a moment's peace before turning their minds to the myriad other details that demanded their attention. The Governor and the Conquian exchanged weary looks. The war was taking its toll on both of them, each in a different way. Ferdinan had been present at all three confrontations with the goruks, and he had an impressive wound on his side to show for it. His stitches itched maddeningly, and after only one day he could already tell that the wound was not healing like it should. That probably had to do with how exhausted he was. How much sleep had he been averaging for the last two weeks? Two hours a night? Maybe three, but no more than that. Yet he really had no desire to sleep, and cursed himself when it became a necessity. There was still so much to do in Tamendad, and nothing had ever been accomplished by sleeping men.

Governor Chamberlain was fairing better when it came to sleep, getting perhaps four or five hours on a good night, but his sleep of late had been so filled with nightmares that it did him little real good. His nighttime hours were consumed by images of howling goruks, and of young men and women, little more than children, bleeding and dying in the streets of Tamendad. He had witnessed none of the actual combat, but he was haunted by the reports of it – cold, emotionless numbers of dead and wounded that did not begin to describe the pain and anguish that his townspeople were enduring.

"You look tired," Ferdinan said.

"You're one to talk," the Governor replied.

Ferdinan shrugged. "Perhaps, but I still have my youth. Es no big deal if I go without sleep."

"Just what are you implying, my good Don Ferdinan?" the Governor asked.

"Oh, nothing at all, Geoffery, just that–"

A knock at the door prevented Ferdinan from completing his thought, which was probably just as well. "Come," both Ferdinan and Governor Chamberlain said at the same time. The door opened and Gunther stuck his head into the room.

"Could I have a word with you, Governor?" the short blacksmith asked. His tone of voice and his expression were equally serious.

"Of course, Gunther, of course," the Governor responded. "Please, come in, have a seat. Whatever it is, I hope you do not mind discussing it in front of Don Ferdinan."

Gunther, who was already making his way toward one of the empty chairs in front of the Governor's desk, looked at Ferdinan. "Oh, no sir, not at all. I've nothin' but respect for Don Ferdinan."

Gunther took a seat and straightened his beard a bit before speaking. He was not visibly nervous, but it was obvious he was reluctant to bring up whatever was on his mind. He cleared his throat, a deep harrumphing sound, and said, "It's about Shield Division, Governor. And the evacuation. I want to request that I be sent along to Tantera."

"Gunther, I can appreciate your desire to see the townspeople to safety, believe me, but we are going to need you here, as a blacksmith as well as a soldier. I have a feeling that this shipment of weapons that Governor Stodlemeyer is sending us will not contain...shall we say...the finest weapons Tantera has to offer, and I need to know I have a good smith available to repair whatever might be wrong with them," the Governor replied.

"I know," Gunther said, "but just hear me out. My boy, Gangis, is a solid blacksmith. He can do just about everything I can, and Colvin will be here to give him a hand. It's important I go, Governor, not just because I wanna make sure everyone gets to Tantera safe. I've got... personal business to see to."

"In Tantera?" the Governor asked.

"Well, not exactly, no," Gunther said, fidgeting with his beard. "Ah, blast it, it has to do with the cave. There, I said it. It's a straight shot south of Tantera, less than half a day on foot, and I can get there without any goruks spottin' me."

The Governor did not look pleased. "Gunther, you know that the cave is off limits to anyone except Ian Morlocke and his scouts," he said. "What reason can you give me for why I should make an exception in your case?"

"I have a reason, Governor, a damn good one, but I can't really say what it is."

Governor Chamberlain sighed. "Then I am sorry, Gunther, but I simply cannot–"

"Governor, may I say something?" Ferdinan interrupted. Governor Chamberlain was obviously not happy about being cut off, but he relented to the Conquian nonetheless.

"I realize I may not be most qualified to vouch for Gunther's character," Ferdinan began, "since I met him such a short time ago, but in that time he has proven himself to be an honorable and selfless man. I am certain that whatever reason compels him to visit the cave, es something he strongly believes will aid the war effort." Gunther nodded enthusiastically at that point to express his agreement. "If he says his reason es one that cannot be discussed," Ferdinan continued, "I believe we should accept that. Sometimes there are certain things men simply cannot discuss, for whatever reason. Es simply a fact of life." Ferdinan gave the Governor a mysteriously telling look once he was done speaking.

"You are suggesting that Gunther be allowed to go, then?" the Governor asked.

"Well, perhaps," Ferdinan told the Governor, then turned to face Gunther and said, "You realize you will be putting yourself in significant danger?"

"Oh, yeah, I know it'll be dangerous," Gunther replied. *No more dangerous than it was any other time*, he thought.

"And you realize if you are captured, may God forbid it, you are bound by honor not to reveal any of what you know as a member of the war council," said Ferdinan.

"Those goruk swine could cut my heart right out of my chest and I wouldn't breathe a word to 'em. I swear it by the soul of my grandfather's grandfather." The look in Gunther's eyes told that he meant every word.

Ferdinan nodded solemnly at Gunther, then looked at the Governor and said, "Sí, I am suggesting that he be allowed to go."

Governor Chamberlain folded his hands together and sighed deeply, alternating his gaze between Gunther and Ferdinan. He was silent for a long while, trying to weigh several factors in his mind and balance them each against the others. At last he said, "Very well, Gunther, you may go, assuming both Colvin and your son agree to assist with weapon repairs."

Gunther breathed deeply, and the short blacksmith looked like a great weight had been lifted from his shoulders. He shook hands vigorously with the Governor from across the desk, muttering, "Thank you, Governor, you won't be sorry, I promise you." Then he turned to Ferdinan and crossed both hands over his own chest, covering his heart, and bowed low. "My debt to you is great, but I swear to repay it best that I can," he told the Conquian, then rose from his bow, which was considerably different than any kind Ferdinan would ever perform, placed a hand on Ferdinan's shoulder, and simply and sincerely said, "Thank you, Ferdinan. Thank you."

"Es nothing, Gunther. I was merely speaking the truth."

Once Gunther had gone, Governor Chamberlain looked and Ferdinan and sighed. "I hate it when you do that," he said.

The corners of Ferdinan's mouth curved ever so slightly upward into an almost imperceptible grin. "I know," he replied.

❖   ❖   ❖

"Prostitution," said Colvin as he and William stepped out of the meeting room.

William's eyes widened in shock, and it took him three tries before he successfully muttered an exasperated, "What?"

"Prostitution is the world's oldest profession," Colvin explained.

"Oh," William said after an extended moment of confusion, and then, "Oh my God, I must have sounded like a fool!"

"Well, yeah, kind of," Colvin agreed, "but I think it's kind of commendable that you didn't know that. Melissa should be pleased to hear it, at least."

William smiled a sheepish smile that was both amused and embarrassed.

"So are you okay with the evacuation?" Colvin asked.

William sighed. "I know it's the best thing for the townspeople. They'll be a lot safer in Tantera. But it's going to be so hard to say goodbye to my friends and family, even if it's just for a little while."

Colvin nodded somberly, not wanting to mention that that was a big *if*. When Tamendad was evacuated, some of the goodbyes said that day would be forever.

Colvin heard McRofaly say, "Excuse me," and realized that the short man had fallen into step beside him without him noticing.

"Yes?" Colvin said.

"I was hoping that I might have a word with you in private."

Colvin genuinely did not want to seem rude, but he just could not keep himself from sighing. It seemed that forces beyond his control were aligning against him with the sole purpose of keeping him from reaching a bed. "Of course," he said, and told William that he would catch up with him later. Once William had disappeared down the hallway, McRofaly and Colvin walked off to themselves a bit, which was a pointless gesture since the two of were alone in the hallway. McRofaly cleared his throat.

"What was that?" Colvin asked.

"That was just me clearing my throat." McRofaly said.

Oh, thought Colvin, *of course it was. How silly of me.*

"Anyway," continued McRofaly, "I haven't had breakfast yet, and I was wondering if you would like to accompany me to the kitchens and we could discuss a few things."

"Sure," Colvin said. *What?* "I'd love to." *No I wouldn't.* "Lead the way."

Colvin sighed once again. He must have been even more tired than he thought. He wasn't even sure what he was saying. But he had agreed, even if it had not been heartfelt, and it would have been rude to renege. Besides, he was a bit hungry. At least he was pretty sure he was.

McRofaly led Colvin down to the kitchens on the first floor. Colvin drug his feet with every step, but perked up a bit once they neared close enough that the smell of sausages frying and breakfast tea brewing wafted down the hallways to greet them. Colvin's stomach rumbled slightly and he thought about what a good idea it was that McRofaly had suggested having breakfast before retiring to bed. He was exhausted, but sleep would come much more easily and would be much more restful with a full stomach churning away at a pile of eggs and sausages and a couple of pieces of toast with jam and whatever else he could find in the kitchens. That turned out to be quite a lot, and when Colvin and McRofaly finally claimed one of the smaller tables in the Governor's common dining room the plate Colvin placed in front of himself was piled near overflowing with eggs and corned beef hash and sausages and toast and roast potatoes with peppers and onions. He eyed it like a wolf that had cornered a chicken. Colvin picked up one of the sausages from his plate and bit half of it off before looking at McRofaly and saying, "So what did you want to talk about?"

McRofaly looked both amused and repulsed, watching Colvin wave half a sausage around like a pointer. "Nothing important, really," the short man said while slicing his egg with knife and fork. "I was just thinking we could discuss the scouting trip, swap some ideas, put our heads together so to speak."

"Gotcha," said Colvin. He was still tired, but his mood was improving by the moment. He shoveled another forkful of eggs in before continuing. "My general feeling," he said with his mouth full, "is that we should probably set out just as soon as it's light, and narrow down the locations we're going to scout so we can be sure to be back here by nightfall. Whether the wall can stand up to an attack or not, I feel a lot safer being inside it when the moon's out."

McRofaly nodded, chewing a bite of egg that was nowhere near as good as what he could have prepared. "A good idea," he said, trying hard not to sound like he would have expected the village idiot to come up with such an obvious suggestion.

"Thank you," Colvin said. "So tell me something, McRofaly. Why did you really want me to be the one to go with you on this scouting mission?"

McRofaly arched an eyebrow. "What do you mean?" he asked, a tinge of defensiveness to his otherwise calm voice. "I already explained my reasons in front of the war council."

Colvin laughed around his mouthful of corned beef hash, which made for a none-too-pleasant image from McRofaly's vantage point. "I'm not saying you were insincere," Colvin said, "but I know when someone is trying to butter me up. You've obviously got another reason for wanting me to go with you, and it's obviously one you didn't want to bring up in front of the council. Since I agreed to go on this mission with you, I think it's only fair we lay all our cards on the table." *Why am I being so straightforward with this man?* Colvin thought. *I hardly know him. God, I need to get some sleep. I'm acting loopy.*

"Captain Jefford was right about you," McRofaly said after a few moments of silence. "You are smarter than you look."

Colvin smirked.

"All right," McRofaly said. "If you honestly want to know why it was you I requested, I will tell you. I meant everything I said in front of the war council about you being an upstanding fellow, but you're right, that is not the only reason. The fact is if I threw a stone in this town it would probably hit three upstanding fellows before it landed. This war, surprisingly enough, has brought out the best in people, including yourself. The reason I requested you specifically is because we have a mutual acquaintance."

"Melinda," Colvin said. It did not even hint at being a question.

"Yes, Melinda," said McRofaly. "She confided in me what happened on your dinner date, and I know any man that reacted as you did to what happened is a man I can depend on when my neck is on the line."

"Well, that's certainly one way to look at it, I guess," Colvin said.

"What are your intentions with Melinda?" McRofaly asked. His voice was serious, though not nearly as serious as it would have been if he had been discussing war matters, and by the look on his face it was evident he expected an answer. A part of Colvin was a little perturbed at McRofaly's bluntness. Oddly enough, though, a larger part of him really did not mind all that much. He was too tired to be concerned with politeness.

"In what sense?" Colvin asked.

"Let me be forthright on this point," McRofaly replied. "I am a man that values his privacy, and as such, there are not many people whom I consider to be friends. Melinda and I are close acquaintances, and out of everyone in this town, if I were going to call someone a friend it would most likely be her. She has confided in me an interest in knowing whether your intentions with her are similar to what they have been with certain other women you have pursued since your arrival in Tamendad."

"You don't do this much, do you?" was Colvin's reply.

"Do what?"

"Favors for other people."

McRofaly sighed. "No," he said. "Is it really that obvious?"

"Painfully," Colvin said, smiling, as he finished off the last of his sausages. McRofaly sighed again, a mildly self-deprecating sound. "Don't worry," Colvin continued, "I think it's a nice thing you're doing. You're a good friend."

"So anyway, your intentions?" persisted McRofaly.

"Well, God, McRofaly, that's a tough question. I barely even know the girl. I've been out with her twice. The first time we hit it off great and almost wound up in bed together. The second time she treated me like I was her cousin. What the twist am I supposed to think about that?"

"Well, Colvin, you must appreciate her apprehensiveness. You have a reputation in this town." McRofaly winked, and by the look of it, it was obvious that that was not something he did very often either. It looked more like he was having an eye spasm.

"I do?" Colvin asked. He was unaware of any reputation he had garnered for himself, besides, of course, the general feeling of respect that McRofaly had mentioned in front of the council. "What kind of reputation, exactly?"

"Well," McRofaly said delicately, "it's widely known that you spend a good amount of your free time with Don Ferdinan, and that the two of you spend a great deal of that time together in the company of various women, pursuing certain unmentionable ends."

"You think I'm a seducer?" Colvin said, a tad bit offended.

"Personally, I don't know one way or the other," McRofaly replied. "But that is the reputation your escapades in the trade district have earned you."

"Well curse me," Colvin muttered to himself. His stomach suddenly felt queasy. It felt like it was Rosie Rothwald all over again. "McRofaly, I've never seduced a woman in my life...well, okay, that's a lie, but I swear I haven't seduced a woman since coming to Tamendad. I've not tried to talk any woman into doing anything she didn't willingly want to do on her own. You believe that, don't you?" *Why should I care if he believes me or not?* Colvin thought. *He's not the one I want to believe me.*

"Actually, I do believe you," said McRofaly. He crossed his knife and fork over his plate, even though there were still a few bites of egg and half a sausage left on it, and crossed his arms over his chest, giving Colvin a thoughtful look. "I don't know why I believe you, but I do. But like I said, you have to understand her reluctance to get involved with you."

"I'll have a talk with her," Colvin said.

"I think that's a good idea," McRofaly replied. "Let me just give you a word of advice about Melinda."

"Please," Colvin said. He was desperate for any advice that might shed some light on the actions of this enigmatic woman.

"She's had a rough time of it when it comes to men. She'd probably kill me if she heard me tell you that, but it's true. I'm not sure exactly what her story is, since she's never told it to me, but it's obvious that romance has never been very kind to her. Even if you do have that talk with her – and I think you should – you should probably expect to still encounter some resistance. She's a pretty private person. That's probably why we get along. Just don't push too hard."

"Understood," said Colvin, nodding. "Now back to the scouting trip, I do have a couple more suggestions now that I think about it."

McRofaly nodded. "Go ahead, I'm listening," he said. Then he sat back in his chair, watched Colvin finish his breakfast, and disregarded just about everything the red-haired young man said.

CHAPTER TWENTY-ONE

THE HIGHLANDS WAY

Very few Turishmen had ever learned why it was that while most of the Dammaugh moved as far south into Glenisle as possible while the kingdom of Tur was being formed, some put down roots in the Highlands. Most Turishmen never discussed the subject, and those few that did offered a wide range of theories as to why some clans decided to stop halfway down the island. Most scholars asserted that those clans assumed the rugged, mountainous terrain of the Highlands would prove easy to defend. Some posited that the Highlander clans believed the land would prove undesirable to Turish conquerors. The official position of Andorius Byrne, Royal Historian to King Archibald Stodlemeyer, was that some Dammaugh clans remained in the Highlands because the region provided ample opportunities to hide from Turish soldiers, even though the Dammaugh had never been known as a people to shy away from a fight. Each of those theories was equally valid, inasmuch as they were all totally inaccurate.

The real story of why some clans remained in the Highlands while others continued southward centered around a man by the name of Kitcher Carlyle. When the men who would eventually call themselves Turish began arriving from across the Melteric Ocean around the third century Posteriori Cataclymian, the natives, who would eventually be called Glenish, rallied together to fight for their homeland. Kitcher Carlyle was the leader of one of the largest resistance movements, and his effort to kick the invaders off the island was very nearly successful, but it ultimately fell short due to the invading forces' knowledge of siege weapons, a military advance that had escaped the clans. Once defeated, Carlyle and his followers retreated south through Tur and across the Taeran, and they were pursued by Turish forces during the entire journey. By the time Carlyle's band reached the Highlands, their pursuers were so close that the banners that flew in their camp were plainly visible on the horizon. Another day and Carlyle and his followers would be routed and slaughtered. With his back against a wall, Carlyle prayed to Rualadgh, Keeper of the Sky and King of the Afterlife, for guidance – this all happened long before the Glenish were converted to the Antrelican faith – and he received a vision that led him to believe that he should lead an attack against the pursuers when night had fallen.

That night, as soon as the sky had turned dark, Kitcher Carlyle and his pursuers discovered the aurora that hung over the Highlands. The luminous, serpentine bands of red and blue and gold that swayed gently through the night sky fascinated Carlyle's men and terrified the Turish forces, and, interpreting the sight as further evidence that Rualadgh was with him, Carlyle sounded the charge. With the aurora hung low in the sky and the sound of war cries echoing all around them, the Turish soldiers called a retreat before they were even engaged in battle. They left everything behind in their camp, many of them fleeing into the night in only their underclothes. Carlyle and his men celebrated their good fortune, and Carlyle declared that his running was over. He would live out his days in the mountains where Rualadgh had led him to face his enemies. Word of his decision and the good omen of the aurora began to spread, and more clans flocked to the area, eventually referring to themselves as Highlanders. Carlyle's escape was not without a price, however. When the pursuing forces returned to the mainland they spread word of what they had witnessed, and for many long years the aurora of the Highlands was interpreted by many as a sign of Glenish pagan magic.

The aurora was barely becoming visible as Gregor MacDugal first caught sight of Duerhein as he led his three companions through the mountain pass. The undulating waves of color seemed to subtly materialize as the sun sank lower and lower on the western horizon, beginning as tiny dancing motes of light. Slowly, methodically, the motes grew and connected, swirling into an ever-expanding prismatic web that branched out in all directions, spreading its ethereal arms over the Highlands like an experienced lover. It was a sight that every Highlander associated with home. Normally, the sight of it, along with the sight of Duerhein, would have done Gregor wonders. As it stood, though, his heart sank to see it. Gregor MacDugal had never been one to skirt his duty, and he would not skirt it now, but he had never been faced with anything like this. His brother was dead. His *comhairadh* were following behind him with weary, doleful expressions, riding horses pressed almost to the breaking point. In front of him lay his city, his castle, his family. He was bringing them word that Angus MacDugal was dead, and he was coming to raise an army. War and death rode with him. War had already begun. Death had already come.

All four men had garnered wounds and scars on their ride south from Tamendad. They had been fortunate in not encountering many goruks, but what few they had encountered no longer walked among the living. A severed goruk head was hanging by the hair from the pommel of Wallace's saddle. Another hung beside Liam's horse, and two dangled from Gabrahn's saddlebow. Gregor's mount sported three trophies, two of them hanging by the hair from either stirrup so that the chins almost dragged on the ground, and the third resting upright on the pommel of his saddle. That one was shorn of all skin, and the eyes and brain had been removed. The skull sat at the front of Gregor's saddle with its hollow sockets staring vacantly forward. It was grisly, and not only in appearance. Although free of skin and organs, the skull still fairly reeked of the sickly-sweet stench of death and decay. Gregor was actually the only man out of the four who did not seem to notice. No one had broached the subject with the big Highlander, not once since he had set about his gruesome task by the fireside the previous night. Liam, Gabrahn and Wallace assumed Gregor had his reasons for doing it, most likely as a warning for other goruks to keep their distance. Gregor himself would have been incapable of explaining why he had decided to use one of his trophies as a macabre saddle ornament. All he knew was that slicing the skin and gouging out the eyes of that goruk's head felt right, and placing the skull on his saddle for all to see served as a message, not for goruks but for everyone: where Gregor MacDugal goes, goruks suffer.

Gregor reigned in as soon as he caught sight of Duerhein, and his companions followed suit. By all appearances, everything was business as usual in the town below. The market was bustling as always, and men and women and children moved this way and that, seeing to whatever business or pleasure held their attention at the moment. In some ways Duerhein was just like Tamendad. In others, it could not have been more different. No wall surrounded the town and everywhere in the unpaved streets men wore kilts and tartans, most in the colors of the Clan MacDugal. A good number of women wore those colors as well, and as many of them wore trousers as skirts or dresses. Highlander women were not nearly so reserved as their Turish counterparts, and a decent number of local Turish magistrates had courted and married Highlander women, finding their fiery, fierce individuality and self-assurance strangely captivating. Whenever such a marriage occurred, it was invariably followed by a change in the politics of that magistrate's jurisdiction. Highlander women were not known to relent to their husbands' decisions just because he was a man, and they often had inventive methods for bringing their husbands around to their own point of view. Kila was that type of woman. She was the perfect compliment to Angus. She and Angus had not had what most people would have called a perfect marriage. They fought. They fought quite a lot, actually. They had a tendency to throw things at each other, and every once in a great while one of them would storm out on the other under the pretense of never coming back. They always came back, though, and they always said they were sorry. And they always walked around with coy, telling smiles after the two of them had participated in the ancient ritual of making up, except when the fight had been serious and the making up even more intense than the fight, after which Kila usually could not walk for a day or two. The truth was that Angus and Kila enjoyed the fighting and enjoyed the making up even more. Kila was the first woman that would ever call Angus's bluff. That was probably the main reason why Angus had fallen so completely, hopelessly in love with her. Kila had no idea that she and Angus would never have another fight. She had no idea Gregor was coming to tell her that her husband was dead. She had no idea she was a widow. Gregor would have probably sold his soul not to be the one to tell her those things.

There was only the one riding path, winding its way lazily back and forth down the face of the mountain until the ground leveled a bit and the path widened to become one of the larger roads running through Duerhein. Calling it a riding path was a bit of a stretch. The path was so perilous in spots, with a single faulty step bring with it a plunge of fifty feet or more, that most people chose to lead their horses down on foot. Gregor was no exception. He and his three companions started down the path leading their horses behind them. The horses, so eager to run just the previous morning, were visibly thankful for the respite. The walk down the mountain was made in silence, since the horses separated the men from one another. They all watched Duerhein grow as they neared it, and it did not take long for the people in the town below to notice the approach of the Highlanders. Gregor was still much too far away to hear, but he knew his name was being spoken. Were they close enough yet for people to realize that Angus was not with them? What comments would their trophies bring? How many would fight to defend a town full of Turishmen? These thoughts followed Gregor all the way down the mountain, and almost before he realized it he stood with his lads at the place where the path widened and became Tramborough Road, on the outskirts of town. They were still alone, more or less. Few people entered Duerhein by Tramborough Road, preferring the easier but longer routes that cut through the valleys. Most people wound up on Tramborough

Road eventually, though, because at the other end of it from where Gregor and his lads now stood lay Castle Duerhein, also called Castle MacDugal by some, the oldest castle in all of Glenisle. Just about everyone who came to Duerhein came to Castle MacDugal. Anyone who had business with the Clan MacDugal that did not require the attention of the *ceann-cinnidh* was usually sent to meet with Gregor MacDugal. With the regularity of such visitors, as well as the numerous people who came throughout the year to pay fealty to Gregor, the township of Duerhein had grown up around the castle to provide for the needs of the men and women who came calling.

The town itself was really little more than an oversized village, a few hundred people spread out across a few acres of land, but it had six inns, four taverns, two bath houses, a set of stables that could hold upwards of a hundred steeds, and a rather impressive church. The great stone edifice of Castle MacDugal towered above the township, its banners proclaiming that this land belonged to the Clan MacDugal in general and to Gregor MacDugal in particular. The castle was austere in appearance, humble as castles went, little more than a four turrets and a central stronghold with a spire, but men and women would come from miles around to marvel at it. It seemed to grow right out of the side of the mountain, an extension of the ground itself. Gregor had lived in that castle his whole life, and the sight of it still amazed him a bit. When he had been young, Angus had said that the castle looked like it had been grown rather than built, and he was exactly right. No one knew exactly how Castle Duerhein had been built, but any fool could have told that it had been around for centuries before the Clan MacDugal had lain claim to it, a forgotten stronghold of a forgotten people. Whatever people had built it, they were a mystery beyond legend now.

"Home," Liam said with a mixture of emotions. Gregor gave him a look that made him shuffle his feet like a child.

"Aye, home, but nae for long. Dinnae get too comfortable."

Liam nodded, as did Wallace and Gabrahn, and that was all that was said on the matter. The men walked together, leading their horses toward the castle that had come to represent not only the Clan MacDugal but the Highland way of life in general. As they drew nearer the heart of the town they could practically feel the increasing number of puzzled looks coming their way. Everyone kept their distance, though. Perhaps it was the severed heads that dangled from the men's steeds that kept them at bay, heads of beasts that no one in Duerhein had ever seen. Just as likely, though, it could have been that no one approached because of the look on Gregor's face. The big Highlander was well known in Duerhein, being the head of the Duerhein MacDugals and something akin to Duerhein's

Governor, and everyone knew that he always had a certain look on his face when he was upset. Walking through his town that evening, Gregor MacDugal had that look in spades. Whatever the cause, the first person to address Gregor was Tanner, head page of Castle Duerhein, when he greeted Gregor and his companions upon entering. Tanner had been page since before Gregor became head of the family, and he had seen just about everything there was to see during his years of service to the Clan MacDugal. The sight of the four Highlanders – battered, injured, thoroughly pissed off – along with the beastly heads dangling from their horses was almost enough to leave him at a loss for words. "God rest ye, Gregor, and welcome home," was all he managed to say.

Gregor only nodded to acknowledge the greeting. "Where's Patricia?"

"Somewhere in th' castle," Tanner replied. "I shall summon her."

"Aye," Gregor replied. "Have her sent t' m' chambers immediately." Gregor continued on into his castle without another word. Nothing further needed to be said. Liam, Gabrahn and Wallace all knew what they were supposed to do, and their requests would be plenty enough to keep Tanner busy for the next few hours.

Gregor walked alone down the familiar stone hallways decorated with tapestries and wall-mounted weapons wielded by previous MacDugals and oil-lamp sconces that bathed the heart of the Castle Duerhein in the soft, warm glow of firelight even when the sun outside was at its noonday harshest. The echoes of his footsteps, the solid *clop* of boots on stone, resounded through the corridors, echoes doubling and redoubling, enveloping him in a steady percussion. The only other sound was the accompanying beat of his heart. The castle was mostly deserted, as always. Its only permanent inhabitants were Gregor, his daughter Patricia, Tanner, the five other pages that answered to Tanner, and the two cooks. A few of the guest rooms were always occupied, either with people calling on business or friends of Gregor who were just stopping in to say hello – Liam, Gabrahn and Wallace all stayed at the castle as much as they stayed in their own homes – but even with those frequent visitors the Castle MacDugal always seemed empty. It was emptier still without Angus.

Gregor found his bedchamber as he had left it. The oversized, overstuffed bed, if not particularly neat and tidy, was at least properly made up. Gregor always made his own bed. He did not believe in making other men clean up after him in his own home. The large wooden wardrobe rested against the south wall with its doors just slightly ajar, a natural result of the warping of the wood throughout the many years. Gregor's big oak desk sat against the north wall, right beside the large window that overlooked the town below. A bottle half-full of whiskey sat on the desk next to an empty glass. Other than that, the desk was bare. The desk was the oldest piece of furniture in the entire castle. His father had sat at that desk, as had his father's father and his grandfather's grandfather, back through the generations. It was simple in design, always smooth and well polished, and sitting at it always made Gregor think about his da. A chair and an end table with an oil lamp on it were the only other pieces of furniture in the room. It was decorated as sparsely as it was furnished. One tapestry, in the colors of the Clan MacDugal, hung on the west wall, an oil painting of Gregor's parents hung above the desk, and two claymores were mounted to the wall above the bed so that their blades crossed in an X. Gregor preferred simplicity in all aspects of his life, and his living space was no exception.

Gregor moved toward his desk with the half-bottle of whiskey in mind. He desperately needed a drink. Patricia entered the room before he even had his glass poured. Her cheeks were the same color as the curly red hair that spilled down her back, and her brow was furrowed in a way that told Gregor he was about to receive a stern talking-to. She was standing in the doorway with her left hand planted on her hip. In her right she held a pitcher of water. She had a tendency to pick things up and walk around the castle with them in hand without even realizing it. It was the only thing that was even slightly absentminded about her.

"So th' vacationer has returned from his holiday," she said in that tone of voice that made her sound eerily like her mother. "So good o' ye t' come back with such promptness, Father. More than two weeks gone and nae so much as a letter, and th' whole time I've been here tending both t' family business as well as our home. And when ye finally do come back, what should I hear but Tanner's voice echoing through th' whole o' th' castle, asking where I am and telling me m' da wants a word with me, just like that, like I have nae been left hanging in th' wind for th' better half of a month." She was tapping her foot rapidly now, and the crimson in her cheeks was beginning to spread down her neck. Pretty soon she would start using language that would make a sailor blush. "And another thing–"

"Uncle Angus is dead, Patricia."

The pitcher shattered as it hit the floor.

"*Dead?*" Patricia said, as though the word was foreign. Gregor nodded somberly. He did not think he could make himself say it out loud again. Patricia looked at her father with wide, disbelieving eyes, eyes that for the first time noticed the cuts and scars and wounds overlaying her father's body. Horror spread across her face as she realized they were far too many and far too serious to have resulted from a lighthearted scuffle or a barroom brawl. They were the mark of a man who had recently fought for his life, and probably more than once. "They *killed* him?" Patricia nearly shrieked.

"Nae," Gregor said firmly. "'Twas nae th' Turish, daughter. They treated us as honored guests."

"Then who?" Her voice was mostly consumed with shock, but even in the midst of such horrible news she had that calm, commanding quality that Gregor probably loved more than anything else about her. Gregor explained it all: the sneak attack, the militia, the battle at the northeast gate, McRofaly's lecture on the goruks. When he was done, both father and daughter had tears in their eyes.

"He gave his life for them," Gregor said. "For a town full o' people he barely knew." There was no holding the tears back then, for either of them. Patricia threw her arms around her father's neck, and although Gregor dwarfed his daughter in size, she was the strong one during that embrace. They hugged for a long, silent moment. When Patricia finally pulled back, she wiped away a stray tear with the sleeve of her dress and said, "What happens now?"

Gregor nodded, as though he agreed with the question. "Liam and Wallace shall ride for Aramarch t' rally men, and Gabrahn shall go t' Kienfallagh. As for m'self, I intend t' visit Padraig, t' call in an old favor. In two days, we march north with as many men as will come, and pray that Tamendad still stands when we get there. But first I shall pay Kila a visit on th' farm."

Patricia delicately place a hand on her father's broad shoulder. "I shall come with ye," she said.

Gregor sighed, and he placed his own hand on top of his daughter's. "I would appreciate that." Patricia smiled back at him, a smile full of pain.

It had been a while since Gregor had visited Angus's farm, not because of distance – it lay less than an hour's ride outside of Duerhein – but because Angus and Kila came to the castle so frequently that there was no need to visit them. The farm was rather modest, considering it belonged to one of the most prominent members of the Clan MacDugal, consisting of a farmhouse and a barn both of two stories, a modest stable housing half a dozen steeds, a dozen acres of vegetables, a couple acres of tobacco, an acre of skunkweed and one thoroughly wicked apple tree. That tree was the reason why Angus had chosen that particular patch of land to start his farm, his infatuation with it lasting long past his childhood. It was half-dead now, and an overgrowth of ivy around its trunk threatened to choke out the other half. Angus had never mentioned that the tree was dying, but Gregor was certain nonetheless that his brother had spent long hours trying to save it. Other than the tree, Gregor found the farm as he had remembered it, and when he finally left the farm that evening with Patricia and Kila on either side, his heart sank as he realized that this visit to the farm would be the one that stood out foremost in his mind.

Kila did not take the news particularly well, but neither did she take it particularly poorly. In all truthfulness, her reaction had been just about exactly what Gregor had expected. Her initial reaction had been incredulity, what with all the talk of goruks and war. When that had worn off there came the moments of silent shock, when Kila had looked from Gregor to Patricia and back to Gregor with pleading desperation, an irrational hopefulness that, as furious as it would have made her, the whole thing was just a twisted, heartless joke and Angus would burst through the door and yell, "Surprise!" at any moment. That was the most difficult for Gregor to watch, because he was all too familiar with that feeling. He had been living with it for three days. Then, with amazing quickness, Kila had realized that it was all really happening, that Angus really was dead, that she was a widow. Oh, how she wept then, and wailed, and screamed, and cursed, and for a moment Gregor thought she was going to turn on him. That thought was not to be taken lightly, not even by a man of Gregor's size and strength. Kila stood six feet tall and weighed at least two hundred pounds, every ounce of it firm, toned muscle. There were few men that could match her physically, and fewer still that could fight with more cunning. Before it ever got to that point, though, Kila regained her composure.

It took only a little coaxing to convince her to return to Duerhein, nothing more than a promise from Gregor that he would send men to look after the farm. Gregor knew that a night alone on the farm with the knowledge her husband was dead would be enough to drive Kila mad. Though she would have sooner died than admitted it, Kila knew it too. Gregor made good on his promise and sent four men to tend Angus's farm as soon as the three of them were back in Duerhein. What he did not tell anyone, even his own daughter, was that the first thing he ordered those four men to do, as soon as they got to the farm, was to uproot and burn that old, diseased apple tree. He would later spend hours wondering why he had done it, but at the time it was the most obvious thing in the world to do.

Liam, Gabrahn, and Wallace made their rides, and word of Angus's death spread throughout Glenisle as only news of a tragedy can. The first wave of visitors arrived in Duerhein the next morning, most coming simply to pay their respects but a good number armed and ready to head north as soon as Gregor gave the word. Gregor made the official announcement that Angus was dead that morning, but by that point it was more of an afterthought, the punctuation on the end of a terrible sentence. By that afternoon, Tavish MacDugal had heard of Angus's passing and pledged a few of his own men to Gregor's cause. Gregor procured more soldiers through his meeting with Padraig McFallagh, and people continued to file into Duerhein, ready to march straight to the battlefield to avenge Angus's death. By the evening of the first day of Gregor's hiatus, Duerhein looked more like a fortified military encampment than a village, and the look of it pleased Gregor as much as it turned his stomach.

The big Highlander sat at his desk under the pretense of looking over the messages that Liam and Gabrahn had sent – Aramarch and Kienfallagh had both been recruited to the fullest extent; Gabrahn was going to ride through the night to reach Glenloch in time; Liam and Wallace were splitting up and going from farm to farm to spread the word. Gregor was thoroughly familiar with those messages, as he had been sitting at his desk with them laid out in front of him for over an hour. Every now and then he would pick one of the papers up and look it over to make certain nothing on it had changed. Mostly, though, he just sat drinking whiskey, alternating his gaze between the view of the campfires in the town below that the window afforded and the portrait of his mother and father. He was so lost in his own thoughts that he did not hear the knock at the door until it came the second time. "Come," he said, grumbling more than he meant to, and did not look around when he heard the door open and shut.

"May God's mercy shine upon ye all th' days o' yer life," Gregor heard the familiar voice say. The big Highlander turned in his chair, and a smile turned up the corners of his mouth when he saw who it was. Carney was a little older, a little balder, and a little paunchier than when he and Gregor were lads, but for that matter, so was Gregor.

"Ye honor me with yer presence, Patrum Gruer." The two men hugged tightly, and all formality passed away. They were no longer priest and practitioner, just two old friends.

"A terrible thing," Carney Gruer said in a whisper. "A terrible thing." When they broke the hug, Carney dabbed at his eyes with the sleeve of his robe.

"Aye, terrible," Gregor said, but there was no emotion in his voice. "Have ye come t' stand postulant for me, Patrum?"

"Just t' talk with ye, really. I suspected I might find ye here rejoicing in th' miracle o' malted barley."

Gregor poured Carney a dram, offering the priest his own glass and taking the bottle for himself. "Beg yer pardon, Carney, but I dinnae feel much like talking about it at th' moment. I'm all talked out."

Carney nodded, sipping his whiskey. "Aye, I can understand. But I dinnae mean I wanted t' talk about that. Just about what ye're intending t' do about it."

"What are ye getting at?" Gregor asked.

"If ye have nae noticed, th' front o' yer castle looks like ye've hired a brute squad, with all th' armed men camped down there, and word is that more are coming from as far away as th' Glens. 'Tis nae a secret what ye're intending, Gregor. Ye're preparing for war."

"Aye, there's nae secret what I'm intending," Gregor replied. "I intend t' exact m' revenge on th' goruks for what th' bastards did t' Angus. This is nae a war I started, but I shall finish it." After a short pause, he added, "Have ye really come t' try talking me out of it?" Gregor could not make himself believe that. He and Carney Gruer had been friends since boyhood. They had so much shared history that they were practically kinsmen, priesthood or no.

"Talk ye out of it?" Carney said incredulously. "Just as well try talking a bear out of eating ye once ye've poked it in th' eye. I dinnae question what ye're doing, Gregor. I suppose ye could say I came t' volunteer."

Gregor looked at Carney with silent stupefaction. "Carney," the big Highlander said at last, "yer fighting days are o'er. Ye're a priest now."

"Aye, m' friend, I cannae fight, and 'tis nae what I'm volunteering for. What ye're doing is a good thing, Gregor, a noble thing, and I know ye enough t' know that ye would still be wrapped up in th' thick o' this, trying yer best t' save Tamendad even if such tragedy had nae befallen ye. 'Tis just yer giving nature. But marching north into Turish territory with an army might be misinterpreted as an act of aggression against th' Turish throne, and I dinnae believe ye would have so easy a time convincing th' king o' yer honorable intentions. Having an ordained priest o' th' Antrelican Church with ye will force people t' listen t' th' truth instead o' jumping t' conclusions. My presence is sure t' lighten yer burden. Besides, I'm sure those Tamendader priests have their hands full tending th' weary and wounded. I intend t' lend them a hand as best I can."

"It shall be good t' have ye, Carney," Gregor said.

"It shall be good t' be had," Carney replied. "M' life has been desperately wanting in adventure o' late. In a way, this will be like one of our boyhood romps."

"Aye, but this time th' monsters we're marching off t' fight are nae make believe."

"Nae, and I suppose they will nae be so easy t' vanquish, either. But then, nothing is e'er so easy as it seemed in childhood. I understand we leave th' day after th' morrow?"

"Aye, that's correct," Gregor said. "At first light."

"That shall give me just enough time t' set th' church in order for m' absence." Carney finished off his whiskey and stood up, handing the empty glass back to Gregor. "Well," the priest said, "I shall leave ye t' yer business. Th' Four Faces o' God smile upon ye, m' friend." The two men embraced once again, and Carney whispered, "I'm here for ye if e'er ye need t' talk or pray." In return, Gregor whispered, "I know." When the hug was over, Carney turned to go. Gregor said Carney's name just before the priest disappeared out the door. Carney looked back at Gregor with quiet concern.

"Aye?"

Gregor cleared his throat before saying, "Well, Patrum…I have made some good friends in Tamendad o'er th' last three weeks, good and honorable people, some o' th' best I have e'er been privileged t' meet, and I was hoping that mayhap, if ye have a chance, ye could pray that Tamendad can hold until we return."

Carney nodded solemnly.

"I already am."

CHAPTER TWENTY-TWO

DIFFICULT GOODBYES

A thick gray canvas of clouds had rolled in through the night and was firmly entrenched by the time the sun began to make its rounds over Tamendad that day. There was a chill in the morning's air, and a light drizzle had been falling since about two hours before sunup, leaving the men and women of the guard damp and trembling. The many bonfires that dotted the hillsides around Tamendad hissed and sputtered as raindrops fell upon them. The rain was too light and too scattered to threaten quenching the flames, just enough to pester them. Colvin and William stood side by side, huddled together by the bonfire closest to the southwest gate of Tamendad, teeth chattering, wet hair matted to their foreheads and damp clothes sticking to their bodies. The conditions were enough to make them thoroughly miserable, and yet they were both in surprisingly good spirits considering their situation. The fire was rapidly warming their bodies and drying their clothes, and the pallid sunlight filtering through the clouds served to announce that their shift was at an end. They had survived a night on guard outside Tamendad's wall, a night that had passed completely without incident. The goruks had not shown their ugly, tusked faces, and there had not been so much as the sound of a twig snapping in the darkness to arouse fear. By all appearances it had been just another rainy night, the type better spent indoors curled up tight in a warm blanket than out in the chill marching around the perimeter of the town wall.

Even better than a night without incident was the knowledge brought by a scout rider that the weapons shipment from Tantera was less than an hour's ride away. Soon the men and women guarding Tamendad against the goruk threat would be resupplied, and the townspeople would be on their way to the relative safety of Tantera. The latter thought was bittersweet, for with it came a host of farewells that no one wanted to bid.

Captain Jefford personally came to dismiss the night watch, and he gave special praise to the men and women who had braved the night outside the city. Once dismissed, Colvin and William said goodbye to one another – the first of many goodbyes that would be said that day – and went their separate ways. William headed home, where he would spend the morning with his family and his betrothed, along with her family as well. Colvin had other matters to attend to that morning, which he had characteristically put off until the last possible moment. Part of that was because he really did not want to butt in on William's last hours with his loved ones, but another part, probably just as large, was that he was not looking forward to his talk with Melinda. When he had discussed the matter with McRofaly over breakfast, it had seemed all too simple. She had some issues with intimacy and she needed reassuring, so obviously Colvin should have a talk with her. It was as simple as that. Now that Colvin was on his way to her house, though, it did not seem nearly so simple. In all honesty, Colvin was more nervous about the conversation he knew was coming than he had been about the prospect of being a member of the first wave of guardsmen to patrol the countryside. That made less than no sense, but Colvin was well aware that the human gut was often governed by forces immune to the powers of logical reasoning.

Each step down the streets that eventually led to Melinda's little three-room house took the greatest of effort and self-will, but strangely enough the trip was completed with lightning quickness and Colvin found himself staring at the sturdy oak door. He knocked quickly, not even giving himself time to think about it. Thinking too much would likely get him into trouble with the business he had at hand. The door opened promptly but only a little, just enough for Melinda to see who it was. By the look on her face she was obviously surprised.

"Oh, Colvin, I wasn't expecting you," Melinda said.

"Yeah, I know, sorry to drop by unannounced. I was kind of hoping I could talk to you. Can I come in?"

Melinda hesitated, and Colvin's heart skipped a beat. "Yeah, sure, come on in," she finally said without enthusiasm, opening the door wide and returning her attention to what she had been doing before Colvin had shown up. "You don't mind if I keep packing while we talk," she said over her shoulder.

Colvin was about to answer until he realized that it had not been a question. He offered to help. She politely declined. Then he said, "McRofaly and I had a talk the other day," and he thought he saw her stiffen.

"Oh really? What about?" She was stuffing various metalworking tools, which were much too fine and delicate to ever be of any use to a blacksmith, into her backpack, and she was concentrating hard on the process to keep from looking at Colvin.

"Lots of things," Colvin replied, concentrating hard in turn to sound nonchalant. "The two of us are going on a scouting mission today. I'm not supposed to tell anyone about it."

She turned to look at him. Their eyes met. Colvin shifted on his feet a little. "Then why did you tell me?" she asked.

"Because I trust you."

Silence.

"Your name came up during our conversation," Colvin continued.

"I never asked him to talk to you," she said defensively. "That was his idea."

"It's okay, I don't mind."

"So what did he say about me?" she asked, turning her attention back to the items that she still had to squeeze into her pack.

"Not much, really. Just that you're still trying to figure me out."

"Well, that's fair to say, I guess. You're not the easiest person to get to know."

Colvin nodded sympathetically. "I just wanted to let you know I understand," he said.

She turned to look at him again. The back of her left hand was pressed against her hip, and her right hand was tucking her hair back behind her ear. At that moment Colvin thought she looked absolutely beautiful. "What do you understand, Colvin?" she asked.

The question took him off guard, and Colvin did not immediately answer. Melinda stared silently at him, still beautiful and in her own way more intimidating than any goruk could ever hope to be. Colvin cleared his throat. "Um, I mean, I understand your apprehensions," he said. "About me, I mean."

Melinda sighed, and nodded, and sort of smiled. "Thank you," she said.

More silence.

"So, hey, congratulations on getting a spot on a ship," Colvin said to clear the air.

"Yeah, that was a bit of good...hold on, how did you find out about that?" She had suspicion in her eyes.

"I put in a good word for you," Colvin said with a smile.

"You rigged the lottery? Colvin, that's horrible. I mean...I'm really flattered that you went out of your way to get me a spot on a ship, but you robbed somebody else of a fair chance."

"Hold your horses," Colvin said, holding up his hands to stay her. "I didn't rig the lottery. I convinced William to lend me some money."

"Huh?"

"I bought you passage on a ship," Colvin said.

Melinda's eyes widened. "Colvin, I...I don't know...how can I ever repay you?"

"You don't have to repay me. Don't worry about it."

"Why?" she asked. "Why would you do something like that for me?"

Colvin wiped his palms on his pants. He found that they had suddenly become sweaty. "Because I care about you," he blurted out, surprised at how easily those words came. The next did not come quite so effortlessly. "In fact," he continued, "it's more than just caring about you. I think I have feelings for you, Melinda. Strong feelings. I think I–"

"Oh, God, please, don't," Melinda interrupted. She had her hand on her chest, and she looked to be on the brink of hyperventilation.

"What?" This was not the reaction Colvin had anticipated.

"Colvin, I think you are a wonderful man, and I very much want to be friends with you, but right now, at this point in my life, friendship is all I can offer. Romance just isn't something I'm looking for right now. I'm really flattered that you feel...whatever it is you feel for me, and if I were looking for a serious relationship, I would jump at the opportunity. But that's not a place I can go. Do you understand?"

"Yes," Colvin lied.

"I'll understand if you want to give the spot on the ship to somebody else."

Colvin hoped dearly that the sting Melinda's words brought did not register on his face. "That's an unconditional gift," he replied.

"Oh," Melinda said. "Well, thank you again. From the bottom of my heart."

"No problem." Colvin forced a smile.

"So when do you and McRofaly leave?" Melinda asked, trying to make it seem not so obvious that she was desperate to change the subject.

"Pretty soon. The weapons shipment from Tantera should be here within the hour. We're going to try slipping out unnoticed during all the commotion with the evacuation."

"Aren't you tired?" she asked.

Colvin shook his head. "I've only been up, oh, maybe six hours. I only put in a half-shift on duty last night. Governor's orders. Or maybe it was Ferdinan's. It's hard to tell."

"Well, be careful," she said.

"Yeah, you too," he replied. "I'd better go track down McRofaly."

She walked up to him, put her arms around his neck, and hugged him tightly. It was the single most confusing thing she possibly could have done. "I mean it, be careful," she repeated. Her body was warm against his, and in spite of everything that had gone so terribly wrong in their conversation, this felt right.

"I will," he said.

He offered once again to help her pack, and once again she politely declined. He left her to her last-minute preparations, letting himself out and strolling more-or-less aimlessly through the streets full of people about to leave their homes. He had not a single thought of tracking down McRofaly. He walked around lost in his thoughts for a while, staring up at the pale gray sky and feeling the drizzle slowly re-soak him.

Who would have ever guessed insanity was such an attractive personality trait? he thought.

Their parents were rather amazed with how well the young couple seemed to be taking the prospect of their separation. Neither William nor Melissa had shed a single tear yet. They did not talk much. Instead they just sat on the daybed in the sitting room of the Stuart-Camen household, holding hands, staring into each other's eyes, taking turns leaning their heads on each other's shoulder and enjoying one another's company. Melissa's family was all packed and ready to go as soon as the word came, as was William's family. Governor Chamberlain had laid down strict guidelines about the evacuation for those people traveling by ship, and one of these was a strict limit of one trunk per person. With Winston Tilman's strong sense of economy and fair play and Jonathan Stuart-Camen's borderline frugality, the two families had managed to pack everything into only three trunks, and that included the belongings of not only the four nobles making the trip but also the six servants who were going with them. Those three trunks stood stacked by the main entrance of the Stuart-Camen household, and Winston was leaning against them with his hands in his pockets, chewing thoughtfully on an unlit pipe. Jonathan sat in his favorite chair, and Lyllian was sitting on his lap. It was the first time in William's life that he could remember seeing his mother sit on his father's lap, the way young girls smitten with puppy love might behave with their first suitor. Julius was sitting against the wall with his legs crossed, spurning the numerous chairs and settees of the sitting room. Jaline, Melissa's mother, was staring out the window of the sitting room, wringing her hands together absently. Out of everyone, she seemed to be taking the evacuation hardest. Melissa was visibly nervous as well, but only to an eye such as William's, which was well trained in picking out subtle peculiarities in her behavior. The delicate way she stroked William's hand or ran her fingers through her hair or the way she would absentmindedly plant a small series of kisses on his forehead while his head rested on her shoulder betrayed her inner feelings through her exterior of forced resolve. If such were possible, William loved her even more because of her inner strength, her ability not to break down and weep like he himself wanted to. He drew strength from her strength.

When the news came that the weapons shipment had arrived from Tantera, William felt Melissa's grip on his hand tighten considerably. They looked into each other's eyes for a long, silent moment. William put his hand against Melissa's cheek, and she closed her eyes and nuzzled against his touch. William sighed, and Melissa did too, and neither of them realized that their parents were doing exactly what they were doing, not through exactly the same gestures but in essence. After about a quarter of an hour, a town crier made his way down the street outside the Stuart-Camen home announcing that everyone who had procured passage on a ship should bring their luggage outside for the carts to pick up. Jonathan, William and Julius all began to move the trunks outside onto the front lawn, and the women all gathered together in the sitting room, arm in arm in arm, pretending that everything was all right. Soon the luggage cart came lumbering down the cobbled street, its two draft horses huffing and puffing against the burden they dragged along behind them. The trunks were loaded on the cart, and then it was time to head to the docks. That journey was surreal, with the streets of the residential district packed with well dressed noblemen and landowners, many openly weeping, all making their way toward the defunct northeast gate. Constables helped keep the crowds of people flowing, kindly but firmly insisting that everyone keep moving along, and more than a handful of people were obviously taken aback by being ordered around like commoners. William and Melissa huddled together under a cloak to stave off the damp autumn chill.

"Bullshit, that's what this is," Winston Tilman's unusually gruff voice carried through the heavy air. Melissa spared a sidelong glance at her father, unaccustomed as she was to hearing profanity from his mouth. "Pure bullshit," Lord Tilman continued. "Tamendad needs every good swordsman it can muster. My knees are not so bad that I can't stand and fight to defend my home."

"When was the last time you climbed a flight of stairs without having to stop halfway up?" Jonathan countered, his voice firm but not condescending.

Winston set his jaw in reply, a small vein bulging in his large forehead as he ground his teeth together. Jonathan and Winston did not look at each other. William felt that he should say something, but he had no idea what so he kept his silence.

"No stairs to climb to kill goruks," Winston finally replied, but it was halfhearted, the response of a man who knew his argument was lost but who took some small measure of comfort in having the last word.

The sight of the northeast gate sent a chill down William's spine despite the fact that he had stood guard at that gate almost every night since its destruction. This morning the carts and wagons had been rolled away to allow men and women to board the ships, and all that remained of the previous night's bonfires were two piles of ash. It made the city look mortally wounded. William said nothing about it. He did not want his parting words to his future wife to be about how easy a target the city had become. Melissa pressed close against him as they walked through the broken gate and onto the docks. They found their ship, the *Stingray*, without much problem, since the only ships docked that morning were the seven that were ferrying passengers to Tantera. The trunks were put onto another ship. To save time during the boarding process, luggage was just carted randomly onto the ships; it would all be sorted upon arrival in Tantera. All too quickly, the time had come for William to say goodbye to his mother, his brother, and his future bride. The knot in his stomach tightened to match the lump in his throat. His hold around Melissa's hip tightened as well.

"If you start to get seasick, remember to go up on deck," he told her. "It helps if you can see where the ship is going." His father had told him that once. He had to assume it was true, since he had never been seasick to find out.

"I will," Melissa said, nodding. "Remember to wear your cloak at night. Autumn's already here, and it will be turning cold soon. I don't want you catching a chill." She shuddered, as if to add emphasis to her words.

"I promise."

"I'll write you every day. Even if I can't send you the letters, I'll write. You can read them all when I get back."

He wanted to say, "I look forward to that," but the words caught in his throat. He felt the warmth of tears welling up behind his eyelids. He hugged her tightly, burying his face in her shoulder, not wanting her to see. She in turn put her head on his shoulder, and he could feel her body tremble with quieted sobs. They stood there for a moment hiding their tears from each other, and when the moment subsided they pulled away and dabbed at their eyes as nonchalantly as they could manage.

"I'll miss you," William told her.

"I already miss you," Melissa replied.

They hugged once more, and then it was goodbye. She turned and boarded the ship with her parents, and she did not look back until she was already on deck. William was thankful for that. It made the cut cleaner, easier to deal with. William turned his attention to Julius and his mother. He embraced both of them tightly, kissing his mother on the cheek and his brother on the forehead. They told him to be careful, and he promised them both that he would. Then they too were gone, onboard the boat that would take them away from Tamendad and the threat of the goruks. That knowledge was what held William together. No matter how terribly he would miss them, they would all be safer where they were going. He felt an arm slide around his shoulder, and when he looked up he saw that his father's face looked as haggard as his own.

"Be brave, William," Jonathan told him. "It may be tough to see them go, but they are sailing to safety."

"I was just thinking the same thing," William said.

"You're wise beyond your years," his father replied, patting him on the back.

"It should be me that was going," said Gangis.

Gunther said nothing, just redoubled his attention on fastening the buckles and tightening the straps on the saddlebags he was securing to his pony. The idea had been hanging insubstantial in the air between father and son all morning, but it had remained unspoken until now, when Gunther was making the final preparations to depart. Now that it was out in the open, Gunther ignored it like a man might ignore a drunkard stumbling in his direction.

"Did you hear me?" Gangis demanded in a tone of voice he rarely ever used with his father.

"I make it a point to ignore nonsense," Gunther grumbled. Gangis had been upset ever since Gunther had told him that he had to stay behind in Tamendad, and he was even more upset after their conversation the night before, when Gunther had finally explained his reasons for escorting the townspeople to Tantera. Gunther had never intended to explain those reasons. It was good enough that he was Gangis's father, and his word was law in the Moragun household. But then at the dinner table last night Gunther had looked at his son, and he had seen the person he sometimes saw when he looked at Gangis – not the sprawling whelp who had once damn near killed himself because he had not heeded his father's warning that he was too young to try smelting on his own, but the intelligent, resourceful young man who stood on the threshold of adulthood, who was quite capable of making decisions on his own, and who at least deserved to know the reasons why he alone out of all of Shield Division was staying behind. Hearing the reasons did little to placate Gangis's anger, but he at least understood. Gunther could tell he understood. And he had not mentioned anything that hinted he disagreed with his father's reasoning until now.

"You're too old to try something like this," Gangis said. "It's too dangerous."

Gunther fixed his son with a steady stare. "Tell you what, boy. If you really believe that, take a swing at me and we'll see how your youth holds up against my experience."

Gangis's eyes widened with shock. The one thing he would never do – never even *dream* of doing – was raise a hand against one of his parents. Gunther chuckled to himself as he looked his saddle over once more. "I didn't expect you'd take me up on that offer," he said. "Now I've already explained myself. It's got to be me that goes. They don't know you, son. They'd as likely kill you on sight as listen to what you have to say."

Gangis began to say something.

"And before you even ask," Gunther interrupted, "the reason you can't help escort the townspeople to Tantera is because Tamendad needs a blacksmith. Colvin's agreed to lend a hand, but he'd be in way over his head if he tried to go it alone. There needs to be someone who knows what he's doin' at the forge."

Gangis crossed his arms sullenly over his chest, as irritated over the fact that his father correctly guessed what he had been about to say as he was at what his father had actually said in response. "I'm not a little kid anymore. I should have a choice."

Gunther patted his pony on the rump when he was finished checking his saddle, and his son's words made him do it a bit more forcefully than he had meant to. The pony brayed and started a bit and gave the appearance that it was seriously considering making a run for it. Both father and son rushed forward to calm the animal, stroking its nose, rubbing its mane, speaking gently to it. Once the animal had been subdued, Gunther looked at his son, who was still scratching behind the pony's ear, and once more he saw the person he had seen last night at dinner. That person seemed to come around more and more often these days.

"You're right," Gunther said to his son.

"What, Dad?"

"You should have a choice. You do have a choice. Whether I like it or not, you're a man now. If you decide to go with Shield Division, I can't stop you."

Gangis was quite close to a state of shock, having won an argument with his father for the first time in his life. "And the cave?" he asked.

"I won't allow you to go to the cave. Not because I think you're still a child. You're my son, and it's my job to watch out for you even after you're grown. But it's your choice to stay here as Tamendad's blacksmith or go to Tantera with Shield Division. I'm askin' you to stay here, if that matters."

Gangis was quiet for a long, thoughtful moment. "Tamendad needs a smith a lot more than it needs one more escort for the townspeople," Gangis said at last. "If it can't have you, I guess I'm the next best thing. I'll stay."

Gunther breathed a sigh of relief and placed a firm hand on his son's shoulder. "You're a good man, Gangis Moragun. A damn fine man."

Gangis suddenly found he could not hold his father's stare. "Thanks, Dad," he said.

"You earned it. Now I've gotta get a move on. Shield Division's meetin' up at the northwest gate."

"Be careful."

"I will. You too. Look after your mother." Gertrude had volunteered to remain in Tamendad as a cook for the constabulary and the Pride. "Oh, and I had a look at the weapons from Tantera this mornin'. There's some nasty-lookin' stuff in there. If anything looks like it's beyond hope, just set it aside and I'll take a look at it when I get back." After mounting his pony, Gunther added, "I love you, son."

"I love you too, Dad."

Gunther righted himself in the saddle and readied the reigns.

"Dad?"

"What is it, Gangis?" There was no impatience in Gunther's voice.

"How do you know how to build a funeral pyre?"

"What?"

"At Angus's funeral, you helped build the pyre, and you looked like you'd done it before. Where'd you learn to do that?"

Gunther slumped visibly in the saddle and sighed. "Son," he said, "there's so much you don't know about our people." Gunther shook his head as he spoke, rebuking himself for a father's failures. "That's my fault. A man should know who he is and where he came from. When I get back, we're gonna have a long talk."

Gangis nodded. He could not think of anything to say in reply, so he simply said, "Godspeed." Then he added, "Ganugamon's pride." Gunther looked at Gangis, and for the briefest of moments Gangis thought he saw a tear come to his father's eye, but in the next moment it was gone and Gangis dismissed it. As far as he knew, his father simply did not cry.

"Ganugamon's pride," Gunther echoed. Then he snapped the reigns and was off, riding toward the northeast gate, toward the cave, toward his destiny.

It was, in fact, only their second kiss – if one counted a kiss on the hand as a kiss at all – and it was the most mind-blowing experience of young Elysia Chamberlain's life. She had kissed her fair share of boys before, but if that had been kissing then this was something completely different, something on another plane of existence. This sent alternating waves of heat and cold throughout her body and a tingle down her spine that made lightning pale in comparison. It curled her toes. It made her tremble like a frightened little girl. This kiss touched her soul. And much too quickly, it was over. She stood in the rain with her eyes closed, the hood of her cloak pulled so far up around her that from a distance it was impossible to tell her apart from any other young lady of high standing, her heart pounding in her chest, licking her lips, trying to savor the taste of the most passionate kiss anyone had ever given her. When she opened her eyes, Don Julio Franco Francisco Ferdinan of Losillas, Ambassador to the Conquian Throne, was smiling that damnable, irresistible smile that made her swoon. She wanted to reach out and grab him roughly by the neck and do things to him that would make the bawdiest harlots in the trade district blush themselves three shades of red, but, being the Governor's daughter and someone quite accustomed to restraining her baser urges, she simply straightened out the ruffles in her cloak and wiped away the moisture around her mouth instead. "If everyone in Conquia kisses like that, I cannot imagine why anyone would ever willingly choose to leave," she said.

Ferdinan laughed softly against the rain. "I beg your forgiveness, my lady," he said. "I was overcome by a moment of passion."

You can overcome me in a moment of passion anytime, Elysia thought. "You are forgiven," she said. "Emotions are running high on all sides today."

"Es a difficult time," Ferdinan replied. "Your bravery es an inspiration to your people."

Elysia laughed softly and was embarrassed by how much it sounded like a giggle. "They are not my people, Don Ferdinan. My father governs them. I am just a noblewoman."

"They look up to you," Ferdinan said. "They have much respect for you. Perhaps in time it will be you that governs them."

Elysia shook her head slightly, still laughing – giggling – and said, "There has never been a woman Governor of Tamendad, or anywhere else that I am aware of. Only men are bestowed that title."

"Things change."

Elysia looked at the docks off in the distance, full of townspeople boarding ships that would bear them away from the only homes they had ever known. Constables and militiamen stood or paced in front of the broken northeast gate with their weapons at the ready. Atop the city wall, lookouts peered off into the distance trying to catch a glimpse of whatever enemy might be lying in wait behind trees or hillsides. Tamendad had turned into a military state right before her eyes.

"That they do," she said, voice raw with emotion. Her eyes stung and her vision blurred with the tears that came to them. She did not want to cry in front of Ferdinan, for reasons that she could not even explain to herself, and she turned her face away so he could not see her. Carefully, gently, Ferdinan placed his hand on her cheek. His touch was soft and warm, much gentler than Elysia would have ever thought a man's touch could be. As he turned her face back toward him, a single fat tear rolled down her cheek and Ferdinan brushed it away with his thumb. Elysia was astonished at how much tenderness and compassion was contained in that one simple gesture, and the way Ferdinan was looking at her made her feel like the butterflies in her stomach were doing cartwheels. Her cheeks colored.

"Es going to be all right," Ferdinan whispered to her, and she wanted nothing more in the world than to believe him. "You must have faith, Elysia. God will see us through."

"It is difficult to have faith at a time like this, when everything looks so hopeless. It feels like God has abandoned us." The words, dangerously close to blasphemy in her own mind, caught in her throat as she spoke them. If Ferdinan was offended by her lack of faith, though, he did not show it. He took her hand in his and gently caressed it. The feel of it made her imagine, against her will, what it would feel like for him to caress other parts of her, and her color reddened even more.

"You must not let yourself believe that, Elysia," he said. "God es with us, now as always. He will see us through this."

Elysia nodded half-believingly. "I will pray for you, Don Ferdinan," she said.

"I would appreciate that very much," Ferdinan replied. Then they were silent together for a moment, looking into each other's eyes, and Elysia thought that he might kiss her again. She wanted that very much, so much that her toes curled a little just thinking about it, but the kiss did not come. Instead, Ferdinan said, "I must ask a favor of you, Elysia."

"Anything," Elysia replied almost before she realized it.

"Do not say that just yet. Es a difficult favor I ask. Es dangerous."

"What is it?" There was a hint of fear in her voice.

Ferdinan reached into his vest and retrieved a folded, wax-sealed piece of paper. "When you arrive in Tantera, find the fastest ship in port and give this to her captain. If he is hesitant to do as the letter says, tell him you are authorized to double the offer. That should be enough to bring any man around."

"I do not understand," Elysia said, looking at the letter in Ferdinan's hand. She could not see how delivering a letter could be dangerous.

"And it must remain that way," Ferdinan said vehemently. "You must promise me you will not read this letter. Es for your own protection. And should the letter fall into the hands of the goruks, may God forbid it, then you must tell them that you knew nothing of the letter's contents, that you were simply paid a small sum by a man you had never seen before to deliver it. Do you understand?"

Elysia nodded. "I understand."

"You will do it?"

"I will." She took the letter from his hand and tucked it securely into the inner pocket of her cloak. She wanted to ask him what it was about and what he was up to, but she knew that he would not answer those questions and that asking them would only make her look like a naive little girl. And in the end it really did not matter what the letter was about. At that moment it could have read, *Kidnap this woman and sail her to Conquia where she is to serve as my personal concubine for the rest of her days, signed Don Ferdinan*, and she would have delivered it. She would have done just about anything he asked at that moment, and again she would not have even been able to explain to herself the reasons why.

"Thank you, from the bottom of my heart," Ferdinan said, the solemness of his voice a stark contrast to the smile on his face. "I am in your debt."

Elysia curtsied formally, and for the first time the gesture made her feel a trifle silly. "My pleasure to be of service," she said. "Now I must take my leave of you, Don Ferdinan, and get to my ship."

That was when Ferdinan kissed her again, and this one blew the first kiss away. Elysia tumbled head over heels into it, heart pounding, palms sweating, body trembling. The kiss set every part of her aflame; body, mind and soul. Until that moment she had no idea that human beings could be made to feel so enraptured. When Ferdinan pulled his lips away from hers sometime later, everything in her world had changed on an essential level. "Oh my," she said absently, breathlessly.

"Sí," Ferdinan replied, equally breathless. They said nothing further to one another; Elysia just turned and walked away, toward the docks. Later she would not even remember doing it. All she would remember was the kiss – the amazing, mind-altering, soul-searing kiss – and then, sometime later, being onboard the ship sailing up the coast toward Tantera. Everything in between was lost in a muddled haze of passions and desires and lusts the likes of which she had never known.

Ferdinan stood and watched Elysia go, absentmindedly trailing his fingers over his own lips. Feelings – strong feelings – were stirring deep within him, feelings he had not felt for quite some time. He watched Elysia until she arrived at the docks and disappeared into the crowd of people waiting to board the ships, the crowd where William was saying goodbye to Melissa. Once Elysia had disappeared from view, Ferdinan straightened and returned his thoughts to the present as though escaping some enchantment she had woven around him. The letter was sent. He had done all that he could by setting his sights beyond the walls of Tamendad. Now it was time to dig in and focus on the here and now and try to hold out as long as possible, until reinforcements arrived. Ferdinan cut down a side street headed for the Governor's house. There was still much work to be done.

CHAPTER TWENTY-THREE

AN EXCURSION IN THE COUNTRYSIDE

As it turned out, it was McRofaly who tracked down Colvin, though to say McRofaly actually did any tracking was a bit of a stretch. Colvin just happened to be wandering haphazardly through the trade district when McRofaly emerged from one of the shops bearing an armload of rope, water skins, saddle blankets, trail rations, maps, books, flint and steel, heavy traveler's cloaks and the first spyglass and compass sold in Tamendad to someone who did not make their living on a ship. The supplies had cost a small fortune, worsened by the fact that any shopkeeper who sold traveling supplies had raised their prices half again over what they normally were. Yet despite the high inflation, the trade district was packed that morning with men and women stocking up on supplies for the overland journey to Tantera, and McRofaly had to fight tooth and nail to come away with what he had. By the time he emerged from the last shop on his list he was about ready to say enough with the whole scouting expedition, but then he spotted Colvin walking dejectedly down the streets, shoulders slumped against the morning's precipitation, and McRofaly left the stresses of the shops behind him.

"Colvin! Oi! Come help me carry some of this stuff," McRofaly called, running as best he could with his arms full to catch up to the red-haired man. Colvin turned when he heard his name and brightened a touch when he saw McRofaly. He took a bit more than his fair share of McRofaly's burden into his own arms and McRofaly helped get one of the traveler's cloaks around Colvin to shield him from the drizzle.

"Didn't expect to find the trade district this busy today," Colvin said.

"Shopkeepers trying to make some last-minute coin," McRofaly replied. "Townspeople making the trip on foot don't have to be ready to go for another hour."

"Looks like they made some pretty decent coin off you. Do we really need all this stuff for a one-day trip?"

"In my experience, one cannot be over-prepared," McRofaly said sagaciously. "Besides, I didn't pay for it."

"No? Who did?"

"William."

"William? Stuart-Camen?"

"The one and only," McRofaly said. "You seem surprised."

"A little, I guess. I figured if anyone was going to front the money for supplies, it would be Governor Chamberlain."

"I tried to hit the Governor up for funding," McRofaly explained, "but the cost of buying up all the extra space on the ships has put a serious dent in the town's coffers. I even tried talking to Ferdinan about it, but he actually sided with the Governor for once. Then I went to William, and he agreed to fund us."

"That was generous of him," Colvin said.

"I found him to be easily persuadable," said McRofaly. "Come on. We're wasting what little daylight there is on this miserable day."

They made their way toward the northwest gate, making small talk as they went. Colvin said nothing about his conversation with Melinda. It was all still too fresh in his mind to discuss it dispassionately. Mostly the two of them just made random comments on how bad the weather was. McRofaly mentioned that he had marked four potential spots on his map that he wanted to scout out. Colvin took up a good amount of time commenting on what amazing devices the compass and spyglass were. In all his years, he had never seen anything like them. The spyglass was quite a trick, but it was the compass that really captivated him. He watched with childlike fascination as the little needle spun to always point in the same direction regardless of which way he turned the compass; and unlike when McRofaly explained that the spyglass worked by bending light through finely ground lenses just like spectacles, none of the wonder went out of the compass for Colvin when his traveling companion started talking about abstract concepts like magnetic north, which Colvin was pretty certain he would never be able to spell, let alone understand. The rest of the gear drew little comment from Colvin, as he was familiar with most of it. A month ago he would have probably thrown a small fit of excitement over the prospect of all the gear he now carried in his arms, but after his time in Tamendad it just did not strike him as anything to get excited about. The saddle blankets, though, caught his attention.

"What are the blankets for?" Colvin asked as he and McRofaly neared the northwest gate. "We're not spending the night out in the country."

"Oh, those aren't for cover," McRofaly explained. "They're saddle blankets for the horses. They prevent saddle sores."

"Horses?" Colvin asked, slightly mortified. It was at that moment he noticed the two beasts tethered to the hitching post up by the northwest gate.

"Of course," McRofaly replied calmly. "We wouldn't be able to cover a quarter of the ground we need to cover today if we tried to make the trip on foot."

"I hate horses," Colvin said.

"How can you hate horses?" McRofaly asked, astounded. "The domestication of the horse represents one of mankind's greatest achievements. If it weren't for horses, men would live out their entire lives within only a few miles of where they were born. Kingdoms could never be maintained. Agriculture would fail. Society would revert back to a loose feudalism, or worse, hunter/gatherer tribalism. Humanity is what it is today because of the horse. Well, that and the written word, but that's an entirely different discussion."

"They're big, dumb, smelly beasts," Colvin said, looking warily at the two horses he and McRofaly were rapidly approaching.

"Well, so are you, but that doesn't keep me from liking you," said McRofaly. Colvin smirked. "But seriously," McRofaly continued, "there's nothing to be afraid of. These are very tame animals." To add emphasis to his words McRofaly walked up to one of the horses, a dark bay stallion that even Colvin had to admit was a beautiful creature, and rubbed his hand along the beast's side. The bay nickered at the touch, and turned its head to look at McRofaly. Colvin jumped slightly at the horse's sudden movement. The bay shook its head, flicking its mane around, and returned its attention to the spot of wall just in front of the hitching post. "See?" McRofaly said. "He's just saying hello. Nothing to be afraid of."

"I'm not afraid of them," Colvin protested, "I just don't like them."

"Well, you're going to have to get over that," McRofaly replied. "Now help me get them saddled."

Saddling the horses was an adventure in itself, and McRofaly soon began to wonder if Colvin was more of a help or a hindrance. Colvin's greater strength and bulk allowed him get the saddles in place and tighten the straps to secure them much more easily than McRofaly could have, but every time one of the horses neighed or moved in the slightest Colvin looked like he was about to jump right out of his skin. Before entirely too long, though, the saddles were secured and the saddlebags were filled with all the gear, and the two men were ready to set off on their expedition. McRofaly claimed the bay for himself, leaving the other horse, a slightly larger but less feisty dun, for Colvin. Coaxing Colvin into the saddle was a bit of work for McRofaly, but in the end it took only about half an hour to get the horses saddled and get underway.

Whatever reservations Colvin had about horses seemingly quadrupled once he was actually on one and riding alongside McRofaly, bouncing up and down in the saddle like a small child on his father's knee. Colvin went on at great length about how little he was enjoying himself. McRofaly for the most part just tuned him out, concentrating instead on navigating the journey.

"Why are we riding up the beach?" Colvin asked once he had tired of complaining about the horse. "All the spots you marked on the map were inland."

"For safety's sake we have to assume we're being watched by goruk spies," McRofaly explained. "If we head straight out of Tamendad toward the cave, the goruks are going to know something's up. If they see us riding up the beach toward Tantera, followed shortly by a host of townspeople with armed escorts, they'll probably just assume we were sent to scout ahead for trouble."

Colvin nodded, but he was bouncing in his saddle too much for McRofaly to notice. "Good thinking," he said.

"Thank you."

They rode up the beach for about an hour, then cut southwest toward the cave. Every now and again McRofaly would stop and check the compass and the map to make sure they were still on course, and whenever they came to an open area they would pause long enough to have a look around with the spyglass, trying to spot any goruks that might be lying in wait ahead of them. As the day approached midmorning Colvin was no longer really commenting on the horse one way or the other, and when McRofaly questioned him about it the red-haired young man just shrugged, which was noticeable now since he was bouncing considerably less while he rode, and said, "Well, they're not as bad as I thought they'd be, but I still don't particularly care for them." McRofaly chuckled at that, though Colvin was not really certain why. The two of them reached the first spot marked on McRofaly's map well before noon, and it took McRofaly less than a quarter of an hour to dismiss it.

"It will never work," McRofaly said after walking around thoughtfully with his hands tucked behind his back for a while.

Colvin, who was keeping a lookout, looked at McRofaly with an arched eyebrow. McRofaly had been studying the little clearing of trees so carefully that Colvin had been certain that the short man was formulating ambush plans. "Why not?" Colvin asked.

"Not enough hiding places for ground troops, not enough sturdy branches to support archers up in the trees, no clear vantage points to place lookouts, too many alternate paths the goruks could take to go around this spot, not enough–"

"Okay, I get it," Colvin interrupted. "Now what?"

"Now we move to the next spot on the map. Mount up."

The next spot proved less promising than the first, and as best the two of them could tell through the thick canopy of clouds it was early afternoon by the time they headed toward the third spot. The horses had begun to tire by that point, and their canter had slowed to a trot, which made it much easier for Colvin and McRofaly to carry on a conversation while riding. They did not really have much to talk about, just a few random comments about whatever caught their attention at the moment, but Colvin was taken completely off guard when McRofaly turned in his saddle to look him square in the eyes and said, "So are you ready to talk about you and Melinda now?"

"What do you mean?" Colvin replied, bemused. "What about me and Melinda?"

"I can't really think of many other reasons why you would be wandering around Tamendad in the rain like a lost puppy. I assume you had your talk with her this morning?"

Colvin sighed. "Yeah. It didn't go particularly well."

"What happened?"

"I'd really rather not talk about it," Colvin said. He felt a little defensive, but he couldn't really say why. McRofaly had been the person to suggest having the talk, after all. It was natural for him to want to follow up on it.

"I don't buy that for a moment," McRofaly said.

"Fine, fine," Colvin said, and then he described his conversation with Melinda in detail, down to every last intonation and facial expression. He was surprised how easily it all came back to him. He did not really want to remember it so clearly.

"That's rough," McRofaly said when he was finished. Silence followed.

"That's rough?" Colvin repeated. "That's all you can think to say? *That's rough?* C'mon, man, I spilled my guts to you. Give me some insight here. You at least know the girl."

"Well, if I had to posit a guess, I'd say you came on too strong."

"What?" Colvin said excitedly. "I did exactly what you told me I should do!"

"I never told you to tell her you were in love with her," McRofaly replied evenly.

Colvin just about exploded. "I never *told* her I was in love with her!" he screamed, startling birds in the nearby trees and flushing them from their roosts.

"Isn't that what you were about to tell her when she interrupted you?" McRofaly asked.

"What? No, I–" Colvin hesitated. Was that what he had been about to say to her? The words had been flowing pretty easily out of his mouth at that point of the conversation, and he had just decided to relax and let them come. With the shock of Melinda's reaction, Colvin really had not spent any time thinking about what he had actually been saying when she interrupted him. It didn't make much sense to Colvin that he would have said that, but the more he thought it over the more plausible it became. "God, maybe you're right," he said at last. "Why would I have said that?"

"Don't ask me," McRofaly replied. "Maybe you're in love with her."

"No," Colvin said quickly. "No way. I've known her, what, a week? People don't fall in love that fast." *Especially not me,* he thought.

McRofaly shrugged. "Well then maybe you think you could fall in love with her in time. I don't know. You're asking the wrong person for advice on your love life. Romance is the subject I know least about. I will say this, though. You've gone farther out of your way and bent over backwards more to pursue a relationship with Melinda than you have with any of your other conquests."

"I do *not* have conquests," Colvin retorted sullenly. "You make it sound like I'm some incurable womanizer."

"No, I think Ferdinan is an incurable womanizer. I think you're a moderate philanderer."

Colvin harrumphed, not wanting to admit he was not entirely certain what that word meant. *F-I-L-L-A-N-D-R-E-R,* he thought, and something clicked in his mind. "Wait, who's going to give me my reading lessons now?" he said with concern.

"What?"

"My reading lessons. Stewart Salvington is being evacuated along with everyone else in Tamendad. What am I supposed to do about my reading lessons?"

"I didn't know you took reading lessons," McRofaly said, that enigmatic *something* back in his voice again.

"Yeah, I've been taking them for the past couple of weeks," Colvin said.

"I could do it," McRofaly said with a disconcerting smile.

"You could? Really? Have you ever given reading lessons before?"

"Well, no," McRofaly admitted, "you'd be my first pupil, but I'm quite well versed on the subject. I've been reading since I was two years old, and I probably read more in a month than any other man in Tamendad reads in a year. And the prospect is too fascinating to pass up."

"Fascinating?" Colvin asked.

"Well like I said, I've never had the opportunity to observe someone learning to read. I only have myself to go by when contemplating how the process works, and even in my earliest childhood memories I was already reading. What mechanics are at work in the human mind when one learns to read? How does one map out all the written symbols in his mind? What cognitive process forever links the written character *a* with the first sound of the word *apple*? Is syntax learned separately, or does it just fall into place when learning how letters fit together to form words? And then words themselves, does the ability to string letters together to form them just grow organically out of a knowledge of letters, or is that a separate skill that must be taught? So many questions about how we learn the written word, and so far only a handful have even been examined, far fewer answered. Fascinating prospect, eh?"

"You're such a damn know-it-all," Colvin said.

"Thank you," McRofaly replied. "So what do you say?"

"Sure, I'm up for it. For the past few days I've been taking my lessons with Master Salvington first thing in the evening, before I go on watch for the night. Will that work with you?"

"Sounds good to me. We'll have our first lesson together when we get back to Tamendad. Say, you're not on watch tonight are you? After scouting with me all day?"

"Yeah, but this scouting expedition earned me a half-pass. I don't go on duty until midnight."

"Sounds good," McRofaly said. "Let's stop and let the horses graze a little while. I want to check the map again. We should be about halfway to the third spot I want to check, but it's so easy to lose your bearings out here."

Colvin kept the laugh that wanted to rise in his throat in check. Only a city boy like McRofaly could have thought it easy to lose his bearings out here. Even with the thick overlay of clouds blocking out the sun, there were plenty of landmarks by which to stay oriented. Colvin did not need the magic compass to tell him that he and McRofaly were headed just about due south, and that they were somewhere between five and seven miles from the third spot on McRofaly's map. The red-haired young man said nothing, though. He was eager to be off his horse, if only for a few moments, and he needed to take a leak. The two of them dismounted next to a small copse of trees. McRofaly pulled his map and compass from one of his saddlebags, and Colvin walked off a small distance to go get acquainted with a bush. They left the horses to their own devices to graze, and Colvin had to admit that the two beasts really were quite well behaved animals. By the time Colvin was finished relieving himself, McRofaly called out, "Yep, still perfectly on course," and Colvin simply nodded in reply, smiling.

McRofaly tucked the map and compass under his arm and retrieved the spyglass hanging from his belt, walking off a bit to have a look around. Colvin contented himself with retrieving a strip of jerky and a bit of hardtack from his trail rations. He munched quietly to himself, taking in the sights around him. The rain had stopped, thank God, and the clouds looked like they might be thinning a little. Every now and then he could make out the position of the sun behind them. The best he could tell, it was about two hours past noon. They were making pretty decent time, considering McRofaly's frequent stops. Colvin gobbled down the last of his jerky and stretched his arms high over his head, twisting his neck this way and that, listening to the snaps and pops it emitted. It was a nice, restful moment.

"Damn it all," he heard McRofaly say.

"What?" Colvin called out.

"Goruks. Five of them. Looks like a scouting party."

"How far?" Colvin asked.

"A little over five hundred feet."

"Do they have horses?"

"No, but they have bows. Here they come. Mount up!"

Screams and howls filled the air as the goruks broke into a charge. Colvin and McRofaly scrambled up onto their horses and broke into a full gallop just as the first arrows came sailing through the air behind them. The arrows fell short by perhaps twenty feet, but they were still too close for comfort. Colvin stole a glance back over his shoulder and saw that all five of the goruks were chasing after them at a full sprint, nocking a second volley of arrows as they came. They were being left behind by the galloping horses, but not nearly quickly enough for Colvin's taste. He had never seen anything run so fast in his life. "We're pulling away slowly," Colvin screamed to McRofaly loudly enough to be heard over the hoof beats. McRofaly gave no sign that he had heard, but his concentration was fully focused on holding on to his reigns and staying in the saddle. Colvin was holding on for dear life as well. He had fairly attenuated himself to the jostling effects of horseback riding while at a trot, but the galloping dun was tossing him around like a sack of potatoes. Somewhere in the recesses of his mind he was certain his balls would ache for a week after this.

Another round of arrows flew through the air, landing thirty, maybe thirty-five feet behind them. The goruks still came on at full charge, readying arrows once again despite the fact that Colvin and McRofaly were pulling steadily away. The goruks seemed to be tiring from their sprint, and Colvin was distantly relieved that they weren't able to keep up that pace for very long. Yet they were still shooting arrows, even though they had no hope of hitting their targets. *What the twist are they doing?* Colvin thought.

"It's a trap!" McRofaly screamed suddenly, and drew up reign. Colvin, taken by surprise, shot quickly past McRofaly and was several feet ahead before he could slow his steed. As Colvin drew up reign his whole world suddenly shifted violently. He had a most horrible sensation of double vertigo as he felt himself leave the saddle at the same time he felt the ground give way from under his horse's hooves. The dun lurched forward into the concealed pitfall, screaming as it went while Colvin was tossed clear. The ground rushed up to meet him with a disorienting thud, and Colvin saw motes of light floating in his field of vision for a moment. The fall had thankfully not knocked the wind from his lungs, and he cried out McRofaly's name in desperation as he climbed clumsily to his feet. Even through blurry eyes he could see that his boot was planted at the very edge of the chasm that now trapped the braying dun. Had he not been just barely starting to draw the horse up when they tripped the snare, he would have been at the bottom of that pit as well.

Colvin shook his head, trying to clear his senses. McRofaly was coming for him, the bay bearing down on him at a gallop, but the goruks were coming for him, too. And they did not look pleased that he and McRofaly had escaped their trap.

"Jump!" McRofaly yelled, barely audible over the din of hoots and snarls. He grabbed the reigns with the same hand that held his walking stick and reached his other out for Colvin. He was ten feet away now... five...three...

Colvin leapt with all the strength left in his legs. He knew this was his only chance to survive. If he managed to actually right himself on the horse behind McRofaly he had a shot, a real shot, at getting out of this alive. If he fell, the goruks would be on him before he even stopped rolling.

Please, Colvin thought distantly.

He felt McRofaly's hand clamp down around his own. He hiked up his left leg, bounced once alongside the horse on his right, and came down hard on the horse's back behind the saddle. Forget a week; his balls were going to ache for a month. But Colvin didn't care. He would be alive to suffer through it. He clenched his arms tightly around McRofaly's waist, and he felt strangely like laughing. He probably would have if he had not felt the pain explode in his leg. He screamed, the sound making McRofaly flinch in the saddle in front of him. Colvin looked down to see the shaft of an arrow protruding from his upper thigh, and suddenly there were more arrows in the air around them, some seeming to miss by mere inches. And yet rather than putting distance between themselves and their assailants, McRofaly was now turning the bay toward the goruks, giving them a head on shot.

"What the twist are you doing?!?" screamed Colvin, quite convinced his savior had now lost his damn mind.

"More traps!" was McRofaly's only explanation, but it sufficed. God only knew what sort of demented, snare filled playground they had narrowly escaped being herded into. They could not press forward, and the goruks lay behind. The only way out was through.

Colvin noticed for the first time that McRofaly had his walking stick in his hand, raised aloft and ready to strike. There was no way they could possibly survive with five goruks shooting at them. The only solution was to take a few of those goruks out. Colvin glanced at his dagger gloves, and he instantly appreciated that they would be worthless from horseback. He drew his sabre instead.

McRofaly closed on the goruks, screaming and holding his walking stick aloft, brandishing it like a sword. One of the goruks leapt for him, trying to tear him from the saddle, and McRofaly let his walking stick fly. It caught the goruk squarely between the eyes and the beast fell limply to the ground, motionless. Another goruk tried the same move from McRofaly's blind side. Colvin's sabre sailed in a graceful arc, and a detached part of him marveled at how there was only the barest moment of resistance before the goruk's head was separated from its shoulders.

"Get down!" screamed McRofaly, leaning so far forward in the saddle that his face was buried in the bay's mane, and it took a moment for Colvin to realize that they were now past the goruks. Their numbers had been reduced by more than a third, but that still left Colvin and McRofaly completely exposed to three bow-wielding goruks. Colvin collapsed himself against McRofaly as best he could, shoving his forehead into the small of McRofaly's back. He was glad no one else could see him.

Colvin heard an arrow zip past his ear, and though he was almost certain his mind was playing tricks on him, he swore it felt as though it had nearly parted his hair. They had to get out of bow range as quickly as they could. "Ride!" Colvin screamed into McRofaly's back. "Ride you son of a bitch!"

McRofaly did exactly as he was told.

The arrow was not deep, but it bled like a mortal wound when

McRofaly pulled it free. At first McRofaly was concerned it had severed an artery, but after a few minutes the bleeding was finally stopped. McRofaly whipped up a quick salve using some aloe leaves, purple coneflower root and woundwort that he said would do the trick until they could get back to Tamendad and get Colvin to a healer. The salve was apparently working, since the wound was no longer hurting as much as it had been. Colvin had to constantly remind himself not to touch or pick at the bandage wrapped tightly around his upper thigh.

The bay was still huffing and puffing, tethered about ten feet from where Colvin sat on the trunk of a fallen tree. The animal had unquestionably saved his life, as well as McRofaly's. He still did not particularly like horses, but he had a newfound respect for them that he knew would be with him for the rest of his life. They bay had borne the two men to safety, evading and outrunning the goruks for the better part of an hour. The poor thing had to be on its last legs after that, and yet it still looked eager to run. That was most likely out of fear, Colvin realized, and once the beast calmed down a bit it would probably become all but impossible to move him. One thing was for certain: there was no way he and McRofaly were riding back to Tamendad. They would have to travel on foot, leading the horse behind them. Colvin saw no sense in breaking the animal that had helped save his life.

A snap of a branch in the nearby trees brought Colvin immediately to his feet and into a defensive stance, and he grimaced at the fresh wave of pain that came as soon as his leg once again bore weight. "It's just me," he heard McRofaly call from the trees, and in the next moment the short man was stepping out from behind a tree trunk into the glade. Colvin sighed and relaxed. McRofaly walked over to Colvin, collapsing the spyglass as he came. "As far as I can tell, we lost them. I can't catch a glimpse of goruks anywhere."

"Thank God," Colvin said.

"Certainly," McRofaly replied. "How's your leg?"

"I'll manage."

"And the horse?"

"Exhausted but okay."

McRofaly nodded. "Well, we've lost half the gear. I'm not going to risk going back for the other horse with those three goruks unaccounted for. Besides, if my guess is right they've probably already had at that horse anyway."

Colvin winced. William had told him the story of what the goruks had done to his father's horse.

"Thankfully we've still got the compass and the spyglass," McRofaly continued. "We'd better get moving. Evening's almost here. We'll have to hurry if we're going to make it back to Tamendad before nightfall, moving on foot." Colvin nodded, silently thankful that McRofaly had come to the same conclusion he had about not trying to ride the horse. McRofaly headed to untie the bay. He stopped suddenly halfway, looking slowly all around him with an unreadable expression on his face. Colvin quickly resumed his stance, bringing up both daggered fists and looking quickly all about.

"What is it?" Colvin asked nervously, ready to pounce on the first thing that moved. "What's the matter?" McRofaly was silent, contemplative. "McRofaly, what is it?" Colvin repeated forcefully.

"Where are we?" McRofaly asked.

"I have no idea," Colvin said. He wasn't sure if he should let his guard down or not. McRofaly hurriedly continued on his way toward the horse, but instead of untying the beast he busied himself retrieving the map and compass from the saddle bags. The horse picked up on his excitement and shifted its weight back and forth on its hooves a bit. McRofaly quickly came back to the center of the glen and sat down on the ground, crossing his legs and unfolding the map on his lap. Colvin took this as an unquestionable sign that there was no pressing, immediate danger, and dropped his stance. He glanced around once more, this time looking not for potential dangers but for whatever it might have been that had so forcefully caught McRofaly's attention about this place. His eyes shifted to the old, moldy tree trunk upon which he had just moments ago been sitting. And suddenly Colvin realized he had lied. He *did* have an idea where they were. In fact, he knew exactly where they were.

"Holy shit," he said. "This is where Lorthok ate the mushrooms!"

"Mmm?" hummed McRofaly, not looking up from the map.

"The gourk that took me hostage," Colvin explained. "I fed it an entire patch of poisonous mushrooms right where we're standing."

McRofaly glanced up at Colvin. The two men held each other's gaze for a moment, and Colvin got the sense that McRofaly was thinking a dozen thoughts at once about what he had just said. McRofaly said nothing, just arched an eyebrow and nodded, then returned his attention firmly to the map. Colvin felt strangely like he had just been weighed in the balance of McRofaly's mind.

"This clearing isn't on the map," McRofaly finally said after a few more minutes of silence.

"I'll kill the mapmaker as soon as we're back in Tamendad," Colvin said dryly.

McRofaly just mumbled to himself, not really even acknowledging Colvin's presence. The short man studied the map silently for a while, looking up occasionally to look around at the trees and up in the sky to catch a glimpse of the sun, which was now finally beginning to peek through breaks in the clouds.

"McRofaly, we really need to be going," Colvin said.

"Just a moment, just a moment," McRofaly said, springing quickly to his feet and pulling the compass out. He slowly spun around in a circle and came to a stop when the little needle was perfectly lined up with the big letter *N* marked on the face of the compass. He looked up into the trees in that direction, and then pointed in various directions, mumbling, "East," or "West," or "North by northwest," as he did so.

"McRofaly?" Colvin said timidly.

McRofaly ignored him and picked up the map from the ground. He studied it intently, frequently looking up at the sun. Finally he jabbed his index finger into the map, making a little crease in the oiled paper. He looked excitedly up at Colvin.

"This is it," he said.

"What?" Colvin asked, and the answer occurred to him before McRofaly could supply it. "The ambush? Here?"

McRofaly nodded and smiled a slightly disturbing smile, all teeth. "This is perfect. Plenty of big, strong trees to support archers and hide foot soldiers. Limited visibility from the ground – we didn't even know this glade was here until we stumbled into it – but from up in the taller trees you can see for miles. And best of all, it lines up almost perfectly with the route the goruks travel to get to Tamendad from the cave. We just have to fell a few trees to ensure they don't go around this spot."

"Won't that be pretty obvious?" Colvin asked.

"We'll uproot them, make them look like they fell naturally. Just send a team of workhorses out here to do it during the day, preferably right after a thunderstorm. The soil will be softened and it'll make it that much more believable." McRofaly's eyes were burning with the fervor of tactical calculation. "It's perfect."

Colvin felt the corners of his mouth curl upward into a wry smile. "Fitting," he said.

"How so?" asked McRofaly.

"I killed my first goruk here. Now I get to kill a bunch more."

McRofaly nodded. "Fitting."

CHAPTER TWENTY-FOUR

BEST LAID PLANS

As if thumbing its nose at the world below, the sun finally emerged from behind its cover of clouds just as it was beginning to hunker down toward the western horizon, when afternoon intersected evening. Colvin and McRofaly walked side by side over the rolling hills toward Tamendad, leading the bay behind them. Colvin was munching on a hardtack biscuit as he walked, and McRofaly was eyeing him with a mixture of disgust and contempt. The short man had tried only a single bite of the hard, flat bread, and it had been enough to turn his stomach. When he asked Colvin how he could possibly bring himself to eat the stuff, Colvin had just sort of shrugged and explained that for the better half of his life he had been surviving on tubers and wild berries, and tree bark when times were really tough, and all of that made hardtack taste like bread fresh from the baker's oven. McRofaly had wasted no time handing over all of the hardtack from the remaining rations to Colvin, telling him to enjoy. Honestly, Colvin had about had his fill of it for one day. The taste was not so bad, but it dried the throat out terribly. The only reason Colvin kept munching on it was because of the amusement he got from watching McRofaly shudder slightly with each bite Colvin took. But that was enough to keep him stuffing it in.

They had been walking for about two hours, keeping a leisurely pace. This allowed the horse some rest, allowed Colvin to adjust to his leg injury, and gave them ample opportunity to be on guard against further goruk subterfuge. So far they had encountered nothing to raise their guard, which in itself was enough to put both men a little on edge. They had seen nothing during their entire morning ride to alarm them until they had nearly been herded into a slaughter. The thought that the same could happen again at any moment kept both men on their toes. They had not really discussed it much, as much out of embarrassment of being taken so completely by surprise as anything else, but McRofaly had mentioned that he did not think that the trap had been set specifically for them. "Goruks have a slave-based society," the short man had explained.

"Slaves?" Colvin asked. "What kind of slaves?"

"Not goruk slaves," was all McRofaly would answer, leaving Colvin to figure the rest out on his own. It hadn't taken him long to do so, and when he realized the fate he had narrowly escaped might very well have been worse than death, he thanked McRofaly anew for rescuing him. The thought of goruks keeping human slaves sickened Colvin. He thought back to his earlier years, years spent in relative safety under the care of Malcomb and Doris. Stories of a man or a woman – or worse, a child – wandering off into the woods never to be heard from again were not common, but they were not nearly rare enough. It was bad enough to think that they had been killed and eaten by a bear or had slipped on a slippery river rock and drowned. The thought that some of those people might still be alive, serving as slaves to the goruks, chilled Colvin to the bone.

"What do you think they do to the people they enslave?" Colvin asked to break the brooding silence, but no answer came. Colvin glanced at McRofaly. The short man had stopped dead in his tracks and was tilting his head slightly to his left with his eyes closed. "What's that sound?" he said quietly.

"What sound?" Colvin asked.

"Shut up and listen."

Colvin closed his eyes and slowed his breathing so he could better listen to whatever it was he was supposed to be listening for. At first he heard nothing, just a light breeze and the bay's breath. Before long, though, he heard it, a steady bass percussion echoing through the hills. It was not a drum beat, though it was reminiscent of one. It was unmistakably the sound of an animal. "Hoof beats," Colvin said.

"That's what I thought," McRofaly replied. He had the spyglass out and extended in an instant, scanning the countryside for signs of movement. Colvin stood with muscles tensed, readying himself mentally for whatever it was they were about to face. He did not have to put on his dagger gloves; he had never bothered to take them off. "There," McRofaly said, pointing into the distance. Colvin squinted and strained, but no matter how he tried he just could not make anything out. Whatever it was, it was too far away.

"Let me see," Colvin said pleadingly. McRofaly reluctantly handed over the spyglass and busied himself looking through the saddlebags for something or other. Colvin paid the short man no mind. He looked through the spyglass in the direction McRofaly had pointed and saw it immediately. It was only the second time he had looked through the

380

spyglass, the first time that he was not just playing around with it, and he was fairly amazed at how well it worked. The horse and rider were entirely too far away to make out any detail, but through the spyglass Colvin could tell that they were there, as plain as day. Whoever it was, whether goruk or man, was wasting no time in coming. If it had not been for the morning's rain, the horse would probably have been stirring up a dust cloud that would have been visible for a mile or more. Colvin took a little comfort in the fact that whoever – or whatever – the rider was, there was no way he could have seen Colvin and McRofaly yet. That, at least, told Colvin that the rider couldn't possibly be coming for them. He still had a difficult time making himself believe it.

"Can you make anything out?" McRofaly called from the horse's side, still rustling around in the saddlebag.

Colvin squinted through the spyglass and was a little surprised to find that it worked to improve his clarity of vision just as it did when he was using his naked eyes. He saw the unmistakable pale pink of flesh tones. "It's human," Colvin said, greatly relieved. A few moments passed in silence, and then Colvin added, quizzically, "It's Morlocke."

"What?"

"It's Ian Morlocke," Colvin repeated. "He's really hauling it, too."

"Oh, good," McRofaly said, glad to hear it was a friendly face. Suddenly the implication hit him. "Wait, no, that's not good."

"Help me flag him down," Colvin said, handing the spyglass back. He waved his arms back and forth over his head. He thought about yelling Morlocke's name, but he thought better of it when he realized anything at all could be pursuing the scout, and yelling would attract its attention as well. McRofaly joined him after securing the spyglass on his belt, jumping up and down and waving his hands in the air and making a general fool of himself. Any doubts the two of them had about whether Ian Morlocke would be able to see them dissolved once they saw the scout turn his horse slightly to ride straight for them.

It did not take long for Ian to join Colvin and McRofaly. The scout's horse reared on its back legs and brayed as it slid to a halt on the wet grass, startling Lucky and making Colvin wince a bit, forcing him to remember the sensation of losing his grip on the reigns and sliding from his horse. Ian had no such trouble staying in the saddle.

"The goruks are on the move," Ian said urgently, not bothering with pleasantries.

"How many?" Colvin asked at the same time McRofaly said, "When?"

"It looked like about a hundred, no more than a hundred and fifty. They left the cave in a march about an hour ago."

McRofaly stole a quick glance at the sun. It would still be a couple of hours at least before it set, and then another hour after that before real darkness fell. "They've been sending out spies," McRofaly said without looking at either Colvin or Ian. "They know when we change the guard. That's when they plan to hit us." He turned quickly to look at Ian, his expression deadly serious. "Were you seen?"

"No chance," Ian replied confidently. "I was a ghost."

McRofaly allowed himself a small, devious grin. "Good," he said. "Do you think your horse can support my weight as well as yours?"

"Midnight can handle it, no problem," Ian said, firmly patting the flank of the black gelding. He extended an arm to McRofaly. "Hop on. What about Colvin?"

"You'll have to ride," McRofaly said, giving the red-haired young man a mildly sympathetic look. "I know you don't want to, but you have to."

Colvin nodded. "Lucky's had a rest. I'm sure he's ready to go."

McRofaly hesitated, arching an eyebrow at Colvin. "*Lucky*?"

Colvin grinned sheepishly. "I named him."

"Wonderful," McRofaly replied, rolling his eyes. He mounted Midnight with Ian's help, then turned to Colvin once more. "Don't try to keep up. I don't think *Lucky* could manage to anyway. Just get back to Tamendad as quickly as you can. You know the way. Hurry." Then, without waiting for any signal from McRofaly, Ian Morlocke dug his heels into Midnight's side, and he and McRofaly were off. Colvin scrambled up into Lucky's saddle and followed after, as quickly as the bay could carry him.

The approach of Morlocke and McRofaly drew a strong reaction from the watchmen at the southwest gate, and the doors of the gate were already opened for the two men by the time they reached it. Ian Morlocke barely slowed Midnight at all as they rode through the gate, quickly drawing reign once they were safely within the city walls. Midnight reared and brayed once again, his hooves sliding across the bricks of the main street, which were worn smooth with age. McRofaly clung tightly to Ian's waist to keep from sliding right off Midnight's back and being dumped to the street below like a sack of potatoes. When Midnight was back on all fours, McRofaly breathed a deep sigh of relief and quickly dismounted. He had a newfound appreciation of Colvin's timidity where horses were concerned.

"Don't shut the doors," McRofaly called to the gatekeepers. "Colvin is right behind us." As if to underscore his words, a lookout atop the wall announced the approach of another rider. "Master Morlocke and I need an audience with Governor Chamberlain," McRofaly continued, focusing his attention on the highest ranking soldier at the gate. Since the skeleton crew of a day guard was still on duty, the commanding officer was not difficult to spot.

"He should already be on his way, Master McRofaly," the constable said. "Word was sent for him as soon as we spotted you."

"Good. Send someone to wake William Stuart-Camen and tell him there is an emergency meeting of the war council. Tell him to come to the church."

"The church?" The constable was clearly confused.

"You heard me, constable," McRofaly barked. "Quickly!" The constable scrambled to flag down a town crier. McRofaly turned to address Ian, only to realize the scout was no longer with him. A quick look around was all it took for McRofaly to spot him, heading quickly up Tamendad's main street with Midnight in tow, hurrying to deliver his news to the Governor. McRofaly smiled in spite of himself. Ian Morlocke was the most singularly determined man he had ever met. In a strange way, Ian reminded him a little of himself. At that moment, Colvin rode in. The gatekeepers quickly started closing and bracing the doors as soon as he was through. Colvin quickly dismounted and made his way toward McRofaly.

"What's the plan?" he asked.

"That remains to be seen," McRofaly replied. "I've called an emergency meeting of the war council. We'll meet at the church while you're getting your leg stitched up, to save time."

"Good thinking," Colvin said. "Just let me find a stableboy to take Lucky."

"That might take a while. All the stableboys were evacuated this morning."

"Oh, yeah," said Colvin, looking around the streets of Tamendad and really appreciating for the first time just how empty they felt. Here and there a town crier hurried on his way to deliver a message to someone somewhere else. The only other presence in the streets were the straw soldiers that McRofaly had set up, spaced out at more or less regular intervals and holding weapons that were too damaged for repair but still looked whole at a distance. Their unmoving forms raised the hair on the back of Colvin's neck. With no one else around, the straw men looked downright eerie, even in broad daylight. *Tamendad's a ghost town,* Colvin thought, and the thought carried a sting. *This is going to crush William.*

Colvin had been in Tamendad less than a month, and he was already falling in love with it. It was William's home. He had grown up here. It was all he knew. Colvin feared that the sight of its empty streets might be enough to send William flying off the edge. McRofaly's impatient stare was enough to bring Colvin back to the moment. A hundred goruks – maybe more – were marching toward Tamendad. William's malaise was going to have to wait. "So what should I do with him?" Colvin asked, nodding toward Lucky.

"Bring him," McRofaly said. "We'll tether him outside the church." When they reached the church they found Ian Morlocke standing in front of it, talking to Governor Chamberlain and Don Ferdinan. All three men wore grave expressions.

"Colvin, McRofaly, es good to see you again," Ferdinan said, bowing in their direction. Governor Chamberlain echoed the sentiment.

"Well this is fortuitous," McRofaly said. "Gentlemen, I suggest we kill two birds with one stone and have the council meeting here while Colvin is attended by a healer." Ferdinan and the Governor both agreed, and after tethering Midnight and Lucky to the hitching post all the men entered the church together, making the Sign of the Compass as they crossed the threshold. Patrum Albermarle saw to Colvin personally, leading him and the other men to a private room large enough to comfortably accommodate all of them. Before the good priest could even thread his needle William Stuart-Camen and Captain Jefford joined them. Both men still had sleep in their eyes. While Patrum Albermarle stitched the wound on Colvin's thigh, Ian filled the two newcomers in on what the rest of the council already knew. Grim looks were exchanged all around.

"Are we sure they're heading for us, and not for the evacuees?" William asked. Colvin sat up when he heard William's words, nearly making Patrum Albermarle miss a stitch. It was a good question, one he cursed himself for not thinking of on his own.

"I trailed them a bit before riding for here," Ian said. "They were headed straight for Tamendad, using the same route they always use. They showed no signs of cutting north toward the townspeople. I left one of my best men behind to trail them. If they make a move to the north, we'll hear it from him long before the goruks reach the townspeople."

"Es my belief they are coming for Tamendad, not the townspeople," Ferdinan said. "From all I have heard, es likely they want to hit the city while the guard es being changed, to take us by surprise."

"An astute assessment, Don Ferdinan," said McRofaly.

"If they know when we change the guard, they probably know other details about our forces as well," Captain Jefford said.

"Like how they are divided," McRofaly added.

"You don't think they plan to attack the northeast gate," Governor Chamberlain said. It was not a question.

"They have seen how well defended it is," McRofaly said. "They have probably also figured out that with all the men stationed there, there aren't many left to defend the other gates. The goruks are smart, smarter than I originally gave them credit for. If I were planning an attack, I would hit the farthest possible point from the northeast gate."

There was a brief silence, broken when Ferdinan said, "McRofaly, could your plan, the one you laid out for us yesterday, be ready to be put into action before the goruks reach us?"

"Now just a moment–" the Governor began.

"Geoffery, please, just hear me out," Ferdinan interrupted. The Governor was glowering, but he allowed Ferdinan to continue. "Es clear the goruks espect to take us by surprise. I know es a risk, but I guarantee you we will not win this war without taking risks. Besides, Lord Governor, you yourself said that once the town was evacuated, all bets were off."

Governor Chamberlain's sigh sounded more like a harrumph. He fixed McRofaly with an even stare that unnerved the short man. "Can we be ready?"

McRofaly ran it all through in his mind: time consideration, manpower, available materials. The goruks would be here in two and a half hours. It was going to be extraordinarily close. "Yes," McRofaly said with a false sense of confidence. "Without a doubt."

"You are in charge of the preparations, McRofaly," Ferdinan said. "As the architect of the plan, you understand the nuances of what must be done better than anyone else. Tell us what to do."

McRofaly was flabbergasted. Even though the Governor had not ruled his first plan out completely when McRofaly had presented it, he had never for a moment believed he would actually have a chance to put it in action. He allowed himself to relish the moment a bit. "All right," he said, clapping his hands together, "here's what we do."

Crouched low, hidden in the tall grass that grew atop the hill, Yargos surveyed the towering edifice of Tamendad's wall, his attention focused on the paleskin sentries atop it. They were bored and lazy now from another uneventful day shift. They had not seen Yargos approach with his warriors, had no idea that more than a hundred of Kor's most loyal followers lay perched and ready to strike just on the other side of this hill. Those inattentive sentries would unknowingly be the ones who gave Yargos the signal to attack. That signal would be coming soon. The sun had set almost an hour ago. The sky's amber-orange hue was quickly receding into the western horizon, being replaced by the deep, dark blue of early night. Kor's plan was working perfectly so far, as Yargos had known it would. Kor's plans were infallible. Kor himself was infallible. He was delivering the reclaiming to his people, just as he had promised.

As Kor had predicted, most of the paleskins had evacuated, and the paleskin leaders had sent many of their warriors along to protect their people, foolishly dividing their forces. Now they were weak, and Kor knew where they were weakest. Tamendad would fall soon. Tonight's raid would cripple the city, and the next would wipe the last traces of the paleskins from it. The honor of commanding this raid had fallen to Yargos. Thinking about it still brought goosebumps. His chance for glory had come. He lay flat and still, barely breathing, focused completely on his target. One of the sentries yawned and stretched. Another looked to be dozing at his post. The third was looking right at where Yargos was crouched in the grass, and still he did not see. This was going to be like killing lurbets.

The warriors remained crouched and silent on the hillside behind Yargos, patiently awaiting the signal. Yargos was less than a hundred feet from them, and yet even when he concentrated all his attention on listening for them he could barely make out the sounds of their breathing. They made him proud. They were fine warriors, and they followed Kor – and by extension, Yargos – with unmitigated devotion. Each knew there was a chance he would not survive the night's raid. The paleskins, while soft and weak, were surprisingly fierce when defending what they had stolen. They would be able to overcome a handful of goruks before Yargos called the retreat. Even with this knowledge, this gamble of life and death, they were resolute in the cause. *Abuneth* was larger than any individual life. It was about the ancestors, and about descendants not yet born. Every goruk warrior was prepared to lay down his life for the reclaiming if called upon to do so. Even Yargos would give his life for the cause, if need be. Commanders and warriors were no different where the cause of *Abuneth* was concerned. The only life that could not be spared was Kor's, for without Kor the reclaiming could never happen. Kor was the cornerstone. He was the all, the only. Kor was *Abuneth* incarnate.

Three new paleskin sentries appeared atop the wall. The dozing one was roused; he and his two companions prepared to depart. The paleskin watch was changing. This was the signal. The time had come. "*Thorak rakuth, Abuneth,*" he whispered, his eyes clenched, his jaw set. He turned to his warriors, perched and waiting behind him on the hill. He nodded to them.

"It is time."

The goruks all sprang to their feet. The ten in front hoisted the battering ram from the ground, five on each side holding it aloft by the metal handles riveted deep into the massive wooden cylinder. Morchas slid free from their sheaths, the ring of steel breaking the silence on the hillside. Together they all broke into a run, cresting the hill and spilling over it, screaming their war cry as they came. Yargos howled at the top of his lungs, and others following behind him did the same. They made as much noise as they could. The time for stealth was over. Yargos wanted to announce their presence to the paleskins, wanted to let them know what was coming for them. He wanted to make them taste fear. From the looks on the faces of the new sentries atop the wall, he was succeeding quite well. There was no resistance to meet them before they reached their target. The nightly patrols had not yet been sent out. With any luck, the warriors would reach the gate just as the keepers were beginning to open it to let the patrols out. The sentries were frantically screaming warnings in their filthy language to whoever was behind the walls, but it was too late. Yargos and his warriors had reached the southwest gate. This was where they would strike, on the opposite side of the city from where the paleskins had their forces stacked to protect the destroyed dockside gate.

The Ancient Ones were smiling on Yargos tonight. The doors of the southwest gate began to creak open after only one solid buffet. No archers were yet upon the walls. It was exactly as Kor said it would be. The paleskins were completely off their guard. With another strike of the ram the doors of the southwest gate swung open three feet. Yargos gave the signal, and the ram was dropped. The goruks pressed forward, pushing the gate open wide as the green wave poured into the city. Yargos had gained entrance to Tamendad. It was his day for glory. He led the charge into the city, his warriors howling and screaming in excitement at achieving their goal. In the bricked street ahead a handful of paleskin soldiers stood staring in flatfooted horror. Yargos could not hold back the laugh that rose in his throat. These soldiers were puny, pathetic creatures, with barely any meat on their bones. One good goruk warrior could rend five of them in half with his bare hands. Yargos howled at them – a deep, booming, guttural war cry that made the paleskins shake in their boots. They did not even bother drawing their weapons. They simply spun on their heels and fled.

"Pursue!" Yargos screamed to his warriors. "Pursue! The paleskins are ours for the taking! *Abuneth kul!*" Yargos broke into a run, following after the fleeing paleskins, his warriors close behind. Archers had finally made their way atop the city wall and now loosed arrows on the goruks, but it they fell several feet short of reaching them. Pursuing the paleskins down the main street of Tamendad, the goruk commander praised the Ancient Ones for blessing him this night.

None of the goruks noticed the southwest gate close behind them.

The puny paleskin warriors might not have been much in a fight, but in a footrace they were all that the goruks could handle. Yargos was accustomed to being able to outrun paleskins without difficulty, but the men he and his warriors were chasing were having no problems maintaining their lead. These had to be the fastest warriors the paleskins had to offer. Something about that thought raised a warning in the back of Yargos's mind, but he did not pursue that line of thinking. Focus was essential for his task. Find the paleskins, kill them, then worry about why they had run so quickly. Within the paleskins' own city, stopping to reconsider something could spell defeat.

The sight of more paleskin warriors standing in the street, neither coming to assist their comrades nor fleeing for safety, confused Yargos at first. Then he realized that what he was seeing was not warriors at all, but merely clothes stuffed with straw and set upright to resemble warriors from a distance. So the paleskins were using trickery to bolster their numbers. That bode well for Yargos's task. Kor had designed this plan around his spies' best estimates of the paleskins' forces. The fact that the paleskins actually had fewer warriors than Kor had planned for meant the job was going to go smoothly. Kor was going to be quite pleased to hear this news, and Yargos salivated at the prospect of being the one to tell him of it. Glory upon glory waited for Yargos back in the Under – assuming he could ever catch up to these damn sprinters. Under the glow of lamps that lit Tamendad, Yargos saw that one reason the paleskins were able to run so effortlessly was because they wore no armor to impede them. Yargos smiled. If the paleskins could not even manage to provide armor to all their warriors, they were truly in a rough spot. A wave of excitement sent chills up Yargos's spine. If all things continued falling into place as they had so far, perhaps this would not have to be a hit and run attack. Perhaps this would be the night that Tamendad fell, and perhaps Yargos would be the warrior who felled it.

Yargos caught sight of the large building that stood in the middle of the town. Kor had said that this was the church where the paleskins worshiped their false god. Little wonder the paleskins were in such dire straits; such blasphemy against the Ancient Ones would not go unpunished for long. Yargos briefly entertained the fantasy of storming the paleskins' filthy church and ransacking it, desecrating the profane temple and claiming it in the name of Kor and the Ancient Ones. It seemed like the right thing to do, even if Kor had not planned it. Perhaps once the raid was over and the paleskins all lay dead in a heap he would do it as an added testament to Kor's greatness. Now, though, it was impossible. The main street was blocked off before it reached the church. Wagons and carts, barrels and crates, all manner of things were stacked high in the street, making passage impossible. The roadblock told Yargos that the paleskins had suspected they might attack away from the northeast gate. It was of little consequence. Kor had prepared him for such an eventuality.

Yargos led his warriors down the much narrower cobbled street that the paleskins had taken upon meeting the roadblock. It raised Yargos's ire that these cowardly wretches were still alive. But the time of their deaths was approaching. They were beginning to tire. Yargos and his warriors were beginning to close the distance. The whooping, screeching war cries increased in intensity as the goruks realized this. The first kill of the night was fast approaching. Paleskin blood would soon be spilled.

Yargos realized that all the alleyways leading off from the street they now ran on had been barricaded in the same manner as the main street. Had all the other side streets been blocked off as well? All but this one? Yargos could not remember – he had been too focused on his task, and too preoccupied with dreams of glory and honor – but for some reason he thought that they had been. Before he could think about what that meant, his eyes widened with glee. This street, too, was blocked a little farther ahead. These infuriatingly quick paleskins were trapped. As they reached the barricade, the paleskins spun on their heels and drew their weapons, heavily winded from their run. So at last they had decided to make their stand, once all other avenues of escape were cut off to them. Cowards. Yargos hated them. He held his morcha high, charging for them. The frenzy of the kill began to take him. The time had come. Glory and honor beyond measure. But a part of him, distant and detached, was ill at ease. There was a smell here that Yargos could not quite put his finger on, a smell that did not belong in a paleskin city. The smell reminded Yargos of home. And there was something about this barricade. It was different from the one back in the main street. This was just a large pile of lumber stacked in the middle of the street. It did not even really look like a barricade at all. It looked like…

It looked like an unlit bonfire.

It was not unlit for long. A scream split the night from atop one of the buildings that lined the street. It was a paleskin scream. It was a battle cry. Flaming arrows zipped through the night from all sides, all shot directly into the heart of the barricade. The wood erupted, flames towering into the air. A raging inferno consumed the street in front of Yargos and his warriors, making passage impossible. The paleskins standing in front of the blaze wore fiendish grins. Yargos felt his stomach lurch. "Back!" he screamed to his warriors. "Back the way we came! Quickly!" His words were drowned out. The screams came from all sides, washing over the goruks in a sea of sound. The goruk battle cries degenerated into howling wails of confusion. Spinning on his heels, Yargos tried to press through the mass of goruk bodies that surrounded him, hoping to lead his warriors out of this trap himself. As he turned, he caught sight of the most terrifying thing he had ever witnessed. The side streets and alleyways all around him were not barricaded. They were filled to the brim with paleskin warriors, armed and armored, bloodlust in their eyes. They poured out of their hiding places like a wave crashing down upon a sandcastle. Yargos's forces were outnumbered almost two to one. Fear reached up from the depths of Yargos's bowels and seized him around the throat. He was overcome with the mortifying yet strangely calming realization that this would be the day of his reckoning before the Ancient Ones.

The paleskins came on, charging headlong into the goruk warriors, overwhelming them, crushing them. The goruks fell back until they reached the bonfire and could go no farther. The paleskins were relentless in their assault; still they pressed forward, and the goruks in the rear were pressed into the flames, screaming as the fire consumed them. Archers perched atop the buildings rained down volley after volley of arrows into the goruk crowd. Yargos howled and screamed orders, trying to recapture the attention of his warriors, trying to regroup. Everything around him was a muddled mass of confusion. Goruks thrashed about madly, swinging morchas at anything that came near, hitting their own comrades as often as paleskins. The paleskins dropped two goruks for every flesh wound they endured. The cause was lost. Yargos's warriors were routed. His glory had been stolen by dirty paleskin trickery.

A group of paleskins began to press directly into the heart of the defending goruks, coming right for Yargos. Their commander was little more than a babe, and his dress marked him as a person of import, a member of the ruling class. He charged with his broadsword aloft, a menacing look on his babyish face. Yargos's blood boiled at the sight of it, at the thought of being challenged with such puerile impudence. He raised his morcha high, screaming at the child. At least before he died, Yargos would have the pleasure of teaching this paleskin pup a lesson he would not forget even in the afterworld. He broke into a charge…and two steps later fell to his knees as the archers from the rooftops riddled his body with arrows. He tasted blood. Breathing brought pain like he could never have imagined. By the time his knees struck the cobblestones of the street he had already lost all sensation in his hands and feet. His vision began to blur, but not before he saw the child close on him, bringing his broadsword to bear.

The last thought that passed through Yargos's head before William Stuart-Camen's blade separated it from his neck was to curse Kor's name for getting him into this mess.

William absentmindedly wiped the blood from his sword, surveying his immediate surroundings. The cobblestones of the street were now a wet, viscous red that gathered in puddles and spread out to fill the cracks and seams. The smell that hung thick in the air was unsettlingly reminiscent of a roast broiling on a spit. The soldiers were wasting no time in throwing the bodies of the conquered goruks into the flames. Some of them were not even dead yet, and these howled and writhed as the flames licked them, but they soon fell still and silent. Many men and women were decapitating the corpses before burning them, saving the heads in a pile off to the side for whatever unfathomable reason. Some men laughed as goruks that were still clinging to life tried to crawl and claw their way back up the street the way they came, trying to escape. Some of the soldiers would allow them to drag themselves a few feet, leaving a trail of blood and entrails behind them, exhausting themselves, before running them through the throat or the eye or the heart. Others screamed profanities as the goruks convulsed and died.

The sights and sounds and smells that enveloped William were grisly and gruesome and disturbing. He did not want them to make him smile, but he was helpless to prevent it. He was glad they were dead. More than that, he was glad they had suffered. That gladness shook him to the core of his soul. He felt dirty. Of course, he was dirty. Filthy, really. He was covered in blood from head to toe, and for once not a drop of it was his. He slid his broadsword back into its sheath, and as he did so he spotted the head of the goruk he had decapitated lying in the street. He was not completely certain, but he had a pretty good hunch that it had been the one in command of the raid. Its armor was a little different than the others', a little more ornamental, and its oily hair was tied back in a ponytail with strips of leather that had feathers and beads on the ends. None of the other goruks had that. William stooped down and picked up the head by the hair and he immediately felt the need to scrub his hands for an hour. He tossed the head into the pile with all the others. He was not certain why. It just seemed like what he should do.

"Lambs to the slaughter," Colvin said, and William turned to look at his friend. Colvin too had escaped unscathed.

"What was that?" William asked.

Colvin noticed the strangely vacant look in the young nobleman's eyes. "Lambs to the slaughter," he repeated. "They didn't even have time to figure out what hit them." William nodded and looked around once more. He tried to stop smiling. He failed.

"Are you all right, man?" Colvin asked.

William sighed. "Yeah," he said. "Just a little tired of being covered in blood and seeing corpses in the street. Even goruk corpses." Colvin put a hand on William's shoulder and squeezed. His steely blue eyes were large and full of concern. He spoke no words, letting the physical contact and the look say all that needed to be said. William put his own hand over Colvin's, then slid his arm around his friend's shoulders. They stood there for a while, embracing as friends, sharing strength, rejoicing that they were still alive and unhurt. "You fought well," William said.

"Yeah, well, look who's talking," Colvin replied. "The man who led the charge right at their commander. That was the craziest damn thing I've ever seen, man. I would've never guessed you had it in you to take a head off with one clean slice like that."

William sort of laughed. "After the story you told today, I couldn't let you show me up."

"That was from horseback," Colvin said. He nudged the headless corpse of the goruk commander with the toe of his boot. "This was all you."

"William, Colvin, es good to see you again," said Ferdinan as he stepped up to both of them. The Conquian did not have to add the word *alive* to the end of his sentence. It was understood. Ferdinan had also escaped the fray without injury. In fact, he did not look to have a hair out of place. By his appearance he might as well have spent the evening dancing and sipping wine instead of fighting goruks to the death.

Ferdinan smiled at William and Colvin, but he was warily glancing at the pile of severed goruks heads out of the corner of his eye. "So tell me, what esactly es this all about?" he asked, gesturing toward the macabre heap.

Colvin shrugged. "Beats me. After the fighting was over, some men just started piling a bunch of heads together over there."

"I see," Ferdinan said, though his tone of voice indicated that he was still rather perplexed. A young constable approached the heap, carrying three heads by the hair in each hand. He dumped the heads onto the pile, then turned and headed back toward the mass of goruk corpses still lying in the street. Ferdinan approached the constable, and Colvin and William followed, curious to hear an explanation. Ferdinan addressed the constable, and the young man snapped quickly to attention when he realized who was speaking to him. "Tell me, constable," Ferdinan inquired, "why esactly are you doing this?"

"Because I'm on head duty, sir," the constable replied.

"*Head* duty? What in the holy name of God es that?"

"Master McRofaly gave a few of us orders, sir, that after the battle was over we were to decapitate the goruk corpses and gather the heads." The constable was obviously not very pleased about being chosen for head duty, but he was following his orders to the best of his ability.

"How many?" Colvin asked.

"All of them," the constable replied. "After we get done with the ones in the street, we have to drag the bodies out of the bonfire with gaff hooks and take their heads too."

"What in the world does McRofaly want with so many goruk heads?" Ferdinan asked with a mixture of incredulity and nausea.

The constable shrugged. "I have no idea. I just follow my orders. But you could ask him, if you want to. He's right over there."

Ferdinan, William and Colvin turned in surprise and saw that McRofaly was indeed there in the street, only a few feet away, looking over the decapitated bodies of fallen goruks and answering random questions from the soldiers about what to do now. The three men walked briskly over to McRofaly. "I'm surprised to see you here," Colvin said, half-smiling, half-smirking "I figured when the real fighting started you'd be in the next town."

"And miss the chance to see my plan in action?" McRofaly replied incredulously. "You must be joking. I was right up there with the archers." McRofaly pointed up to the roof of the tallest building. "I had a bird's eye view."

"Well I am certainly glad that your plan worked so well," said Ferdinan. "What es the phrase you Turishmen use? Everything came off without a hitch."

McRofaly nodded. "An overwhelming success. I won't lie to you, I never expected it to work this well. The preliminary count is one hundred seventeen fallen goruks, compared to a loss of twelve of our soldiers." Everyone stood in amazement. The numbers were astounding. Through his elation of victory, though, William Stuart-Camen felt a pang of remorse at the thought that times were so dark that he felt relieved when only twelve of his fellow Tamendaders were killed on a given day. "An impressive victory indeed," McRofaly continued, looking around at the carnage. He was smiling, but his voice almost sounded rueful. "This changes things, of course."

Ferdinan arched an eyebrow. "What esactly es going to change?"

"Everything," McRofaly replied evenly. "Tonight's victory carries with it a multitude of complications."

"How so, if you do not mind my asking?"

"We have tipped our hand to the goruks," said McRofaly. "When they learn that we were prepared for this attack, they will know that we have been watching them. Ian Morlocke's job is about to become considerably more difficult and dangerous. It is also likely that the goruks will now abandon stealth tactics and hit and run strikes, since their past two attempts have been easily thwarted. They now know what we are capable of. From now on, when the goruks attack I suspect they will rely more on force than the element of surprise."

Ferdinan nodded. "You have a gift for military strategy. Those are esactly the ramifications I espected when I recommended your plan."

"Hold on," William interrupted, "you knew all that would happen if we did this?"

"Sí," Ferdinan said, nodding.

"Then why do it?" William asked. "If you knew McRofaly's plan would give our spies away, why didn't we try something different? It doesn't seem worth it."

"McRofaly's plan did not give our spies away," Ferdinan insisted. "The goruks will not know who es watching them, or how they are being watched. All they will know es that we knew what they were planning to do before they did it. Es going to cast a shadow of doubt on whatever else they may have planned."

"Well that's smart," said Colvin. "But what about the other part, about the goruks relying on force? Aren't we trying to buy time for Gregor to get back with reinforcements? What's the sense in getting the goruks to attack us with bigger numbers when we're trying to hold out?"

"Don Ferdinan understands, as I do, that the time for subterfuge is at an end," McRofaly said, eyeing the Conquian with a hint of suspicion. "So far the goruks have teased us and tested us to see what we were capable of, and we have allowed them to do so. We could have done nothing, as you suggest, Colvin, and allowed the goruks to continue with their hit and run tactics, and they would have drained the well of our resistance a cupful at a time. The alternative, which we have chosen here tonight, is to make our stand and demand the goruks take us seriously, and in so doing perhaps buy ourselves a measure more of the most precious resource to be had in any war."

"What's that?" asked Colvin.

"Time," said McRofaly simply. "The goruks no doubt had a thousand schemes of how to pick us off a few at a time. I doubt they have any strategies on how to confront us head on. And developing those will take some time. During that time, we are as safe as any side can ever hope to be during a war."

"Sí," agreed Ferdinan, "McRofaly, I am very grateful that you and I are both on the same side."

"As am I, Don Ferdinan. As am I."

"My only question es what you plan to do with all the goruks heads," Ferdinan said.

McRofaly chuckled quietly to himself. "Ah, of course. You must think me quite mad. Don't worry, I don't plan to use them to decorate my home or anything like that."

"I am glad to hear that," Ferdinan said, but if the news really was a relief his voice did not show it. "But what do you plan to do with them?"

"I'm going to hang them from the city wall, for the goruks to see."

Ferdinan's usually calm demeanor faltered for just a moment, and his eyes widened in disgust. "What?" he asked, voice thick with repulsion. "Why?"

"Isn't it obvious? McRofaly replied. "I want to send the goruks a message."

"What in the world kind of message would that be?" William asked.

"Simple, William," McRofaly replied. "You wanted a war? You got a war."

CHAPTER TWENTY-FIVE

THINGS IN THE DARKNESS

The next two days were pure, raw torture.

McRofaly had the goruk heads hung from atop the city wall as soon as they were all collected, so that they would be visible at first light. When it was over, everyone who had been assigned to head duty had vomited at least once and was covered in gore from head to foot. Ferdinan had given those poor souls an hour's break, ordering them to get cleaned up and put some food back on their stomachs. The Conquian, who had made sure to stand upwind while giving the orders, felt certain that while the young men were obviously eager to bathe, few if any of them would follow the order to eat something. After the task they had just completed, Ferdinan could not blame them.

The headless goruk bodies had been disposed of in the bonfire, and the stench of charred flesh and burnt hair hung so thick in the air that it threatened to become a permanent fixture in Tamendad. Once cleanup was over, the constables and militiamen were put back on regular duty guarding the gates or patrolling around the city; all except Colvin, who was given his richly deserved half-night off. That left William, who was stationed at the northeast gate that night, without anyone to talk to to pass the time, and as the small hours melted away toward morning the young nobleman's thoughts turned inward and began to wander. It was his first night in an evacuated Tamendad – a dead, deserted Tamendad – and the sight of row upon row, street upon street of abandoned buildings and darkened windows gave him a case of the shudders that had nothing to do with the night's chill. He remembered an evening about two weeks ago, an evening from another life, when he had experienced a feeling similar to this. It had been the first evening Gregor and his lads had spent in town, at the Crown Rose. Then, the drunken chorus of a trade district full of revelers had worked to counteract the loneliness and melancholy that threatened to encroach upon young William's soul. Now there was no chorus, no revelers, no sound, nothing at all. Tamendad really was empty, and although he was surrounded on all sides by constables and militiamen stationed with him at the northeast gate, William Stuart-Camen was alone. By the time his shift was over, William felt like locking himself in his bedchamber, pulling his blanket up over his head, curing up into a little ball, and not coming out for a long, long while.

At first light, a goruk spy showed itself out in the open for the first time. It came howling and jabbering like a rabid dog from behind a low-lying hill to the south. It was obviously none too happy about the heads, since that was what it spent most of its time pointing and screaming at. It stood there ranting and raving in its incomprehensible language, flailing its fists wildly about, making gestures obscene enough to transcend any language barrier until one of the patrols that had not yet made it back into the city rounded on it and it fled. A few of the soldiers joked that McRofaly's message had been delivered, but most were too unsettled by the fact that even under the current levels of heightened security a goruk had managed to sneak its way within a hundred yards of the city wall completely undetected.

The morning hours passed without incident. As the sun approached its apex, Ferdinan showed up at the northeast gate. The members of the day guard stationed there were a little puzzled by his presence. It was widely known that Don Ferdinan slept during the day. When the commanding officer at the gate asked, nonchalantly, what was keeping the Conquian up so late, Ferdinan smiled wearily and explained that he was looking for something. The officer left it at that, and Ferdinan spent the next half-hour strolling around the gate with his hands thoughtfully tucked behind his back, occasionally glancing up at the sun or out toward the empty docks. Shortly past noon a ship passed Tamendad sailing southeast, a rare sight of late. Just as it was passing by, someone on board shot a single flaming arrow straight up into the air. A number of quizzical looks were exchanged among the day guard, and when the commanding officer turned to ask Ferdinan what he made of it, he found that the Conquian was already on his way back toward the Governor's house.

That evening, Colvin received word that he was being temporarily pulled from guard duty. Gangis had had a chance to look over the weapons shipment from Tantera, and found it an absolute mess. He informed Governor Chamberlain that he desperately needed Colvin's help. Colvin had been adamant in his opposition to the idea at first, insisting that he had given Gregor his word he would look after Fist

Division. He softened a bit when told that he and Gangis would be working at night so that they would be available at a moment's notice during an emergency. His last objection died away when Governor Chamberlain and Don Ferdinan agreed that Fist Division could call on him if they ran into any problems in training the new volunteers. Gangis and Colvin got to work in the forge that night, and Colvin found out for himself just how much of a nightmare the shipment from Tantera really was. About half of the weapons were in decent, usable condition, requiring nothing more than a little while at the grinding wheel and a polish. The other half, though, was nearly enough to make the two surrogate blacksmiths weep. There was rust, there were dents, there were nicks, and there were complete breaks. Some of the swords looked like they had been run over by a wagon train and then pissed on for good measure. The heads of the polearms were in a little better condition, but of the ones with wooden hafts a disheartening number had rotted clean through. The first half of that night had been spent separating the salvageable weapons from the hopeless ones.

Around midnight, the goruks exacted their revenge. The alarm bells caused a stir of anxiety among the soldiers, since the lookouts had not announced spotting anything. Word soon spread throughout all of Tamendad by way of town crier that an entire patrol, twenty trained soldiers, had come up missing. Ferdinan personally led a search for the missing men, and within an hour he had found where it had happened. It was the furthest point from the city wall that a patrol covered, on the crest of William and Melissa's hill. Ferdinan found signs of a scuffle there, along with a few discarded weapons, but no blood. The men had been taken alive, probably by surprise, by goruks lying in wait just on the other side of the hill. That it had been done so silently that no other patrol had heard sounds of the assault sent a chill up Ferdinan's spine. The Conquian bitterly cursed himself. He had believed, as McRofaly had, that the goruks would abandon sneak attacks and trickery when they learned what their last attempt had earned them. Ferdinan searched for the missing patrol all through the night, assisted by thirty soldiers who had not hesitated in volunteering despite the dangers involved.

Early the next morning, when the sun was not yet up but its light had begun to brighten the eastern sky, Ferdinan found them – what was left of them – in the copse of trees where the logging party harvested lumber for the bonfires. They had all been decapitated, their heads arranged in a circle on the ground, all facing Tamendad. Their bodies had been mutilated, ripped brutally into pieces and the remains strung up in the trees. Blood was everywhere, splattered all around. The trees were covered in blood as well, but not splattered like everything else. The trees had been intentionally marked, painted with blood. The message was clear: *We have been watching you, too.*

Ferdinan fell to his knees at the sight and wept. That reaction was common among the soldiers as well, and a few lost whatever food was on their stomachs. It nearly killed Ferdinan to leave the men there like that, but he knew there was nothing he could do for them at that moment except pray for their souls. The collection of their remains would require ladders and saws and at least one large wagon to transport it all back to Tamendad, and it could not even be touched until a priest performed the last rites. Ferdinan convened the war council as soon as he was back in Tamendad, hesitating only long enough to commission thirty strong men and a priest to gather supplies and go bring the soldiers home. Governor Chamberlain immediately terminated all night patrols despite McRofaly's insistence that they were necessary.

"The purpose of the patrols is to give us advance warning of a goruk attack," the Governor said. "If the goruks can snatch a patrol right from under us without us even noticing, then so far as I can tell they serve no purpose except endangering the lives of the men and women on patrol." For once, McRofaly had nothing to say in response to that.

The war council was in session for a long time that morning. They grieved for the lost patrolmen, of course, but more than that they discussed the implications of the kidnapping beyond the loss of twenty good soldiers. The event was terrifying enough in itself, but it was made worse by the fact that none of Ian Morlocke's men had reported seeing goruks on the move. That left two possibilities. Either Morlocke and his men had been discovered and eliminated, or there were goruks on the loose that were unaccounted for. Neither possibility was desirable, but the prospect of losing Tamendad's best spies threatened to deal a death blow to the war effort.

They were not made to ponder which undesirable fate they faced for very long. Close to midmorning one of Morlocke's men arrived in Tamendad to report no unusual activity had been spotted.

"There is likely a second entrance into the goruks' underground lair that we don't know about," McRofaly reasoned. "One small enough or remote enough to make it impractical for moving large numbers of troops through, but useful for sneaking a few goruks out unnoticed. That would explain the goruks that tried to ambush Colvin and myself while we were scouting."

Ferdinan charged McRofaly with searching the maps in the Governor's library for this purported second entrance, but it was quickly decided that if McRofaly's search turned up nothing they were not going to devote any serious manpower to discovering the location of the entrance. It could have been anywhere, and sending out scouting parties blindly into the countryside was much too dangerous.

The remains of the patrolmen were brought back to Tamendad early in the afternoon and buried in another communal grave. Just about everyone that was not on duty attended the funeral and burial, even though it meant giving up a couple of hours of precious sleep.

That evening the clouds opened and the rains came, soaking everything far beyond the possibility of making a bonfire. The storm lasted only a couple of hours after dark, but by the time it subsided the entire night watch was soaked to the bone and low in spirits. This was especially true of the men and women who would have been assigned to patrol duty that night. Instead of being sent on patrol they were all gathered together and stationed in formation at the southwest gate, ready to march forward to meet whatever enemy might be spotted. All they could do was stand there, huddling together for warmth, letting the rain soak them, praying for the lookouts atop the wall not to catch a glimpse of anything.

Around midnight the clouds broke up and the moon came out. It was a waning half, more than enough to see by after the eyes had become attenuated to the blackness of the cloud-covered night, and it was not a quarter hour later that a lookout spotted something. It was a lone goruk, and it had something large slung over its shoulder. The goruk drew within a few hundred feet of the wall, paused, and dumped its cargo thoughtlessly to the ground. It hit with a dull thud and sprawled out limply in a way that left little doubt to what it was. The goruk then turned back into the cover of night, leaving whoever it was lying silently motionless on the ground. Word was immediately sent for Don Ferdinan, who was overseeing the northeast gate that night. The Conquian came with uncharacteristic swiftness, and his quickness of breath said that he had been running. He climbed up to the lookout platform so he could have a look for himself.

"This reeks of a trap," Ferdinan said once the lookout had brought him up to speed. "Of course, that does not change the fact that I am going out there."

"Why go out if you think it's a trap, sir?" asked the lookout.

"Es possible that person es still alive. If you were in such a position, would you not want someone to come after you?"

The lookout nodded. "I've got your back, Don Ferdinan," he said. "If it is a trap, I'll let you know before anything gets within five hundred feet of you."

"Thank you, constable," replied Ferdinan, patting the lookout on the back.

Once he was back on the ground, the constables and militiamen who had less than an hour ago been soaked and dispirited to the brink of misery were falling over themselves to accompany Ferdinan to rescue whomever it was the goruk had left behind. Ferdinan selected ten good soldiers to accompany him, to watch his back and keep a lookout for anything unusual. Ferdinan drew his sabre, and with his accompaniment in tow began to cautiously inch toward the unmoving humanoid shape. After about a hundred feet it became clear that it was indeed a person, a man from the look of it. Ferdinan had to keep a tight hold of himself then to fight the urge to rush to the man's side. He would be of little use to anyone, he told himself, if he got himself killed trying to help someone who was very likely dead anyway.

After about another fifty feet, any hope Ferdinan had of saving the man's life vanished as the outline of a dagger protruding from his chest materialized in the moonlight. "Stay alert," Ferdinan told his companions. "If this es a trap, it will be sprung soon." He sheathed his sabre as he crept near the dead man and knelt softly in the grass beside him. Whoever he was, he was young and had been good looking before the goruks had gotten hold of him. Now he was missing his eyes, and most of his fingers. His flesh had been cut in multiple places, in multiple ways. With all that had been done to him, the dagger in his chest looked more like an added touch than a killing blow. The dagger was plunged through a piece of paper, holding it in place against the man's breastbone. The paper looked to have little if any blood on it. It was folded, but Ferdinan could still tell that it bore writing. It was a letter.

"Send for a priest," Ferdinan said, his voice full of urgency. "This man needs last rites."

The priest came, dressed in full vestments and prepared to perform the rites, less than a quarter of an hour later, and Ferdinan appreciated his haste greatly. Once the rites were performed, Ferdinan and the soldiers that had accompanied him carried the body back inside the city wall. When they gently laid the body on the bricked street, Ferdinan heard someone gasp. He turned to see a constable rushing toward him to get a better look.

"Oh my God," the constable said. "That's Edgar."

"You know this man?" Ferdinan asked.

"He's my cousin," the constable said, not looking away from the body. Tears were welling up in his eyes. "He's in Shield Division."

Ferdinan gently placed a hand on the man's shoulder. "You have my deepest sympathies," he said. "Your cousin has scaled the summit." Ferdinan ordered the constable to take a few moments to collect himself and light a candle at the church. He did it partly out of compassion for the man, but mostly because he did not want the man to see what he had to do to his cousin's body. Once the constable was out of sight, Ferdinan planted a boot firmly on the dead man's chest, gripping the handle of the dagger tightly in both hands. He pulled with all the strength that he had, and when the dagger finally came free Ferdinan nearly fell over backward from the force it required. He quickly discarded the dagger, wiping his hands on his pant leg, and unfolded the letter. He called for a town crier before he was even finished reading it.

"Wake McRofaly and summon him to the Governor's house, along with William Stuart-Camen and Colvin," Ferdinan told the messenger. "I am calling an emergency meeting of the war council."

The forge was considerably cooler now, after the rain had ended and the vents on the roof could be opened again, letting some of the heat escape. Colvin and Gangis were still dripping with sweat, but the night breeze felt wonderful against their damp skin and it had helped them find their second wind. They were making good progress. The weapons in need of a spit and polish job had already been seen to, and they were making steady headway with the more seriously damaged weapons. The "hopeless" pile, as Colvin had come to think of it, was slowly growing, expanding to fill the corner of the workshop as Colvin and Gangis encountered weapons that at first glance appeared salvageable but were found to be beyond repair once they were on the anvil. The thing that really gnawed at Colvin's brain was the certainty that a number of those "hopeless" weapons would be repaired to like-new condition as soon as Gunther got his hands on them. It wasn't resentment, not by a far cry. It was more like wonderment, a sense of awe that anyone could be as good at anything as Gunther was at what he did. Colvin wanted very much to be that good at something, anything, before he died. Reaching that level of skill at something had to bring a sense of meaning to a man's life.

Colvin's thoughts were a muddled mess tonight. The shadowy illumination of the forge, supplied by the oil lamps hanging from the hooks in the ceiling, gave the workshop an ominous, brooding cast that made the mind wander in strange directions. He thought about the kidnapped patrolmen. What had their last moments been like? Had they struggled to the bitter end against their captors, or had fear rendered them helpless long before the killing blow had come? He thought about

William, and hoped that the young nobleman really was holding up as well as he seemed to be. Colvin had a feeling his friend had a tendency to keep his feelings – his real, true feelings – bottled deep down inside, stored securely in some often overlooked and forgotten corner of his mind. He thought about Gunther, off on some self-appointed quest to save Tamendad, the details of which he steadfastly refused to divulge under the harshest scrutiny. The short blacksmith was probably in Tantera by now, or had already moved on from it to whatever the next leg of his journey required of him. Each strike of hammer against glowing metal reminded Colvin of Gunther. He was the most giving, selfless person Colvin had ever met. Colvin also thought about Gregor, and wondered where he was. It was difficult to keep track of the days lately, but Colvin felt relatively certain that the big Highlander was probably making final arrangements to depart his home and return to Tamendad. If he decided to come back at all, now that he was safely within the confines of his own home. Colvin shook that thought off and bit at himself for allowing it to play across the stage of his mind. Of course Gregor would come back. Gregor MacDugal was a man of his word, and he valued honor as highly, in his own way, as Ferdinan did.

Colvin's mind was tugged in these directions and a hundred more, and while the thoughts all seemed random and disjointed, thoroughly unconnected, each in fact led progressively down a chain to the next logical link, and at the center all these chains orbited around a single name, and that name was Melinda. Her raven hair and green eyes and secretive smile were stamped firmly on the depths of Colvin's mind, like a rivet in a breastplate. No matter which direction Colvin turned his thoughts, her name haunted him from the dancing shadows that played out like a demented puppet show on the walls of the workshop. In this shadow he saw the thoughtful way she had looked him over, appraised him, at their first encounter. In that one was the shape of their bodies as they had tumbled into bed together, before she had suddenly and violently decided that she wanted nothing to do with him. In most of them was a memory of the kiss that by all rights she should have never given him, that he should have never taken. Melinda had invaded his brain and made a nice little nest for herself there, hooking her fingers delicately into fabric of his mind and tying it in knots. Worse, she had done it almost entirely unawares, and without him noticing until now, when she was gone. And holy God, was she gone. Even if she hadn't been in Tantera tonight, even if she was standing right here beside him at the forge, she would still be gone, emotionally distant beyond measure. Ferdinan had called this *el prím amor*, first love. If this was love – this infuriating fixation, bordering on obsession, that was growing worse by the day instead of better, that was beginning to invade his sleeping thoughts as well as his waking ones – well then deal him out. He would stick to harmless one night stands.

He focused all his attention on the blade of the sword he was coaxing back to straightness, hoping to push aside all thoughts of the whirlwind he had become wrapped up in. It worked, marginally. This was perhaps the tenth sword he had repaired, the third that was in need of serious work. The blade was nicked in two places and had a bend about halfway up its length that was so subtle you didn't even notice it until you tried to swing it and felt for yourself how loopy it made the balance. Thankfully the blade had not been in such bad condition that it needed to be melted down and reforged from scratch. If it had been, it would have tumbled headlong right into the "hopeless" pile. Neither Colvin nor Gangis had the skill or the time to try reforging a sword blade. They both had to work with what they could manage, and Colvin found he could manage this sword just fine. That thought pleased him quite a bit, really, because he felt rather certain that when he had first come to Tamendad he would have probably chucked this sword right into the "hopeless" pile as well. He had picked up a handful of highly useful tips and pointers just by watching Gunther work, and the short blacksmith had explained to him another handful in vivid detail. He could do more now than he could do before, understood more now than he had understood before.

The most important thing he understood, a thing that had never been spoken aloud at the forge but was the first thing he had learned from Gunther nonetheless, was that you could not hope to force the sword back into shape. It was a horrible misconception that blacksmiths *forced* metal. Blacksmiths worked *with* metal, shaped it, tempered it, sharpened it. The only force involved was the brute force involved in swinging a hammer against an anvil, but even that was not raw, unchecked force. You couldn't just swing that hammer away to your heart's content, or you would wind up with a mangled hunk of useless scrap. You had to see the sword within the metal, see where the metal needed to be struck, changed, altered, to make it whole and perfect. Repairing a sword was the same way, perhaps even more so. The sword had at one point been whole and perfect, and now it was damaged. You couldn't just force it back into wholeness. You couldn't just blindly hammer its perfection back into it. You had to watch the sword, feel the sword, let it tell you what needed to be done to mend its wounds. The sword told the blacksmith what needed to be done, and the greatest blacksmiths, like Gunther, were the ones who listened completely, wholeheartedly, and provided exactly what the sword needed.

A woman is like a sword.

The thought screamed into Colvin's mind from the depths of his subconscious. The progressive chains of thought shattered, leaving only Melinda's face, and she was smiling that secretive smile. The hammer in Colvin's hand dropped to the floor with a loud *clang* that echoed through the workshop. Gangis jumped a little, turning in surprise to look at Colvin with wide eyes. Colvin just stood there. He was smiling. He felt like laughing.

"What the twist is wrong with you?" Gangis asked.

"Nothing, I'm fine. I'm gonna take a break. I need to talk to Ferdinan."

"Yeah, do that," Gangis muttered, turning back to his anvil. "I think the heat's starting to get to you."

Colvin wiped the sweat from his body and quickly pulled his shirt back on. He stepped out of the workshop into the cool, damp night and shuddered slightly at the chill of the wind against his still-damp body. It was only the first day of autumn, but the temperature was already beginning to dip significantly at night. The first frost would come early this year. It was probably going to be a rough winter. But none of that mattered to Colvin at the moment. In fact, the entire war effort did not really matter much to Colvin at the moment. He had had what he could only refer to as a moment of insight, a sense of clarity like he had only felt once, maybe twice before in all his life. He had to talk to Ferdinan about this. Only Ferdinan would understand, and Ferdinan had understood the whole time. That thought made Colvin want to laugh all the more. His Conquian friend had laid it all out right in front of him, everything he needed to know, but not in a way that would simply lead Colvin around by the nose. His riddle had forced Colvin to figure it out on his own, and Colvin had done it. It took him what now felt in retrospect like a day more than forever to do it, but he had finally figured it out, and now he understood. He wanted so badly to find Ferdinan and explain it all to him, to let Ferdinan know that he really understood it all, that he had really figured it all out on his own. And then...

His smiled faltered a little. And then...what? Melinda? She was in another city, and he was right in the middle of a war for survival. There were no guarantees here.

Colvin did not allow himself to go very far down that avenue of thought. He knew from experience that it only led to self-pity and a sense of resentment toward things he had no control over. Of course there were no guarantees here. There were no guarantees anywhere, ever. Life was a game of probabilities; he understood that as well as anyone. He also understood that he had a much better shot at survival here, in Tamendad, than he would have had wandering about the countryside alone. It had taken pure, blind luck to rescue him from Lorthok's clutches. Colvin had little doubt that if he hadn't come to Tamendad he would have wound up dead by now, or worse, a goruk's slave. There was no guarantee that he would ever see Melinda again, but Colvin's gut told him that he had a pretty good shot at it. At least fifty-fifty. Colvin tended to trust his gut. It had rarely steered him wrong in the past. Besides, even if he never saw Melinda again, for whatever reason, he was still excited about talking to Ferdinan, about telling his instructor that he had figured out the riddle. That accomplishment was in itself something to brag about.

The rain had gathered in an interconnected latticework of puddles around the cobblestones of the street, and Colvin's boots splashed through them as he hurried down it. The clouds were gone now, thankfully, and the position of the moon in the sky told him that it was close to midnight or shortly after. Half the night had been swallowed up by the fires of the forge. Colvin realized with mild surprise that he was hungry. He had not eaten since his reading lesson with McRofaly, and since then he had had his fencing lesson with Ferdinan and spent four hours at the forge. Strangely enough, he was finding it pretty easy to forget to eat now that food was available on demand. Well, he would grab a bite to eat after he found Ferdinan. With any luck, Gertrude would be making one of her wicked stews for the night watch's lunch, which actually occurred around one or two in the morning, and he could get dibs on a bowl while it was still scalding hot, and maybe half a loaf of crusty bread fresh from the oven with butter and honey, and a tall tankard of milk, so cold that little drops of water would form on the outside of the cup. Colvin's stomach growled, and he patted it absentmindedly. Maybe he'd grab a bite to eat *before* finding Ferdinan.

Colvin rounded a corner, and collided head-first with a town crier. Colvin staggered back a few steps and reached out to grab hold of the building beside him to steady himself. The town crier tumbled backward, falling flat on his back with his legs up in the air. He stared up at Colvin with wide, confused eyes, blinking rapidly. "Oh, Master Colvin, it's you!" the crier said after a few disoriented moments. "I'm glad I ran into you…oh, I mean…not that I literally ran into you…in the physical sense, I mean…"

"Don't worry about it," Colvin said, stepping forward and extending a hand to the prone messenger. He helped the man to his feet. The crier swayed gently back and forth once he was again upright, not having fully regained his sense of equilibrium yet. Colvin patted him gently on the shoulder, careful not to do it too forcefully. "You all right?" he asked.

The crier nodded. "Yes, sir," he replied. "I think you knocked a few cobwebs loose."

Colvin laughed. "So what's the message?"

"Message, sir?"

Colvin arched an eyebrow. "Don't you have a message for me? I just assumed, since you said you were glad you ran into me."

"Oh!" the crier said suddenly. "Right! The message! Don Ferdinan wants you to come to the Governor's house on the double. He's called an emergency meeting of the war council."

"What's happened?" Colvin asked, concerned. The messenger gave him the condensed version, which was as accurate as any account from a man who was not physically present to witness the actual events could be. The most dubious part of the story, so far as the town crier was concerned, was that the whole thing probably had something to do with whatever had been written on the piece of paper stuck to poor young Edgar's chest, and he was very straightforward with Colvin that this was only conjecture on his part. Colvin thanked the messenger, checked once more to make sure he was okay, and then quickly proceeded on his way to the Governor's house.

Colvin was the next to last person to arrive in the big room on the third floor of the Governor's house with the table built for ten people. McRofaly was the last. Although the meeting was held at nearly one in the morning, McRofaly was the only man who had sleep in his eyes. Ferdinan began to address the war council as soon as McRofaly took his seat, as though McRofaly's rear end touching his chair was a starter's signal in a race. Ferdinan's perceptible anxiousness, bordering on impatience, was unsettling to the other men on the war council. The Conquian was usually as calm in his approach to the war council as he was passionate in pretty much every other aspect of his life.

"We have received a message," Ferdinan said, not looking at anyone, rubbing the slightly damp grain of the paper between his fingers. "Two messages, actually. One from Shield Division and one from the goruks."

"What are you talking about, Don Ferdinan?" asked the Governor.

Ferdinan recounted his experiences outside the city wall earlier in the evening. Everyone except McRofaly had heard some streamlined version of it, but Ferdinan's retelling filled in various missing details and undid some falsehoods that had slipped in as word had spread. When he was finished, Ferdinan said, "This es what was stuck to the young man's chest." He laid the folded piece of paper flat on the table and slid it over to Governor Chamberlain. "I would appreciate it if you would read it, Geoffery. I can speak Turish quite well, but the reading sometimes presents difficulties."

Governor Chamberlain nodded and picked up the letter. He ran his thumb across the place where a wax seal had once been, but was now gone. The letter looked naked without it, indecent. What obscenity was contained within? He cautiously unfolded the paper. Everyone else except Ferdinan inched forward on their seats. Geoffery Chamberlain found that the letter did indeed contain two messages, as Ferdinan had said. The first one, underneath, was written in ink. It was from Shield Division. The other one, the one on top, was unmistakably written in blood. Governor Chamberlain read them both aloud, though it was often difficult to decipher exactly what each said. The first message was addressed to the Governor. It read:

It is my pleasure to report to you that Shield Division has successfully completed its assignment and safely escorted the evacuated townspeople to their temporary refuge in Tantera. We will be returning to Tamendad with all possible haste, where we greatly anticipate helping defend our home from the goruks. All Shields except Gunther Moragun will be returning. Gunther personally requested, rather enigmatically, that I inform you he has set about his "business." We anticipate our return to be swifter than our journey here, since our progress will not be slowed by the evacuees. With a little luck we will be back in Tamendad by nightfall tomorrow, 17th Anteron.

I pray this letter finds Your Lordship in good health. There was much debate over its sending, but the general consensus is that it might do Your Lordship well to know that reinforcements are on the way. We have selected our best rider to bring it to you on our fastest horse. Both rider and horse deserve a king's welcome, if I may say so. May the Face of Beneficence smile upon Your Lordship during these trying times. I look forward to returning home.

Signed,

Aiden Thalison

Representative of Shield Division

The second message, the one written in blood, was superimposed over the message from Shield Division. The script was scratchy and irregular, and it reminded Governor Chamberlain of how a rather slow child might write. It read:

>*Paleskins, your time is ending. What was stolen will be reclaimed. Your sins will not go unpunished. Your acts have made this a vendetta. Your suffering is necessary, now, but your deaths are not. You have a choice. Surrender and you will live. Refuse, and you will die. Our victory is certain either way. Choose with wisdom.*
>
>*Kor*

William Stuart-Camen exhaled a long, slow breath, the first sound to penetrate the silence after Governor Chamberlain had finished reading. The young nobleman realized that his fists were clenched, his knuckles white with tension. White hot rage boiled in his veins, kindled by the words he had just heard. He was shaking, only a little but uncontrollably. "Who – or what – is Kor?" he asked.

"Es most likely the name of the goruk who es masterminding this assault against us," Ferdinan said. "Thank you, Governor Chamberlain, for reading that. Hearing it spoken aloud has cleared up much for me that I could not reason out while trying to read it myself."

"You're very welcome, Don Ferdinan," the Governor replied. "So, we have our first communique from the goruks."

McRofaly yawned. "They must have seen the heads."

"Indeed. Now, gentlemen, how do we respond to this?"

"We ambush the bastards," William growled. Everyone looked at him, and they were all surprised by the fire that burned in the young nobleman's eyes. "Sorry, please excuse my language," William added, "but it seems to me that the line's been drawn. Every time the goruks have come against us, they've expected us to just roll over and die like... like...like I don't *know* what!" William slammed his fist against the table, hard. A couple of the other council members jumped in surprise.

"I agree with William," Ferdinan said. "Our only hope es to meet aggression with aggression. Appearing weak or indecisive to the goruks could be very costly."

"I also agree with William on this matter," the Governor said. "This conflict is rapidly escalating. It is time, I feel, for us to take a more proactive stance and make a move against the goruks, instead of waiting to react to their next move against us. Master McRofaly, tomorrow you are going to take a small detachment with you and begin making preparations at the ambush site. I want to move on this as soon as Shield

Division is back among us."

"Yes, Lord Governor," McRofaly replied. "I would personally prefer a little bigger of a storm than we had tonight, just to make the felled trees a bit more believable, but things are just moving too quickly for that. Everything will be ready in two days."

"Exercise the greatest possible caution, Master McRofaly," Captain Jefford warned. "If the goruks spot you, it would deal an irreparable blow to our plans."

McRofaly nodded. *What kind of idiot do you take me for?* he thought.

"What exactly is Gunther's business?" asked Colvin out of blue. He had been thinking about this ever since the Governor had read the message from Shield Division. Governor Chamberlain and Don Ferdinan exchanged a look.

"I am afraid es known only to Gunther himself," Ferdinan said. "Es something Gunther believed was very important to the war effort, but he did not give specifics."

"Okay," said Colvin," just wondering. We could really use his help at the forge."

"I can imagine," Governor Chamberlain said. "Those weapons did not look very promising."

Colvin just nodded.

About an hour later, after a few specifics and minor details were seen to, the war council adjourned and everyone dispersed back to what they had been doing before the meeting. Colvin caught up with Ferdinan in the hallway leading to the central stairway. Other than the two of them, the hallway was deserted.

"I figured it out, Ferdinan!" Colvin said. "I figured out how a woman is like a sword!"

Ferdinan crossed his arms over his chest. "All right, tell me," Ferdinan said. "How es a woman like a sword?"

"I figured it out while I was at the forge," Colvin began. "I was fixing swords, obviously, and I started thinking about how you can't just force a sword back into shape. You have to figure out what's wrong with the sword, and once you've figured that out you know what the sword needs. And I was thinking about how the really great blacksmiths, not just the good ones but the master smiths, like Gunther, get to be so good because they've learned how to feel out a sword and realize what it needs. And then it just hit me, out of the blue. That's what *you* do with a woman, and it's what you've been trying to teach me to do all along. You listen to a woman. You feel her, until you know exactly what she needs to make her whole. Then you give it to her."

Ferdinan stood still with his arms folded over his chest. He had not made a move, not so much as the subtlest nod of the head, the whole time Colvin was speaking. Once Colvin finished, his words echoed slightly in the empty hallway and died away, and silence engulfed both men. Yet still Ferdinan stood still as stone. Colvin nervously shuffled his feet a little.

"Selflessness," Ferdinan said at last.

"Selflessness," Colvin agreed.

Ferdinan embraced Colvin suddenly, moving with the quick, catlike fluidity that Colvin swore only Ferdinan could manage. Ferdinan kissed Colvin on each cheek, which was just about the strangest thing Colvin thought Ferdinan could do under the circumstances. *Must be a Conquian thing*, he thought.

"Well done, Colvin," Ferdinan said. "Well done."

"I got it right?' Colvin asked excitedly. "All of it?"

"Well, no, not all of it. But the part you did get, you got esactly right."

A puzzled pause, and then Colvin said, "Huh?"

"Colvin, when I was a little boy growing up in Conquia, the first thing my father – may God rest his soul – told me about women was that a woman es like a sword. That was years ago, and still I am finding ways in which es true, ways I had never thought about before. Es not something you figure out in a few days. Some of the greatest sages in Conquia dedicate their lives to pondering that old riddle, yet still men – some younger than you – discover new truths in it."

"Wow," said Colvin.

"Sí. And this truth you have discovered, while not new, es one of the most deeply meaningful truths known. It does not deal with a simple amorous encounter. Es the sort of truth that applies to a woman you commit yourself to completely, a woman you wish to make happy for the rest of her life. I do not have to ask who you were thinking of when you made this discovery."

Colvin said nothing. He smiled a little sheepishly.

"Be mindful of your feelings, Colvin," Ferdinan continued. "Do not let your head get in the way of your heart. Remember, passion above all else."

Colvin nodded. Ferdinan embraced him again, and he embraced back.

"Ferdinan, can I ask you a personal question?" Colvin asked.

"Of course," Ferdinan responded.

"This is the first time I've ever heard you mention your father. What did he do?"

"He played the mandolin in a whorehouse."

Colvin nearly choked. "Wh-what?!?" he sputtered.

Ferdinan repeated himself. There was no mistaking what he said.

"Wow," Colvin said absently. "So, your mother…was she…?"

"No," Ferdinan said quickly. "My mother was the daughter of a farmer. The two of them ran away together because her father forbid her to marry him, because of who he was and what he did. I never met my grandfather. He died several years ago."

"Wow," Colvin said once again, sounding rather stupid but unable to help it. "I'd just sort of assumed you were, you know, of noble birth or whatever."

"Colvin, you of all people should know better than that," said Ferdinan.

"Better than what?" asked Colvin.

Ferdinan gave Colvin a pat on the back. "Es a man's life, not his birth, that makes him noble."

CHAPTER TWENTY-SIX

REVELATIONS AND ESCALATIONS

The visions would not cease. Undeniable in their authenticity, they came nightly, bombarding the ardah's mind while he slept. He could smell the stench of burning flesh, could hear the wails of his people burning alive. Above that, he could hear the war cries of the paleskins as they continued to pour out from their hiding places among the shadows. There was a seemingly endless sea of them, and blood lust was in their eyes. The ardah watched helplessly, bound captive by the power of the visions, as the paleskins mowed down his people like grain at the harvest. But it was more than a vision. It was worse than that. The ardah was there with them, standing among his people as the paleskins massacred them. He felt his flesh cut open by the paleskin blades, tasted the metallic bite of his own blood in his mouth. He felt his organs rupture as his body was riddled with the paleskins' arrows. He felt his own life force slipping away from him like sand through the fingers of a fist that grips too tightly. And he felt his flesh begin to burn as the paleskins threw his body into the flames before his life had fully slipped away from him.

The ardah sat bolt upright, crossing the gulf between deep sleep and full, waking consciousness in the briefest of moments. The sound of his scream hung in the air, echoing off the stone walls of his quarters. This was the third successive night he had awoken screaming. His oil lamp, the only oil lamp among his people, was turned down to just the barest flicker of a flame. What little light it produced cast long, dancing shadows across the walls of the ardah's chambers. As the haze of sleep receded from his vision, the ardah could clearly make out faces peering at him in those shadows, eyes burning, mouths open in silent howls of rage. The faces of the Ancient Ones surrounded him.

The Ancient Ones were furious.

The visions had never been this frequent before, or this vivid. It had always been an honor to receive visions from the Ancient Ones. It was a sign that their favor was upon you. Those with the greatest propensity for receiving visions were chosen to study under the ardah, and the most talented initiate one day was chosen to cast off his given name and rise to the level of ardah himself. Now, though, the visions had become a nightmare. They were filled with violence, and suffering, and death. They were nearly constant, and if they became any worse they would be crippling.

The first vision had come two nights ago, and it had been the worst. The ardah had known then that he was experiencing the massacre of his people as it happened. He knew that Yargos, the fool, had led his warriors into a trap before Yargos himself knew it. The only pleasant thing about that first vision was experiencing firsthand the painful, bloody price Yargos had paid for his stupidity. The rest of it had been sheer terror, watching his people being wiped out like children standing against seasoned warriors. Worse than that had been seeing – *feeling* – what the paleskins had done to the bodies of the dead. Long before the spy had returned with his urgent message, the ardah knew that the walls of Tamendad bore the severed heads of the fallen.

That was unforgivable. That was why the Ancient Ones demanded restitution.

But therein lay the ardah's problem.

Who was he to punish?

His instinct, naturally, was to direct his wrath at the paleskins, to censure them for the unforgivable atrocity they had perpetrated. They had committed the crime, after all. They were the criminals. It was intuitive that they were the ones who would be made to pay dearly for this unrequitable act. Why else would the Ancient Ones be giving the ardah visions, if not to say, "Look at what these paleskin swine have done. Witness their crimes against our people. They must be made to suffer."

Yet the ardah, incensed though he was, could not bring himself to place the blame of what had happened squarely and solely on the shoulders of the paleskins. *Who is the instigator?* the ardah asked himself again and again. *Who set all this in motion?* From a strictly historical context, the ardah supposed the answer to that question was the paleskin conqueror who had originally wrenched control of the land out of goruk hands, the man whom the stories passed down through the generations, from ardah to ardah, had named *Dan*. He had begun the rivalry between paleskin and goruk. Before Dan, the goruks had maintained an unspoken, mutual agreement with the paleskins who dwelt in the mountains to the south not to interfere in the others' business. The mountain men had no interest in the northern lands, and the goruks saw nothing to gain from the mountains. But the arrival of Dan from across the sea plunged the goruks into a savage battle with these new paleskins, a battle to hold control of the northern lands, a battle the goruks lost. Dan set the war machine in motion. He struck the first blow.

But that was so far in the past.

Dan was long dead now, dead before the ardah's great-grandfather was even born. To the paleskins who now held the northern lands, Dan was a figure of the distant past, a history lesson. They swore no allegiance to him. If the ardah's suspicions were correct, most of them would not even be able to recall his name on command. If the Ancient Ones wanted the instigator punished, Dan was out of the question. It was impossible to punish a ghost.

Besides, even though the goruks had lost control of the northern lands, they had gained the whole new world of the Under. The Under provided all they needed to survive, and it provided a place to hide from their enemies. The goruks had adapted quite nicely into their new environment, and now they thrived in it. The Ancient Ones had provided. The only undesirable aspect of the Under, so far as the ardah was concerned, was having to exist in such close proximity to the filthy, despicable Ganugamosh. But even as for that, there had been no contact between goruks and Ganugamosh for generations. Life in the Under was not so bad. In the ardah's opinion, all the tyrannical Dan had really done, when the dust settled, was open the goruks to a new way of life.

Who was the instigator?

The paleskins had desecrated the bodies of the fallen warriors, had prevented them from finding the glory accorded by the Ancient Ones to those who fell in battle. That sin was unforgivable. The paleskins had to be censured for that. It was beyond question. Wrongdoing against the Ancient Ones did not go unpunished. But were the paleskins the instigators?

No.

The paleskins had transgressed, certainly, but the ardah could not deny that what they did, they did as a reaction. There was no excusing the act itself, but their reasons for doing it had to be considered. What the paleskins had done was not an isolated incident, existing alone in a vacuum. It was one link in the complex chain of events in the struggle for control of Tamendad. That was what disturbed the ardah the most. His people were wrapped up in the middle of a war with the paleskins, a war the ardah did not know was coming until it was upon him. His people called it the reclaiming. *Abuneth.* As though the goruks who came to him to ask for guidance in pleasing the Ancient Ones had suffered any loss to the paleskins. As if they personally had been driven into the Under by Dan and his army, not their long dead, long forgotten ancestors. The thought of *Abuneth* was like a fever spreading among his people. It affected their reasoning, made them delirious. The paleskins had committed the actual crime – that much of the blame was theirs alone, and they would pay the terrible price for it – but they had been driven to their crime by the cruel machinations of *Abuneth*. And behind *Abuneth* stood a single soul.

Kor.

Kor the great general. Kor the fearless leader. Kor the revolutionary. Some of this, the ardah knew, was Kor's own fault. Kor was the instigator. Part of the punishment belonged to him. But Kor had made himself untouchable. He had won the support, and perhaps the love, of his people. If the ardah made a move against Kor, some of Kor's followers would side with him even over the ardah. Their loyalty was that fierce. And even if their numbers were insufficient to overwhelm those who remained loyal to the ardah, the battle that was sure to ensue would do irreparable damage to the goruks.

How bad had it become, that goruks would openly revolt against the ardah? How blind had the ardah allowed himself to become, that he had not noticed it happening until he found himself surrounded by it on all sides? Kor was playing the game brilliantly.

Politics. That was what the ardah had become wrapped up in. Stupid, simple, mundane politics. Kor wanted to bring about a revolution, to reshape their society with himself at the top. There was little doubt in the ardah's mind what place was reserved for him in Kor's new society. For all his sworn devotion to the Ancient Ones and the old ways, there was an unmistakable desire in Kor's heart to break with tradition and remake all things anew.

And Kor despised the ardah.

It had taken the ardah a long time, far too long, to realize this. At first even the ardah was persuaded by Kor's talks – not speeches; Kor rarely ever made speeches – about making life better for their people. Kor wanted to improve the quality of life of the goruks, and in that the ardah was firmly with him. The Ancient Ones wanted them to be contented; not so contented that they forgot that they relied on the Ancient Ones for all things – a little suffering helped keep the mind clear – but contented nonetheless. But while Kor was talking openly and publicly of making life better in a vague, undefined sense, in private he whispered to a select few about strength and readiness to serve and dedication. About *Abuneth*. Those whispers spread like a fire, like a cancer, throughout their people, and by the time those whispers reached the ardah's ears it was too late to circumvent it. By that time, *Abuneth* had become an Idea. It had become an Institution. It had become Something Worth Dying For. And before long, the ancient goruk mantra of *Thorak rakuth, Rikolatha* – what I do, I *do for the Ancient Ones* – had somehow become *Thorak rakuth, Abuneth*. Just like that, the ardah had found his people in a war with the paleskins for control of Tamendad, and found himself in a personal war with Kor for control of their people.

The ardah had no gift for politics. There was no politicking with the Ancient Ones. There was only subservience and gratitude for being chosen to serve. If the ardah enjoyed luxuries that none of his people enjoyed, it was just a part of the unparalleled honor of the title. If he had to answer to no authority save his own, it was because the ardah answered only to the Ancient Ones. Politics were as alien to the ardah as intelligence was to the Ganugamosh. Yet here he was, locked in a political struggle with Kor that he had no desire to fight. No matter how much of the blame rested on Kor – and the ardah was certain a good portion of it did – he could not come down publicly against Kor. That would cause a rupture that would likely never heal. There were really only two possibilities left, then. Either he could remain neutral, say nothing, and let *Abuneth* run its course, or he could aid Kor, minimally, in the hopes of forestalling further atrocities against his people. Down the first path lay the certainty of his eventual casting out from his people and perhaps even his own death and the death of the old ways. Down the second lay the potential for incurring the wrath of the Ancient Ones, assuming it really was Kor the Ancient Ones desired to see punished. It was, in essence, choosing the lesser of two evils.

The ardah sighed. He was supposed to be a spiritual leader and advisor, a guide to his people. He was not supposed to become involved in matters such as this. The problems he faced were greater than those that had been faced by any ardah in a thousand seasons. His head swam from all his guessing and second-guessing, and his eyelids had once again begun to droop. Tomorrow he would make a blood sacrifice to the Ancient Ones and ask them for guidance, and hope that they offered more help than they had so far.

The ardah laid back down. Slowly, and with great difficulty, he found his way back to sleep, where the visions were waiting for him.

❖   ❖   ❖

"Three o'clock and all's well!"

"Now there's a bullshit statement if I ever heard one," William muttered under his breath.

"What was that, sir?"

William jumped a little bit, startled at being addressed. He had walked off a little ways from the northeast gate to take his lunch alone. He sat on the ground, his back resting up against the wall of a deserted shop, his legs crisscrossed with an empty bowl resting on his lap. His lunch of fish stew and bread, delicious as usual from Gertrude's kitchen, was long since finished, and his full belly had helped his mind to wander. As a result, he had lost track of time.

The person who had addressed him, it turned out, was a Sword. His name was Tad. He was at least three years older than William, but whenever Tad addressed the young nobleman he did so with a reverence William felt should have been reserved for the eldest, bravest war heroes.

"Nothing, Tad," William said while getting to his feet. "Didn't really even mean to say it out loud."

"Are you all right, sir?" Tad asked. That was another thing about Tad. He was much too perceptive for his own good.

"Just got a lot on my mind. The look of this town at night just doesn't sit right with me."

"I know what you mean," Tad said. "It feels so empty it's just... wrong."

William nodded. Tad was one of the very, very few people William felt he could talk to, on very rare occasions, about how he felt. Out of Tad's entire family, he was the only one left in Tamendad. All the rest had been evacuated. Tad was alone. William sometimes wondered to himself whether he or Tad had the worse lot. William could not imagine what it would be like to be completely cut off from his family. At the very least William could take comfort in the fact that his father, the man he respected most in all the world, was still here with him. But when it came down to it, his father was not really as with him as William would have liked. Not since Jonathan Stuart-Camen had been put in command of the day guard, a position surpassed in authority only by Captain Jefford, Governor Chamberlain and, to hear some people tell it, Don Ferdinan. William was both happy and proud over his father's appointment; it was quite an honor. But it also meant that William had seen very little of his father since the duty roster for the guards had been rearranged, when McRofaly's suggestions had been implemented. The only real time father and son saw each other these days was at the breakfast table – which was really the dinner table to William – when Jonathan was just beginning his day and William was just ending his. And even then, during that little precious time that they got to spend together, an odd emotional distance had set in between father and son that disturbed William deeply. Worse was the certainty that the distance had arisen through no fault of Jonathan's. Every morning at breakfast he would ask William how his shift had gone, talk at length about whatever subject came up, and make sure William had a good meal to finish up his day with – a task not taken lightly by a man who had never had to cook for himself. Jonathan Stuart-Camen was as attentive and loving a father as he had ever been. It was William who had changed.

There had been a time, not very long ago at all, when William had not been able to make a real decision without first conferring with his father. Jonathan's opinion had been everything to William, his presence a beacon of wisdom and guidance in William's life. In some ways that was still true. William still respected his father more than anyone in the world. But now, instead of pouring his heart out to his father without Jonathan even having to ask, William was holding his thoughts and fears in even under the scrutiny of his father's most pointed questions. The silence as they sat at their dining room table together, alone in a house much too large for just a father and his son, unsettled both men visibly, but still William would not – perhaps could not – bring himself to discuss his fears, his uncertainties and the dark desire that had been growing in William's heart lately to kill as many goruks as he possibly could, to cause as much pain to the goruks as he possibly could. There was a barrier between William and his father that he had erected himself, a barrier as invisible as the air but as impenetrable as a wall of bricks and mortar. William could not explain why he was drawing into himself more and more these days except that the feelings that had arisen in him since the beginning of the war felt so deeply personal that he did not feel comfortable discussing them with anyone, not even his father. A part of William supposed that it was just a natural part of growing up, to become a more private person, but another part of him believed that if this brooding, secretive person he had become was a natural result of entering manhood, he was not entirely certain he wanted anything to do with it.

William brushed the dust from his pants and straightened to look at Tad, focusing on the here and now, putting his wandering thoughts aside for later exploration. Tad stood raptly at attention, although William did not insist on his men doing so every time they addressed him. William often mused that Tad would make an excellent career soldier. "So, Tad, what can I do for you?" William asked.

"Well, sir, it's the new recruits. We're trying to give them a few tips on parrying, and we were hoping that you could give us a hand. None of us are quite as good at explaining it as you are."

William reddened a bit around the cheeks. He felt competent at giving lessons in swordsmanship, but he did not feel particularly gifted at it. He was often concerned that he was being either too vague or too belaboring. His men, however, seemed to enjoy his lessons quite a bit, and that made William feel quite proud of himself whenever he let himself dwell on it. "Sure thing, Tad," William said, starting back toward the northeast gate. "Glad to be of service."

When he arrived at the wounded gate, he found a group of about thirty new volunteers spread out more or less evenly, listening intently to whichever of William's men happened to be speaking at the moment. Everyone seemed to be wearing the same expression of slight frustration, the instructors because they just could not quite find the correct words to express their ideas, the students because they could not quite follow what their instructors were trying to tell them. As William approached, people began to turn their heads in his direction and whisper to one another with a certain level of excitement. It made William feel somewhat like a celebrity, a feeling which the young nobleman did not particularly mind but did not particularly care for, either. He assumed there was no harm in it, though, and it was sometimes good fun to play the war hero, especially when people were literally lining up to play the part of adoring admirer.

"Parrying lessons, eh?" William said to another of his men when he came within speaking distance. "Tad tells me you've been having some problems putting it into words."

"Yes, Lord William," the Sword said. "I just don't think we have the knack for instruction that you do, sir."

William just nodded politely to avoid having to take credit for something he did not feel particularly gifted in. He turned his attention to the new volunteers, who seemed extremely interested in hearing what he had to say to them. A few of them positively beamed when they saw him draw his broadsword from its sheath at his side.

"Well now, gentlemen," William said, speaking up so his voice would carry, "I suppose the first thing you need know about parrying is that it's more about stance than technique or specific maneuvers."

"See, George, that's what I was trying to tell you," William heard Tad whisper to another Sword. George made no reply, so William continued.

"The most important aspect of parrying is the defensive stance, which differs from the basic swordsman's stance in really only one key way. Whereas with the basic stance you lean your body weight slightly forward on your dominant foot, in the defensive stance you want to balance your weight equally on both feet."

"Why is that, Lord William?" one of the new volunteers spoke up, then hastily added, "If you don't mind me asking, sir."

"No, no, please, ask questions," William said. "It's the best way to learn. Now the reason for the difference in balance is because when you're on the offensive, you're constantly pressing forward toward your opponent, trying to push him back and off guard. But when you're concentrating on defense, you need to be able to move in whatever direction necessary to get out of the way of your opponent's attack. The best way to manage that is to have your body weight balanced in a neutral state, evenly on both feet." William was met by a good number of understanding nods.

"Now pay close attention here, because this is an important point," William added, and some of the men and women he was addressing actually stood tiptoe and craned their necks to better hear. "A lot of people make the mistake of shifting their weight back onto their off foot when they go on the defensive. This is a good way to get yourself killed. The assumption is that when parrying, you will be backing away from your opponent. Sometimes that's true, but just as often you'll need to duck left or right, and sometimes even forward, to evade an opponent's attack. So remember, keep your weight equally balanced on both feet.

"That brings us to how to use your sword while parrying. The thing to remember here is—"

"Lord William, message for you from Don Ferdinan, sir."

William turned to see a town crier hurrying toward him. A wave of murmurs spread through the crowd of volunteers. Everyone knew that William Stuart-Camen was a member of the war council, and when he received messages from Don Ferdinan it usually meant something exciting was about to happen, or already had. William approached the messenger, coming close enough that he could speak without being overheard by the crowd. "What's the message, Alaister?" William asked under his breath. William was on a first name basis with all the messengers in Tamendad these days.

"Come to the church, quickly, sir," the messenger said. "Something about Ian Morlocke, but I'm not certain what. Whatever it is, it's urgent."

William nodded, and said, "I'm on my way." Alaister returned the nod and hurried back the way he came. William quickly returned to the new volunteers. "I have to go," he told them. "Official war council business. But I have all the faith in the world that my men will be able to instruct you on the finer points of defensive swordsmanship. Always keep in mind that while parrying, you should use your sword as a barrier between you and your opponent. The safest you can ever be in a sword fight is when your opponent is out of range to strike you." William was met once more with a host of nods and a number of appreciative looks. The young nobleman turned to go, but hesitated before he had taken two steps and turned back toward the volunteers once more. "Oh, and one more thing," he added, recalling the sight of his own broadsword sailing through the night air. "Above all else, always keep a firm grip on your sword."

From the feel of Don Ferdinan's message, William expected to find the church abuzz with activity. When he arrived, though, it seemed downright docile. Very few people were around, since just about everyone who was not on duty was asleep. William hurried inside, and was met just inside the doors by Master Postulant Dunleavy.

"Ah, William, you are expected," the Master Postulant said. "You will find the others in the room Colvin was attended to the other day." William nodded his thanks and hurried down the corridor leading to the room. The church was eerily silent, not so much as a devotional hymn from a stray priest to break the silence. The only sounds were the occasional hiss and sputter of prayer candles struggling to remain lit against the numerous drafts in the old church and the echoes of his own footfalls against the stone walls. For all the silence that pervaded the air, the church might as well have been a tomb.

William hastened down the corridor, passing several private rooms on his way. All the doors were drawn shut, but as he neared his destination a door just in front of him opened and Patrum Albermarle stepped into the hallway. William nearly collided with the Master Healer, who gave an uncharacteristic yelp over the near miss. William began apologizing profusely right away, but he fell silent as he caught a sidelong glance into the room from which Patrum Albermarle had just emerged. It was the briefest of glances, as Patrum Albermarle quickly drew the door shut behind him, but it was long enough for William to get a look at the man sitting inside, sporting a good number of fresh stitches. It looked like one of Ian Morlocke's men.

"Was that–?"

"Best hurry along, William," Patrum Albermarle interrupted, a telling look in his eyes. "You're expected."

William nodded and said no more, continuing down the corridor. When he entered the room he found what he had feared. In the middle of the room sat Ian Morlocke, being tended by a healer. He had his shirt off, and the broken shaft of an arrow was protruding from his left shoulder. He had been nicked and scraped in several other places, and sported a particularly nasty gash down the side of his right calf. Governor Chamberlain, Captain Jefford and Colvin were sitting around Morlocke. Don Ferdinan was standing. They all looked grim. Everyone in the room except the healer looked up at William when he entered.

"William, es good to see you again," Ferdinan said, but there was no pleasantness to his voice. Colvin waved. The Governor and Captain

Jefford, who had been whispering to one another, simply nodded.

"What happened?" William asked.

"We are waiting to find that out ourselves," Ferdinan replied. "I thought it would be best to wait until we were all here before we began, so Ian Morlocke would not have to esplain himself more than once. Besides, I thought it would do him well to see a healer before we began drilling him with questions."

William nodded and quietly took a chair next to Colvin. Governor Chamberlain continued speaking in hushed tones with Captain Jefford. Ferdinan stood with his hands tucked behind his back, occasionally pacing back and forth but usually just standing still and looking thoughtful. The healer continued to work on Ian Morlocke, and the only noise the master scout made was a sharp intake of breath when the healer removed the arrow from his shoulder. Morlocke avoided eye contact and did not speak except when the healer asked him a question. No one spoke to Morlocke, either. The tension was thick in the air. After a little while, the healer packed his bandages and salves back into his bag and let himself out without a word or a backwards glance.

Not five minutes later, the door opened and McRofaly walked briskly inside. "I don't know what the point of going back to bed is when you're just going to call for me again an hour later," he muttered testily, mostly to himself. Colvin sort of chuckled. No one else made any response at all. McRofaly glanced quickly around the room. When his eyes took in the sight of Ian Morlocke, wounded and battered, McRofaly's face went pale. "You were spotted?" he asked, almost demanded.

"Sí," Ferdinan interrupted before Morlocke had an opportunity to respond, "we are all here now, so we best be underway with our business. Ian, could you please tell us what happened?"

Morlocke slumped his shoulders, looking as though he bore a great weight upon them. With great difficulty he managed to glance around the room, meeting everyone's gaze, before he spoke. There was sadness in those eyes, a deep, terrible sadness, but there was something else as well. There was shame.

"I take the blame," Morlocke began. "I should have known they would have found our outpost. They're damn good scouts, goruks. Just because we hadn't seen any close to us, I assumed they hadn't discovered our camp. It's my fault."

"What es your fault, Ian?" Ferdinan said delicately. "What happened?"

"It was a setup. A damn brilliant one. The goruks marched a few of their soldiers out of the cave, looking like they were heading for here. I dispatched a rider immediately, then circled back to follow after the goruks. By the time I realized they were breaking for our encampment it was almost too late. I had to break cover to reach camp before they did; that's how I earned the arrow. We barely made it out in time. Still, we lost a man. Two, if you count the rider I sent out. He was ambushed. I'm still not sure how they snuck the goruks past us to set up the ambush. We never saw any come out of the cave before they marched their soldiers out." Ian looked like he was torn between beating himself or weeping. It was obviously killing him inside.

"We think there might be another cave somewhere else," William said. "Not big enough to move a lot of soldiers, but good for sneaking a few goruks out undetected. Like to set up a small ambush." William felt a little awkward talking about the purported second cave. It was technically secret war council information, but William could not stand to see Ian tormenting himself for something that was most likely not his fault. Apparently everyone else felt similarly, because no one objected to William sharing this knowledge.

"That's probably how they got past you to set up the ambush for me and McRofaly," Colvin added. "It's not your fault, Ian."

Morlocke shook his head. "It doesn't matter how they were getting out. We should have noticed the activity. I should have noticed it."

"No one es blaming you," Ferdinan said. "Es regrettable that this has happened, but there es no need to place blame. You thought your outpost was safely secluded from goruk eyes. If something seems to be working, you do not stray from it. Es human nature." If Ferdinan's words did anything to comfort Ian, though, it did not show on the scout's face.

"So we have lost our biggest tactical advantage against the goruks," Governor Chamberlain said. "The goruks are going to have a stranglehold on that cave after this. Intelligence is going to be hard to come by from this point forward."

"I'll bring you regular scouting reports," Morlocke said with steely determination. "You can count on me."

"I know I can," Governor Chamberlain said with a small, troubled smile. "You're invaluable to this war effort, Master Morlocke. You are without question the best scout we have. So you can understand that we don't want to take unnecessary risks with you. You'll be back on scouting duty as soon as you're ready to ride, but I don't want you or any of your men nearing within five miles of the cave. Best to keep a safe distance and stay out of harm's way."

"But Governor, that will seriously shorten our response time!" Morlocke protested. "I know I can safely get within a mile or two of the cave, and a couple of my men are capable of the same. We can't afford–"

"What we cannot afford," interrupted Ferdinan, "es to lose any more scouts. Information es our most precious commodity in this war, and you and your men are our esclusive scurce of it. I agree with the Governor in this matter."

Ian Morlocke looked at Don Ferdinan, then to Governor Chamberlain, and finally nodded reluctantly. "Yes, sir, five miles."

McRofaly, who had been deathly silent up until now, cleared his throat. "Ian, I have a question about the two men you lost tonight," he said.

"Yes, sir?" Morlocke replied.

"Did you see them die?"

No one spoke right away. Ian looked as though he had just swallowed something that had turned his stomach. William and Colvin exchanged a confused glance. Ferdinan arched an eyebrow. Governor Chamberlain straightened in his chair. Captain Jefford looked as though he was about to say something, but then thought better of it.

"What?" Ian asked at last, his voice a bit shaky.

"The two men you lost, Ian. Did you personally witness their deaths?"

Ian looked like he was about to be sick.

Colvin straightened, taking pity on the scout. "McRofaly, c'mon, lay off..." But McRofaly silenced him with a raised hand, not even looking in the red-haired young man's direction.

"This is a very important point," McRofaly continued calmly. "Either you saw them die, or you didn't. Which is it?"

William and Colvin were looking at McRofaly with something bordering on disgust. McRofaly, however, was staring intently at Morlocke, as were Ferdinan, Governor Chamberlain and Captain Jefford.

Ian took a deep breath and cast a long glance at the floor before answering. Timidly, he met McRofaly's gaze and began to speak, his voice quavering. "Franklin, the rider I sent out," he said, then hesitated, shuddering. After another deep breath he continued, saying, "I know Franklin's dead. We found him...what was left of him...during our escape. God, what they did to him..."

McRofaly nodded. "And the other?" he said. There was a factual, distanced quality to his voice, a lack of respect for the dead that made Colvin clench his fists and William fume. Ferdinan obviously did not think much of McRofaly's method of questioning, either, but the Conquian said nothing; he simply placed a reassuring hand on Ian shoulder.

"The other one we lost...Rodney...the goruks got him while we were making a break for it. They took his horse down with arrows. He tried to run for it. I wanted to circle back and pick him up but...there was no time. They were already on him. They swarmed him like...like vultures.

It was horrible. He was only eighteen…"

"Did you see him die?" McRofaly repeated.

"No!" Morlocke said forcefully, almost yelling. "No, I didn't see him die! I didn't want to hang around to watch that! And I still had four men I had to see to safety!"

"So you are not completely certain what fate befell young Rodney?" McRofaly asked, and finally there was at least a hint of compassion in his voice.

"The goruks had him," Ian insisted. "There was no way for him to escape…"

"But you did not actually witness his death."

After a long, agonizing hesitation, Ian whispered, through clenched teeth, "No."

"Let's hope he's dead."

The next moment the room was in an uproar, Colvin and William on their feet screaming at McRofaly, McRofaly on his feet screaming back, Ian Morlocke with his head buried in his hands, sobbing. Ferdinan and Captain Jefford quickly stepped between McRofaly and Colvin and William, helping them back to their seats.

"That's a damn cold thing to say, man," Colvin yelled at McRofaly from his chair. "Damn cold."

"Colvin, restrain yourself." Colvin looked at Ferdinan, and found the Conquian's face as stern as he had ever seen it. Colvin fell silent, partly out of respect for Ferdinan and partly out of being intimidated. "I believe I know what McRofaly es trying to say, though his method leaves something to be desired." Ferdinan raised his voice somewhat while saying the last bit, so that McRofaly was sure to hear it.

"What's he trying to say, Ferdinan?" William demanded, still glaring at McRofaly.

"What I'm trying to say, Lord Stuart-Camen," McRofaly said icily, "is that we had better hope he's dead for the sake of the war effort."

Aside from the sound of Ian Morlocke weeping, the room fell silent.

"If Rodney is dead," McRofaly continued, "then we lost a fine scout. If he is alive, however, we might have lost a damn sight more than that. Outside of the war council, Morlocke's scouts know more about what's going on with the war than anyone else. Dead men can't tell their secrets."

"He wouldn't…" William began, but there was a marked lack of certainty in his voice.

"You heard Don Ferdinan tell, not two hours ago, what the goruks did to the rider from Shield Division. If they're capable of that level of brutality, don't you think they're capable of torturing whatever information they want out of a man?"

"Indeed I think," said Governor Chamberlain, "that we should pray Rodney died a quick death tonight. That would be the best fate for him as well as for us. But we cannot be sure of his fate either way, and that leaves us in a most unenviable position. In its own way, uncertainty can be as troublesome as defeat."

Ferdinan nodded. "We must press ahead with the ambush, Geoffery, while we still have what little advantage remains to us. The scouts knew nothing of those plans."

"I agree," the Governor said. "Master McRofaly, I want everything in place by sundown tomorrow. We will make our move the day after."

"That doesn't leave much room for error," Captain Jefford said.

"What else is new?" said Colvin.

Captain Jefford nodded. "Indeed."

"I want to volunteer for the ambush," William said suddenly, and everyone looked at him. "I want my fair shot at these bastards," he added firmly.

"Yeah, I'm in too," said Colvin. "And before anyone even says anything, it's not open to question. I helped find the spot, so I get to be there. No point debating this one with me."

Ferdinan chuckled very softly, and Colvin thought he heard the Conquian say, "Passion es the most important virtue," under his breath.

"Very well," Governor Chamberlain said, "consider yourselves the first two men assigned to the task."

"Mark me down as the third, Geoffery," Ferdinan said. Governor Chamberlain nodded somberly.

"Well, let me know how it goes, gentlemen," said McRofaly, heading for the door. "I'm going back to bed."

CHAPTER TWENTY-SEVEN

INTO THE BREACH

It had thus far been a most eventful night, but the rest of it passed without incident. Early the next morning a funeral was held for young Edgar of Shield Division, and his body was buried in Tamendad's graveyard. Memorial services were also held for Franklin and Rodney, though neither of their bodies were present to be interred. The exact nature of the scouts' deaths was not made public knowledge; Governor Chamberlain and Don Ferdinan both still believed it unwise to divulge information about the cave, especially now that the war was escalating. Still, it was easy enough to explain the deaths of two scouts without mentioning the cave and without deliberately misleading anyone. The scouts died in the line of duty, just like Edgar. That was the official word on the matter, and no one in the know on the subject did anything to dissuade the assumption that spread throughout Tamendad that Franklin and Rodney had been killed while on routine scouting missions.

The town square was packed for the services; all of the night watch attended, and more than a few members of the day guard attempted to attend as well before Captain Jefford personally got on them about trying to skirt their duties. Ian Morlocke attended the service, and he appeared tragically statuesque throughout. The service was overseen by the Master Postulant, who delivered a moving eulogy of the three young men. Don Ferdinan also spoke, and those who had managed to keep their eyes dry during the eulogy found them wet once the Conquian had finished speaking. Gangis, who was the only Shield left in Tamendad, and thus the only Shield able to attend the funeral, mourned the death of his brother at arms with a dirge on the pipe flute. Then, after the Master Postulant led all those in attendance in the Prayer for the Fallen in Battle, came the burials: a simple wooden casket for Edgar, two long-stemmed white roses for Franklin and Rodney. When it was all over, Ian Morlocke looked to be on the verge of throwing up. No one had an opportunity to console him, though, as he immediately left the square, mounted

Midnight, and rode off into the countryside to resume his scouting duties.

McRofaly was the lone member of the war council remaining in Tamendad who did not attend the funeral. He left the city just after sunrise, taking with him twenty strong soldiers, two scouts, and a team of five stout workhorses. Their departure was met with great excitement. It was not common knowledge exactly what their mission entailed – details of the ambush were classified – but there was no mistaking that whatever McRofaly was up to, it was quite likely to score a major blow against the goruks. McRofaly's ideas were thought of quite highly, since so far they had all seemed to work quite well.

The morning hours drifted lazily by. It was bright and warm, to contrast the previous day's dreariness. There was no denying that autumn was coming quickly along and that the weather would soon be turning cold, but for the moment, at least, summer seemed to be sticking around for a little while longer. Lunch came and went, leaving the day guard full and contented; Gertrude was rapidly becoming the most popular woman in Tamendad. Jonathan Stuart-Camen, commander of the day guard, visited each of the four gates after lunch, to make sure Gertrude's fine cooking had not taken the lookouts off their edge. As usual, he found everything to be in order.

By all appearances, it was going to be a fine, lazy sort of day, the kind that creeps past at a snail's pace but that seems, upon reflection, to have blazed by in a hurry of uneventfulness. That was the general feeling that hung in the air, at least, until early in the afternoon, when Ian Morlocke was spotted riding bent for leather back toward Tamendad, screaming at the top of his lungs as he came that the goruks were coming.

Don Ferdinan was dreaming, and it was a good dream. He was back in Losillas, having left the war-torn Tamendad long behind him. His city was as breathtakingly beautiful as he remembered it, with the sun reflecting brightly off the streets and limestone buildings. The scent of lavender and honeysuckle hung thick in the autumn air, just enough to mask the underlying scent of grapevines that the wind blew in from the many vineyards that covered the surrounding countryside. Young, beautiful *velabaílaras* danced in the streets to music from the many mandolin players and flutists and guitarists who lined the ways, their instrument cases lying open on the street before them so that passers-by who enjoyed their performance might drop in a coin or two. Ferdinan always made it a point to give liberally to these musicians. He loved his city best when it was set to music.

Don Ferdinan was standing before the Palace in the heart of the city, the bright autumn sunlight reflecting brightly off its edifice, the sweet and savory mixture of botanical scents wafting out from its many gardens. The fountain outside the main entrance was bubbling wine, not water. Ferdinan felt like dancing, he was so happy to be back in Losillas. In fact, he *was* dancing, right there in front of the Palace, holding a goblet filled to overflowing from the fountain. He was laughing so hard that tears streamed down his cheeks. He was laughing because the music he was dancing to was all wrong, completely inappropriate for the *arasta noche.* How was one supposed to dance such a sensual, passionate dance to the sound of bagpipes? But Gregor was having such a wonderful time playing the pipes, sitting on the wall of the Palace with another overflowing goblet of wine by his side, that Ferdinan just could not bring himself to ask for a change of tune. And Elysia did not seem to mind dancing to such unusual music, either. She was laughing as well between sips of wine, as beautiful as ever, the dry heat of Conquia bringing a fine sheen of sweat to her supple skin. Standing off to themselves a bit, Colvin and William were laughing as well and clapping boisterously to keep the time of Gregor's performance. They both wore broad smiles, and both were dressed in the latest Conquian fashion. Ferdinan was glad to see Colvin wearing such nice clothes. He deserved nice things. He had had such a hard life.

He was home. He was home and his foreign friends were all here with him. The happiness washed over him like a wave, and it was almost too great to bear, almost enough to steal his breath away. He wanted to stay here forever, just he and his friends, together, dancing and laughing. Forever. But he knew that was not possible. He knew it was a dream, and he knew it would be ending soon, because someone was banging roughly on the door.

Ferdinan came reluctantly back to consciousness, taking a moment longer than was really necessary to rise from his bed, basking in the warm afterglow of such a particularly fine dream. The muddled haze of sleep began to recede from the corners of his mind, and an urgency set in in its place. A quick, cursory glance revealed that his bedroom was still brightly lit by the afternoon sunlight streaming through the windows, and this told Ferdinan that whoever it was banging away like mad on his chamber door carried with him a most urgent message. Otherwise no sane person would ever dream of rousing Don Julio Franco Francisco Ferdinan prematurely from his sleep.

Ferdinan jumped hurriedly from his bed, rubbed his eyes quickly, pulled his robe around him to cover his nakedness and opened the door. Standing just the other side of it was Ian Morlocke, eyes wide, sweaty, breathing hard.

"Goruks," the master scout said breathlessly.

"How many?" Ferdinan asked.

"Two, maybe three hundred."

"So the storm es finally coming," Ferdinan said, through he sounded more as though he was talking to himself than to Ian.

"What was that, sir?" Morlocke asked.

"Nothing," Ferdinan said. "Es nothing. Have you woken Geoffery?"

"No, I came to you first, Don Ferdinan." Morlocke looked a little sheepish upon saying this, but there was an unspoken understanding shared between himself and the Conquian. Don Ferdinan just seemed more comfortable and natural in heading up a war than Geoffery Chamberlain ever did.

Ferdinan nodded. "How long now?" he asked quickly.

"An hour, maybe an hour and a half."

Ferdinan cursed bitterly, furrowing his brow. Ian flinched a little at the sight of it, how angry Ferdinan had become in the turn of a moment. "Es going to be cutting it very close," Ferdinan said. "We have to warn McRofaly."

"I already have, sir," Ian replied quickly. "On my ride back. They're lying low, taking cover in the forest. The goruks should march right past them without noticing, as long as they can keep the horses quiet."

"Good man!" Ferdinan said, clapping Ian on the shoulder. "Now, to the matter at hand."

"Should I call the war council?"

Ferdinan shook his head. "Es no time. Rouse everyone. I mean *everyone*. Get the town criers and the day guard to assist you. I want every standing soldier up and at arms. Assemble in the town square. I will wake the Governor and the Captain of the Guard, leave that to me. Go now. Quickly."

Ian nodded and sped off down the hallway. Ferdinan shut the door and dressed quickly, taking far less than the usual amount of time he allowed himself to ensure the quality of his appearance. When he was dressed he strapped his sword belt around his waist, and before exiting the room cast one long, wistful look back toward his unmade bed. The dreamworld Losillas was now as far away as the real thing, and he was once again right in the middle of this accursed war. *Men who follow the path of decusé do not question where it leads them, Julio*, he told himself resolutely, drawing himself up to full measure. He was here, now, and the war was here with him. It was his duty to do as honor demanded of him. He could do nothing less and still be able to call himself a man. He left his bed and his dreams behind him, and hurried to awaken the Governor.

❖   ❖   ❖

A quick quarter of an hour later Don Ferdinan was making his way toward the town square alongside Governor Chamberlain and Captain Jefford. None of them looked more than three-quarters awake at most. All three bore the appearance of men hastily dressed and moderately frazzled. As they neared the town square, they heard the ever-increasing sounds of men and women gathering there, nervously discussing the situation. Morlocke had certainly wasted no time. The square already looked to be half full, with more soldiers arriving by the moment. The anxiety was palpable.

"You're certain about this, Don Ferdinan?" Captain Jefford asked quietly. "They're coming now?"

"I have no reason to doubt Morlocke's word, Captain," Ferdinan replied.

"No, no, nor do I," Jefford quickly added. "It's just…McRofaly told us that they despised sunlight."

"Indeed he did, Captain," said Ferdinan. "But if you will also remember, Colvin encountered a goruk out in the countryside first thing in the morning. Obviously es not like the goruks are incapable of coming out during the day. They are flesh and blood. Es not like we are talking children's stories, like vampires and such. Sunlight does not kill them."

"It makes sense," Governor Chamberlain said groggily, still having some obvious difficulties waking up fully. "They have had numerous opportunities to see what our defenses are like at night. They even know when we change the guard. They surely must realize our day guard is little more than a skeleton crew. If I were them, that knowledge would certainly tempt me to come out during the day."

Ferdinan nodded his agreement, but said nothing. The three men had arrived in the town square, and a hush immediately spread over the ever-enlarging crowd. Don Ferdinan, Governor Chamberlain and Captain Jefford ascended the steps of the church and turned to face the crowd. They were not surprised to see William and Colvin hurrying up the steps toward them.

"Is it true?" William asked quietly once he was in their presence. The look on Colvin's face told that he had been about to ask the same thing. Don Ferdinan nodded somberly.

"During the daylight?" William asked incredulously.

"Daylight didn't really seem to bother Lorthok that much," said Colvin. "They might not care for it, but from what I could tell, it's really not much of a hindrance to them."

William sighed, looking troubled. "So now what?"

"Now we fight," Ferdinan said, as though he thought that much was obvious. "Go back to your men, try to reassure them. We will make the

435

announcement soon." William and Colvin nodded and turned to go, but before they had descended more than a couple of steps, Ferdinan called Colvin back. The red-haired young man turned to face Ferdinan. Ferdinan pointed questioningly at Colvin's hip, where hung his sabre.

"What about your gloves?" Ferdinan asked.

Colvin shrugged. "I want to try out some of those new moves you've been showing me in practice. I think I'm getting good enough to use them."

Ferdinan said nothing, just nodded. Colvin returned to his men. After a few more minutes the town square appeared sufficiently full, and Governor Chamberlain began to address the soldiers. He did not mince words and he did not sugarcoat it, partially because there was little time and partially because he was not yet quite fully awake. The weary faces of the soldiers stared back at him with shock and surprise. A good number of people protested that it was still daylight, as if reminding the goruks of this fact would make them turn around and go back where they came from so the Tamendaders could get a few more hours of sleep before having to defend the town. The ruckus died down quickly, much to the Governor's chagrin, when Don Ferdinan raised a hand to still the crowd.

"The goruks know most of you are on duty during the night. Es why they have chosen to attack now, during the day, in the hopes of catching you at a weak moment, still sleepy and disoriented. *But*," Ferdinan said, pausing for emphasis, "do not fail to take into account that goruks are also nocturnal creatures. They as well will be fighting when they should be sleeping. They have miscalculated. The time of their attack will give them no advantage."

Murmurs ran through the crowd, intermingled with occasional yawns.

"If anything," Ferdinan continued, his dander rising, "their mistake will give us the advantage, because we are best suited to fighting in the daylight. Make no mistake, this will be difficult. I espect they will attack with a ferocity we have not seen from them since the night they almost took the city, the night Angus MacDugal died."

A noticeable change swept over the crowd at the mention of Angus's name. Angus MacDugal had become something of a martyr to the members of the Pride, especially Fist Division, and members of the constabulary thought most highly of the fallen Highlander as well. Invoking his name as Ferdinan had was akin to kindling a fire in their souls. It was, of course, exactly the effect Ferdinan had intended.

"What are our orders?" a voice rang out loud and clear from the heart of the crowd, and Ferdinan was relatively certain it belonged to William Stuart-Camen. Ferdinan glanced quickly at Governor Chamberlain and

Captain Jefford. Both men met his gaze in equal measure, their faces hard and stern. Governor Chamberlain nodded. The Captain drew himself up to attention, his hands clasped behind his back. Ferdinan returned his attention to the soldiers waiting anxiously before him.

"You will be led into battle by the Captain of the Guard and myself."

Stunned silence followed. It was no great surprise that Ferdinan would be leading them. The Conquian had been right in the thick of things from the very beginning, placing himself in harm's way to defend Tamendad more often than many of the soldiers who lived there. Captain Jefford leading men into battle, however, was a rare occurrence indeed. Legend had it that Amon Jefford had been quite the swordsman in his day, but now as Captain of the Guard his duties were primarily bureaucratic and organizational. His coming out of retirement, so to speak, was obviously a move meant to boost morale, but the certainty of this fact did not preclude it from actually working. It seemed to bolster the constables most, understandably, but everyone seemed to gain some measure of courage from the fact that probably the two most accomplished swordsmen Tamendad had seen in a generation were going to be leading them against the goruks in a little less than an hour.

Captain Jefford walked briskly down the steps of the church, and the throng of makeshift soldiers parted to accept him into their midst. He crossed his arms over his chest and surveyed the standing forces of Tamendad, and suddenly he felt the old flame of a soldier's spirit rekindled within him. "I am not a man for speeches," he said. "I leave that to our Lord Governor and our Conquian friend. I am a man for action."

Amon Jefford drew his sword. It felt so very right in his hand.

"Those bastards are coming. I say let them come, and we'll give them what for."

Half an hour later, every armed man and woman Tamendad had to offer was standing in formation with their backs to the closed southwest gate, all except the archers who had been positioned along the town wall. They stood, for the first time in a long while, separated into constabulary and militiamen. Captain Jefford was in charge of the constables, and Don Ferdinan had temporarily assumed command of the Pride of Tamendad. No one in the Pride complained about this, though a good number of Fists showed Colvin the same measure of deference as they showed Don Ferdinan, and a few Swords expressed similar sentiments toward William. They stood waiting with weapons drawn and arrows nocked, nervously counting the seconds that passed without sight or sound of approaching goruks. Ian Morlocke had ridden back out into the countryside to keep an eye out for the goruks, saying he would return when they neared within a mile. There was nothing left to do except wait, and try to wake up a little more before plunging headlong into battle. The tension was broken only by the occasional yawn of the bleary-eyed soldiers still trying to shake off sleep.

"Do you think this is a good idea?" Colvin whispered to William while they both stood waiting. They had positioned themselves next to each other when the Pride fell into formation, to have someone to talk to while they waited as well as to know that they would be fighting alongside someone they could count on if things took a turn for the worse. "Leaving the northeast gate unguarded, I mean," Colvin added.

William shrugged. "The gate's barricaded more heavily than usual, and the bonfires are lit. And really, if the goruks get through all of us to reach the gate, it's kind of a moot point, isn't it?"

"Good point," said Colvin, looking around at all the soldiers standing ready to engage the enemy. What William said was true; if the goruks reached the northeast gate, the war would most likely be over anyway. "Still, throwing everything we've got against the goruks like this? Seems a little...I don't know...desperate, don't you think?"

William shook his head subtly, and replied quietly so as not to be overheard. "I don't think it's got anything to do with desperation. It's about meeting force with force. That's been Ferdinan's plan from the start, I think. This war's starting to heat up, and we have to show the goruks we're not going to back down from the fight. We're drawing a line in the sand."

Colvin laughed softly to himself. "How the twist did I get into this mess?"

"Wrong place at the right time, my friend," William replied with a rueful grin.

Colvin nodded. "Wouldn't miss it for the world," he said. "I just hope McRofaly didn't get discovered. I kinda lashed out at him last night when he wouldn't lay off of Ian. I'd hate for the last words I said to him to be out of anger."

"McRofaly's a smart man. Almost too smart, if you ask me. If anyone could avoid getting caught–"

Before William could finish his sentence, Ian Morlocke came galloping over the hill and down toward Tamendad, waving frantically as he came. When he was close enough to be heard, he shouted, "The goruks are within a mile! Godspeed! Tamendad stands!" Then, as there was no time to open the gate to allow him to enter, he sped off down the beach to distance himself from danger. Murmurs spread throughout the crowd and then fell silent. Soldiers tightened grips on weapons or readjusted armor, exchanging glances with their fellows. There was fear, undeniably, but atop that fear there existed the stronger emotion of anger. Men and women prepared, once again, to defend their homes.

Then, in the distance, they could be heard coming, the unmistakable snarling, whooping screams of the goruks carried on the wind. It was quiet at first, little more than an echo – a whisper – but it grew, and grew, until the sound was right on top of them.

"I guess this is it," Colvin said without looking at William.

William simply nodded.

"Archers! Ready!" boomed the voice of Captain Jefford, and all the archers atop the wall drew their bowstrings and waited.

The goruks cleared the hill. Morlocke's estimate looked to be accurate; the goruk army pouring down the hillside looked just a bit smaller than the one that had attacked the night the northeast gate had been destroyed. The goruks came in a steady stream, scimitars brandished high, charging straight toward the soldiers standing in formation outside the southwest gate. There was no way to be certain, since the goruks were still much too far away to be able to discern the expressions on their ugly, tusked faces, but Colvin swore they looked a bit surprised to find all the Tamendaders standing at arms, waiting for them. That thought pleased Colvin greatly.

The archers atop the wall loosed their first volley of arrows at Captain Jefford's signal, when the goruks were about halfway down the hill. A few scattered green forms dropped to the ground under the barrage and did not move again, but the overall result was like taking a bucketful of water out of a small lake.

The goruks came streaming down the hill toward Tamendad without any semblance of organization, except that the entire swarm seemed to center around a single goruk who stood a good deal taller and broader than the rest. In truth, it was the largest goruk any of the Tamendaders had ever seen. While all the goruks were screaming and howling, this one seemed to be doing so at the surrounding goruks rather than the soldiers assembled outside Tamendad's southwest gate. It was clear that this was the leader of this raid, but there was something more to it. While the archers' volley had been in the air, the goruks nearest this one had fallen over themselves to shield their commander from the arrows with their own bodies. The impression was that this was more than just the goruks' commander, this was their leader.

"That's Kor," William said breathlessly. "That has to be Kor."

Captain Jefford signaled for another volley of arrows as the goruks reached the base of the hill, where the land flattened out as it approached the shore. A few more goruks stumbled and fell, but not enough to make a serious dent in their forces. There was no time for a third volley. The goruks were quickly closing the gap. Captain Jefford and Don Ferdinan gave the command to advance, and suddenly the air was filled with a cacophony of screams that drowned out even the loudest goruk as every man and woman with a weapon bellowed a war cry at the top of their lungs and broke into a run. Captain Jefford was in the lead, the constables surrounding him closely, longswords high and ready to strike. Behind them, Ferdinan led the charge of militiamen as the Pride swarmed forward.

The lines met with the piercing ring of steel on steel, and screams of pain began to intermingle with the war cries that rose from both sides. Goruks and humans both began to stumble and fall, clutching bleeding wounds. The forces continued to pour into one another as those who brought up the rear joined the fray. The battle spread out as the front line grew. Sword rang against sword. Weapons on both sides sliced flesh and broke bone. Blood splattered the grass. The specter of war descended once again like a shadow over Tamendad. It had all become terrifyingly familiar.

It was difficult to tell what was going on elsewhere on the battlefield when there were bloodthirsty goruks to deal with in the immediate vicinity, but from the sound of things Captain Jefford was obviously making quite a stir and having none too many issues working out whatever rust had accumulated during his more peaceful days. The constables, inspired by their commander's efforts, fought like lions, sticking close to Captain Jefford, pressing right into the heart of the goruk forces. There was no mistaking that the goruks were falling back from the constables, not wanting to make a stand against them. Refusing to be outdone by their counterparts in uniform, the Pride circled around the constables, Fist Division going one way and Sword Division the other to keep the goruks from trying to skirt past Captain Jefford and his men. Ferdinan helped William lead Sword Division in the maneuver, leaving Colvin to command Fist Division. Colvin had not anticipated how awkward it would feel leading Fist Division in battle while brandishing a sabre, but none of the Fists really seemed to be paying attention to what weapon he was using.

The next moment everything changed. The largest goruk drew the twin scimitars crisscrossed over his back and launched himself into the battle, moving with an alacrity that was rivaled only by Ferdinan. His swords were little more than blurs, and as he began to press forward toward the human soldiers the goruks around him erupted with frenzied howls of what in goruk circles might have passed for ecstasy. The goruks redoubled their efforts in the assault, and concentrated everything on the constables standing in their path. Where they had fallen back from the constables a moment before, now the goruks actually flung themselves into their midst. They jabbered like lunatics as they came. "*Thorak rakuth, Abuneth!*" they screamed as always, but now they sometimes added the chant of, "*Kor! Kor!*" Most soldiers were indifferent to what the goruks were screaming as they attacked, but the new chant seemed to light a fire under the members of the war council.

Kor broke through a line of constables with little difficulty and found himself face to face with Tamendad's Captain of the Guard. The two seasoned warriors eyed each other, Kor with his dual morchas, Captain Jefford with his longsword. Kor snarled. Surprisingly enough, Captain Jefford snarled back.

"Kor," Jefford spat, sneering. "I'm going to enjoy watching you die."

"Let us see how easy you bleed, paleskin," Kor growled.

Kor leapt, both morchas swinging in wild streaks of steely blue. Jefford was ready, his longsword an almost imperceptible blur of defensive maneuvers. Goruks and humans alike gave the combatants wide passage, not wanting to find themselves on the wrong end of an errant swipe of a sword.

Back and forth they fought as the battle raged all around them, neither Kor nor Jefford able to hold an advantage for any length of time. Sweat poured down their faces, stinging their eyes. Jefford fought with both hands firmly wrapped around the hilt of his longsword, swinging with every ounce of strength he could muster, hoping to knock one of Kor's swords free and level the playing field. Kor, however, maintained a firm hold on his morchas, spinning and slashing them with dizzying, disconcerting effect. He could sense Jefford was beginning to tire; the Captain's age was beginning to catch up to him. His defenses were slipping. Kor was sneaking attacks past him now – nothing major, just a few nicks and cuts on the arms and face, but it signaled that Jefford was beginning to falter. Then the opening came.

Kor grinned wickedly at Jefford. There was a glint of steel in the early evening sunlight, and Captain Jefford found his longsword trapped between Kor's morchas. Kor pulled Jefford forward by his sword, until their faces were mere inches apart. Captain Jefford grimaced. Kor's breath stank.

"Bow to me, paleskin," Kor taunted through a wide smile. "Save yourself."

"Not in this life," Jefford growled.

"So be it." Kor twisted both morchas quickly, and Jefford's longsword was pulled free. It landed only a couple of feet away, but it might as well have been a mile for all the good it could do to its owner. Jefford sighed, and he had the most unusual sensation of being deflated. His shoulders slumped. His legs went numb. Thoughts raced through his mind at lightning speed.

> *May the Four Faces of God smile upon you.*
> *May He hold you tight in His arms.*
> *May He lift you up and exalt your name.*
> *May you find peace forever,*
> *Now that your suffering is at an end.*

Amon Jefford, Tamendad's Captain of the Guard, gasped, and his eyes widened as he felt Kor's morcha slide up underneath the bottom of his breastplate, through his abdomen, and out the top of his back. An unnatural, sickly warmth spread throughout his body and little motes of light began to dance frenziedly in the corners of his vision. He tried to take another breath and found it choked him to do so. He could taste blood.

"How does it feel, paleskin?" Kor snarled, smiling. Jefford stared into the maw of his murderer. He had had a good, long life, with enough happiness to fill two lifetimes. His only regret about dying for Tamendad was that this ugly son of a bitch was going to be the last thing he saw in this world.

Kor twisted his morcha, and a pain unlike anything Amon Jefford would have thought possible wracked his body. "I asked how it felt," Kor growled. Jefford could not reply. He could take in no air. So to answer Kor's question, he summoned what little energy remained in him and spat in the goruk's ugly face.

Kor, no longer smiling, slid his morcha free of Jefford's body, and the Captain fell to the ground in a heap. There was a great eruption of noise as the goruks howled in victory and the constables screamed in terror. Kor glared down at the fallen Captain, who looked back at him with glazed eyes. Kor raised one of his morchas high.

"Now you die, paleskin."

Kor's sword sliced the air as it flew toward Captain Jefford's neck… and was stopped a foot shy of its target with the resounding *clang* of metal on metal. Kor stared in momentary surprise at the blade that had intercepted his own. It was as much like his own morcha as it was unlike it, curved similarly but with a significantly different taper to the blade. And it was beautiful, so beautiful that it put Kor's swords to shame. In fact, it was quite possibly the most beautiful thing Kor had ever seen, and from the moment he saw it he wanted it very much. Kor trailed his eyes along the blade, past the gilded handle, up the arm of the wielder to his face, and found himself staring eye to eye with Don Julio Franco Francisco Ferdinan.

"Your leader is dead," Kor snarled. "You are beaten."

"You just made a terrible mistake, Kor," Ferdinan whispered, his voice soft and ominous, "and now you pay."

Ferdinan sprang, throwing himself completely into his attack. Sabre connected with morcha again and again as Ferdinan struck with a graceful celerity that exceeded even Kor's. Kor railed against Ferdinan, his morchas swinging wildly in all directions. Some of these frenzied attacks found their way past Ferdinan's defenses, but the Conquian was adept enough with sabre and parrying dagger to ensure that he sustained no injury more grievous than a flesh wound. To Ferdinan's consternation, though, Kor was also capably fending off incoming attacks, suffering only superficial injuries when most men would have taken a sword through the heart or the eye.

"You fight well, dark one," Kor growled, his sweaty green face screwed up in fierce concentration.

"I wish I could say the same for you," Ferdinan replied, not relenting his assault. "Perhaps you goruks are just too stupid to learn the finer points of swordplay."

Kor's upper lip curled in anger. "Your words are going to get you into trouble," the goruk snarled.

"Es going to take a much larger threat than what you present to get me into trouble, you miserable waste of flesh."

Kor screamed, his eyes burning with rage, and launched himself at Ferdinan. This was, of course, exactly the effect Ferdinan was aiming for. He fell back into a defensive posture, pushing Kor's attacks aside – admittedly with no small degree of difficulty – and studied the goruk. There was a flaw in Kor's method of attack. Ferdinan had caught glimpses of it while they had fought, but Kor attacked with such intensity that Ferdinan had not been able to really focus on what it was he was seeing, or to devise a method to exploit it. Now, though, he was ready. His mind was focused, his senses honed. As Kor came on, flailing like a cornered animal, Ferdinan was paying meticulous attention to even the subtlest of his opponent's moves.

Until his attention was wrenched away by something else.

"Ferdinan! Help! Please!"

Under Kor's barrage, Ferdinan could not even steal a glance in the direction of the voice, but he did not have to. He already knew. It was Colvin.

Kor hesitated. The goruk glanced around quickly like he was waking up from a dream, or coming out of a trance. A subtle grin turned up the corners of his tusked mouth. He began to back slowly away. Ferdinan cursed. His opportunity was lost. But he had other, more pressing matters on his mind. Colvin was in trouble. Ferdinan had to help him, just as soon as Kor was far enough away for Ferdinan to safely turn his back on him. The goruk's withdrawal seemed to take an eternity, hours seeming to pass between each measured step. Ferdinan told himself that one more step would be far enough. Just one more...

But Kor stopped backing away. He raised his sword, pointing it menacingly at Ferdinan. "This was just a taste of what is to come, paleskin," Kor said evenly. "We will meet again."

"You can count on it," Ferdinan hissed. He could wait no longer. He spun on his heels and ran, searching frantically for Colvin. He found him almost immediately, surrounded by three goruks that looked to be toying with him before moving in for the kill. Ferdinan broke into a sprint, approaching the goruk closest to him from behind. Colvin did not see him coming. The red-haired young man's attention was focused completely on trying to keep his distance from three circling goruks at the same time.

Ferdinan reached the closest goruk still at full sprint. He leapt. The sole of his left boot connected with the goruk's sloped back, and Ferdinan pushed off to propel himself forward. His right foot came down on the crown of the goruk's head. Ferdinan used the goruk's cranium as a springboard, leaping through the air toward a very surprised Colvin. Ferdinan landed in a crouch beside Colvin, whose jaw dropped open slightly. The next moment Ferdinan was up, his sabre extended, his back against Colvin's. The goruks, more surprised by the recent turn of events than even Colvin, fled. The one Ferdinan had trampled was running with a bit of a stagger. As Ferdinan watched them go, he realized that they were not the only goruks on the run. Kor was leading all of his warriors in a withdrawal.

"Let them go!" Ferdinan yelled. "We must not leave Tamendad undefended!" The soldiers who had looked to be about to give chase obviously did not think too highly of this order, but they obeyed it all the same.

Ferdinan turned to Colvin and quickly looked him over. He did not look to be badly injured, nothing more than a few minor cuts. "Colvin, are you all right?" Ferdinan asked quickly.

Colvin was looking at Ferdinan like the Conquian had just walked on water. "Ferdinan," he stammered, "that...what you just...holy–"

"Are you all right?!?" Ferdinan screamed. "Quickly!"

444

Colvin blinked his wide eyes rapidly. "Yeah," he said. "Yeah, I'm okay."

"Thank God," said Ferdinan. "Help whoever needs helping. I must tend to Captain Jefford." Ferdinan left Colvin standing there looking dumbfounded, hurrying back to where Captain Jefford was laying. The Conquian slid to a knee beside the fallen Captain of the Guard, his hands quickly probing Amon's face, his throat, his chest, desperately searching for any sign of life. Blood was everywhere, and Ferdinan was quickly covered in it.

"Don Ferdinan!" yelled a young constable, rushing forward to help. "How bad is it? Should I get a healer?"

"Es not necessary," Ferdinan said quietly, bowing his head. "The Captain es dead."

It was like they had lost the war. At least that was how it felt to the constables, and the militiamen were not taking it much better. The loss of Captain Jefford was the most demoralizing thing they could have endured, except perhaps the loss of Governor Chamberlain or Don Ferdinan. As far as that went, though, the general feeling was that if either of those two men were lost, so was the war.

Captain Jefford received his last rites from the Master Postulant. His body was then carried back into Tamendad by a group of constables and laid on the steps of the church, where men and women immediately began to form a long line, waiting to pay their respects. Governor Chamberlain was already waiting at the church, and he was the first to kneel beside the body of the fallen Captain of the Guard. The Governor's face was etched with concern and despair as he whispered to his old friend, and several people later agreed that it was at that moment that Geoffery Chamberlain looked the weakest he ever looked during the entire war.

As soon as Governor Chamberlain rose from beside Jefford's body, the Governor and Don Ferdinan quickly disappeared into the church. No one was invited to accompany them. Outside, in the slowly failing autumn sunlight, Colvin and William lined up together to wait their turn to kneel before the Captain's body. William had also been skilled enough – or lucky enough – to have avoided serious injury.

"This is not good," William whispered to Colvin, taking great care not to be overheard. The young nobleman craned his neck and peered up along the line of soldiers waiting ahead of them. "Not good at all."

Colvin nodded grimly and sighed. He was trying very hard to be respectful, but his thoughts were still consumed by what he had seen

Ferdinan do. There was no doubt that Colvin was still alive because of Ferdinan coming to his rescue, in Ferdinan's inimitable style. Colvin was burning to tell William all about what Ferdinan had done, every mind-blowing, death-defying detail of it. But now was not the time.

"This is really going to hurt the war effort," William continued, now shifting his attention to the men and women standing in line behind them.

"Yeah," replied Colvin quietly, "he was an important part of the war council. We're gonna have our work cut out for us without him."

William gave Colvin a look that bordered on incredulity. "This goes a lot deeper than the war council," he said. "Captain Jefford's been Captain of the Guard since my father was my age. He's one of the most respected men in Tamendad, right up there with Patrum Albermarle and the Master Postulant and the Governor. This is going to hit a lot of people hard."

"Yeah," Colvin said. It was a lame reply, he knew, but he could not think of anything else to say. Not having grown up in Tamendad as William had, Colvin had not quite grasped the magnitude of Captain Jefford's passing. "Still…"

William waited a few moments for Colvin to continue his thought, and when it became clear this was not going to happen, he said, "Still what?"

"Well, don't get me wrong, I respect Captain Jefford to no end, but when it's all said and done, it's just one more soldier lost, isn't it? God, I know that sounds horrible, but I mean so many good people have already died. Why is Jefford's death more important?"

William looked amazed, and not in a good way. "It's not…it's not like Captain Jefford's death is more *important* than anyone else's…I mean, not on its own, but…Captain Jefford was a symbol of the constabulary. He was a symbol of the war."

"Symbols can be dangerous," Colvin said. "Sometimes people think losing a symbol is the same thing as losing what it stands for."

William's brow furrowed. He opened his mouth, then closed it, opened it again, then closed it once more. He looked highly perplexed and deeply troubled. He said nothing else to Colvin the entire time they stood in line together, and Colvin worried that he might have deeply upset his friend. But once they had both knelt beside Jefford's body and paid their respects, then moved off to themselves a little ways so they could talk more easily, William said, "I think that's the wisest thing anyone has ever told me, Colvin."

Colvin, who had never been given a compliment even approaching this one, looked thunderstruck. He did not get a chance to respond, because at that moment Governor Chamberlain and Don Ferdinan appeared at the top of the church steps. Both men wore unreadable expressions. Everyone in the square – which was actually just about everyone left in Tamendad – gathered closely around to hear what the two men had to say.

"There is no need to dress it up with fancy words, Tamendad has suffered a great loss in the death of Captain Amon Jefford," the Governor said grimly. This pronouncement was followed by a silence so absolute that if a man standing there had closed his eyes, he would have thought himself alone in the town square.

"BUT – THIS – WAR – IS – NOT – OVER!!!" Governor Chamberlain screamed suddenly. Several people started at the sound of it, surprised both by the outburst and by the fact that it had come from the usually reposed Governor.

"I suppose I might have known Captain Jefford better than anyone else in this town," Chamberlain continued. "He was a good man. And a good friend. His loss will be felt in Tamendad for years to come.

"But if there is one thing I know about Amon Jefford, one thing I am certain of over all else, it is that if he were capable of sending us all a message right now, that message would be, 'Fight on! Fight for your homes! Fight for your families! Fight for Tamendad!' That is what Amon Jefford would want to tell us above all else. That is the kind of man he was."

Governor Chamberlain paused for a moment to let his words sink in. There were murmurs of agreement throughout the crowd, most strongly discernible from the constables.

"Perhaps the most damnable thing about war is that there is rarely time to mourn those lost," the Governor went on. "Under the current circumstances, I am afraid that Captain Jefford cannot receive nearly the fitting tribute he deserves. He will be buried in the town graveyard, of course. His grave is being dug as we speak. He will be buried this evening, as soon as it is ready.

"But in a way, I am glad that it must happen like this. The grand procession that usually follows a great man's death usually brings with it some small amount of closure over the loss. I do not want any of us to find that closure. I want the thought of Captain Jefford's death to burn and ache within us like a wound that will not heal. I want it to stoke the flames of fury within our souls. I want it to seethe within us until we feel we might break from it.

"I want the loss of Captain Jefford to fuel us in our struggle against the goruks. Just like the loss of Angus MacDugal. Just like the loss of young Edgar of Shield Division, and of the scout riders Franklin and Rodney. Just like the loss of every good soldier who lays down his or her life to defend Tamendad."

There was a long, unbroken silence.

William and Colvin glanced sidelong at one another.

"Now to more practical matters," said the Governor. "Don Ferdinan has been appointed Tamendad's acting Captain of the Guard. It is, obviously, a temporary appointment, but Don Ferdinan has assured me, on numerous occasions, that he intends to stay the course with us and see this war through to the end. We are all very fortunate to have a man of such selfless devotion to take up the post left vacant by Amon Jefford."

Ferdinan looked neither pleased nor apprehensive, standing stoically upon the church's top step with his hands tucked behind him. He looked out over the men and women gathered together in the square. Ferdinan's appointment to Captain of the Guard simply made official what everyone already knew: he was an integral, indispensable part of the war.

Ferdinan stepped forward, drawing even alongside Governor Chamberlain, and as if on cue the Governor fell back a couple of steps.

"There are no words to espress my deep respect and admiration for Captain Jefford. He was a good and honorable man, one of the finest I have met during my stay in Tur. Es with deepest heartfelt remorse that I assume the post he has departed. I do not espect to command the respect you felt for Captain Jefford. Although we have fought together for a good while now, I am still a newcomer to your land and your ways, and it takes years to establish a reputation such as that of Captain Jefford, may God rest his soul.

"What I do espect to command, however, es the military resistance against the goruks. I swear to you, one and all, and God es my witness, I will devote myself completely to my duties as Captain of the Guard, and strive during my every waking moment to live up to the high standards set during the tenure of my predecessor."

Ferdinan paused. A few quiet murmurs rippled through the crowd. Colvin and William spared another glance in the other's direction.

"My first act as Captain of the Guard es to make a solemn vow to you all," continued Ferdinan. "We will win this war."

There were a few cheers and a round of applause, but it seemed underinflated, uninspired. Ferdinan appeared not to be perturbed by this.

"The goruks committed a serious error here today," he continued. "If they had followed through in their assault, es possible they might have overwhelmed us while the initial shock of Captain Jefford's death took hold–"

"He's got a funny way of rallying the troops," Colvin whispered to William.

"Shh!" William replied harshly.

"–but instead they decided to pull back as soon as they had struck a major blow. As usual, they espect us to become demoralized, to lose the will to fight. Well, you have to hand it to the goruks, just when you think they could not possibly get any stupider, they top themselves."

Some of the soldiers laughed.

"You would think the goruks would learn that we are not going to break, and that they would alter their strategy to fit this knowledge, but instead they stick to their hit and run tactics. Well, I suppose I overestimated them. Thankfully, es an escusable mistake to overestimate an enemy. What es inescusable es to underestimate an enemy, and, *compagnos*, the goruks have grievously underestimated us, for three reasons:

"First, they must be aware that Shield Division will soon be back among us. Instead of trying to overwhelm us while our forces are still divided, they allow us to regroup and strengthen our defenses.

"Second, they do not know that Gregor MacDugal es bringing reinforcements from the south, and that they will be here perhaps as soon as two days from now. Obviously this tells us the goruks have failed to plan for the unespected.

"And finally, McRofaly and the men who accompanied him this morning will be returning soon, after setting up an ambush for the goruks which we will spring on them tomorrow."

Excited whispers spread quickly through the crowd. After all that had happened, the soldiers responded to the opportunity of striking back at the goruks like Winterfeast had come early.

"Both Colvin and Lord Stuart-Camen of Sword Division have already volunteered to help lead the ambush–"

"Lead?" Colvin whispered to William. William shrugged, looking surprised.

"–and I will be joining them in the effort, but we still are in need of a good number of volunteers…"

Hands began to raise all over the town square, and William and Colvin, who were right in the midst of the crowd, were bombarded by people eagerly trying to get their attention so that they could volunteer. Atop the church stairs, Ferdinan fought off the urge to smile.

McRofaly returned about an hour before dusk, and he was surprised to find that he was greeted like a hero. People pressed around him on all sides asking for details about the ambush, so that by the time he finally arrived at his prearranged meeting with Governor Chamberlain and Don Ferdinan in the Governor's study he was looking decidedly frazzled.

"Let it slip a bit early, did you?" he said by way of greeting. It had been decided that word of the ambush would not be made public until after McRofaly had returned to verify that everything was prepared.

"It was necessary, given the situation," Ferdinan said, no hint of apology in his voice. "The situation has changed." Don Ferdinan and Governor Chamberlain gave McRofaly a quick rundown of the day's numerous events – the goruk attack, Kor's appearance, Captain Jefford's death, Ferdinan's appointment – before interrogating him on how the setup went.

McRofaly reported that it all went remarkably smoothly, all things considered. They only had to fell four trees to completely cut off all feasible alternate routes around the clearing, and McRofaly had managed to sketch a detailed diagram showing all the best positions to place archers in the trees and hide foot soldiers among the foliage. The only real hitch McRofaly and his crew encountered was having to take cover for about three quarters of an hour while the goruks marched past, but McRofaly insisted that even that had its benefits. For one thing, the goruks had marched straight through the clearing even though the fourth tree had yet to be felled and the goruks could have chosen to bypass the clearing and go another way. For another, twenty-three men and four thoroughly exhausted draft horses had easily concealed themselves from the passing goruks, which indicated that the soldiers lying in wait should have no problem remaining hidden from sight until the ambush was sprung. And as an added bonus the goruks had seen the fallen trees on their march toward Tamendad, and were thus less likely to be suspicious of them tomorrow.

"Long story short," McRofaly concluded, "the site is ready when you are."

"Very good, McRofaly," Ferdinan said, looking pleased. "Now, all that remains es–"

Ferdinan was interrupted by a knock at the door. A timid-looking guard, whom Ferdinan and McRofaly both recognized on sight with no small degree of displeasure, stuck his head into the room when beckoned and sheepishly muttered, "Urgent message, sirs, sorry to interrupt."

"What?" Ferdinan snapped.

"A goruk, sir, approaching from the southwest."

"The goruks are coming back?" said Governor Chamberlain, springing to his feet behind his desk.

"Well, yes and no, Your Lordship," the guard replied. "You see, there's only the one."

"A single goruk?" asked Ferdinan. "You are certain of this?"

"The message from the southwest gate was very specific on this point, Don Fer...I mean, Captain Fer–"

"*Don* es appropriate," Ferdinan interrupted.

"Yes, sir," the guard replied meekly.

"I suspect I know what this is about," interjected McRofaly. "I suggest we go have a look."

They found the southwest gate abuzz with the excited chatter of the night watch, which had just arrived for its shift. The chatter fell hushed as Governor Chamberlain, Don Ferdinan, and McRofaly made their way through the crowd and ascended a ladder up to the lookout's platform. By the time McRofaly reached the top, Governor Chamberlain was already shading his squinted eyes from the setting sun, peering out into the countryside. Ferdinan stood with his arms crossed over his chest, his brow furrowed, staring in the same direction as the Governor. There was indeed a lone figure in the distance, moving out there among the corpses of the goruks, but it was impossible to tell exactly what it was doing.

"Here, use this," McRofaly said, handing his spyglass to Governor Chamberlain. The Governor accepted it gratefully and peered through it, stared for a moment, then turned a slight shade of green. He handed the spyglass to Ferdinan without a word, looking as though he was fighting back the urge to vomit. Ferdinan gave the Governor a curious look, then peered through the spyglass himself. It took about ten seconds for a look of utmost revulsion to spread across Ferdinan's face.

"What in the holy name of God es it doing?" said Ferdinan as he handed the spyglass to McRofaly.

McRofaly fixed the spyglass on the goruk. It was dressed in a flowing patchwork garment of animal skins, and it had beads and feathers tied at the ends of its numerous braids of hair. It was carrying a sack made of what looked to be blood-soaked burlap. The sack was still wet. McRofaly could see it dripping.

The goruk knelt beside the body of one of its fallen brethren and laid the sack aside, retrieving something from its belt. As the sunlight struck the object the goruk now held, McRofaly could tell that it was a wicked-looking knife, all serrated edges and barbs, the kind that would be of absolutely no practical value in combat. The goruk raised the knife high, clenching the handle in both hands, and brought it swiftly down into the corpse's chest, just left of center. The goruk worked the handle of the knife back and forth, twisting it in a nauseating fashion, and then began the unmistakable motions of sawing through the corpse's ribs. McRofaly's mouth went dry, and his stomach lurched a bit.

Once the hole in the corpse's chest was sufficiently wide, the goruk plunged its free hand through it, into the chest cavity, and when it pulled its hand back out it was clenching what could only be the corpse's heart.

The goruk swiped its knife in an arc under the heart, severing the arteries that held it in place. It then returned its knife to its belt, retrieved the burlap sack, and deposited the heart into it before moving on to the next corpse.

"It's freeing the souls of the dead goruks, in case we decide to sever their heads," McRofaly said, collapsing his spyglass. "That is the ardah, sort of a shaman or witch-doctor. He acts as a sort of intermediary between the goruks and the gods."

"Gods?" said Ferdinan. "Plural?"

"The goruks worship many gods," replied McRofaly. Ferdinan did not look pleased at this. "They also believe that if the head is severed before the heart is removed, a goruk's soul is forever imprisoned in the body and cannot reach the afterworld."

"Where did you learn all of this?" said Ferdinan incredulously.

"I read a lot," McRofaly replied.

"Should we attack it, Lord Governor?" called an archer from the next platform over. Governor Chamberlain glanced at McRofaly and Ferdinan.

"Killing the ardah would have about as much effect as killing a priest," McRofaly said quietly. "There would be no military gain from it, and all we would accomplish is infuriating the goruks."

Ferdinan looked hesitant, casting a quick glance out over the wall toward the ardah, but mumbled a half-hearted, "Agreed," nonetheless.

"It presents no danger to us at this time," Governor Chamberlain called back to the archer. "If it comes within a hundred feet of the wall, shoot it."

The three men descended the ladder, leaving the ardah to its grizzly business. "We should have a drink, gentlemen," said the Governor once they were back upon the ground, "to toast tomorrow's ambush. And to be frank, after what we just witnessed, I think I could simply use one."

They returned to the Governor's house and settled into the Governor's study, and the Governor himself doled out snifters of brandy. Each man held his drink high as the Governor said a few words of praise for McRofaly's strategies and Ferdinan's leadership, and they finished the toast off by all exclaiming, "To the ambush!" And after that the conversation died as each man fell to his own unshared musings. Each man looked thoughtful, but Ferdinan was downright brooding.

"Something vexes you, Don Ferdinan?" the Governor finally broke the silence.

The Conquian looked for a moment like he was not going to say anything, but then with a subtle shrug explained, "Es something that Kor said to me on the battlefield today, just after he had murdered Captain

Jefford. I keep playing it over and over in my mind."

Geoffery did his best to mask the revulsion that came with the idea of conversing with the goruk leader. "What did he say?" he asked. McRofaly straightened in his chair, obviously interested in hearing for himself.

"He said to me, 'Your leader es dead. You are defeated.'" Ferdinan arched an eyebrow as he said it.

"Well," said the Governor, "Captain Jefford was the most highly decorated soldier on the battlefield today. It would not be difficult to identify him as the commander of the forces, especially since you yourself bore no military insignia, Don Ferdinan."

"If I may?" came McRofaly's voice. Both the Governor and Don Ferdinan turned to look at him, and the diminutive tactician had a most peculiar look on his face. With a nod, the Governor told him to continue.

"I believe it's safe to assume Kor was implying a great deal more than that our commanding officer had been slain. You have to realize, the goruks know next to nothing about our society and our culture. They've scouted the city, to be certain, and they understand the methods we are utilizing to defend it, but as to how we live and interact, the nuances of our society, they are completely ignorant. Goruks have a much simpler social setup than we do. To them, there is no distinction to be made between a military leader and a political one. In Kor's mind, Captain Jefford would be not just the leader of Tamendad's forces, but of Tamendad entire."

"Amon was the target," said Geoffery. There was no masking the cold hatred in his voice.

"I believe you would be safe to make that wager," replied McRofaly. "In Kor's mind, he decimated our command structure today by killing the Captain."

"Es why he retreated as soon as the Captain was dead," Ferdinan said. "He met his objective. He espects us to languish before he moves in for the killing blow."

"Indeed," agreed McRofaly. "You and I both expected the goruks to escalate the war. Well this is how they do that. I must confess I made the error, as I'm certain did you, that this would mean the goruks attacking us with traditional military formations and strategies, banners unfurled. In this we made the exact same sort of mistake that the goruks have made: we failed to appreciate that their society is completely different from our own. They have no knowledge of how to wage a war as we wage it. Kor thought he was meeting the chieftain of Tamendad in battle. The fact that you were waiting for him outside the gates probably fed into his faulty reasoning. In Kor's mind, our leader *is* dead, because if the tables were turned and Captain Jefford had won the day, the goruks would have lost their one and only leader. The goruks cannot appreciate that in our society, it can sometimes be a bit more difficult to ascertain who is actually in charge."

At this the Governor glanced at Don Ferdinan, and found the Conquian glancing right back at him. Neither man acknowledged the other with words.

"Kor believes we are defeated?" the Governor asked, turning his gaze back toward McRofaly.

McRofaly nodded. "In his mind, he won Tamendad today. I would bet your life on it."

Governor Chamberlain refilled each man's snifter. "Gentlemen," he said, "we have something else to drink to."

PART III

THE BATTLE OF TAMENDAD

CHAPTER TWENTY-EIGHT

OF FIGHT AND FLIGHT

They had set out from Tamendad at first light, all one hundred and twelve soldiers. Twenty-three archers, eighty-nine foot soldiers. No horses. Horses were dangerous. One errant whinny or nicker could have doomed the whole thing. McRofaly had been emphatic on that point. He had also been emphatic that one hundred twelve was the perfect number of soldiers for the ambush. He had pages and pages of esoteric calculations and incomprehensible diagrams to illustrate his point, and to further prove that this proportion of archers to foot soldiers was ideal. Even with all his arithmetic and geometry, all his numbers and angles, McRofaly still had a difficult time selling this point to the Governor and Don Ferdinan. A hundred and twelve soldiers, while nothing to sneeze at, would not be of much use if the goruks marched three or four hundred toward Tamendad. The clearing could safely hide another fifty soldiers, close to a hundred if they really pushed it – Ferdinan had discerned that much by perusing McRofaly's diagrams. But McRofaly was indefatigable. He had looked at the problem from a number of different angles, approached it from various perspectives. Always his conclusion was the same: one hundred twelve was the magic number. So finally, and with no small degree of reluctance, Governor Chamberlain and Don Ferdinan acquiesced. One hundred and twelve it was.

They had traveled at such an infuriatingly slow pace that even the sturdiest soldiers were frustrated by the time they had reached their destination. The greener troops seemed almost mutinous in their eagerness to just get on with it. But every precaution had to be taken to ensure that they reached the forest clearing undetected. If those precautions included moving at a snail's pace, so be it. Better to have to endure creeping along with mind-numbing slowness and arrive at the clearing frazzled than to give their presence away and ruin their opportunity to deal a major blow to the goruks. So a snail's pace it was, all one hundred and twelve soldiers inching their way across the countryside, spending several minutes at a time standing completely stationary while Ian Morlocke and his men scouted the land ahead. Not another step was taken until the all clear came in from the scouts, and it often took a quarter of an hour to scout a quarter of a mile.

The first couple of hours were really not so bad. It was, after all, the first trip out of Tamendad in weeks for many of the men and women chosen to be part of the ambush, and the fresh air and rolling hills of the northern Glenish coast were enough to keep them pacified. Some of the soldiers chatted quietly, when talking was permitted, about how only a few days into autumn some of the leaves had already begun to change color and how by all appearances winter would be coming early this year. But the thrill of a rare trip outside the city walls eventually wore thin, and the frustration of moving so slowly began to take hold. As the hours wore on, Ferdinan, William and Colvin had an increasingly difficult time pacifying the soldiers' grumblings, often having to endure the added stress of doing so without being able to make any noise themselves.

But now all one hundred and twelve soldiers were safely hidden in the forest clearing. The archers were in their spots among the branches of the trees, the foot soldiers were concealed by the underbrush and tree trunks. Ian Morlocke and his men had ridden ahead to watch for signs of movement from the goruks. It was a tense moment, undeniably, but the long morning coupled with the prospect of having to wait God only knew how many more hours before the goruks showed themselves had given rise to a sense of idleness that undermined the tension.

Hidden among the leaves and brambles, crouched down behind the trunk of a large cedar, William Stuart-Camen silently surveyed the men and women around him. He had to hand it to McRofaly, these hiding places were nearly perfect. William could clearly make out the faces and forms only of people within ten feet of him. Beyond that range, for all William could tell by sight alone, he was surrounded by empty forest. He looked to his right, where he knew but could not see that Colvin was waiting, crouched down and hidden like himself. Ferdinan was somewhere on the other side of the clearing; William was not entirely certain where. One thing he was certain of, though, was that he would be willing to pay a hefty sum for the opportunity to talk to either of them, just to have something to do to pass the time. But talking was strictly forbidden except when absolutely necessary. They had not come this far to ruin it all just because someone was feeling chatty.

As for the other soldiers hidden around the forest clearing, William had to commend them. Despite the frustrations of the journey, they were as still and as silent as a sleeping babe now that they were hidden and waiting. Of course, William was not surprised by this very much. He had come to realize over the course of the last few weeks that his fellow Tamendaders were capable of extraordinary things when circumstances demanded it. The fact that these men and women were here at all was a testament to that. The constables, who composed a little more than half of the fighting force, had watched their beloved Captain fall under the blade of the commanding goruk less than twenty-four hours ago, and yet the entire constabulary had volunteered for the assignment without hesitation. Meanwhile, the members of Shield Division had not arrived back in Tamendad until nearly midnight after a long and arduous journey from Tantera, only to find their brother in arms, Edgar, dead and buried along with the Captain of the Guard, but that did not keep them from volunteering in such numbers that some had to be sent away. No, the men and women of Tamendad were made of sterner stuff than even William would have imagined. Still, none of that made the time pass any quicker.

An hour passed with mind-numbing slowness, followed by another. The shadows were pointing in the other direction now. All around the clearing men and women had given up crouching for sitting on the ground, to salvage their leg muscles. Even William had taken a load off, sitting behind a thicket with his legs crossed, peering between the leaves for the subtlest sign of movement So far there had been nothing, not so much as a hint of activity. The entire forest was dead, and it was beginning to resemble William's mood.

William felt a hand gently grip his shoulder, and his heart leapt into his throat. He turned quickly, half-startled, half-furious that someone had broken cover, and saw Ferdinan crouching behind him, his finger over his lips urging William to remain quiet.

"I have just had a word with Ian Morlocke," Ferdinan whispered, barely audible.

William stared in disbelief. "Ferdinan?" he whispered, forgetting himself. "Wha–? Where did you come from?"

The look on Ferdinan's face told that he thought this a very silly question. "From the other side of the clearing, of course," he replied.

"But I didn't hear a thing!"

"Well I should hope not," replied Ferdinan. "I was very careful not to make noise."

William was at a loss for words. He had been intently watching and listening for any hint of movement, any indication that anything at all was amiss, and yet Ferdinan had managed to sneak all the way around the forest clearing undetected until the moment he had literally tapped

William on the shoulder. Either William was terribly inattentive, or Ferdinan was the stealthiest man he had ever met. Biased though he may have been, William suspected that he had not been guilty of inattention. "Wait a moment," he said, as Ferdinan's words began to sink in, "did you say you've been talking with Ian Morlocke?"

"Sí," whispered Ferdinan.

"Where?"

"On the other side of the clearing. I believe we have been over this."

"But I didn't hear–"

"Ian can also be rather quiet when he needs to be," said Ferdinan impatiently.

"Sorry. What news?"

"He says there es activity among the goruks."

"They're coming?!" William said excitedly, his voice much louder than he had intended. The look Ferdinan gave him in return made him want to curl up and die.

"Not yet," Ferdinan whispered. "Morlocke said they look to be preparing to move. Es most likely they are going to try to hit Tamendad during the changing of the guard again."

"They just don't learn, do they?" said William. "Hold on. How does he know they're getting ready to move? He'd have to be practically on top of the cave to see that."

"He seems to believe that the current situation justifies actions that would otherwise be prohibited," said Ferdinan. The disapproval was obvious in the Conquian's voice, even though William could barely hear what he was saying.

"Right. So what do we do?"

"Spread the word. When Morlocke brings word that the goruks are moving, I will make a sound like a lark. You know what a lark sounds like, no?"

"Yes."

"Good. When you hear the signal, make a noise like an owl to let me know you have heard it. After that, absolutely no noise of any kind. Once the goruks are in the clearing, charge them once the archers have gotten off a round of arrows. Understand?"

"Absolutely."

"Good. I am going to tell Colvin. God goes with you, William." Ferdinan began to slink away into the woods, but William called softly after him and Ferdinan looked back.

"See you on the other side," William whispered.

Ferdinan nodded. Then he was gone, disappearing completely into the foliage of the forest without a sound. He did it, William noted, with considerably greater ease than William himself could ever have managed. The young nobleman stared for a few moments in the direction Ferdinan had vanished, then began whispering instructions to the soldier nearest him.

It was that time of day when afternoon had not yet fully conceded defeat to evening and shadows were just beginning to creep longer than the objects that cast them. In a small forest glade southwest of Tamendad, all was quiet. There was no sign or signal of danger, nothing that would have put even the jumpiest person on guard. By all appearances, everything was peaceful and calm on this early autumn afternoon.

It was, in fact, too peaceful, too calm. Nothing stirred in the forest clearing, not the tiniest sound. Animals were keeping their distance. That in itself would have been enough to signal that something was amiss, but it would have taken a master woodsman to notice it. Besides, the clearing was obviously not completely devoid of animal life, as a lark's song rose high and clear through the trees, and it was met by the hooting of two owls from the other side of the glade. The birdsong drifted away into the autumn breeze, and once again all was consumed by silence. Time drifted lazily by, unaware or unconcerned with what was about to happen. There was no way to be certain exactly how much time passed. The trees were still in possession of the entirety of their leaves, and they blocked the sky just enough to make it impossible to follow the movement of the sun. But some amount of time later – perhaps an hour or two by the feel of it – the silence of the woods began to give way to the unmistakable sounds of movement. Mass movement. The goruks were coming.

The sounds of their marching carried far on the autumn wind, and what felt like perhaps another quarter of an hour passed before the rustling of branches and the snapping of twigs told that they were near. They did not hesitate when they reached the clearing but continued right into it. They moved in an unorganized pack, without form or rank. This made them difficult to count, and all that could really be discerned quickly was that there was less than a hundred, and perhaps just a bit more than fifty. Not nearly as many as there might have been. It was difficult to decide if that was a good thing or a bad.

One hundred and twelve people held their breath as the goruks entered the clearing. One good thing about the goruks' number was that they would all be able to fit inside the clearing; they would be surrounded. The goruks made their way across the glade, moving more quickly than a man would have but apparently without any sense of urgency. That made sense. It was wise to conserve energy during an overland march when a battle lay at the end of it. Of course, these goruks had already reached the end of their march. They just were not aware of it yet.

The goruks at the front of the pack had just reached the other edge of the clearing as the goruks bringing up the rear stepped into it for the first time, and it was at that moment that the trap was sprung. Arrows flew from the trees, dropping goruks at the front and the rear. Screams shattered the tranquility of the afternoon, screams from both the goruks who were realizing what was happening and from the Tamendaders who were emerging from their hiding places with weapons held high, Ferdinan, Colvin and William in the lead.

Another volley of arrows zipped through the air, and then the foot soldiers met the goruk line. The goruks had not yet even had time to draw their weapons. The Tamendaders crashed into them, making short work of the first goruks they encountered. By the time the goruks were able to draw swords, their numbers had nearly been cut in half.

"Tamendad stands!" William screamed as his broadsword slid through a goruk's heart. He twisted the blade sharply and the goruk slumped to the ground, like the three before it. All around him men and women vented their frustrations. They were merciless, cutting through the tusked monsters with an almost frightening zeal. William heard his battle cry echoed by Colvin, who stood no more than twenty feet away, sabre clenched tightly in his right hand, dagger-glove worn on his left. Two goruks lay dead at his feet, both of his blades shining a brilliant, wet crimson in the sunlight filtering through the forest canopy. Colvin turned and met William's gaze. William smiled savagely, but Colvin's eyes widened in horrified surprise.

"William, watch out!" Colvin screamed, pointing over the young nobleman's shoulder. William spun on his heels, and as he did so he heard the quiet scream of an arrow flying true and the dull *thunk* of it finding its target. Turning, William saw a goruk standing before him, not five feet away, its curved sword held high. William instinctively raised his broadsword to defend himself before he realized that the goruk was not moving; it was apparently held in the grip of paralysis. Once more William heard the *ziff* of a flying arrow, the *thunk* of it striking its target, and the goruk fell face-forward to the ground. One arrow protruded from its upper back, the other out of the back of its head. William stared at it for a moment with wide eyes, then snapped back to reality, called out a word of thanks to the archers in the trees, and turned his attention to the goruks that were still up and moving.

In the course of perhaps a minute or two it had become a cleanup operation, only a handful of goruks still standing. William, Colvin, and Ferdinan now stood together, mostly just supervising, attacking only when a goruk came too close. The foot soldiers were primarily herding the goruks, preventing them from escaping while the archers picked them off from the trees.

"That went well, I think," said Colvin, still tensed and bouncing slightly on the balls of his feet, ready to pounce at any moment even though the nearest goruk was twenty feet away and surrounded by three soldiers. "Too bad Kor wasn't leading them."

"Es just what I was thinking," Ferdinan said, looking over the carnage. The Conquian looked to be completely at ease, totally relaxed, except that his eyes were darting in all directions with the speed and intensity of a hawk. His calm demeanor fooled neither of his companions. William and Colvin both knew that if a crisis arose, Ferdinan would leave them both flatfooted and be halfway through dealing with it before they even realized anything had happened.

"A victory's a victory," said William, who looked back over his shoulder every few seconds. "We'll get Kor in time."

"Agreed," said Ferdinan, not looking at William.

"Yeah," said Colvin, "I just wish I could see the look on Kor's face when–"

Ferdinan's head snapped to his left, and he raised his sabre and parrying dagger into a defensive stance in one quick motion. Colvin and William jumped from the suddenness of it.

"What–?"

The surrounding forest erupted with howling, snarling screams. The woods were suddenly alive with movement, goruks appearing from behind trees and under bushes in all directions, all breaking into a sprint toward the glade. Arrows filled the air, streaking from the forest floor into the trees. The arrow-riddled bodies of archers began to fall from their perches.

"Es an ambush!" Ferdinan screamed.

"They're ambushing the ambush!" echoed Colvin.

"Run! Run for your lives!"

But there was nowhere to run. The goruks were closing in on all sides, hundreds of them. They were surrounded.

"To me!" Ferdinan screamed at the top of his lungs. "Soldiers of Tamendad to me if you want to live!" They gathered around Ferdinan as the goruks closed in around them. Ferdinan was as close to frantic as anyone in Tamendad had ever seen him. "We have one chance! Follow me! Kill any goruks that get in your way! *Do not stop running!* Es the only way we are going to live!" Ferdinan turned and ran at full sprint toward the approaching goruks, into the forest. Everyone followed without hesitation. It was better than just standing around and waiting for them to come.

The goruks came on, and the lines met only a few feet outside the clearing. As Ferdinan commanded, no one stopped running, not unless they fell down and did not get up again. Some of the goruks were actually bowled over as men literally ran them down. Everyone scattered, finding holes here or there in the goruk line to slip through. They ran, and they did not look back, the goruks right behind them.

William and Colvin sprinted deeper into the woods together. They had become separated from Ferdinan, and everyone else for that matter. The goruks, hundreds of them, were following close behind. Here and there William or Colvin would occasionally catch a glimpse of someone sprinting through the trees in roughly the same direction they were heading, but they dared not call out to them, and risk the goruks hearing and figuring out where they were. All around them the woods were filled with the howls of goruks, and here and there the sounds of skirmishes breaking out where they had managed to corner a human or two. William and Colvin did not dare stop running, even when their legs threatened to fold under their own weight, not when it became an epic struggle just to breathe, not even when the wailing screams of pain they heard echoing through the forest sounded like people they knew. As long as they were running, they were alive.

"Where...are we...going?" William huffed. His lungs felt like they were about to shrivel up under protest, and it was all he could do just to get four words out.

"Don't...know," Colvin gasped in reply. There was no sense of direction here in this accursed forest. Colvin kept looking for a sign, any sign, that told him where they were headed, but for all he could tell it was just as likely that they were heading straight toward the goruks' cave as toward Tamendad.

A goruk suddenly emerged from the other side of a tree, standing right in Colvin and William's path. It might as well have materialized out of thin air for all the time they had to react. There was no time to think. Colvin acted on instinct. He dove straight for the goruk, burying his shoulder in its sternum. He felt the goruk go limp beneath him, the wind knocked from its lungs, as they both fell to the ground. One quick motion and Colvin had plunged the entire length of his dagger-glove blade into the goruk's ear. Its eyes rolled up into its ugly head, and its whole body convulsed in death spasms.

One down. The thought brought no comfort to Colvin. Goruks wouldn't be alone in these woods.

Colvin glanced up at William. The young nobleman was a few feet ahead, having run past when Colvin dove, but now he was slowing down and looking back over his shoulder. "Run!" Colvin screamed, frantically waving William on. A look of pained indecision spread across William's face. "GO!!!" Colvin shouted more forcefully. "I'll catch up!" *What the twist is he thinking?* thought Colvin frantically. *What the twist am I thinking?* Colvin scrambled back to his feet, and finally William had begun running again in earnest.

But it was too late.

Goruks began emerging from the trees all around them, five, ten, twenty or more in total. A snare sailed twirling through the air, a sturdy strap of leather with a weight attached to each end, and Colvin could only watch as it entwined itself hopelessly around William's legs. William went down hard; his head collided with an exposed root of a gnarled tree. A chill wrapped its icy fingers around Colvin's spine as he saw William's body fall limp as a rag doll. *Don't let him be dead*, Colvin thought. *Please, God, don't let him be dead.*

Another voice in Colvin's brain replied, *Who are you kidding? You're both dead.*

Colvin ignored this voice, ignored the bitter irrefutability of it. He might well have been about to die, but he wasn't going out like that, on his knees bemoaning his fate. He was going to die on his feet, with a sword in his hand. He was going to die fighting.

Run! screamed the voice inside his head. *You can still save yourself! You got away once! You can do it again!*

No, Colvin told the voice, *not while there's still a chance to save William.* If he was going to die, he was going to die following the path of *decusé*. He stood, his right hand clenching the handle of his sabre so tightly that he might have left indentations where his fingers gripped it. He flexed his left hand in the dagger-glove, the stiff leather now worn in enough to fit the contours of his fist perfectly. The goruks approached. Fifteen? Twenty? No time to count. Most of them closed in on Colvin, but a group of four was heading for William's prone form. Colvin's heart skipped a beat. He had to make it to William, protect him somehow, some way. He couldn't just watch his friend die.

Another snare came whipping toward him. He had the briefest of moments to react. He dove to his right, rolling on the ground, standing again. A few of the goruks laughed. They obviously thought it funny that this paleskin still had fight left in him. They closed in around him. Colvin assumed the stance.

He sprang like a cat at the nearest goruk, one that had been laughing at him. The grin slid from the ugly monster's face as Colvin ran it through the throat with his sabre. It was a perfect thrust. Ferdinan would have been proud. *If I ever see him again, I'll tell him all about it.* The goruk collapsed, clenching its throat, gurgling and sputtering. With it out of the way, Colvin had an almost straight shot to William. He could reach his friend before the goruks did. He knew he could. He ran with everything he had left. There was a moment of hesitation, like an instant frozen in time, when the goruks realized what had just happened and Colvin was the only thing moving. The four goruks that had been going for William turned around at the sound of their companion's death rattle and stood staring at the goruk that lay twitching in the ever-expanding puddle of blood. The laughter died away and an eerie silence replaced it, the silence of shock that is destined to end in an explosion of rage. As Colvin ran, he could hear the sounds of fighting echoing through the woods all around him. It was like the forest had come alive under the possession of some ancient, violent demon. But somehow the sound was different than before. It was the sound of a full-on fray, not a lopsided massacre. It sounded as though, somehow, the Tamendaders were fighting back and holding their own. Colvin chalked it up to wishful thinking.

The goruks screamed. They howled. They snarled. And they all started moving for Colvin. He was almost to William, just a few feet away, but the four goruks that had been going for William rounded on him. They were on him in a heartbeat. He jumped, dodged, leapt wildly. He felt a sword pierce his side and another slice into the back of his calf. How bad was it? No way to know. No time to check. Colvin punched frantically and flailed his sabre at anything that came near him. There was no method or style to his attack. He had become a cornered animal, fighting for survival. He bled, and was splattered with blood that was not his own. He was cut, and punched, and clawed, and was vaguely aware of his own blades cutting open flesh and of the wails of pain and anger in his ears. Everything was a muddled blur of violent confusion. Then he was standing above William.

He wanted to check for a pulse, breathing, anything that would tell him whether his friend was alive or dead. There was no time. If William was dead, he was dead. If he was alive…then he'd most likely be dead in a few moments anyway. *Not before me*, thought Colvin. That was what it had come down to now. He was going to fight to his last breath trying to save his friend. He was going to follow the path of *decusé* right into his own coffin, where he would be buried alongside the rest of Tamendad's martyrs.

Once again, Colvin assumed the stance.

The goruks narrowed in around him, a look of bloodlust and vengeance in their eyes. Their razor-sharp scimitars were all pointing right at his heart. Colvin backed against the gnarled tree. At least he wasn't going to die from a sword through the back. He looked over his attackers. At least twenty. At least. A handful were bleeding, weakened, but most where whole. Whole and furious and approaching in a narrowing circle like a noose tightening around Colvin's neck. A peculiar sense of calm overtook Colvin, spreading through his body and mind as he watched his assailants approach, and with it came clarity, understanding, acceptance. He smiled in spite of his fate, or perhaps because of it. It was, after all, as good a day as any to scale the summit. Colvin drew himself up to full measure against the tree and readied his sabre and his bladed fist. He spoke with a surprisingly level voice. "All right, you ugly bastards. Let's do this."

As if in reply there came a whirling, pulsating sound, something strangely familiar yet unidentifiable. Something – a spinning blur – came flying from among the trees. A goruk landed face-down, convulsed for a moment and lay still. Screams filled the air once more, coming from among the trees, where now *something* was moving. They were not goruk screams. They weren't human, either. They were deep and booming and guttural.

Given a brief stay of execution, Colvin stared at the object protruding from the dead goruk's back. It looked like a hatchet, but not like any hatchet Colvin had seen before. It looked to be made of a single piece of metal and streamlined for throwing. The craftsmanship was reminiscent of an axe Colvin had seen before…

And then Colvin no longer stood alone against the goruks. They came at a run, ten of them, moving with surprising agility, screaming at the top of their lungs. Colvin's eyes widened. His jaw dropped. He wasn't seeing this. He was dead. He was dying, and this was his mind's way of deluding itself, a concocted fantasy too implausible to be true. It couldn't be true. It was just too good.

"Gunther?"

The short blacksmith hurled another hand-axe, and this one caught a goruk standing five feet to Colvin's left squarely between the eyes. Gunther then retrieved his battleaxe from his belt, the wicked double-headed weapon, and charged. His nine squat, stout, bearded companions were already swarming, drawing the goruks' attention away from Colvin and William. Gunther alone was moving toward the two men, cleaving his way through goruks as he came. As for the goruks, Colvin might as well have ceased to exist for all the attention they showed him. They railed against Gunther and his companions with an intensity that stunned

Colvin, and he had seen goruks seriously riled on more than one occasion. Gunther and his friends were having no problems holding their own, though. In fact, they moved so deftly against their foes, dodging and weaving, infuriating the goruks all the more, that it seemed as though fighting goruks was second nature to them.

Gunther emerged from the fray. There was now only one goruk separating Gunther from Colvin and William; the rest had turned their attention to Gunther's nine companions. The lone goruk charged Gunther, its scimitar held at the ready. Gunther rushed it, holding his axe high, ready to strike. Colvin had the distinct impression of two rams about to butt heads. For a moment it appeared that Gunther and the goruk were actually going to collide. As they neared, the goruk slashed its scimitar in a downward arc, right at Gunther's face. Gunther was rushing right into it. Colvin wanted to scream a warning, but there was no time. At the last possible moment, Gunther ducked. He did more than duck, really; he fell face-down, flat on the ground, and rolled. The goruk's momentum carried it right over Gunther; it had to high-step to avoid being tripped. For a horrifying moment Colvin thought Gunther had been hit, but in the next moment the short blacksmith was up on his feet, spinning, swinging his axe. One smooth slash of his weapon took the goruk's legs out from underneath it, literally. The goruk collapsed, howling in pain, its amputated legs lying limp and useless a couple of feet away. Gunther wasted no time. He closed on his prone opponent and with one clean swipe of his axe separated the goruk's head from its body. With no hesitation to consider his kill, he hurried to Colvin.

"Is he alive?" Gunther asked quickly with a nod toward William.

Gunther's scratchy, sandpaper voice sounded so wonderful to Colvin, so much like the sweet sound of salvation, that it took a moment for the words to really sink in. Colvin looked down at William's motionless body and his overwhelming sense of relief at still being alive abated somewhat. Now that he actually had a chance to check William for signs of life, there was nothing in the world he wanted to do less. He didn't want to find out for sure, to face the possibility that William really was dead. But he had to know. Colvin reached down, gingerly placing his fingers to the side of William's neck. The world had suddenly stood still. His fingers probed William's neck. For a moment he could find nothing, and his heart plummeted from his throat to his stomach. William was dead. But then, shifting his fingers slightly to the left, hoping against hope, he found it: the steady, rhythmic beating of William's heart. It pulsed steadily against Colvin's touch, if a bit slowly. The passage of time resumed its normal velocity.

"He's alive," Colvin said. He wanted to scream it.

"Can you carry him?"

"Yes," Colvin replied, without even thinking about it. He began hoisting William's unconscious form onto his shoulder. "Where's Ferdinan? Is he…?"

"He's leadin' a group of about twenty out together," Gunther said, his hand clenched tightly around the haft of his axe, his eyes scanning in all directions for approaching danger. "Most of the others are helpin' him."

"Others? How many of you are there?" Colvin's words came out in a grunt under William's added weight.

"Just over a hundred." A wave of goosebumps spread from the pit of Colvin's stomach to the tips of his fingers and toes. They might actually make it out alive. They honestly might. "We're gonna meet up with 'em," Gunther continued in his rough growl, "and get you outta here. C'mon, and try to keep up."

"What about the goruks?"

Gunther chuckled roughly, once. "What goruks?"

Colvin looked around. Gunther was right, there was not a single goruk to be seen, at least none that were alive. Scattered here and there on the forest floor were goruk corpses, all of them beheaded, but not enough to account for the number that had cornered Colvin and William. The only things still standing were the nine squat, stout, bearded men – not men, exactly; Ganugamosh – holding axes and picks and hammers, looking ready to strike at any sign of movement. A Ganugamosh with a braided black beard that came to his knees approached Gunther and Colvin, though like Gunther he too was glancing all around, attentively but not what Colvin would have called warily. The way he carried himself almost suggested eager anticipation.

The black-bearded Ganugamosh said something incomprehensible as he approached. It sounded so gruff it was nearly comical, but Colvin was in no mood to laugh. Both heads of the military pick held firmly in the black-bearded Ganugamosh's hands were thoroughly soaked with blood, as was a majority of his body, even though he sported no visible wounds.

"He says the goruks that didn't die hightailed it as soon as it started to look like a fair fight," Gunther translated with a bit of a smile. He looked squarely at Colvin for only the second time since coming to his rescue, and the smile slid right off his face. "You're bleedin'," he said. It was a statement of both fact and concern.

"I'm fine," Colvin lied. In fact, he had no idea how bad his wounds were. Judging by how they felt, he had suffered worse, but judging an injury's severity by feel could be misleading. A simple flesh wound could ache and sting like it was mortal, while a life-threatening injury might not hurt much at all. But Colvin could walk, and that was all that mattered at the moment. Let the healers deal with mending him when – if – he got back to Tamendad.

The ten Ganugamosh encircled him as they cautiously made their way through the trees together, Gunther in the lead. Colvin was straining under the weight of William's limp body but he kept putting one foot determinedly in front of the other, only distantly aware of the flaring pain in his left calf every time he took a step. It was slow going, and Colvin was thankful for that. He had learned that Ganugamosh could really move when they wanted to, and he was not certain that he could walk any faster than he already was. The Ganugamosh, however, looked ready for anything. But for all they saw and heard, they might have been alone in the forest. The sounds of fighting had subsided, and the only sign of goruks they saw was the occasional decapitated corpse. The calm did not exactly raise Colvin's spirits; while it might have indicated that the goruks had fled, it might also have meant that they had wiped out the Tamendaders' resistance.

The calm did nothing to put the Ganugamosh at ease, either. They walked with their weapons ready and their eyes peeled. Every now and then they would stop dead in their tracks, sometimes so abruptly that Colvin nearly stumbled into Gunther from behind, and together they would stand peering around into the woods for some length of time before moving again. The frequency of the stops seemed completely random, as did the length of time they remained stationary. Sometimes it was the briefest of moments, little more than a hesitation between steps. Other times they stood still as statues for several minutes, visibly straining to hear the slightest sound, and did not move again until they were absolutely certain nothing was amiss. Neither way presented Colvin with much of an opportunity to rest. He had come fully down from his battle high, and William's dead weight was draining his remaining strength a little more with each passing step. His wounds were no longer bleeding freely, but what blood he had lost only made the toll of his exertion all the worse. He was stumbling as much as he was walking now, and he very nearly fell once, dropping to a knee and forcing himself back up at the cost of that much more of his precious strength. He did not dare set William down and take a rest, though, for fear that he would not be able to hoist William's limp body back onto his shoulders when he was finished. Gunther was looking back over his shoulder at Colvin as much as he was scanning the surrounding woods, and when Colvin dropped to a knee the short blacksmith said in a concerned voice, "Colvin, why don't you let me–"

"I'll manage," Colvin snapped in reply, much more roughly than he had intended. Gunther said nothing further about it, but the backwards glances continued, and with increased frequency.

Colvin was on the verge of collapse, each step a test of will, when they found the others. They were huddled closely together in a place where the trees thinned a bit, about thirty Tamendaders and twice as many Ganugamosh by the look of it. Everyone had weapons drawn and looked ready to attack at a moment's notice, but there was an unmistakable sense that the Ganugamosh were the protectors and the Tamendaders the protected. For one terrifying moment Colvin thought he and his Ganugamosh guard were going to be attacked just for emerging unannounced into the others' presence, everyone seemed so tense and ready to strike at anything, but comprehension quickly dawned on human and Ganugamosh faces alike and people were rushing forward to lend assistance. William's dead weight was lifted from Colvin's shoulders – who had done this Colvin could not say – and the red-haired young man collapsed to his hands and knees, breathing raggedly, on the verge of passing out. He heard someone calling for water and immediately recognized the concerned voice of Ferdinan. He was rolled gently onto his back and gazed up into the Conquian's surprisingly gentle face. Without a word, Ferdinan pressed the spout of a water skin to Colvin's lips and cool, wonderful, life-giving water ran down his throat. He could have drank it all, could have drank rivers dry at that moment, but too soon Ferdinan pulled the skin away and delicately wiped the excess moisture from Colvin's chin. A very strange thought ran through Colvin's mind: *This must be what it's like to have a father.*

"Colvin," said Ferdinan, smiling, voice wavering and full of emotion, "es good to see you again."

Colvin laughed weakly. "Right back at you, Ferdinan."

"Es William–?"

"He's alive. He got tripped up and banged his head pretty good against a tree root, but he's got a good, strong pulse. I think he's just out cold." Ferdinan nodded, looking relieved. "Ferdinan, you should have seen it" Colvin said with as much enthusiasm as he could muster. "I got one of them. One of the goruks. With my sabre. It was a perfect thrust, Ferdinan. Just like you taught me. I got him right through the throat. You would have been so proud."

"I am proud, Colvin," Ferdinan said. "You fought bravely, and with great honor."

Colvin sat up slowly and took the water skin back from Ferdinan, lifting it to his lips and taking a long drink. He looked around disconsolately. The men and women huddled together there constituted barely more than a quarter of what had departed Tamendad that morning. "Is this it?" he said, finding the question difficult to ask. "Is this all that made it out alive?"

Ferdinan wore a pained expression. "Most of our men scattered into the woods, much like you and William did. Most of the ones you see here I managed to keep together, in the hopes of fighting our way out. How does the old saying go in Turish? Numbers have strength? Anyway, when Gunther and his people arrived, we were the first ones they found, probably because we were making the most noise. Together we drove the goruks back. Most of the credit for that must go to Gunther's people. Most of them remained with us once the goruks had gone, but some went out into the woods to search for more survivors. Gunther's party es the first to come back."

So there was a chance that more than this had survived. That should have consoled Colvin, gave him some glimmer of hope, but it didn't. It had taken the leadership of Ferdinan and the arrival of the Ganugamosh to save these thirty or so. William and he himself were alive only through the good fortune of Gunther showing up in time. Anyone left completely on their own would almost certainly have been slaughtered like cattle by now. A wave of hopelessness threatened to wash over Colvin, to consume him. He fought it back as best he could. Now was no time to brood, but the feeling did not relent easily. "So what's the plan?" he asked, trying to focus on something – anything – else.

"To get our asses outta here as soon as we know it's safe," came Gunther's rough voice in reply before Ferdinan had a chance to respond. The short blacksmith walked up and clapped a hand on Colvin's shoulder. "How you feelin'?"

"Like shit," Colvin answered.

Gunther nodded and grunted. It was so good to see Gunther again that the looming wave of hopelessness receded into the corners of Colvin's mind. Gunther looked to the men and women gathered together among the trees, and Colvin appreciated the lines of worry on Gunther's face for the first time. "Colvin, was…was Gangis a part of this?" Gunther asked in a voice close to breaking.

Colvin could have kicked himself for not thinking to tell Gunther earlier. "Oh, God, no, Gunther. Gangis stayed in Tamendad. He's safe."

"Sí," added Ferdinan, "we did not want to put all of our best soldiers in one place, in case something like this happened."

Relief spread over Gunther's face, and ten years seemed to melt away from him. He laughed, a deep guffaw that drew the attention of some of the other Ganugamosh, and said, "I bet that irked him somethin' terrible, havin' to stay behind. That boy can get downright sullen when he feels like he's bein' left out of somethin'."

Colvin nodded in agreement. Gangis could indeed be obstinate and bullheaded when the mood struck him. He took after his father in that regard. "He's been working his butt off at the forge while you've been gone," Colvin said.

"And he has fought fiercely and courageously when the need arose," Ferdinan added. "He has been a great asset to Tamendad."

"I knew he'd do me proud." Gunther said with unmistakable satisfaction. "Now that I'm back, I expect I might have to wrestle control of the forge away from him."

"I doubt it," said Colvin. "We've got a whole pile of weapons that we can't do a damn thing with waiting for you when you get back. We've done about all that we can."

"I'll take a look at 'em as soon as there's time," Gunther said, unable to hide his anxiousness to get back to work at his forge. Colvin wondered if Gunther had ever gone this long without doing some sort of metalwork in his life. "It'll be good to get back to work," Gunther added with a gleam in his eye.

"Tell me, Gunther," said Ferdinan, "however did you manage to reach us in time? Did you know what the goruks were planning? If your arrival had been delayed a quarter of an hour, I espect you would have found a forest full of corpses."

Gunther shifted on his feet a bit. Whatever the explanation was, it was clear he did not want to discuss it then and there. "Ah, well, there's a long story behind it, and this isn't the time or the place to start tellin' it. I'll explain everything when we're back in Tamendad. I hate havin' to tell a story twice, and I'm sure the Governor's gonna want to hear all about it too. Right now we need to be worryin' about getting' outta this forest as soon as the others get back. Do you think you can walk, Colvin?"

"I think so," said Colvin. Slowly, he tried to stand, and immediately fell back down again. His legs felt like they had turned to jelly.

"I'll take that as a no," Gunther said. "That's all right. Help's not gonna be hard to come by." He was definitely right about that. Ten different people volunteered to help him walk as soon as they heard he needed it. Over the course of the next half an hour, three more groups of Ganugamosh emerged from the forest, each group containing ten Ganugamosh and escorting a handful of humans. By the time the last group of Ganugamosh returned it had become clear that the goruks had withdrawn back to the cave. William had finally begun to stir by then, able to communicate fairly lucidly but incapable of doing anything more with his limbs than flail them around limply. One of the Ganugamosh, whom Gunther called Jorvin, slung William over his broad shoulders the same way a hunter might carry a dead deer. If William's added weight was any burden on him, Jorvin did not show it.

Finally, when all the Ganugamosh and all the survivors that could be found were gathered together, and when all the injured were given the necessary help, they began the slow, difficult journey back to Tamendad, wounded, dispirited, but alive to fight another day.

CHAPTER TWENTY-NINE

GANUGAMOSH

The journey back to Tamendad was quicker than the morning's had been, but only just. Even with help, Colvin could only manage to walk about half as fast as a healthy man, and it took effort to maintain even that. He found his legs again after about an hour and was able to walk unassisted, but still he could do no better than a meandering pace and he required rest and water often. During that same hour, William came fully back to his senses and regained the use of his limbs. He had a sizable knot on the side of his head and complained of a headache that hurt all the way down to his toes, but he could at least walk on his own, even if it was more slowly than Jorvin could carry him. And then there were the seriously wounded, those that had to be carried all the way back to Tamendad. Some of those would not walk under their own power for several days, if ever again. Gunther and some of the other Ganugamosh had fashioned pallets to carry them on, taking turns at dragging them. The pallets were well-made, and the Ganugamosh seemed well-suited to the work, but it was still enough of a burden to slow them down. Added to that were the numerous people with sprains or strains or some other mundane but hobbling injury. Even the people that were whole and well were quickly worn thin from helping all those that could not manage on their own. It was a slow, tedious, generally unpleasant trip. The only highlights were that there was no sign of goruks, and the rare but wonderful occasions when they met up with others who had managed to escape the goruk ambush.

After about two hours, Ian Morlocke found them. He had returned to Tamendad along with the rest of his scouts after informing Ferdinan that the goruks were on the move, but he had become concerned over not hearing anything after so long a time, and he persuaded Governor Chamberlain to let him ride back out to see what was going on. His initial incredulity over the Ganugamosh quickly subsided as Ferdinan recounted the ambushing of the ambush. It was immediately apparent that Morlocke blamed himself, and that no amount of argument would shift his opinion. It did not help matters that judging by the looks some of the soldiers were giving him, they felt the same way. Even Ferdinan, Colvin and William, who held Morlocke in the highest respect, had to admit that the soldiers had good reason to feel that way, at least in their own minds. Perhaps the whole thing could have been averted, perhaps dozens of lives could have been saved, if one of the scouts had managed to catch a glimpse of the second troop of goruks bringing up the rear. That was the thought going through the mind of Ian Morlocke, along with a fair number of soldiers, and it was such a persuasive thought that the fallacy within it was well concealed. The goruks had gone to great lengths to set up their ambush, greater lengths than perhaps even the Tamendaders. There was no way to know how long the second troop of goruks had waited to depart after the first had already started marching, but it would have been a comfortable cushion of time to be sure. They had to make it look like the first troop was all that was coming. The only way Morlocke could have discovered the ambush would have been if he had circled around to tail the goruks and been fortunate enough to catch a glimpse of the second group coming along from behind. Trying to circle a scout around the goruks to trail them would have risked detection, and detection would have doomed the ambush. Deep down, everyone knew that. Even Ian Morlocke. But that knowledge still wasn't enough to keep such an easy, persuasive idea from surfacing at least a little.

Morlocke wanted them to stop and rest while he rode back to Tamendad to fetch help, but Ferdinan and Gunther would have none of it. The goruks had withdrawn, but a withdrawal was not the same thing as a retreat. Each moment that passed was another moment that the goruks had to regroup, and no one particularly felt like sitting around and waiting for them to come back and finish the job. So Morlocke hastened back to Tamendad, and the soldiers kept moving, slowly but steadily. The sun had halfway buried itself in the horizon by the time the convoy from Tamendad found them. Governor Chamberlain had sent thirty armed soldiers and twenty horses. Ferdinan was torn as to how to feel about that. It was a blessing, almost a miracle, and it practically guaranteed that some of the seriously injured would get back to Tamendad in time to benefit from a healer's care when they otherwise might not have. On the other hand, Ferdinan appreciated that Tamendad could almost certainly not spare thirty guards, not with the number they were already doing without because of the ambush. Tamendad was seriously undermanned because of sending this many soldiers out. In the end, Ferdinan decided to be thankful and to do all he could to get these men and women – and

Ganugamosh – back to Tamendad as quickly as possible. The pallets were hitched to some of the horses, and the mounts that were leftover were given to soldiers with injuries that impeded movement. That meant both Colvin and William rode, while Ferdinan remained on his feet. Colvin protested this decision a bit, insisting that he was feeling better, but he eventually succumbed to reason and allowed himself to be helped into the saddle.

Governor Chamberlain was waiting at the southeast gate for them when they arrived, a little over an hour after the sun had gone down. The ghostly post-sunset illumination was barely enough to see by, and it cast Tamendad in a sickly blue glow that was a perfect accompaniment to the mood of the city. Word had spread about the events of the day, and spirits were low. The survivors rode back into a Tamendad dominated by silence, facing the somber stares of soldiers who were struggling with the guilt of feeling relieved that they had not been chosen to take part in the ambush. Out of all, though, the Ganugamosh received the most stares by far, and they did their fair share of staring back. It was plain that they did not know quite what to make of the buildings of brick and wood, or the bricked and cobbled streets, or the thick wall that separated Tamendad from its surroundings. Most of them looked something between astonished and uncomprehending, but a good few just shook their heads and a handful exchanged comments in their unintelligible language that did not sound very appreciative.

Healers from the church, headed by Patrum Albermarle, began tending the wounded as soon as they were safely within the city walls. The injured were escorted to the church, many of the less seriously wounded protesting all the way. These included William and Colvin, who insisted that they had urgent war council business with the Governor. Neither were in much condition to resist, however, as Colvin was so weary he could barely keep his head up in the saddle and the ache in William's head was such that the slightest sudden movement sent nauseating waves coursing through his body. Gunther and Ferdinan bade a hasty goodbye to Colvin and William, telling the two young men that their top priority was to let the healers mend them, then strode quickly to the Governor. Everyone else gave the men room. "Governor, we need to talk," Gunther said, the note of urgency in his gruff voice sounding quite out of place.

"I was just thinking the same thing, Gunther," the Governor replied. "Somewhere private. McRofaly should be waiting for us." And indeed he was, sitting at the round table built to seat ten in the meeting room on the third floor of the Governor's house, a look of anxiousness on his face and a black cat hanging limply over his left shoulder, purring softly.

Everyone paused when they saw the cat, but no one mentioned it as they took their seats.

"What the twist happened?" McRofaly asked anxiously, worriedly, before they had even made it to their chairs. "What went wrong?"

"Yes," said Governor Chamberlain, "that is exactly what I was about to ask."

Ferdinan sank wearily into his chair and sighed deeply, rubbing his eyes with his palms before beginning the story. He told the most of it, Gunther filling in points here or there. When it was told, McRofaly looked beside himself, though it was difficult to say whether it was because of the losses Tamendad had suffered or because the goruks had found a way to thwart his seemingly perfect plan. McRofaly's discomfiture was contrasted by Governor Chamberlain's icy-calm demeanor. The Governor had said not a word, made not a single sound, not so much as raised an eyebrow the entire time that Ferdinan and Gunther had laid out the events of the evening. After Ferdinan was done, the Governor sat in contemplative silence for a long moment.

"Our best plans are continuously undermined by the goruks," he said at last. His voice was cold and even, containing no hint of anger. What it contained, in ample amount, was contempt. "Their tactics have chipped away at our defenses and our resolve again and again, until now we find ourselves backed into a corner. We must be vigilant. We cannot afford to be tricked like this again."

"I don't think you have to worry about it happenin' again, Governor," said Gunther. "From here on out, the goruks aren't gonna waste their time with ambushes and sneak attacks and the hit-and-run crap we're used to from 'em. They're gonna come right at us, and they're gonna fight to the last one standing."

"Gunther, I mean no offense by this, " Ferdinan said, "but we have thought that before, and still the goruks adhere to their same old tactics. What makes you think es going to change now?"

Gunther actually looked amused. "Because now you've got about a hundred Ganugamosh with you." He sounded like he was explaining that things fell down when you dropped them.

McRofaly straightened in his chair. Sococo raised his head at the disturbance and looked around with droopy eyes for a moment, then licked his chops and went back to sleep. "It's true?" McRofaly asked excitedly. "You're really...a Ganugamosh?"

"In blood and spirit," Gunther replied. "I follow He Who First Carved the Way."

"HA!" McRofaly exclaimed wildly. "I knew it! I *knew* it! This is fantastic! I have so many questions..." McRofaly fell silent as the

Governor cleared his throat. This was neither the time nor the place, but a million questions were welling up inside McRofaly's brain, threatening to burst the dam of his restraint. Sococo, who had had quite enough excitement, jumped down from McRofaly's shoulder and curled up on the table in front of him. McRofaly absentmindedly stroked him behind the ears.

"Well, Gunther, your story is as good a place as any to begin, I think," said Governor Chamberlain. "Please enlighten us as to what these last few days have held for you."

Gunther cleared his throat and took a deep breath, giving the other three men at the table the impression that they were in store for a long story. "Well, you already know I followed the refugees to Tantera with the rest of Shield Division. As soon as we got there, I headed south. It was a rough trip. The goruks had scouts out everywhere, and I had to do my fair share of fightin' 'em off. The bastards killed my horse, too, which slowed me down. It took me about half the day to get to the cave, and I spent the other half tryin' to find my people."

"Your people live with the goruks?" McRofaly asked with a mixture of academic interest and simple incredulity.

"Bite your tongue!" Gunther replied. "Not if the world depended on it. We'd never be able to stand the stench. No, I told you before, that cave opens up into caverns that cover just about this whole island. You think the goruks take up all that space themselves? If they did, they wouldn't have to piss around with hit-and-run bullshit. There'd be enough of 'em to wash over all Glenisle like a wave, and crush any resistance we put up. There's other things down there than just goruks, and you'd better be thankful for that. Some of what's down there helps keep the goruks in check, most of the time."

"Like Ganugamosh?" said McRofaly.

"Well, that used to be the case," answered Gunther. "I've heard the stories about how the goruks started showin' up, around Isaac Dan's time and the foundin' of Tamendad. That was the first time in a long time that my people had any contact with goruks at all, and even then it was just a few skirmishes. The fightin' went back and forth for a while, and then the goruks were gone. Well, we thought they were, at least. Seems they just found themselves a decent hidin' place. But I'm gettin' ahead of myself.

"Like I said, it took me half a day to find my people. Ganugamosh are miners, mostly, stonemasons and metallurgists. We stay in one place only while there's good ore and stone to be harvested. If you find a good spot, that can be generations, but usually it means movin' around every few years. Well, it'd been a while since I'd visited, and all I found where the Ganugamosh had been the last time I was there was a bunch of hollowed out rock. I'd been expectin' that, really, but I had no idea where to start lookin'. I suspect I was halfway to the Highlands when I found 'em. They patched me up, and–"

"Patched you up?" Ferdinan interrupted. "Why did you need patching up?"

"Oh, well, things can get pretty hairy in those caverns. Lots of nasties down there. Lot of stuff that just lives to fight, more muscle than brains. And I'm not just talkin' about the goruks. There's stuff down there that makes goruks look like kittens. That's what I meant when I said there were things that kept the goruks in line, incidentally," Gunther added with a nod in McRofaly's direction. McRofaly was positively salivating over the prospect of adding a whole slew of questions about these *nasties* to his list.

"Well, anyway, I had to fight my way through a few holdups in my search for my people," Gunther continued, "and by the time I found 'em I was pretty hard up for a healer's care. But they took good care of me. Ganugamosh always take care of their own. As soon as I was up and around again, I met with the Ganugamosh-Morga–"

"The *what*?" asked McRofaly, Ferdinan and Governor Chamberlain simultaneously, McRofaly by far the most fervently.

"The Ganugamosh-Morga," repeated Gunther. "It's the title of our leader. Anyway, the last time I visited, Maerngrymm was Ganugamosh-Morga, but it turns out he broke the stone about ten years ago. Died of the sleepin' sickness, and his nephew Grumlah had assumed the title. At that point I knew I was in luck. I've known Grumlah since he was a pup. His family and mine go back generations. His dad was my biggest supporter when I married Gertrude. He was one of the only ones that argued I shouldn't be exiled from the homeland because of it.

"Grumlah was eager to see me, no doubt about that. The first thing he said to me when I sat before him was, 'Is it true?' Not, 'Good to see you, Gunther. How's the wife?' Not, 'Ganugamon favor you, Brother of the Stone.' No, just, 'Is it true?' And I could see in his eyes that whatever it was he was talkin' about, he was worried sick over it. So I asked him just what the twist he was talkin' about, and he said, 'Have the goruks attacked the lightsiders?' Well, I was floored. I tried to ask him how he knew about the goruks, but he wouldn't say a damn word about anything until I answered him. So I told him it was true, and that was why I'd come. I didn't wanna get right to it like that – there's just certain times in life that a man's gotta display a little tact and patience, and sittin' in front of the Ganugamosh-Morga is way up there on that list – but he was the one who brought it up. Then, finally, he started answerin' some questions.

"Turns out the goruks had carved out a place for themselves in a spot that no one in their right mind would choose to call home, and they'd just been lyin' low all this time, livin' on bat shit and fungus. Well, you are what you eat, I guess. Anyway, the goruks had recently started comin' out of hidin', sneakin' up above ground, spyin' on lightsiders. And apparently they'd got themselves a new leader, too, a goruk that calls himself Kor."

"We have had communication with him," Ferdinan said, spitting the words like they left a bitter taste in his mouth. He explained about the unfortunate end Edgar had met, as well as the ill fate of Franklin and Rodney. When Ferdinan was finished, Gunther looked ready to chew nails.

"Scurvy, no-good, pig-lickin' sons of whores," growled Gunther, slamming his fist on the table. "Give me a pickaxe, a branding iron and a quarter-hour alone with Kor, and I'll make him curse his bitch of a mother for bringing him into this world, that contemptible, goat-sucking piece of..." Gunther hesitated, looking around the table at the stares sent his way, and reddened a bit. "Sorry," he mumbled. "Temper..."

"Es okay," said Ferdinan. "Es pretty much how we all feel about him. Please go on."

Gunther forced himself to take a deep, calming breath before continuing. It was difficult keeping his anger in check. He had gotten to know Edgar pretty well during the ride to Tantera. "Yeah, well, like I said, Kor's leadin' the goruks now. Has been for at least five years now, from what I heard. At least, that's how long it's been since they've started pokin' their heads outta their shit-smellin' corner of the Under. Grumlah's been keeping a close eye on 'em, see. At first he thought they were plannin' on attackin' the Ganugamosh, try to drive 'em out of their homes and take it over for themselves. Ganugamosh are a damn sight better at pickin' places to live, as you can probably imagine. Well, an attack on the Ganugamosh never came, and as the years passed it became pretty clear what the goruks were plannin'. They'd set their sights aboveground. Grumlah wasn't sure where, but he had a pretty good guess that it would be Andoria, Tantera or Tamendad.

"Recently the goruks have been more active than usual, more trips to the surface in bigger numbers. And they've been heard talkin' about what they call the reclaiming. Then I showed up, and Grumlah knew it was all really happenin'. And he wasn't pleased."

"So he pledged assistance?" asked Governor Chamberlain, a note of incredulity in his voice. It did seem a little far-fetched that the Ganugamosh, who had never had contact with Tamendad – or any other human city – would lend aid at the drop of a hat. Aid had been hard to come by from Tamendad's own neighbors.

"Well, not so simple as that, no," replied Gunther, scratching at his beard. "It's complicated. Normally, Ganugamosh don't meddle in human affairs. We're a people that value our privacy. We usually don't mess in anyone else's business, and we expect everyone else to stay outta our own. But just before I arrived in the homeland, Grumlah made a discovery that brought him into the middle of this."

"What was the discovery?" Ferdinan asked, unconsciously scooting onto the edge of his seat. Gunther certainly did have a knack for telling a good story.

"That's the most complicated thing of all," Gunther said. "At least, it's the most difficult thing to explain to anyone that's not of the Ganugamosh. But here goes. Legend has it that before the Great Burden, the Ganugamosh had knowledge of metalworking and stonemasonry that puts what we know now to shame. That knowledge was lost during the Great Burden, during the Gamugamosh's fight for survival. Part of that knowledge, accordin' to legend, was the creation of *Lugosh-Alogar*, World-Forges, forges that harness the heat from the world's core. *Lugosh-Alogar* could produce the finest steel the world's ever seen, in half the time of any other forge. There're stories of whole cities being crafted from *Lugosh-Alogar*, before the Great Burden. When the Ganugamosh were at our peak, there was nothin' we couldn't do.

"But like I said, that knowledge was lost during the Great Burden. Only a handful of *Lugosh-Alogar* have been found, and every single one of 'em is across the Melteric, on the Continent. Well, under it, really. Until now."

A lingering silence fell over the room as the members of the war council exchanged glances. "You found one?" McRofaly asked at last, excitement plain in his voice. He had never heard legends of *Lugosh-Alogar* – he felt relatively certain that no human ever had before – but a subject so shrouded in the mysterious fog of lost history intrigued him to his core.

"Yeah," Gunther said, rather anti-climactically. "Yeah, we found one," he added, "but the goruks found it first." Wide-eyed stares met the short blacksmith, and he worked hard to avoid meeting them. "The *Lugosh-Alogar* is what's been supplyin' the goruks with weapons for the war. Ganugamon only knows how they found it, or when. They had slaves down there churnin' out those dirty morchas day and night. From what Grumlah's spies told him, they've got enough to outfit more than two thousand standin' soldiers."

"Could they honestly have that many?" Ferdinan asked in a voice that was barely more than a whisper. He was putting great effort into maintaining his outward calm, but there was no masking the underlying sense of pleading in his voice, or the hint of fear.

"Oh, I seriously doubt it," Gunther replied. "Not much chance of goruk numbers gettin' that high. No, goruks seem to have the knack for limitin' their own population. They're violent as all get out, always have been, and they'll fight each other as soon as they'll fight anyone else, if they start to get on each other's nerves. Of course, this Kor seems to be keepin' 'em pretty focused, but still I'd be downright shocked if he could manage to have anywhere near two thousand warriors to command. I don't know what the actual number is, but Kor would be doin' an amazin' job if he managed half that."

Another heavy silence. The prospect of possibly facing an army of one thousand goruks did not lift the spirits of the other war council members nearly so much as it did Gunther's, it seemed.

"So did Grumlah pledge assistance in the hopes that we will defeat the goruks and your people can take back the World-Forges?" asked Governor Chamberlain. That didn't seem to make any sense either.

"Oh, no, we've already taken back the *Lugosh-Alogar*. We took it back as soon as we found out about it. I was a part of that raid." Pride was thick in Gunther's voice, and his eyes had a far-away look to them as he remembered reclaiming what rightfully belonged to the Ganugamosh. "The World-Forges are back in Ganugamosh hands, where they belong," he continued. "But that doesn't undo the damage that's been done. Kor used the *Lugosh-Alogar* to make weapons to use against Tamendad in the war. You gotta understand, the *Lugosh-Alogar* are sacred to us. Ganugamon himself taught us how to make 'em and use 'em, if you believe the stories. And I do. *Lugosh-Alogar* are as much a part of the Ganugamosh as our beards are. They're a part of our history. Part of our souls. And they've been used against Tamendad. That wrong is marked on all our hearts, on Grumlah's heart most of all. Grumlah had to make amends for it, so he sent as many Ganugamosh warriors as he could spare, and since I'm a Tamendacer he put me in charge of 'em. So, Lord Governor, we're here to serve."

"Your people are an honorable people, Gunther," said Ferdinan, his voice thick with reverence. "Es an honor to fight alongside you."

"Just doin' what we can," Gunther replied. "No more, no less. That's the way of the Ganugamosh."

"I would greatly enjoy hearing more about this Ganugamon you speak of," said Ferdinan. "He sounds like an estraordinary individual. But now there are more pressing matters. How did you learn that Kor was planning to ambush the ambush?"

"Well, that was dumb luck, really," Gunther said, tugging at his beard.

"See, Grumlah's got spies out tryin' to figure out what Kor's up to, while Kor's got out spies of his own, makin' sure that nobody else in the Under is plannin' on makin' trouble for the goruks. Well, yesterday one of our spies managed to sneak up on a couple of theirs. Kor never sends out goruks alone, see. It's always two at a time, at least. Well, goruks are impatient bastards, and when they don't have anything to kill they usually set their tongues to flappin' when they're bored. Kor's own spies let word slip of the ambush, talkin' about how much it pissed 'em off that they got stuck on watchman's duty while everyone else was off killin' humans. When Grumlah got word of what the goruks were plannin', he knew we had to act. And we've already been over the rest."

"But how did the goruks discover what we were planning?" asked McRofaly in a pained voice. "It should have been foolproof. They didn't even give the felled trees a second glance when they passed through the clearing two days ago."

"As to that, I don't know," Gunther said with a sigh. "Could it've been leaked somehow? Did…did Edgar know about the ambush? Or either of those two scouts?"

"No," said Governor Chamberlain, "we kept word of the ambush secret until we drafted volunteers for it the night before. No one who knew about it ever came into contact with the goruks except for Don Ferdinan, Lord William and Colvin."

Ferdinan sat up a bit in his chair. "You did not speak of the ambush to anyone else, did you McRofaly?"

McRofaly straightened indignantly. "Not a word!"

"Of course," Ferdinan replied. "No offense, but you understand I had to ask." McRofaly nodded curtly in return.

At that moment, the door flew open without a knock. A member of the Governor's personal guard strode quickly into the room, excited and out of breath, and exclaimed one word. "Goruks!" The war council was already on their feet. Ferdinan, who already had his sabre halfway out of its sheath, slammed it back home.

"How many and where?" Ferdinan demanded.

"The first report was fifty, give or take," the guard replied quickly, "and they're heading for the northeast gate."

Ferdinan cursed. "Geoffery, stay here," he said with a glance in the Governor's direction. "Your safety es of the highest importance. You as well, McRofaly." Gunther was already out the door, and Ferdinan hastened to catch up with the short blacksmith in the hallway. As they descended the stairs together, Ferdinan said, "You know, Gunther, I heard a very interesting saying the other day, one that I had never heard before. *Trial by fire*, I believe it was. Are you familiar with it?"

"Yeah, Ferdinan, I believe I am," Gunther said with a sneer.

❖   ❖   ❖

They were met by a sea of insanity at the northeast gate. A handful of goruks had managed to get past the bonfires and the barricade and enter Tamendad, while a few Ganugamosh had achieved the same goal in the opposite direction. Mostly, though, the battle was taking place right at the gate itself, where goruks, Ganugamosh and Tamendaders were all scrambling over obstacles to reach each other. The battle was still fresh when Ferdinan and Gunther arrived, but already any semblance of military strategy was lost on both sides. The goruks were incensed, consumed with a battle rage rare even for them, railing against Ganugamosh with all their strength and practically ignoring the Tamendaders. The Ganugamosh were dodging and weaving, interspersed in the fighting, calling out what were unmistakably taunts and jeers in that unintelligible language of theirs. More than two Ganugamosh fighting side by side was a rarity. And as for the Tamendaders, at first glance it seemed that they had all just simply gone mad. They threw themselves into the attack without any structure or form, more of a lynch mob than a military unit, but by God they fought with an intensity that they had never displayed before. They fought like men who had lost all that they had, save the overwhelming thirst for revenge.

There was neither time nor opportunity to bring structure to the Tamendaders' defensive stand, and the Ganugamosh seemed to know what they were doing, so there was little for Ferdinan and Gunther to do except just jump headlong into the fray. Gunther disappeared as soon as they were in the battle, ducking, dodging, jumping, weaving, doing all the things that infuriated the goruks. Ferdinan moved through the battlefield, going wherever he was needed, which was wherever the goruks outnumbered the humans, but always he kept his eyes peeled for Kor, for the opportunity to finish their duel. But it soon became evident that Kor was not leading this assault. In fact, it did not appear that anyone was leading it. The goruks were simply throwing themselves against Tamendad, fighting tooth and nail against whatever got in their way, actively seeking out Ganugamosh targets. They most certainly did not look like they were planning to run away any time soon.

Soldiers were arriving from the other gates with each passing moment. Arrows began to fly as archers found safe spots from which to pick off goruks here and there. Still the goruks showed no signs of breaking their attack. As Ferdinan danced among them, turning scimitars aside with his parrying dagger, his sabre making short work of any goruks that came too close, he knew that Gunther had spoken the truth.

The goruks had finally abandoned stealth and trickery in favor of overwhelming brute force. Even as he stood defending Tamendad from this onslaught of goruks, Ferdinan felt his stomach tighten with a sense of foreboding that had nothing to do with this assault on the town. This tide could be turned; of that Ferdinan felt confident. These goruks were blind and stupid with rage, walking into their own deaths as quickly as Tamendaders and Ganugamosh could dispatch them. Ferdinan's sense of trepidation was directed toward the future, based in the certainty that both sides in the war were approaching the final, deciding confrontation after so long and agonizing a buildup.

Kor sat enveloped in a darkness so complete even his eyes could not pierce it. He came to this place sometimes, to think, to rage, to be alone. It was far from his people's place in the Under, isolated from the rest of existence by the eternal night that ruled here.

The silence was as complete as the darkness. So far as Kor could tell, he was alone for miles around. His thinking place was deep underground, not as deep as the forges but deep enough that no living thing would ever choose to make its home here. In fact, Kor suspected the forges might be the nearest sign of civilization.

The forges. That was one of the things that had driven Kor to his thinking place. His forges. His no more. The filthy Ganugamosh had risen up like phantoms from the past to steal them from right under his nose. With those forges, the Ganugamosh had stolen his people's only means of producing weapons for *Abuneth*. Their supply chain had been broken, and by the Ganugamosh of all people. Generations without so much as the sight of one of their scuzzy little beards, and now they had reappeared in an attempt to sabotage *Abuneth*.

It was not as though the forges were necessary for taking Tamendad. Kor had more than enough morchas to carry his warriors through their objective. But *Abuneth* did not end with the fall of Tamendad. That city was merely the first stage in a much larger campaign. *Abuneth* would not be complete until the goruks had reclaimed not only what had once been theirs, but what had always been meant to be theirs, that which Kor's people had never been given a rightful chance to claim because of paleskin ambition and greed. That was the dream of *Abuneth*, Kor's dream. But reality was proving to be considerably more complicated than the dream. The forges were lost. Worse, the Ganugamosh were now standing with the paleskins and defending Tamendad. That more than anything was what vexed Kor. The loss of the forges was regrettable, but there were other forges to be found and taken. The paleskins had been weakened. Their chieftain was dead, felled by Kor's own morchas. They were ready to crack, susceptible to a killing blow. The ambush in the forest should have been enough to crush them at last, but instead the Ganugamosh had bolstered the paleskins in both numbers and spirit. Now Kor found himself back at the beginning for what felt like the hundredth time since starting this war. Worse, the warriors were livid. Some had already defied Kor's order and attacked Tamendad as a mob out of their hatred for the wretched Ganugamosh. That rag-tag band of would-be mercenaries had no doubt met their bitter end by now, and accomplished little besides perhaps killing a handful of Ganugamosh and costing Kor more warriors he could not spare. His army, which had seemed so grandiose, so unconquerable at the beginning, was now beginning to dwindle. He still outnumbered the paleskins, but he was going to have to take great care and exercise the greatest caution to win this war. He could not succumb to his instincts, driven by hatred of the Ganugamosh, to attack Tamendad in an all-out direct assault, relying on sheer numbers and brute strength to carry his side to victory. That would work if the felling of Tamendad were the end goal of *Abuneth*, but *Abuneth* was more. *Abuneth* demanded stealth, demanded that Kor not reveal himself fully until the last paleskin city was toppled. If the dream of *Abuneth* were to be realized, Kor needed fear and uncertainty to remain his allies on the battlefield for the duration.

Now more than ever Kor needed a plan, and he knew it had to be a damn good one. Because Kor also knew that no matter how much he loathed them, no matter how much he cursed their names, no matter how much he did not want to admit it, a hundred Ganugamosh were worth a thousand paleskins. That was what had driven Kor to his thinking place, and that was what Kor sat thinking about now, consumed by darkness.

"May I entreat a word, Kor?"

The impenetrable darkness was a blessing, for it prevented the ardah from seeing Kor jump nearly a foot off the ground in his discovery that he was not alone. The ardah could move like a cat, and Kor hated being snuck up on. "Have you had another vision you would like to share?" Kor asked, his voice cold and laced with venom.

"The Ancient Ones reveal what the Ancient Ones decide," came the reply from out of the darkness. "It is not my place to question the will of the Ancient Ones. Nor is it yours."

"Of course," said Kor with a smirk the ardah could not see. It felt like he had heard that line a thousand times. "The Ancient Ones had their reasons for not mentioning that a hundred Ganugamosh would be in that forest with the paleskins when they sent you their vision. Perhaps it was a practical joke. Do you suppose the Ancient Ones have a sense of humor?"

"I will not abide blasphemy, Kor."

"Be gone, then," Kor snapped with a growl. "You find me with patience worn thin and close to breaking. Take your leave of me before I say – or do – something we both regret."

There was a long silence, broken when the ardah said, "I bring a message, Kor."

"What is this nonsense?" Kor asked tentatively. "The ardah is no messenger."

"Who can say with any certainty what the ardah is under your rule, Kor?" the ardah sighed. "That which has endured for generations among our people, you change at your whim. Under you, even I question my own role among our people. Besides, it is a most important message. I alone knew where to find you, and even if such were not the case, I alone would dare approach you when you come here to brood."

"I am not brooding," Kor snapped. "I am thinking."

"A fine distinction, to be certain. Will you hear the message?"

"Tell it."

"The mountain men from the south are marching an army toward Tamendad."

Kor was on his feet in an instant, and pain exploded in his hand as he slammed his fist into the wall of the cave. His growl echoed throughout the darkness for what seemed an eternity. He could feel the blood flowing from his knuckles, and smell it, even if he could not see it. "Now do you see?" Kor demanded. "Now do you understand? Not only have the paleskins formed alliance with the Ganugamosh–" Kor hesitated to spit at naming them, "–but now they bring the paleskins from the south into this as well. Do you see their trickery? Their deception? We must crush them, now, quickly. Our window swiftly closes, ardah. We cannot hold back, waiting passively for signs from below. The time is upon us. Join me. Together we will lead our people into a new era of prosperity, wealth beyond our wildest dreams!"

A heavy sigh from the darkness was the ardah's only reply at first. Kor clenched his hand out of frustration, forcing more blood to flow from his opened knuckles. The soft patter of his blood dripping against stone was the only sound to be heard. At last, the ardah spoke.

"With every step you take, you leave a wake of change behind you, Kor, and you leave our people struggling to maintain a hold on what we have always known. You murder the old ways without thought of what you are killing. Would you murder me as well? Perhaps, if it suited your needs. And yet now you ask me to support you, to pledge to you like one of your young, impassioned warriors. I am too old, Kor. Too old, and too tired. You have exhausted me. All my energy is spent trying to preserve what little I can under the new ways you usher in."

"And so here we have it, then," said Kor, softly yet menacingly. "Our impasse has come fully to the surface, for both of us to see. For you are devoted to the old ways, while I seek to make things new for our people. Why do you resist the changes I seek, ardah? Can you not see that my aim is the betterment of all our people? Even you can prosper under my rule. My dream is only to take back what was rightfully ours from the beginning. Will you not join me now, as this conflict draws to a head?"

"I cannot join you," came the reply, so quickly that the words clipped Kor's. "I am ardah. My role is intercessor between this world and the world of the Ancient Ones. I cannot become involved in matters such as these. You have brought this conflict upon us, and it is your burden alone to lead us out of it, or to lead us to our doom. Which it will be, only the Ancient Ones know. But know this, Kor: I do not support you, but neither do I oppose you. I will abide your rule, as I have abided the rule of those who came before you. And I will do all that I can to ensure that our people survive this war you have brought down upon us. I will find what place I may to do what I must, while you lead our people away from all they have ever known."

There was silence long after the ardah's words faded into darkness. At last Kor spoke, saying, "What was that last part, again, ardah?"

"I will find what place I may—"

"To do what you must," Kor interrupted, speaking in a voice that sounded far away, "while I lead our people away..."

For a moment there was silence again, and then Kor's laughter echoed through the Under.

It was in all actuality one of the toughest battles the Tamendaders had fought throughout the entire war. The goruks were relentless, never backing down. They fought through injuries that would have normally sent goruks scurrying for cover of darkness. They forced even the sturdy Ganugamosh back, fighting their way inch by inch past the carts and wagons and other obstacles that blockaded the northeast gate, coming farther than any previous goruk force had managed – save, of course, the one they had opened the door for. Though their push never really threatened to break the defenders' line, the fact that the goruks had managed to gain entry to Tamendad – at least technically – unnerved the soldiers. The goruks had indeed fought to the last warrior, and when only that lone goruk remained it still fought as though it could not see the bodies of it comrades strewn about on the streets. It met its death at the head of a Ganugamosh's axe, and went raving and slavering into the afterworld.

Now Tamendad was quiet again, the streets inside the northeast gate strewn with the carcasses of goruks and debris, splattered red with the blood of friend and foe. The bodies were already being piled by the guards – the goruks in a haphazard heap, the humans and Ganugamosh laid delicately and peacefully in a row. Gunther stood a few feet away from the pile of goruk corpses, wiping the blood from his axe, casting an eye all around. Ferdinan was overseeing the cleanup effort, giving orders in that way of his that demanded compliance without coming across as too overbearing or imperious. The Conquian had fought well, and as for that Gunther was entirely unsurprised. His style was nothing at all like how the Ganugamosh were trained to fight, much more rhythmic and flowing than anything a Ganugamosh would ever deign to attempt, but it suited him well. And he fought with heart. In the end, Gunther Moragun respected anyone you could say that about.

"Dad!" Gangis's voice cut through Gunther's musings like a knife. Gunther turned and saw his son rushing toward him, and his heart leapt into his throat. Father and son embraced in a tight hug that lasted a long while. When they finally pulled away, both found their eyes misted and glassy.

"I came as soon as I heard," Gangis said in a rush. "I was at the forge. I heard you were back, but you were meeting with the Governor so I just waited at the forge for you. I didn't even know we were under attack til just now. I would've come sooner…"

Gunther placed a firm hand on his son's shoulder, and Gangis fell silent. "Son, it's okay," Gunther said. "There wasn't time to raise the alarm. But everything's fine. We made short work of 'em."

Gangis looked all around, saying nothing. His eyes were wide, his mouth slightly open in a look of stupefaction. At first Gunther thought his son was focusing on the bloody aftermath of the battle, the corpses of the goruks piled haphazardly, but it became apparent that Gangis's attention was fixed not on the dead but upon the living. He eyed the Ganugamosh all about him, then turned his gaze upon his father. The sparkle of incredulity and wonder was in his eyes. Gangis gestured vaguely toward the numerous men who looked so much like his father. "Dad," he said, "are these…?" His question trailed off into silence. Father and son stared at each other, neither able for the moment to find quite the right words.

"These are our people, Gangis," Gunther said at last. "The Ganugamosh." Gangis said nothing, just stared in wide-eyed wonder at the enigmatic people who represented his father's side of the family.

Physically, every last one of them could have passed for Gunther's own brother. Not one stood taller than five feet. Hair color ranged only from dark brown to black, or the grayness that comes with age, and all wore their hair either braided or tied back. All had beards to at least their bellies, and all wore well-tailored but austere clothes of simple, neutral tones. But all this sameness with his own father underscored the fact that they were entirely different from anyone else Gangis had ever met. These people were truly from a different world, one which Gangis had only heard stories about and which – although he was now ashamed to admit it – he had never really felt an interest in learning about. Until now. Now that he was surrounded by them he burned with a desire for knowledge about them, for an understanding of this side of his bloodline. And yet he stood silent, unable to ask the multitude of questions that were welling up within him. He stood surrounded by Ganugamosh, and yet in a strange way he felt more separated from them, more cut off, than he ever had.

Gunther threw an arm around his son's shoulders. "C'mon, boy," he said, the growl of his voice at odds with the grin on his face, "there's someone I want you to meet." Gunther pulled Gangis along more than guided him as they made their way toward the Ganugamosh. It was just about all Gangis could do to put one foot in front of the other, though had he failed to do so his father would have probably just dragged him along behind. Together they approached a Ganugamosh standing off to himself. Streaks of black still showed in his gray hair. He was the same height as Gunther, which meant that Gangis stood half a head taller. The lone Ganugamosh eyed Gangis with interest as he approached, looking him over in a way that was not unfriendly but made Gangis feel like a cow being inspected at market nonetheless. Gunther spoke to the Ganugamosh in the strange language Gangis sometimes heard his father use, and Gangis sorely wished that he had paid more attention on the occasions that Gunther had tried to teach it to him. Whatever Gunther was saying, it was making the Ganugamosh's eyes light up.

"Gangis, this is Wulfric," Gunther said, and Gangis was a bit startled at the sudden switch back to a language he knew. "If anything'd happened to me while you were growin' up, Wulfric would've seen to it that you were raised right."

Gangis looked at Wulfric. Wulfric was smiling warmly at him. Gangis smiled back. "I'm pleased to meet you," Gangis said, feeling extremely awkward. Wulfric stepped forward and placed his hands upon Gangis's shoulders. Gangis returned the gesture. This custom, at least, he knew. Gunther still used it frequently as a gesture of greeting.

"Ganugamon favor you, Brother of the Stone," Wulfric said in a heavy, muddled accent, obviously struggling with the Turish.

Gangis, unable to come up with any response he felt was appropriate, said, "Thanks."

"C'mon," Gunther said, clapping Gangis and Wulfric on the shoulders. "I've got a quarter-keg of stout in my basement, and we've got a load to discuss. I've let you go way too long without learnin' about your roots, Gangis."

Gangis just nodded, smiled eagerly and walked with his father and Wulfric toward what he knew was a new chapter in his life.

CHAPTER THIRTY

DAMMAUGH OFF TO WAR

Colvin awoke on a cot in the church. A damp cloth was pressed against his forehead, and he was naked save for a loincloth. He was bathed in soft, filtered sunlight. For a moment he lay motionless, blinking his eyes to clear the haze of sleep from them. The world reluctantly came into focus. It took Colvin a moment to realize where he was. At first he thought it a small room with a very high ceiling, but now he realized what he first took for walls were actually just curtains drawn up to afford some privacy. He was in the healers' hospital in the back of the church, and he was not alone. The curtains had been drawn up around two cots, and in the one opposite Colvin's, William was stretched out and sleeping, also nearly naked. Between the cots, propped back against the small table the healers used to prepare their elixirs and poultices, was a straight-backed wooden chair, and on that chair sat Jonathan Stuart-Camen, his chin on his chest, snoring lightly.

Colvin was in no hurry to get out of bed. He wasn't in pain – not exactly – but every muscle in his body felt sore and lethargic, and he had a faint headache. It was like a hangover without the benefit of actually having been drunk. But even in his discomfort Colvin had to admit he felt a hundred times better. The healers had taken good care of him. They had dressed his wounds and bathed him. Then they had given him a tonic that tasted like honeyed water and put him to bed. Twice during the night they had woken him long enough to pour more tonic down his throat, which had resulted in some very peculiar dreams. It had done its job, though, taking him from the verge of collapse – the healer's words – and leaving him with only a mild hangover.

Colvin sat up slowly and stretched, finding that a good deal of the soreness departed his muscles as he did so. The movement roused Jonathan. He sat up quickly, bringing the front legs of his chair down on the stone floor with a loud *clack*. He looked first to his son, then to

Colvin. Then he smiled.

"Oh, Colvin, good morning," he said, wiping his bleary eyes with the back of his hand. "How are you feeling?"

"Better," Colvin said quietly, so as not to wake William.

"Good, good. Patrum Albermarle was concerned it might take you a couple of days to recover from the exhaustion. He said you worked yourself right to the brink."

"Well, whatever was in that tonic worked wonders," Colvin said. "Gave me some weird dreams, though. I dreamed that goruks were surrounding the city, and the wall was just falling down right in front of them to let them in."

Jonathan gave Colvin a grave look. "The goruks *did* attack last night," he said. "It was right after you were put to bed. They tried to hit the northeast gate again. But there's nothing to worry about. They were put down quickly, mostly by Gunther and his...ah...*kin*. William and I were talking about it when the healers woke you to give you your medicine during the night. You must have overheard us."

Colvin nodded blankly. "Was Kor with them? Or that...*other* one?"

"What other one?"

"The one McRofaly saw cutting the hearts out of the dead goruks outside the wall."

Jonathan shook his head. "No, neither of them were there."

"They were in my dream," Colvin said. "Both of them."

"It's all right, Colvin. With all you've been through, it wouldn't surprise anyone to hear you're dreaming about goruks. I think we all are."

"Yeah," said Colvin after a pause. "So what were you and William doing up so late? I'd have thought the healers would've sent him to bed too."

"No, they wanted him to stay awake for a while. If you fall asleep after a blow to the head, apparently you might never wake up again. Did you know that?"

Colvin shook his head.

"Nor did I, but the order came from Patrum Albermarle himself, and he has forgotten more of the healer's art than most healers are ever fortunate enough to learn."

Colvin glanced briefly at William's sleeping form. "So he's going to be all right, then?"

"He's going to be fine," Jonathan said, trying and failing to mask the raw emotion in his voice. "Patrum Albermarle said that his is the sort of injury that, if it doesn't kill you, you're fully recovered in no time. He'll be as good as new as soon as he's rested. And I've got you to thank for that."

Colvin and Jonathan looked at each other for a long, silent moment.

"I heard about what you did, Colvin," Jonathan said. "What you did for William. He and Ferdinan told me most of it. The rest I picked up from the stories Gunther's people are telling. I am forever in your debt. If there is every anything you need – anything at all – just ask, and if it is within my power it will be done."

Colvin shifted uncomfortably on his cot. "I didn't really do anything, Lord Stuart-Camen," he mumbled.

"Yes you did, Colvin. You brought my son back to me."

"No I didn't," Colvin said more forcefully. "Gunther saved William, not me. We'd both be dead if it wasn't for Gunther. I had nothing to do with it."

Jonathan shook his head. "You stayed with him. You protected him when he was defenseless. You had no way of knowing that Gunther would show up when he did, and still you were going to take on all those goruks by yourself when you could have just run away and saved yourself. You bought my son time, and that saved his life. For that I can never thank you enough."

Colvin blinked. "You're welcome," he said. After a short pause, and eager to change the subject, he added, "I'm gonna get dressed and get out of here, I think. William needs his rest."

"It's okay, I'm up," came a groggy voice from the other cot. William slowly sat up and placed a hand gingerly on his forehead. The knot had already gone down considerably, but he still winced when he touched it.

"How are you feeling, son?" Jonathan asked. "Do you need anything?"

"I'm fine," William replied. "I'm hungry enough to eat a horse. Where are my clothes?"

"Under your cot. As are yours, Colvin. Do you need any help putting them on?"

"Um, no, thanks," Colvin replied. "I can manage." That was the first time in Colvin's life that someone had suspected he might need assistance getting dressed. A few women had offered to help him get undressed before, but that was a different matter altogether.

After William and Colvin had both dressed, and after repeated assurances by William that he felt fine, Jonathan left them to return to his duties as Captain of the Day Guard. William and Colvin were eager to leave the church, but they took the time to light a candle in the sanctuary and express their thanks to Patrum Albermarle for taking such good care of them.

"It's gonna be downright impossible to get our schedules turned back around to night duty," Colvin said to William as together they emerged from the church into the brilliance of the midmorning sunlight.

"Who's to say we're even going back on night duty?" replied William. "The goruks have obviously gotten over whatever reservations they had about attacking during the day. I would say there's a good chance that Ferdinan and Governor Chamberlain will decide to increase the day guard."

Colvin sighed and ran his fingers through his hair, fighting a losing battle to untangle the knots that had accumulated in it since last he had washed it. "God, let's not think about that right now," he said. "We just got released from the healers. Let's give ourselves a quarter of an hour to unwind and relax. That's all I need, just a quarter of an hour to not think about goruks or killing or war."

"That sounds good to me," said William. "What do you want to do?"

Colvin pulled his fingers free from the tangled mess of his hair and said, "I'm going to have to have a bath at some point, but first I want something to eat. I'm starved. I've not had a bite of decent food since yesterday morning." As his own words sank in, Colvin had to chuckle at himself. He had gone days without a square meal before. He had subsisted on dry twigs that cut his mouth and wild berries sour enough to blister his tongue. He had once eaten nothing but moldy tree bark for three consecutive days during a particularly nasty winter. Yet now going twenty-four hours without sitting down at a proper dinner table was enough to make him feel famished. The abounding comforts of Tamendad were making him soft. Strangely enough, he felt not one bit guilty about it. The way he looked at it, he had endured more than enough hardships to earn himself a bit of softness. Besides, there were plenty of things keeping him from growing too soft. A war for control of Tamendad, for example.

"I'm with you on that one," William replied. "I could really go for some steak and eggs. Let's drop by the Governor's house and see if Gertrude is still in the kitchens."

But Gertrude was not still in the kitchens, as they both soon discovered. She was, in fact, sitting beside her husband in a small garden in the town square, as was Gangis and about thirty Ganugamosh. They were all sitting on the ground in a disorganized cluster, and they all had their attention focused intently upon Gunther, who was speaking rather animatedly about something Colvin and William could not quite overhear. The thought of a meal departed the two young men for a moment. They swapped a curious glance with each other and stole a bit closer so that they might catch a listen.

"And so, Ganugamon," Gunther was saying, "knowing he had been betrayed by Thindrel, took up his hammer and descended into the World Under the World. 'Let Thindrel think I am defeated,' he said. 'Let him think he has me out of his hair. I will bide my time and regain my strength and use his overconfidence against him.' And Ganugamon left the Land of Light and made a place for himself in the eternal night of the World Below. His wounds were deep and his strength was all but gone. A hundred days he rested in the darkness, and still he lacked even the strength to stand. 'And so it comes to this,' said Ganugamon at length. 'Here I will die, for I cannot even find water for myself.'

"And then it was that the dragon found him, and Ganugamon, whose eyes could see even in the darkness, said, 'So at last you have come to end me. Well, be of haste, for all you do is exchange a quick death for a slow one.' But the dragon was still and did not strike, saying, 'I told you when next I saw you I would kill you. But how was I to know then that this would be how I found you, weak and pitiful? And I do take pity on you.' And the dragon picked up Ganugamon gently in his mouth and took him deep into the World Under the World, deeper than anyone who had ever stepped foot in the Land of Light had been, and they came at last to the dragon's den. There Ganugamon found it was light, for the very rocks glowed with heat and flowed as a river.

"The dragon cared for Ganugamon, and after another hundred days Ganugamon found his strength again. Once Ganugamon was healed, the dragon came and laid his head at Ganugamon's feet and begged Ganugamon to kill him. 'What is this?' Ganugamon asked in his astonishment. 'It is a poor patient who murders his nurse as soon as he is well. What reason have I to slay you?' The dragon responded, 'I have broken my pledge. I swore to kill you when next I saw you, yet I have not done it. I am an oath-breaker, and my life is forfeit.'

"Ganugamon replied, saying, 'Your oath was made in haste and anger, gentle dragon, and only a fool would follow out such an oath. You are no fool, and so when the time came to make good on your promise you faltered, and I am much the better off for it. If your life is forfeit, I refuse to claim it over so paltry an offense. Stand, dragon. You have spared my life, and I now spare yours.' And the dragon wept at Ganugamon's great kindness and boundless wisdom, and said, 'Now I see you for who you are, oh great Ganugamon, and I name you friend. Forever will my kind and yours enjoy peace and prosperous relations, and I will help you all that I can, even in your revenge on Thindrel Bloodtongue.'

"Now Ganugamon flew into a rage at hearing the name of his betrayer and smote the walls of stone with his hammer, and even the mighty dragon was cowed by the anger of Ganugamon. Such was

Ganugamon's fury that when he had calmed, he found his hammer warped beyond repair, and his heart was filled with sadness. 'I am weaponless,' he said in his despair. 'How now might I bring my vengeance to bear on Thindrel's head? Surely not with hands bare.' The dragon then became most excited and said, 'I have pledged aid to your quest for revenge, Ganugamon, and this pledge I made not in haste. You will make a new weapon, a weapon unlike any the Land of Light has ever witnessed, and I shall help you. We will make a forge together, you and I. We will make a forge that draws upon the perfect heat that flows here, at the Heart of the World.'"

And so on the story went, and Colvin and William stood listening, transfixed by it. They had never heard Gunther talk like this, more like a priest delivering a sermon than a grizzled old blacksmith. Together they stood there listening to the story of Ganugamon and his quest for revenge against Thindrel. As with all good stories it was impossible to say exactly how long it took to tell. The telling seemed to last for hours while it was going on, but once it was over it seemed to William and Colvin that they had always known the story, that they had heard it in their cribs as infants, and had just spent a moment reminiscing on it.

Together Ganugamon and the dragon, whose name was never given, created the first *Lugosh-Alogar*. When it was ready they collaborated on the making of the perfect weapon, which turned out to be the very first axe. The dragon even donated one of his own scales to the effort, which according to the story made Ganugamon's axe the strongest weapon ever forged. Exactly why the dragon had sworn to kill Ganugamon, William and Colvin never found out, nor exactly how Thindrel had betrayed him. But after yet another hundred days Under the World, Ganugamon's axe was finished and he set out to kill Thindrel Bloodtongue. The dragon flew Ganugamon to Thindrel's palace, which was set atop the highest mountain in the world. There Ganugamon found Thindrel sharing a feast with the people to whom he had apparently betrayed Ganugamon, and all sorts of madness broke loose. The dragon took on Thindrel's dinner companions while Ganugamon and Thindrel fought an epic battle that lasted – indeed – one hundred days. Ganugamon was victorious. When it was over, he cast Thindrel's body down from the mountain, and where it landed, no living thing would ever grow again.

"Thus is told the tale of *Ganugamon and Thindrel Bloodtongue*, being the first part of *Ganugamon and the Dragon*," Gunther said to conclude, and as soon as it was done a visible change came over him. It was as though the gruff, cantankerous Gunther both William and Colvin knew was coming back to his senses after being possessed by the spirit of a long-dead orator. "Now somebody pass me a skin," he growled in a voice even scratchier than usual. "I'm 'bout all dried up." Gertrude handed her husband a water skin and he drank deeply from it. Gangis applauded eagerly. The other Ganugamosh nodded in approval and pounded their fists against their thighs. "All right now, fellas," said Gunther, "I'm all told out. I'm goin' home and gettin' some sleep." Gunther stood, groaning as he stretched out his muscles, and dusted himself off. Slowly, somewhat reluctantly, the crowd of Ganugamosh began to disperse. Soon all that remained in the little garden in front of the church were Gunther's family and Wulfric.

"Well you boys are certainly lookin' better," Gunther said when he noticed Colvin and William. "How you feelin'?"

"Not bad," said Colvin at the same time William said, "Bit of a headache."

Gunther introduced them to Wulfric, who stumbled his way through the greetings in Turish. Before William and Colvin ever had a chance to get out a word about food they found themselves invited to breakfast at Gunther's home. "It'll be a nice change to cook for five instead of hundreds," Gertrude said.

"Actually, Mom, make that four," said Gangis. "I'm going to go with Wulfric." Both Gunther and his wife did their best to restrain their grins as they said that was all right. As they watched their son and his godfather walk away, Gertrude and Gunther both slid an arm around the other's waist. Gunther actually locked on the verge of tears.

McRofaly had not slept. His hair was a disheveled mess; his mind was the same. He sat alone in the Governor's library, his only company the various tomes, scrolls and codices splayed across all the flat surfaces of the room. He had been there since the moment the Governor's guard had announced the return of the goruks the evening prior. When Ferdinan and Gunther had departed the meeting room to go and save Tamendad, McRofaly had done likewise. But whereas men like Ferdinan and Gunther proved their mettle on the battlefield, McRofaly demonstrated his worth academically. The Conquian ambassador and the Ganugamosh smith flew off to save the city from the latest wave of attack. McRofaly was playing for much higher stakes.

McRofaly had a problem. Really, all of Tamendad had a problem. And it was the sort of problem that could really make things go a bit fig shaped. It was also the sort of problem that McRofaly alone, out of the entire population of Tamendad, was qualified to solve. So Tamendad's problem had become McRofaly's problem, and McRofaly did what McRofaly always did when confronted with the sort of problem he alone was qualified to solve: he studied.

Men of intelligence, such as McRofaly, were aware not only of the various subjects of study they had mastered through the exercise of their prodigious mental acuity, but also of the nature of intelligence itself. And the more you had, the better you understood it. McRofaly had, by all reasonable methods of reckoning, more than his fair share, and as such, he was aware that what the common layman called *intelligence* – usually with the same sort of uncertain, reverential inflection used when discussing tenuous, mythical constructs like sanctity – was, in fact, a dualism. What the general populace would lump together under the standard banner of intelligence was really two distinct, though interrelated, faculties: intellect and knowledge. Intellect was power of the mind, the ability to reason coherently and derive logical conclusions. Knowledge was book learning, education, the possession of information. With insufficient intellect, knowledge was trivial. With insufficient knowledge, intellect was impotent.

Of the multifarious thoughts flittering through McRofaly's mind – and there were always many when he studied – one of the ones further toward the back was a consideration of the misconception many people had of academicians as stodgy do-nothings of questionable worth to society. On their scouting expedition for the ambush, Colvin had leveled the phrase *know-it-all* against him with a derisive tone, intending it as an insult. It was not the first time McRofaly had encountered the phrase, but it made no more sense now than it had upon first hearing. There was in McRofaly's mind no loftier, more desirable goal than knowing it all. To a man of sufficient intellect, infinite knowledge was tantamount to infinite power.

A lack of knowledge was what vexed McRofaly presently. That was why he had thrown himself so wholeheartedly into study. There was some bit of information that he was missing, and that missing bit had rendered him paralyzed. Somehow, without any seemingly rational explanation, the goruks had known about the ambush. Not simply known about it, but had a knowledge of it sufficient to devise and implement a counter to it. They knew what was coming, and they were ready for it, and McRofaly was still, after a full night of contemplation, completely at a loss as to how.

With no other plausible alternatives, McRofaly was forced to consider the possibility. And the possibility terrified him.

For the first time in enough hours to lose track of, the door to the Governor's library opened, exhuming McRofaly from the depths of his musings. Don Ferdinan entered, glanced around the room, glanced at McRofaly, and smirked. He said nothing, not wanting to disturb, turning his attention to the shelves that lined the walls, seeking out something or other. McRofaly was glad to see the Conquian, since it meant that he had survived the latest skirmish with the goruks.

"Good morning, Don Ferdinan," McRofaly said.

Ferdinan spun on his heels with sufficient urgency to wrest McRofaly's attention fully away from the book that laid open before him. The Conquian's eyes were large, his stare incredulous. What had captured his attention so forcefully was not McRofaly's salutation, but the fact that the merchant tactician had said it in Conquian.

"You speak Conquian?" Ferdinan implored.

To drive home his affirmation, McRofaly responded in the language. "I am fluent in all the Continental tongues. I find Conquian to be little more than a dialect of Prima Tonce."

"Come with me!" Ferdinan exclaimed, lunging for McRofaly and seizing him by the arm, pulling him from his chair and out the door of the library. At first McRofaly wanted to protest, but he had never seen Ferdinan act with such urgency, and to be honest he was ready to take his leave of the written word for a while. All his night of study had taught him with any certainty was that the secret he was missing was most likely not to be found in any of the Governor's book.

Ferdinan dragged McRofaly by the wrist down to the kitchens, which was about the last place McRofaly expected to be dragged. Ferdinan deposited McRofaly into a chair at a smaller table on the outskirts of the hall, then moved with all deliberate haste to one of the undercooks working breakfast duty.

"Red wine. Now."

The undercook had obviously not been expecting this during breakfast, but the fierceness of the request coupled with the importance of the man who made it compelled him to fulfill it quickly. Ferdinan accepted the goblet full of red with the curtest of nods, the returned promptly to McRofaly's table. He mounted the chair more than sat down in it. His look was frenzied, and it made McRofaly most uncomfortable to be on the receiving end of it. He took a sip of wine.

"Now, talk."

McRofaly blinked his eyes beneath a furrowed brow. "About what, exactly?"

"I have no preference," replied Ferdinan. "Talk about the weather. Recite the oracles. Question the purity of my lineage. Just do it in Conquian."

McRofaly's stared. "What is this about?" he asked.

The look that Ferdinan gave McRofaly was sufficient to convey the magnitude of the pressure that bore down upon the Conquian's shoulders, but he explained it in words regardless. "I am miles from home, in a strange land with a stranger language, the ranking commander in a war with questionable prospects for success. I am cut off, isolated, orphaned. I am alone. But when I talk to you...when you talk to me...I am home. I need this moment, to quicken me. So, I say again, talk."

And so, with a subtle grin and a sense of compassion, McRofaly began to talk.

As soon as they were all back at Gunther's house, Gertrude immediately set to work in the kitchen. The three men gathered around the table over mugs of mulled cider. Mostly Gunther and Colvin just discussed what had been going on at the forge, and together Colvin and William filled in Gunther on some of what he had missed while he had been away. To William's delight Gertrude served up heaping plates of steak and eggs and fried potatoes. Colvin and William ate ravenously, and William found that his headache had been at least partially due to hunger. Once the plates were about halfway cleared, the act of eating became less frenzied and again conversation broke out.

"That was quite an audience you had, Gunther," Colvin said between bites. "I didn't know you were such a storyteller."

Gunther chuckled. "I've been known to spin a yarn every now and again."

"Especially when you've had a couple of mugs," added Gertrude.

"Hush, woman," said Gunther. "Never a man was made whose lips weren't loosened after a drink. Anyhow, that whole thing in the square was spur of the moment. Last night Wulfric and I sat Gangis down and started tellin' him a little of his people's history. Somehow word got out that we were tellin' some of the old legends, and pretty soon just about every Ganugamosh in town that could speak a lick of Turish was showin' up at my door. None of 'em have ever heard the legends told in anything but our own language, see. Well there was no way I was gonna fit all of 'em in my house, so we decided to go to the town square."

"You were out there telling stories all night?" asked William.

"Once I got started they wouldn't let me stop. They kept askin' for another story as soon as the last one was told. I knew I had to bag it in when they asked for *Ganugamon and Thindrel Bloodtongue*, or they'd want to hear all of *Ganugamon and the Dragon*, and it's got fourteen parts."

"Where did you learn all these stories, Gunther?" asked William in amazement.

"Every Ganugamosh grows up hearin' the legends, William, just like every Antrelican learns about Hidalgo Sanctus. The stories are part of our history. They're our heritage. Any Ganugamosh can tell 'em. I just happen to know how to tell 'em in Turish, which around here is apparently good enough to draw a crowd."

"I've just got one question," Colvin said around a mouthful of steak.

"What's that?" said Gunther.

"Why'd the dragon swear to kill Ganugamon in the first place?"

Gunther broke out into guffaws of laughter. "I'm glad to see I tell a good enough story to hold the attention of a couple of young men like yourselves," he said. "But I've been tellin' all night, and like I said, I'm all told out. Especially when we're talkin' about a story I just got done tellin'. Ask me again sometime."

"All right," Colvin said dejectedly and returned his attention to his rapidly disappearing breakfast.

After the dishes were cleared away Colvin shared a pipe with Gunther while William had a second mug of cider. Then Gunther went to bed and Gertrude returned to the kitchens at the Governor's house to oversee the preparation of lunch for the day guard. William and Colvin were left on their own. They walked together out of the trade district, surrounded by closed up storefronts and merchants' apartments bearing black funeral swaths. The two of them did not feel very much like sticking around. They passed *McRofaly's Magnificent Keepsakes and Aureate Regalia.* Colvin was going to suggest stopping in to say hello but the doors and shutters were closed and no one looked to be home.

"So should we grab those baths now?" asked William as they neared the outskirts of the trade district.

"God, no, I'm way too full," said Colvin, rubbing his stomach. "I need to walk for a while until my food settles."

"If I didn't know any better," said William, "I'd think you were trying to avoid getting anything done today."

Colvin grinned sheepishly and shrugged his shoulders. "Well, it's not really like we've got anything to do. I mean, technically we're off duty right now. I've got a feeling I won't be getting my reading lesson today, and I don't know about you but there's no way I could sleep right now. So the way I look at it, if we feel like taking a walk, what's stopping us?"

"Okay, where do you want to go?"

"I don't know. Everywhere I look it's death and war. I wish we could just get out of town for awhile."

"Okay," said William. "Let's get out of town."

Colvin gave him a suspicious look. "We can't."

"Sure we can. You're in charge of Fist Division, at least in name. I'm in charge of Sword Division, and a nobleman besides. Do you really think anyone's going to refuse to let us out if we press the issue?"

Colvin was silent a moment. "You know, William," he finally said, "I don't think I've ever seen this side of you before."

"I don't let it out much," the young nobleman replied. "Now come on."

It turned out to be surprisingly easy to get outside the city wall. They barely had to pull rank at all. The hardest part turned out to be clambering over the obstacles barricading the northeast gate, but soon that was behind them and they found themselves alone on the beach. They walked together in silence, two friends enjoying each other's company without feeling the need to muddle things up with unnecessary conversation. They watched for dolphins, though it was late in the year to see them, and they breathed deeply of the salty-sweet sea breeze. It was strange; it was exactly the same air they breathed in Tamendad, but out here it smelled sweeter, felt somehow less heavy. The early autumn sun glinted off the rippling waves of the Taeran. Seagulls coasted lazily overhead, occasionally giving them reason to be quick on their feet. It was a good day. Yet Colvin felt troubled. At first it was a vague and indistinguishable sense of unease in the pit of his stomach that he misidentified as indigestion, but soon it began to grow and formulate itself into something tangible and within only minutes had made the transition from Colvin's stomach to his conscious mind. He missed Tamendad. This realization was made all the worse by the accompanying realization that what he missed was not the war-torn Tamendad he and William had just left, but the Tamendad he had stumbled across mere weeks ago. Mere weeks and a lifetime ago. He was a different person now than he had been on the day he had cleared the hill and discovered the city by the sea. He had long since given up trying to fight it or deny it. He had changed, and he was pretty sure there was no going back to the way he had been before. He had friends and acquaintances and a handful of romantic interests now, the vast majority of which were at the moment up the coast in Tantera. He had ties that bound him to Tamendad and the people who lived there, for better or worse. And he felt no desire to leave, to run away and wash his hands of his responsibilities. That more than anything else was proof that he had changed. All he wanted was his Tamendad back, and the source of all his emotional discomfort was the knowledge that he couldn't have it.

You're just reevaluating your life. It's a natural thing to do after facing the genuine prospect of death, he thought, and wasn't entirely sure where the thought had come from. Still, he found some small, strange measure of comfort in it.

"Do you believe Gunther's story?" William asked suddenly, drawing

Colvin's thoughts outside of himself.

"What?"

"Do you believe there really was a Ganugamon and a Thindrel and a dragon and all that?" It was obvious William was having some difficulty making up his own mind on the matter.

Colvin mulled the question over a moment. "I don't know," he said, disappointed by the anti-climactic sound of his own words. "Who can say? We know the world-forges really exist, and they had to come from somewhere. And is it really so far-fetched to believe there was once someone named Thindrel who double-crossed someone named Ganugamon?"

"But a dragon?"

Colvin shrugged. "Who knows what the dragon really was? Stories have a way of getting twisted around so the heroes look larger than life. For that matter, who's to say there weren't really dragons back in the day? A month ago I probably wouldn't have believed stories about goruks."

"So you believe it, then?"

"Well I'm not saying that, exactly. I think it's possible, but I don't know if I think it's true or not. I mean, do I really believe Hidalgo Sanctus rose from the dead, for that matter? I guess it could've happened, but who knows for sure?"

William was silent for a while thereafter. The two of them stopped and threw stones into the sea, then just stood and watched the water. After a very quiet quarter-hour, William finally said, "I want to go up on my hill."

"Come again?" asked Colvin.

William pointed to the hill overlooking Tamendad from the southwest, the tallest hill around, the hill from atop which Colvin had discovered Tamendad, and said, "Melissa and I go on picnics up there. Sometimes I think of it as our hill. I want to go up there. Do you want to come with me?"

"Sure," said Colvin.

They waved to the lookouts atop the city wall as they passed and began climbing the hill. It was not so steep that they had to use their hands, but they were frequently doubled-over as they went, throwing their weight forward to keep their momentum going up. About halfway to the top William suddenly reached out and clasped Colvin's shoulder, which nearly sent him back down the hill the hard way. Colvin did not even have time to curse. "Do you hear that?" William said in a near-panicked whisper. Colvin stopped dead in his tracks and listened. He heard it then, too: a low, warbling sound. Slowly and steadily the sound began to grow.

"Is it a horn?" Colvin asked.

William shook his head uncertainly and strained to listen. Then suddenly his eyes lit up and the hand he still had on Colvin's shoulder began to shake with excitement. "That's no horn," he said. "It's pipes!"

Together they sprinted up the hillside, their feet not carrying them nearly quickly enough. They crested the hill, and then they saw it. Making its way over and around the hills from the south was an army, and it bore the colors of the Clan MacDugal. The sound of Highland pipes was clearer atop the hill, as was the accompanying sound of drums, which they had not been able to hear while climbing. The army was still too far away to clearly make out individuals, but both William and Colvin knew that at the head of the procession rode Gregor MacDugal, making good on his promise.

"There are *hundreds* of them," said William. "Hundreds!" Colvin said nothing in return, and William almost didn't notice when he made to run down the hill toward the marching Highlanders. William quickly reached out and stopped him, and Colvin did not look pleased about it. "Wait!" William said hurriedly. "If the lookouts see us start sprinting down the hill out of sight they might think something's wrong."

A pained look flashed across Colvin's face, his desire to rush down and welcome Gregor conflicting with the logic of Williams words. "Right," he said, logic winning out. "Let's go tell them." William nodded, smiling like a madman, and together they ran down the hill toward Tamendad, yelling at the top of their lungs that the Highlanders were coming.

Gregor drew up rein as he crested the final, tallest hill before Tamendad. Liam, Gabrahn and Wallace rode with him, as did Carney Gruer. Behind them the pipers blared *Dammaugh Off to War* to lift the spirits of the men who had marched a very long way in a very short time. Down below, the gates of Tamendad stood open and people were amassing before it to welcome the Highlanders. Gregor breathed a deep sigh of relief. Tamendad still stood. His nightmares of returning to find it a graveyard overridden with goruks had proved at last to be nothing but dreams. Yet war had taken its toll on her. She looked a ghost town, a shell of her former self, and the faces of those who waited just inside the open gate, while presently alight with excitement, showed the unmistakable signs of stress and fatigue. The town still stood, but she was on her last legs.

"Back at last," said Wallace from over Gregor's shoulder. "And nae too soon, from th' look of it."

"Aye, ye spoke true there, lad," said Gregor without removing his gaze from Tamendad. "If she were a lass I'd say she needed a week o' rest and some good cooking t' put meat back on her bones. What do ye make of it, Patrum Gruer?"

Carney was quiet for a moment, his attention focused not on the town but upon the many freshly dug graves just outside it. "We shall all do well t' beseech th' Face o' Consonance for fortitude," said the priest at length. "I believe we all have more than a fair share o' work cut out for us before this struggle finds an end."

Gregor and his lads found no comfort in these words. Gabrahn, Liam and Wallace exchanged unsteady glances. Gregor, meanwhile, kept his eyes locked on the town where his brother had died. "All right, lads," the big Highlander said, "let's be about it, shall we?" Then he turned his head and called out to his men, his voice booming over the pipes and the drums. "Step lively, lads! Remember, this is what we came all this way for!"

The procession of Highlanders started down the hill. The colors of the Clan MacDugal flew proudly. The pipers and drummers kept a brisk pace in their playing to match that of the march. Gregor was pleased to find that two of the first faces he saw belonged to William and Colvin. The big Highlander dismounted as he reached the gate, as did every other Highlander with a horse upon seeing this, and he motioned his two young friends over, walking into Tamendad with them. Colvin and William both immediately threw their arms around Gregor's neck in a hug, and with his bulk he easily accommodated both of them.

"It's so good to see you again, Gregor." said William, his eyes glassy.

"Tough up there, lad," said Gregor. "There shall be plenty o' time for tears later, and time alone shall tell whether they be o' joy or sorrow."

"Sorry," said William, wiping his eyes with his sleeve.

"Gregor, how many did you bring?" asked Colvin as he watched the Highlanders continue to stream through the gate into Tamendad.

"Two score and three hundred marched from Duerhein four days gone," said Gregor, "but a score and three we lost along th' way."

Colvin spent a moment doing the math. "Three hundred and seventeen?" he said to himself, and he sounded like a boy who had awoke on the first day of Summerfeast to find that he had not received the bow he had asked for, but instead a much better one. But no one was listening to him.

"Was it goruks?" William asked in a hushed voice.

"Aye, 'twas, and there's a story t' tell in all o' that, but 'tis a matter best saved for th' war council. Where are th' Governor and—"

"Gregor!" exclaimed Colvin. Gregor turned to find the red-haired young man standing frozen in mid-word, mouth agape, eyes wide, pointing into the crowd of Highlanders pouring into the town. It was impossible not to see what he was pointing at. In the midst of the tartan throng was a man who stood head and shoulders above even Gregor, with whole hams for biceps and a tree trunk for a neck. On his back he wore what had to be the largest sword in the world, simply because it was inconceivable that a sword bigger than that could ever be made. If Gregor was a giant among men, then this man was a giant among giants. William tore his wide eyes away from the behemoth of a man and looked at Gregor.

"Hamish?"

"Aye. He and Angus were fast friends. They learned t' farm t'gether."

"But I thought you said he would never leave Rebecca behind."

"He dinnae," said Gregor. "She was fast with Angus as well, and she's nae too bad with a sword or bow, truth t' tell."

"I've gotta get me one of those!" said Colvin, paying zero attention to what William and Gregor were saying. He was pointing at the sword hanging on Hamish's back. Gregor just laughed.

"Colvin, it's as big as you are!" said William. "You couldn't even swing it."

"I could learn," insisted Colvin.

"Start with a claymore, lad," said Gregor. "'Tis more yer size. Now back t' th' matter o' th' war council. Where are th' Governor and Ferdinan?"

"We sent word to them when we saw you. They're probably on their way," said William.

"Aye, well, let us meet them halfway, shall we? There's much t' discuss, and I need t' know what I've missed in m' absence."

As they walked away from the southwest gate together, leaving Gabrahn, Liam and Wallace the hopeless task of giving the inflow of Highlanders into Tamendad some semblance of order, Colvin said, "You know, now that you and Gunther are back, the war council's all back together again." After a brief hesitation he added, ruefully, "Well, almost, anyway."

"That statement raises a pair o' questions, lad," said Gregor. "First, where has Gunther been, and second, what do ye mean, almost?"

William and Colvin exchanged a glance. After filling in Gunther on the goings-on of Tamendad earlier that morning and now facing the prospect of doing the same for Gregor, they both were starting to understand what Gunther had meant by *all told out*. They took it in turns together, explaining Gunther's journey to the cave bit by bit, one picking up where the other left off, doing the best they could to remain true to what the short blacksmith had told them. When they finally reached the part of the story where Gunther and the Ganugamosh turned the tide of the goruk ambush, Gregor said something that left them both speechless.

"Aye, so th' wee bastard finally came clean about being a 'Nugermosh?" he said.

"You knew?" stammered William, whose eyes were just as wide as Colvin's.

"Oh, aye, I've known for years, e'er since Gunther came t' Duerhein looking for work as a smith. I was a wee lad, then, mind ye, but I had heard m' da tell stories o' th' little men under th' mountains. There's been a strain o' 'Nugermosh living in th' mountains 'round Duerhein for generations, as th' stories go. But 'twas easier t' pull a bull's back tooth than get Gunther t' talk about his people. It took me three years just t' get it out o' him that he was a 'Nugermosh at all. And he asked me nae t' speak of it t' people who dinnae already know. Highlanders would nae much mind, o' course, but he felt it easier that way."

"Well shit," said Colvin, "and here I've been thinking I'm special because he told me what he was before he left for the cave."

"He told you before he left?" said William in an accusatory tone of voice.

"Lad, if he told ye what he was, after knowing ye for a matter o' weeks, I would say that marks ye special for sure," said Gregor. "Now what o' this almost business? Who are we missing from th' council?" And for the second time that day William and Colvin told of how Captain Jefford had met his end. A solemn look spread across Gregor's face as he listened to the tale, and when it was finished he bowed his head and sighed. "A good death for a good man," he said. "We should be so fortunate that he be th' last good man we lose."

They were approaching the church now, and before Colvin even had a chance to respond to Gregor's statement they noticed a man coming down Tamendad's main street toward them. It was Ferdinan, and he was running. Gregor's face nearly split in two, he was smiling so broadly, and when the short, wiry Conquian finally reached the big, burly Highlander it was impossible to tell who was hugging who harder. "Ah, lad, good t' see ye," said Gregor as he broke the hug with Ferdinan. "A sight for sore eyes, ye are."

"The same goes doubly for you, Gregor," said Ferdinan. "Praise God you return to us safely. You have been constantly in my prayers. Your coming es a good omen."

"Aye, well, as for that, lad, let us nae be too hasty. 'Tis a relief t' be back, and t' find th' town still t'gether, nae doubt there, but nae all th' news o' m' coming is good."

"It sounds as though you have a story to tell, *compagno*."

Gregor nodded, and there was something unpleasant in the way he did it, something that raised the hair on the back of Colvin's neck.

"Well then," said Ferdinan, "the war council es assembling as we speak. Let us go and hear this story you have to tell."

CHAPTER THIRTY-ONE

DANCE BEFORE THE DARKNESS

"Thank God you have returned to us safely, Gregor!" said Governor Chamberlain, rushing forward to clasp the big Highlander's hand as he entered the meeting room. Gregor returned his smile, but it was markedly less enthusiastic.

"'Tis good t' be back, Governor, but th' pleasantries shall have t' wait for later. We have much t' discuss." Gregor took a seat at the table built for ten. McRofaly was already seated, his trusty *Compendium* lying in front of him on the table and his trusty cat lying on his trusty *Compendium*. He had the look of a man who had been up all night. Ferdinan took the chair next to Gregor, and the Governor the one next to Ferdinan. When William and Colvin were also seated, Gregor looked around the table and said, "Where's Gunther?"

"On his way," said Ferdinan. "We sent word for him as soon as we heard you were back."

"He was up all night telling stories in the town square," added William. "He just went to bed about an hour ago. That's probably what's keeping him."

"God help whoe'er ye sent t' rouse him," said Gregor.

It was a matter of mere minutes before the door of the meeting room opened and a very tired and grumpy-looking Gunther entered. The short blacksmith collapsed into a chair and said, "Glad you're back, Gregor. Let's get through this so I can get some sleep."

"Right," said Gregor, stifling a chuckle. "Down t' business. I have brought three hundred and seventeen souls with me. Out o' that, about an even three hundred would be ready t' charge th' field if th' goruks attacked right now. Th' rest have injuries, but naught so bad they would nae be useful at least for defending th' gates from within. That's th' good news. Th' bad news is that we marched from Duerhein two score and three hundred strong, and those that were lost, were lost t' goruk blades."

"You were attacked?" asked the Governor.

"Nae rightly. Th' goruks we came across we discovered by chance. They have scouts out in th' countryside, probably t' get wind of another shipment like th' one from Tantera. 'Twas we who did th' attacking whene'er we stumbled across goruks, and we put all we had into killing th' lot o' them. But those green bastards are as crafty as they are cowardly. In th' end, we let a couple o' them slip away."

Ferdinan's brow furrowed. "So what you are saying es—"

"The goruks know we're here," said Gregor.

"Maybe this won't be so bad," said McRofaly. "Our forces have to at least be close to equaling the goruks', and now Kor knows it. That might intimidate them enough to make them back down."

"Normally I'd agree with you," said Gunther. "The last thing goruks want is a fair fight. But Kor's gotta still be pretty pissed about the ambush goin' wrong, and I'd bet it won't sit well with him that Gregor's brought the Highlanders into this, either. We'd be hopeful borderin' on foolish if we let ourselves think we might still get outta this without a fight."

"Aye, and I shall tell ye plain, I've got a load o' people who shall be feeling pretty sore if they came all this way and dinnae get a chance t' kill something," added Gregor. "Now permit me a question, if ye would. Who exactly is this Kor fellow ye mention? William and Colvin filled me in on Gunther's return and Captain Jefford's passing, but aside from that I'm still clueless about what I've missed."

"Of course, *compagno*," said Ferdinan. "Forgive us for not informing you of everything earlier, but we were all caught up in the escitement of your return. Let us esplain." And they took most of the next hour to tell Gregor every noteworthy thing that had happened while he was gone. It was Ferdinan who explained who Kor was, going into great detail on the fate of poor Edgar of Shield Division and making the Sign of the Compass repeatedly throughout. Governor Chamberlain proffered the blood-scribbled note written by Kor's hand. Gregor read it several times, then crumpled it in his fist so tightly that his knuckles turned white and the veins on his forearm were clearly discernible.

"Let them come and try t' claim their prize," he said through clenched teeth, "and they shall discover th' wrath o' th' Clan MacDugal."

"All right," said Governor Chamberlain once Gregor was brought up to speed, "as of this moment Tamendad is on high alert. With Kor knowing what he's facing, we can be sure that the next time we face a goruk attack it will be the battle that decides the war."

"If Kor's nearly as hot as I'd guess he is, that attack's as likely to come in daylight as in darkness," said Gunther.

"We'll need to rearrange the guard schedule," said McRofaly, "to even out our defenses." William and Colvin exchanged a look.

"Agreed," said Ferdinan. "Gregor, since your kinsmen are already accustomed to being awake during the day, I want to put them on day watch. Sword and Fist Divisions will back you up."

"Sure thing," said William and Colvin.

"Good," replied Ferdinan. "It looked to me like most of the town was awake and coming out for a look at the Highlanders, so es just a matter of not letting some of them go back to bed. The constabulary and Shield Division will maintain the night watch."

"What about us?" said Gunther.

"That decision I leave in your hands, Gunther. You and your people have demonstrated that you are of the greatest aid when you are allowed to decide for yourselves where and when you are needed."

Gunther swelled with pride upon hearing this. "We'll be ready for anything," he said.

"The scouts need to be made aware of what's going on," said McRofaly.

"Agreed," said the Governor. "They will be informed as soon as they check in. And we will need to make arrangements to quarter your kinsmen, Gregor. Under the circumstances, I doubt we will have much problem finding space for them."

"I would appreciate that, Governor," said Gregor. "O' course, m' lads and I shall be staying in th' Crown Rose, so 'twould be helpful if we could keep th' rest close by there."

"Of course. Filing up the inns in the trade district will be the easiest way to quarter that many people. That leaves only one issue unresolved. Master McRofaly, have we yet discovered how the goruks knew our plans for the ambush?"

McRofaly tensed visibly when the Governor called on him. "Nothing so far," he admitted, slumping a little. "As far as I can tell, it's just as likely it was a lucky guess as anything else."

"No, they knew," said Gunther. "They knew what you were plannin', when, and where."

"But the question es how," said Ferdinan.

"As to that, I haven't even a suspicion," McRofaly lied.

There were surprisingly few complaints from the militiamen about going back on day duty, owing to the fact that everyone was excited about standing guard with the Highlanders. Gregor, Colvin and William found the Highlanders in more or less the same disorganized condition they had left them, though a good number had migrated from the southwest gate to the church while the war council had been meeting. When they arrived at the church, William and Colvin immediately noticed Patrum Albermarle talking with a priest they had never seen before who was wearing considerably simpler robes than the Tamendader priests. "Ah!" said Gregor upon noticing their stares, "o' course. All th' bustle has made me forget m' manners. This is Patrum Carney Gruer, priest o' Duerhein and m' own personal religious adviser when I'm fortunate enough for him t' spare some time for me. Carney, this is William o' th' House Stuart-Camen, and this is Colvin."

"Th' light o' God shine 'round ye," Patrum Gruer said with an endearing smile. "Dinnae listen t' Gregor, m' lads. I always make time for anyone who has need o' counseling in matters religious. Gregor's told me much about ye both. At th' moment m' attention's turned t' assisting th' good Patrum Albermarle and his healers in tending th' injured, but I hope I have th' chance t' get t' know ye personally."

Colvin and William shared the sentiment, then left the Highlander priest to his providential business.

The majority of that day's watch, if it could really even be called a watch, consisted of getting the Highlanders settled into Tamendad's inns, which were filled to capacity for the first time during the war. Wallace spent the afternoon picking the lock on the front door of the Crown Rose. He was overheard around the four o'clock hour muttering under his breath in frustration about how Torrance Mayhew should have had the common courtesy to leave it unlocked anticipating Gregor's return, and something unfavorable about Mayhew's mother and a donkey which everyone assumed he did not really mean. By five o'clock the lock was picked, the door was open, and the Crown Rose was once again open for business. The Highlanders and the militiamen finished their shift without incident. Most of the militiamen immediately retired for the evening, being exhausted from their move from night duty to day. The Highlanders, however, had no intentions of turning in early.

That night a miracle happened. The trade district of Tamendad was once again filled with lights and music. The sound of bagpipes and pipe flutes, drums and voices drifted over the city like an ethereal haze. No sound so festive and cheerful had been heard in Tamendad for what seemed like an age, but tonight the celebration was such that an onlooker would have thought the war had already been won. Gregor had the wine cellar and liquor cabinet of the Crown Rose emptied, and there was a barrel at every street corner for revelers to refill their empty mugs. Fiddlers played in the cobbled streets and pipers played on rooftops, and a dozen different songs were sung completely out of time and tune by the masses, mostly wearing tartan plaid, who made their way from alehouse to alehouse and inn to inn. Most of the Tamendaders did not know what to make of the festivities, but the sounds of merrymaking were a comfort that uplifted the spirits of the night watch.

A few members of the day guard joined the Highlanders in their revelry. These were mostly the younger militiamen, and Colvin and William were among them. William initially expressed some hesitation, but Gregor eventually overcame the young nobleman's protestations and soon they were sitting together at a table in the main dining room of the Crown Rose with three different varieties of Highlands whiskey laid out in front of them, tapping their feet in time with the music of the pipers and fiddlers on the balcony. Ferdinan arrived shortly after sundown, and Gregor had the finest bottle of wine in Mayhew's cellar waiting for him. He accepted it graciously, and soon he was holding a full goblet and dancing a Conquian flatfooted dance with a pretty Highlander lass. As the hour neared ten o'clock there came quite a stir in the main dining room, though from where Gregor, Colvin and William were sitting they at first had to crane their necks to see why. Gunther and a handful of other Ganugamosh had arrived at the Crown Rose. Their arrival was met with excited jubilation – many Highlanders believed the "little people" to be bringers of good fortune. Gunther wasted no time, cutting a straight path through the boisterous crowd toward Gregor's table.

"There's some mighty foolish talk goin' around town, Gregor," Gunther said in a serious tone. The short blacksmith wore a grave expression, but there was a sparkle of mischief in his eyes.

"I shall have t' apologize if any o' m' lads have said something t' upset ye, Gunther," Gregor said. "What's th' rumor?"

"I've heard it said more than once tonight that a Highlander could drink a Ganugamosh under the table," Gunther said with a smirk, "and that's just plain bullshit."

"Well, I'm afraid I cannae apologize for m' kinsmen speaking th' truth," responded Gregor with an even, but playful, look.

"Care to put that to a test, Highlander?" said Gunther.

"Ye and I, 'Nugermosh?"

"First one under the table's the loser."

"Consider it a done deal. And dinnae worry, I shall make sure m' lads see ye put safely t' bed once ye've lost."

"Just be careful not to hurt yourself fallin' outta your chair."

And so it was on. Ganugamosh and Highlanders crowded around the table. Liam and Wulfric were put in charge of keeping count of drinks; it was a foregone conclusion that Gunther and Gregor would soon be incapable of doing so for themselves. Full whiskey bottles and empty glasses were set in front of the big Highlander and the short blacksmith, and they each poured their first round while staring holes through the other.

"Gregor, is this smart?" said William in a whisper after Gregor had slammed back his first dram of Highlands whiskey. "We could fall under attack at any moment. I don't know if now is the time to be drinking and making merry."

"Now's exactly th' time, lad," said Gregor. "There's a saying in th' Highlands. Better dance before th' darkness comes, if ye plan t' dance at all. Th' attack won't come t'night, lad, ye can be pretty sure o' that. Whate'er Kor's planning after what he's learned t'day, 'tis going t' take time for him t' put it in action. But it might damn well come on th' morrow, so t'night might be th' last opportunity some o' these men will e'er have t' make merry."

William stared blank-faced at Gregor, thinking about what the big Highlander had just said. "Take it as it comes," he whispered to himself.

"What was that, lad?" asked Gregor.

"Nothing," said William, taking a sip of his whiskey. He sat in silent introspection as Gregor and Gunther matched one another shot for shot. He sang along with some of the tunes he recognized, slipping in a bit of the old tongue whenever he came to a word that he knew, but his mind was always somewhere else. When the town criers called that it was eleven o'clock and all was well, the young nobleman politely excused himself and retired for the evening.

At first Colvin was thoroughly involved with the drinking contest between Gunther and Gregor, alternately cheering on each of his two friends as they hammered back drams, but he soon realized that the entertainment value of watching a Highlander and a Ganugamosh getting piss drunk only extended so far. There had to be far more enjoyable things he could be doing in a trade district populated almost entirely by Gregor's people, he reasoned, and shortly after William headed home, Colvin headed out into the town to see what mischief he could get into. For about half an hour he walked the streets of the trade district, dropping into random alehouses and common rooms to see what was going on inside. He danced a little and drank a little, won a few coins at arm wrestling and lost it at throwing dice. He met so many people it was impossible to remember all the names, Highlanders tall and fat, short and skinny, and every imaginable combination in between. There were about a quarter as many women as there were men, and every single woman Colvin met looked ready to fight, which was something he found a little difficult to get used to. He had met his fair share of hard women in his life, but these Highlander lasses took it to the next level.

Eventually Colvin found himself sitting at the bar of the *Sailor's Song*. As with every other tavern in the trade district that night, the *Sailor's Song* had no bartender. Kegs of beer stood open around the barroom and various bottles of harder stuff lined the bar, and a person helped himself to whatever he wanted. Colvin sat sipping a mug of beer, watching a Highlander and a member of Fist Division wrestling around on the cleared barroom floor. He had a couple of coins on the Fist, a wager he had placed to show confidence in his own division of the militia and which he fully expected to lose. The young man was doing surprisingly well, though, and Colvin couldn't help but grin whenever he noticed the Fist using a move he had taught him.

Colvin was riding a high fueled both by alcohol and the exhilaration of festivity, and it took him a while to notice that the hand that had gripped his shoulder lingered a bit too long to be the incidental contact of a man refilling his drink at the bar. "Excuse me, lad, but would yer name by chance happen t' be Colvin?" came the voice from beside him in a decidedly more sprightly accent than most Highlanders possessed. Colvin turned and found himself looking into the soft eyes of a man of middle years and medium build wearing nicely tailored trousers and a leather jerkin. His look was friendly, and he withdrew his hand as soon as Colvin looked at him. Colvin found it impossible to be put on his guard by the man, even though this stranger knew his name.

"Yeah, I'm Colvin," he said, his voice a blend of friendliness and measured distance. "You have the advantage on me, sir. Who might you be?"

"My name is Padraig McFallagh, a friend o' Gregor MacDugal. My apologies for startling ye, lad, but Gregor has spoken to me mighty highly o' ye and I dinnae wish t' miss the opportunity t' meet ye in the quick."

"How did you know it was me? If you don't mind me asking, sir."

"Well, 'tis nae difficult t' find a man with red hair like yers among Highlanders, but the eyes were a dead giveaway," Padraig said with a wink.

Colvin laughed and extended his hand. "A pleasure to meet you, Padraig. Any friend of Gregor's is a friend of mine. So you aren't from the Highlands?"

"Nae, I hail from further south on the island, closer t' the Glens. My family has long held ties with the Duerhein MacDugals. We share a common ancestor if ye trace the family trees back far enough. And where d'ye hail from, Colvin? That's one matter on which Gregor was nae very clear."

"Oh, here and there," said Colvin. "I move around a lot."

"A wanderer," said Padraig. "'Tis nae so terrible a life. I spent a good deal o' my younger years in the same manner. Eventually a man needs to find a place he can call home, though."

Colvin just nodded.

"So tell me about yerself, Colvin, if ye dinnae mind. What Gregor has told me makes ye out t' be a most interesting fellow, but alas, he has only known ye for a month, so there is much t' tell that he dinnae know."

So Colvin recounted the story of his life to Padraig as they sat together at the bar of the *Sailor's Song*. His words came easily, much more easily than they ever had before when talking about himself. Part of it was Padraig's easygoing attitude, and part of it was the fact that his glass seemed to be refilled much more frequently when sitting next to Padraig, but Colvin allowed himself to really open up to the kindly Glensman. He even told Padraig about Loran Rothwald and his very curious daughter Rosie, and how Colvin's apprenticeship under the blacksmith had ended with a broken jaw and a weeping girl. If Padraig passed any judgment on Colvin's misbegotten deeds, it did now show on his face or in his manner.

It was after midnight when the young lady joined them, and Colvin's tale was almost told. He was just coming to the point in his story when Gregor asked him to watch over Fist Division when he noticed her sitting at the bar beside Padraig, listening to Colvin's story with interest. She was close to Colvin's height, with curly brown hair spilling down her back and a face made striking by green eyes and high cheekbones. She wore a skirt divided for riding and a man's shirt, and she had a longsword strapped to her back. Colvin was instantly taken by her.

"Ah," said Padraig, noticing Colvin's stare, "o' course, beg yer pardon, Colvin. Allow me t' introduce my daughter, Rebecca. Rebecca, this is Colvin, Gregor's young friend he was telling us about on the journey."

Rebecca stepped closer to Colvin, a little closer than was really necessary, and said, "'Tis a pleasure t' meet ye, Colvin," in a voice that sent chills up Colvin's spine. "Gregor MacDugal speaks highly o' ye, sir, and any man that can be said about must be on the level." Her breath smelled slightly of whiskey, but Colvin didn't mind.

"A pleasure, Rebecca," Colvin said, grasping her hand lightly and kissing where her index and middle fingers met the knuckles. He was impressed to see that she did not blush or make any other show of embarrassment. She simply smiled.

"Please dinnae allow me t' interrupt," Rebecca said, resuming her place beside her father at the bar. "'Twas a most entertaining story ye were telling, what little I heard."

"Of course," replied Colvin. "I'm not one to keep a lady waiting. Just let me refill my glass." His head was really spinning now, adrift on currents of wine, whiskey and beer. He spent the next quarter of an hour wrapping up the tale of his life, getting the facts more or less straight and jumping around only slightly in the chronology. When he was done he gave a bow grand enough for a bard at court, and had to reach out and take hold of the bar to prevent himself from continuing all the way down to the ground. Padraig and Rebecca both laughed and clapped.

Time began doing very strange things after that. Great chunks of it would rush by in a hazy blur, leaving Colvin with only fragmented memories of what transpired, only to be followed by a few minutes that took a small eternity to pass. Through the inebriated fog of Colvin's mind, which was now floating upon a small ocean of drink, he became aware that Padraig was gone, and had been for some time, but Rebecca was still with him. He remembered walking through the streets holding her hand, dancing with her in a couple of different taverns and having his arms around her waist a couple of times. There were other memories that were lost in a scattered jumble of inebriation, like the circuit they made of the trade district or the sense that something important was said. Now that he was in the grip of another lucid moment – this one a bit more enduring; he had stopped drinking a while ago – he found himself back in the common room of the Crown Rose standing in a corner with Rebecca. She was looking at him with a strange smile curling her lips.

"Aye," she said. "I'd love to."

It took a moment for Colvin to remember what he had just asked her. It came to him in a flash of clarity: he had asked her if she wanted to go upstairs to one of the guest rooms with him. So up the stairs they went, arm in arm, and disappeared together behind the privacy of a closed door. Colvin was never quite certain whether he kissed her first or she kissed him, but soon her divided skirt and man's shirt lay discarded on the floor along with Colvin's clothes. Rebecca made love wildly, enthusiastically and with the hint of experience that Colvin found most endearing of all possible feminine traits. They made love until their bodies were sweaty and sore, and the room was filled with the musky, unmistakable scent of their union.

After, they lay naked together, limbs entangled, sweat drying on their bodies, feeling their hearts beat together. The exertion had driven some of the drunken murkiness from Colvin's brain, and he stared fixedly at the ceiling as Rebecca stroked her fingers through his hair. "We probably shouldn't have done that," he said.

Rebecca propped herself up on her elbow and looked at him with a hint of concern. "Why d'ye say that, hon?"

"There's something I need to tell you, Rebecca. I should have told you before."

"Like that ye're married, perchance?" She arched an eyebrow, but the smirk on her face did not suggest anger. It was more like a peculiar playfulness.

"No," said Colvin quickly and adamantly, "nothing like that. Just someone that I might be interested in…I think."

"That dinnae sound too serious if ye ask me, Colvin," she said with a smile.

"Well, it's not really, I guess. But I still should have told you. I would really hate for you to think my intentions were more than they were. I mean, you're an amazing woman… really amazing…but this was just…"

"A tryst," said Rebecca, still smiling. She patted his hand. "'Tis all right, dear Colvin. I expected nae more than what I got." She winked at him. "Well, actually I expected a bit less than what I got, if ye take my meaning."

"Thank you," he said with a laugh.

"But dinnae worry about that. I already told ye, there is someone in my life as well."

"Oh," said Colvin. "All right then." He made to wrap his arms back around her, but she got up from the bed and began to dress. "Where are you going?" he asked.

"I have t' be going now, hon. Something I have t' attend to. Enjoy yer rest, Colvin." And with that, Rebecca took her leave of her conquest.

Colvin smiled and sighed, basking in the warm, inebriated, post-coital glow that enveloped his body and his mind. It was not long now before a dawn that would bring what could well be the hardest day Tamendad had ever known. Colvin curled himself into a ball beneath the blankets and drifted off to sleep.

❖   ❖   ❖

Dearest Melissa,

You told me that you would write, and I thought it would be nice if you had a letter waiting on you as well when you returned home. To be honest, I had meant to write you a letter before now, but I found myself continually putting it off. Part of it was because I have been extraordinarily busy during your absence, but another part of it is because I have been avoiding it. Not that I do not enjoy writing you letters. Far from it. But even now I find writing these words difficult because each letter is a reminder that you are far away from me. I miss you so very much, my love.

I almost died on the day before yesterday. I hate to be so blunt about that, but it is a subject I have been dwelling upon quite a bit recently. When I say I almost died, I do not mean it in the sense that any man on a battlefield comes close to death simply by placing himself in a dangerous situation. I have been that close to death since this war began, and though it feels peculiar to admit it I have grown accustomed to it. But on the day before yesterday I found myself lying unconscious in a forest, surrounded by goruks who wanted to kill me. There are two men responsible for my still being alive to write you this letter. One is Gunther Moragun, Tamendad's blacksmith. The other is Colvin. What I know of the details come strictly from second-hand accounts, as I have already mentioned that I was unconscious at the time. Essentially, when I was knocked out by the goruks Colvin had a choice between running and saving himself, which would have left me for dead, or standing over me and trying to fend off an incomprehensible number of goruks by himself in the unlikely hopes of saving my life. He made the latter choice, and through nothing short of a miracle Gunther and his people arrived in time to help Colvin deal with the goruks. There's a story to tell about Gunther there, but I will save it to tell you in person when you return to me.

I find I am having quite a difficult time dealing with the fact that I could very well be dead and gone right now. The thought is eating my brain. I cannot shake it. Even when my mind is completely focused on my duties it is still there in the background, whispering to me in a chill voice. I am consumed by thoughts of all that I would have missed if Colvin had made the other decision, or if Gunther had not arrived in time. The greatest loss I would have suffered is that I would never marry you. I would have been robbed of our life together, our happiness, our growing old. I find I cannot conceive of a life which ends before you become my bride and bear my children, and yet I am faced with the undeniable fact that it very well could have happened, and worse, that it still might.

I miss you so much, my love. I have endured torture being away from you, thinking of you, your face, your laugh. I think I would sell the world for just a moment of time together with you right now. Just a glimpse of you. A single touch. It drives me mad.

If I were to die, there would be certain things that my soul could never rest easy if you did not know. The first is that never have I felt love as I feel it for you. You have taught me the meaning of the word. The second is that you have my undying admiration, not simply because you are my betrothed but because you have earned it. And the last is a discovery I have made only recently, that I will never be complete so long as you are not with me. That, I believe, will ring true even in death.

I must away now, my love. The sun has risen, and my shift on the guard is soon to begin. I send my undying love to you across the miles that separate us, and I constantly pray for our safe reunion. My mind and body are in Tamendad, but my heart remains forever with you. I love you.

Your beloved,

William

William sat back in his chair and stared out the window of his bedroom. The world outside was shrouded in the pallid gray of early morning mist that the newly risen sun had not yet gotten around to burning off. William sighed and stretched his arms high above his head, flexing out a few of the knots that had accumulated in his back over a night of tossing and turning. His neck hurt as he leaned forward to blow on the ink. He sprinkled the letter with sand, folded it and tucked it securely into the drawer of his writing desk. He was not certain if he would ever actually let Melissa read it; it might upset her too greatly. He thought he would feel better for having written it. He found such was not the case.

He came downstairs to an empty kitchen. Even though he and his father were now once again both on the day shift they still saw almost nothing of each other. Jonathan, being in charge of the day guard, left the house about an hour before dawn to give himself time to look over the report from the night watch and to oversee the changing of the guard. In fact, the night William had spent under the healers' care after the ambush had been the most time he had spent with his father in what felt like forever. William spooned himself out a bowl of the porridge his father had left for him. It was lukewarm, but he did not feel like kindling a fire to heat it. He drank water with it; no merchants in town meant no milk.

He could have had a considerably better breakfast simply by walking up the street to the Governor's house – Gertrude and her undercooks would be serving in the main dining hall by now, of course – but the thought barely skittered across his mind. This was the breakfast his father had taken the time to make for him, prepared with the care and concern only a parent could manage, and William ate it without complaint.

The knot on his head ached. His scars itched, and his fresher wounds stung. There were bags under his eyes, and his whole body was filled with the overwhelming sense of lethargy that seemed to await him every time he awoke these days. He finished his breakfast and stacked his bowl atop the heap of dirty dishes that had piled up since the servants had been away. Eventually someone was going to have to do something about them, but at the moment they barely registered in his mind. He washed himself quickly from a pitcher of water, deciding to forgo a bath. He had never appreciated how much work went into drawing a bath until the first time he had tried to draw one for himself. One of the first things he was going to do when Reynolds and Nelsie returned was sit them down and thank them for all the work they did to keep the household running smoothly.

He was out the door of his house and halfway down the walk before it dawned on him that he had no idea where he was stationed today. The previous day's watch had been the most disorganized thing he had ever been a part of, consisting mostly of just getting all the Highlanders moved into the inns and settled, and it had left him with absolutely no idea of what his duties would be now that he was back on day guard. A grin spread across his lips as he realized that meant he would have to meet with the commander of the day guard to receive his assignment. William savored any opportunity to spend a little time with his father, even if it was only to discuss to which gate he had been assigned. But his smiled faded when he arrived at the Governor's house and was told that his father was in a meeting with Don Ferdinan and could not be disturbed. A lieutenant gave William his assignment – the southwest gate today – and sent him on his way.

He stopped at the church on his way to the gate. He intended to go in and make his morning devotional, a practice he had been neglecting of late, but instead he sat down on the steps outside. A sense of despair washed over him. He sat with his head in his hands, staring at the polished stone of the steps. The tears came. There was no holding them back; they were upon him so suddenly that they were streaming down his cheeks before he even realized he was crying. Besides, he had no desire to hold them back any longer. He had been holding them back for weeks. He had come close to breaking down when Gregor returned, but somehow he had managed to keep a firm hold on himself. Now every hurt and sorrow and worry of the past month flowed out of him. Great sobs wracked his body. A few passers-by stopped to look at him a moment, but no one said anything. He felt embarrassed to be behaving like this in public, but he was powerless to stop it so he just let himself cry. He was thankful that it did not take long to cry himself out, and soon he sat wiping his eyes and sniffling.

"Ye have th' look of a man who bears too many burdens, m' lad," came a voice from over his shoulder.

William turned to find Carney Gruer standing on the steps behind him. "Forgive me, Patrum," he said, rubbing his cheeks dry. "I was overcome for a moment."

"'Tis nothing t' apologize for, lad," said Carney. "All of us are strong at times and weak at others. 'Tis th' way th' Creator made us, and there is nae fault t' be found in th' divine design. Might I join ye, William?"

"Of course," William said, and he stared in amazement as Carney came and sat beside him on the steps of the church. He had never seen a priest behave in such a way, but something in Carney's manner allowed him to do it without embarrassing himself.

"Rough night?" asked Patrum Gruer.

"Rough month," replied William.

Carney nodded. "I have heard mention o' how much ye have done for Tamendad. 'Tis a full plate for any man, especially one so young as yerself."

"Sometimes I feel like the whole world is pressing down on me," said William, his voice close to breaking. "I give and I give and I give, but it never seems like enough. I don't feel like I've accomplished anything. If this is what it means to be a man, I don't think I want to do it anymore."

Carney put an arm around William's shoulders, a gesture which would have seemed extremely awkward coming from any other priest. "I have bad news, lad," said the Highlander clergyman. "This *is* what it means t' be a man."

William stared at him. That had not been the answer he was expecting.

"At least, 'tis part o' being a man," Carney continued. "Perhaps th' worst part. Ye see, William, when we leave childhood behind, we open ourselves up t' problems we ne'er had t' face as children, problems that often dinnae appear t' have a solution regardless o' what we do. 'Tis th' other side o' th' responsibilities and privileges that come with being a man, and 'tis a side o' manhood that nae many people talk about."

"I never imagined it would be this hard," said William.

"Well, normally 'tis nae, William. Ye just happened t' come of age under very peculiar circumstances. What ye have dealt with in th' past month, some fortunate men dinnae have t' deal with in their entire lives."

"But why?" William demanded. "Why am I the one that has to deal with it? It's not fair!" He felt a little guilty for speaking to the Highlander priest so angrily, but things he had kept bottled up for too long were finally bubbling to the surface.

"Ye must have faith 'tis all part o' God's plan," said Carney softly.

"But how could God let this happen?" The question that had been burning him up inside was finally out there.

Patrum Gruer looked thoughtful for a moment. "William," he said, "Which is the Face o' God that we as good, Architessera-abiding Antrelicans discuss th' least?"

William paused for a moment. His brow furrowed. "Paraxis."

"Aye," said Carney, "and why do ye suppose that is? What is it that makes th' Face o' Strife smile?"

"Violence," whispered William in reply. That world had never tasted so cold coming out of his mouth.

Patrum Gruer shook his head, subtly, not unkindly. "'Tis th' common misconception on th' matter. We shy away from the Face o' Strife because we dinnae comprehend it. 'Tis nae th' violence that makes th' Face o' Strife smile."

"Then what is it?"

"In true Highlands fashion, I shall once again answer yer question with a question, William. What would ye say is th' greatest gift God gives us?"

William thought it over for a few moments. He really was not very good at questions like this. "Life?" he replied a bit timidly.

"Well, there could be a good argument made for that answer, and a good number o' priests would agree with ye. But personally, I would say 'tis free will. If we lacked free will, what kind of existence would that be, mindlessly doing whate'er we're compelled t' do? Free will is our freedom, William. 'Tis our spiritual liberty. 'Tis what makes us individuals. Do ye follow me?"

"I think so," said William. It made sense.

"But as with manhood, 'tis another side t' free will that most people dinnae discuss. Th' divine gift o' free will is absolute, meaning we can do with it what we choose without fear o' rescission. Unfortunately, some creatures, like th' goruks, exercise their free will t' pursue evil ends. 'Tis why things like this happen, William, nae because God dinnae care but because at times some misuse th' precious gift God gives them. And at those times good men – men like yerself, William – must rise up against th' evil that would be wrought. And what ye have had t' endure oe'r th' last month is th' result.

"That is what makes the Face o' Strife smile. Nae th' violence itself, ne'er violence for its own sake. The Face o' Strife smiles when good men and women rise up against those who would do evil, when we exercise th' greatest gift we're given in pursuit o' sanctity. Ye must always have faith that God sees all that goes on, and that He cares."

"That's so hard to remember sometimes," said William.

"Aye, it can be hard t' keep th' faith when our troubles seem t' be multiplying around us. We must learn from those who came before us. What I suggest whene'er someone comes t' me in Duerhein with tested faith is for them t' choose one o' th' oracles – it dinnae matter which – and learn how they dealt with their struggles o' faith. I think 'twould do ye much good t' do th' same."

"The oracles' faith was tested?" William asked. That was something the priests had never taught him during all the time studying about them. The oracles always seemed superhuman.

"Oh, aye, William, just like you or I. They were men and women, and all men and women struggle with their faith at times. They are also th' best source of inspiration and knowledge about how t' deal with struggles o' faith in our own lives."

"I think I'll do that," said William. "It sounds like it would help."

"'Twould, I suspect," said Carney with a smile as he rose to his feet and dusted off his robes. "Well, there's healer's work t' be done, and ye have guard duty t' report for. But allow me t' bless ye before we part."

"I would be honored, Patrum Gruer."

Carney placed his hand on William's head. "*Tessera et Unum*, sanctity flows from th' Four Faces o' God t' all living things. May th' Face o' Beneficence smile upon ye this day, William Stuart-Camen, and th' Face o' Strife as well, and may that smile be a light t' warm ye against th' cold and darkness that abounds. May sanctity guide yer footsteps and lead ye down th' path o' righteousness. God's healing hand embrace ye and hold ye safe against injury and despair. As it was, so it is, so shall it fore'er remain."

It was a trick of the mind. It had to be. Yet it felt so real. William felt warmth pour into his body, filling him completely, and it was flowing into him from Carney's hand. For a moment every wound and scar on his body seared. Then the warmth washed the pain away. The lethargy that filled his muscles evaporated. He felt like he was waking up from a very long, restless sleep. His head was spinning slightly as Carney took his hand away.

"Wh-what was th-that?" gasped William.

Carney smiled at him. "Th' Four Faces o' God are always watching,

William," the Highlander priest said, then turned and walked up the steps into the church.

❖   ❖   ❖

Gabrahn Cowan was in charge of the Highlanders at the southwest gate, and this morning like many others he wondered to himself whether his kinsmen's eagerness to follow his commands was due to his ability to lead or to the fact that Angus MacDugal's claymore was hanging on his back. Either way, they followed what he said to the letter, and that was what mattered in the end.

It was a fine day. The sun had burned off the morning fog. Now it was clear and pleasantly crisp, and Gabrahn had only a hint of a hangover. He felt good. He felt alive. The incessant marching and the piddling skirmishes with handfuls of goruks were finally at an end. He was back in Tamendad, and now all that was left was the thing they had come here to do.

William was prompt in his arrival at the gate if not exactly early. Gabrahn spotted the young nobleman walking down the main street from the church and waved. It took William a moment to see Gabrahn, and then another moment to respond. There was obviously something on the young man's mind. "Top o' th' morning, commander," Gabrahn said.

William looked confused. "Huh?" he said.

Gabrahn chuckled. "Ye've been placed in command o' th' members o' Sword Division here at th' southwest gate. Dinnae anyone tell ye?"

"Oh," said William. "No, nobody said anything to me about it." After a few moments' silence, he added, "Who's in charge of the Fists?"

"'Twould be Colvin, but I suspect someone shall have t' go fetch him from th' Crown Rose if we want t' see him before midday. He was out late last night doing th' sorts o' things that make a man want t' sleep away most o' th' next morning."

"Oh," said William once more. "I can go get him," he added absently.

"Lad, what's troubling ye?" asked Gabrahn. "'Tis like ye're half in another world."

The question made William focus on Gabrahn, and he seemed to notice the Highlander for the first time. "Something happened just now at the church," he said with a great deal of seriousness.

"What was it, lad?"

William talked as though in a daze. "I was talking with Patrum Gruer about…certain things, and when our conversation was over he blessed me, and when he did it something strange happened. It felt like my whole body was on fire, but it didn't hurt at all."

"Ye beheld Agathas," Gabrahn said with a grin, as though that solved everything.

"What?"

"Th' Face o' Beneficence. Have ye ne'er beheld one o' God's Faces before?"

William stared at Gabrahn in silence. The Four Faces of God were something that priest talked about from the altar, a way of describing the all-encompassing scope of the Divine. He had never taken the notion literally, yet here was Gabrahn insisting that William had just beheld an actual Face of God. And what seemed craziest of all about the entire thing was that William could think of no better description for what he had just experienced on the steps of the church. He had no idea what to say. He never had an opportunity to say anything, though, because at that moment a lookout atop the wall yelled out, "A rider approaches!"

"Human or goruk?" Gabrahn yelled out in reply.

"Human," said the lookout, and then after a little while, "It's Ian Morlocke! He's badly hurt!"

"Open the gate!" William screamed, but the gatekeepers were already turning the winch. The doors creaked open, and after a moment Ian Morlocke rode through them. He was slumped in the saddle. The broken shafts of three arrows protruded from his body at odd angles in different places. He looked dead. In an instant a crowd was around him, pulling him from the saddle and laying him gently on the bricked street. William leaned over him, checking for a pulse while Gabrahn inspected his wounds. The grim look on the Highlander's face told the tale. He was not yet dead, but he would be soon and nothing could change that.

Ian's eyes fluttered open. He was obviously having a great deal of trouble focusing them. Gabrahn and William leaned close so that Ian could see them. The scout summoned what energy he had left and reached out to them, taking their hands in his. "A…trap," he whispered, and blood trickled from the corners of his mouth as he spoke. A hush spread over the southwest gate like a wave. "The…other…scouts," Ian whispered. "All…dead…" His eyes began to roll back in his head.

"Stay with me, lad," said Gabrahn, squeezing his hand. "What happened?"

"They're coming," whispered Ian, his eyes wide with urgency.

"The goruks?" said William. "How many?"

"All…of…them…"

William and Gabrahn looked at each other. There was only a hint of fear in that look, a tiny hint. Mostly it was filled with a simple acknowledgment that the inescapable conclusion of this standoff had finally arrived.

"Lad, I need a number," Gabrahn urged gently.

"Hundreds," whispered Ian. "A...thousand."

Murmurs spread throughout the hushed crowd gathered around the dying scout. Runners sprinted up the bricked main street without being sent. Tamendad began to prepare for war.

"Fight them..." Ian whispered, his voice full of both encouragement and pleading. "Fight..."

"We will," said Gabrahn with a soft smile. "Ye've done yer duty, lad."

Ian smiled as well, weakly. His eyes had lost their focus. He tried to say something, struggling against his failing body, but the words would not come.

A long, slow exhalation, and Ian Morlocke was gone.

CHAPTER THIRTY-TWO

BLOOD HILL

Colvin was having a very good dream that involved both Melinda and Rebecca, but not a stitch of clothing, and he was a little perturbed when he was violently shaken awake. It was already daylight, which immediately told Colvin that he was late to report for guard duty. At first he assumed that was why he had been roused, but Wallace's demeanor was much too excited and urgent to be attributable only to Colvin's tardiness. Colvin sat up quickly in the bed and rubbed his eyes. His head was swimming a little and his mouth was terribly dry, but his hangover could have been considerably worse, no doubt would have been considerably worse if he had been allowed to sleep much longer. He smelled like whiskey and sex, both of which smelled considerably worse now than how he remembered them from the night before.

"What is it?" Colvin asked groggily, the haze just beginning to clear from his vision.

"Th' goruks are coming, lad," said Wallace quickly. "Th' whole lot o' them. This is it, th' final dance."

Colvin was up in an instant, not bothering to cover his nakedness. Wallace did not seem to think anything of it. "Where am I going?" Colvin asked.

"Emergency meeting in th' town square, lad," replied Wallace. "As soon as ye can get there. Be quick about it, and dinnae forget yer weapons." Then Wallace was gone, leaving Colvin to the business of dressing himself. It took frustratingly too long to find all his clothes, and he never did exactly figure out how one of his boots wound up on top of the wardrobe, but finally he was dressed. He paused only long enough to guzzle down half the water pitcher and then he was out the door.

The Crown Rose was empty except for him, but he found plenty of company in the streets. Everyone was hurrying toward the church. Excited chatter hung in the air, and in this part of town it was colored by

Highlander accents. Colvin picked up on a little apprehension and much anxiousness, but he did not dally to take part in any of the conversations he overheard. He was not entirely certain if he was still technically in charge of Fist Division now that Gregor was back, but the possibility spurned him onward and he was quickly dodging around people to get to the town square.

The entire war council was already congregated together on the steps of the church when Colvin arrived in the town square. Colvin hastened to join them, but his progress was hampered by the large crowd that was gathering in the square around them. Colvin dodged and weaved his way through constables and militiamen and Highlanders, and he was nearly to the bottom step of the church when he suddenly found himself face to face with Rebecca. She reached out and touched his forearm, and she wore a nervous smile. For her, he hesitated.

"Time for th' reckoning," she said.

"Looks like it," he replied. "At least you didn't have to wait long."

She laughed. "Aye, 'tis true. I do so hate t' wait."

"I noticed," Colvin said. At that moment he became aware of the gargantuan Hamish moving through the crowd, though it was actually more like the crowd was parting itself around Hamish for fear of being crushed by him. Colvin stared in spite of himself. The fact that he had seen the mammoth Highlander before was not enough to curb his sense of awe seeing him among more normal-sized people. There was a good chance, Colvin believed, that the goruks would turn around and run away as soon as they laid eyes on Hamish.

Rebecca noticed Colvin's stare. "Ye've met Hamish, have ye?" she asked.

Colvin tore his eyes away from the giant and looked at her. "No," he said, "I saw him when Gregor arrived yesterday, but I haven't met him yet. You know him?"

"Aye," Rebecca said. And then Hamish was there with them, emerging from the surrounding crowd as though he had failed to notice that it was there. If possible, he was even bigger close up. He bent down and kissed Rebecca on the lips, then wrapped an immense arm around her waist.

"Who be this, wife?" he said in the thickest and most muddled of accents.

Colvin's whole body went numb. He thought for a moment that his knees were going to buckle and he was going to fall flat on his face. He could barely process the thought that he had slept with this man's wife. His mental image of Hamish ripping goruks limb from limb transformed suddenly into Hamish doing the same to him. He swallowed hard as he felt all the color drain from his face.

"This is Colvin, husband," Rebecca said with a pleasant smile that in no way fit with the death sentence she had placed upon his head. "M' father and I met him last night. He is a friend o' Gregor's."

A light of comprehension dawned on Hamish's large face, and he reached forward to clasp Colvin's forearm. Colvin braced for the savage beating that he was sure would follow, but it did not come. Hamish just shook his forearm, a bit violently but no more so than was attributable to his size. "Gregor's spoke o' ye," Hamish said with a smile. "Says ye're a good man. Pleasure t' meet ye."

Colvin's heart sank like a stone. If anything, Hamish being nice to him was worse than the beating that he thought was impending. "Yeah, well, same to you," Colvin mumbled, gesturing over his shoulder toward the steps of the church. "If you'll excuse me, I've gotta... um..."

"Go?" Rebecca suggested, still wearing that infuriatingly pleasant smile.

"Um, yeah. Go. Nice to...um...meet you." Colvin felt like he might pass out. He turned and started up the steps. His whole world was reeling, and when he finally reached the top his heart was about to pound right out of his chest.

"Did we have some trouble deciding when to call it a night last night?" Ferdinan said with an arched eyebrow, looking him over from head to toe. "You are as pale as a ghost."

"I have to talk to you right now, Ferdinan," Colvin whispered. If anyone would understand this, it was Ferdinan.

"I am kind of busy at the moment, Colvin," Ferdinan replied. "You see, we are about to go to war, and–"

Colvin grasped Ferdinan's shoulder. There was plain desperation in his eyes. "Please," he begged. "It's urgent."

Ferdinan sighed. "All right," he said. "I can spare only a moment." He and Colvin stepped away from the rest of the crowd atop the steps, a little closer toward the church. "Now what es the matter? It had better be important."

"I slept with Hamish's wife."

Ferdinan had a look of confusion which very quickly changed into wide-eyed shock. He looked at the crowd that was filling the town square and found Hamish without difficulty. No one had difficulty picking Hamish out of a crowd. Then he looked back to Colvin.

"You are kidding," he said. "Please tell me you are kidding."

"I'm not," Colvin said, and again he felt the bile rising. "I didn't know. She never told me. You can appreciate that, can't you?"

Ferdinan calmed a little, and there was sympathy in his eyes. "Dear

God, Colvin," he said. "Does he know?"

"I don't think so. I hope not. I just talked to him and he didn't let on like he did."

Ferdinan shook his head angrily. "Es no time to deal with this. The timing es terrible." He seemed to be talking more to himself than to Colvin. "You must not tell anyone of this. Not a soul. If his wife has not told him yet, she probably es not going to do so now. What kind of wife would tell her husband she has been unfaithful as they march onto a battlefield together?"

"Not her," said Colvin. "She's way too nice for that."

"Yes, she es a real angel, I am sure," replied Ferdinan. "Now I mean it, Colvin, you must not speak a word of this to anyone. He might not hear it from his wife, but the more people you tell, the more people there are that can tell him."

Colvin nodded soberly. "Right. Sorry to spring this on you right now, Ferdinan. I just didn't know who else to talk to about it."

"Es all right, Colvin," said Ferdinan with a forced smile. "We will deal with this further after the battle es over, you and I. Until then, we have more important things to focus on."

"Yeah," said Colvin.

"I would suggest staying away from him while the fighting es going on, though, just to be safe," Ferdinan added as he walked back toward where the Governor and the others were standing. Colvin's eyes went wide as saucers, but he said nothing.

"All right, lads, ye heard what th' Governor said." Gregor MacDugal paced back and forth in front of his kinsmen outside the southwest gate, looking them over. They looked lean and hungry, and a tad bit hung-over. "We're meeting th' goruks head-on. Those green bastards wanted a war, and when they get here they're going t' find a war like nothing they could e'er fathom."

The Highlanders, all three hundred and seventeen of them, voiced their agreement.

"All right then," said Gregor. "Th' most important thing t' remember is that we cannae let th' goruks get inside th' city. We have t' hold them outside th' gates. Those green bastards will have too many places t' hide in th' streets o' Tamendad.

"Remember why we're here, lads. Remember why we're fighting this day. 'Tis nae just about revenge. If these goruks are nae checked, they shall keep taking and taking until there's an army o' them knocking on th' door o' th' Highlands, coming t' take our towns and our farms right out from underneath us. They're a plague that needs stopped now, before it spreads and gains strength. We're nae just fighting t' avenge a death, but t' prevent more innocent men and women and children from dying."

Nods of agreement from the mass of Highlanders, but Gregor was certain they believed the words as much as he himself did. It was true that the goruks were a threat that needed to be put down now, before they could gain momentum in their war against mankind, but the principal reason that over three hundred Highlanders stood together ready to draw and shed blood today was because Angus MacDugal was dead. It was not that they did not care about Tamendad or the people who called it home, but first and foremost Highlanders looked after their own.

Gregor went over the instructions once again, just to make sure everyone had them down. It was going to be quite a fight, whenever the goruks showed up. The Highlanders were going to charge headlong into the goruk army, along with most of Fist Division, Sword Division and the constabulary. Shield Division was holding back at the fractured northeast gate to deal with any goruks that splintered off from the main army and tried to gain entry to Tamendad on their own, and to protect what few civilians remained in the city. The small number of constables, Swords and Fists that were not outside the city walls awaiting the goruks' arrival stood with them. Everyone who was not a soldier was in the Governor's house with the Governor's personal guard forming a protective ring around them, the last line of defense.

Gregor felt a hand on his shoulder. He spun on his heels quickly, ready to attack whoever – whatever – the hand belonged to. He was ready for bloodshed, but he quickly pulled back when he saw it was Ferdinan standing behind him. The Conquian looked a little jumpy, no doubt because Gregor had almost lunged for him. Gregor smiled.

"Ah, lad, good t' see ye."

"The same goes for you, as always, *compagno*," Ferdinan said. "I was hoping to have a word with you, if you could spare the time."

"O' course, lad. Always got time for a friend. What's on yer mind?"

Ferdinan sighed, the look on his face making evident the internal struggle he was having over whatever it was he wanted to talk about. "Gregor, you are a wise and honorable man," the Conquian said, "and I would never presume that you need advice on how to live your life..."

"Lad, spit it out," said Gregor. "Whate'er's on yer mind, 'tis obviously something ye believe important."

"All right then," said Ferdinan. "Please do not feel insulted by this, but I wanted to tell you, please do not let your emotions get the best of you against the goruks."

Gregor looked a little suspicious. "What do ye mean, lad?"

"Gregor, there es no hiding what you are fighting for. I do not have a brother, so I cannot imagine what it would be like to lose one. But I can imagine what it might do to a man. And in some situations, it might drive a man to be reckless."

"I appreciate yer concern, m' friend," said Gregor, "but dinnae waste yer worry on me. I can take care o' m'self."

"I know," said Ferdinan. "Just be careful out there."

"I will lad."

A long, low howl pierced the air, and everyone outside the southwest gate tensed anxiously. Ferdinan and Gregor looked at each other. "I suppose this es it," Ferdinan said.

"Ferdinan?"

"Sí, Gregor?"

"Do me a favor, would ye, lad, and take yer own advice?"

"Whatever do you mean?" replied Ferdinan.

"Well, ye have a tendency t' go o'er th' edge on occasion. I dinnae want t' see ye get hurt, lad. Just be careful."

Ferdinan smiled. "I will, *compagno*."

"All right then," said Gregor with a nod. "I shall see ye on th' other side."

The forces of Tamendad stood ready. Gregor MacDugal stood in command of the Highlanders. Ferdinan commanded the constables. William stood with the Swords, and Colvin with the Fists. Together they awaited the signal from the lookouts atop the city wall. Everything had led up to this moment. All that had yet transpired was but a precursor to the battle at hand. This was the battle for Tamendad.

The goruks were coming, and from the sound of it there was a lot of them. Their howls and snarls could be heard echoing through the hills, growing louder as they came. Now it sounded like they were right on top of Tamendad. Men and women gripped weapons anxiously, nervously, waiting for the chance to use them. Then that chance came.

"NOW!"

The scream poured down from every lookout on Tamendad's wall, and all the soldiers below reacted. Together Highlander and Tamendader, constable and militiaman advanced from the barred southwest gate. They began at a walk, but by the time they reached the base of the hill overlooking the city they were at a run. The enemy could be heard on the other side of the hill, snarling and hooting like rabid beasts. Screams went up to drown the filthy noise out. From the constables and militiamen rose the familiar cry of *Tamendad stands*. From the

Highlanders came a different noise, unidentifiable to anyone who had not grown up in the Highlands. It was a war cry and a mourning wail all wrapped up into one, and to anyone who could identify it, it meant that vengeance was at hand for Gregor MacDugal.

They met at the top of the hill, with the Highlanders at the head of the charge. The goruks showed little surprise at being met head-on, and they did not back down as the Highlanders and Tamendaders crashed into them. The fighting spread as more from both sides continued to join the fray. The bedlam consumed the hillside. Soon there was no distinguishing among Highlanders, constables, militiamen. There were only humans and goruks, all killing each other. The lookouts atop the city wall watched in horror, waiting to send word to the Governor if the goruks broke through the line.

In the midst of the battle Gregor carved his way through the sea of goruks that surrounded him, his claymore cleaving through green bodies, leaving a trail of carnage in his wake. He cut through them in a violent frenzy, his mind consumed with rage and thoughts of revenge. Around him on all sides were screams both human and inhuman, and the grass was becoming slick with blood. Suddenly Colvin was there with him, and William too, fighting alongside him, pushing into the oncoming goruks. He was glad to see them, glad to know they were still alive and well, but a nagging thought came to him. "Did Ferdinan send ye t' keep an eye on me, lads?" he yelled, mostly in jest, as he split a goruk's head in two.

"Yes," said William, running a goruk through the stomach, then slashing it across the throat. "But don't take that the wrong way. We both thought we'd be safest wherever you were."

Gregor laughed. "Dinnae be so sure about that, lads!" he screamed, then planted his shoulder into the sternum of a charging goruk, bowling it to the ground then taking its head. "This day th' Clan MacDugal's out for blood!"

But despite the warning, William and Colvin stayed with Gregor. Whenever they came across a Sword or a Fist they joined up until the current of battle separated them again. There was little sense trying to stay with their divisions in this blitzkrieg. This was every man for himself, and if a man stopped moving – or hesitated for someone else – it would probably be the last thing he ever did. So Colvin and William did their best to keep up with Gregor and never looked back.

Chaos reigned. There was little if any strategy, just an all-out assault of goruks against humans. And at the heart of the battle, the mountain of a man known as Hamish was carving his way through green bodies with an ease that even the humans found frightening. Every swipe of his mammoth sword laid waste to the goruk line, a reaper's scythe that slashed through bone and flesh as easily as it sliced the air. And the truly disturbing thing about the sight was the steady-handed placidity with which Hamish fought. This giant was slaughtering goruks by the dozen, his man-sized sword spilling a torrent of blood that soaked the very ground, and yet his face never changed. His square jaw was rigid, his teeth clamped firmly together, his protruding brow furrowed to a squint. He made not a sound, not so much as a grunt even when his sword dropped two and three goruks at a time. He was a statue, a monument to pain and death. And if the humans who fought alongside him found him frightening, the goruks were nothing short of terrified by him.

Suddenly someone was screaming. That in itself was not unusual. Everyone was screaming. But this one person, whoever he was, was actually saying something. "It's Kor!" came the voice. "It's Kor!" And then William and Colvin could not keep up with Gregor any longer. It was like some long-dormant beast had stirred within him. He was off in the direction of the voice as fast as his legs could carry him, which was faster than either William or Colvin could move. They were left behind, fending for themselves, watching as Gregor charged toward his destiny.

Then they saw him up ahead, the cause of all their pain. Surrounded by a swarm of goruks, Kor was fighting his way through the battlefield, his scimitars a blur around him. He cut through humans without pause or remorse, and it was straight for him that Gregor was running. But he was not the only one. A gargantuan blade cleaved into the goruks surrounding Kor from behind, and they were felled so quickly they did not have time to scream.

Hamish had gotten there first.

The whole mass of goruks turned on the giant. Hamish squared himself against them, and another swipe of his sword dropped four more. He screamed as he brought his sword around for another attack, the first sound he had made since the battle began, and then they were on him. They did not try to take him with swords. They knew that was a hopeless battle. Instead they literally flung themselves upon him, casting their swords down as they leapt. They clung to his back, around his arms, his legs, wherever they landed. Hamish managed one more swipe of his blade, dragging along a goruk clinging frantically to his forearm, and then they took his legs from under him. They clawed and bit and kicked at him, and then more goruks were there, stabbing at him with their swords. Colvin could just watch in horror. Then Gregor was there.

The first goruk was cut cleanly in half. The second lost its head, the third both its legs. Blood splattered. Howls filled the air. Gregor was getting very close to Kor, and the goruks around him knew it. They turned on him with a viciousness that would have impressed even Gunther. But it was nothing to match the viciousness with which Gregor attacked them. Another goruk went down holding its own intestines. A fifth lost an arm and half its head. "Ye bastards took m' brother!" Gregor screamed. His eyes were glazed. He was frothing at the corners of his mouth. He cursed them in the old tongue. Suddenly he became aware that he no longer held his claymore. They had wrestled it from him. He was surrounded.

Somewhere far away, Colvin screamed. He and William stared in horror, gripped by the paralysis of shock. They were going to watch Gregor MacDugal die, just as they had watched Hamish die, and Angus, and far too many others. But someone had apparently failed to inform Gregor of that. The big Highlander lunged for the nearest goruk. One swift motion, Gregor locked his fingers around the creature's throat and pulled. It came away in a spurt of blood. Gregor tossed it aside, reaching forward again quickly with both hands. He gripped the tusk of the dying goruk tightly in his right hand, bracing its forehead with his left. He pulled with all his might. The sound was sickening, like the creaking, groaning sound of a board of wood being bent out of shape. A loud crack. Gregor held the thing's broken tusk in his hand. He spun and drove it through the next goruk's eye. Its body stiffened. In one smooth, surging motion Gregor had the beast in the air, above his head. He threw it the way a willful child might toss her rag doll in frustration, and bowled down two more goruks with it. He reached out and clenched two more by their necks, ramming their heads together, savoring the sound of their skulls caving in. William and Colvin could not believe what they were seeing.

"Come on, son!" Jonathan Stuart-Camen screamed to William, rushing past with his broadsword held aloft. William snapped back to reality. Gregor needed help. He grabbed Colvin by the arm and started running.

"Did you see that?!?" Colvin screamed as they ran. William just nodded.

Kor had already moved on by the time Gregor had been rescued – if one could really call it that. By the time the big Highlander had his claymore back in his hands there was a pile of ten dead goruks around him, and all he had to show for it was one significant wound, a nasty gash across his back. "Thank ye, lads," he said quickly to the men who had come to his aid.

"Th' bastards got Hamish!" yelled Gabrahn, who had also come to help Gregor. "Where is he? Where's Kor?"

"There he is," said Jonathan, pointing with his broadsword. Kor was backing away toward the bulk of his own forces, nearing the other side of the hill. In fact, it looked like most of the goruks were doing the same, not exactly retreating but withdrawing. William glanced quickly around. The hillside was soaked red with blood, and bodies were strewn everywhere. The carnage was overwhelming, but even a cursory glance revealed that there were more dead goruks than humans. The Tamendaders were winning.

"He's trying to regroup!" William shouted. "Hurry! Get them!"

"Forward, lads!" Gregor screamed, holding his claymore high and breaking into a run. William and Jonathan followed close behind. The forces of Tamendad pushed forward and the goruks began to fall back, some spilling back down the hill the way they had come. The goruks were fighting in a single large pack now, with Kor in the middle of it calling out orders in his incomprehensible language. Slowly, methodically, the pack of goruks was backing away.

"They're withdrawing!" Jonathan Stuart-Camen yelled. "Forward!" Those words seemed to spread through Tamendad's forces like wildfire. They redoubled their efforts, throwing themselves against the goruks over and over again, never backing down, never giving an inch, always pressing forward. And they were backing the goruks down the hill. They were going to win the day. The thought began to take hold, and it drove the soldiers forward like a whip. They were going to win the war. The front line of goruks began to founder. The goruks in the rear began to move down the hill more quickly. Their resolve was breaking. It was time for the death blow.

"Taste th' wrath o' th' Clan MacDugal!"

The Highlanders erupted at Gregor's words, drowning out all other noise. The ruckus was deafening, and every Highlander charged forward once more into the goruk hoard. They penetrated the line. Kor's forces were routed.

"Retreat!" Kor screamed at the top of his lungs, turning even as he spoke and breaking into a run down the hill. "Retreat, retreat, retreat!"

The goruks broke rank and ran for it, moving in a disorganized jumble down the hillside. Many slipped and fell on the slippery red grass, where they never got up again.

"We've got them now, lads!" yelled Gregor. "After them!" He led the Highlanders in a charge down the hill after the goruks, toward what was an assured victory. Many of the constables and militiamen followed close behind, some pursuing a sense of destiny, others simply looking for revenge. It was a beautiful moment, one that no one there would ever forget.

Something made Colvin hesitate. He could not quite put his finger on it, but something just felt wrong, out of joint. William had already started down the hill with his father. Just about everyone who was not injured was following Gregor after the goruks. But Colvin remained on top of the blood-slicked hill for a moment, some great struggle he could not even identify raging in his brain. It felt like he was screaming at himself through a foot of water; the message was obviously urgent, but it was impossible to decipher.

Colvin spotted Ferdinan running toward him. The Conquian was not injured, and he was not following after Gregor either. He had a look of concern in his eyes which Colvin was certain was in his own as well.

"Do not pursue!" Ferdinan was screaming, not to Colvin but to the people running down the hill. "Something es wrong! Come back!"

"What is it?" Colvin said when Ferdinan was close enough.

"He spoke Turish!" Ferdinan yelled. "Why would Kor order his own people in Turish? That was for us to hear! To goad us into a pursuit!"

Colvin's hands went cold and his stomach tightened. "But why?"

"There are not enough of them!" Ferdinan replied quickly. "Morlocke said they were marching close to a thousand toward us. We are lucky if we faced five hundred on this hill. Where are the rest?"

Something clicked into place in Colvin's brain. His heart plummeted. Something made him turn back toward the city.

"GORUKS IN TAMENDAD!!!"

God only knew where such a noise had come from. It drifted up from the town like the voice of a thunder god. But wherever it had come from, the voice told the truth. Colvin could barely see the southeast gate from his vantage point, but he could see it clearly enough to know that it was no longer there, and that goruks were pouring through it into the city.

"It's a setup!" Colvin screamed, frantically trying to capture the attention of the men and women charging down the other side of the hill. Some of those had already halted, having heard the voice as well. They turned with faces full of shock and ran in the other direction, back toward Tamendad. But not all turned around. Many – too many – were too far gone, either in distance or in mind, to hear.

Tamendad's forces were divided.

CHAPTER THIRTY-THREE

THE BATTLE OF TAMENDAD

He was supposed to be in the Governor's house just like everyone else, but McRofaly had no desire to lock himself in a building that would be impossible to escape from if the goruks somehow managed to get inside the city. Not that he really expected the goruks to win the day, but he had no plans to just lie down and die in the event that they actually did. It had not taken much effort to slip past the Governor's guards, which made him feel that much wiser about his decision not to entrust his wellbeing to them, and now he was hurrying down the cobbled street that led to the southeast gate. The soldiers were going to be engaging the goruk army to the southwest, and any goruks that happened to make it past the fighting would most likely try to enter the city through the broken northeast gate. That left the northwest and southeast gates open to McRofaly as possible avenues of escape. The northwest gate was entirely too close to the Governor's house, which was certain to be the goruks' principal target if they ever made it into the city, so McRofaly decided to take his chances with the southeast gate.

Getting past the lookouts at the gate would prove no more difficult than getting past the Governor's guard, McRofaly assumed. He was, after all, a member of the war council and if he told the lookouts they were needed elsewhere in the city they would have no reason not to believe him. And it wasn't like he was actually going to leave the southeast gate unmanned once the lookouts had been sent on their way. He was not about to make a run for it. Not just yet. He would only exercise that option if it was necessary to save his own life. He wasn't a coward, after all. Sure, he was invested in seeing Tamendad defended from the goruks, but he was no soldier. He never had been, and he never would be. He was a strategist, and no good on a battlefield. If the goruks stormed the city, his usefulness would be immediately used up and under those circumstances who would blame him for making a run for it? It was a simple matter of self-preservation. Yeah, that was it.

"Master McRofaly, what are you doing here, sir?" called one of the lookouts from the platform atop the wall as McRofaly arrived at the southeast gate. "Aren't you supposed to be at the Governor's house?"

"Yes, well, I was," replied McRofaly confidently, "but they sent me with an urgent message. More lookouts are needed at the southwest gate, to help keep an eye on the battle and make sure no goruks get through the fighting. Very important assignment."

"I was not informed of any change of plans, sir," called down another lookout, and McRofaly immediately recognized that this was the man in charge here.

"No, you wouldn't, now would you, considering that the decision just came down from the war council? Well, those members of it who aren't out on the battlefield already."

"And we are just supposed to leave the southeast gate unmanned, sir?"

"Oh, absolutely not, commander! Don't be ridiculous! That's why they sent me."

"You, sir?" replied the commander. "You don't have any training as... Excuse me, sir? You're going to have to speak up."

"I said, tell me, commander," McRofaly called up, "were you in a terrible rush when you shaved this morning? You must have missed a small patch on your chin. You have some stubble growing there."

The commander rubbed at his chin, looking McRofaly over thoughtfully. Anyone with eyes good enough to spot an uneven shave on a man from that far away would doubtless have little problem keeping an eye out for anything unusual.

"All right, men," said the commander at length, "you heard Master McRofaly. We've been reassigned to the southwest gate. Quickly, now. Hustle." All the lookouts atop the platform began down the ladder, followed by the commanding officer. The nod the commander gave McRofaly as he passed by was rather curt, bordering on impertinence, but McRofaly let it slide. After all, it was a pretty implausible story. But it got the lookouts out of McRofaly's hair and opened up his avenue of escape. He breathed easier as the lookouts disappeared down the street. He was alone, unwatched, and could get away with anything.

The distant, echoing sounds of armed confrontation met McRofaly's ears, and he knew the fighting had begun. He nervously tapped his foot against the cobblestones of the street. He did not want to leave Tamendad, and he hoped he would not have to. It was home, and it had been pretty good to him over the years. It would be difficult to leave it behind, if the need came. It would be especially difficult to leave Sococo.

McRofaly had never had another living thing be dependent upon him, and he found now that he was experiencing the most peculiar sensation of guilt as he thought about leaving the cat behind. For a moment he considered running back to his house and fetching Sococo, but he quickly dismissed the notion. Sococo was locked safe and sound in the kitchen with enough food and water to last a month and a large pan full of sand in which to do his business. He was much safer there than he would be with McRofaly during an escape from attacking goruks. It would be hard to leave him behind, but McRofaly knew it was the right thing to do.

It would be even harder to leave behind his secret basement. How bad would it be if – when – someone finally discovered it and all its incriminating contents? McRofaly could watch the scenario play out in his own mind detail by detail. It would probably be some elderly woman, a grandmotherly type, who would rent the place once McRofaly had abandoned it and turn it into a tea room, where the specialty was grandmother's very own handmade sweets. And then one day grandmother would trip over the seam of the trapdoor while she was busy in the kitchen making her wares. "Oh, what do we have here?" she would say to herself in her own grandmotherly fashion, just tickled pink at the discovery of a basement she never knew she had. And then what would happen once she descended the stairs into that chamber? Would she drop dead of fright when she realized what she was seeing, what terrible secrets had lain right beneath her floorboards for God only knew how long? Probably. And what a macabre tableau that would be when her friends – grandmother would have all kinds of friends – came to check on her. They would demand to know who was responsible for killing such a kind, gentle old woman, and of course it would not be long before people began to remember the man who lived there before. "Abandoned us all during the war, that McRofaly did. Never cared for the chap myself. No, sir, something just wrong with the man. I say we all go find him and burn him at the stake." Oh well. By that time he would be far away, living under a different name and appearance, probably somewhere far north on the mainland. He had been a little foolish to stay in Tamendad so long anyway. Esten always encouraged moving around a lot, to keep them off the trail.

The sounds of conflict were louder now. The battle was escalating. McRofaly needed to see what was going on. All his scheming to ensure the possibility of escape would be in vain if he did not have a way to know that it was actually time to escape. But the vantage point was going to be a problem. At the southeast gate as he was, it was going to be impossible to get a clear view of the battle. Then again, he did not really need a clear view, he reminded himself. All he needed was a notion that things were going wrong, a very general indication that Tamendad's defenses were beginning to break. He eyed the lookout platform. It would do, and it was relatively safe behind a wooden parapet more than thick enough to stop arrows and, McRofaly felt certain, more than tall enough to keep him from falling off. He still hated heights, though, and he stood for a long moment with one hand wrapped tightly around the third rung of the ladder leading up to the platform. Then he started to climb.

When he reached the top, his heart plummeted all the way to his feet. There, coming at a march toward Tamendad from the southeast, were goruks. Hundreds of goruks. As soon as McRofaly regained his powers of speech he cursed himself bitterly. It was brilliant, and there was no reason so far as he could see that he should not have thought of it before. The oldest military tactic in the world, after all, was divide and conquer.

He wanted to run, to sprint as quickly as he could across the town, out the northwest gate, and not stop running until he reached Tantera. But he could not do it. He would not make a run for it now, not like this. It was one thing to bolt when defeat was already assured, but McRofaly found himself now in the position of being the only thing standing between Tamendad and an army of goruks. He had to get to the northeast gate and let Shield Division know they were coming. There was no one else who could do it. Except...

Except the goruks were not heading toward the northeast gate. They were heading straight toward him. They were planning to come through the southeast gate, where no one was waiting to face them. And they were too close for McRofaly to summon soldiers to fight them. He was going to have to face them alone.

"Oh shit," McRofaly whispered to himself.

The ardah was leading them, moving confidently if not eagerly toward the city wall. They had spotted McRofaly, but if there were archers among the goruks they obviously did not think him enough of a threat to waste arrows on. But as for that, who could blame them? What was one short, slight man against several hundred armed goruks? They did not know his secret, though.

The ardah led his people right up to the gate, where he hesitated. He did not even bother to spare a glance up at McRofaly. He just stood staring at the gate as though in deep concentration, like he expected the gate to simply disappear if he thought about it hard enough.

"Who goes there?" McRofaly called down in the most authoritative voice he could manage. He was not entirely certain how well he pulled it off. He thought he might wet himself at any moment.

There was no immediate reply from the ardah, and after a few moments McRofaly repeated himself more forcefully. This time the ardah acknowledged his presence by glancing upward and snarling, "Be gone, worm."

McRofaly took a deep breath and glanced around quickly, just out of habit, to make sure no one else was nearby. *Well, it's now or never,* he thought. He drew himself up to full measure, wishing for once that he measured a little more, and pointed forcefully at the ardah. In his other hand he held his walking stick aloft, pointing skyward, trying to make himself appear the way the great artists always depicted the oracles. "You be gone, ardah!" he yelled down, his voice booming. For the first time, the ardah took a genuine interest in him, eyeing him warily and with no small amount of curiosity . There was no turning back now. "This city is under my protection. Your filth is unwelcome here!"

"Fool paleskin, what powers bring you against so many?" The intrigue that showed plainly on the ardah's face told that this question was not rhetorical.

The time had come. McRofaly was about to stick his neck out for Tamendad in a way that Esten would have killed him for, had the paranoid old bastard still been alive.

"*Ardos,*" McRofaly whispered, and in his cupped hand there appeared a little flame, no larger than that of a torch. It danced and flickered on his palm but did not burn his skin. He extended his hand so that all the goruks could see. "If you wish to discover my powers," said McRofaly, "come and test them." There were uneasy mutterings among the goruks. McRofaly could not understand their language, but he knew what they were saying nonetheless: this paleskin had magic, and that changed things.

"Calm yourselves!" barked the ardah crossly in his own language. "It is a simple bit of trickery he is using. Any fool could learn it. Where is your loyalty to the Ancient Ones?" This seemed to calm the goruks a bit. Then the ardah turned back to McRofaly and said in Turish, "Very well, wizard. Let us test your magic against the power of the Ancient Ones." The ardah closed his eyes and began to chant softly. He lurched forward, extending both arms toward the gate. His fingers were tightly clenched, not into fists but as though gripping some invisible object. Slowly, laboriously, he began to wrench his arms as though turning a great unseen wheel. The southeast gate began to shake and groan.

"Oh *shit,*" said McRofaly.

He was down from the lookout platform in an instant, running away at full speed. Behind him the rumbling, creaking sounds grew continuously louder. Then the southeast gate ripped itself apart. The explosion was as spectacular as the one that had claimed the northeast gate, yet completely different. The blast that took down the northeast gate had been a blazing inferno, like it had been swept away by the wrath of a fire god. This was as though the southeast gate had simply lost the will to exist and obliterated itself in a terrifying suicidal moment. McRofaly stopped and stared in wide-eyed horror as goruks began to file through the rended gate. The certainty of his own death washed over him, nearly suffocating him. He was operating on pure survival instinct now, all his cunning reduced to the simple, primordial act of fighting to stay alive. He began weaving an incantation almost before he realized what he was doing. It was a simple spell, one of the first Esten had taught him, just an elementary warping of sound. Usually it was used to muffle noise, but it could swing the other way as well. Concentrating entirely on the message, McRofaly threw everything he had into it. The sound was deafening, coming from everywhere and nowhere, reverberating out of the very air itself.

"GORUKS IN TAMENDAD!!!"

Even the ardah was halted for a moment by the shock of it, the impossible volume, and McRofaly took full advantage of the goruks' hesitation. He ran faster than he had ever run in his life. The goruks' shock at the explosive noise soon subsided as it became clear that it was an isolated occurrence, not the precursor of some horrible doom about to be rained down upon them, and once again they began to flood into the streets of Tamendad. McRofaly could hear them closing in behind him, gaining ground with every step. They were mere feet behind now. The noose was tightening around his neck. He had just one option left, one more thing he had never tried before and the hope that it would be enough to spare him from so ill a fate. He ducked down a narrow side street, but instead of continuing to run he turned and stood fast.

"*Arcoos Nargai,*" McRofaly intoned, and at once he felt the power surge into him, filling every fiber of his body to the saturation point. His whole being was effused with it, and he felt as though he might wash away on its current. The waves of power began to flow within him, coursing through his veins like precious lifeblood, flowing down his arms, concentrating in his hands. All of this happened in less than a heartbeat. This was the first offensive incantation he had ever learned, and until now he had never used it against a living thing. His fingers glowed and crackled with the power. That was the one shortcoming of the spell, and the reason McRofaly had never used it openly before: its effects were visible to the naked eye, which was tantamount to screaming, "Get the stake ready, boys, we're gonna burn ourselves a warlock!" Under the present circumstances, however, McRofaly was more than willing to take a chance on it.

A goruk turned the corner mere moments after McRofaly had, holding its scimitar high and jabbering like a rabid dog as it came. Its eyes widened in surprise as it found itself rushing toward a paleskin that was not running away, but patiently awaiting it with glowing hands. McRofaly lunged, driving both palms hard into the goruk's sternum before it had a chance to swing its sword, and at once he felt the power surge out of his fingertips and into the goruk's body, scrambling its brains and roasting its organs. The monstrosity's eyes widened further, its mouth went slack, and a gurgling sound came from the back of its throat. McRofaly was aware of it slumping helplessly to the ground, and of the putrid stench of charred flesh and burnt hair, but distantly, as though through a dizzying cyclonic haze. Something was wrong. Something very strange was happening. McRofaly had the sensation of falling, not to the ground but *through* himself, *outside* himself, outside reality. He closed his eyes and found he could not open them again. The world around him fell away, and...

Red is the color. But not just red. Scarlet. Crimson. Red the color of blood, the color of life, the color of death. The blood flows and eddies like a river, and the River runs in a place where time means nothing. Red is the only color, for all else is monochrome, all the shades of grey. The Grey encompasses all except the River. The Grey communicates the essence of oblivion better than oblivion itself ever could. This place was once alive. It is impossible to say how that is known, but it is known all the same, with as much certainty as that it is now dead. Spires reach toward the pallid sky, spires black the color of soot, trying to escape the emptiness that encompasses this place. The spires were once trees. That, too, is known. They are all that remain of the life that once thrived here. Now they are hollow, devoid of soul, a testament to death's triumph over life. Everything died with the River, but only the River was able to transcend death. Now it alone thrives in this ashen landscape, this barren world that is not a world, this emptiness given form. The River is the End, the place where all paths eventually converge. It is a crossroads. A nexus. It is where they all end up, sooner or later. They come willingly but unknowingly to this place, just as McRofaly has come here now. McRofaly will go back from whence he came, for this is but his first visit and he does not yet understand. But some who travel the River never leave again. The River is the End. The River is not the Source, but it is the

Key. The River is the Path of Understanding. The River is eternal, for the River flows from the Word, and the Word is...

KALATHEPTORIS

McRofaly wretched. He felt like his whole body was crawling with maggots and flies and lice and spiders and all manner of unmentionable, nasty things. He felt soiled to his core, and he wretched up what food was in his stomach all over the body of the dead goruk that lay at his feet. He knew – he did not know how he knew, but he knew – that he had only been gone for the briefest of moments. But he also knew that he really had been gone, that he had traveled somewhere else, somewhere very far away, and that he had not traveled there in body. He had gone there only in mind. And he never, ever wanted to go back there. *I'm never using that spell again,* he thought. *Not if that's what happens.*

His senses cleared a bit, and he became aware once again of the imminent danger he was in. Another goruk had come around the corner and was now staring at him, an indescribable look of horror mixed with revulsion firmly entrenched on its face. McRofaly was not particularly surprised. The thing had just come around the bend to witness McRofaly drop its comrade with some brilliant flash of light, then go cross-eyed for a moment and throw up all over its comrade's dead body. It was enough to cause anyone's brain to stick for a moment. But McRofaly appreciated that the moment would soon be over, and he was hopelessly overmatched. He had been a fool to try to turn and stand against this. He had nothing approximating the sort of power it would take to contend with this goruk threat. Against one or two he would be invincible, especially with subterfuge as his co-conspirator. Against hundreds of armed and enraged goruks who already knew the truth of what he was, he would be dead. Esten was right again.

Without hesitation he gripped the end of his walking stick firmly in both hands, bringing it down swiftly and cracking it over the goruk's skull. The goruk dropped to its knees and once again McRofaly ran, but by now the goruks were swarming the streets. Every way he looked he saw goruks up ahead, spreading out across the city like a plague, and he was right out in the middle of it. He had been spotted from numerous directions, and now they were closing in to finish him off. McRofaly exercised the only option he had left. He screamed.

"Help me, dear God, please, somebody help me!" To his great surprise, he received an answer.

"Over here! There's one over here! C'mon!" And suddenly there was screaming and yelling going on all around McRofaly, and the sound of fighting, and Gunther was leading a band of Ganugamosh through the street toward McRofaly, cutting down the goruks that stood in their way. The goruks quickly lost interest in McRofaly, focusing instead on the short, stout newcomers. "McRofaly!" Gunther yelled over the din of battle. "Stick close to me, boy! I'll make sure you don't get skewered!" And then the short blacksmith laughed like a madman as he split the skull of a goruk in two with his axe. As McRofaly fell into the midst of the Ganugamosh, he thought it was the most beautiful sight he had ever seen.

Ferdinan and Colvin came running down the hillside toward Tamendad as quickly as their legs would carry them, calling out all the while for the gatekeepers inside the southwest gate to open the doors. In their panicked return to the city, they had failed to notice that the doors of the southwest gate were already creaking open. The gatekeepers had heard McRofaly's magical warning even more clearly than had the soldiers atop Blood Hill, and the lookouts had already noticed Ferdinan and Colvin urgently leading the charge back to Tamendad.

Ferdinan and Colvin hurried through the gate, followed by the seventy or so constables and militiamen that had followed them. Now for the first time Ferdinan spared a moment to look them over, and he cursed under his breath as he did so. Not that there was anything wrong with these men and women – they were all fine soldiers – but they were hardly enough to hold Tamendad, and there was not a single person of rank among them. Everyone of importance or considerable skill had followed Kor's army in a wild goose chase far away from where the real battle was going to take place.

"Es no good," Ferdinan whispered. "We cannot win like this."

"That's the spirit," said Colvin, who was standing close enough to overhear.

Ferdinan shook his head. "No, I mean we cannot hope to hold the city with only these soldiers. We cannot accomplish anything with barely seventy men. We must go to the northeast gate and join up with Shield Division."

"But if we do that, the southwest gate will be undefended. If Gregor can't hold against Kor's army–"

"If Gregor cannot hold, we are all dead," said Ferdinan.

"Good point," said Colvin. "Come on, let's get to the gate."

But they had not made it three blocks down the main street before they were blindsided by a pack of about twenty goruks. Normally a group of seventy constables and militiamen would have made short work of so few goruks, but they came at full sprint, seeming to just appear right out of the shadows of a blind alley, and they never stopped running. They just attacked as they rushed by, and they were gone before the Tamendaders even had a chance to set themselves for an attack. When it was over, mere moments after it had begun, the goruks had dropped ten men and lost only two of their own in the process.

"You must stay alert at all times!" commanded Ferdinan. "There are too many places for goruks to hide! An attack can come from anywhere!" The soldiers took Ferdinan's words to heart, but two blocks farther up the street the same thing happened again. This time they fared a little better, losing only seven of their own and dropping three goruks.

"Es not going to work," Ferdinan said, glancing at the dwindling number of troops he now led. "They are using hit and run tactics."

"So what else is new?" said Colvin as he wiped the goruk blood from the blade of his dagger-glove.

"Sí, but es much too easy for them to run and hide, fighting in the streets like this," said Ferdinan. "We will never be able to engage them, and our men simply are not trained for this sort of fighting."

"So what are we going to do?" said Colvin. To him it sounded an awful lot like Ferdinan was giving up, but he just could not make himself believe that.

"We have one chance," said Ferdinan, looking simultaneously thoughtful and skeptical. "Es a long shot, but perhaps es a day for miracles."

Before Colvin had a chance to ask Ferdinan what the twist he was talking about, he was interrupted by the frantic tolling of bells from deeper within the city. "Kind of late to be sounding the alarm now, isn't it?" said Colvin.

Ferdinan's brow was furrowed as he listened intently to the bells for a moment, and then a look of horror spread over his face. He broke instantly into a sprint down the main street. "Es not the alarm!" he screamed over his shoulder. "Es coming from the church!"

It was an honest mistake, but a potentially disastrous one. Everyone in Tamendad incapable of fighting had been shut up tight in the Governor's house for their own protection. This included people like the Governor's stablemaster, the cooks and most of the town criers. It also included McRofaly and the Governor himself. But it did not include the priests, nor the people who were too badly injured to be transferred from the healers' hospital to the Governor's house. No one had really given that much thought during the hasty preparations for war after Ian Morlocke had delivered his final report. Priests were never evacuated during a war, because no one ever attacked a church. There was nothing to gain from it. The Antrelican Church remained neutral in political affairs. The most involved it ever became was participating in the coronation of kings. So the church had been overlooked, as had the fact that the goruks might consider it a target worthy of their attention.

The scene at the church was straight out of a nightmare. Goruks were pushing their way up the steps toward the entrance. The heavy brass doors of the church looked like they had been battered open by a ram, though there was no ram anywhere to be seen now. Two priests lay dead, their blood trickling slowly down the steps, consecrating the place of worship with their sacrifice. Just outside the doors, a handful of priests stood shoulder to shoulder clenching makeshift weapons, trying to hold off the goruks and having about as much success at it as priests would be expected. Carney Gruer was among these priests and was having by far the greatest success against the goruks, using his walking staff as a shillelagh against them. In the whole horrible scene, Gruer was the one uplifting sight. He had a cut across his cheek and another down his side, and his simple vestments were now blood-soaked, but he had a look about him that reminded those who saw him of an oracle calling down fire from the heavens. Three goruks lay unconscious at his feet, and it was obvious that the only reason the goruks had not just bowled right through the priests and into the church was their reluctance to draw too near to Carney's stout shaft of poplar. But from the looks of it, even with Gruer's courageous stand, Ferdinan and Colvin were mere moments from being too late.

"Es *him*," spat Ferdinan, pointing into the crowd of goruks at the base of the church steps. Colvin tore his eyes away from the horror at the church doors and realized at once what Ferdinan was pointing at. Although he had never seen the beast with his own eyes before, Colvin knew that the goruk leading this assault against the church, clad in skins, with feathers in its braided hair, was the one McRofaly called the ardah.

Ferdinan screamed. It was not a scream of fear, but the sound of unbridled rage. Then he charged the goruks. Alone. He did not even bother to command the soldiers to follow him, but they followed nonetheless, as did Colvin. The sight had stirred up similar emotions in them all. The goruks, who were intently focused on the church, were surprised to find themselves suddenly being charged by over fifty thoroughly pissed off Tamendaders, led by one completely livid Conquian, and it was amazing how quickly they shifted from pillaging terrors to trembling cowards. Ferdinan moved like lightning, screaming something in Conquian at the top of his lungs that he would have never dared, under normal circumstances, to utter in the presence of priests. His sabre struck with such swift, deadly accuracy that three goruks had been downed by it before anyone else even had the chance to join the fighting. From goruk to goruk the Conquian danced, killing without mercy and shouting at his victims as they died, always fighting his way closer and closer to the ardah. Colvin was right behind him, not as swift but just as deadly, mercilessly plunging the blades of his dagger gloves into any goruk that came close enough for him to pounce on. The goruks fell back into a tight ring around the ardah, though whether they did this to protect him or because they just wanted to get away from their assailants, it was impossible to tell. One more frenzied push, and the goruks, led by the ardah, retreated hastily up the main street, leaving the church be.

"Do not give chase!" Ferdinan yelled to the soldiers. "We are needed here!" Then he hurried up the blood-slicked steps of the church to check on the priests.

"'Tis a good thing ye came when ye did, brother, or there would have been a lot more blood shed here this day," said Carney Gruer upon seeing Ferdinan.

"Be careful not to speak too quickly, Patrum," said Ferdinan. "The day es just begun. There es plenty of time still for more blood to be shed."

"Well spoken, lad. Where's Gregor?"

"The goruks tricked us into following them by showing signs of retreat. Gregor es still out there fighting them. These are all the men we managed to bring back with us when we realized the deception."

"God be with us," said Patrum Gruer. Ferdinan nodded, making the Sign of the Compass.

"Ferdinan," said Colvin, who had just joined them atop the church steps, "what's that smell?" At first, Ferdinan thought his friend's mind had snapped, asking about smells at a time like this. But as he sniffed the air, Ferdinan smelled it: the acrid, slightly musty smell of wood smoke.

"They are burning the town," said Ferdinan.

"The wall!" exclaimed Colvin. "If it goes up—"

"No, no," said Ferdinan, "they will not burn the city wall. They will want it whole. Es one of the biggest reasons they want Tamendad, because es easily defended."

"Yeah," said Colvin. "Real easy."

"My guess es they are setting fire to some of the houses to confuse and demoralize us," Ferdinan said.

"We have to stop them."

"Es nothing we can do. Even if we could spare the men to form a fire brigade, they would never be able to put the fires out with goruks swarming all over the city."

"Perhaps 'twould be best for ye t' regroup here," said Patrum Gruer. "Rally as many men as ye can and lead them all out t'gether against th' goruks."

Ferdinan sighed. "It cannot be done. Everything es moving too quickly. By the time we found enough men, I am afraid the goruks would already have stormed the Governor's house. I have to get in there and speak with Geoffery before this goes any further. Es still a chance we all might get out of this alive. I will leave these men with you to defend the church."

"Ferdinan," said Colvin, "is that a good…" He trailed off into silence as Ferdinan gave him a look that made his blood run cold.

"I will not leave the church undefended," the Conquian said levelly.

"Right," said Colvin. "What do you want me to do?"

"I need you to get to the northeast gate and meet up with Shield Division. No doubt they have already pulled away from the gate by now to try to engage the goruks, but they should not be difficult to find. I need you to slow the goruks down any way you can. Every moment you buy me could be the difference between life and death."

"Oh, well, no pressure then," said Colvin.

Ferdinan smiled that damned roguish grin that always made Colvin laugh, even now. "What es a life without pressure?" he said.

"I'll do my best," said Colvin with a determined nod.

Ferdinan hugged Colvin tightly and kissed him on either cheek. "God goes with you, *compagno*," he said. "God willing, we will get drunk together on the finest wine and boast of our adventures."

"Who needs to boast?" said Colvin.

They went their separate ways, uncertain if they would ever see each other again, leaving the church behind them and plunging, alone, back into bedlam.

Somewhere along the way, things had started to go wrong. William could not pinpoint exactly when it had begun to happen. It had been simple enough at first, just running after the goruks and trying to get close enough to slide a sword through one's back. The goruks had barely tried to defend themselves; all they had been concerned with had been putting distance between themselves and Tamendad. But the farther they got away from the city, the more they began to engage their pursuers. It began with just a few goruks, the ones bringing up the rear of the pack, turning suddenly and taking a few swings at the nearest humans before turning and fleeing again. The more ground they covered, the more the goruks started fighting back against the humans, until now it had become less of a retreat and more of a strategic withdrawal. The goruks were still backing away, but that was exactly the problem: they were *backing* away, inching backward through the hills while concentrating on fighting the forces of Tamendad. And they weren't backing away very quickly at all. Now whenever the soldiers would push the goruks back, they would push them right up a hillside. This gave the goruks the advantage of higher ground, so that every step the Tamendaders backed the goruks up proved more difficult than the one before it. It also seemed that the goruks were fighting more fiercely and intelligently now, harder even than they had fought atop the hill. It was not just that each individual goruk was fighting harder or smarter. All of them together were fighting more cohesively as a group. In the middle of it all Kor was quickly barking orders here and there, commanding his warriors this way and that in his own language. He had also lost the frantic, panicked demeanor with which he had given the order to retreat, now issuing his commands with a cool confidence that William, at least, found unnerving.

William fought alongside his father, leading an assorted group of about twenty Swords and constables in a push against an equal detachment of goruks that had been giving them problems. Both he and his father were bleeding. The wounds were superficial but numerous, and there had been far too many close calls and near misses for William to feel like his side had any genuine advantage in this confrontation. Whenever William thought he and his father were finally about to rout them, the goruks would do something – usually something unorthodox – that salvaged their hides. It was never enough to swing the balance in their favor, just enough to make William's side have to regroup and try again. That seemed to be the story all over the battlefield. The momentum had shifted away from the assured victory of the forces of Tamendad and into the tedium of a stalemate. Only Gregor seemed not to be having any trouble handling the goruks, cutting through them as easily as always. Then again, William assumed Gregor would have had no problem dealing with anything, the state that he was in. The big Highlander could have probably carved his way through a mountain.

It had been a while now since they had pursued the goruks down the hillside away from Tamendad. The withdrawal had ground to a standstill, and now they fought in a bowl of land between two hills. It had become apparent to the Tamendaders by this time that a good portion of their number was missing. All the Highlanders appeared to be here, but many of the constables and militiamen were nowhere to be found. They were not dead – really very few people were dying at the moment in this standoff. They were simply missing. Foremost of these in William's mind, and quite a few others', were Ferdinan and Colvin. William was relatively certain that Colvin was okay. At least, that had been the case when William had last seen him, right before following the retreating goruks down the hillside.

He had not seen Ferdinan in quite a while, but he felt certain that the news of anything happening to the Conquian would have spread quickly even in the confusion of battle. It was inconceivable that they would not be here if they were still able to fight. William could not imagine where they might be. Almost involuntarily he turned for a moment back in the direction of Tamendad, and he almost expected to see them leading a charge of reinforcements toward them. What he saw instead made his breath catch in his lungs. Over the hills in the distance, pillars of smoke were billowing their way heavenward. The city itself was concealed from view by the hills here, but the source of that smoke was unmistakable and inescapable.

Tamendad was burning.

William pointed, in much the same way that a little boy might point to a shadowy corner of his bedchamber in the hopes that his parents will assure him that there are no monsters lurking there, and he screamed.

"LOOK!!!"

In his shock he could manage that single word, and yet still his command was easier said than done. There was, after all, a battle going on at the moment, and if everyone had stopped fighting to turn around and look when William said to look, the results would have proven disastrous. But slowly, one by one, men and women began to sneak a glance behind them when the opportunity presented itself, and word of what they saw there began to spread.

"It's a damn ruse!" Jonathan Stuart-Camen screamed. "Pull back! We've got to get back to Tamendad!"

And then the goruks went stark raving mad.

It happened so suddenly, after such a long back-and-forth parlay, that the humans were almost overwhelmed in an instant. The goruks came on like rabid, ravenous dogs that had suddenly slipped the leash, and even Gregor had to draw back from them. The goruks swarmed, spreading out in all directions, herding and encircling their opponents, their weapons moving in a blur of all-out assault. A good number of goruks died doing that, going completely on the offense without any concern for defending themselves, but they took down a fair number of humans with them. They also ensured that the humans were not going anywhere, which had been Kor's aim all along. The forces of Tamendad soon found themselves huddled together in a jumbled mass against the surrounding goruks, doing all they could just to keep the green monsters at bay. All sense of order was lost. It was a bitter realization that the battle had finally come full circle.

"What the twist are we going to do?" screamed William. In all the chaos and confusion he had to yell at the top of his lungs just to be heard. "We have to get back and help defend the city!" There was no longer any doubt in his mind where Ferdinan and Colvin were.

"Aye, and good luck with that, lad!" cried some random Highlander. "I'm sure if ye explain it t' them like that, they'll be sure t' let ye pass by."

William had no time for a retort. A pack of goruks, maybe forty in number, were spearheading their way right into the heart of the Tamendad forces. "Stick close to me son," he heard his father say with surprising confidence, and then the goruks were upon them. William did as he was told, pressing his back against his father's as the goruks engulfed them. William's blade carved out a halo of safety around him, pricking any goruk that came too close, but he knew there was no way he could keep it up forever. He and his father were backing away from the oncoming goruks, but soon they would reach the tightly packed nucleus of their own soldiers and there would simply be nowhere left to go. They would be cornered. For a moment William thought that the goruks would push their way right through the cluster of Highlanders and constables and militiamen, dividing the forces of Tamendad and routing them. It was the first time since the very beginning of the war that the certainty of defeat had welled up in William's heart, and it threatened to smother him. But just as William grew certain that all hope was about to break, the goruks hit a wall – quite literally. That same packed nucleus that the goruks had backed William and Jonathan into prevented them from going any farther. They could not wedge their way through it or risk becoming surrounded and crushed. And then, using their own density, the forces of Tamendad began to push back, some Highlanders literally pushing on the backs of those in front of them to force the goruks to concede ground. The goruks were forced to withdraw. The same thing happened from the other side of the circle, more goruks trying to wedge their way into the huddled Tamendaders and Highlanders, and with the same result. This attempt did not even reach William and his father before being pushed back. Another wave of goruks came in from another side only to be pushed back in the end, and another, and another, and never did the goruks succeed in pressing their way completely through, but the strategy was having some success nonetheless. Each time a wave of goruks would press its way forward and fall back, it left a trail of human bodies in its wake. Apparently the goruks were content to take down their opponents a handful at a time.

There was activity among the goruks. It was not another press into

Tamendad's forces. There was movement along the perimeter of the goruk circle, something that looked like a division of forces. William and Jonathan watched along with everyone else as a group of about fifty goruks broke away from the rest, not coming toward the Highlanders and Tamendaders but moving farther away from them. William could not see what was happening very well, but it was obvious that something important was going on. He craned his neck in hopes of catching a better view. He failed at that, but in his attempt he spotted Gregor standing about twenty feet away. William had to scream three times, each at the top of his lungs, to catch the big Highlander's attention and ask him what was happening.

"Some o' th' goruks are pulling away and heading back toward Tamendad," said Gregor. "That bastard Kor's leading them out!"

"We can't let him get into Tamendad!" William yelled. But there was nothing that could be done about it, because at that moment the circle of goruks surrounding them began to tighten. It no longer came on as a series of waves. All the goruks began to advance at once, clamping down around them like a vice. The Highlanders and Tamendaders, who were already crammed together, began to fall back more, until those at the fringe had nowhere left to retreat, and those in the center were packed together so tightly they could not even ready their weapons.

"This is it," Jonathan said as he and William stood shoulder to shoulder, watching the goruks approach. "They're going to try to squeeze us like a cider press. Stay alert."

William felt more alert than he had felt in a long time, more alert than perhaps he would have chosen to be as he watched the goruk circle contract tighter around them. He and his father were close to the edge of the pack, and soon the goruks were upon them. William stayed close to his father, both men's broadswords working frantically to hold the tusked monsters at bay. They were doing fairly well at first, it seemed, managing to take a few good chunks out of some goruks' hides, pushing them a step backwards or at least to the side. But every time a goruk dropped or pulled away, two more were there to take its place. The circle of goruks deepened as it constricted, and it was now six or eight bodies deep. The holes William and his father cut into it closed up right before their eyes. They tried to back farther away but it was quickly becoming too crowded to maneuver. They were stuck.

As he tried to take just one more step backward, Jonathan stepped on the body of a fallen Highlander. His foot slipped. He teetered for an agonizing moment as he lost his balance, then took a tumble to one knee. It was all so quick that William did not even notice it happen. But the goruks did. Two of them were there in an instant, pouncing on Jonathan like lions on a sick and weakened antelope. The first goruk slashed him across the chest from shoulder to shoulder, a deep gash that spurted blood. Jonathan screamed out in pain and tensed, and as he did so the second goruk slid its scimitar into his abdomen. William screamed as for the first time he realized what was happening. It was a scene that would haunt his dreams forever, his father collapsing in a bloody heap, both goruks raising their scimitars for the death blow. There came a sound from William's mouth that could not be rightly called a scream. It was more than a scream, beyond a scream, a sound originating from the deepest, most bestial part of his soul. He was not aware of taking his father's broadsword in his left hand, nor was he aware of turning on the two goruks that had felled his father, but he was aware, then and forevermore, of every cut he bestowed upon those two goruks. And there were many. Never had he savored cutting open flesh and muscle more than he did at that moment, never had he so thoroughly enjoyed causing such pain to another living thing. The howls and screams of the two goruks were the sweetest sounds his ears had ever known, but instead of satiating his desire to cause them harm each scream made him want to hurt them all the more. His swords twirled in a blur of slashes and thrusts as piece by piece he cut his enemies down. He even cut himself once or twice during his assault, though he never knew it. At the time he was immune to the pain, and later there was no way of knowing that some of his wounds were self-inflicted.

Sometime later, both goruks were dead. In truth, dead was an understatement. They were mutilated, dismembered, eviscerated. William stood over what was left of them, both broadswords still held high and ready to swing, wishing the goruks were not dead so he could cause them more pain. He was not aware that there was a battle raging all around him. He was not aware that goruks were closing in on him with a look of bloodlust in their eyes. He was not aware that someone was screaming his name. When he was grabbed from behind he spun without thinking, letting both blades fly wildly, and he would have decapitated Gregor had the big Highlander not grabbed both of his arms and pinned them to his sides. In his state, William did not even realize what he had been about to do.

"Grab yer da, lad," said Gregor, releasing William and taking his claymore in his hands. "Follow close." Gregor's words jarred something in William's brain. He realized people were stepping past him, past his father, keeping the goruks back long enough for William to get his father out of there. Sheathing his swords in an instant, he hoisted his father into his arms. Jonathan opened his eyes and looked at him, and William felt indescribable relief to see he was not dead. Jonathan gave William a look that only can pass between parent and child, the kind that asks all questions and gives all answers in a single glance.

"William," Jonathan whispered, "I don't ever want to see you do anything like that again."

Gregor pushed his way farther into the crowd of Highlanders and Tamendaders, toward the middle. When they were a few good feet removed from the fighting, Gregor helped William lay Jonathan delicately on the ground and looked him over quickly. "'Tis serious," he said gravely, "but from th' look of it, I think 'tis nae mortal. How do ye feel, Jonathan?"

"Cold. I need a healer."

Gregor nodded. "Aye, lad. We'll get ye t' one. In th' meantime, I need ye t' put yer fist inside yer wound. Th' deep one. Can ye do that? Do ye have th' strength?" Jonathan nodded, and Gregor nodded in return. Then he turned to William and said, "We have t' end this. Now. We have t' get back t' Tamendad."

"I'm with you," said William, pulling both his swords again.

"Nae, lad, ye need t' stay here."

William shook his head vehemently. "No, Gregor," he protested. "I have to kill them. All of them."

"Ye're talking crazy, lad. I need ye t' keep yer wits about ye. Ye have t' stay with yer da. He needs ye. This fight's about t' grow intense, and yer da cannae defend himself if a goruk reaches him."

"Right," said William, looking down at his father. "Right."

"All right, lad. Be careful, and stay on yer toes. M' lads and I are going t' end this thing." Then Gregor held his claymore high and called out in an impossibly loud voice, "*Eyre Dammaugh meínar go Angus bràidir gabrach!*" The reaction this evoked in the Highlanders was the same as if the goruks had gone up to every single Highlander there and called his mother a whore. Some dam that held back the full extent of the Highlanders' rage and bloodlust – even now, in the heat of battle – burst, and suddenly the Highlanders were no longer men but great wild beasts. William did not know all the words Gregor had spoken, but he had learned enough of the old tongue to piece together the general meaning: *The wrath of the Highlands for the wrongs done to brother Angus.*

William crouched low over his father, trying to watch in all directions at once for any goruks that happened to make it through the Highlanders and Tamendaders. Around him, the battle had reached its zenith. The Highlanders were exploding through the confinement of the goruk circle, bowling their way through, many dying in the process. It was as though they had been waiting all along for Gregor's signal that it was past time to care whether they lived or died.

Governor Chamberlain stared out of the window of the meeting room, the same room in which the war council met. He was on the third floor, along with every citizen remaining in Tamendad, because it was, according to Don Ferdinan, the most strategically sound place for him to be in the event that the goruks breached the perimeter of the city wall. The iron gate leading to the courtyard of his house was locked and barred, as was every door and window on the first floor. All the stairways up from the first floor had been barricaded and members of the Governor's guard were posted at each barricade. Two archers stood at either end of the third floor hallway, ready to pick off any goruks that did manage to make their way up the stairs. Then, inside the locked and barred door of this meeting room, two more guardsmen stood with Governor Chamberlain as the last line of defense. Geoffery could definitely see the good Don's point, at least from a military point of view, but now that the goruks had actually gotten into the city he felt as though he was trapped in a burning prison tower. Goruks were beginning to gather in front of his house like some monstrous constituency come to claim the head of their king. At the moment it looked like there were no more than fifty goruks out there, but more were arriving all the time. Geoffery knew, of course, once he had heard that the goruks were in the city it was only a matter of time before they found him. His house was the most conspicuous building in Tamendad besides the church.

He watched silently as down below in the courtyard the majority of his personal guard busied themselves with repelling the goruks who managed to climb the ten-foot stone wall that was, for the moment at least, managing to keep most of them at bay. There were not yet enough goruks gathered there to overwhelm the guards, and most of them were not even bothering to attempt scaling the stone wall yet, so the Governor's guards were not having too terribly difficult a time doing their jobs for the moment. Most of the goruks down there were just standing and waiting, with weapons drawn and a look of anxious impatience in their eyes. They looked like they were waiting for something, and Geoffery could guess what it was. Kor was not down there yet. The goruks were waiting for their great general to lead them into the glory of victory.

Governor Chamberlain turned away from the window. It was like a bad play out there, the sort of melodramatic nonsense that kept the audience on the edge of their seats right up to the end. That seemed fitting. All that Tamendad had been through over the last few weeks would have been enough to make the worst hack of a tragedian rich beyond his wildest dreams. Geoffery poured himself a glass of brandy and found that his hand shook as he did so. He was so unaccustomed to being frightened that he was uncertain exactly what he was supposed to do. Part of him wanted to crawl under the table, while another part wanted to take one of his guardsmen's swords and leap right out the window into the middle of the goruk mob and not stop hacking away until every last one of them was dead as a doornail. So he compromised at last on a nip of brandy to settle his nerves.

"It does not look good out there," he said offhandedly to his two guards. They looked at him with nervous eyes.

"No, sir," they said in unison, neither relaxing their attention, both trying their best, and failing, to promote a sense of confidence.

Geoffery sighed as he slid into his usual chair at the table. Everyone else who usually sat at that table with him was out there right now fighting to save him and his town. Everyone except Amon Jefford, who had already given up his life for that cause. That thought made him wonder if any of the other members of the war council had already made that same sacrifice today. Under the circumstances, it appeared entirely likely. He sighed.

"Do you know what separates a good leader from a bad one?" Governor Chamberlain asked his two guards.

"What's that, sir?" they replied, looking at him. This track of conversation seemed to interest them a bit more than commenting on what was going on outside.

"One will follow a good cause all the way to the end, no matter the cost, while the other will abandon it when the cost grows too high." The guards nodded with feigned thoughtfulness. Governor Chamberlain sank back into his chair.

I just wish I knew which was which.

Colvin snuck through the streets alone, edging his way toward the northeast gate. He stuck to side streets and alleyways, doing his best to avoid the main street; its width and openness just made him feel too exposed. A haze of smoke was beginning to settle over the city. It was not enough to reduce visibility, but it made Colvin's eyes water and his throat feel like it was about to seize up and in general added one more annoyance to an already frustrating situation. With his dagger gloves, Colvin had to be careful when he rubbed his eyes in the smoke. The first time he had done it he had not been thinking, and he had come damn close to maiming himself. That was all he needed now that everything was on the line, to die by running himself through the eye.

He had not seen a single soul since leaving the church, but he knew they were out there. He could hear them, and by the sounds of it they were somewhere close by. The sounds of fighting echoed through the streets, a mishmash of human and goruk voices shouting commands and obscenities mixed with the ring of steel against steel and the screams of the wounded and dying. But Colvin could tell that what he was drawing nearer to was not a major standoff. The sounds were too isolated and spread out for that. It sounded like Shield Division was having the same problems Colvin and Ferdinan had experienced. The need for haste pressed down on Colvin's mind, and Ferdinan's words – *every moment you buy me could be the difference between life and death* – kept echoing in his brain. But he had to be careful. One hasty, careless step could potentially open him up to sneak attack by unseen goruks, and then where would Ferdinan be? Probably in the same place as Colvin: atop the summit, recounting how good a try they made of it against such overwhelming odds. He had not come this far and survived for this long only to die when the war was on the line just because he had been too hasty to see the danger coming.

Colvin crept down an alleyway so narrow that the walls brushed his shoulders as he walked. It was difficult to keep track of his location, skulking like he was, but by his best guess he was more than halfway to the northeast gate. About fifteen feet ahead, where the alleyway emptied into a street, there came the unmistakable sounds of conflict. What was more, Colvin could make out shadows gliding across the ground in a dance of violence. He stooped down low in the alleyway to conceal himself. It was still a few hours before noon and the sun was only about halfway into the eastern sky, which meant the alleyway was still shadowy enough to obscure him until he was at the very edge of it. With a spot of luck he would be able to introduce himself into the fray completely undetected and take the goruks by surprise. He crept forward in an awkward, stooping walk, his arms held tensed in front of him, ready to strike with his dagger-gloves at a moment's notice. He was within mere feet of the alley's end before he got a look at the action. It was the closest thing to a real battle he had yet seen in Tamendad that day, about thirty goruks squared off against twenty Shields, with neither side giving an inch. At first Colvin was surprised to find goruks standing fast against odds so nearly even, but he quickly realized the reason why. Gangis was among the Shields, his single-hafted axe soaked and gleaming with goruk blood. The goruks could obviously tell that he was part Ganugamosh, because they were singling him out. At the moment he was fending off three goruks, and doing surprisingly well at it.

Colvin's opportunity came so quickly it almost passed him by. Gangis was backing away from the goruks and toward the alleyway Colvin was hidden in, trying to get his back against a wall to keep the goruks from surrounding him, when the heel of his boot caught on an uneven cobblestone. He tripped and fell flat on his back, losing his grip on his axe, not ten feet from where Colvin was hidden. The three goruks were around him in an instant, moving in for the kill. In the process, two of the goruks turned their backs to the alleyway. Colvin cursed as he sprang forward out of the shadows, driving the blades of his dagger gloves through the base of the two goruks' necks and up into their skulls. They dropped into a twitching heap just as the third goruk took a swipe at Gangis's head with its scimitar. The blade seemed to move in slow motion, gliding through its arc at a snail's pace, yet Colvin moved more slowly still. Less than three feet away from the assailant, he was powerless to save Gangis's life. Thankfully Gangis was capable of saving his own. He rolled aside at the last moment, and the goruk's scimitar struck only cobblestone. Colvin lunged, putting everything he had into the punch. The blade of his dagger-glove pierced the goruk's throat and his fist crushed its windpipe. It fell immediately into a fetal position, kicking its feet wildly, clenching its throat, gurgling and gasping wetly as it died. Colvin kicked it hard in the abdomen; why, he never exactly knew. He chalked it up to simple frustration.

"Thanks," said Gangis, still lying on the ground, looking up at Colvin with wide eyes. "I owe you one."

Colvin extended a hand to offer Gangis a lift up. "Don't mention it. I–"

"Behind you!" Gangis screamed, pointing frantically. Colvin spun in one fluid motion before his conscious mind had even registered what Gangis had said, some primitive part of him deep down inside, a part that had been tempered at the forge of war, reacting involuntarily to the threat of danger. A lightning-quick arc as he pulled his sabre from the sheath at his side, a flash of steel, a spray of blood, the sound of the goruk's severed head hitting the ground: every moment, every detail of it no matter how minute was burned forever into Colvin's memory. The goruk's decapitated body remained standing for the briefest of moments, then fell limply beside its head. Colvin's heart was in his throat. His fingers were clenched so tightly around his sabre that his hand was going numb. He looked back to Gangis, who was just getting to his feet.

"We're even," said Colvin.

"Are you all right?"

"No harm done." Colvin glanced around quickly and saw that the same could not be said for many of the other combatants. Most of the goruks were dead, as were most of Gangis's companions. Five Shields remained standing including Gangis. It looked like about ten goruks had decided that a halfblood was not worth dying for and made a run for it. "Where's your father, Gangis?" Colvin asked. "We could use him right now."

"He led the Ganugamosh into the residential district against the goruks," Gangis said. "It looked like that was where most of them were headed."

"Good," said Colvin, distantly, as though to himself. "Good. We've got that going for us. That should already have made a difference."

After a moment of hesitation, during which Gangis looked uncertain about which of the numerous questions going through his head he should ask first, he said, "What are you doing here? Not that I'm not thankful," he added hastily, "I just thought–"

"It was a setup," Colvin interrupted. "There's no time to explain. Ferdinan and I figured it out before it was too late. Now he's trying to get into the Governor's house, and he needs us to hold up the goruks to buy him some time."

Gangis nodded, suddenly understanding. "Right," he said. "Let's round up a few more Shields and get to the residential district."

"No, there's no time," said Colvin. "I took too long getting here as it is. It's going to have to be us."

Gangis looked at Colvin like he had just asked him to move the world. "How are we supposed to hold back the goruks? There's six of us."

Colvin stared blankly at Gangis for a moment, and at the four other Shields who now stood around him. "I don't know," he said at last. This did nothing to improve the spirits of the Shields. "We can't just try to fight them," he added. "For one thing, we'd get slaughtered, and for another, goruks would just slip past us through the streets. We have to think of something else."

"Like what?" said one of the Shields.

"I said I don't know!" Colvin snapped. "A moment to think," he whispered to himself. "Just one moment to think. That's all I ask." He threw his head back and gazed up at the blue morning sky as though he expected the heavens to offer up a solution, but all he could see of the heavens was the narrow strip that ran between the tightly clustered buildings that crowded this narrow side street. His brow furrowed as he focused on those buildings.

"Archers," he said, turning his gaze from the sky.

"What?" asked Gangis.

"We didn't use any archers against the goruks today. Why?"

"There aren't enough arrows left to outfit them," said another Shield.

"But there are still *some* arrows left?" said Colvin.

A couple of the Shields looked at each other. "I think so," said one of them.

"And bows?"

"Plenty of bows," said Gangis. "A ton of bows."

"Where?" asked Colvin.

"There should be some in the guardhouse at the northeast gate."

They ran at a sprint to the guardhouse. It was locked, but Gangis had a key. Inside they found at least thirty bows, but only thirty-seven arrows. Not even enough to fill a single archer's quiver. Colvin did not look troubled by that at all. "That's six arrows for each of us," he said. "I'll take the extra one. Everyone grab a bow."

"What good are six arrows going to do against all those goruks?" asked one of the Shields. "There's hundreds of them. It won't even make a dent."

"We're not trying to kill them," Colvin explained. "We're trying to intimidate them. Look, the Governor's house is in the corner of the town, right? There's only two streets you can come down to get to it. All the houses on those streets have balconies and decks, and a lot of them have flat roofs. Plenty of places to position archers. As the goruks come down those streets, we loose a few arrows on them. They'll have no way of knowing that we've only got a few arrows apiece."

"Sounds good," said Gangis. "But our deception won't last long."

"It won't have to last long. Just a few minutes should be enough time. Now come on, Ferdinan's probably to the Governor's house already. We have to hurry. Grab a bow."

They felt a little like goruks, sneaking quickly through the residential district, staying out of the way of the fighting that was going on. They made good time, but some of the goruks had beaten them and were already amassed in front of the Governor's house. There was around a hundred of them, by the look of it, but apparently the Governor's guard was holding. "No time to worry about that," said Colvin. "Find a good spot, and hold your arrows until you know you've got a good shot. We have to make every one count." They split up. Three Shields set up on the street that cut across from the main street. Colvin, Gangis, and the other Shield took the street that came up from the northwest gate. They formed a triangle around a section of street about four blocks from the Governor's house. Colvin positioned himself on the roof of the Stuart-Camen home, Gangis two houses up on a balcony of the Dalsandrian household, and the Shield across the street atop the home of the Tamendad Moricans.

They did not have to wait long before the goruks began coming up the street in force. It looked as though Tamendad's final stand against the goruks was finally breaking. Colvin nocked an arrow, his eye on a group of about forty goruks walking briskly up the street toward him. They goruk in the lead of the pack was most definitely in charge. It was bigger and stronger than its companions, and it kept yelling out what Colvin assumed were orders to the others, spurring them along up the street. Colvin drew back his bowstring, taking aim at the lead goruk. He held still as a statue, waiting with bated breath for the right moment to loose.

What the twist are you doing? You've never shot a bow in your life.

Colvin released the bowstring. The arrow zipped away, silently slicing the air as it flew. The arrowhead must have caught the morning sunlight just before Colvin shot, because the goruk commander turned in his direction just as he was releasing the string as though something had caught its attention. The arrow flew right through its eye. There was no scream, no blood, no agonizing death. The goruk just fell down and did not move again.

"Wow," whispered Colvin to himself. "I did it."

Another arrow zipped into the pack of goruks, shot by Gangis. It took another one through the throat. The rest began to back down the street, away from the Governor's house. It was working. More goruks were coming down the street, but they were hesitating now as word spread of what had happened and they saw the two dead goruks in the street with their own eyes. A few goruks tried to creep closer, trying either to sneak by unnoticed or to fetch the bodies of their two fallen comrades. An arrow from the Shield across the street struck one in the chest, and the others pulled back. The confusion would not last long, Colvin knew, but it was buying precious time.

Colvin heard someone scream his name. He turned and saw Gangis pointing at something.

"Look!"

Colvin looked. Ferdinan was walking across the top of the city wall, toward the Governor's house. "What the twist is he doing?" Colvin said to himself, turning back and shooting another arrow into the goruks.

Ferdinan left the church behind him, hurrying into the residential district. It did not look like many goruks had made it into this part of the city yet, but there were enough to make him have to stay alert. The caution he was forced to exercise slowed him down, and every moment that slipped away from him was a moment that brought Tamendad that much closer to defeat. He had to make it to the Governor's house, and quickly, before the goruks took it by force. If the Face of Consonance smiled on him this day, there was still a chance that Tamendad might be saved.

The sounds of fighting became discernible as he drew farther into the residential district, nearing the noblemen's houses. The smoke began to grow thicker, too. He could see two houses ablaze from where he stood, and he was certain there were more burning elsewhere. None close enough to the wall to endanger it but all close enough to the Governor's house to send a message. There were times that the smoke was so thick that Ferdinan had to cup his hand over his mouth to breathe. It was like this, with his eyes watering so much that he could see no farther than ten feet in front of him, that he came around a corner and found himself in the heat of battle. Ganugamosh and goruks fought all over the street, railing against each other with axes and scimitars and, just as frequently, with bare hands. Bodies were strewn about the street, and the cobblestones were slick with blood. Only now did Ferdinan understand the enmity between the two races. Several on both sides were maimed, some having lost limbs, others partially disemboweled, but they fought on. One Ganugamosh that had lost both his legs was literally pulling himself up the street with one hand and swinging his axe in the other, leaving a trail of blood behind him. A goruk was using its own severed arm as a makeshift club against the Ganugamosh. In the midst of the carnage, Gunther was screaming orders to his kinsmen. The short blacksmith was covered in blood from head to foot, his beard tangled and partially ripped out, and he was busying himself with pulling the intestines from the opened abdomen of a screaming, convulsing goruk. The scene turned Ferdinan's stomach. He ducked into the yard of a modest landowner's house and convinced himself not to throw up. There was no way he was going to get through the massacre in that street. He had to find another way.

"Psst," someone whispered. "Ferdinan! Ferdinan, over here!" Ferdinan looked all around, and he almost did not notice McRofaly peering out at him from the window of the house. The short man had stuck his head up just enough to be able to see, and his nose was resting on the windowsill. "Hurry, Ferdinan!" McRofaly whispered. "The door's unlocked!" Ferdinan arched an eyebrow, but he took McRofaly's invitation. As he stepped through the front door into the common room of the house, McRofaly came rushing up to him. "Thank God you're alive, Ferdinan," he said. "We've got to get out of here."

"McRofaly, why are you not at the Governor's house?" said Ferdinan.

"I slipped past the Governor's guards," McRofaly said. "It's a good thing, too. That's where they're all heading. I'd be trapped like a rat."

Ferdinan looked thoughtful for a moment. "I need you to do me a favor, McRofaly. I need you to deliver a message."

"Are you crazy? The only way I'm leaving this house is to get out of the city."

"Es esactly what I have in mind," said Ferdinan.

"Okay, I'm listening."

"I need you to get a message to Gregor, outside the city. Tell him that no matter what it looks like, he must trust me."

"What are you going to do?"

"I am not quite certain yet. I have to get into the Governor's house first."

"That's crazy, Ferdinan! It's suicide! Look around. It's over. The war's lost. We have to get out of here. Together. We'll meet up with Gregor and go to the Highlands. The goruks won't dare come that far south. At least not for a while."

Ferdinan grabbed McRofaly by the collar and pulled him in until their noses were an inch apart, staring into his eyes with an intensity that made McRofaly want to shrink away. "I am not about to leave this city, not while there es even the slightest chance left to save it."

"Okay," said McRofaly. "All right. Suit yourself. I'll get your message to Gregor, but how am I supposed to get out of the city?"

"Over the wall," said Ferdinan. "You do not happen to have a grappling hook on you, by any chance?"

"No, sorry, I left it in my other pants," McRofaly replied with a smirk.

"Well, we will just have to improvise. What about your spyglass?"

"Now that I can help with," said McRofaly as he pulled open his belt pouch. He handed the compact leather case to Ferdinan, who tucked it inside his shirt.

"Right," said Ferdinan. "Stay close to me, and try not to make any noise. We cannot be spotted if we are going to get you over the wall." Ferdinan led a trembling McRofaly out of the safety of the house. They bypassed the street that held the showdown between Ganugamosh and goruks, doubling back the way Ferdinan had come a little bit and taking an alternate route. They had a couple of close calls, having to duck behind a fence or tree as a small band of goruks came running suddenly up the street in their direction, but they made it to the outskirts of the nobility's homes undetected.

"Keep your eyes peeled for a house with a garden shed," Ferdinan whispered to McRofaly as they crept along the street. McRofaly looked confused at this command, but he followed it. It did not take long to find one. They ducked inside the shed, and Ferdinan immediately began taking inventory of its contents.

"What are you looking for?" McRofaly asked, nervously peering out of the shed.

Ferdinan hoisted a coil of rope from a peg on the wall, running his hand along a small length of it. "This should be sturdy enough," he said, disregarding McRofaly's question. Then he began sorting through the various gardening tools until he found a hand rake. He looked it over and smiled. "We are in luck. I believe es Gunther's handiwork. It should be more than strong enough to hold." He began tying one end of the rope securely around the rake.

"What are you doing?" asked McRofaly.

"I am making a grappling hook," Ferdinan replied without looking up.

"Not in this life," said McRofaly with an edge of panic in his voice. "I'm not shimmying down a rope tied to a garden rake."

"The rake es strong enough to hold," said Ferdinan. "I would stake my life on Gunther's skill. Or, in this case, your life."

"I'm not worried about the rake breaking. What if the rope slips off?"

"Do not worry about that. I learned all about knot-tying during the time it took to sail from Conquia to here. The rope will hold. And es either the rope or stay in the city and take your chances with the goruks."

McRofaly stared long and hard at the makeshift grappling hook. His basic instinct of self-preservation, honed to perfection during his formative years by Esten, was at war with itself in his mind. If he followed Ferdinan's plan, he might very well wind up killing himself. If he stayed in Tamendad, though, his death was assured. Too many goruks had seen his incantations at the southeast gate. "I'll take my chances with the rope," he said at last.

Ferdinan nodded. "All right, we have to make it to the closest lookout platform without being seen. Stay close." It was a straight shot across a few lawns to the wall. They stayed off the streets as much as possible, sticking close to trees and bushes so they could hide if the need arose suddenly. When they reached the wall and began climbing the ladder up to the platform McRofaly felt like he could burst out in song. He was slipping the noose.

Ferdinan secured the hand rake on one of the platform's supports, then wrapped the rope around his forearm a couple of times. "I will help lower you down. Remember, tell Gregor he has to trust me, no matter what. Es imperative that he does nothing rash."

McRofaly nodded. "I'll tell him. Good luck, Ferdinan. With whatever it is you think you're doing."

Ferdinan smiled. "Thank you, *compagno*. Now get moving. Time es precious."

McRofaly held on to the rope with a death grip, rappelling down the city wall with his eyes tightly shut until he reached the ground. Once he felt his feet touch, he could not contain his laughter. Overcome for a moment, he actually bent down and kissed the soil. He stood and waved up at Ferdinan, then began running away from Tamendad. Ferdinan wasted no time watching him go. He pulled the rope back up quickly and turned toward the Governor's house. Already from his vantage point he could see goruks gathering outside it. Time was running out. Without hesitation, Ferdinan stepped off of the platform and onto the wall itself. Balancing himself with his arms held out, he put one foot in front of the other, making his way along the wall toward his destination. The wall was more than thick enough to provide a foothold, but the top of it was dreadfully uneven as he moved from timber to timber. If he lost his balance it would mean a twenty-foot drop; plenty enough to kill a man if he went head first. But his balance never faltered in the slightest.

The wall came within forty feet of the Governor's house at the nearest lookout platform, and it was upon this platform that Ferdinan eventually stopped. He stood staring at the building's facade. Forty feet. It might as well have been forty miles by the way it looked. He chose his spot on the house, the metal railing of the balcony off the master bedroom on the third floor. That was his best bet. He raised the makeshift grappling hook above his head, gripping it firmly, lining up his shot. He flung it as hard as he could manage and still maintain any control. The rake sailed through the air in a graceful arc, pulling the rope along behind it. Ten, twenty, thirty feet it sailed as Ferdinan watched. It hit its mark, sailing onto the balcony. Ferdinan tugged the rope as hard and as fast as he could, snapping the slack back toward him. The rake shot backwards for an instant, then entangled itself on the balcony's railing. Ferdinan gave the rope a couple of tugs to ensure it was a good hold, then pulled it as tight as it would go and tied the other end around a support beam on the platform. He took a deep breath as he stepped out onto the rope.

The rope tensed a bit under his boot, but it held. Ferdinan took another slow, steady step forward. Just like on the wall, he continued to put one foot in front of the other. His hands were spread out from his body to balance himself. He was ten feet away from the wall now. The Governor's house drew nearer. Another step. Left foot in front of right, right back in front of left. Having never done this before, Ferdinan thought himself pretty good at it. Fifteen feet away from the wall. Twenty. He was halfway between the wall and the house when his foot slipped. There was nothing he could do about it. The bottom of his foot slipped right off the side of the rope, and he fell. The sickening sensation of weightlessness gripped his stomach, and he was brought to a brain-rattling halt as the rope met him between the legs. He clenched the rope in both hands and crossed his legs around it, hanging upside-down, staring at the ground. The nauseating pain welled up in him. Spots danced in front of his eyes. Everything between his lower abdomen and his upper thighs was numb. It was the most embarrassing position he had ever been in in his life, and he was dearly thankful that no one was there to witness it.

He gave himself a moment, waiting until the pain receded a bit, thankful that he was in the back of the house, where no goruks had congregated. He began to pull and shimmy his way across the rope, still upside down. There was no way he was going to get back to his feet. He could actually go faster this way without fear of falling, and he cursed himself for not thinking to just try it this way from the start. Soon he was at the balcony. He pulled himself up onto it and wiped away the sweat that had broken out on his forehead. From here he could see over the city wall to the northwest, but he needed a better view. He climbed up the balcony and took hold of the edge of the roof, pulling himself onto it. The view was incredible; the entire Taeran stretched out before him. He took McRofaly's spyglass from his belt, extending it and aiming it east, out into the sea. He found what he was looking for. Hope was not yet fully lost.

A raucous sound from down below brought his attention back to Tamendad. He drew closer to the edge of the roof and peered down, and saw immediately what the commotion was about. Kor had arrived at the Governor's house, and the goruks had begun laying siege to it. Ferdinan was encouraged by the fact that Kor looked to have only brought about fifty goruks with him. That meant there was a good chance Gregor and the others were still alive.

Ferdinan walked along the edge of the roof until he came to the window of the meeting room in which Governor Chamberlain was locked. In one smooth movement he dropped off the roof, turning as he did so and grabbing hold of the edge of it. He kicked his legs forward, shattering the glass and carrying himself through the window. Nonchalantly brushing a few shards of glass from his shoulders, he stepped further into the room. The Governor's two guards looked like they were about to faint at the sight of it, both holding swords in their shaking hands. Ferdinan paid them no attention, walking directly to the Governor, who was seated at the table. The Governor looked at Ferdinan as though he was seeing a ghost.

"Geoffery," said Ferdinan, "I believe es time to signal our surrender."

Chapter Thirty-Four

Terms of Surrender

Colvin's heart sank. He could not believe his eyes. He stood on the roof of the Stuart-Camen household with his last arrow nocked loosely in his bow, staring at the Governor's house where Ferdinan had just emerged onto a balcony waving a white flag. His mind could not process the sight. He looked over at Gangis, who was still perched on the balcony of the Dalsandrian house. Gangis was staring as well, and though Colvin was too far away to tell, he was certain Gangis's expression was just as shocked as his own. He had to call Gangis's name twice before catching his attention.

"What's he doing?" Colvin asked, gesturing toward the Governor's house.

"I think he's surrendering," Gangis called back.

It wasn't possible. This was why it was so important Ferdinan got into the Governor's house? This was the one chance to save Tamendad? To surrender it into goruk hands at the final moment? Colvin felt used. He felt worse than used. He felt betrayed. He had risked his life to hold back the goruks for just a few moments, to give Ferdinan just a little more time, in the hope that the Conquian could pull off some sort of miracle and save the day. Instead Ferdinan had folded and personally handed the town over to Kor himself. Colvin felt nauseous. He wanted to scream. He snapped his bow over his knee in a rage and cast the pieces to the ground. He wanted to kill Ferdinan, to throttle his skinny little neck with his bare hands for what he had done.

It was the only way.

"No it wasn't!" Colvin told himself. "There had to be some other way. Ferdinan said there was still a chance."

He said there was a chance we might all get out of this alive, not that Tamendad might be saved. This was the only way to save the people.

"But…but…"

But nothing. That was the plain and simple fact. There was no saving the town, but the people could still be saved. Those people were obviously more important to Ferdinan than the city itself. And when it was put like that, Colvin couldn't blame him.

"So what do we do now?" called Gangis from his balcony.

Colvin shrugged. "Wait and see, I guess," he said. "It's all in Ferdinan's hands now."

Ferdinan stepped off the balcony and rejoined the Governor in Elysia's bedchamber, the only room on the third floor with a balcony overlooking the courtyard. Ferdinan regretted that he was seeing it for the first time under such circumstances. It would have been a considerably lovelier place with some candlelight, a bottle of wine, a book of Conquian sonnets, some heated oil... *Later,* Ferdinan told himself. *Later.*

"Well, they have seen it," said Ferdinan, laying the makeshift flag – a pillowcase tied around the end of the fire poker – on Elysia's writing desk. "Now we just have to hope they know what a white flag means."

The Governor's nod was accompanied by a sigh. "You are certain this is the only way?" he said.

Ferdinan gave him a compassionate look. "Es the only way, Geoffery. The city es lost. Our forces are divided. We have been...what es the word?...*outfoxed.* At least this way we can save as many people as possible."

"It feels wrong, Ferdinan," said Geoffery. "To fight so long and so hard for something, and sacrifice so much, only to fail. It just feels wrong."

"I know, Geoffery. You must trust me. Es the only way."

The Governor nodded once again, this time a little more resolutely. "All right, Ferdinan. You have never led me astray before."

"The goruks are standing down," said one of the Governor's guards, peering out the window. "Their leader is coming to the front, and the one with feathers in its hair."

"Right," said the Governor. "Looks like they got the message. So what happens now? I have never surrendered my city before. I am unfamiliar with the protocol."

"We meet with them to negotiate terms," said Ferdinan. "You will be there, of course, but as Captain of the Guard es probably a good idea to let me do most of the talking. I have esperience negotiating treaties."

"You do?"

"Sí. Es part of my duties as an ambassador of King Altores. I have never negotiated a treaty of surrender, but I am educated on how to do so, and most of the basic principles are the same."

"I thought you were just a dignitary," said the Governor.

"Ah," said Ferdinan. "You thought wrong. Now, choose ten of your best guards to accompany us out to meet Kor."

"Is it a good idea for us to go out armed?"

"It would be a horrible idea for us to go out unarmed. Negotiations begin, and often end, with first impressions. We must let Kor know from the start that we are willing to discuss the option of surrender, but that we are not going to lie down like dogs and give him everything he demands."

Governor Chamberlain chose ten of his guards as an accompaniment, an easy decision since there were only twelve guards inside the house with him. The barricades were removed from the front door, and together Ferdinan and the Governor went out to meet their conquerors. There was an eruption of noise as they emerged from the house, a chorus of raucous cheers and insults in an incomprehensible tongue. Surrounded by their guards, Ferdinan and the Governor approached the iron gate. Kor and the ardah were waiting on the other side.

"Kneel, paleskins," said Kor through the gate once they were within speaking distance. This brought a new wave of noise from the surrounding goruks.

"Patience, Kor," said Ferdinan. "We have not yet discussed terms."

"There are no terms," growled Kor.

"There are always terms," replied Ferdinan. "Let us meet together to discuss them."

"What trickery is this?" demanded Kor. "Your leader is dead! I killed him myself."

"You are wrong, Kor," replied Ferdinan. "Captain Jefford was not our leader. He was our champion. You bested our most decorated warrior, but our leader still lives."

Kor roared, a sound so fierce that Ferdinan nearly took a step backward. He forced his boots to remain planted where they were. Such trifling displays of weakness could be enough to sabotage negotiations.

"No matter!" said Kor. "I won this city on the battlefield. Champion or chief, he is dead by my hand!"

"The city was not Jefford's to give. Es ours. Come, meet with us, let us end this."

"Luring me inside so that you can corner me with your warriors?" Kor said. "Do you take me for a fool?"

"Es no trickery," said Ferdinan. "There are certain customs that must be followed. I am sure you can appreciate that. Es no need to fear for your safety. We have ten guards with us. You choose fifteen of your own. The advantage of numbers will be yours."

Kor thought this over for a moment. "Let us discuss these terms of yours here, in the open," he said at last, "so all can hear."

"Alas, es not possible," said Ferdinan. "Negotiations of surrender require a certain level of privacy."

"The paleskin speaks the truth, Kor," said the ardah in his own language. "This is business for the chief, not for all our people."

Ferdinan had no way of knowing what the ardah had said, but he could tell by the look on Kor's face that it had been a challenge to his authority. Ferdinan noted that with interest. If there was tension between these two it could work to his advantage.

"Very well," said Kor after shooting a spiteful glance at the ardah. "But I will bring twenty warriors with me."

"Of course," said Ferdinan, bowing in a manner that could have almost been called subservient if it had been anyone else doing it. "You are the victor, Kor. Your entourage can be whatever you choose."

Kor selected his twenty warriors, and the gate was unbarred and opened. When the ardah stepped through the gate alongside Kor, Kor shot him another scathing look. "I will accompany," said the ardah without even acknowledging Kor's scowl. "It is my right." Kor concentrated so hard on saying nothing in reply that he might as well have blown up in a rage. They withdrew into the Governor's house. The goruks surrounding it did not attempt to follow, but neither did they disperse.

In spite of himself, McRofaly found himself wondering what Ferdinan was up to. The situation in Tamendad was hopeless. It was unsalvageable. But there was something in Ferdinan's eyes when he lowered McRofaly from the city wall, an inflection in his voice as he insisted Gregor must trust him that told he really believed he could win the day. Was Ferdinan mad? That was no small possibility in McRofaly's mind. With all the stress the Conquian had been under, it was entirely plausible that his mind had simply snapped. But McRofaly could not quite make himself believe it. There was something Ferdinan knew that McRofaly did not, and it was driving McRofaly insane trying to puzzle out what it was. But whatever it was, it was back in Tamendad, and so far as McRofaly was concerned it could stay there. Nothing was going to get McRofaly back into the city now that he was safe, not even his own unquenchable curiosity.

Every step carried McRofaly further from assured death. Behind him lay a Tamendad overrun with goruks, led by an ardah who knew McRofaly could use magic. Somewhere ahead of him was Gregor, who McRofaly was certain was big enough and strong enough to keep him safe. And if there were goruks wherever Gregor was, so what? At least those goruks did not know McRofaly for what he was. To them he would be just another short, skinny human, certainly no threat and nothing to worry about. And McRofaly had no plans to draw attention to himself should he come across any goruks. He had done plenty of that in Tamendad. A lifetime's worth, so far as he was concerned. Now he clung to the tenuous safety of being separated from those goruks that knew his secret.

Finding Gregor and the others was no challenge. It was simply a matter of beginning atop the bloody hill overlooking Tamendad and following the trail of carnage from there. But nothing prepared McRofaly for the sight that met him as he cleared a small hill about half a mile from Tamendad and found them. The broken corpses of goruks and humans littered the ground, strewn haphazardly about. The stench of death and the metallic tang of blood hung in the air. The only redeeming quality of the sight, if one could be found at all, was that while a number of Highlanders and Tamendaders were still up and moving, pulling themselves back together and tending to the wounded, all the goruks were dead.

McRofaly pushed his way into the jumbled throng, dodging this way and that around a multitude of bloodied faces and battered bodies. At last, when he was finally beginning to wonder about Gregor's fate, he felt a strong hand on his shoulder and turned to find himself staring up at the big Highlander.

"McRofaly, what th' bugger are ye doing here?" Gregor demanded. "Why are ye nae in th' Governor's house?"

"I have a message for you from Ferdinan," explained McRofaly. Pain shot through his shoulder as Gregor tightened his grip.

"What is it lad? Is he in trouble? Does he need help?"

"He says you have to trust him," said McRofaly, worming his way out of Gregor's grasp.

"Trust him t' do what?"

"I'm not sure. He just said you had to trust him."

"I dinnae like th' sound o' that," said Gregor. "Sounds like he's going t' need some help."

McRofaly's eyes widened. "Wait a minute, Gregor," he said excitedly, "We can't go back! The city's overrun with goruks!"

"That settles it, then," replied Gregor. "Give William a hand with his father, will ye?" He turned and began to bark orders at his kinsmen to make ready to move. McRofaly was left by himself, standing in wide-eyed shock, mumbling incoherencies.

"But...but...they'll recognize me," he said to no one in particular. "And Ferdinan said not to do anything rash."

"McRofaly, help me," came a voice from behind him. McRofaly turned and saw William kneeling beside his wounded father.

"Good God, what happened?"

"They almost got him," replied William. "He needs to get to a healer. Can you get his feet?"

McRofaly stood still as stone. "I...I can't, William," he said, and found the words surprisingly painful. "I can't go back to Tamendad. The goruks have seen my face. They'll be looking for me."

William stared at McRofaly, and never had McRofaly seen such anguish in a face so young. "McRofaly, please," said William, and there was no mistaking that he was on the verge of tears. "I can't get him back to Tamendad alone."

"Can't someone else do it?" said McRofaly.

"There is no one else."

And looking around, McRofaly realized William was right. Every Highlander and Tamendader capable of walking under his or her own volition was already moving away back toward Tamendad at a trot.

"If my father doesn't get to a healer soon he's going to die," said William. "You're the only one who can help me, McRofaly. *Please*."

McRofaly felt more conflicted at that moment, standing rigid above the semi-conscious form of Jonathan Stuart-Camen, than he had ever felt in his entire life. "All right," he sighed after a moment of indecision. He moved around and took hold of Jonathan's ankles. "But at the first sign of trouble you're on your own."

William fought back tears as he and McRofaly hoisted Jonathan up and began to move him over the blood-soaked grass. "Thank you," he said, the words almost catching in his throat.

"You can thank me if I survive," grumbled McRofaly.

"We are prepared to offer you the city," said Ferdinan as he and the Governor took their seats across the table from Kor and the ardah. Kor refused to go any higher than the ground floor, so they met in the dining room, the only room large enough to comfortably accommodate the thirty various bodyguards. "We will hand it over to you as soon as our people are evacuated."

Kor stared in silent contempt, his upper lip curling around his tusks. "There will be no evacuation," he growled. "You are beaten. Those of you that are spared will live only to serve us."

"You intend to go back on your word, then?" said Ferdinan. "I warn you, such an act carries grave consequences. I urge you to reconsider."

"Do not try to fool me, paleskin worm," said Kor. "I gave my word on nothing."

Ferdinan reached inside his vest. The twenty goruk warriors lined up behind Kor tensed, their hands darting to the hilts of their scimitars, which in turn made the guards behind Ferdinan and the Governor go for their own weapons. Before it could come to blows Ferdinan pulled out not a dagger but a crumpled piece of paper, unfolding it delicately and laying it on the table. On it were written two messages, one in ink and one in blood.

"*Your suffering es necessary, now, but your deaths are not. You have a choice. Surrender and you will live,*" recited Ferdinan as he slid the paper across the table. "Your words, Kor. Are you now going back on them?"

Kor stared at the paper like it was a dead fish. He made no move to inspect it, but the ardah reached forward and took it from Ferdinan's hand. He read it over for a while, then turned and spoke with Kor in their own language. "Is it true, Kor?" he asked. "Was this written by your hand?"

"What of it?" replied Kor. "That was written days ago. The offer has passed."

"You must honor this," said the ardah. "If you do not, you risk incurring the wrath of the Ancient Ones. You have given your word as chief, and now you must follow it. Otherwise I shall be forced to come down against you before our people."

Kor grinned wickedly, holding back a laugh. "Do you really believe our people will side against me now that I have won the day, you old fool? The reclaiming has tasted its first victory. You hold sway over them no longer, ardah." He had saved these words for so long, and they tasted so very sweet coming out of his mouth. The ardah, however, was unshaken.

"Our people have twice witnessed the power of the Ancient Ones this day, once to tear down the city's gate and once to cast open the doors of its blasphemous church. I believe this has been sufficient to restore their faith in the Ancient Ones, as well as their respect for my opinion. If you disagree, though, then challenge my authority and we shall see together in which direction our people lean."

Kor was speechless. He turned to look at the goruks standing in file behind him. They tensed uncomfortably under his gaze, and he knew the ardah was right. His people would never side with him, even now that

Tamendad was theirs, after witnessing the ardah's magic firsthand. He had allowed an error to slip into his strategy, that was plain. But it was of little consequence. "Very well," said Kor in Turish, turning back to Ferdinan and the Governor. "You will be spared, as I told you you would. But not all of you. The one responsible for the heads that hang from the wall will not survive his crime."

"Es fair," said Ferdinan. "You will have your justice."

"Bring me this man now, before we go any farther with this," demanded Kor.

"He es already here, Kor. I am that man."

Kor was on his feet in an instant, both morchas drawn and ready to strike, but Ferdinan was quicker still. The Conquian had both sabre and parrying dagger readied in a defensive stance before Kor took his first step around the table toward him. The goruk warriors and the Governor's guards drew weapons as well, and for a terrifying moment it looked like the whole thing was going to end in a bloodbath right then and there. But then Ferdinan was yelling, "Wait, Kor! Not like this! Wait until we are finished here and I will give myself up willingly!" His words did not stay Kor, but they seemed to satisfy the ardah, who reached out and grasped Kor's forearm.

"Patience," said the ardah. "We have him. There is no need for haste." Kor turned on the ardah with venom in his eyes, looking for a moment like he was going to cut him down. "His crime is too great to be dealt with like this," the ardah added. "Our people deserve to witness his punishment."

This, at least, made sense to Kor. He lowered his swords. "Surrender your weapons," he growled at Ferdinan.

"Only with your word I will live until this es over," Ferdinan replied.

Kor hesitated for a moment, glancing sidelong at the ardah before he agreed. Ferdinan laid his sabre and dagger on the table and slid them across to Kor. Everyone began slowly putting their weapons away as they saw Kor resheathe his scimitars and return to his seat. Ferdinan did the same, delicately sinking back into his chair beside the Governor. Geoffery cast a questioning look in his direction, and it was clear he could not decipher why Ferdinan had decided to take the fall for McRofaly. Ferdinan did not acknowledge the Governor's look, but he stepped firmly on Geoffery's foot and shook his head ever so slightly to tell him to drop it. The Governor complied immediately, and the entire exchange was over before Kor or the ardah could notice it.

"You will die a very painful death," Kor told Ferdinan, running his clawed fingers up and down the length of the duelist's sabre. "Your people will be spared, as I have promised. But I said nothing of setting them free. They will watch you die, and then they will live out the rest of their lives as our slaves, to atone for the wrongs they have committed against my people."

"Es unacceptable," Ferdinan replied flatly.

"What?" demanded Kor.

"Es unacceptable," Ferdinan repeated. "I will never agree to those terms."

"You have no choice!" screamed Kor.

"Oh, but we do," said Ferdinan. "We still have many soldiers in Tamendad, many of whom no doubt have had time to position themselves behind your warriors outside this building and ready themselves for a fight. If we cannot come to terms here, I am certain it would be no problem to go back to killing each other."

"You are overwhelmingly outnumbered," said Kor. "Attacking us now would be suicide."

"I believe you will find," said Governor Chamberlain, "that our people will fight to the last man rather than live in slavery."

"Very true," said Ferdinan. "And I also believe you will find that we still have more than enough men left to make life very difficult for you. You have seen how hard we can fight when backed into a corner. How many soldiers have you lost already, Kor? How many more can you afford to lose and still be able to withhold the counterattack that will come once word spreads that Tamendad has fallen? Es no secret that Tamendad was merely a stepping stone for you. This es an opportunity to secure that stepping stone while maintaining what forces you have left. Es in the best interests of everyone to stop fighting now, Kor. Our people escape with their lives, while you get Tamendad and my head."

"It is not enough," said Kor. "You paleskins have been a thorn in my side for the duration of this war. I will not come away from it with only the city and your head to show for my troubles."

"Then take me," said Governor Chamberlain.

"What?" said Kor and Ferdinan simultaneously.

"I am offering myself as part of the deal," said Governor Chamberlain. "I will submit to you, Kor, and serve as your personal slave, if you agree to let the rest of my people go."

"What about fighting to the last before living in slavery?" said Kor with a smirk.

"This is a different matter. I am exchanging my life for the lives of my people. Think of it, Kor. Having the Governor of Tamendad as your own personal whipping boy. I represent all the people of Tamendad, so with me as your slave it would be like having the entire city in servitude to you."

"Are you certain about this, Geoffery?" asked Ferdinan.

"If my Captain of the Guard is willing to sacrifice his life for this, I should be willing to do the same," replied the Governor.

Ferdinan nodded solemnly. "There you have it," he said to Kor. "These are our terms: our people will be allowed to leave Tamendad without further threat of harm, and in return you gain the city, the Governor's servitude and my head."

Kor did not say anything at first, though it was obvious by both the poorly concealed grin on his face and the absentminded way he caressed the blade of Ferdinan's sabre that his hesitation was for purely dramatic purposes. "Agreed," he said at long last. "The other paleskins will be allowed to leave peacefully. My warriors will accompany them to the gate to ensure they go without causing more trouble."

Ferdinan shook his head. "Our soldiers are war-weary, and many of them are seriously injured. Many of them would not survive a long march, especially now that the weather es beginning to turn. They must be allowed to travel by ship."

"You must take me for a great fool," said Kor. "I will not be stalled for days while you arrange for ships to carry your people away. I will not give you time to scheme in hopes of devising a plan to save your city."

"Es no need to wait," replied Ferdinan. "I already arranged for transport ships several days ago. I saw them sailing up the coast before I signaled surrender."

"You did what?!?" demanded Governor Chamberlain, and by the look on his face it was plain to see he was livid.

Ferdinan had not been looking forward to this moment. "I sent a letter with Elysia," explained Ferdinan, "to arrange for more passenger ships at my own espense. I knew there was a good chance we would need to make a hasty withdrawal from Tamendad. I had hoped they would arrive before the deciding battle began, but this es just as good to everyone escept you and myself."

"You had absolutely no right," said the Governor in an icy voice.

"As Captain of the Guard es my duty to prepare for every eventuality."

"You told me you would see this war through to the end," said Geoffery. "I trusted you."

"I kept my word," replied Ferdinan. "I had to accept that this war might end in defeat, and prepare for that possibility."

"These ships are here now?" interrupted Kor, who had lost interest in the spat.

"They should be arriving at the docks shortly," said Ferdinan.

"Very well," said Kor. "We will round up the survivors and escort them to the docks. There they will board your ships and leave Tamendad to me."

"We will have to send someone to gather the survivors outside the city, the ones who pursued you down the hill," said Ferdinan. "And I am certain some people will need to be seen by a healer."

"Yes, yes," said Kor impatiently. "All will be accounted for. If my warriors left any survivors outside the city, we will collect them. And before your people leave, they will watch you die as a reminder of what punishment awaits those who stand against us."

"Then it is agreed," said Ferdinan solemnly. "When our remaining soldiers are evacuated, this city es yours."

"I dinnae believe it," said Gregor. He stood in the town square beside William, who in turn was kneeling beside Jonathan, who in turn was being attended by a healer. All the injured had been brought to the church, but there were entirely too many of them to all fit inside, so the healers had laid them out in the square and attended them there. The square was surrounded by armed goruks that stared malevolently at the injured and at the priests who were tending them. Gregor shook his head at the sight. "I dinnae believe Ferdinan would give up th' town like this, after all we've fought for."

"Ferdinan said we had to trust him," said McRofaly, who stood close by with his head downcast, doing his best to obscure his face from the goruks. So far none of them seemed to have recognized him, and there had been no sign of the ardah. "From a strategic standpoint the city was already lost. At least this way Ferdinan saved as many lives as possible."

"There are worse fates than dying, lad," said Gregor.

"Speak for yourself," said McRofaly.

William was oblivious to the conversation. All his attention was focused on the unconscious form of his father. Jonathan had passed out once William and McRofaly had gotten him back to Tamendad. He was still alive, though, and the healer who now tended him seemed as optimistic as Gregor that his wounds, while very serious, were not mortal. The deep gash across his chest had already been stitched up. The healer was now applying a dressing to the puncture in his abdomen, which was too deep for stitches. William held his father's hand, staring at his expressionless face. He focused intently on his father mostly out of deep concern, but also partially because it helped him block out the reality of what was happening. Even with his incredible worries consuming the majority of his mind, though, some thought of the situation still managed to sneak its way into his brain. The war was over.

His side had lost. Ferdinan was going to die. Governor Chamberlain was going to become Kor's slave. Soon William and his father were going to board a ship and leave Tamendad for what would probably be the last time ever, and Jonathan would not even been awake to realize it. "Where did Ferdinan get the ships, again?" William asked absentmindedly.

"Details on that are sketchy," said McRofaly. "From what I can piece together, he sent a letter to Tantera when the city was evacuated."

"They took their sweet time getting here," said William. "It's less than a day's sail up the coast."

"My guess is it took a while to find captains willing to take such a risk," said McRofaly. "They were asked to sail into a war zone, remember."

"My work is done," interrupted the healer as he gathered up his ointments and bandages. "He needs bed rest and sunlight, and I would suggest a tea of coneflower and golden seal twice a day. The healers in Tantera will know what to do for him."

"Thank you, Patrum," said William.

"Well, I suppose we should get to the docks," said McRofaly. "No point in prolonging the inevitable."

"Aye," said Gregor, eyeing the sword-wielding goruks with contempt. "I could do with a change o' scenery. Do ye need any help carrying yer da, William?"

"I can manage," huffed William as he hoisted his father's body into his arms. "It's not far to go."

The sight at the docks was worse, if anything. Kor and the ardah were both there under the pretense of overseeing the departure of the Tamendaders, and they were accompanied by just as many goruks as there had been in the town square. Ferdinan was there as well, unarmed, doing his best to organize the many people huddled together around the docks. The first of the ships – and there were many – were just beginning to come into harbor. The mood was sullen, even more sullen than in the town square. Gregor spotted Colvin in the crowd, and he, William and McRofaly made their way toward him. Colvin did not notice them until they were almost beside him, and when he greeted them he had about him a look of shock that at any moment might degenerate into tears. In that place, at that moment, it was a common look. Colvin looked over Jonathan's prone form with as much concern as he could manage. "Is he all right?" he asked in a voice not far from monotone.

"The healer said his wounds weren't mortal. He should recover with bed rest."

"Good," said Colvin. "Gunther lost a hand."

"What?" said William and Gregor at the same time.

"His right hand," said Colvin. "Cut clean off at the wrist." His voice was emotionless, but there was a bitterness behind his words that had never been there before. Never had he tasted defeat like this. Never had he invested himself so much in anything as he had invested himself in Tamendad, and so never had anything wounded him so deeply as its falling.

"How will he be able to work at a forge?"said William. Colvin stared at him incredulously.

"I believe that's the point, lad," said Gregor.

"Oh," said William, and then with dawning comprehension, "Oh, God! That'll be enough to kill him, having to give up being a blacksmith."

"Where is he?" asked Gregor.

"At the Governor's house with the rest of the Ganugamosh," said Colvin. "Kor isn't letting them leave."

"Ferdinan agreed t' that?" asked Gregor, hovering somewhere between outrage and disbelief. Colvin nodded, and outrage surged to the forefront. "What th' bugger is th' bastard thinking?" Gregor said in a voice loud enough to carry all the way to Ferdinan. "I dinnae march three hundred o' m' kinsmen north for this, t' tuck tail like a whipped bitch and betray m' friends while I did it." At this Kor began to laugh heartily, until Gregor pointed fiercely at him and said, "I suggest ye shut yer mouth, ye bastard cur. Nae all of us here have lost our resolve, and I for one am nae afraid t' put ye in yer place." Kor's expression became deadly serious, and he took a step in Gregor's direction. Ferdinan was there before the situation could escalate, doing his best to hold the big Highlander back and calm him down.

"Es not worth it, *compagno*," Ferdinan said in a carrying voice, and then added in a whisper, "Trust me, Gregor. When have I ever led you astray?" His look was mysterious, but it pleaded for Gregor's trust.

After a long, silent moment, Gregor sighed, "All right, lad, I trust ye."

"Your friend should watch his tongue before he loses it," growled Kor. He sneered once at Gregor, then turned his attention elsewhere.

"Aye, I'm sure ye'd have a much better go at it than th' green bastards we left lying in th' mud," said Gregor, but if Kor heard he did not acknowledge it.

During all the commotion, McRofaly snuck up beside William and elbowed him lightly in the ribs. William, who was not having an easy time supporting the dead weight of his father's limp body, grumbled, "What was that for?"

"Shh," whispered McRofaly harshly, still doing his best to evade the attention of the ardah and any of the other goruks who might have seen him at the southeast gate. He gestured toward the docks. "The ships," he said.

William looked. The first ships had arrived in the docks, and the crews were beginning to secure the moorings. "Yeah," he said dejectedly, averting his eyes from the sight. He would see plenty enough of those ships as they carried him away from his home, forever. He had no desire to look at them right now.

"No," said McRofaly, again jabbing William in the ribs. "*Look* at the ships."

William looked again, and as if a fog had lifted from his eyes he saw what McRofaly was referring to. Having spent his whole life in a port city, William had developed a natural familiarity with ships. Though he could count on one hand the number of times he had actually been on a ship himself, not a day of his life had gone by without witnessing ships of all sorts and sizes coming and going in the Taeran. That William's mind had been consumed by brooding thoughts of defeat and his father's injuries was the only reason he had not noticed what was peculiar about these particular ships, but now with McRofaly's prodding he saw it. All the ships docking in Tamendad had the deep keels of ocean-faring vessels. There was not a single shallow-keeled schooner or flat-bottomed coastrunner in the whole lot. Stranger still, every ship was identical to every other, exact copies not only of design but of materials and craftsmanship. Now that he was aware of it, William realized it was the strangest sight he had ever seen in Tamendad's harbor. Ten eerily similar ships sat anchored at the docks, with at least as many still out coasting on the Taeran awaiting their turn, and not a single one sailed with colors hoisted. William wanted to ask McRofaly what it meant, but the look McRofaly gave him told him in no uncertain terms to hold his tongue.

Kor, who had lived his life far away from the sea, and so had no way to know that anything peculiar was afoot, surveyed the ten ships that occupied the docks. "The bargain is met," he said. "Tamendad is mine. Your people will be allowed to depart as soon as they witness justice served." He raised Ferdinan's sabre and grinned menacingly.

"Es still one unresolved issue to be dealt with before that happens," said Ferdinan, and before Kor could get a word out, the Conquian screamed, "NOW!" There was upon the decks of the ships a flurry of activity, dozens of men springing up from hiding places, and Kor and the other goruks at the docks found themselves targeted by crossbows. Lots and lots of crossbows.

"Allow me to present the Royal Armada of King Altores," announced Ferdinan.

Colvin burst out laughing. He could not contain it. It was just too beautiful a thing to witness, Ferdinan grinning like a rogue and Kor staring wide-eyed with mouth hanging slack. Cheers erupted from the Tamendaders, and the goruks howled with rage. Kor advanced on Ferdinan, but Ferdinan was quicker. He sprang backwards out of harm's way and yelled something in Conquian. At his words there was a shuffle of movement aboard the ships as at least thirty men all turned their crossbows on Kor. "I told them to shoot you if you take another step, Kor!" Ferdinan shouted, and Kor stopped dead in his tracks. He growled, and Ferdinan smiled.

"We will not evacuate," said Ferdinan evenly. "We will not surrender the city."

"Paleskin scum!" said Kor. "You will pay dearly for this. None of your wretched ilk will survive. We will crush you like gnats."

"If you so much as raise a hand against us, you will be wiped out like the stain that you are," said Ferdinan evenly. "You are beaten. Stand down."

"Never," said Kor. "Death before surrender."

Although the Tamendaders were all cheering as though the war was won, Ferdinan realized that they now in fact stood in its most critical moment. So far Ferdinan's wager had worked, but now with sides evenly matched and facing one another in a standoff the whole thing could very easily blow up right in Ferdinan's face. If Kor and his goruks were really willing to fight to the death against such odds for their cause then a lot more people were going to have to die before the war was over. Ferdinan's mind raced, searching for a way to prevent that from happening.

"Challenge him to a duel!" shouted William from the crowd. Ferdinan and Kor both turned to look at him, as did just about everyone else who understood Turish. William gave Ferdinan an encouraging nod.

"An escellent idea," said Ferdinan, turning his attention back to Kor. "You are willing to risk the lives of all your underlings to achieve your ends. Are you willing to risk your own?"

"What?" spat the goruk.

"A duel, you brainless son of a goat. For control of Tamendad. If I win, you and your...*people*...will go back from whence you came and swear to never again show your ugly faces near Tamendad. If you win, the city es yours. Forever."

There was a tense moment of silence during which nobody moved and very few people breathed, and at the end of which the ardah turned to all the goruks gathered at the docks, raised both hands high, and said in his own language, "Our chief has been challenged to do battle!" The goruks erupted in cheers and whistles, and Kor looked at the ardah with daggers in his eyes. There was little doubt in his mind who the ardah wanted to see victorious. But he knew he no longer had a choice in the matter.

"Very well," Kor told Ferdinan. "A fight to the death."

"As you would have it, Kor," replied Ferdinan. He turned and beckoned Colvin from the crowd. "Colvin, you will be my second," he said. Colvin blinked in confusion.

"What is this *second*?" asked the ardah.

"Es someone who stands behind me during the duel, both literally and figuratively, to ensure the rules of the duel are followed," explained Ferdinan.

"Then I shall stand as Kor's second," said the ardah. Once again Kor shot the ardah a scathing look but said nothing.

"So what do I do?" Colvin asked Ferdinan quietly. "I've never done this before."

"Stay behind me," said Ferdinan. "At least a few feet back. I do not want you to get hurt. Keep an eye on me, and pay attention to the tactics I am using. If I do anything that goes against the tenets of *decusé*, kill me."

"Wh-what?" stammered Colvin.

"If I fight dishonorably in this duel, kill me," repeated Ferdinan.

"Ferdinan, I can't do that," said Colvin.

Ferdinan patted Colvin's shoulder reassuringly. "You will not have to," he said.

"Are we ready?" demanded Kor, his voice thick with impatience.

"Almost," said Ferdinan. "I will be needing my sword."

"Take it, then," said Kor with a sneer. He cast the sabre away as though, after caressing it like a lover since receiving it, he was now loath to touch it. It landed at Ferdinan's feet. Ferdinan made no immediate move to pick it up, and that probably saved his life, because as soon as it came to rest Kor drew both morchas and charged headlong at Ferdinan. Ferdinan moved like lightning. Instead of stooping down to pick up his sabre he quickly hooked his foot under it and kicked it upward, grabbing it in midair. Kor was upon him as soon as his fingers closed around the handle, one of the goruk's swords aimed straight for his heart. One quick flick of Ferdinan's wrist pushed Kor's sword high and aside, but it was too little, too late. Ferdinan screamed in pain as he felt the cold bite of sharpened steel sliding into his left shoulder. He felt the warmth of his own blood trickling down his chest and back. The Tamendaders gasped in horror, and the goruks howled excitedly. Kor grinned, his snout-like nose almost touching Ferdinan's. "Now you die," he said.

Ferdinan's reaction came in an instant. With all his strength he drove his sabre up through Kor's outstretched arm, piercing it cleanly through the biceps. Kor screamed, and Ferdinan screamed with him from the pain that consumed his shoulder as he moved to strike. Kor pulled quickly away, leaving one of his morchas still embedded in Ferdinan's shoulder. Ferdinan pulled his own sabre free of Kor's arm as the goruk chieftain withdrew.

"Get this thing out of me," Ferdinan growled to Colvin without ever taking his eyes off Kor. Colvin stepped forward quickly and without warning pulled the scimitar out of Ferdinan's shoulder. Ferdinan screamed, and blood gushed from the wound. For a moment Colvin thought Ferdinan might actually run him through. He quickly ducked back out of the way.

Kor stood a few feet away gripping his arm, trying to staunch his bleeding. His eyes were locked on Ferdinan. "You are going to pay for that, paleskin," he said. Ferdinan made no reply, advancing with sabre at the ready, left arm dangling loosely.

"Get him, lad!" screamed Gregor. "Give him what for!" Gregor's words began a wave of cheers and encouragement from the Tamendaders, which was met with an opposing chorus of grunts and howls from the goruks. But Ferdinan seemed oblivious to the cacophony. He struck, his sabre slashing high for Kor's head. The noise of the crowd drowned out the ring of steel on steel as Kor's blade deflected the blow. Ferdinan doubled back on his attack, swinging low for Kor's abdomen, but Kor managed to bring his own sword down in time to push Ferdinan's sabre side. A thrust of Ferdinan's sabre, aimed for Kor's heart, was likewise deflected. But Ferdinan never faltered in his assault, bombarding Kor with a barrage of attacks, wielding his sabre in one fluid, never-ending blur of motion. Kor was not overwhelmed having to defend himself with only one sword and the use of only his left hand, but he had to concentrate fully on parrying Ferdinan's blows, having no chance to mount a counteroffensive. The cheers of the Tamendaders grew louder and more boisterous as Kor began to back away from Ferdinan, and likewise the howls and snarls of the goruks gained a desperate, anxious quality they had previously lacked. But just when it looked like Ferdinan was on the verge of breaking through Kor's defenses, he backed down a step. His entire left side was blood-drenched, and his breath was coming in quick, ragged gasps.

Kor was immediately on the offensive, his lone morcha slicing in long arcs for Ferdinan's head, his heart, his abdomen. Ferdinan parried each attack masterfully, but now it was he who was backing away, pushed backward by Kor's onslaught. The goruks waved their fists in the air, howling excitedly as they watched their chief turn the tide and advance on Ferdinan. The Tamendaders' cries, so raucous and confident a moment before, were now tinged with fear and panic. The war that seemed so easily won a moment ago now looked to be tilting in the enemy's favor. William alone seemed unafraid. Concern lined his face, but he watched with great concentration as Ferdinan pushed each of Kor's attacks away. He had seen Ferdinan fight like this once before, on a night spent on duty at the very spot where they now stood.

"Find it," William whispered. "Find his weakness. Please, God, let him find it."

And then the unthinkable happened.

Ferdinan's sabre, the most beautiful sword in Tamendad, sailed gracefully through the air, twirling magnificently end over end and away from its owner. It landed a mile away, in another universe, and the sound of it striking the bricks of the street was the death knell for all of Tamendad. A collective gasp from all the Tamendaders was met in reply with an explosion of noise from the goruks, howls and screams of ecstasy at witnessing the victory of their chief. Ferdinan's whole body slumped, a marionette's puppet with strings severed. Without his sword he looked small and pitiful. He watched his opponent with wide, hollow eyes. Kor gave a baleful grin.

"Filth," the goruk spat, raising his morcha. "NOW – YOU – DIE!!!"

Kor leapt.

And so did Ferdinan.

The Conquian dodged sideways, away from Kor's sword, ducking and twirling, stepping in toward his fellow combatant. Kor cursed as his morcha sliced only air, the blade sailing high above Ferdinan's ducked head. Ferdinan lunged, spinning on his heels as he brought his shoulder into Kor's abdomen, raising up, his hand snaking quick as lightning for Kor's sword, plucking the blade from the goruk's loose grasp. One more spin with everything Ferdinan had and a spray of blood as Kor's throat was opened with his own morcha.

Kor's eyes widened in shock, and he made a sickly sputtering sound as blood began to pour from the gash. Ferdinan dropped the sword, grabbing Kor by the tusks, bringing the dying goruk's face within inches of his own. "It ends here," Ferdinan whispered. "All your plans die with you at the end of your own sword. You have failed." He said nothing further, just stood holding Kor's face in his hands, watching the beast bleed. When he finally let go, Kor fell limply to the ground, where he died staring up at the sky over Tamendad.

"Always keep a firm grip on your sword," whispered William to himself.

The explosion of noise that came from the Tamendaders was met by the stunned silence of the goruks. They stared at their fallen chief in wordless shock, and of all the goruks who had witnessed it only the ardah bore an expression that in any way resembled a smile. A single goruk broke free from the crowd, a young one by the look of it, and charged at Ferdinan. It was immediately put down by bolts from seven different crossbows, which served to its comrades as a sufficient deterrent against trying the same thing. Ferdinan barely glanced at the dead beast as he stepped over it to retrieve his sword. Once he had it in hand again, he rounded on the ardah. The ardah watched him approach and did not flinch until the point of Ferdinan's sabre was pressed against his throat.

"I hold you to Kor's promise," said Ferdinan, his eyes cold and his voice even. "You will lead your people out of Tamendad and never return."

"The bargain will be honored," said the ardah with an only slightly quavering voice. "Your grandchildren's grandchildren shall live out their lives without ever laying eyes upon one of our people."

Ferdinan nodded. "And in case you are ever tempted to go against your word, remember this: you attacked a church. Two priests are dead on your orders. I should kill you myself for such an offense, but I gave my word that you would be allowed to leave, and I am always a man of my word. But rest assured that if you ever show your face in the light of day again, there will be a whole legion of the Church's knights-militant looking for you, and the punishment they will have in store for you will be far worse than anything I could ever do. Am I understood?"

The ardah nodded, but the look in his eyes alone was enough to tell that he understood quite well.

"Good," said Ferdinan. "Now get out of my sight."

The ardah's gaze was locked with Ferdinan's for a long, silent moment. Ferdinan's upper lip quivered in a snarl and his hand shook slightly, causing the point of his sabre to vibrate against the ardah's larynx. The whole of the Conquian's will was bent on resisting the urge to plunge his blade through the green bastard's throat. The ardah slowly backed away from Ferdinan, then bowed his head low, bending himself into a submissive posture.

"The bargain will be honored," the ardah repeated in a whisper, then turned and addressed the goruks in their own language. The specifics of what was said, no human ever knew. The ardah led his people out of Tamendad, a procession of broken spirits, back down into the only world they had ever known.

CHAPTER THIRTY-FIVE

A PARTING OF THE WAYS

McRofaly was the onetime apprentice of Esten, the self-proclaimed greatest arcanologist – what the common folk would call a wizard – in all of Glenisle until his untimely death. Deposited on the old sage's doorstep at an early age, McRofaly had no memories of a life before his introduction to the arcane. His formative years, which other boys devoted to the usual sorts of things boys tend to enjoy, had been spent pouring over ancient, musty texts, delving the depths of the arcane arts and mastering the rudiments of magic. He had grown into manhood under Esten's stern and ever-present gaze, and even now, years after the old sage had left this world, McRofaly still lived his life by the ironhanded and often paranoid principles his mentor had instilled in him. His magic had served him well through his years, and now it had even saved his life. Well, his magic and an angry mob of Ganugamosh out for goruk blood.

Now McRofaly sat at a table in the Crown Rose with an inebriated smile firmly entrenched on his face. He clenched a wine goblet in his right hand. It was half-full at the moment, but it had already been filled and emptied many times tonight. He was, for the first time in a very long time, thorough soused. He tended to avoid heavy intoxication, but tonight was an occasion to celebrate, for various reasons. First and foremost, the war had been won. Tamendad was safe; Kor's severed head atop a pike in the town square attested to that. But no less amazing a fact, at least in McRofaly's mind, was that he had used his magic overtly and had suffered none of the horrible fates Esten had always assured would befall him if he did so. There was no burning stake with his name on it, no gallows awaiting him, no heretical inquisition in hot pursuit. In fact he had been congratulated and personally thanked by Governor Chamberlain, Ferdinan, Colvin, William and no fewer than a hundred other random fellows for his contributions to the success of the war effort. He felt quite like a rooster that had snuck a visit to the hen house, then had a parade thrown in his honor for it.

McRofaly was not alone in the Crown Rose, and by no stretch of the imagination was he the most inebriated. The house was packed from wall to wall with Highlanders and Tamendaders all drinking and singing and dancing, so many that the party had spilled out onto the lawn of the Crown Rose and into the street. Never had Tamendad seen such a celebration, and at the heart of it, sitting at the largest table in the main dining room, was Gregor MacDugal. People toasted his health at random intervals and fought their way through the crowd to draw close enough to pat him on the back or shake his hand, and he received them all with a smile and a kind nod. But all the well-wishers passed by him in a blur. His mind was far away from them, drawn inward to the only place where Angus still existed in this world. His thoughts were on his brother, as they had continuously been since watching Ferdinan kill Kor. Angus's death seemed complete now that it had been avenged. It no longer burned and seethed within him like an open sore on his soul. Now it was just there, a simple fact: his brother was dead. The time for revenge had come and gone. Now came the time to grieve. But not just yet. Grief could wait a while longer. There was too much to celebrate.

A hand clapped Gregor's shoulder. The big Highlander had been clapped on the back so many times he barely even noticed it. "Thank ye, lad," he said absently to whoever the hand belonged to. "Hope ye're enjoying yerself."

"Not a bad party you put on, Gregor," said Colvin as he slid into the chair next to the big Highlander. "I doubt this town's ever seen its equal."

Gregor's smile broadened. "Colvin! Good t' see ye!" he said, slapping Colvin's back in return. "I was beginning t' wonder when one o' ye would come around. McRofaly's here, but he says he prefers t' drink alone, th' unsocial bastard. Where is e'eryone? 'Tis nae right for men who stood t'gether in battle t' nae drink t'gether afterwards."

Colvin nodded in agreement, then shrugged. "Ferdinan went straight from the healers to the Governor's house, William's still at the church with his father, and Gunther's shut himself up in his house and won't come out."

"Aye," sighed Gregor. "I tried calling on him earlier m'self, and he would nae even answer. I hope th' bastard dinnae do anything daft."

"Gangis says he's drinking himself stupid, but Gertrude's keeping an eye on him. I can't imagine what he's going through. Blacksmithing is his life."

"He's always been one t' keep his emotions inside. 'Twould nae be a bad idea for ye t' visit him once he starts t' come 'round. Th' company would do him some good."

"Yeah, I was planning on it," said Colvin. He sighed and looked pensively around the crowded dining room.

"Something on yer mind, lad?" asked Gregor.

"Have you seen Rebecca?" Colvin asked. "I've been looking for her all afternoon."

"Nae since th' battlefield," said Gregor. "Th' lass has reason t' keep t' herself."

"Yeah," said Colvin. "I still can't believe Hamish is dead."

"'Tis nae just Hamish, lad," said Gregor gravely. "She lost Padraig as well."

"No!" said Colvin, his eyes wide with shock. "They got Padraig?"

"Aye. They found his body this even. Th' Glens have suffered quite a loss. Padraig McFallagh was a damn fine man. He'd been m' friend for nigh on thirty years."

"Her husband *and* her father?" said Colvin in a whisper.

"Aye, lad. I cannae begin t' imagine th' pain she's enduring, even having lost Angus like I did. Th' goruks stole her whole life from her." There was a long silence, filled with heavy-hearted looks from both men. "Tell me, lad," said Gregor at last, "why were ye looking for her? I dinnae even know th' two o' ye had met."

Colvin's expression turned grave, and he glanced around the dining room to make sure no one was listening in on the conversation. Then he leaned forward until he was less than a hand's width from Gregor and whispered, "Promise me you won't tell anybody what I'm about to tell you."

"I swear it, lad. On m' honor, and th' honor o' th' Clan MacDugal."

"Okay, well, last night I met Rebecca, and...well...we, uh...we sort of...wound up sleeping together." Gregor eyed him curiously. "We had sex, all right?" Colvin added in consternation.

"I know what sleeping t'gether means, lad," said Gregor. "And?"

"And what?" asked Colvin.

"That's what I'm asking ye, lad."

"Gregor, I slept with a man's wife, then watched him die on the battlefield. He died without ever finding out his wife cheated on him. I betrayed him."

"Ye dinnae betray him," said Gregor.

"I did," insisted Colvin. "I had a chance to tell him, and I didn't do it."

"M' guess is he already knew."

"How would he have found out?"

Gregor replied, "Rebecca would have told him, I'm sure."

"No way. I saw Hamish this morning before the battle and he didn't try to kill me. If Rebecca had told him, I wouldn't be sitting here now. I'd be out there in pieces with Hamish and Padraig, and honestly I'm not sure that isn't what I deserve."

"Lad, Hamish would nae have tried t' kill ye for sleeping with his wife. Hamish held close t' th' old ways, as does Rebecca. 'Tis th' old custom t' share yer bed before battle. There are stories from th' auld of entire armies falling t' th' deed together, passing wives around like wineskins. I'm sure while ye were with Rebecca last night, Hamish was with a lass o' his own, and when they were done with that they laid together."

"Oh," said Colvin, his expression blank. "So I didn't do anything wrong."

"I would nae go so far as that," said Gregor. "Personally, I think th' practice is distasteful. If ye're nae going t' foreswear sleeping with whoe'er suits yer fancy, what's th' point o' getting married? But ye need nae worry about betraying Hamish. He would have expected Rebecca t' do exactly as she did. If I were ye, I'd be more worried about what someone else thought about it."

"Who?"

"Melinda, lad."

Colvin sighed. "Yeah, I've thought about that, too. But Melinda's made it abundantly clear she just wants to be friends."

"Well," said Gregor, "if ye believe that, ye've nothing t' worry about."

Colvin's brow furrowed. "What do you mean, *if*–"

Before Colvin could finish his sentence there was a raucous eruption of cheers in the crowded dining room. Ferdinan had just arrived at the Crown Rose. His shoulder was heavily bandaged and his left arm was in a sling, but it did nothing to dampen the smile on his face. He bowed graciously at the hero's welcome he was receiving, hampered slightly by his immobile left arm.

"Well if 'tis nae th' man o' th' hour," said Gregor with a smile as he made his way through the crowd toward Ferdinan. He grabbed the Conquian and pulled him into a hug, careful not to hurt his shoulder. "Glad t' see ye finally decided t' show yer face in public."

"Please escuse my tardiness, *compagno*," said Ferdinan. "I had to meet with Geoffery to relinquish my position as Captain of the Guard and help him make plans to get Tamendad back in order. He es going to have his hands full for a while, I am afraid."

"Th' savior o' Tamendad need make nae excuses. He can come and go as he pleases. I'm just glad ye finally came t' have a drink."

Colvin already had a glass of wine poured for Ferdinan when he reached the table. "It's Conquian," Colvin said with a smile. "The Armada was kind enough to donate a couple of casks to the celebration."

"Ah!" said Ferdinan with a gleam in his eyes. "The king's ships carry only the finest wine. Have you sampled it?"

"No," said Colvin, "but I think McRofaly has." He gestured over his shoulder, where McRofaly was now standing on top of a table.

"Look!" McRofaly yelled to the crowd. "I'm a bird!" He jumped off the table, flapped his arms wildly, crashed to the floor in a heap, and began to snore loudly.

Ferdinan nodded thoughtfully. "Conquian wine es a bit stronger than other varieties," he said. "It can have that effect on the uninitiated."

"I shall try a nip o' that," said Gregor.

"So how es my brave second faring?" Ferdinan asked Colvin as they took their seats.

"Just happy to be alive," replied Colvin.

"Well spoken," said Ferdinan.

"So what shall we drink to, lads?" said Gregor, pouring himself a dram.

Ferdinan thought for a moment, then raised his glass high. "To brotherhood."

Gregor and Colvin smiled, raising their glasses as well.

"To brotherhood."

Days rolled by, but the celebration in Tamendad refused to wane. The Highlanders, when they were not making merry, assisted with the laborious process of cleaning up the city and burying the dead. Only one ship of the Conquian Royal Armada remained docked, waiting to bear their esteemed ambassador back to his homeland as soon as he was healed enough to travel. Ferdinan ordered the other ships to sail out of Turish waters, not wanting their continued presence to cause a political stir. Gregor, Colvin, McRofaly and Ferdinan spent their evenings together at the Crown Rose, graciously accepting and enduring the vast amounts of praise and gratitude that was showered on them. William came around once in a while, but the young nobleman spent most of his time at the bedside of his father. The healer's prognosis seemed to be accurate; Jonathan was showing daily improvement. He was confined to his bed, of course, but by the second day he could manage a coherent conversation and by the third he could prop himself up on his pillows without the pain being too great to bear.

On the fourth day after Kor's death, the first ships full of evacuated townspeople arrived in the harbor. The docks were overflowing with people awaiting their reunion with loved ones, and as soon as passengers began to disembark from the ships the scene degenerated into a confused mass of hugs and tears of joy. William stood amid the emotional tumult outside the defunct northeast gate, craning his neck in hopes of catching a glimpse of a familiar face. He had no idea if his family was even on one of these first ships, but the promise of seeing the people he loved kept him frozen there on his tiptoes, straining hopelessly to peer through the chaos and spot his mother, his brother, or – *Oh, God, please let it be* – Melissa. But sight of those faces evaded him. All around him were people he knew, and he was glad to see them, but never the people he searched for. The first ship emptied, and then the second. The moments crept by with agonizing slowness, yet before he knew it he had been standing at the docks looking for his family for half an hour. He began to resign himself to the idea that he might have to wait for other ships to arrive before being reunited with his family when to his right the crowd parted just a little and suddenly someone was hugging him tightly around the waist.

"Julius!" William cried out, and threw his arms tightly around his brother's neck. Then the tears came, hot and salty, streaming down his face.

"I missed you, brother," said Julius, his voice muffled since his face was pressed firmly into William's abdomen.

"Oh, God, I missed you too," replied William, wiping his tears away. And then before he could ask where everyone else was, they emerged from the crowd, his mother anxiously pulling at her shawl, Melissa shrouded by her parents on either side. William felt as though his heart might burst, and finally, *finally* he remembered what life was like without the goruks.

Melissa began to sob the moment her eyes met William's, her hand pressed delicately over her mouth, and it was the most beautiful William had ever seen her. They fell into each other's arms and the world fell away from them. All that was real was their embrace, their two hearts beating in steady accompanying rhythm. They kissed, and it was as if new life had been breathed into them. Never had there been such a perfect kiss, and forevermore their kisses always held a hint of that perfection.

"I love you," Melissa told him.

"I love you," William replied.

It was a perfect moment, and in a perfect world it would have lasted forever. The world in which William and Melissa lived, however, was imperfect, and all too soon the moment passed away. William felt a delicate touch on his shoulder, and he turned to see his mother standing there with a most anxious look on her face. "William, where is your father?" she asked, and William knew at once what horrors were racing through her mind. All around them on the docks were people receiving the news that their loved ones were gone.

"It's okay," said William, taking his mother into his arms and hugging her tight. "Father was injured, but he's going to be okay. He's under healer's care at the church, but he'll be able to come home soon. He's doing better every day."

"What happened?" gasped his mother, the shock of hearing that her husband had been wounded competing with her relief to hear he was still alive.

"It was during the battle. What's important is that he's okay. We'll go and see him together. All of us. He asked me to bring you all as soon as I found you."

As William and his family left the docks together and headed toward the church, Melissa once again slid her arms around him. She walked with her head nuzzled against the crook of his neck. "I missed you, my love," she said. "Each day I felt my heart break a little more without you."

William sighed contentedly, savoring the warmth of her so close to him. "There were times I thought I'd die, I missed you so," he said. "But now we're together again. Forever."

"Forever," Melissa echoed in a whisper. "I wrote you every day," she added in a less daydreamy tone. "I have so many letters for you to read."

William smiled. "I have one for you to read as well, my love."

"I wish I could go with you."

It was the sort of romantic nonsense that a woman of Elysia Chamberlain's stature could only get away with saying while lying naked beside her lover. Ferdinan propped himself up on his good arm and smiled at her. "As do I," he said. "You must come to Conquia whenever you get the opportunity. You would fall in love with it."

"I do not doubt it," Elysia replied. She snuggled up against him, nuzzling his chest, careful not to press against his injured shoulder. "Everything I have heard of it sounds wonderful."

"Words cannot do it justice," he said. "It must be seen to be believed."

"You will be going back soon." Her words hung unpleasantly in the air, met only by a mutual silence. She looked up at him, and he saw that her eyes were wet. "If it is such a wonderful place you are going back to, whatever could I hope for to bring you back to me?" she whispered.

If Ferdinan could have moved his left arm at all, he would have thrown his arms around her and held her tight. Instead he inched closer to her on the bed, until every possible part of their bodies was touching. The effect it had on her was the same. "We knew this would be difficult," said Ferdinan softly. "Es why we fought it for so long."

"But I never knew how difficult it would really be until this moment," Elysia replied, and her voice almost broke.

"Hear me now," said Ferdinan. "We will see each other again. I promise it."

"I hope so," said Elysia. "From the bottom of my heart I hope so. Now that you've come into my life, I don't know how I could ever go back to living without you."

Ferdinan nodded, grinning roguishly. "I seem to have that effect on women."

Elysia slapped at him playfully. "Oh, shut up. You know what I mean."

"Indeed I do, Lady Chamberlain," said Ferdinan. Still grinning, he rose from the bed and walked to the door of Elysia's balcony, where four days ago he had feigned surrender to Kor's army. He stared out at a Tamendad that was slowly, steadily coming back to life. The war was over; townspeople were beginning to return to their homes. Life was returning to normal, or as close to normal as could be expected after all that Tamendad had been through. A grin turned the corners of Ferdinan's lips. He had done his job.

From the bed, Elysia Chamberlain studied her lover's naked form. Her eyes drank in the way the early evening sunlight illuminated every curve and line of Ferdinan's body. Even with his arm in a sling, he was the image of masculine perfection to her. Elysia felt feelings stirring within her she had never felt before. "Answer me one question," she said, trying to take her mind off her emotions.

"I am an open book to you," Ferdinan replied. "Ask."

"How did the ship from Tantera – the one whose captain I gave your letter to – reach the Armada in time?"

Ferdinan gave her a thoughtful look. "So you figured it out, then."

"It was simple enough to piece together," replied Elysia. "The only part I cannot quite figure out is how the ship made the journey to the Armada and the Armada made the journey back here before it was too late. It takes almost a month to cross the Melteric."

Ferdinan sat down on the edge of the bed. His manner had turned gravely serious. "What I am about to tell you must remain with you," he said.

"Of course."

"You must swear it."

"I swear on the soul of my mother," she said without hesitation, "I will never speak a word of what you tell me to anyone."

Ferdinan nodded. He took a moment to gather his thoughts. "Relations between our countries have, at various times throughout history, been tense," he began. "While Conquia and Tur have never been openly hostile toward one another, we often fail to see eye to eye on many issues. In many ways, my visit to this kingdom was seen as a turning point for both our countries. A single ambassador of the Conquian crown to be the personal guest of King Stodlemeyer, then tour the entire kingdom. If it went well, the hope was it would be reciprocated with a Turish ambassador visiting Conquia, and eventually lead to trips across the ocean for both kings."

"But what does this have to do with the Armada?" Elysia asked.

"I am coming to that. You see, as with all ambassadorial visits, there was a great fuss made about how I would get from Conquia to Tur. King Altores demanded I be escorted by the Royal Armada all the way to the shores of Tur. King Stodlemeyer relented, on the condition that the Armada would return to Conquia as soon as I was safely on Turish soil, and I would return to Conquia as a guest of the King Stodlemeyer's navy. It was agreed, escept for one thing which nobody knew: the Armada was under orders from King Altores not to return home.

"What?"

"For months prior to my arrival, the Armada had charted how the Turish navy patrols their waters. There were areas found...blind spots, no? Routes ships could sail and never be discovered by the patrols. Upon my arrival in Tur, the Armada was to give the appearance of sailing back toward Conquia until they were out of sight, then circle around and remain hidden at arm's length during the whole of my visit."

Elysia looked at Ferdinan with eyes wide. Lesser acts had begun wars. "Why would King Altores do such a thing?" she asked.

"To protect me. It took a great deal of good faith for King Altores to send an ambassador alone into a foreign land. He wanted his Armada close enough to react in case anything happened. As it turns out, that was our good fortune."

"It was still quite a risk," said Elysia, somewhat shaken.

Ferdinan nodded. "Es why I hesitated to call the Armada into Turish waters for so long." After a pause, he smiled. "Besides," he added, "we Conquians have a reputation for taking calculated risks."

Elysia sighed. She had to admit, to herself at least, that was one of the qualities that so strongly attracted her to him. "When will you leave?" she asked.

"Possibly tomorrow, but most likely the day after. Your father wishes to hold a grand banquet tomorrow celebrating our victory, and he insists I attend. I doubt we will have a chance to sail until the following morning."

"And what are your plans for this evening, Don Ferdinan?"

"I promised your father I would assist him with settling the returning townspeople and bringing them up to speed on what has transpired during their absence. Why do you ask?"

"Well," she said, smiling, casting her eyes downward in uncharacteristically girlish fashion, "I was wondering if we had time to make love again."

Ferdinan caressed her cheek with his good hand, and almost instinctively Elysia closed her eyes and nuzzled her face against his gentle touch. "For you, my lady, es time enough."

The Governor's banquet, the first official city function in Tamendad since the beginning of the war, was as grand and formal an event as the city had ever witnessed. More than two hundred people were in attendance, representing every noble house and landowning family in Tamendad. All were dressed in the finest clothes, and they ate the finest food off the finest porcelain plates and drank the finest wine from the finest crystal goblets. They talked, they toasted, they danced, they sang, and most of all they applauded and adored the Governor's guests of honor. Almost all surviving members of the war council were in attendance, and they did their best to ignore all the people of high standing who were continuously fawning over them. It was a gala event, and guests boasted for years to come that it was the finest party Governor Chamberlain ever put on, but to those who had fought in the war there was a sense of artificiality about the whole affair. The fighting, the killing, the *blood* was just too fresh on their minds and hands to adjust themselves to the niceties of a formal banquet.

Not to say that they did not enjoy themselves. William and Melissa spent almost the whole of the night in each other's arms, whether on the dance floor, at the dinner table, or mingling with guests. Colvin, who had never attended a formal dinner, savored every course of the meal, packing away enough to feed a small cow. Gregor made the most of the open bar before thrilling the guests with an impromptu pipes concert and serenade, accompanied by Liam, Gabrahn and Wallace. Ferdinan, of course, was like a fish in water the whole evening, completely at ease with his surroundings. He toasted, he mingled, he made eloquent speeches off the cuff about the bravery and resolve of Tamendad and the hope that his involvement in the war against the goruks might pave the way toward improved relations between Conquia and Tur. But by far his most notable act of the evening was the dance he shared with Elysia Chamberlain, the sort of slow, sensual, almost erotic dance that was all too common in Conquia but that most Turishmen had never seen in their lives. The dance drew a good number of stares, none more prevalent than the Governor's.

As a counterpoint to Ferdinan's sociable nature, McRofaly was very elusive throughout the evening, keeping to himself and conversing only with those people he already knew. Whenever someone would approach him to shower praise on him, as was being done to everyone who had played a part in the war, McRofaly would smile and say thank you, then quickly find an excuse to move to another part of the room. Yet McRofaly, for all his aloofness, enjoyed the affair perhaps most of all. Every bite of food, every drink of wine, every note the band played he enjoyed as he had never enjoyed anything before. His life, it was now plain to him, had been divided into two parts: that which had occurred before he had used his magic in public, and that which had occurred after. He was at a new beginning in his life, and where he went from here was anybody's guess.

For all its grandeur, though, an unmistakable something was missing from the banquet: Gunther Moragun was not in attendance. The short blacksmith spent the evening in his workshop, where he had been practically since losing his hand. He was alone except for a barrel of beer; he wouldn't even let Gangis or Gertrude visit with him. He sat in the dark, staring at the forge, trying – and failing – to drink the pain away.

Torrance Mayhew stood alone in the center of the main dining room of the Crown Rose, purveying the destruction with wide eyes and an expressionless face. He had returned from Tantera that morning to find his beloved Crown Rose in complete disarray. His pantries were bare, his wine cellar emptied. Much of the furniture in the main dining room was beyond repair. The railing along the balcony needed some work. And, of course, he still needed a new chandelier. He wanted to believe that goruks had done this. At least then it would be a culprit he was comfortable with hating. But the goruks were not accountable. The damage was too vast, too random and too obviously caused by revelry to be attributable to goruks. No, something far more dangerous and destructive had happened to the Crown Rose.

Gregor MacDugal had happened.

"Aye, Master Mayhew, I've been expecting ye," came Gregor's booming voice as he descended the stairs from the second floor. "M' kinsmen and I are set t' return home t' th' Highlands this morn. Th' only business I've left in Tamendad is t' settle m' bill."

Mayhew turned and faced the big Highlander. The proprietor's face was pale. He looked like he might faint.

"You've killed it," he said. "You've killed my business."

"Well, now, that's o'erstating it a bit, don't ye think?"

"It's dead," said Mayhew without hesitation. "I'm ruined."

"Torrance, I told ye I'd be held responsible for all damages," said Gregor in a moderately exasperated tone. "I intend t' honor m' word. I've already had someone inspect th' place." Gregor handed Mayhew a folded piece of paper. "Th' estimate," Gregor explained.

Mayhew took the paper from Gregor apprehensively. He unfolded it and looked it over. His eyes widened, his mouth fell open and his face turned the color of a beet. His eyes shot from the incomprehensible paper to the incomprehensible Highlander, and it took a moment for him to realize that Gregor was offering him a bulky sack of coins.

"There's an extra fifteen percent in there," said Gregor, "t' cover th' ten I told ye t' add and anything th' appraiser might've missed." Mayhew took the sack cautiously, as though he expected it to explode at any moment. When it was firmly in hand, he marveled at the weight of it. "And this," continued Gregor, pulling another, much smaller coin purse from his belt, "is t' cover our meals and boarding."

A flabbergasted Mayhew took this second bag of coins in his other hand, shifting his gaze back and forth between the two and occasionally up at Gregor. "Ah, well, I suppose this settles your bill, Master MacDugal. Yes, indeed. I hope you have enjoyed your stay at the Crown Rose. Please come again." After a brief hesitation, he added, "But do take your time."

Gregor laughed and patted Mayhew on the back. "Ye're a credit t' yer kin, sir. I've ne'er met a Turishman who could suffer me and m' lads like ye have. God bless ye."

Ferdinan was waiting outside when Gregor emerged from the Crown Rose. The Conquian was busying himself with a leisurely stroll through one of the gardens, which was not much entertainment since everything was either dead or dying from the coming cold season. He joined Gregor and together they left the Crown Rose behind them.

"How did he take it?" asked Ferdinan.

"Rather well, I have t' say. I suspect he'll be in shock for a while, though."

"Es understandable. You did quite a number on the place."

608

Gregor shrugged. "'Tis his own fault for being foolish enough t' rent t' me."

They crossed the town in silence, walking in step beside each other, two friends bonded by the horrors of war and the elation of victory. It was time for them to part now, for Gregor to return to Duerhein and Ferdinan to cross the ocean back to Conquia, and they found themselves in a moment where words were an intrusion. They simply walked and shared the morning. Children followed behind them in the streets, excitedly whispering that these were the men who saved their homes and how they wanted to be just like Gregor and Ferdinan when they were big. Gregor and Ferdinan pretended not to hear, but they allowed themselves to smile nonetheless. It had been so long since smiling came so naturally.

They passed the church and made the Sign of the Compass together. The battered doors had been removed, and a team of carpenters were busy replacing them with sturdy wooden ones that would suffice until another pair of bronze doors could be cast. All the debris and all the blood had been cleared away. It was once again sacrosanct.

They continued down the main street, the same stretch of street that Gregor and his lads had explored for nearly an hour upon first arriving in town, before William had come to their aid and filled in as tour guide. That memory was so distant in Gregor's mind now, so cloudy, like trying to see the bottom of a muddied stream. Gregor MacDugal was a different man now. A little older, not much wiser, but different through and through. Violent conflict changed a man, and Gregor had endured enough of it to last ten lifetimes. Worse, he knew there would be more to come, sometime, waiting for him on a hopefully distant day. But that was Gregor's lot, and he did not resent it. Such was the life he had chosen for himself, the life of a Highlander.

They came at last to the southwest gate, which now stood beautifully, inspiringly open. This afforded a perfect view of the tallest hill overlooking the city, where the forces of Tamendad had charged to meet Kor's army and where the grass was still stained red from the blood of those who had died atop it. Gregor's kinsmen were amassed on that hill, waiting for their general to lead them back home. But Gregor did not rush to join them. He paused for a moment at the gate, as did Ferdinan, and together they turned back for one more look at Tamendad. Neither man spoke of what he felt at that moment, but whenever either of them thought of Tamendad, that was the moment that first came to mind. Not the fighting and the bleeding and the dying, not goruks, not the agony of what they had endured, but the simple view of the bricked main street of a small but bustling port city. And in that moment, everything was all right.

"Well," said Gregor in a sigh, "time t' be going."

Ferdinan hesitated. "Gregor, before you do, es something I have to say to you. Es something I have been intending to say for days now, but I have put it off until the last possible moment like a coward."

Gregor eyed his Conquian friend curiously. "Aye, lad?"

"Es about Kor," said Ferdinan. "I hope...I hope you bear me no ill will for being the one who killed him."

"What th' bugger are ye talking about, lad?"

"Of everyone in this war," explained Ferdinan, "you had the greatest cause for revenge. Kor's head should have rightfully been yours, to avenge the death of your brother. I hope you do not...what es the word? ...*begrudge* me for being the one who killed him."

Gregor placed a big hand on Ferdinan's shoulder. "There could ne'er be hard feelings 'tween us, m' friend. When Angus was killed, Kor signed his own death warrant. I dinnae care if I was th' one who did it, or one o' m' lads, or a Tamendader, or a falling rock. Th' bastard had t' die. And ye saw t' it that he did. And for that I shall always be indebted t' ye."

Ferdinan nodded, smiling. "If there es one thing I have learned during my travels in this country, Gregor, es that the Turish are fools to not heed the wisdom of your people."

"Been saying that for years, lad," replied Gregor with a wink.

Together they exited Tamendad through the southwest gate and found that a crowd had amassed there. As Gregor and Ferdinan passed through, the townspeople cast flowers at their feet and cheered them. When they were through the crowd they began to climb the hill that would forevermore be known to Tamendaders and Highlanders as Blood Hill. Three hundred and forty men and women had set out from Duerhein with Gregor MacDugal. On this crisp Anteron morning, less than two hundred prepared to return with him. Liam, Gabrahn and Wallace already had them organized – as organized as Highlanders got, at any rate – and ready to march. And atop Blood Hill, Gregor also found two who were not making the journey with him.

"William! Colvin! Good t' see ye this morning!"

"We weren't about to let you leave without saying goodbye," said William.

"Ah, thank ye, lads. That means a lot t' me."

"So are you excited to be going home?" asked Colvin.

"Might as well ask if a groom's excited on his wedding night, lad," replied Gregor with a gleam in his eyes. "It shall be good for life t' return t' normal."

"Amen to that," said William. "And don't forget, Melissa and I are getting married in less than a year. You'll have to make the journey north for that. It just wouldn't be right if you weren't here."

"Would nae miss it, lad. Ye can tell me all about it when ye come visit Duerhein. I shall expect ye at th' spring thaw."

William laughed. "Be there with bells on! Me and Colvin both."

"Shit yeah!" echoed Colvin.

"Aye, and McRofaly too. Speaking o' which, where is that wee bastard?"

"He wanted to come see you off," said William, "but he's back open for business. Quite a few people are buying expensive gifts to celebrate our victory."

"Ah, well, glad t' see he's turning a profit again. Tell him I said fair ye well. Now I've got t' get m' horse ready t' ride. I've a journey ahead."

"I'll give you a hand with that," said Colvin, giving Gregor a look the big Highlander could not mistake.

"Aye, I shall be glad t' have th' help," Gregor replied.

Together they walked to Gregor's horse, which gave them some privacy to talk. They busied themselves with checking straps and securing saddlebags and brushing the great beast's coat, though Colvin admittedly had no idea what he was doing. "Still no word from Rebecca?" he said sidelong to Gregor in a voice too low to be overheard by others.

Gregor sighed, grimly shaking his head. "She's up and disappeared. But with what she's been through, who could blame her? M' guess is she's gone off somewhere t' start a new life for herself. I'd likely nae want t' go home either, were I in her boots."

"Yeah," said Colvin dejectedly. "I just wish I'd had a chance to talk to her after it happened."

"Aye, lad. Me too."

Gregor and Colvin finished up with the horse and returned for one last round of goodbyes. Liam, Gabrahn and Wallace had joined Ferdinan and William and were exchanging farewells. "Well now, 'tis pointless t' draw this out," said Gregor when he and Colvin rejoined the others. "We shall be seeing each other again soon enough."

"Well spoken," said Ferdinan. He embraced the big Highlander, kissing him once on either cheek. "Safe journey, *compagno*. God goes with you."

"Same t' ye, m' friend," replied Gregor.

Gregor and his lads mounted their horses, and with a wave goodbye began to lead the Highlanders down Blood Hill and away from Tamendad. William, Colvin and Ferdinan watched them go, saying nothing to each other, until Gregor's army was but a cluster of specs on the distant hills. And with that, Gregor MacDugal was gone from

Tamendad.

"Es time for me to be going as well," said Ferdinan at length. Would you care to accompany me to the docks?"

"Sure thing," said Colvin.

They were saluted as they re-entered the city, and all traffic on the main street stopped to let them pass. The trade district was bustling as they passed by, and that was a wonderful sight. When they came to the northeast gate they found another small crowd had gathered there, and the street was littered with rose petals. The ship that was to carry Ferdinan back to his home was anchored in the docks, colors flying high.

"No need for long goodbyes," said Ferdinan. "William, send me a letter with the details of your wedding. Just put my name on it and send it to Losillas. It will find me. Colvin, keep practicing the sabre. You have great potential at it. And I espect a letter from you as well."

He embraced them both, then boarded his ship and went below deck without looking back. The flagship of the Conquian Armada cast off, sailing down the Taeran Sea toward the Melteric Ocean.

"There goes one of the cockiest bastards in all the world," said Colvin as he and William watched the ship sail away.

William burst out laughing. "Yeah, but he's a great man."

"Most of the great ones are, I suspect."

"True enough," said William. "Well, I'm having lunch with Melissa and then going to visit with Father at the church. Would you like to join me?"

"Nah," said Colvin. "I think I'm going to take a walk on the beach."

"All right, then, I'll see you at home," said William, turning and leaving Colvin at the docks.

Colvin chuckled to himself as he watched his friend go, then left the docks and walked along the beach. He took off his boots and walked barefoot, feeling the sand sift through his toes as he wiggled them. He walked along the shore, letting the waves crash over his feet until they were frozen. He tossed some rocks into the sea, watching the small explosions of water as they plunked into the wash. Then he retreated up the beach a bit and built a fire with his bare hands, a skill he had picked up during his wandering years. He sat in front of the little driftwood fire with his legs crisscrossed, staring out at the sea, watching ships come and go. The sun was behind him now. He tended the fire. He thought.

Who are you?

He wasn't really sure. He wasn't the same person he'd been a month ago; that much he knew. He was calmer now, more trusting, perhaps a bit saner. He was softer now, too. That was undeniable. Though not in the physical sense – a month and more of fighting coupled with the full meals he had been eating had gotten him in the best shape he'd been in since being Loran Rothwald's apprentice. But emotionally he was softer. His walls had come down a bit. Things got to him a bit more easily. He cared more. That, he thought, was really at the heart of the matter. And it didn't bother him as much as he thought it perhaps should.

He was a new man. He was Colvin. Colvin of Tamendad.

Suddenly Melinda was there, plopping down in the sand in front of him on the other side of the fire, sitting with her knees bent up to her chest. She brushed her hair back behind her ear and smiled at him.

"Oi," she said.

"Oi," he replied, smiling. "Just get back?"

"Yeah. I decided to save my money and make the trip on land."

"Wise," said Colvin. "So how are you?"

"Tired. I'm going to sleep like a baby tonight in my own bed." After a brief pause, she added, "How are you?"

"I'm okay."

She smiled coyly. "From what I hear, you're more than okay."

Colvin arched an eyebrow. "Come again?

"A few of my female shipmates on the trip to Tantera had apparently gotten to know you…intimately. Your name came up, and some of them exchanged stories."

Colvin couldn't keep from cracking a grin. "Oh really?" he said, suppressing a laugh. "That must have been interesting."

"And informative," Melinda retorted. "You're quite popular. Well, maybe not anymore."

"Yeah, well, no regrets, right?"

They looked into each other's eyes for a long, silent moment. Melinda wanted to look away, but Colvin's steady gaze prevented it. "There's something I have to tell you," he said at last. "During the war, about a week ago now, I met someone. She was Glenish. We wound up sleeping together. It didn't mean anything."

"Why are you telling me this?" Melinda asked. She looked uncomfortable.

"I don't know. I just thought you should know."

"Colvin, we're not married. We're not courting. You don't have to explain yourself to me. What you do, and with who, is your own business. And whatever you do, it won't change the fact that we're friends."

"There's something else I have to tell you," he said.

"Oh God," she replied, rolling her eyes.

"No, no, it's nothing bad. It's something I figured out while you were gone, about us being friends."

"I'm listening," she said, a little apprehensively.

Colvin cleared his throat and scratched the back of his neck. His walls might have come down a bit, but it still wasn't easy wearing his heart on his sleeve. "Being friends with you is really important to me," he began. "More important than just about anything else, really. And I wouldn't want to do anything to hurt our friendship. I guess that's why I told you about Rebecca. I wanted to make sure you were okay with it."

"Colvin, it's okay," she said.

"I know," Colvin replied. "There's more. I have feelings for you."

Melinda looked as though she was about to interrupt him, but he didn't let her. "I tried to tell you this before you left," he continued, "but you said it was the wrong time. Well, I'm making this the right time. I have to get this off my chest. I have to be honest with you. You're not like anyone I've ever met. But I know you're not interested in romance or courtship, so I'm okay with that. I have feelings for you, but I respect where you are in your life and what you need right now. I'm not offering anything but friendship, and I don't expect anything more than that."

There was a silence that followed Colvin's words, and he and Melinda sat looking at each other from across the fire. He longed to know what she was thinking, and he wished he was better able to express in words the revelation he had had at Gunther's forge. But he had expressed it as best he could. Now he awaited her reaction. The silence stretched out to the threshold of awkwardness, and Colvin wondered if he had blown it. Then the corners of Melinda's mouth curved slightly upward, and for once Colvin thought perhaps he understood her secret just a little.

"Thank you," she said.

"You're welcome," he told her.

Melinda stood up and stretched, and her back popped loudly. "Oh God," she said, wincing. "I think I'm going to take a hot bath and sleep for about twelve hours."

"That sounds like fun."

"Lunch tomorrow?"

"Sure thing. I'll meet you in the marketplace around noon."

They said goodbye. Melinda walked up the beach back toward Tamendad. Colvin watched her go, and when she was gone he lay down in the sand and stared up at the sky. The clouds swirled by overhead, resembling a thousand different things. Curious seagulls hovered nearby. The afternoon was cool, but his feet were warm in his boots by the fire. The fragrance of the sea was sweet. He drifted into unconsciousness and dreamed good dreams, free of the bad things. He dreamed of Gregor and Ferdinan, of William, of the Crown Rose. He dreamed of a happy and vibrant Rebecca, with Hamish by her side. He dreamed of Gunther with two hands. He dreamed of Melinda's smiling face.

He woke at dusk, slightly chilled, slightly stiff. The fire was reduced to embers. The seagulls were gone. No ships were sailing, only sitting quietly anchored in the harbor. He was very hungry.

Colvin stood up, brushed the sand from his clothes, and started for home.

GLOSSARY

Agathas (AG-a-thas) – the Face of Beneficence; one of the Four Faces of God as described in the Architessera; believed to be the supreme or purest face of God

Animas (AN-e-moss) – the Face of Dissonance; one of the Four Faces of God as described in the Architessera

Antrelican Church – a monotheistic faith founded approximately 3,000 years ago by the ancient oracle Antrelus; reformed around the time of the Great Burden by Hidalgo Sanctus; the predominant religion of Tur and the Continental Kingdoms

Architessera (ark-i-TESS-er-a) – the holy scriptures of the Antrelican church, which describe the Four Faces of God

Arcumore (ar-coo-MOR-ay) – a high-ranking priest in the Antrelican church who oversees religious matters in a large area

Andoria – the largest Turish city in Glenisle

ardah (AR-da) – literally "seer"

compagno (com-PAN-o) – Conquian word meaning "close friend"

Conquia (CON-kwee-a) – one of the three Continental Kingdoms; it is the wealthiest country in the world and considered by many to be the most powerful; it is currently ruled by King Carlos Altores

Dammaugh (DAM-ow) – the proper, self-given name of the people who have come to be known as Highlanders or Glensmen; Dammaugh culture predates the founding of Tur by hundreds, perhaps thousands of years

Dan, Sir Isaac – the founder of Tamendad

decusé (de-coo-SAY) – the philosophical foundation of Conquian swordplay and the Conquian way of life in general

devotional – ritualistic prayers that members of the Antrelican church perform before a priest to rededicate themselves to the faith, as opposed to petitioning for sanctity or favor

duál (DWAL) – a braid of hair worn by Highlanders; the side of the face it hangs on and the color of the leather that wraps the end are symbols of rank and importance

Duerhein (DAIRN) – an ancient castle in the Highlands that is a stronghold of the Clan MacDugal; also, the name of a town that has grown up around the castle

Four Faces of God – an Antrelican conceptualization of God, in which it is said that God has four faces that represent four seemingly incongruent qualities; it is said that at all times and under all circumstances at least one face of God is smiling; each face is given a name and a title; it should not be inferred that the Architessera espouses a polytheistic doctrine; each of the four faces describes a different aspect of the same God

Ganugamon (ga-NU-ga-mon) – the mythological progenitor of the Ganugamosh; also referred to as He Who First Carved the Way

Ganugamosh (ga-NU-ga-mosh) – a short, stout, subterranean people, renowned by those few who are aware of their existence for their skill as stonemasons and metallurgists; their life span exceeds that of a normal man, and they tend to be a little rough around the edges

Glenish – a general Turish term describing any native of Glenisle; it is a term that no self-respecting Highlander or Glensman would ever self-apply

Glenisle – an island-colony of Tur off the southern coast of the mainland and separated by the Taeran Sea

Glens, the – a series of farming towns in southern Glenisle from which the island derives its name; the food production and trade of the Glens supports the economic infrastructure of the entire island, and much of southern Tur

Glensman – a member of the Dammaugh people who makes his home in far-southern Glenisle, in or around the Glens; note the significant difference between *Glensman* and *Glenish.*

Great Burden – a cataclysmic event that occurred almost one thousand years ago; very few details are known

healer – an Antrelican priest devoted to the study of medicinal herbs and remedies

Hidalgo Sanctus – the reformer of the Antrelican Church; lived during the time of the Great Burden; the only oracle ever to be canonized; is said to have performed many miracles, including building the Cathedral of San Hidalgo in two days and rising from the dead after his own assassination; known as the Great Benefactor

Highlander – the offshoot of the Dammaugh people who years ago settled in the mountain range that cuts its way across the middle of Glenisle

Kalatheptoris (kal-a-thep-TOR-is) – meaning unknown

Losillas (lo-SEE-as) – a city in western Conquia famous for its master swordsmen and swordsmiths; it is the second largest city in the kingdom

Lugosh-Alogar – literally "world-forge"; forges built by the Ganugamosh that harness heat from the world's core

lurbet – a race of small, sightless, rather stupid creatures that live underground

Master Postulant – the head of a church with multiple priests

morcha – a curved sword, very similar in design to a scimitar

Paraxis (par-AX-is) – the Face of Strife; one of the Four Faces of God as described in the Architessera

Parland – one of the three Continental Kingdoms; Parlandian traders are world-renowned

Parlandis – the native language of Parland; the suffix –*is* is appropriate under the language's grammatical rules; referring to the language as *Parlandish* is incorrect

Patrum – a priest of the Antrelican church; note that the term is masculine; a female priest, though quite rare, is known as a Matrum

Posteriori Cataclymian – literally "after the cataclysm"; a method or reckoning years from the Great Burden; years preceding the Great Burden are recorded as Ante Cataclymian, though recorded history predating the Great Burden is essentially lost

Prima Tonce (PREEM-a TAHN-say) – literally "first tongue"; the official language of the Antrelican Church and the preferred language of scholars and sages; the root of all languages spoken in the Continental Kingdoms and one of the root languages of Turish; also called the Holy Tongue and the Academic Language

Royal House – a noble house that has held the Turish throne at any point in its history; the noble house that currently holds the throne is referred to as the Reigning Royal House

Sacred Compass – the symbol of the Antrelican faith, resembling an equilateral cross with its points connected to form a diamond that is in turn enclosed in a circle

San Hidalgo – the capital city of Conquia; also, the Conquian name for Hidalgo Sanctus

sanctity – in the Antrelican faith, the physical manifestation of God's will

scale the summit – an Antrelican conception of death; it is believed that the soul ascends to a state of perpetual attunement with Agathas, the Face of Beneficence

Sign of the Compass – touching, in succession, the left shoulder, the sternum, the right shoulder, and the forehead, all with the right hand

Summerfeast – a seven-day festival ending on Midsummer's Day

Tactus (TAC-tus) – the Face of Consonance; one of the Four Faces of God as described in the Architessera

Tamendad (tahm-in-DOD) – the principle Turish port city on Glenisle

Tantera (tan-TARE-a) – a smaller port city up the coast from Tamendad

Tur – an island nation separated from the Continental Kingdoms by the Melteric Ocean; it is currently governed by King Archibald Stodlemeyer

Westerland – one of four cities, known as the Four Corners, that surround Wexford in each of the principal directions of the compass

Wexford – the capital city of Tur

Winterfeast – a seven-day festival ending on the first day of the new year

Appendix A

Antrelican Calendar

Twelve Months
Altor (AL-tor)
Ralmon (RAL-mon)
Tinction (TINK-shun)
Daimont (DIE-mont)
Forteris (for-TARE-is)
Bonavent (BON-a-vent)
Luthane (LEW-thane)
Anteron (AN-ter-on)
Corazon (kor-a-ZON)
Hidal (HI-dal)
Oridandum (or-i-DAN-dum)
Rotharus (ro-THAR-us)

Each month has 30 days.

Seasons

Spring: 16th Ralmon – 15th Forteris
Summer: 15th Forteris – 15th Anteron
Autumn: 16th Anteron – 15th Oridandum
Winter: 16th Oridandum – 15th Ralmon

Festivals and Events

Summerfeast: 25th Bonavent – 1st Luthane
    Day of Rememberance: 28th Bonavent
Winterfeast: 25th Rotharus – 1st Altor
    Day of Rememberance : 28th Rotharus

Years

- A year is measured from Winter Solstice (1st Altor) to the day before the next Winter Solstice (30th Rotharus).
- Years are recorded either after the Great Burden (*Posteriori Cataclymian*), or before (*Ante Cataclymian*).

APPENDIX B

NOBLE HOUSES OF TUR

Bancroft*
Bastion-Ayers
Burgess
Chamberlain*
Coulings
Dalsandrian
Dordanmeyer
Jameson
Lancaster*
Magnus-Courtwright
Morican
Stodlemeyer†
Stuart-Camen
Thalison
Tilman
Wayneswright*

* Royal House
† Reigning Royal House

ABOUT THE AUTHOR

Shannon Matthew McNally was educated at Virginia Tech. He currently lives in Illinois with his wife, his kids, his dogs and his overactive imagination.

For more information, visit www.smatthewmcnally.com